Ildefonso Falcones' first novel, *Cathedral of the Sea*, became a publishing legend with over a million copies sold in Spain alone. It has since been published in over forty countries, becoming a European bestseller. In his latest blockbuster, *The Hand of Fátima*, Falcones marks the four hundredth anniversary of the expulsion of the Moors from seventeenth-century Spain. Falcones is a practising lawyer in Barcelona, where he lives with his wife and four sons.

Nick Caistor is an award-winning translator of more than thirty books from Spain and Latin America. He has edited the *Faber Book of Contemporary Latin American Fiction*, and has translated other Barcelona-based writers such as Eduardo Mendoza, Juan Marsé and Manuel Vázquez Montalban.

Also by Ildefonso Falcones

CATHEDRAL OF THE SEA

and published by Black Swan

THE HAND
OF FÁTIMA

Ildefonso Falcones

BLACK SWAN

TRANSWORLD PUBLISHERS
61–63 Uxbridge Road, London W5 5SA
A Random House Group Company
www.transworldbooks.co.uk

**THE HAND OF FÁTIMA
A BLACK SWAN BOOK: 9780552776462**

La Mano de Fátima, first published by
Random House Mondadori, S.A. in 2009

First published in Great Britain
in 2010 by Doubleday
an imprint of Transworld Publishers
Black Swan edition published 2011

Addresses for Random House Group Ltd companies outside the UK
can be found at: www.randomhouse.co.uk
The Random House Group Ltd Reg. No. 954009

The Random House Group Limited supports The Forest Stewardship Council®
(FSC®), the leading international forest certification organisation. All our titles that
are printed on Greenpeace approved FSC® certified paper carry the FSC® logo. Our
paper procurement policy can be found at www.rbooks.co.uk/environment

Typeset in 11/12.5pt Minion by Falcon Oast Graphic Art Ltd.
Printed and bound by CPI Group (UK) Ltd, Croydon, CR0 4YY

2 4 6 8 10 9 7 5 3 1

To my children: Ildefonso, Alejandro, José María and Guillermo

If a Muslim is fighting or travelling in pagan territory, he has no obligation to appear differently from those around him. In such circumstances, Muslims may prefer or be obliged to adopt a similar appearance, always provided that this supposes a religious benefit, such as being able to preach to the infidel, discover their secrets and transmit them to other Muslims, to avert harm, or for any other useful end.

Ahmad ibn Taymiya (1263–1328), famous Arab jurist

PART ONE

IN THE NAME OF ALLAH

And so, fighting each day against enemies, the cold, heat, hunger, a general lack of arms and equipment, fresh disasters, and continual deaths, we finally saw that warlike nation, once so solid, well-armed and defended, favoured by barbarians and Turks, now defeated, subjugated, driven from their lands and dispossessed of their homes and goods; made prisoner, their men and women in chains; captive children sold at auction or taken to live in lands far from their own. A dubious victory, and full of so many dangers that we at times doubted whether it was us or the enemy whom God sought to punish.

Diego Hurtado de Mendoza, *The War in Granada,*
Book the First

1

A BELL CALLING the faithful to ten o'clock mass rang out through the icy air of a small village perched on one of the many spurs of the Sierra Nevada. Its metallic echoes drifted down the slopes, crashing against the hills of the Contraviesa, the mountain chain enclosing the fertile valley to the south. Three rivers, the Guadalfeo, Adra and Andarax, and their many tributaries flowed down from the snowy peaks to water the valley. Beyond the Contraviesa, the lands of the Alpujarra stretched to the Mediterranean. In the weak winter sun, almost two hundred men, women and children – most of them dragging their feet, almost all of them without a word – headed towards the church and pressed round its doors.

The building was a simple rectangular block made of ochre stone, bare of all external decoration. The bell was housed in a sturdy tower to one side. Next to the church stood a square built over the streams crisscrossing the valley from the Sierra Nevada. Leading off the square towards the mountains were narrow lanes bordered by a maze of houses with walls covered in crushed slate, one- or two-storey dwellings, with tiny doors and windows, flat terraced roofs and round chimneys topped by mushroom-shaped crowns. Peppers, figs and grapes were laid out on the terraces to dry. The streets wound their way up the mountainsides, so that the roofs of those down below were level with the foundations of those above, as though they were built one on top of the other.

In the square beside the church, a group of children and some of the score of old Christians* living in the village were gazing at an old woman perched atop a ladder leaning against the church's façade. The woman was shaking with cold, and the few teeth she had left chattered. The Moriscos† slipped into the church without casting a glance at their sister in faith, forced to stay up there since dawn, clinging to the top rung and suffering the winter cold with no protection. The bell pealed again, and one of the children pointed at the old woman as she trembled with each clang, trying desperately not to fall off. Laughter broke the silence.

'Witch!' someone shouted amid the guffaws.

One or two stones hit the old woman, and the foot of the ladder was covered in spittle.

The bell ceased to ring; the Christians left outside rushed to enter the church. Inside, kneeling bare-chested a step or two from the altar and facing the congregation, was a burly, dark-haired, weather-beaten man. He had no outdoor clothes on to protect him from the cold; a rope hung round his neck and he held his arms outstretched, a lighted candle in either hand.

A few days earlier that same man had given his wife's smock to the old woman on the ladder, for her to wash it in the waters of a spring reputed to have healing powers. No one ever washed clothes in that small natural spring, hidden among the rocks and thick undergrowth of the rugged sierra. Don Martín, the village priest, caught the woman by surprise while she was rinsing the garment, and had no doubt it was some kind of sorcery.

*Old Christians were those who had practised their religion throughout the Moorish occupation of Spain.
†Moors forced to be baptized as Christians after the Reconquest; also known, together with Jewish converts, as new Christians.

Punishment was swift: the old woman was to spend Sunday morning at the top of the ladder, exposed to public scorn. The naive Morisco who had asked for the magic cure was condemned to do penance while listening to mass on his knees, an example to the entire congregation.

As soon as the villagers entered the church, the men split off from the women, who went to the front with their daughters. The kneeling penitent stared straight ahead of him. They all knew him: he was a good man who looked after his land and his two cows. He was only trying to help his sick wife! The men gradually took their places behind the women. When everyone had settled, the priest, Don Martín, his deacon, Don Salvador, and the sacristan Andrés appeared at the altar. Don Martín, plump, pale-skinned and red-cheeked, was decked out in a white, gold-fringed chasuble. He sat on his throne facing the congregation, flanked by the other two men. The main door was shut. The draught subsided and the candles stopped flickering. The coffered mudéjar* ceiling glowed in the darkness, vying with the sober, tragic altarpieces.

The sacristan was a tall young man dressed all in black. Thin-faced and as dark-complexioned as most of the congregation, he opened a ledger, cleared his throat, and began to read: 'Francisco Alguacil.'

'Here.'

After checking where the answer came from, the sacristan made an entry in his book.

'José Almer.'

'Here.'

Again, the sacristan jotted something down. 'Milagros García, María Ambroz . . .' Each name was answered with a 'Here' that, as Andrés went down his list, sounded more and more like a grunt. The sacristan continued to check who had spoken and noted it down.

*Architecture of Moors living in Christian territory, but not forced to convert.

'Marcos Núñez.'

'Here.'

'You did not attend mass last Sunday,' said the sacristan.

'I was . . .' The man tried to explain, but could not find the words. Waving a piece of paper, he ended his sentence in Arabic.

'Come closer,' Andrés ordered.

Marcos Núñez slipped through the congregation until he reached the foot of the altar.

'I was in Ugíjar,' he struggled to explain this time, handing the paper to the sacristan.

Andrés glanced at it, and then passed it to the priest. Don Martín read it through carefully, verified the signature, and nodded his approval with a twist of the mouth: the head abbot of the collegiate church in Ugíjar certified that on 5 December 1568 the new Christian by the name of Marcos Núñez, from the village of Juviles, had attended the mass celebrated in his church.

Smiling almost imperceptibly, the sacristan wrote again in his book before continuing with the interminable list of new Christians – those Muslims ordered by the King to be baptized and to profess Christianity – whose attendance at services had to be confirmed every Sunday and on all holy days of obligation. Some of the names he called out drew no answer, and their absence was duly recorded. Unlike Marcos Núñez with his certificate from Ugíjar, two women could not explain why they had not been at mass the previous Sunday. They both hurriedly tried to excuse themselves. Andrés let them talk, but glanced sideways at the priest. When Don Martín raised his hand imperiously, the first woman fell silent; the second however went on insisting she had been ill on that day.

'Ask my husband!' she screeched, searching nervously for him among the men at the back of the church. 'He will—'

'Silence, you devil worshipper!'

Don Martín's roar cowed the woman into silence. The

sacristan wrote down her name: both women were to pay a fine of half a real.

When the lengthy roll-call was over, Don Martín began to say mass. Before starting, he told the sacristan to make sure the penitent lifted his arms holding the candles higher in the air.

'In the name of the Father, of the Son, and of the Holy Spirit . . .'

The rite went on, although few in the congregation could understand the readings from the Scriptures or follow the frenetic pace or the constant reproaches with which the priest admonished them throughout his homily.

'Do you really believe that water from a spring will cure you of an illness?' Don Martín pointed at the kneeling penitent. His forefinger shook, and his face was contorted with anger. 'This is your penance. Only Christ the Lord can free you from the wretchedness and hardships with which he punishes you for your dissolute lives, your blasphemies and your sacrilegious attitudes!'

Most of those present did not speak Spanish. Some of them communicated with the Spaniards in *aljamiado*, a dialect that was a mixture of Arabic and the Romance language. Nevertheless, they were all obliged to know the Lord's Prayer, the Hail Mary, the Creed, the Hymn to the Virgin Mary and the Ten Commandments in Spanish. The Morisco children were given lessons by the sacristan; the men and women were taught Christian doctrine on Fridays and Saturdays in sessions that they missed on penalty of being fined or refused permission to marry. Only when they could recite the church prayers by heart were they excused from classes.

Some of the congregation prayed during the mass. Keeping a watchful eye on the sacristan, the children did so out loud, almost shouting, as their parents had encouraged them to do. Under cover of this noise, the adults could avoid the attentions of the deacon as he walked up and down among them, and recite under their breath: *Allahu Akbar*. Many of them whispered it, eyes tight shut, with a sigh.

'O Compassionate and Merciful One! Free me from my sins and vices . . .' could be heard from the lines of men as soon as Don Salvador moved away. He never went too far from them, fearful lest they defy him by calling on the Muslim god in this Christian temple during high mass.

'O Almighty One! Guide me with your power . . .' a young Morisco man called out several rows back, his plea masked by the children shouting the Lord's Prayer.

Don Salvador turned furiously towards him.

'O Giver of Peace! Allow me into your glory . . .' another man risked saying from the opposite side of the church.

The deacon turned scarlet with anger.

'O All-merciful . . .' a third man prayed.

Then suddenly, when the Christian prayer had finished, the priest's rasping voice rang out again.

'His name be praised,' came the chant from one of the last rows of men.

Most of the Moriscos stood still, erect, unmoving. Some of them stared defiantly back at Don Salvador, but many lowered their eyes. Who had dared praise the name of Allah? The deacon pushed his way through the men, but could not identify the heretic.

Halfway through the mass, while Don Martín looked on closely from his seat, his deacon and the sacristan, one clasping his book and the other a basket, stood to receive the offerings of the faithful: copper coins, bread, eggs, linen . . . Only the poor were exempt from making a donation; if those who were better off gave nothing for three consecutive Sundays, they would be fined accordingly. Andrés took careful note of who gave what.

When the bell the Moriscos called 'the death knell' sounded for the consecration of the host, they reluctantly knelt while the old Christians professed their faith. The bell tinkled as the priest, back to the congregation, raised the host; it sounded again as he held the chalice aloft. He was about to pronounce the sacrament when all of a sudden, enraged at the muttering disturbing the church's silence, he turned furiously to face the worshippers.

'Dogs!' he shouted. His curse spattered the holy vessel with saliva. 'What are you muttering about? Be quiet, heretics! Kneel as you should to receive the body of Christ, the only God! You!' he said, pointing to an old man in the third row. 'Straighten up! Do not prostrate yourself in front of your false idol! Look up! Raise your eyes when you are being offered the holiest of sacraments!'

His eyes blazed at two more Moriscos before he proceeded with the mass. Men and women went up in silence to eat 'the cake'. Many of them would try to keep the wafer of wheat in their mouths until they could spit it out at home; all of them without exception washed out any crumbs that were left.

After receiving the blessing, the villagers filed out of church. The Christians received the blessing devotedly; the great majority of the others scoffed at it either by crossing themselves backwards and silently affirming that there was only one God, not the Christian trinity. Then the Moriscos rushed home to spit out the remains of the host. The few Christians in the village gathered at the church door to talk, ignoring the insults their children were shouting at the old woman, who had finally fallen from the ladder. She lay on the ground, numb and terrified, her lips blue as she struggled to draw breath. Inside the church, the priest and his assistants prolonged the penitent's punishment, rebuking him for his sinful ways while they cleared away the ceremonial dishes.

2

It is true that the Moriscos have risen up in rebellion, but it is the old Christians who have driven them to despair by their arrogance, larcenies, and the insolence with which they seize their women. Even the priests behave in a similar manner. When an entire Morisco village complained to the archbishop about their pastor, an investigation was made into the reasons for their complaint. Take him away from here . . . the faithful pleaded . . . or if not, let him be married, because all our children are born with the same blue eyes as him.

Letter from Francés de Álava, Spain's ambassador in France,
to Philip II, 1568

JUVILES WAS THE centre of a district made up of some twenty villages scattered round the foothills of the Sierra Nevada. A quarter of the land was irrigated, the rest dry earth. Wheat and barley were the main crops, and there were more than four thousand *marjales** planted with vines, olives, figs, chestnut and walnut trees, but above all with mulberries, fed on by the silk worms that were the area's main source of wealth, although silk from Juviles did not enjoy the same prestige as that from other parts of the Alpujarra.

On those heights, at more than a thousand yards above sea level, the long-suffering, hard-working Moriscos cultivated

*A Moorish measurement, equivalent to 441.75 square metres.

even the steepest plot of land that could produce corn. Wherever the mountain slopes were not bare rock, they were filled with small terraces, carved out of even the remotest corners. That Sunday, with the sun already high, the young Hernando Ruiz was returning to Juviles from one of these terraces. He was fourteen, with dark-brown hair but a much lighter complexion than the burnished olive of the other villagers. His features were mostly similar to the other Moriscos, but beneath his thick eyebrows shone a pair of big blue eyes. He was of average height, thin and wiry.

He had just finished picking the last olives from a gnarled old tree that could withstand the cold of the mountains and grew protected beside the terrace planted with wheat. He had harvested them all by hand, climbing up the tree without using a pole, and had picked even the olives that still looked unripe. The sun tempered the cold breeze from the Sierra Nevada. Hernando would have liked to stay up there longer to hoe the weeds, and then visit another terrace, where he guessed his friend Hamid would be working the tiny parcel of land he owned. When they were on their own together on the mountainside, at work or roaming the hills in search of the herbs the modest older man used for his remedies, he called him Hamid rather than Francisco, the Christian name he had been baptized with. The majority of the Moriscos used two names: their Christian name and, within their own community, their Muslim one. Hernando, though, was simply Hernando, although in the village they often made fun of him or insulted him by calling him the 'Nazarene'.

Remembering this nickname, the youth instinctively slowed down. He was no Nazarene! He kicked an imaginary stone, then continued towards his home: a house on the outskirts of the village where there had been enough room to build a stable for the six mules his father-in-law used to ply up and down the tracks of the Alpujarra, together with his favourite, La Vieja, the Old One.

It had been almost a year since his mother had been obliged

to tell Hernando the reason for his nickname. One morning at dawn Hernando had been helping his stepfather Brahim – José to the Christians – to harness the mules. When he had finished, he was giving La Vieja an affectionate pat on the neck when a hefty blow to his head sent him sprawling.

'Nazarene dog!' Brahim shouted angrily. The lad shook his head to clear his thoughts, and raised a hand to his ear. Beyond his stepfather, who was standing threateningly over him, he caught a glimpse of his mother disappearing head down back inside their house.

'You've not tightened that mule's girth properly!' his stepfather bawled at him, pointing at one of the animals. 'Do you want it to rub all the way, so the mule won't be able to work? You're nothing more than a useless Nazarene, a Christian bastard,' he said, spitting at him.

Hernando had crawled out from under his stepfather's feet, then hidden in the straw in a corner of the barn, his head between his knees. As soon as the sound of the team's hoofs announced Brahim's departure, his mother Aisha appeared outside the stable, and then came in to find him, a glass of fresh lemonade in her hand.

'Does it hurt?' she asked, bending down and stroking his hair.

'Why does everyone call me Nazarene, Mother?' he sobbed, raising his head. Seeing her son's face bathed in tears, Aisha closed her eyes. When she tried to wipe her son's tears away, he jerked his head to one side, and insisted: 'Why?'

Aisha sighed deeply, but then nodded and settled back on her heels in the straw. 'All right, you are old enough now,' she said sadly, as if what she was about to say took a huge effort. 'You should know that fifteen years ago the village priest where I used to live in the parish of Almería took me by force ...' Hernando was so startled he stopped crying. 'Yes, my son. As our Muslim law demands, I screamed and resisted, but there was little I could do against the strength of that – that brute. He came up to me in the fields a long way from the village, mid-morning one sunny day. I was only a child!' she protested. 'He ripped off my tunic, then threw me to the ground, and . . .'

Aisha stopped; the scene faded in her mind as she drifted back to reality. She found her son staring at her, his blue eyes wide open.

'You are the fruit of that abomination,' she said sadly. 'That's why . . . that's why they call you the Nazarene. Because your father was a Christian priest. I am the one to blame . . .'

For several long seconds, mother and son stared at each other. Fresh tears streamed down the boy's cheeks, this time caused by a different kind of pain. Aisha fought back her own tears until she realized it was impossible. She dropped the glass of lemonade and held out her arms to her son. He rushed into her embrace.

Even though the young Aisha had salvaged her honour by fighting her attacker, as soon as the pregnancy became obvious, her father, a poor Morisco muleteer, realizing that shame could not be avoided, tried at least to avoid having to witness it. He found the solution in Brahim, a young, good-looking muledriver from Juviles whom he often met on the mountain trails. He offered marriage to his daughter in exchange for two mules as dowry: one for the girl, and the other for the child she was bearing. Brahim hesitated, but he was young and poor and needed animals. Besides, who knew if the child would be born? Or perhaps it would only live a few months? In those inhospitable lands, many children died in infancy.

And so, although Brahim found the knowledge that the girl had been violated by a Christian priest repugnant, he accepted the offer and took her with him to Juviles, where, despite his hopes, Hernando was born a strong, healthy baby with the blue eyes of the rapist. He also survived his early infancy. The details of his origin were soon common knowledge, and although the villagers pitied the raped girl, they did not feel the same towards the illegitimate fruit of the crime. Their attitude became even harsher when they saw how Don Martín and Andrés favoured him. These two paid him even more attention than they did the Christian children, as if wishing to protect this priestly bastard from any influence of the followers of Muhammad.

The half-smile with which Hernando gave his mother the olives did not fool her. She gently stroked his hair as she always did when she knew he was sad. Even though his four stepbrothers and -sisters were in the room, he let her caress him: his mother could seldom show her affection openly, and then only when his stepfather was absent. Brahim had no qualms about joining in the Morisco community's rejection of Hernando. His hatred of the blue-eyed Nazarene, the Christian priests' favourite, had only increased when Aisha gave birth to their legitimate offspring. When Hernando was nine, he was pushed out into the stable with the mules, and only ate in the house when his stepfather was absent. Aisha was forced to follow her husband's wishes, and could only show her love for her son through surreptitious but heartfelt gestures.

The food was ready and his four half-brothers and -sisters were waiting for him. Even the youngest, four-year-old Musa, scowled at him.

'In the name of all-merciful God,' Hernando prayed before sitting on the ground.

Little Musa and his brother Aquil, who was three years older, did the same. The three of them dipped their fingers into the pot and pulled out pieces of the lamb their mother had prepared with thistles cooked in oil, mint, coriander, saffron and vinegar.

Hernando glanced up at his mother. She was watching them eat, leaning against one of the walls of the small but clean room that served as kitchen, dining room and temporary bedroom for the other children. His two half-sisters, Raissa and Zahara, stood next to her, waiting for the males to finish eating before they began. Hernando chewed on a piece of lamb and smiled at his mother.

After the lamb dish, his eleven-year-old half-sister Zahara

brought a platter of raisins. Hernando scarcely had time to try one or two before a muffled noise in the distance made him cock his head to one side. The other boys saw him and stopped eating, wondering what he had heard; neither of them had ears sharp enough to tell when the mules were arriving.

'La Vieja!' Musa shouted when the noise of her hoofs became obvious to them all.

Hernando's mouth tightened as he looked across again at his mother. Her expression seemed to confirm that what they had heard was indeed La Vieja's hoofs. He tried to smile, but could only twist his mouth sadly in the same way as she did: Brahim was on his way home.

'Praise be to God,' Hernando said, putting an end to the meal. He got up resignedly.

Outside, La Vieja stood waiting patiently for him. Her ribs stuck out from her dusty, sore-covered hide, but she was not carrying any load.

'Come on, Vieja,' Hernando said, and led her towards the stable.

The clip-clop of her hoofs followed him as he walked round the house. When they had reached the stable, he forked some hay for her and patted her neck affectionately.

'How was your journey?' he whispered as he examined a fresh sore that had not been there when she had left.

He watched her chewing the hay for a while, and then ran out up the mountainside. His stepfather would be in hiding, waiting for him well away from the Ugíjar road. Hernando ran for some time across open country, careful to avoid meeting any Christians. He skirted the cultivated terraces or anywhere someone might be working even at that time of day. Almost out of breath, he reached a rocky, inaccessible spot on the edge of a precipice, where he saw Brahim waiting for him. His stepfather was a tall, strong man with a beard. He was wearing a green broad-brimmed cap and a half-length blue cape under which a pleated tunic came down to his thighs. His legs were bare, but he wore leather shoes tied with laces. Like all the Moriscos in the kingdom of Granada, once new laws came into force at the start of the following year, Brahim would have to give up these clothes and wear Christian apparel. Even now he was defying the ban on carrying weapons by sporting a curved dagger at his belt.

Behind him, standing in line – there was no room for them abreast on the rocky outcrop – were the six loaded mules. In the cliff wall there were entrances to several small caves.

When he caught sight of his stepfather, Hernando slowed to a walk. The fear he always felt on seeing him gripped him once more. How would he be received this time? The last time he had cuffed him round the ear for taking so long, even though he had run all the way.

'Why have you stopped?' Brahim growled.

Hernando scurried towards his stepfather, instinctively shying away as he reached him. This did not save him from another cuff round the head. He stumbled, but then made his way up to the leading mule, squeezing between the animals and the rock face until he was at the mouth of one of the caves. Without a word, he began stuffing the bundles his stepfather unloaded into the cave.

'This oil is for Juan,' Brahim told him, passing him a jar. 'Aisar!' He shouted the Muslim name, seeing doubt flit across his stepson's face. 'This other one is for Faris.' As he stacked the goods inside the cave, Hernando tried to remember to whom each one belonged.

When half the bundles had been unloaded, Brahim started off down to Juviles, leaving the boy at the cave entrance, staring out at the vast expanse of countryside that stretched as far as the Contraviesa in the distance. He did not stand there for long: he knew the landscape by heart. He turned back into the cave, and spent some time examining the goods he had just hidden and the many others stored there. Hundreds of caves in the Alpujarra had been turned into storehouses where the Moriscos hid their possessions. Before nightfall, the owners would appear to carry off whatever they needed. Every trip was the same. Wherever he came from, before reaching Juviles his stepfather would unhitch La Vieja and order her to find her way home. 'She knows the Alpujarra better than anyone. I've spent my whole life on these trails, but she has got me out of a tight spot more than once,' the mule-driver used to say. When La Vieja arrived on her own back in Juviles, that was the signal for Hernando to run up to the caves to meet his stepfather. By unloading half of the goods there, they also halved the high taxes that Brahim had to pay on the profits from his work. The buyers did the same with a large proportion of the goods they received from Hernando before they reached Juviles. The endless stream of collectors of tithes and tributes, as well as the bailiffs who imposed fines and penalties, would burst into the Moriscos' homes to seize whatever they could find, even if it was worth more than what was owed. They never disclosed how much these goods fetched at auction, and so the Moriscos were robbed of their property. The community had made numerous complaints to the mayor of Ugíjar, the bishop and even the chief magistrate in Granada, but these protests always fell on deaf ears and the Christian officials went on stealing from them with impunity, which was why everyone adopted Brahim's plan.

Seated with his back to the cave wall, Hernando crushed a dry twig and played half-heartedly with the pieces of wood; he had a long wait ahead of him. Looking at the piles of goods around him, he told himself these subterfuges were necessary: without them, the Christians would have left the Moriscos in absolute poverty. Hernando also helped the villagers hide their sheep and goats from the tithe. Although the Moriscos spurned him, they were willing to accept him as their accomplice. 'The Nazarene', one old man commented, 'knows how to write, read and count.' It was true: from his early childhood, the sacristan Andrés had paid great attention to his education, and Hernando had shown himself to be a good pupil. Someone with a head for numbers was essential to fool the tithes collector who appeared every spring.

The tax collector demanded that the animals be herded together in a flat field and then made to file through a narrow corral of branches. Out of every ten animals, one was for the Church. The Moriscos argued that they should not have to pay a tithe on flocks of thirty or fewer animals, but should pay a fixed amount instead. As a result, when the official appeared, the village agreed between themselves to divide the flocks into groups of thirty or fewer, a ruse that afterwards demanded considerable skill when it came to re-forming the original groups.

Yet the cost had been very high for Hernando. As he recalled the evening when he had been chosen to help fool the Christians, he hurled the pieces of twig at the cave wall. They all fell to the ground before they reached it . . .

'Many of us know how to count,' one of the Moriscos had protested when it was suggested Hernando take the lead in this way. 'Perhaps not as well as the Nazarene, but—'

'But all of you own goats or sheep, which means the Christians are suspicious of you,' insisted the old man who had proposed Hernando. 'Neither Brahim nor the Nazarene has any interest in livestock.'

'What if he betrays us?' said a third man. 'He spends a lot of time with the priests.'

Everyone fell silent.

'Don't worry. I'll make sure he doesn't,' Brahim had assured them.

That same night, Brahim took his stepson by surprise while he was settling the mules.

'Woman!' the muleteer shouted.

Hernando was bewildered. His stepfather was only a couple of steps away from him. What could he have done wrong this time? Why was he calling his mother? Aisha appeared in the stable doorway. She hurried over to them, wiping her hands on the cloth she wore as an apron. Before she could say a word, Brahim whirled round and gave her a tremendous slap across the face. Aisha stumbled; a trickle of blood appeared at the corner of her mouth.

'Did you see that?' Brahim growled. 'Your mother will get a hundred of the same if you ever take it into your head to say anything to the priests about what we are doing in the caves or with the livestock.'

Hernando spent the whole afternoon in the cave, until the last Morisco arrived shortly before dusk. At last he could return to the village to look after the mules: he had to treat any scrapes and see they were all in good condition. In the corner of the stables where he slept, he found a bowl of gruel and some lemonade. He made short work of both. As soon as he had finished with the animals, he rushed out of the shed.

As he passed in front of the small wooden door of the house, he spat on the ground. Inside, the rest of the family were laughing. His stepfather's penetrating voice could be heard above all the cheerful noise. Seeing Hernando from the window, Raissa smiled fleetingly; she was the only one who occasionally showed him any affection, although her guarded gestures, like Aisha's, had to be kept hidden from Brahim. Hernando speeded up until he was running as fast as he could to Hamid's house.

The wizened old holy man had a lined and weather-beaten face. He was lame in his left leg, and since his wife had died had lived on his own in a hovel that had been patched up a thousand times without much success. Hernando was not sure how old Hamid was, but thought he must be one of the oldest men in the village. Even though the door to the shack was open, Hernando knocked three times.

'Peace,' Hamid replied at the third knock. 'I saw Brahim return to the village,' he said when the lad had crossed the threshold.

The room was lit by a smoky oil lamp, the only one in Hamid's dwelling. In spite of the peeling walls and the leaks from the roof, the room was as neat and tidy as all the other Morisco homes. The fire in the hearth was out. The single tiny window was blocked up to prevent the frame collapsing.

The boy nodded and sat on a threadbare pillow next to Hamid.

'Have you prayed?'

Hernando knew he would be asked that. He also knew what the next words would be: 'The night prayer . . .'

'. . . is the only one we can perform with any degree of safety,' Hamid always said, 'because the Christians are asleep.'

Whereas Andrés the sacristan was determined to teach Hernando Christian prayers and to count, read and write, the poverty-stricken Hamid, who was respected as a holy man in the village, did the same with Muslim beliefs and teachings. He had taken this task upon himself ever since the other Moriscos had rejected the priest's bastard, as though he felt the need to compete with the sacristan and all the rest of the community. He also got Hernando to pray while he was working the land, safe from prying eyes, and the two of them would chant the suras together as they roamed the hills in search of medicinal herbs.

Before Hernando could answer Hamid's question, the old man stood up. He shut and barred the door, then they both stripped off in silence. The water was ready for them in clean earthenware bowls. They turned to face Mecca, the kiblah.

'O God, my Lord!' Hamid intoned, dipping his hands into the bowl and washing them three times. Hernando accompanied him in his prayers and also washed his hands. 'With your aid I preserve myself from the filth and evil of accursed Satan . . .'

They then proceeded to wash their bodies as prescribed by law: their private parts, hands, nose and mouth, their right and left arms from fingers to elbow, their heads, ears and feet down to their ankles. They accompanied each ablution with the corresponding prayers, although occasionally Hamid's voice dropped to an almost inaudible whisper. This was the sign that the boy should take the lead in saying the prayers; Hernando smiled as he did so, the pair of them still with their eyes fixed on the kiblah.

'. . . that on the Day of Reckoning you give me . . .' the boy prayed out loud.

Hamid half closed his eyes, nodded contentedly, then took up the prayer again:

'... my scroll in my right hand, and that you judge me leniently and kindly.'

After their ablutions, the two of them recited the night prayer, bending forward twice and then crouching down to touch their ankles.

'All praise be to Allah ...' they began in unison.

Just as they were prostrating themselves, kneeling on the only rug Hamid possessed, their foreheads and noses pressed against the cloth, their arms outstretched in front of them, they heard knocking at the door.

They fell silent, motionless on the mat.

The knocking came again, louder this time.

Startled, Hamid turned towards the boy, seeing his blue eyes glint in the candlelight. 'I'm sorry,' the old man seemed to be saying. He was old, but Hernando ...

'Hamid, open up!' they heard from outside.

Hamid? In spite of his lame leg, the Morisco jumped up and went to the door. Hamid! No Christian would have called him that.

'Peace.'

The visitor came in to find Hernando still kneeling on the mat, feet pressed downwards.

'Peace,' said the stranger. He was a small, bronze-skinned man, considerably younger than Hamid.

'This is Hernando,' Hamid said. 'Hernando, this is Ali, from Órgiva. He's my sister's husband. What brings you here at this time of night? You're far from home.' Ali's only reply was to lift his chin in the direction of the young boy. 'You can trust him,' Hamid said. 'See for yourself.'

Ali studied Hernando as he got to his feet, and then nodded. Hamid gestured for his brother-in-law to sit down, and then did likewise. Ali sat on the rug, Hamid on the threadbare pillow.

'Bring some fresh water and raisins,' he asked Hernando.

'The end of the year will bring a new world,' Ali announced

solemnly, without waiting for the boy to carry out the request.

The twenty or so raisins in the bowl that Hernando left between the two men must have been charity from the villagers. Hernando had even brought gifts for the old scholar from his stepfather, who did not exactly have a reputation for being generous.

Hamid nodded at what his brother-in-law said. 'So I have heard.'

Hernando, who had sat down again on one corner of the mat, looked quizzically at him. It was a surprise to him that Hamid had relatives, but it was not the first time he had heard what Ali had said: his stepfather kept repeating something similar, especially when he returned from Granada. The sacristan Andrés had explained it was because the turn of the year was when the new royal decree came into force, obliging the Moriscos to dress like Christians and to abandon the use of Arabic.

'There was a failed attempt at Easter this year,' Hamid went on. 'Why would it be any different this time?'

Hernando cocked his head to one side. What was Hamid saying? What failed attempt was he talking about?

'This time it will succeed,' Ali assured him. 'Last time, the plans for revolt were on everyone's lips throughout the Alpujarra. That's how the Marquis of Mondéjar got to hear about them, and the people of the Albaicín pulled out.'

Hamid encouraged him to say more. When he heard the word 'revolt', Hernando was all ears.

'This time, it's been decided that those in the Alpujarra will not be told until the moment has come to take Granada. Precise instructions have been given to the Moriscos in the Albaicín, the plains and the valley of Lecrín and Órgiva. Married men have been recruiting other married men, and the unmarried and widowers have been doing the same. There are more than eight thousand ready and waiting to launch the assault on the Albaicín. Only once that has happened will the people of the Alpujarra be informed. A hundred thousand men could rise up in arms.'

'Who is behind it this time?'

'The meetings are held at the house of a candle-maker in the Albaicín called Adelet. Those who attend are the men the Christians call Hernando el Zaguer, a town councillor from Cádiar, Diego López from Mecina de Bombarón, Miguel de Rojas from Ugíjar, as well as Farax ibn Farax, El Tagari, Mofarrix, Alatar . . . and there are many Morisco outlaws who support them,' Ali explained.

'I don't trust those bandits,' Hamid interrupted him.

Ali shrugged. 'As you know,' he said, 'many of them were forced to go and live in the mountains. They don't give us any trouble! You yourself would have gone with him, had it not been for . . .' Ali averted his eyes from Hamid's withered leg. 'Most of them became outlaws because of the same injustices you have suffered.'

Ali said no more, waiting for his brother-in-law to react. For a few moments Hamid seemed lost in memories, but eventually he pursed his lips in agreement.

'What injust—?' Hernando started to ask, but a brusque gesture from Hamid silenced him.

'Which bands of outlaws have promised their support?' the old scholar wanted to know.

'Those of El Partal of Narila, El Nacoz of Nigüelas, and El Seniz of Bérchul.' Hamid was listening closely as Ali insisted: 'It's all been planned. The men in the Albaicín are ready to rise up on New Year's Day. As soon as they do, the eight thousand outside Granada will scale . . . we will scale the Alhambra walls on the Generalife side. We'll use seventeen ladders that are already being put together in Ugíjar and Quéntar. I've seen them: they are made of strong, tough hemp ropes, with rungs of hard wood that can support three men at a time. We'll have to attack disguised as Turks, so the Christians think we are being supported by the Berbers or the Sultan. Our women are working on the disguises. Granada can't defend itself. We will retake it on the same day it surrendered to the Christian monarchs.'

'And once Granada has been taken?'

'Algiers will come to our aid. The Great Turk will support us. They have promised to do so. Spain can't cope with more wars. It can't fight on more fronts – its armies are already engaged in Flanders, the Indies and against the Berbers and the Turks.' Ali raised his eyes to the roof. 'Allah be praised,' he murmured. 'The prophecies will be fulfilled, Hamid!' he shouted. 'They will be fulfilled!'

At this, silence filled the room, broken only by Hernando's agitated breathing. The boy was trembling from head to foot, looking compulsively from one man to the other.

'What do you want me to do? What can I do?' Hamid asked all of a sudden. 'I'm lame . . .'

'As a direct descendant of the Nasrids, you should be present at the taking of Granada as a representative of the people it has always belonged to and should still belong to. Your sister is willing to go with you.'

Hernando was almost on his feet by now, desperate to ask more questions, but Hamid stretched out a restraining arm, as though begging him to be patient. The boy sat back down on the mat, but could not take his eyes off the humble old scholar. He was a descendant of the Nasrids, the Kings of Granada!

3

HAMID BEGGED Ali to stay the night, but he declined. He knew his host had only one bed, but to avoid offending him claimed he had to see someone else in Juviles who was waiting for him. This excuse satisfied Hamid, who went to the door to see him on his way. From the mat, Hernando watched the two men take leave of each other. The old man waited until his brother-in-law had disappeared into the darkness, then barred the door again. When he turned back to the boy, the lines seemed more deeply etched on his face, and his normally calm eyes had a new glint to them.

Hamid remained at the door for a few moments, lost in thought. Then he slowly limped over to the boy, holding up his hand for him to be quiet. To Hernando, the seconds before he dropped it seemed endless. Finally, Hamid sat down and smiled openly at him. The thousand questions crowding into the boy's mind – Nasrids? What uprising? What was the Great Turk going to do? And the people from Algiers? Why should you have become an outlaw? Are there Berbers in the Alpujarra? – resolved into a single one: 'How can you be so poor if you are a descendant of—'

Before he had even finished his question, the old man's face darkened. 'They took everything from me,' he replied shortly.

Hernando looked away. 'I'm so sorry . . .' he managed to blurt out. To his surprise, the old holy man seemed to want to explain.

'Not long ago, since you were born, in fact, there has been an important change in the administration of Granada. Until then, we Moriscos were governed by the captain-general, the Marquis of Mondéjar, the representative of the King and lord of almost all these lands. But the host of officials and legal clerks in the chancery of Granada insisted they should have control over the Moriscos and, despite the marquis's opposition, the King agreed. From that moment on, the Christian clerks and lawyers began to dust off old lawsuits aimed at the Moriscos.'

It had long been the custom that any Morisco who accepted the King's rule was pardoned any offence he might have committed. This benefited everyone: the Moriscos could settle peacefully in the Alpujarra, while the King received workers who paid much higher taxes than if the lands had been in the hands of Christians. The only ones who did not benefit were the chancery.

Hamid took a raisin from the bowl. 'Don't you want one?' he asked.

Hernando was impatient. No, he did not want one . . . He wanted Hamid to give him answers, to go on talking! So as not to offend him, he stretched out his hand and chewed silently on a raisin.

'Well,' Hamid continued, 'the chancery clerks used the excuse of pursuing the Morisco outlaws to create squads of soldiers who were in fact almost always their servants or relatives . . . and who received the best pay ever known in the King's armies. They were paid more than the Germans in the Flanders regiments! While these men did their fighting for them, the jumped-up officials, instead of using their swords against the brigands, used their legal chicanery against peaceful Moriscos. Those who had lawsuits brought against them were forced to pay to defend themselves, with the result that many had to abandon their homes and join the outlaws. Yet the officials' greed did not end there: they began to question the Moriscos' property deeds, and anyone who did not have written proof of ownership was forced to pay the

King or to leave his lands. Many of us had no such proof...'

'You didn't have titles to your property?' Hernando asked when the scholar paused in his explanation.

'No,' Hamid said sadly. 'I am a descendant of the Nasrid dynasty, the last to reign in Granada. My family, my clan' – the sudden note of pride in Hamid's voice gave Hernando a jolt – 'was one of the noblest and most prominent in Granada, and a miserable Christian clerk took all my lands and possessions from me.'

Hernando shuddered. Overwhelmed by these sad memories, Hamid's voice trailed off. He recovered quickly though and went on, as if wanting at least this once to be able to tell someone the story of his ruin.

'When Abu Abdallah, whom the Christians called Boabdil, surrendered to the Castilians in Granada, they offered him the Alpujarra as his fiefdom in compensation. He withdrew there with his court, one of whom was his cousin, my father, a renowned scholar. But those deceitful monarchs were not content with this: behind Boabdil's back, they used an intermediary to buy back the lands they had awarded him shortly before, and then expelled him from them. Almost all the Muslim nobles and grandees left Spain with the "Little King". My father was one of the few who decided to stay on with his people, those who needed his protection and advice. And then Cardinal Cisneros, betraying the terms of the Granada surrender which guaranteed the Moors the right to live in peace and enjoy their own religious beliefs, convinced the Spanish kings to expel all those who did not convert. How could they want to leave their lands, where they were born and had raised their children? The Christians sprinkled holy water on hundreds of us at a time. Many left the churches claiming that not a single drop had fallen on them, and that therefore they were still Muslims. When I was born, fifty years ago—' Hernando looked startled. 'Did you think I was older?' The boy lowered his eyes. 'In those days, we lived quietly on the lands that Boabdil had verbally ceded to the Christians. No one disputed our rights until that army of officials and legal clerks set out on the march. Then . . .' Hamid fell silent.

'Then they took all you had,' Hernando finished the sentence for him, almost choking with emotion.

'Nearly everything.' The old man took another raisin. Hernando leant closer to him. 'Nearly everything,' Hamid said again, still chewing the raisin. 'But they could not take our faith from us, although that was what they wished for most of all. And they could not take from me . . .' Hamid struggled to his feet and went over to one of the walls. He dug in the dirt of the floor with his right foot until he uncovered a long plank of wood. He pulled at one end, then bent down to pull out something wrapped in cloth. Hernando did not need to be told what it was: its long, curved shape spoke for itself.

Hamid unwrapped the scimitar carefully and showed it to the boy. 'This. They couldn't take this from me either. While bailiffs, clerks and officials were carrying off silk clothes, precious stones, animals and grain, I managed to hide my family's most precious possession. This sword was in the hands of the Prophet, the peace and blessings of God be upon Him!' he said solemnly. 'According to my father, his father told him that it was one of many Muhammad received as ransom from the infidel Quraysh whom he took captive when he conquered Mecca.'

The golden scabbard was hung with strips of metal inscribed in Arabic. Hernando shivered again, and his eyes shone like those of a young boy. A sword that had belonged to the Prophet! Hamid unsheathed the scimitar, which glittered in the smoky air.

'You will be there when we recover the city that we should never have lost. You will be a witness that our prophecies are fulfilled and that true believers reign once more in al-Andalus.'

4

THE RUMOURS flying round the village for two days were confirmed by a band of armed outlaws who rode through on their way to Ugíjar.

'All the armed men of the Alpujarra are to meet in Ugíjar,' they told the Juviles villagers from on horseback. 'The uprising has begun. We will win our lands back! Granada will be Muslim again!'

In spite of the hope of the leaders in the Albaicín of Granada that they could keep the revolt a secret, the news that 'at the end of the year there will be a new world' spread like wildfire through the mountains, and the armed bands and the men of the Alpujarra did not wait for New Year's Day. One group attacked and butchered several Christian officials as they were crossing the Alpujarra on their way back to Granada to celebrate Christmas. As usual, these officials had been stealing indiscriminately and with impunity as they passed through villages and farmsteads. Other bands attacked a small detachment of soldiers, while the Moriscos in the village of Cádiar rose en masse, sacked the church and the Christians' houses and slaughtered them all.

After the armed band had passed through Juviles, the Christians barricaded themselves in their homes. The rest of the village was a hive of activity. The men armed themselves with knives, daggers and even some old swords and harquebuses they had succeeded in zealously hiding from the Christian officials. The women donned veils and colourful silk, linen or woollen dresses embroidered with gold and silver and went out into the streets wearing these very un-Christian garments, their hands and feet tattooed with henna. Some of them wore blouses, others long cowls ending in a point in the middle of the back, with embroidered tunics underneath; they wore baggy trousers pleated at their calves and thick stockings rolled up to their knees, where they were tucked under the trousers. On their feet they wore clogs with laces or slippers. The entire village was an explosion of colour: greens, blues, yellows . . . There were women dressed in their finery everywhere, although without exception they kept their heads covered: some only concealed their hair, but most of them hid their faces as well.

Hernando had been in the church since first light, helping Andrés to prepare the Christmas Eve mass. The sacristan was checking a magnificent gold-embroidered chasuble when the doors of the church were suddenly flung open, and a group of shrieking Moriscos burst in. The priest and his deacon, who had been dragged out of their house, were thrown to the floor by the gang, then kicked and prodded until they got to their feet again.

'What are you doing?' Andrés managed to say from the sacristy door before being seized and thrown to the ground by the Moriscos. The sacristan fell at the feet of Don Martín and Don Salvador, who were still being beaten and punched.

At first Hernando made to follow Andrés, but when he saw the enraged mob surging into the sacristy he cringed back. The attackers were howling, shouting, kicking out at anything in their way. One of them swept all the objects off the table with his arm: down went paper, inkwell, quills . . . Others headed for the cupboards and began to pull out everything they found. All at once a rough hand gripped Hernando by the throat and dragged him out of the sacristy, pushing him towards where the priest and his assistants were cowering. Hernando's face was cut as he fell to the floor.

Several other groups of Moriscos started manhandling the village's Christian families into the church. They pushed them up towards the altar where Hernando and the three churchmen were being guarded. By now, all Juviles was gathered inside the church. The Morisco women began dancing around the Christians, chanting their keen, ululating cries. In utter bewilderment, Hernando watched as one man urinated on the altar, another slashed the rope to silence the bell, and still others hacked at the holy images and altarpieces.

All the church's treasures were piled in front of the priest and the other Christians: chalices, patens, lamps, gold-embroidered robes; and, all the while, there was a deafening noise as the Morisco men shouted and the women whooped with delight. Hernando watched as two burly men tried to rip the gold door off the tabernacle. All at once, the noise of the chanting died away as his senses became fixed on a single image: his mother's ample breasts swaying to the rhythm of a wild dance. Her long black tresses hung loose over her shoulders; her tongue flicked in and out of her gaping mouth.

'Mother,' he whispered. What was she doing? This was a church! And . . . how could she show herself like that in front of all the men?

As if she had heard his frightened whisper, Aisha turned her face towards him. To Hernando it seemed she was doing this painfully slowly, but before he knew it, she was standing right in front of him.

'Let him go,' she ordered the Morisco men standing guard over him. 'He's my son. He's a Muslim.'

Hernando found it impossible to take his eyes off his mother's breasts, which now hung down limply.

'He's the Nazarene,' he heard one of the men shout behind his back.

Hearing his nickname brought Hernando back to reality.

The Nazarene again! He turned and saw who it was: an ill-tempered blacksmith his stepfather often quarrelled with. Grabbing her son by the arm, Aisha tried to drag him away, but the Morisco stopped her.

'Wait for your man to come back with the mules,' he said slyly. 'He will decide.'

Mother and son exchanged glances: her eyes had narrowed, and her mouth was drawn in a tight, tremulous line. All of a sudden, Aisha turned on her heels and ran off. Next to Hernando, the sacristan tried to put his arm round his shoulder, but the terrified boy instinctively backed away, and pushed against the guards to catch a glimpse of his mother. As soon as Aisha's black head of hair had disappeared beyond the church door, he became aware once more of the tumultuous noise inside.

Juviles became one huge celebration. The Moriscos sang and danced in the streets to the sound of pipes and tabors, rattles, drums, flutes and *dulzainas*. The doors to the Christian houses had been wrenched off their hinges. Brahim entered the village sitting proud and handsome on a dappled horse at the head of a band of armed Moriscos. His followers had difficulty pushing through the rejoicing crowd: all around them, men and women were celebrating the uprising.

The muleteer had been working in Cádiar when the revolt caught him by surprise. He had fought side by side with El Partal and his men against a company of fifty Christian harque-busiers, whom they had wiped out.

Brahim asked after the village's Christians, and several people paused in their rejoicing to point towards the church. He rode up to it on his horse. As he paused in the doorway while the horse panted nervously, the tumult inside died down sufficiently for the sound of Don Martín's feeble protest to be heard: 'Sacril—!'

A flurry of blows and kicks silenced the priest. As the noise swelled up again, Brahim urged his mount on over the debris of altarpieces, crosses and holy images that littered the church floor. Shihab, the village constable, waved from the altar where the Christians were gathered, and Brahim headed for him.

'The whole of the Alpujarra is up in arms,' Brahim shouted when he reached him. 'El Partal ordered me to bring the women, children and old Moriscos who cannot fight to seek refuge in Juviles castle. I have also left the booty we took in Cádiar there.'

Juviles castle was almost within gunshot range to the east of the village, perched on a rocky outcrop almost a thousand feet high. Built in the tenth century, its walls and several half-ruined towers were still standing, and it was big enough to contain all the refugees from Cádiar, as well as the spoils they had taken from that rich town.

'There are no Christians alive in Cádiar!' Brahim shouted exultantly.

'What shall we do with these?' Shihab asked, pointing to the captives by the altar.

Brahim was about to reply, when somebody shouted another question: 'And this one? What shall we do with him?' The blacksmith came out from behind the group of Christians, dragging Hernando with him.

Catching sight of his stepson, a cruel smile flitted across Brahim's face. Those blue Christian eyes of his! How he would love to tear them out . . .

'You've always said he was a Christian dog!' the blacksmith insisted.

It was true Brahim had said so a thousand times . . . but now he needed the lad. When Brahim had asked for the sword, harquebus and dappled horse that had belonged to Captain Herrera, the commander of the Christian garrison at Cádiar, El Partal had said straight out: 'Your job is as a mule-driver. We need you to transport the goods we take from these infidels to exchange for arms in Barbary. You won't need a horse to lead your mule teams.' But Brahim wanted that horse. And he burnt with desire to use the sword and the gun against the hated Christians.

'My stepson Hernando can look after the mules,' he had told El Partal almost without thinking. 'He is capable of it: he knows how to shoe and look after the animals, and they follow his commands. I will be in charge of whatever men you give me to guard the baggage and the spoils we transport.'

El Partal stroked his beard. Another of the Morisco leaders, El Zaguer, who knew Brahim well, spoke up on his behalf.

'He could be more useful as a soldier than a muleteer,' he said. 'He is brave and capable. And I know his child: he is good with the mules.'

'Very well,' said El Partal after a few moments' reflection. 'Take the people to Juviles and guard the possessions we have taken. You and your son will answer for them with your lives.'

And now here was the blacksmith insisting Hernando be kept captive as a Christian. Brahim muttered a few unintelligible words from the saddle.

'Your stepson is Christian!' the blacksmith shouted again. 'You have said so yourself time and again.'

'Tell him, Hernando!' Andrés said. The sacristan had struggled to his feet and approached the boy. One of the guards was about to throw himself on the sacristan, but Shihab held him back. 'Proclaim your faith in Christ!' Andrés cried, arms outstretched.

'Yes, my son. Pray to the one and only God,' added Don Martín, his bloody face bowed in pain. 'Commend yourself to the true—' A fresh blow cut him short.

Hernando surveyed the crowd of Muslims and Christians in front of him. What was he? Andrés had always paid more attention to him than to any of the other village boys. The sacristan had treated him better than his stepfather. 'He can speak Arabic and Spanish, he knows how to read, write and count,' was the extent of the Moriscos' interest in him. Yet Hamid had also taken care of him, and in the fields and his hovel had patiently taught him the Muslim prayers and doctrine. There were no more Christians alive in Cádiar! That was what Brahim had said. Drops of cold sweat pearled

Hernando's brow: if they decided he was a Christian, he would be condemned to . . . The shouting in the church had died down, and a small group of Moriscos were muttering amongst themselves by their captives.

Brahim's horse pawed the ground. Hernando was a Christian! his rider's eyes seemed to be saying. Wasn't he a priest's son? Didn't he know more about Christ's teachings than any Muslim? Perhaps his second son, Aquil, could take care of the mules? El Partal did not know his children. What if he told him . . . ?

'Make your mind up!' Shihab pressed him.

Brahim sighed; an evil smile appeared on his handsome face. 'You decide . . .'

'What is to be decided? What is going on here?'

Hamid's voice silenced the muttering voices. The old holy man was wearing a simple robe that showed off the gold sheath of the long scimitar hanging from a cord he wore as a belt. He was walking as upright as his withered leg allowed. The tinkling of the strips of metal hanging from the sword sounded through the church. Some of the Moriscos seemed to be trying to read the inscriptions.

'What is to be decided?' Hamid repeated.

Aisha was panting for breath behind him. Knowing Hamid's affection for her son and how respected the old man was in the village, she had run all the way to his hovel. Only he could save Hernando! If they were waiting for Brahim's decision, as the blacksmith had suggested . . . The boy's origins were never mentioned, but that was not necessary. Brahim never concealed his hatred: he treated Hernando badly and always talked contemptuously to him. If anyone in the village wanted to anger him, they had only to mention the Nazarene. Her husband always flew into a rage and cursed, and later the same night would take it out on Aisha. The only response she had found was to remind him time and again that she was the mother of his other four children. By devoting herself to them and winning their loyalty, she aroused in her husband the atavistic sense of a family clan that every

Muslim respects. As a consequence, Brahim yielded reluctantly to her. But at a moment like this . . . at a moment like this it would be not merely her husband, but the entire village in the grip of battle frenzy who would take it out on the Nazarene.

At the sight of the bare-breasted Aisha at his door, Hamid had lowered his eyes to the ground. 'Cover yourself,' he begged, as troubled as she was when she suddenly became aware of her half-naked state. He tried to understand what she was saying, holding up his hands for her to calm down and speak more slowly. When Aisha finally managed to explain herself, the old man did not hesitate for a second. The two of them rushed back to the church, Hamid limping along behind her as best he could.

'The boy is Christian!' the blacksmith insisted, still shaking Hernando roughly.

Hamid frowned. 'You, Yusuf' – he pointed to the blacksmith – 'recite the profession of faith.'

Many of the Moriscos in the church lowered their gaze, and the blacksmith hesitated.

'What has this got to do with—?' Brahim started to protest from his horse.

'Be quiet,' Hamid commanded, raising an arm. 'Pray!' he urged the blacksmith.

'There is no god but God, and Muhammad is the messenger of God,' Yusuf intoned.

'Go on.'

'That is the profession of faith. That's enough,' the blacksmith argued.

'No, it's not. In al-Andalus, it is not enough. Say the prayer of your forefathers, those you say you wish to avenge.'

Yusuf looked the holy man in the eye for a few seconds, but then looked down, as did most of the others.

'Say the prayer you should have taught your children, but which you have forgotten,' Hamid reproached him. 'Can anyone here recite the attributes of Allah, as is the custom in our lands?'

The old man surveyed the group of Moriscos. No one answered.

'You do it, Hernando,' he told the boy.

Hernando wriggled free from the blacksmith's grasp. He picked one of the gold-embroidered chasubles from the pile in front of the altar, hesitated for a second, then turned towards the kiblah and knelt on the silk garment.

'No!' shouted Andrés, but the guards around him pummelled him into silence. The sacristan raised his hands to his face and sobbed at the way his pupil was about to betray him.

Hernando began to recite: 'There is no god but God, and Muhammad is the messenger of God. He knows that all people must understand there is only one God in His kingdom. He created everything that exists in the world, the high and the low, the throne and the footstool, the heavens and the earth, and all that is in them and exists among them.' Hernando had begun uncertainly, but as he went on, his voice grew ever firmer. 'All living beings have been created by Your power; nothing moves without Your permission . . .'

Even the dappled horse stood quiet while Hernando prayed. Hamid listened contentedly with half-closed eyes. Aisha stood anxiously wringing her hands, as if trying to force the right words out of her son's mouth.

'He is the first and the last, He who shows Himself and conceals Himself. He knows everything that exists,' the boy concluded.

No one spoke until Hamid broke the silence: 'Who now dares maintain that this boy is Christian?'

5

ALL THE Christians from Juviles were locked in the church under Hamid's watchful eye. He was to try to get them to renounce their religion and convert to Islam.

Brahim set off north, towards the mountains, where El Partal had promised he would encourage the Moriscos to revolt. Brahim led a motley band consisting of half a dozen men, some armed with the guns they had seized from the harquebusiers of Cádiar, others with nothing more than sticks or slings. In the rear came Hernando. He was in charge of the mule team, augmented by six sturdy animals chosen by Brahim from those taken from Cádiar.

Hernando had been forced to run behind his stepfather's horse. When nobody in the church had dared challenge the old scholar, Brahim had spurred his mount out of the church, and ordered his stepson to follow. Hernando could not even say goodbye to Hamid or his mother; all he had managed was to smile at them as he went past. In the square outside, he found men and mules waiting.

'If you lose an animal or any load, I'll tear your eyes out.'

These were the only words his stepfather said to him before they all set out.

From then on, the boy's only concern was to keep the mules in line behind his stepfather's horse and the marching men. The Juviles mules obeyed his instructions; the new ones had minds of their own. The tallest of them snapped its teeth at him when he tried to force it into line. Hernando jumped nimbly aside, but when he went to punish the animal he found he was empty-handed.

'I'll see to you,' he muttered to himself. The mule trotted on unconcernedly while Hernando searched round for a weapon. A stick will do, he thought. The mules were not stupid, but that one in particular needed to be taught a lesson. With his stepfather so close by, he could not allow any of them to disobey him or he would be the one to be punished. He picked up a good-sized stone and ran back to the mule's right-hand side, concealing his arm behind his back. As soon as it realized he was there, the animal tried again to bite him, but Hernando struck it hard on the jaw with the stone. The mule shook its head and brayed loudly. Hernando gave it a push, and it submissively rejoined the line. When he looked up, he saw his stepfather had turned in the saddle and was watching him closely, ready to punish him immediately if he did anything wrong.

They continued climbing towards Alcútar. They were advancing in single file along a narrow track with Juviles still in sight down below when the sound of a loud voice echoed across the ravines, streams and hillsides. Hernando came to a halt. A shiver ran down his spine. How often he had heard Hamid! Even in the distance, the boy could recognize the old holy man's voice as it rang out proud, strong and defiantly, as happily as on the evening Hamid had shown him the Prophet's sword.

'Come to prayer!' they all heard Hamid calling, probably from the church tower.

The call to prayer bounced off cliffs, rolled among the boulders and penetrated the thick vegetation, until it filled the entire valley of the Alpujarra, from the Sierra Nevada to the Contraviesa, and then rose up to the heavens. It had been more than sixty years since the call of a muezzin had sounded here!

The group came to a halt. Hernando looked up at the sun. Then he stood upright to make sure his shadow was twice his height: it was the exact moment for prayer.

'There is no strength and power but in Allah, the excellent and great,' he murmured, joining in with the others. This was the response they had given every day in their homes, either at night or noon, taking the utmost care to make sure no Christian could hear them from the street.

'Allah is great!' Brahim shouted, standing upright on his stirrups and brandishing an harquebus high above his head.

At the sight of his stepfather's ruthless face, Hernando shrank back in fear.

Brahim's shout was taken up by all the men following him. Brahim waved his harquebus for them to set off again. Before he renewed his march, one of the men wiped the back of his hand across his eyes. Hernando heard him snuffling and clearing his throat, as though trying to keep back tears. He urged the mules on again, Hamid's call to prayer still echoing in his mind.

In Alcútar, situated at a little more than a league from Juviles, they were received with the same dancing, chants and celebrations as they had left behind in their own village. El Partal, after encouraging the villagers to rise up, had moved on with his men to nearby Narila, where he had been born.

Like all the villages in the high Alpujarra, Alcútar was a maze of narrow streets that crisscrossed the mountainside, lined by small, whitewashed houses with flat roofs. Brahim headed for the church.

A group of between fifteen and twenty Christians were gathered in front of it. They were closely guarded by Moriscos armed with sticks who shouted at them and beat them into line, like shepherds with their flocks. Hernando could see the terrified eyes of a young girl whose straw-coloured hair stood out among the Christians; she was staring at the body of the deacon, which lay riddled with arrows by the church front. As the Moriscos passed by, they spat on it or scornfully kicked the slumped body. Next to him on his knees was a young man whose right hand had been sliced off. He was trying in vain to stop the blood haemorrhaging as his life drained away. The blood stained the sleet-covered ground, while nearby, to the delight of some Morisco children, a dog was playing with the severed hand.

'Load up the booty!'

Brahim's voice rang out just as the most daring of the children stole the hand from the dog and threw it at the feet of the mutilated Christian. The dog ran after it, but before it could reach the stricken man, a woman cackled, spat on him, and kicked the severed hand away again, for the dog to do its worst with.

Hernando shook his head and followed the armed men into the church. The straw-haired Christian girl, her hair soaked by the falling sleet, was still staring wide-eyed at the deacon's body.

Soon afterwards, he re-emerged, his arms laden with the gold-embroidered silk vestments and a pair of silver candelabra. Hernando threw them on to the heap of goods piling up outside the church. He bent down to pick up a woollen cape that had been looted from one of the Christian houses. Brahim frowned at him from atop his horse.

'Do you want me to die of cold?' Hernando said, anticipating his stepfather's reprimand.

By the time the sun began to set and a red line was painted above the peaks surrounding the Alpujarra, the twelve mules were weighed down with the spoils. The body of the young Christian who had bled to death lay on top of the deacon's. The other Christians remained huddled together nervously outside the church. The voice of the village muezzin rang out, and the Moriscos laid out the silk and linen garments in the freezing mud and prostrated themselves in prayer.

The red sky had turned to black and the sunset prayers had been said when El Partal and his men returned to Alcútar. His band of thirty ruffians – some of them on horseback, others on foot, all of them well wrapped up and armed with crossbows, swords or harquebuses, and all wearing daggers at their belts – had been joined by some armed villagers from Narila, who were now trying to control the line of Christians they had brought with them. El Partal's men did not seem to mind the cold or the falling sleet: they were talking and laughing among themselves. Beyond them, Hernando saw there was another mule team loaded with the spoils from Narila.

The new prisoners joined the already numerous Christians outside the church. The Moriscos lashed out if any of them attempted to talk to the newcomers, so that in a short while silence reigned once more. The Morisco children ran in among the armed band, admiring their daggers and swelling with pride if any of them ruffled their hair. Brahim and the Alcútar constable welcomed El Partal, and then withdrew to one side to talk with him. Hernando saw his stepfather pointing in his direction, and noticed how El Partal nodded. El Partal then pointed to the mules carrying the booty from Narila, and gestured as if to call their mule-driver over, but Brahim was obviously against the idea. In spite of the distance and the fact that only a few torches pierced the gloom, Hernando realized that the two men were arguing. Brahim was gesticulating and shaking his head: it was plain they were discussing the new muleteer. El Partal seemed to be trying to calm things down and to convince Brahim of something. Eventually they appeared to reach an agreement, and the Morisco leader called the recently arrived mule-driver over to give him instructions. The man offered Brahim his hand, but the other refused, and stared at him warily.

'Have you understood what your place is?' Brahim growled at him, glancing at El Partal out of the corner of his eye. The Narila mule-driver nodded. 'Your reputation goes ahead of you: I don't want any problems with you, your mules or your way of working. I hope I won't have to remind you of that,' Brahim said by way of farewell.

The man's name was Cecilio, but on the mountain trails he was known as Ubaid of Narila. That was how he proudly presented himself to Hernando, after he had followed Brahim's orders and led his team of mules over to join the young lad.

'I'm Hernando,' he replied.

Ubaid waited.

'Hernando?' was all he said when it became obvious the boy was not going to add anything more.

'Yes. Just Hernando,' he replied firmly, although Ubaid was several years older than him and a professional muleteer.

Ubaid laughed sarcastically, then immediately turned his back to attend to his animals.

If he heard what my nickname was . . . thought Hernando, feeling his stomach muscles clench. Perhaps I should adopt a Muslim name.

That night the Moriscos feasted on food and grain looted from the Christians' houses and celebrated the success of the uprising in the Alpujarra. All the Morisco villages in the region had joined them, El Partal said joyously. Now there was only Granada!

While the leading men of the village looked after the armed bands, the Christians were shut in the church under the care of the village scholar. Like Hamid in Juviles, he was charged with attempting to convert them to Islam. Hernando and Ubaid stayed with the mules and the booty, protected from the sleet in a rough shed. The women of the village did not forget them, however, and brought them quantities of food. Hernando quickly sated his hunger, and so did Ubaid, but once his stomach was full, he wanted to satisfy his other appetites, and Hernando noticed him pawing any woman who came near. Some of them sidled up to him as well, sitting next to him and encouraging his advances. Hernando shrank back and looked away, until the women left him alone.

'What's the matter, boy? Are you scared of them?' asked his companion. The food and the women's company seemed to have put him in a better mood. 'There's nothing to be afraid of, is there?' he said, addressing one of them.

The woman laughed out loud, and Hernando blushed. The muleteer from Narila sneered: 'Or are you afraid of what your stepfather might say? You two don't seem to get on very well.'

Hernando said nothing.

'Well, there's no surprise in that,' Ubaid concluded. His mouth twisted in a complicit smile that in no way improved his filthy, slovenly looks. 'Don't worry, he's too busy playing the big man ... but you and I are far closer to what really matters, aren't we?'

At that moment, the woman pestering Ubaid demanded more attention from him. The muleteer shot Hernando a glance he did not fully comprehend, and then sank his head between the woman's breasts.

Later on, Ubaid went off with another woman. As he watched them leave, Hernando recalled what the Juviles sacristan had told him: 'The new Christians, those Morisco women,' he had explained in one of the many doctrinal lessons he had given the boy in the sacristy, 'indulge in the arts of love by disporting themselves shamelessly with their husbands ... or with those who they are not married to! Of course, marriage does not mean much to the Moors: it is nothing more than a contract similar to that for buying a cow or renting a piece of land.' The sacristan treated Hernando as though he were an old Christian, descended from a long line of Christians, rather than the son of a Morisco woman. 'Both men and women indulge in the vices of the flesh, in a way that is repellent to our Christ the Lord. That is why they are all so fat, so dark and fat, because their only wish is to give their men pleasure, to sleep with them like bitches on heat. And if their husbands are away, they turn to adultery; they fall into the sins of gluttony and sloth. They spend the whole day gossiping; all they want to do is pass the time until they can receive their men again with open arms.'

'Christian women can be fat too,' Hernando had been tempted to reply, 'and some of them have far darker skin than the Morisco women,' but in the end he had kept quiet, as he always did with the sacristan.

Christmas Day dawned cold and clear in the Sierra Nevada.

'They will not renounce their faith,' the Alcútar scholar told El Partal and the other Moriscos gathered outside the church.

'If I talk to them about the true God and His Prophet, they reply by saying their Christian prayers together. If I threaten to punish them, they commend themselves to Christ. We have beaten them, but the more we do that, the more they call on their god. We have taken their crosses and medallions from them, but they go on crossing themselves.'

'They will give way,' El Partal growled. 'Cuxurio de Bérchules rose up last night. El Seniz and other leaders are expecting us there. Gather up the spoils,' he said, addressing Brahim. 'And bring the Christians out of the church. We'll take them to Cuxurio.'

About eighty people were dragged out of the church with shouts and blows. When they saw the furious mob outside, the women and children began to cry, and many raised their eyes to the heavens and prayed; others made the sign of the cross.

El Partal waited until all the Christians were outside, then went to look them over.

'May Christ bring down—'

The bandit leader silenced the Christian's threat with a violent thrust from his crossbow. The thin, small man fell to his knees, blood trickling from his mouth. A woman who must have been his wife ran to help him, but El Partal sent her sprawling too. He screwed up his eyes until his dark brows formed a single menacing line. All the Moriscos of Alcútar were present. The Christians remained silent.

'Take off your clothes!' El Partal commanded. 'All men and boys aged over ten are to strip!'

The Christian men looked at each other incredulously. How could they strip off in front of their wives, their neighbours' wives, their daughters? There was a rumble of protest.

'Take off your clothes!' El Partal ordered an old man with a straggly beard who was standing in front of him, a whole head smaller than he was. The man's only reply was to cross himself. The outlaw slowly drew his long, heavy sword. He pressed the sharp point on the old man's Adam's apple, until a drop of blood appeared. He insisted: 'Obey me!'

Defiantly, the old man dropped his hands to his sides. Without hesitation, El Partal plunged the sword into his throat.

'You. Strip!' he ordered the next man, raising his bloody sword again. The Christian turned pale. He looked at his neighbour choking to death beside him, and slowly began to undo his shirt. 'All of you,' barked El Partal.

Many of the Christian women lowered their gaze or covered their daughters' eyes. The Moriscos burst out laughing.

Ubaid, who had been closely following what had happened, walked off towards the mules. Hernando followed him; they had to prepare for departure.

'The poor things are going to be really weighed down!' the muleteer observed ironically. 'Nobody knows exactly what they are carrying. Perhaps that's just as well; if by chance something were lost, nobody would notice . . .'

Taken aback, Hernando turned to look at him. What had he meant by that? But Ubaid seemed to be concentrating on his task, as though what he had said had been nothing more than a stray comment. Yet, almost without thinking, Hernando heard himself reply in a stronger voice than usual: 'Nothing is going to get lost! All these spoils belong to our people.'

Neither of them said anything more.

The procession finally left Alcútar; Brahim, El Partal and his men led the way. Behind them came a line of more than forty Christian men. They were naked and barefoot, shivering from the cold, and had their hands tied behind their backs. Their terrified women and Christian children under ten brought up the rear, together with the twenty or so mules carrying the booty Hernando and Ubaid were keeping a watchful eye on. Scattered among the others were the village lads who had decided to join the uprising. They cursed the Christians, and threatened them with a thousand horrific tortures if they did not renounce their faith and convert to Islam.

Even though Cuxurio de Bérchules was less than a quarter of a league from Alcútar, the harsh terrain soon began to cut the

Christian men's bare feet, and Hernando noticed several stones stained with blood. All of a sudden, one of the line fell to the ground: to judge by his thin legs and lack of hair in the groin, he must have been a young boy. Their hands tied, none of the other men were able to help him. When some of the women tried to do so, the Moriscos pushed them away, kicking out at the fallen boy. Hernando saw the straw-haired girl fling herself on him.

'Leave him alone!' she cried, kneeling beside the boy and shielding his head with her arms.

'Ask your god to help him up,' shouted one of the youths.

'Renounce your faith!' another one hissed.

The small group formed by the fallen boy, the girl and the four armed youths was preventing the lead mule from advancing.

'What's going on?' Hernando heard Ubaid calling from behind.

Hernando reached the group just as one of the Morisco men added his voice to Ubaid's: 'If you don't move on, we'll kill you!'

Hernando saw the boy's huddled body, and the look of terror on his face, even though his eyes were tight shut. He spoke without even thinking: 'If you kill them you won't be able to . . . we won't be able to . . .' he said, instantly correcting himself, '. . . we won't be able to convert them to the true faith.'

All four Moriscos turned to confront him. They were much older and stronger than him.

'Who are you to tell us what to do?'

'Who are you to kill them?' Hernando said defiantly.

'Look after your mules, boy—'

Hernando cut him short, and spat on the ground. 'Why don't you ask him what you should do?' he said, pointing to El Partal's broad back as he rode at the front of the line. 'Don't you think he would already have killed them in Alcútar if that's what he wanted?'

The four young men looked uneasily at each other and finally decided to move off, though not before they launched a few more kicks at the fallen Christian. With the girl's help, Hernando moved the boy off the path so that the mule team could get by; held under the arms by Hernando and the straw-haired girl, he was gasping for air. Ubaid had watched the scene without comment, seeming to be weighing up the situation. So Brahim's stepson had more guts than he had at first thought . . . At that moment, Hernando was helping the girl lift the boy on to La Vieja's back.

'Why did you defend him?' Hernando asked her. 'They could have killed you.'

'He's my brother,' she replied, her face bathed in tears. 'My only brother. He's a good boy,' she added, as if begging for mercy.

As the pair of them walked alongside La Vieja, she told him her name was Isabel and her brother was known as Gonzalico. She did not say much more than that, but it was enough for Hernando to realize the great affection they had for each other.

The scene in Cuxurio de Bérchules was similar to that in all the villages where the revolt had broken out: the church had been sacked and desecrated; the Moriscos were celebrating; and the Christians were being held prisoner. Another armed band under the command of Lope el Seniz was waiting there for them. The outlaw leaders decided to give the Christians one more chance, but this time, given the lack of results in Alcútar, they instructed the scholars to threaten to abuse, violate and kill their women if they refused to convert to Islam.

'He is like a young religious teacher,' Brahim blustered to El Partal and El Seniz when they were surprised at the sight of his stepson, La Vieja with the Christian boy on its back, and Isabel walking into the village. 'Do you know Hamid from Juviles?' The two men nodded. Who in the Alpujarra had not heard of the lame Hamid? 'He has taken the boy under his wing. He has taught him the true faith,' Brahim explained.

El Partal narrowed his eyes and watched Hernando, the mule and the boy arrive. Seeing such a young boy convert could do more to undermine the faith of those stubborn Christians than any threat, he thought to himself.

'Come over here,' he ordered Hernando. 'If what your step-father says is true, tonight you will stay with the young Christian boy and make him renounce his faith.'

While the rebellious Moriscos were attempting to convert the Christians, the uprising in the Alpujarra suffered its first important setback. On that same Christmas night, neither the Moriscos in Granada nor those on the plains joined the uprising. Farax, the rich dyer who was leading the rebellion, entered the Albaicín at the head of 180 armed men, all of them disguised as Turks to give the impression that reinforcements had landed. They ran through the Morisco quarter of Granada calling for the populace to join them. But while they chased up and down the twisting streets, the few Christian soldiers in the garrison barricaded themselves in the Alhambra. Worse still, the doors and windows of the Morisco houses stayed shut.

'How many of you are there?' someone demanded through a gap in a window.

'Six thousand,' Farax lied.

'There are too few of you, and you've come too soon.'

At that, the window slammed shut.

6

W HEN GONZALICO was forced to hand back the blankets that had protected him during the night, he began to tremble.

'Has he renounced his faith?' one of El Seniz's armed followers asked Hernando at first light.

Hernando and Gonzalico had talked long into the night beside a bonfire in the field where the mules were resting. The outlaw's question surprised them as they sat quietly beside the fire, staring at its embers. Renounced it? No: Gonzalico had proclaimed his faith with a child's voice but an adult's conviction. He had prayed to his God. He had entrusted his soul to the Christian Lord.

Hernando shook his head sadly. The soldier roughly dragged Gonzalico off. All Hernando could see were his tiny feet scurrying away towards the village.

Should he follow them? What if the boy renounced his faith in the end? He raised his head from the embers, which were now dying. 'Like Gonzalico's life!' he said to himself. Perhaps the boy would not live long enough to burn as brightly and as passionately as the fire had done that night. He was only a boy! He watched Gonzalico trotting along, trying to keep up with the Morisco, stumbling as he trod on a rock, or falling and being dragged along for a few steps before he could recover his feet. Tears welled up in Hernando's eyes. He stood up to follow the pair.

'Your kings forced us to give up our faith,' Hernando had tried to explain to Gonzalico. 'And we did so. They had all of us baptized.' Gonzalico did not take his huge grey-brown eyes off him. 'So now that we are going to reign—'

'You will never reign in heaven,' the boy interrupted him.

'If that were true,' he remembered saying, without wanting to get drawn into any discussion about it, 'why does it matter if you renounce your faith here on earth?'

The boy looked startled. 'Renounce Christ?' he said, in the faintest of voices.

Why were these Christians so stubborn? Hernando told him of the fatwa decreed by the mufti of Oran when the Spanish Muslims were forced to convert: 'If they force you to drink wine, then drink it, but do not make a vice of it,' the Muslim scholar had instructed his brothers in al-Andalus, a ruling which all the Moriscos had accepted. 'And the mufti said: "If they force you to eat pork, eat it against your will and in the knowledge that it is forbidden." All of which means that if you are forced to do something against your will,' Hernando explained, 'you are not in fact abandoning your faith – provided you remain true to your God.'

'You are admitting your own heresy,' Gonzalico insisted.

Hernando sighed and looked away at La Vieja, who was still close by them, dozing as she stood upright.

'You will be killed,' he declared eventually.

'I will die for Christ,' the boy exclaimed, with a shudder that neither the darkness nor the blanket wrapped around him could hide.

At this, they both fell silent. Hernando heard Gonzalico crying softly. *I will die for Christ!* But he was no more than a boy! Hernando looked for another blanket to cover him with, and although he knew he was not asleep, stretched out beside him.

'Thank you,' Gonzalico snuffled.

Thank you? Hernando said to himself as he felt the boy's hand reaching out from under the blankets to clutch one of his own. He let him hold on tightly until the sobs gave way to the sound of regular breathing. For the rest of the night he stayed next to Gonzalico, not daring to let go of his hand in case he woke up.

They had woken shortly before El Seniz's armed bandits arrived. Gonzalico smiled at Hernando, but when Hernando tried to respond, the smile froze on his face. How could Gonzalico smile? He's only an innocent child! he told himself. The night, their talk, the danger, the different gods: all that was in the past, and now he was simply a little boy again. Wasn't this a new day? Wouldn't the sun shine just as it always did? Hernando did not insist again that he renounce his faith, and now smiled openly at him.

They had nothing to eat.

'We'll eat later on,' Gonzalico said in his childish voice.

'Yes, later,' Hernando forced himself to agree.

Not a single one of the Christians had renounced their faith. *I will die for Christ . . .* Hernando recalled the boy's defiant affirmation as he saw him being thrown into the crowd of Christian men who had been herded naked outside the church in the centre of Cuxurio. The wild ululations of the Morisco women mingled with the tears of the Christian women, who were kept at a distance from their fathers, husbands and sons. If any of them looked down or closed their eyes, the Moriscos immediately beat them and forced them to watch. All the Christian men from Alcútar, Narila and Cuxurio de Bérchules were there: more than eighty of them, from old men to children over ten. El Seniz and El Partal were arguing with the scholar who had been with the Christians all night. El Seniz was the first to move away: he headed straight for the group of Christians. He stood in front of them, lit the fuse on his ancient gold-inlaid harquebus and placed it in the serpentine.

Everyone in the square fell silent. All of them were staring at the sputtering linen rag soaked in saltpetre.

El Seniz leant the gun butt on the ground, and then poured

gunpowder into the barrel. He put a small piece of rag in and tamped it down with a ramrod. El Seniz was concentrating entirely on his weapon. He dropped a lead ball in, and rammed that down too. He raised the gun and took aim.

A cry went up from the group of Christians. One woman fell to her knees, hands raised in prayer, but a Morisco pulled her by the hair, forcing her to watch. El Seniz did not even turn his head, but poured fine powder into the flash pan. Then, without warning, he shot a Christian straight in the chest.

'Allah is great!' he cried. The sound of the shot echoed in the air. 'Kill them! Kill them all!'

The outlaws, youths and Morisco villagers flung themselves on the Christians, wielding harquebuses, lances, swords, daggers and even farming tools. Cuxurio was in uproar. The Morisco women and youths held back the Christian women and forced them to witness the massacre. Naked and over-whelmed by the enraged mob, their men could do nothing to defend themselves. Some of them knelt down, making the sign of the cross. Others tried to protect their sons in their arms. Hernando watched the scene with the Christian women. A huge Morisco woman thrust a knife in his hand and urged him to join the killing. The knife-blade glinted as the woman pushed him forward. Hernando took a step towards the men under attack. What was he to do? How could he kill anyone? As he advanced, Gonzalico's sister Isabel rushed forward and gripped his hand.

'Save him!' she begged.

Save him? He was supposed to kill him! The enormous Morisco woman was staring at him, and . . .

He seized Isabel by the arm and moved behind her. Pressing the knife to her throat, he forced her to watch the massacre, as other men were doing with their captives. This seemed to satisfy the Morisco woman.

'Save him,' Isabel said over and over between her sobs, with-out making any attempt to free herself.

Her pleas seared Hernando's chest.

Still he forced her to watch and, over her shoulder, he did the same. Ubaid had headed straight for Gonzalico. For a moment the mule-driver turned to look back at Hernando and Isabel, then he seized the little boy by the hair and twisted his head until his throat was exposed. The boy did not resist. Ubaid slashed his throat, silencing the prayer forming on his lips. Isabel stopped pleading with Hernando, and seemed to stop breathing too. Ubaid let the dead boy's body slump forward, and then knelt down to plunge his dagger in the back. He searched until he found the heart, pulled it out, and with a triumphant shout raised it high in the air as the blood streamed down his arm. He rushed back towards Isabel and Hernando and flung it at their feet.

Hernando had relaxed his grip on the girl, but she still clung to him. Neither of them could bear to look down at the heart, but kept their eyes on Ubaid as he rejoined the slaughter. The deacon Montoya had one eye gouged out before the mob stabbed him time and again; another two priests were martyred with crossbow bolts fired at them until their bodies bristled with arrows; still others were hacked to pieces before they expired. One man was frenziedly plunging a hoe into an unrecognizable bloody mass. A Morisco ran over to the captive Christian women brandishing a head on a pole, then he danced about, waving it in their faces. Eventually, the shrieking turned into chants of celebration at the cruel massacre. *I will die for Christ.* Hernando could not take his eyes off Gonzalico's mutilated body, piled with the others in front of the church in a sea of blood. He forced back his tears. A few armed Moriscos clambered over the bodies, finishing off any they thought might still be alive; the rest were laughing and talking among themselves. Somebody began to play a clarinet, and the Morisco villagers started to dance. Nobody paid any attention to the captive Christian women. The same enormous Morisco woman who had given Hernando the dagger pulled Isabel away from him and shoved her with the others. Then she demanded the dagger back.

Hernando was still clutching it. He could not tear his gaze away from the pile of bodies.

'Give me the dagger,' the woman insisted.

Hernando did not move.

She shook him roughly. 'My dagger!' Hernando mechanically passed it to her. 'What's your name?'

When his only reply was a confused stammer, she shook him again.

'What's your name?'

'Hamid,' said Hernando, coming back to reality. 'Ibn Hamid.'

The same day as the massacre at Cuxurio de Bérchules, El Seniz, El Partal and their men received orders from Farax, the dyer from the Albaicín who was one of the leaders of the uprising, to take the booty and the female Christian captives to the castle at Juviles. On Christmas Day at Béznar, a village at the western entrance to the Alpujarra, the Moriscos proclaimed Don Fernando de Válor as King of Granada and Córdoba.

Like Hamid, the new King was a descendant of the Muslim royal house of Granada. Unlike the scholar of Juviles, however, he claimed to descend from the Umayyad dynasty of the caliphs of Córdoba. And again unlike Hamid, his family had integrated with the Christians after the fall of Granada. His father had become a councillor, forming part of the group of nobles who dominated and ran the city government, until he was condemned to the galleys for a crime. His son inherited his position, but was soon also put on trial, accused of killing the man who betrayed his father and several witnesses to the crime. Don Fernando de Válor then sold the councillor's position to another Morisco who had been his guarantor at the trial, but this man, who did not entirely trust Don Fernando and was afraid he might lose his surety, arranged things so that at the moment he paid for purchasing the right to be councillor, the authorities immediately seized the money on his behalf. On 24 December 1568, learning of the uprising in the Alpujarra,

Don Fernando de Válor y de Córdoba fled Granada, no longer a councillor and no longer a rich man. With only a lover and a negro slave for company, he went to join those who, he argued, were his true people.

The new King of Granada and Córdoba was twenty-two years old. His skin was a dark olive colour; his dark eyebrows formed one solid line above his big dark eyes. Courteous and distinguished-looking, he was loved and respected by all the Moriscos, both for the high position he had held in Granada and for his royal blood. He was proclaimed King at Béznar, under an olive tree, surrounded by a huge gathering of Moriscos. Farax was violently opposed to the idea, as he claimed the title for himself, but the new monarch silenced him by appointing him his chancellor. The dyer kissed the ground beneath the new King's feet after Don Fernando, dressed in purple, had prayed on four banners laid out to the four cardinal points, and had sworn to die in his kingdom and in the faith and teaching of Muhammad. He was crowned King with a tin crown stolen from a statue of the Virgin, and given the name Muhammad ibn Umayya (which the Christians turned into Aben Humeya) to the acclamation of all those present.

7

ABEN HUMEYA'S first measure was to send Farax through the Alpujarra at the head of an army of three hundred battle-hardened men. They were to gather all the booty so that it could be traded for weapons from the Berbers. This meant Hernando had to set off once more with his mule team to the castle at Juviles. He dreaded being with Ubaid again: he could not erase the image of the mule-driver's crazed features as he joined the slaughter at Juviles. He also remembered what Ubaid had said about how some of the spoils might accidentally be lost.

'I have to keep an eye on La Vieja,' Hernando told him. 'She's always lagging behind.' Hernando wanted to make sure he brought up the rear: he did not like the idea of having Ubaid behind his back.

'An old mule eats as much as a young one,' Ubaid retorted. 'Kill it.' Hernando did not reply. 'Do you want me to do that for you too?' the muleteer added, moving his hand towards the dagger at his belt.

'This mule knows the trails of the Alpujarra better than you do,' Hernando blurted out.

They stared at each other; Ubaid's eyes flashed with hatred. He was muttering something under his breath when a shout from Brahim made him turn his head. The line of captive Christian women had already set off, and it was time for the mules to get under way too. Ubaid frowned, shouted back at Brahim, then made his way to the front of the mule team, glaring angrily at Hernando as he did so.

It was then that Ubaid decided he had to get rid of the lad. After all, he represented Brahim, the muleteer from Juviles with whom he had had so many problems on the trails of the Alpujarra ... as he had with most of the other drivers. The gold and other valuables they were carrying had aroused Ubaid's greed. Who would notice if some went missing? Nobody was checking what they loaded the mules with. Yes, his people's fight was important, but some day it would be over, and would he then still be nothing more than a poor mule-driver forced to roam the snowy peaks to scrape a miserable living? He had no desire to do that. The Moriscos' victory would not be threatened if they had a little less treasure. He had tried to enlist Hernando on his side, to win him over by reminding him how badly they both got on with his stepfather, but the stubborn fool had not shown any interest. So be it! Too bad for him! Now was the time, at the start of the uprising, before everyone became more organized. Later on ... later on, who knew how many muleteers might join them, or what arrangements the new King might make? Anyway, it was obvious that nobody, not even his stepfather, would miss this boy they called the Nazarene.

Ubaid knew the trail well. He chose a bend in the narrow track winding along by the mountainside. Rocky outcrops made it impossible to see who was in front or behind, and it was so narrow that no one could turn round: nobody could catch him by surprise. The mules were at the back of the line; last of all came La Vieja and Hernando. It would be easy for Ubaid: he could hide round the bend, slit the boy's throat when he appeared, put him on a well-loaded mule, then hide the body and the animal in one of the many caves in the mountain. He would not even have to slow up. Everyone would think that Hernando had gone off with part of the spoils. It would be Brahim's fault for trusting in a bastard Nazarene; all Ubaid needed to do was return after nightfall and hide his share of the booty until the war was over.

He put his plan into practice. He urged his mules forward. Used to these trails, the animals moved on obediently. He drew his knife and raised it as the first mules of Hernando's team came round the bend. Ubaid knew there were twelve of them. He counted as they went past, pushing them on without a word. When the eleventh mule appeared round the corner, Ubaid stiffened: after the last one had gone by, it was the boy's turn.

But La Vieja halted. Hernando shouted for her to continue, but the beast stubbornly refused: she knew there was someone lurking round the corner.

'What's wrong, Vieja?' Hernando said, making his way round her to see what . . .

As the boy approached the bend, the mule backed into him, as if trying to prevent him going any further. He stood rooted to the spot. All at once, Ubaid appeared on the path, brandishing his weapon; the other mules were some distance away, so he had to finish it quickly. Protected behind La Vieja, Hernando at first made to run, but then changed his mind, and instead seized a big silver five-branched candelabrum from one of the bags.

The two faced each other, the mule between them. Hernando, his back covered in a sweat that was colder than the mountain air, tried desperately to keep his arms and body steady as he threatened the Narila mule-driver with the heavy candelabrum. To their right lay a bottomless ravine. Ubaid glanced down at it: one blow with that candelabrum . . .

'Just you dare!' Hernando shrieked nervously at him.

Ubaid weighed up the situation, then stuck his knife back in his belt.

'I thought you were being pursued by Christians,' he said cynically, before turning his back and striding off.

Hernando did not even watch him go. The candelabrum was suddenly so heavy he had to struggle to get it back in the saddlebag. He was trembling even more now than he had done when he confronted Ubaid. He could scarcely control his hands. He leant against La Vieja's hindquarters and gratefully patted her haunch. Then he slowly continued on his way, making sure that the mule went round every bend ahead of him.

It was late evening on Saint Stephen's Day by the time that, accompanied by a gaggle of young children, they climbed the steep slope up to the castle at Juviles. Hernando was still keeping a watchful eye on Ubaid, who was at the front of the mule teams. As they approached the castle, they could hear music and smell the food being cooked inside. When their fathers, husbands or sons had joined the revolt, the women, children and old people from Cádiar had taken refuge here, together with many more from all over the Alpujarra. Inside the fortification, some of whose nine defensive towers still rose high above the plain, dozens of stalls and shacks made from branches and cloth tarpaulins made it seem like a colourful fair. Camp fires had been lit in the spaces between the stalls; animals, children and old people were all packed in together, while the womenfolk in their bright Morisco robes were all busy cooking. The cheerful noise and the cooking smells helped Hernando relax: the food was nothing like the stews and soups the Christians made from their vegetables and pork; here everything was cooked in oil. They were warmly received by everyone as they went by. One woman offered him a sweet made of almonds and honey; another a fried dumpling; and a third a pastry with preserves dusted in flour. There were groups of musicians playing pipes and tabors, drums, *dulzainas* and rebecs. Hernando took a bite of the pastry, and his mouth was filled with the flavours of sugar, starch, amber, red coral and pearls, deer's heart and orange-blossom water. Soon afterwards, floating on the air among the women, the singing and the dancing, he could make out the aroma of lamb, hare and venison, as well as the herbs and spices they were being cooked in: coriander, mint, thyme, as well as cinnamon, aniseed, dill and a thousand others. The mules threaded their way laboriously through the crowds to the far side of the castle yard, next to the ruins of the former citadel where the booty seized in Cádiar was being stored. The Morisco women threw themselves on the new female Christian prisoners, stripping them of their few possessions before setting them to work.

With the help of the men Brahim had ordered to guard the booty, Hernando and Ubaid began to unload the mules and store the valuables. They watched each other warily as they did so. They were busy transporting the spoils into the citadel when they heard the noise of singing and dancing gradually die away. Hamid's voice could clearly be heard, calling everyone to prayer from the bell tower at Juviles, now transformed into a minaret. There were two wells inside the castle, providing clean, pure water from the mountains. The two men performed their ablutions and said their prayers, and then went back to the unloading: inside the citadel was a considerable treasure of all the valuables, jewellery and money seized from the Christians.

Hernando gazed at all the piled-up gold and silver. He was so absorbed he did not realize Ubaid was close behind him. After the night prayer, the gloom in the citadel was pierced only by the light from a pair of burning torches. The din in the courtyard had started up again. Brahim was talking to the guards at the entrance to the citadel.

Ubaid jostled Hernando as he passed by. 'Next time, you won't be so lucky,' he growled.

Next time! Hernando said to himself. The man was a thief and a murderer! They were alone together. He looked at Ubaid, and thought for a few moments. What if . . . ?

'You dog!' Hernando insulted him.

The mule-driver turned in surprise, to find Hernando flinging himself on him. Ubaid knocked him away with a powerful blow. Hernando stumbled more than necessary and landed on the Morisco spoils, right on top of a small cross with gold and pearls that he had spied shortly before. Their scuffle attracted the attention of Brahim and the soldiers.

'What . . . ?' Brahim started to say, striding into the citadel. 'What are you doing with our booty?'

'I fell. I tripped over,' Hernando stammered, shaking out his clothes as he concealed the cross in his right hand.

Ubaid was looking on in bewilderment. Why had the boy suddenly attacked him like that?

'Clumsy oaf,' Hernando's stepfather rebuked him, coming over to the heap of treasure to make sure nothing was broken.

'I'm going down to Juviles,' Hernando told him abruptly.

'You're staying here . . .' Brahim objected.

'What do you mean?' Hernando raised his voice and flung his arms out. He had stuffed the cross in his belt, and concealed it behind a smock he had grabbed from the pile of Christian clothing from Alcútar. 'Come and see!'

He marched out of the citadel and went over to the teams of mules. Confused, Brahim followed close behind.

'This one has a shoe loose.' Hernando lifted the front leg of one of the mules and shook the iron shoe. 'That one over there is starting to get a sore on its back.' In order to reach the animal, Hernando slid in between Ubaid's mules. 'No, not that one,' he said from in among the animals.

He stood on tiptoe, arms by his sides, as if looking for which animal was the injured one. As he did so, he slid the cross into the saddlebag of one of Ubaid's mules.

'That one, yes, that's the one.' He went over to the mule and lifted her bags. His hands were trembling and sweaty, but the wound he had spotted earlier was clear for his stepfather to see. 'And this one here must have something wrong with her mouth, because she refuses to eat,' he lied. 'My tools and medicines are down in the village.'

Brahim glanced at the animals. 'All right,' he agreed after

considering them for a few moments. 'You can go down to Juviles, but be ready to come back at once if I say so.'

Hernando smiled at Ubaid, who was standing with the guards in the citadel doorway. The muleteer glowered at him, and narrowed his eyes when he saw the youth smile. He raised a warning forefinger in Hernando's direction, and then disappeared off among the stalls, where the Morisco women were starting to serve food. Brahim made to follow him.

'Aren't you going to check?' his stepson said, holding him back.

'Check what?'

'I don't want any problems over the booty,' Hernando interrupted him, looking solemn. 'If anything were missing...'

'I would kill you.' Brahim leant towards the boy, his eyes screwed up into two narrow lines.

'Exactly.' Hernando had to struggle to keep a tremor out of his voice. 'These are the spoils our people have won. The proof of our victory. I don't want any problems, so check my mules!'

Brahim did so. He made sure all the saddlebags were empty, examined the harnesses, and even made Hernando take off the smock so that he could search him before he allowed him out of the castle.

Once he was free, and was leading his mule team through the maze of stalls, Hernando looked back: Brahim was busy checking Ubaid's animals.

'Get on with you!' he urged his mules.

By the time Hernando and his team reached Juviles it was completely dark. The sound of their hoofs broke the village silence. Some of the women came to their windows, wanting to ask for news of the uprising, but when they saw it was the young Nazarene leading the mules, they ducked back inside. Aisha was waiting at her door; as usual, La Vieja had gone on ahead. Hernando encouraged the other mules to carry on to the stable, and halted in front of his mother. The flickering light of a candle inside the house played on his mother's face. Hernando suddenly remembered the sight of her huge breasts swaying in the church to her ululating cries, but then the image was replaced with one of her begging Hamid to come to his aid.

'Where's your father?' she asked.

'He's stayed at the castle.'

Aisha said no more, but opened her arms wide. Smiling, Hernando stepped forward to receive her embrace.

'Thank you, Mother,' he whispered.

As he hugged her, he suddenly realized how tired he was: his legs were almost giving way under him, and all his muscles felt weak. Aisha held him more tightly and began to sing a lullaby, rocking him gently back and forth. How often he had heard that song as a child! But then . . . then Brahim's children had come along, and he . . .

A lantern flickered up by the last houses of the village. Aisha turned nervously towards it. 'Have you eaten?' she asked, trying to push Hernando away from her. He resisted. He preferred the warmth of her embrace to any food. 'Come on!' she insisted. 'I'll make you something.'

She strode purposefully back inside the house. Hernando stood where he was for a few moments longer, still drinking in the perfume of her clothes and a body he had so few opportunities to cling to.

'Stir yourself!' his mother hissed from inside the house. 'There's lots to do, and it's late.'

Hernando unharnessed the mules and filled their trough with barley. Aisha soon came out with egg, breadcrumbs and orange juice. Mules and master ate together in silence. Sitting next to him and softly stroking his hair, his mother listened to the story of all that had happened to him since he had left Juviles. When he told her, voice choked with emotion, how Gonzalico had died, she kissed him on the top of his head.

'He had his chance,' she said, trying to console him. 'You gave it him. This is a war; a war against the Christians. We will all suffer because of it, I am sure of that.'

Hernando finished eating and his mother went back inside. He inspected the mules: now they had eaten their fill, they all stood resting, their heads and ears drooping. For a minute he closed his eyes as well, overwhelmed by tiredness. Almost at once, though, he got to his feet: Brahim could call him at any moment. He shod the mule that needed it. The sound of hammering echoed across riverbeds and gullies as he hammered the soft iron on the anvil and beat the shoe back into the four-pointed shape the Berbers favoured. Brahim insisted on continuing the Arab tradition, and refused to use the semicircular ones the Christians preferred. This was something about which Hernando agreed with him: the overlap of the shoes gave the mules a better grip on steep slopes. Once he had repaired the shoe, he cut the hoof around it: something the Christians would not do either. When he had finished, he checked all the other mules' hooves, and then turned his attention to the sores he had pointed out up at the castle. He had asked his mother to build up the fire before going to bed. He went into the house, ignoring his four half- brothers and sisters, who were stretched out on the floor of the room that was both kitchen and dining room. They would soon be sleeping upstairs again, like his mother and Brahim. That would be after the almost two thousand silkworm cocoons clinging to the rows of mulberry leaves hanging from the walls had spun their thread; for now, the worms had to be left to eat quietly, and his stepbrothers and -sisters had been obliged to give up their bedrooms. Hernando heated some water and warmed up a mixture of honey and euphorbia, leaving it on the fire while he returned to the stable to soften the mule's back with the water. He returned to his mixture, and added salt in a cloth. When he thought the remedy was ready, he applied it to the wound. That mule would not be able to work for several days, however unhappy Brahim was about it. He surveyed the animals, satisfied with his work. He filled his lungs with the freezing night air, and then looked up at the outline of the mountain ranges around Juviles: they were all deep in shadow apart from the hill where the castle stood, which was lit by the camp fires still burning inside the yard. I wonder what happened to Ubaid? thought Hernando as he returned to the stable to sleep for what little remained of the night.

8

THE NEXT morning, Hernando was up at dawn. He washed and answered Hamid's call to prayers. He bowed twice and recited the first chapter of the Koran, then the prayer, before he sat on the ground leaning on his right side to continue the blessing and finish with the call to peace. His brothers and sisters, only half awake, tried to copy him, stammering prayers they did not properly know. He applied some more lotion to the injured mule's back and headed for Hamid's shack. He had so much to tell him! So many questions to ask! The Juviles Christians were still locked in the church on bread and water; Hamid still insisted they be converted to Islam. When Hernando passed by the church, he found a crowd of women, children and old men talking noisily outside. He joined a group gathered around the remains of the church bell.

'Hamid knows our laws very well,' one of the old men was saying.

'It has been many years since a Muslim was judged according to our own justice. In Ugíjar—'

'In Ugíjar we have never known any justice!' the first man protested.

A murmur of assent ran through the group. Hernando looked at the villagers, the old men, children and women who had played no part in the uprising, but now were starting to head off up towards the castle. Aisha was one of them.

'What's going on, Mother?' Hernando asked when he caught up with her.

'Your father has summoned Hamid to the castle,' Aisha said, striding on. 'They are going to try a muleteer from Narila who stole a cross.'

'What will they do to him?'

'Some say they will flog him. Others that his right hand will be cut off, and others still that he will be put to death. I don't know, my son. Whatever happens, he deserves what he gets,' said his mother, still striding along. 'Your stepfather has often mentioned him: he stole from the goods he transported. He has had many problems and complaints from Moriscos, but the mayor of Ugíjar always defended him. The shame of it! It's one thing to steal from Christians, quite another from your own people! It's said he was a friend of . . .'

Hernando's attention drifted away from his mother. He was recalling the argument Brahim had had with El Partal, and the way Ubaid had looked at his stepfather when he refused to greet him. Brahim was capable of many things, but he would never steal from a Muslim! Aisha had gone on ahead; she was talking and gesticulating with the other women, who were all as stirred up as she was.

Hernando did not follow them. He had no wish to be present at the trial. He was sure the Narila muleteer would publicly try to place the blame on him.

'I have to look after the mules,' he said as a group of the village children ran past him. A shudder ran through him. Put him to death . . . ! Then again, why not? Wasn't that what Ubaid had tried to do to him? If it hadn't been for La Vieja . . . and hadn't he threatened him again? And Gonzalico? He had wreaked a cruel revenge on the little boy, even if he had been no more savage than the other Moriscos.

Hernando chased away these thoughts. It was for Hamid to decide: he was bound to choose an appropriate punishment.

* * *

The trial began immediately after the noon prayer and lasted all afternoon. Not only did Ubaid deny having stolen the cross, but he also questioned Hamid's right to judge him.

'It's true I am not a qualified legal person,' said the old man, holding up the cross found in the mule's bags. 'And after all these years perhaps I am not a scholar either. Would you prefer someone else to judge you?'

The muleteer saw some of the men surrounding Hamid lift their hands to their daggers and swords and step towards him: he immediately said he would recognize the old scholar's authority. Ubaid could find no one willing to speak in his favour. No one gave positive responses to Hamid's opening questions: 'Do you testify that the person known as Ubaid, a muleteer from Narila, is an upright man of whom nothing bad can be said, and that he carries out his faith and his purifications as he should, and is a true follower of Muhammad, just in his dealings with others?'

Instead, everybody there spoke of the many problems the muleteer had caused in his dealings with his brothers in faith. Two women even came forward on their own account and, as if to support their menfolk's accusations, said they had seen Ubaid committing adultery the previous night.

Hamid paid no attention to the charges a desperate Ubaid made against Hernando. He sentenced him to have his right hand chopped off for theft. However, since the accusation of adultery had not been proven by four witnesses, he also ordered that the two women who had given testimony to this effect receive eighty lashes as stipulated under Muslim law.

Before carrying out the sentence on the muleteer, Brahim turned his attention to the two women. He had found a slender rod, and when Hamid led them before him, looked at the wise man enquiringly.

Hamid asked if they were pregnant. When they both shook their heads, he said to Brahim: 'Go gently with the lashes, restrain yourself. That is what the law requires.'

The two women gave sighs of relief.

'Take their smocks and tunics off, but do not strip them naked. Don't tie their hands or feet either . . . unless they try to run away.'

Brahim did his best to follow Hamid's counsel. Even so, eighty strokes with the rod brought thin bloody lines to the women's undershirts, and the blood soon covered their backs.

That evening at dusk, in front of hundreds of Moriscos gathered in the castle courtyard, Brahim took out his scimitar and chopped off the Narila muleteer's right hand with one blow. Ubaid's arm was placed outstretched on the stump of a tree that served as a chopping-block, and he shut his eyes to avoid seeing the blow. When his hand was cut off, and a tourniquet applied, Ubaid did not utter a sound. It was only when his arm was thrust into a cauldron full of vinegar and crushed salt that he howled with pain.

His howls made everyone present shudder.

Hernando heard all the details later that night, when his mother came back down to the village and made him supper.

'At the end the muleteer kept saying that you were the one who had stolen the cross. He kept shouting and calling you the Nazarene. Why did the scoundrel say that?' asked Aisha.

'Because he's a vile liar!' Hernando replied, still chewing on his food. He quickly pushed another piece of meat into his mouth.

That night he did not dare go to Hamid's house, and he could not sleep. What could the old man have thought of Ubaid's accusations? He had ordered them to chop off his right hand! The mule-driver would not let things lie there. He knew it had been Hernando. Of course he did. But now . . . now Ubaid had no right hand, and that was the one he had used to raise the dagger against him. Still, he had to be careful. Hernando tossed and turned on the straw. What about Brahim? His stepfather had been surprised when Hernando insisted he check the mules. And the others who had been there? That accursed nickname of his! Before he had only been the Nazarene to the people of Juviles, but now that was how he would be known throughout the Alpujarra.

The next morning he could not bring himself to visit Hamid either, but at midday the old man sent for him. Hernando found him sitting in the winter sun beside the church. He was perched on the largest fragment of the bell that had been smashed in the revolt, with the Prophet's sword at his feet. Seated in rows in front of him was a large group of children, from Juviles or the castle. A few women and old men stood nearby. Hamid gestured to Hernando to approach. 'Peace be with you, Hernando,' he greeted him.

'Ibn Hamid,' the lad corrected him. 'That's the name I've adopted . . . if you have no objection,' he stammered.

The holy man stared into Hernando's blue eyes. He only needed a moment: he could read the truth there. Hernando hung his head in shame; Hamid sighed deeply and looked up at the sky.

Making sure that one of the children looked after the precious sword, Hamid drew Hernando a few steps away from the group.

For a while, he said nothing.

'Are you sorry for what you did, or simply afraid?' Hamid eventually asked.

Hernando had expected a much harsher tone. He thought about the question, then he replied: 'He tried to persuade me to steal some of the spoils. He tried to kill me once, and threatened to do so again.'

'He might try it,' Hamid admitted. 'You will have to live with that. Are you going to face up to him, or run away?'

Hernando glanced at him: it was as though the old man could read his innermost thoughts.

'He's stronger than me . . . even without one of his hands.'

'But you're more intelligent. Use your intelligence.'

They stared at each other for a long while. Hernando wanted to speak, to ask Hamid why he had protected him. He hesitated. Hamid did not move.

'According to our customs, a judge cannot commit an injustice,' the old scholar said at length. 'If he alters the truth, it is in order to do something useful. And I am sure I did something useful for our people. Think of that. I trust you, Ibn Hamid,' he whispered. 'I know you had your reasons.'

The lad tried to say something, but the old man stopped him.

'Well,' he said. 'I have a lot to do, and those children need to learn the Koran. We have to make up for all the lost years.'

He turned back to the group of children, who were already shifting restlessly, and asked: 'Who among you know the first sura, *al-Fatiha*?' he asked as he hobbled back over to them.

Quite a few of them raised their hands. Hamid pointed towards one of the older ones and told him to recite the prayer. The boy stood up:

'*Bismillah ar-Rahman ar-Rahim* . . . In the name of God, the Compassionate and Merciful—'

'No, no,' Hamid interrupted him. 'Slowly . . .'

Nervous, the boy began again. '*Bismillah—*'

'No, no, no,' the old man interrupted him again. 'Listen. Ibn Hamid, recite the first sura for us.'

Hernando obeyed, and started the prayer, rocking gently back and forth as he did so: '*Bismillah* . . .'

He finished the sura, and Hamid let a few moments go by. He rotated his hands, fingers bent, in a slow rhythmic movement at both sides of his head, as if the prayer had been music. None of the children could take their eyes off those skinny hands caressing the air.

'You should know that the Arabic language is the language of the entire Muslim world,' he explained. 'It is what unites us wherever we come from or are living. Through the Koran, Arabic has become a divine language, holy and sublime. You need to learn to recite the suras rhythmically so that they resonate in your own ears and in those of anyone hearing them. I want the Christians in there' – he pointed towards the church – 'to hear this celestial music from your mouths and become convinced that there is no god but God, and no other Prophet but Muhammad. Show them, Hernando . . .'

For two days after that, Hernando had no chance to talk to

Hamid. While waiting for instructions from his stepfather, he looked after the mules, did what little work there was to do in the fields at that time of year, and spent the rest of the time teaching the Morisco children.

On 30 December, Farax came through Juviles at the head of a band of armed Moriscos. Before leaving, he ordered the immediate execution of all the Christians held in the church.

Farax the dyer not only followed King Aben Humeya's instructions to bring him all the booty taken from the Christians, but took it upon himself to decree death to all Christian males aged over ten who had not already been killed. He further ordered that their bodies were not to be buried, but left out in the open to be eaten by wild animals. He also declared that any Moriscos who hid or protected a Christian would themselves be put to death.

Hernando and the members of his improvised school watched as the Christian men were led out of Juviles church. Many of them looked ill, and shuffled along naked, hands tied behind their backs. They were taken to an open field nearby; as he stumbled along with the priest and the deacon, Andrés the sacristan turned towards Hernando, who was seated on a piece of the smashed bell. Hernando stared back at him until a Morisco jabbed his gun butt into the sacristan's chest and forced him on. Hernando could almost feel the blow in his own body. He's not a bad man, he told himself. Andrés had always been kind to him . . . The villagers joined the procession. They shrieked and danced around the Christian men. The children watched silently, until one of them shouted out and they all ran off to the field to join in the celebration.

'You must not stay here,' Hernando heard a voice behind him say.

He turned, to find that Hamid had come up to him.

'I don't want to see them die,' the lad confessed. 'Why do we have to kill them? We've lived together . . .'

'I don't like it either, but we have to go and witness it. They forced us to become Christians under threat of expulsion, and that is another form of dying, to be sent far from your homeland and family. They have refused to recognize the one true God; they have not taken advantage of the opportunity they were given. They have chosen to die. Come on.' Hamid was insistent, but Hernando still hesitated. 'Don't risk your own skin, Ibn Hamid. You could be next.'

The first to be stabbed to death were the deacon and the priest. As he watched from a small terrace some distance away, Hernando was horrified to see his mother go up to Don Martín as he lay in his death agony on the ground. What was she doing? He felt Hamid put his arm round his shoulder. The Morisco women pushed and shoved until their menfolk moved away from the bodies. Silently, almost solemnly, one of them handed Aisha a knife. Hernando watched as she knelt beside the priest, raised the weapon high above her head, and then plunged it into his heart. The ululations rang out again. Hamid squeezed the boy's shoulder tightly as his mother slashed at the priest's lifeless form. Before long, his body was nothing more than a bloody mass, but his mother, still on her knees, kept stabbing at it, as though with each blow she were avenging part of the fate that the other priest had condemned her to many years before. Eventually some of the other women came up and lifted her by the arms to drag her away. Hernando caught a glimpse of her contorted face covered in blood and tears. Aisha pushed the women off, dropped the knife, lifted her arms high in the air, and shouted as loudly as she could: 'Allah is great!'

The Moriscos killed two more men, the most prominent Christians in the village, but before they could dispatch the rest, including Andrés the sacristan, El Zaguer from Cádiar appeared with his men. He told them to stop the killing.

Hernando could only guess at the arguments going on between Zaguer's soldiers and the Moriscos who wanted blood. His attention was divided between his mother, who by now was sitting on the ground with her head between her knees, and Andrés, who was next in line to be slain.

'Go to her,' Hamid said, pushing him forward. 'She did it for you,' he added, seeing the boy resist. 'Your mother took her revenge on a man of Christ, and part of that revenge is yours too.'

Hernando walked towards his mother, but came to a halt some way off. The other Moriscos were slowly drifting from the field, and some animals began to investigate the four bodies on the ground. Hernando watched as two dogs started to sniff at the deacon's bloody form. He was wondering whether he should drive them off, when Aisha stood up.

'Let's go, my son,' was all she said.

From that moment Aisha behaved as if nothing had happened; that day she did not even change her clothes, as if the bloodstains on them were perfectly natural. It was Hernando who was much more affected: Ubaid was waiting for him up at the castle. The muleteer might even decide to come down to the village to look for him. When he was in the stable with his mules, Hernando kept a constant lookout. He had to be on his guard. Hamid knew he had set a trap for the muleteer. *I trust you*, the old man had said, but what did he really think of him? *A judge cannot commit an injustice. If he alters the truth, it is in order to do something useful.* The scholar had assured him this was what he really felt. Still, Hernando looked carefully all round the stable, his ears pricked for the slightest noise.

He slept badly, and the next day as he recited the Koran even the children could tell he was distracted. This was the first day of the year according to the Christian calendar, and as was the custom, the women had gone to spin silk under the mulberry trees. They had painted their hands with henna, which they had also daubed on the doors of their houses. They had prepared dry bread and garlic and set off for the fields where they had built some clay ovens. Here they drowned the silkworm cocoons in a copper cauldron, and then cooked them with soap to get rid of the grease. While they stirred the cocoons with a small broom made of thyme, they spun the silk on crude wheels set up under the mulberry trees. The Morisco women were very skilful, and had all the patience needed to spin the slender threads. They sorted the cocoons into three categories: the almond ones, which gave the most valuable silk; the twin cocoons, which provided round silk, which was stronger and rougher; and the damaged ones, which gave thread used for lace and poorer quality weaves.

Hernando wondered what they would do with the silk that year. How could they transport it and sell it in the silk market at Granada? According to Morisco spies in the city, the Marquis of Mondéjar was still gathering an army to set off into the Alpujarra.

'And the Marquis of los Vélez has told King Philip he will put down the revolt in the Almería region,' some old men were saying in the square by the church, where Hernando was teaching the children. He gestured to the boy reciting the suras to go on, and went over to the group.

'The Devil Iron Head,' he heard one old man say fearfully. That was the Moriscos' name for the cruel and bloodthirsty marquis. 'They say his horses urinate in panic the moment he climbs on their back.'

'We will be crushed between the two marquises,' another man said.

'Things would have been different if the people of the Albaicín and the plains had joined us,' a third man declared. 'If that had happened, the Marquis of Mondéjar would have had problems in his own city, and would not have been able to come out to the Alpujarra.'

Hernando saw several of the others nod in agreement.

'The Moriscos in the Albaicín are already paying for their betrayal,' the first man said, spitting on the ground. 'Some of them have realized their mistake and are heading for the mountains. Granada is full of Spanish nobles and soldiers of fortune, and although the hospitals have offered to pay for their food and lodging, the Marquis of Mondéjar has ordered that they stay in houses belonging to Morisco families. They steal, and rape the wives and children. Every night.'

'They say that more than a hundred of the most prominent and richest Moriscos have been locked up in the chancery,' another man said.

The first old man nodded.

The group fell silent.

'We will be victorious!' one of them shouted. At his sudden roar, the boy reciting the suras fell silent. 'God will be with us! We will triumph!' the man insisted, with such conviction that the other men and the children all began to cheer with him.

On 3 January 1569, Hernando was told by Brahim to report to Juviles castle. The Moriscos were heading out to meet the Marquis of Mondéjar's army as it entered the Alpujarra.

His hands were trembling so much he could not even tighten the girth on the first mule. The harness slipped to one side and fell to the ground. Hernando looked anxiously down at his hands. What was Ubaid going to do? He would kill him. He would be waiting for him . . . No. What could a one-armed muleteer do in the castle? How could he work with mules? A cold sweat broke out on Hernando's back: Ubaid would lay a trap for him. He would not try anything in the castle. That was not the place . . .

Hernando harnessed the mule team as best he could, said goodbye to his mother and set off. What if he ran away? He could . . . he could join the Christians, but . . . he would never succeed in crossing the Alpujarra! He would be stopped. If he did not turn up at the castle, Brahim would send people looking for him, and he would know that Ubaid had been telling the truth. He remembered Hamid's advice, and the trust the wise old man had placed in him. He could not fail him.

Hernando made his way up to the castle, staying in the middle of the mules for protection, and keeping a good look-out. Despite his fears, Ubaid was not lying in wait for him. The castle was a hive of activity, as the Moriscos prepared for their march to Pampaneira, where Aben Humeya was waiting for them with his army. Hernando looked for Brahim. He found him next to the citadel, talking to some of the leaders of the Morisco bandits.

'We are leaving unloaded,' his stepfather announced. 'Get my horse ready . . . and the Narila mules too,' he added, nodding towards Ubaid.

The Narila muleteer's stump was swathed in filthy bandages. His clothes were in tatters, and his face seemed gaunt and pale as he tried without success to harness his mules.

'But—' Hernando started to complain.

'As you will have heard, he has paid for his crime,' Brahim said, cutting him short, and stressing the last two words. He leant towards Hernando, eyes narrowed, as if challenging him to complain again.

He knew! His stepfather knew as well! And yet he was the one who had wielded the sword to cut off Ubaid's hand.

Brahim watched his stepson walk towards the mules. A satisfied grin appeared on his face. He was glad Hernando and Ubaid were enemies: he hated them both.

'I'll harness your animals,' Hernando told the muleteer, unable to take his eyes off the bloody bandage wrapped round the stump of his arm.

Ubaid spat at the lad, who turned to his stepfather in protest.

'Get them ready!' Brahim shouted. He was no longer smiling.

'Move away from the mules,' Hernando told the mule-driver. 'I'm going to harness your animals whether you like it or not, but I want you well away from me.' Seeing a big stick on the ground, he picked it up in both hands and threatened Ubaid with it. 'Get away from me!' he repeated. 'If you come near me, I'll kill you.'

'I'll kill you first,' growled Ubaid.

Hernando thrust the stick at him, but Ubaid grabbed it with his left hand and parried the blow. Hernando could not believe how strong the muleteer was after all he had suffered. Brahim seemed to be enjoying their tussle, which lasted several moments. What can I do? Hernando wondered. *Use your intelligence*, he remembered. He took his right hand off the stick and raised it high in the air. Reacting instinctively to the threat, Ubaid tried to ward off the blow – with his stump! The sight of his bloody, mutilated arm confused the muleteer, and Hernando took advantage to thrust the stick hard into his stomach with his left hand. Ubaid staggered back and fell to the ground.

'Don't come near me! I want you far away from me at all times!' Hernando shouted, threatening him again with the stick.

Unable to conceal how much his arm hurt, the muleteer crawled away.

Aben Humeya had set up headquarters in the fortress of Poqueira, perched on the top of a rocky outcrop that controlled the gorges of the Sangre, Poqueira and the river Guadalfeo. Hernando made his way there from Juviles together with almost a thousand other Moriscos. Some of them were armed, but most were simply carrying their agricultural tools; all of them were desperate to join the fight against the marquis. Ubaid stayed at the head of the mule team. He managed to make the journey leaning on them for support, although he did not have the strength to mount one. The men from Juviles were not alone: a throng of Moriscos had answered the King of Granada and Córdoba's call. There was no more room in the fortress for them, so they spilled down into the small town of Pampaneira, where all the houses were soon filled as well. The late arrivals considered themselves lucky to be able to shelter from the cold under the broad balconies lining the narrow, crooked streets.

Hernando and the others arrived at night. Soon afterwards, a band of Moriscos trooped back defeated to Pampaneira, leaving behind some two hundred dead. Hernando was put to work at once: several horses had returned wounded, and Brahim offered his son to treat them.

Before the revolt, only a few of the outlaws had had horses, because Moriscos were forbidden to own any. Even if they wanted to put a donkey with mares or a stallion with jennies to produce mules, they had to obtain special permission. Thus they had no experts who could look after horses. By daylight the next morning, Hernando found himself in a field close to the one where he kept the mules, examining the injured horses. He stood there silently for some time, unprepared for what he was seeing: these were not the usual problems he met with his animals. He could not imagine how some of the horses had managed to get this far with the wounds they'd suffered. It was icily cold, and two horses lay in their death throes on the frosty ground. Others stood upright, but were obviously in pain from wounds left by lead harquebus balls, swords, lances or halberds wielded by the Christian soldiers. Clouds of vapour rose from their nostrils. Ubaid was a few paces away from him, also looking from horse to horse. The previous night, Hernando had made sure they slept well away from each other. He'd lain down next to La Vieja, and tied a rope from her to one of his legs: he knew she was always suspicious of anyone who tried to come close.

'Get to work!' he heard the order ring out behind him. Hernando turned to see Brahim and several of the armed bandits looking at him. 'What are you waiting for? Look after them!'

Look after them? How? He was on the point of answering his stepfather back, but thought better of it. A gigantic Morisco fighter, armed with an harquebus that had a fine gold inlay and was twice as long as a normal one, pointed to a chestnut pony. He lifted the weapon with one arm as though it weighed no more than a silk handkerchief.

'That one is mine, lad. I will need it soon,' said the warrior, who was known as El Gironcillo.

Hernando glanced at the pony. How could the poor thing take all his weight? The harquebus alone must be a heavy load.

'Get on with it!' Brahim shouted.

Why not? thought Hernando. He could start with any of the injured animals.

'You examine those two,' he told Ubaid, pointing to the horses stretched out on the grass. He made his way over to the chestnut, all the time checking out of the corner of his eye that the Narila muleteer was obeying his instructions.

In spite of the hobbles on its legs, when Hernando tried to approach the horse it limped off a few paces. A bloody wound was slashed across its right hindquarters down to its haunch. He won't get far at that speed, thought Hernando. If he wanted to, Hernando could seize the horse's bridle in two bounds, and yet . . . He pulled up some dried grass and held it out in his hand, whispering to the horse. The chestnut did not even deign to look at him.

'Get hold of him!' Brahim shouted behind him.

Hernando was still whispering to the horse, reciting the first sura as rhythmically as he could.

'Grab him!' his stepfather insisted.

'Be quiet,' muttered Hernando, without turning round.

Brahim leapt towards him, but before he could land a blow El Gironcillo grasped him by the shoulder and forced him to be still. Hernando heard the scuffle and waited, the muscles on his back knotted. When nothing happened, he began whispering again. After a long pause, the chestnut pony turned its head towards him. Hernando stretched his arm out further, but the horse made no attempt to reach for the grass. Many more anxious moments went by, and Hernando had almost come to an end of the suras he knew. At last, when the horse was breathing steadily once more, he went quietly up to it and gently took hold of the bridle.

'How are the other two?' he asked Ubaid.

'They will die,' the muleteer responded gruffly. 'One has lost all its guts, the other's chest is shot away.'

'Let's go,' El Gironcillo said to Brahim. 'Your boy seems to know what he's doing.'

'Finish them off,' Hernando said, pointing to the horses on the ground. 'They should not suffer any longer.'

'You do it,' replied Brahim, still scowling at him. 'At your age you should be killing Christians.' He burst out laughing, threw Hernando a knife, and then walked off with the other soldiers.

9

Puente de Tablate, gateway to the Alpujarra
Monday, 10 January 1569

HERNANDO WALKED down from Pampaneira to the bridge at Puente de Tablate. He had no mules with him, and, like all the more than 3,500 Moriscos heading to meet the Marquis of Mondéjar's forces, he was on foot. Thanks to bonfires his scouts had lit on the tallest peaks, Aben Humeya had learnt of the Christian army's movements, and had given orders that the marquis was not to cross the bridge that gave access to the Alpujarra.

Before leaving, El Gironcillo had examined the silk thread stitches that the lad had used to sew up his pony's wound. He had nodded approvingly as he clambered on to his mount.

'You are to stay beside me,' he ordered Hernando. 'In case my horse needs you.'

So Hernando trotted alongside him, listening to El Gironcillo talking to other Morisco leaders.

'They say there are only two thousand Christian infantry,' one of them remarked.

'And a hundred knights!' added another.

'There are a lot more of us . . .'

'But we don't have weapons to match theirs.'

'We have God on our side!' roared El Gironcillo.

As he said this, the Morisco commander thumped his saddle. Hernando shrank back in alarm, but the horse and the stitches over the wound both held firm. He looked among the few horses of the Morisco cavalry, but could not see the other three animals he had treated. Then he looked down at his clothes, caked in blood.

As soon as Brahim and the bandit leaders had left that morning, Hernando had decided to put the two other wounded horses out of their misery. He strode resolutely up to the first of them, the one whose stomach had been ripped out by a lance.

He was a man now! he told himself over and over. Many Moriscos of his age were already married and had children. He must be able to kill a horse! He reached the animal, lying motionless on the ground. Its forelegs were bent under its body, so that its abdomen was pressing against the frosty ground as if in an attempt to relieve the pain from the savagely deep wound. Hernando had often seen slaughterers kill cattle in his village. The Christian butcher did it in public. He slaughtered the animal in such a way that its Adam's apple came away with the windpipe and lungs. The Muslims were forced to carry out their prohibited rites in secret outside the village. They lined the animal up facing the kiblah, then slit its throat so that the Adam's apple stayed with the head of the beast.

Hernando stood behind the dying horse. He took its mane in his left hand, and encircled its neck with his right arm. He hesitated. Above or below the Adam's apple? The Moriscos were forbidden to eat horse meat, so what did it matter how he killed it? He exchanged looks with Ubaid, who was scowling at him from some way off. He had to show him . . . Hernando closed his eyes and drew the knife across the horse's neck as hard as he could. As soon as it felt the knife cutting into it, the horse threw back its head, striking Hernando in the face, and struggled to its feet, whinnying loudly. It wasn't hobbled, and galloped off in panic across the field, blood spurting from its jugular and its guts hanging out. It seemed to take an age before it finally bled to death. Pale-faced, bile rising in his throat, Hernando watched the animal breathe its last. And yet . . . he looked round for Ubaid. It was amazing what Nature could do: even when fatally wounded the horse had fought until its final breath! He realized yet again how careful he must be: the muleteer had only lost a hand.

To dispatch the second horse, Hernando first found a rope and tied the animal's legs. It did not have the strength to resist. As before, he slit the beast's throat with all the strength he could muster. This time, he managed to avoid the head as it jerked back, and went on plunging the knife in until nearly all his body was covered in warm blood. The horse died swiftly, without moving from the spot.

The sweet smell of the second horse's blood filled Hernando's nostrils as he returned to the others. He listened to what a group of them were saying.

'The marquis could not wait for more reinforcements to arrive,' one of them said. 'In Órgiva the Christians have been besieged in the church for two weeks already, resisting all attacks. He has to enter the Alpujarra as soon as he can to go to their rescue.'

'Let's give thanks to the Christians of Órgiva then,' laughed a brigand who must have just joined the group. Hernando saw he was riding another of the mounts he had treated.

They camped for the night on top of the bluff above Puente de Tablate. Under the bridge ran a deep rocky gorge, and on the far side were the slopes of Lecrín valley. When he dismounted and saw that the stitches on his pony had resisted the tough day's ride, El Gironcillo rewarded Hernando with a dark smile and a powerful slap on the back. Hernando spent much of that night tending to the horses once more.

At first light the Morisco scouts announced that the Christian army was approaching. Aben Humeya ordered his men to destroy the bridge. Hernando watched a party demolishing the wooden structure until all that was left was the arches and a few planks, which they had to use to return to the Morisco ranks. Three of the men fell through the skeleton of the bridge; their cries gradually tailed off as they plummeted down the apparently bottomless ravine.

'Come,' El Gironcillo said to him, forcing him to look away from the chasm where the last of the Moriscos had perished. 'We need to take up our positions to give those infidels the reception they deserve.'

'But . . .' Hernando protested, pointing towards the horses.

'The children can look after them. Your stepfather is right. You're old enough to fight, and I want you by my side. I think you bring me luck.'

Hernando followed El Gironcillo down the mountainside. In a few minutes, the slopes were covered with more than three thousand men, all of them waiting joyfully and confidently for the clash with the Christian army. The ravine of Tablate was in front of them, and beyond that the slopes down which the marquis's army would have to advance.

Somebody began a song, and then a drum sounded. Another Morisco stood up and waved a huge white banner. Further on a red one suddenly appeared, and then another, and another . . . a hundred of them! Hernando could feel the hairs rising on his arms as three thousand Moriscos sang as one. The drums resounded, and hundreds of banners turned the mountainside into a vast red-and-white carpet.

And so they met the army commanded by the Marquis of Mondéjar, captain-general of the kingdom of Granada. Hernando was swept along by the Moriscos' enthusiasm. Standing beside the huge figure of El Gironcillo, he shouted his defiance of the Christian army with all his might.

His armour gleaming in the sun, the marquis took up his position at the head of his troops. He ordered the cavalry to the rear, deployed the footsoldiers across the slopes, and gave the order for the harquebusiers to advance. The Moriscos took up their positions.

They responded to the attack by firing what few guns and crossbows they had. Their main weapons though were the stones they rained down with their slings on the Christian forces across the narrow ravine. Hernando could smell the gunpowder from El Gironcillo's harquebus. He himself did not even have a sling, so had to throw stones as hard as he could, yelling all the while. His aim was good: he had thrown stones at animals, and had also practised out in the fields. He struck one footsoldier, and this encouraged him to get closer and closer, exposing himself to the enemy fire.

'Take cover!' The Morisco reached and tugged him down. Then he began loading his gun once more. Hernando stood up to throw another stone, but El Gironcillo stopped him. 'I am a target among the thousands of us here,' he said. 'My harquebus attracts their fire.' He slipped a lead ball into the harquebus's muzzle and rammed it in as hard as he could. 'I don't want you to be killed because of me. Throw your stones but do it without standing up!'

The exchange of stones and gunfire did not last very long. The Moriscos could not withstand the Christians' superior firepower. The marquis's men loaded and fired repeatedly, causing many casualties. El Gironcillo ordered his men to withdraw to higher ground, out of range of the harquebus balls.

'They won't be able to cross the bridge,' the Moriscos consoled themselves as they withdrew.

When he saw that the harquebuses were having no effect, the marquis ordered a ceasefire. At this, the Moriscos started singing and shouting once more. Many of them went on firing missiles from their slings, thinking they could reach further than the Christian guns, but they did little damage. Helmet in hand, the marquis and his uniformed captains came down to examine the ruined bridge. Impossible for an army to cross it!

Both sides fell silent, and they all saw the marquis shake his head. The Moriscos burst out yelling again, and waved all their banners. Hernando shouted as well, raising his fist to the sky. The Christian captain-general was walking away disconsolately when all of a sudden a Franciscan friar ran out of the infantry ranks. He was carrying a cross in his right hand, and his habit was tucked up to his waist. Without so much as looking back at the marquis, he started to run across the dangerous bridge. The Moriscos' triumphant chants died away. The marquis ordered covering fire for the man of God. For a few moments everyone on both sides of the ravine had eyes only for the friar as he advanced precariously across the bridge, holding the cross proudly up for the Moriscos to see.

Before he reached the far bank, two more footsoldiers had followed him. One of them missed his step and fell into the void. As his body crashed into the side of the ravine, it was as though his death was a rallying cry to his companions: the shout went up from the Christian soldiers: 'Santiago!'*

The battle cry was still echoing as a long line of soldiers rushed to the end of the bridge and began crossing it. The friar had almost reached the far end. The Christian sergeants urged the harquebusiers to fire as quickly as they could to prevent the Moriscos coming down from the heights and attacking the soldiers on the bridge. Although many tried, the fire from the Christian guns proved effective. Within a few minutes, a squad of soldiers, together with the friar who by now was on his knees praying, the cross held aloft, were able to defend the bridge from the Alpujarra side.

Aben Humeya ordered the retreat. A hundred and fifty Moriscos had lost their lives at Puente de Tablate.

'Get on,' El Gironcillo told Hernando, pointing to a horse. They had both reached the summit of the mountain. 'His rider is dead,' he explained when he saw the lad hesitate. 'We mustn't leave the horse for the Christians. Cling to its neck and let it carry you,' he added, galloping off.

---

* According to legend, Saint James the Apostle came to Spain to evangelize soon after the death of Jesus. In the ninth century, Saint James/Santiago is said to have appeared to Christian troops at the battle of Clavijo, the beginning of the 'Reconquest' of Spain by the Christians. In later centuries, the battle cry of 'Santiago y cierra' was commonly used to rally Christian forces. The remains of Saint James are said to be buried at Santiago de Compostela.

10

A BEN HUMEYA fled with his men towards Juviles. The Marquis of Mondéjar pursued him and took all the villages between Puente de Tablate and Juviles. His army looted the houses, took the Morisco women and children who had stayed behind prisoner, and seized a large amount of booty.

In Juviles castle, the Moriscos argued about their situation and what they could do. Some wanted to surrender; the outlaws, who knew they would be punished without mercy, were all for a fight to the death; still others were in favour of fleeing to the high mountains.

When their scouts announced that the Christian army was no more than a day's march from Juviles, the Morisco commanders quickly adopted a compromise solution. The armed men would take flight with the spoils, after first releasing the more than four hundred Christian captives they were holding. They would do this as a goodwill gesture, in the hope of continuing with the peace negotiations that some of their leaders had already begun. Their terrified wives were forced to say goodbye to their husbands and wait in dread for the arrival of the Christians.

'Do you want my children to die?' Brahim shouted to Aisha from the saddle of his dappled horse when she suggested they escape from Juviles with him. 'They would never withstand winter in the mountains. This is no picnic. It's war!'

Aisha lowered her eyes to the ground. Dazed by all that was

going on, Raissa and Zahara were sobbing. The boys, although they could feel the tension in the air, stared up at their father admiringly. At the head of his team of mules, which were laden down with all the booty from the castle, Hernando could feel his stomach churn. 'We could—' he tried to say.

'Be quiet!' His stepfather silenced him. 'I know you wouldn't care if your brothers and sisters died.' Then he barked at Aisha: 'Stay here and take good care of them!'

Brahim spurred his horse on. The mules followed him. Even Ubaid started on his way, but Hernando was still waiting for his mother to look up again. When finally she did so, there was a determined look in her eye.

'Peace will come,' she reassured her son. 'Don't worry.' His eyes misting over, Hernando tried to embrace her, but she pushed him away. 'Your mules have already gone,' she said. 'Go after them.' She stretched up and ruffled his hair, as though to make light of the situation. When she saw the pained look in Hernando's face, she repeated: 'Go on!'

But the lad was still not ready to set off after them. He found Hamid at the ruins of the castle gate wishing the fighters well. He was encouraging them, telling them God was with them, and would never abandon them.

'Hurry up!' Hernando said. 'Why are you still standing there?'

'This is where my journey ends, my son,' the old man said.

Son! That was the first time Hamid had called him that.

'But you can't stay here,' Hernando protested.

'Yes. I have to. I have to stay with the women, children and old men. My place is here. Besides . . . what would a lame old man like me do chasing around the mountains?' Hamid forced a smile. 'I would only be a burden.'

His mother, Hamid . . . Perhaps he should stay as well? Hadn't she told him peace would come? As dozens of Moriscos streamed past them out of the castle, the old scholar seemed to read his thoughts.

'Fight for me, Ibn Hamid. Here.' The old man unbuckled the

precious sword hanging from his belt and offered it to him. 'Always remember, it once belonged to the Prophet.'

Hernando received it solemnly, holding out both arms so that Hamid could lay it in his outstretched palms.

'Don't ever let it fall into Christian hands. And don't cry, my boy.' Unlike his mother, the old man allowed Hernando to embrace him. 'Our people and our faith matter more than any one of us alone. That is our destiny. May the Prophet guide and be with you.'

The Christian army entered Juviles, and more than four hundred Christian women, set free by their captors, came out to greet them.

'Kill them! Kill the heretics!' they demanded of the soldiers.

'They slit my son's throat,' one cried.

'They killed our husbands and sons,' sobbed another woman with a baby in her arms.

'They desecrated the churches!' a third one tried to explain above the uproar.

Some of the women were from Cuxurio and Alcútar, but others came from all over the Alpujarra. When the soldiers had dispersed through the village streets and square, they listened with horror to the stories the captive women related. In every town and village where the Moriscos had revolted, there had been brutal killings and massacres, most of them on direct orders from Farax.

'They amused themselves torturing the Christians,' one woman told them. 'They cut off their forefingers and thumbs so they could not make the sign of the cross before they died.'

'They hoisted the deacon on a rope up to the top of the bell tower,' another one said, sobbing. 'They tied him to a piece of wood with his arms outstretched, to mock the crucifixion of our Lord Jesus. When he reached the top, they let go of the rope, and he came crashing down to the stones of the square. They did the same four times over, clapping and laughing each time. Then, when he was still alive, though all his bones were broken, they handed him over to the women for them to stone him to death.'

The same scene was repeated all over the village. The soldiers, once they'd heard the women's terrible stories, were soon crying out for vengeance. A young girl from Laroles said that the Moriscos, after accepting the Christians' surrender, went back on their word. They seized the priests and daubed their feet with oil and pitch before burning them on a bonfire, executing them, and then dismembering their bodies. Another woman from Canjáyar told how in her village the Moriscos had pretended to hold a mass. The deacon and sacristan were made to stand naked on the altar. Then they forced the sacristan to read out the list of Moriscos, and whenever someone heard their name called, they went up to the altar and took revenge on the two Christians with stones, sticks or their bare hands, making sure they did not kill them outright. Finally, still alive, they were cut into pieces, starting from their toes.

While all this was going on amongst the soldiery, however, a party of sixteen Muslim scholars went to petition the Marquis of Mondéjar. They threw themselves at his feet, begging him to pardon them and all the men in the villages that had surrendered. The marquis yielded, and promised clemency for all those who laid down their arms. He made no such promise with regard to Aben Humeya and the armed bandits. Instead, he ordered his army to advance on the castle at Juviles.

News of the marquis's terms spread like wildfire through the Christian ranks. After all they had seen and heard, after the grief and tears of their women, after marching endless leagues to defend the Alpujarra without receiving pay or reward of any kind, they refused to accept them. The Moriscos had to be punished, and their possessions shared out among the soldiers!

As the army approached Juviles castle, they were met by Hamid and two other old men waving a white flag. They said they wanted to hand over the fortress to the Christians, and begged for mercy for the more than two thousand women, children and old men still seeking refuge inside.

The marquis accepted. He issued a decree pardoning the men and declaring that the women and their children be set free. To calm his soldiers' anger, he authorized the looting of any valuables they could find in the castle and village. He also ordered that the men who had surrendered be held prisoner in the village. As many Morisco women and children as possible were shut in the church; the rest were herded into the main square, guarded by soldiers still indignant at his decisions.

The marquis's clemency and the discontent among the Christian army soon came to the ears of the long column of Morisco fighters fleeing towards Ugíjar. Hernando smiled openly at three old men who had refused to stay in the castle, and were now struggling to keep up with the others.

'Nothing will happen to the women,' Hernando said, raising his clenched fist.

None of them replied. They plodded forward, a grim look on their faces.

'What's wrong?' Hernando asked. 'Didn't you hear that the marquis has pardoned all those who stayed behind?'

'It's one man against an army,' the oldest-looking of the three said, without glancing back. 'It won't happen. The Christians' greed will be too strong for any command he may give.'

Hernando went up to him. 'What do you mean?'

'The marquis has a vested interest in pardoning us: it will bring him a lot of money. But as for the soldiers with him – they're no more than mercenaries! People with nothing who enlisted to seek their fortunes. Christians only respect whatever brings them money. If the women had been taken prisoner, they would have been respected, because there is money involved. But since they are not, no decree or ruling by any noble will prevent . . .' Hernando's smile was wiped from his face. He gripped Hamid's scimitar at his belt. '. . . the soldiers doing their worst,' the old man finished wearily.

Without a second's thought, Hernando started to run. He avoided the Moriscos in the column behind him, and gave no answer when they asked what he was doing as he bumped into them. Juviles! All he could think of were his mother and Hamid. Hearing the protests as Hernando pushed his way through the men, Brahim wheeled his horse round. When he reached the three old men, one of them stopped him with a gesture.

'Where is he going?' Brahim asked.

'I imagine he is going to do what all Muslims should have done: to fight. To give up his life for his people, his family, and his God.'

The muleteer scowled. 'That is what we are all fighting for. This is war, old man.'

The Morisco agreed. 'More than you can know.'

By the time Hernando reached Juviles night had fallen. Christian soldiers were everywhere. He skirted the village along the terraces, and approached the church where the women and children were being held from the south side of the square. By now it was completely dark; the only points of light came from the soldiers' camp fires. Hernando crossed the same open plot of land where his mother had stabbed the priest: the church and square were up above him. *She did it for you,* Hamid had told him on this very spot as they stood watching his mother wreaking her revenge. Now the soldiers' conversation came to him as a distant murmur, occasionally broken by a laugh or loud curse.

He was straining to hear beyond the soldiers when somebody leapt on his back, then held him down with his knee. Hernando had no time to cry out; a hand immediately covered his mouth. He felt the steel of a knife at the back of his neck. Exactly as he had killed the horses, he thought. Was he going to die the same way?

'Don't kill him,' he heard someone hissing in Arabic just as the blade was about to slit his jugular. There were several men around him. 'I thought I saw something glistening . . . Look at his scimitar.'

Hernando felt a hand grabbing the sword. When the metal ribbons jangled, they all held their breath, but down in the square the Christian soldiers went on talking apparently unawares.

'He is one of us,' another of the men said as his fingers explored the metal ribbons on the curved scimitar.

'Who are you?' whispered the man holding him down. He took his hand from Hernando's mouth, but pressed his blade more firmly into his neck.

'Ibn Hamid.'

'What are you doing here?' a third man enquired.

'The same as you, I should think,' replied Hernando. 'I came to rescue my mother.'

Still pressing the knife to his throat, they turned him over. None of them could see each other's face in the dim glow from the Christian fires.

'How do we know he isn't trying to fool us?' Hernando heard them discussing amongst themselves.

'He speaks Arabic,' one of them said.

'Some Christians know our language too. Would you send a spy who did not speak Arabic?'

'Why would the Christians send a spy here?' asked the first man.

'Kill him,' the other one said dismissively.

'There is no god but God, and Muhammad is the messenger of God,' Hernando recited. The pressure from the knife immediately lessened. He went on with the Muslim profession of faith.

Gradually, as he repeated the same prayer that only a few days before had saved him when the Moriscos of Juviles had wanted to hand him over, the knife was lifted from his throat.

He soon discovered they were three Moriscos from Cádiar who had come to free their wives and children.

'A lot of them are being held in the church,' one of them

explained. 'Others are out in the square, but there's no way we can find out where our women are. There are hundreds of them with their children, and no one can see a thing! The soldiers would not allow them to light fires, so they are nothing more than a mass of shadows. If we move forward now we won't be able to find them, and the soldiers would hear the noise.'

What about the men? thought Hernando. And Hamid? They had only mentioned women and children.

'What about the men who stayed in the castle?' he asked.

'We think they're being held in the village houses.'

'How can we free them?' Hernando whispered.

'We have time to think of a way,' another of the men rejoined. 'We'll have to wait until first light: we can't do anything until then.'

'In daylight? What chance will we have in daylight? What can we do?' the lad said, surprised.

There was no reply.

The chill of the night gripped them as they hid in the bushes waiting for dawn. They went on talking in hushed voices. Hernando learnt what had happened to the women and children from Cádiar, and explained that in the church and on the terrace where they were hiding he had discovered how intense his mother's suffering had been. As the night wore on, the village fell silent. The soldiers were dozing by their fires. The four Moriscos could feel their muscles seizing up with the cold. The Sierra Nevada had no pity on them.

'We'll freeze to death.'

Hernando could hear one of his companions' teeth chattering. He himself could feel the cramp in his fingers as he grasped the scimitar: they seemed stuck to the scabbard.

'We need to find shelter until dawn—' one of them began, when suddenly he was interrupted by a woman's shriek from the village square.

Her scream was followed by a second, and then a third.

'Halt! Who goes there?' They heard a soldier on guard next to one of the fires call out.

'There are armed Moors in among the women!' came the shout from another fire.

Those were the last words they heard with any clarity. The Moriscos stared at each other. Armed Moors? Hernando peered over the top of the bushes protecting them. The screams of women and children mingled with the soldiers' shouted orders. Dozens of them ran from their camp fires towards the square, swords and halberds at the ready. Everything was a jumble of shadows. Then the first harquebus was fired: Hernando saw the spark, then the flash, followed by a cloud of smoke that hovered above the black mass of shapes outside the church.

More shots. More flashes of light in the darkness. More shouts.

Hernando was the first to jump up and run towards the square. He raised the scimitar above his head, clasping it in both hands. The Moriscos from Cádiar followed his lead. After a few moments' hesitation, the women in the square began trying to defend themselves from the soldiers who were lunging at them from all sides.

'There are Moors here!' More cries from in among the tangle of people.

'They're attacking us,' shouted the Christian soldiers from all sides of the square.

Everywhere was in total darkness.

'Mother!' Hernando began to shout.

In the dark, the Christian harquebusiers were firing in all directions. Hernando nearly fell over a body on the ground. Close by him on the right there was the flash of another gunshot, and he was engulfed in smoke. He wheeled the scimitar through the dense cloud and could feel his weapon sink into flesh. Then he heard a shriek of a man mortally wounded.

'Mother!'

He still had the scimitar raised above his head. He could not see a thing! He could not recognize anyone in this chaos. A woman jumped on him.

'I'm a Morisco!' he shouted at her.

'Santiago!' came the shout from behind his back.

The halberd grazed his side and plunged into the woman's stomach. She clung to him, and he felt her warm breath on his face as she expired. Struggling free of her dying embrace, he wheeled his sword through the air. It bounced off a metal helmet and sank into the Christian's shoulder. Hernando felt the woman's body slip down his legs.

'Mother!' he shouted again.

He stumbled over more and more bodies of women and children. He was splashing through blood! The church doors remained shut. What if Aisha was inside? Although the army captains were ordering their men to stop firing, the soldiers paid no attention. They were so afraid and furious that they went on slaughtering anyone they ran into. No one could halt the killing.

Hernando still could not see. How was he going to find Aisha? What if she were one of the bodies lying in the blood-soaked square?

'Mother,' he groaned, his sword lowered.

'Hernando, is that you?'

Hernando raised the scimitar again. Where was she? Where had the voice come from?

'Mother!'

'Hernando?' A shadow reached out to grasp him. He drew his arm back to strike. 'Hernando, it's me,' Aisha said, shaking him.

'Mother! Praise be to God! Let's go. Let's get out of here,' he replied, taking her arm and pushing her . . . but where to?

'Your sisters! Your sisters are missing!' she insisted. 'Musa and Aquil are already with me.'

'Where are the girls?'

'I lost them in the tumult.'

Two shots were fired in their direction. On the left close by them, a body sank to the ground.

'There's a Moor!' they heard a Christian soldier roar.

Thanks to the flashes from the guns, Hernando could make out a shadow next to him. It was a small figure . . . perhaps it was Raissa? He thought it was a girl. Raissa? They would all be killed. He grabbed the figure by the hair and pulled her towards him.

'Here's Raissa,' he told his mother.

'What about Zahara?'

This time three shots were fired directly at them. Hernando pushed his mother forward, and dragged the girl along with them.

'We have to go!' he shouted.

He guided himself by the outline of the church tower, where someone had lit a torch, pushing his mother in front of him. She had hold of her two boys, and he pulled the girl along with him. Crouching down, they reached the terrace. Then they ran along it, stumbling, falling, getting up again, gradually leaving behind the gunfire and the terrified screams of women and children.

They only came to a halt when the gunfire was a distant echo. Aisha collapsed in a heap. Musa and Aquil started sobbing, while Hernando and the girl said nothing, trying to get their breath back.

'Thank you, my son,' Aisha said, suddenly standing up again. 'We must get on. We can't stop here. We're still in danger. Raissa?' Aisha ran over to the girl and caught hold of her chin. 'You're not Raissa!'

'My name is Fátima,' the girl panted. 'And this is Salvador,' she said, showing them a baby she was clutching to her breast; he was only a few months old. 'Humam, I mean.'

Hernando could not see Fátima's huge black almond-shaped eyes, but he did notice a gleam that seemed to pierce the darkness around them.

That night, more than a thousand women and children were killed in the church square at Juviles. Those who had sought refuge in the church survived, because the doors were barred, but daylight revealed the ground outside littered with the corpses of defenceless women and children, together with the bodies of several Christian soldiers who had been killed by their colleagues in the confusion. Only one dead Morisco male was discovered. He was identified as a villager from Cádiar. The Marquis of Mondéjar launched an investigation into the mutiny, which concluded with the execution of three soldiers who, under cover of darkness, had attempted to rape a woman: it was her cries that had caused the confusion that sparked the massacre.

11

SHE WAS thirteen and came from Terque, in the district of Marchena, on the eastern slopes of the Alpujarra. Fátima explained this to Hernando as they made their way to Ugíjar. And no, she had no idea where her husband was. Humam's father had joined the men who rushed to fight the Marquis of los Vélez in the far east of the region. Like so many other Morisco women, she had ended up in the square at Juviles.

'I saw you were armed, so I got as close to you as I could. I'm sorry . . . I couldn't allow the soldiers to kill my boy,' Fátima went on. There was pain in her black eyes, but a determined glint as well. The two of them were walking ahead of Aisha, who had not said a word since she realized the mistake they'd made as they were escaping the massacre.

Hernando's two stepbrothers were struggling to keep up with the adults, complaining the whole time.

Day dawned. The sun began to shine on mountainsides and ravines as if nothing had happened during the night. The cold and snow created such a sense of clean freshness that the killing at Juviles seemed like nothing more than a macabre fantasy.

But it had been real, and Hernando had achieved what he had set out to do: he had rescued his mother. His stepsisters though . . . and Hamid? What could have happened to him? Hernando clasped the scimitar to him, and turned to look at Aisha. She was walking with her eyes lowered to the ground. Earlier, he had heard her weeping, but now she simply followed them in silence. Hernando also took advantage of the sun's first rays to glance at his new companion. Her black hair hung down to her shoulders in tight curls. She was dark-skinned, with sharply defined features. Her body was that of a girl who has given birth at a tender age, and despite her exhaustion she walked with great dignity. Sensing his gaze on her, she turned to him and smiled slightly. For the first time, he noticed her sparkling, wonderful almond-shaped eyes. Hernando saw a flush spread across her cheeks, and then Humam started to cry. Fátima cradled him, but kept on walking.

'Let's stop so that the baby can have some milk,' Aisha suggested from behind.

Fátima agreed, so they all stepped off the path.

'I'm so sorry, Mother,' Hernando said while Fátima sat down to breastfeed the baby. His two stepbrothers looked on, fascinated. Aisha did not reply. 'I thought . . . I thought she was Raissa.'

'You saved my life,' his mother said. 'Mine and those of your two brothers.' As she said this, Aisha broke down and pulled Hernando to her. 'You have no reason to be sorry,' she sobbed, still clinging to him. 'But you must understand how I feel about your sisters. Thank you . . .'

Fátima stared at them, her face sombre. Humam was greedily taking her milk. On her bare breast, Hernando caught sight of a golden necklace: the *al-hamsa*, the hand of Fátima, an amulet warding off evil that the Christians had forbidden the Moriscos to wear.

It took Hernando and his little group the whole morning to cover the three leagues between Juviles and Ugíjar. This was the most important Christian village in the Alpujarra, but Farax had ordered all Christians slaughtered, and now it was in the hands of the Moriscos. Set in the valley of the Nechite, it was some way from the heights of the Sierra Nevada, so that the landscape was not as harsh as that of the high Alpujarra. Not only was the village rich in vines and cereals, but it also had ample pasture for livestock. When Hernando and the others arrived, Aben Humeya's army had already made camp there. Ugíjar was bustling with activity.

The King of Granada had installed himself in the house that had once belonged to Pedro López, the chief bailiff of the Alpujarra. The building was situated in one of the defensive towers in the village. The three towers formed a triangle: most of the Morisco army had taken shelter in between them. Hernando found his team of mules outside the collegiate church. Ubaid was looking after his stepfather's dappled stallion. Although Hernando had been afraid of him before, he now addressed him without a qualm: 'Where is Brahim?' he asked.

Ubaid shrugged, and stared at Fátima. Musa and Aquil tried to approach the mules, but were stopped by some soldiers. Even when little Musa was pushed away from the plunder and fell at his feet, Ubaid could not take his eyes off Fátima. Intimidated, she moved closer to Hernando.

'What are you looking at?' he growled at Ubaid.

The muleteer shrugged, gave one last lascivious look at the girl, and turned away. Hernando, who had instinctively dropped his hand to his sword hilt, relaxed his grip.

He asked one of the soldiers where his stepfather was, then led his little group to Pedro López's house. They found Brahim in the doorway, with some of the commanders and a host of Morisco soldiers. Aben Humeya was inside with his advisers.

'What does this mean?' his stepfather exclaimed when he saw Aisha and his two sons, but El Gironcillo, who was standing nearby, forestalled him.

'Welcome, my boy!' he greeted Hernando. 'I think we're going to need you. We have a lot of wounded animals.'

El Gironcillo went on to explain to the other soldiers how Hernando had treated his pony. Choking with rage, Brahim waited until the Morisco leader had finished singing his stepson's praises.

'But you abandoned the mules!' he protested as soon as El

Gironcillo fell silent. 'And why did you bring my sons here? I already told you—'

'I have no idea if we will all die here, or if something will happen to your sons,' Aisha cut in, surprising her husband with her forceful tone, 'but for the moment, Hernando has saved their lives.'

'The Christians . . .' the lad started to explain. 'The Christians have slaughtered hundreds of our women and children outside Juviles church.'

The Moriscos crowded round as he told the tragic story.

'Come with me,' El Gironcillo said before Hernando had even properly finished, 'you have to tell Ibn Umayya what happened.'

The soldiers on guard at the doors let them through without any question. Hernando went in with El Gironcillo, and when the men tried to keep Brahim out, he managed to convince them he had to accompany his stepson.

It was a large, whitewashed house of two storeys, with wrought-iron balconies on the upper floor and a sloping tiled roof. Even before the heavy wooden doors to the room where Aben Humeya was holding court had swung open, Hernando could smell a cloying perfume. When the guards knocked and then opened the door, the scent of musk mingled with the sound of an ud, a short-necked lute. The young, imposing-looking King was lying back on a wooden couch draped with red silk, surrounded by his four wives. His figure loomed over the others present, who were all seated on the floor on silken cushions woven with gold and silver thread and goatskins embroidered in a thousand colours. More carpets and rugs were spread across the room. In its centre, a woman was dancing.

The three of them stood on the threshold, gazing in: Brahim could not take his eyes off the dancer, while El Gironcillo and Hernando stared all around them. In the end it was Aben Humeya who raised his hand to silence the music and then signalled for them to enter. Miguel de Rojas, the father of the

King's first wife, who was a wealthy Morisco from Ugíjar, several of the prominent men of the village, and some of the outlaw leaders, among them El Partal, El Seniz and El Gorri, turned to stare at the newcomers.

'What do you want?' Aben Humeya asked directly.

'This lad has brought news from Juviles,' El Gironcillo said without hesitation.

'Speak,' the King ordered.

Hernando hardly dared raise his eyes to look at him. As if by witchcraft, the new confidence he had found the night before vanished. He began to stammer out his story, and it was not until the King smiled openly at him that he regained his composure.

'Murderers!' El Partal cried when he had heard all the details.

'They slaughter women and children!' shouted El Seniz.

'I told you we should make a stand here in Ugíjar,' Miguel de Rojas protested. 'We have to fight to protect our families.'

'No! We would not be able to halt the marquis's army here,' argued El Partal.

Aben Humeya commanded them to be quiet. He held up his hand to calm the other bandit leaders, who all wanted to leave the town at once and go on the attack.

'I have already said that for now we will stay in Ugíjar,' the King declared, despite the mutterings of some of the Morisco leaders. 'As for you,' he said, addressing Hernando, 'I congratulate you on your bravery. What do you usually do?'

'I am a muleteer. I look after my stepfather's mules,' he explained, pointing to Brahim. Aben Humeya nodded in his direction. 'And I look after your spoils.'

'He's also a magnificent horse doctor,' El Gironcillo added.

The King thought for a few moments, and then said: 'Will you take as good care of our people's money as you did of your mother?' Hernando nodded. 'Then you can stay by my side with all our gold.'

Next to his stepson, Brahim shifted uneasily.

'I have asked for help from Uluch Ali, the beylerbey of

Algiers,' Aben Humeya went on. 'I have promised to become a vassal of the Great Turk, and I have learnt that in one of the mosques at Algiers they are collecting weapons to send to us. As soon as the sailing season begins, they will reach here . . . and we will have to pay for them.'

The King fell silent again. Hernando was wondering whether what he had said included his stepfather as well, when Aben Humeya went on.

'We need harquebuses and artillery. Most of our men are fighting with nothing more than slings or their farming tools. But I see that you at least have a worthy scimitar,' he said, pointing to the sword hanging from Hernando's waist.

Hernando unsheathed it to show the King. The blade was stained with blood. He remembered wielding it the night before, and the wounds he had made in Christian flesh. He had not had time to reflect on it before, but he did now as he stood there, staring at the dried gore on his blade.

'I see you have used it too,' said Aben Humeya. 'I trust you will continue to do so, and that many Christians fall beneath its steel.'

'I was given it by Hamid, the Muslim holy man of Juviles,' Hernando explained. He did not say that the sword had once belonged to the Prophet: he was afraid it might be taken from him, and he had promised Hamid he would take care of it. The King nodded as a sign that he knew who Hamid was.

'Hamid was with the men in the village . . .' the lad said unhappily.

With this he fell silent. Aben Humeya joined him in this mark of respect for the old man, but one of the outlaw leaders stood up, intent on taking the sword. The King saw the avaricious glint in his eye and said in a loud voice: 'Hernando, you are to take care of it until you can return it to Hamid. I, King of Granada and Córdoba, so decree. I am sure you will be able to give it back to him one day, my boy,' he added with a smile. 'When the janissaries and Berbers are here fighting alongside us, we will reign in al-Andalus once more.'

* * *

Hernando and his companions left Aben Humeya's house and found something to eat. The men sat on the ground to make a start on the strips of cooked lamb.

'Who is she?' muttered Brahim, pointing at Fátima.

Before Hernando could reply, Aisha said: 'She escaped with us from Juviles.'

Brahim's eyes narrowed. He stared hard at the young girl, who was standing next to Aisha. Humam was asleep in a wicker basket between the two women. Clutching a morsel of lamb, Brahim eyed her up and down, his gaze lingering on her breasts and her wonderful black eyes. Uneasy, Fátima looked down at the ground.

Clicking his tongue shamelessly as if in a sign of approval, the muleteer bit on his piece of meat.

'What about my daughters?' he asked as he chewed.

'I don't know.' Aisha choked back a sob. 'It was night. There were so many people . . . it was so dark . . . I couldn't find them. I was trying to protect the boys!' she said apologetically.

Brahim looked at his two sons and nodded, as if accepting Aisha's apology. 'You!' he said to Fátima. 'Bring me water.'

As she fetched him the jug, Brahim undressed her with his eyes. He kept his cup by his side so that she would have to come close to him.

Hernando found he was holding his breath as he watched Fátima try to avoid coming into contact with his stepfather. What was Brahim trying to do? Out of the corner of his eye, he thought he saw Aisha poke Humam's basket with her foot: the baby began to cry.

'I have to feed him,' Fátima said, embarrassed.

The muleteer followed her every move, trembling as he thought of her young milky breasts.

'Hernando,' Fátima whispered once she had breastfed her baby, and he was fast asleep again in her arms.

'Ibn Hamid,' he corrected her.

Fátima nodded. 'Will you come with me to try to find news of my husband? I need to know what happened to him.' Fátima cast a sideways glance at Brahim.

They left Aisha looking after Humam and made their way through the tents and crowds of people, seeking any information they could about the men from the Marchena region who had fought with the armed outlaws against the Marquis of los Vélez. He was governor of the kingdom of Murcia and captain-general of Cartagena, and was known to be a cruel soldier who fought ruthlessly against the Moriscos. He had begun his attack even before the Spanish King had appointed him, sweeping from the eastern coast of the old kingdom to the south and east of the Alpujarra, where the Marquis of Mondéjar could not reach.

It was not hard for them to discover the news they were seeking. A band of the men who had fought with El Gorri against the Marquis of los Vélez told them what had happened.

'But my husband was not with El Gorri,' Fátima interrupted them. 'He went with El Futey. He's . . . he is his cousin.'

The soldier who had been speaking sighed deeply. Fátima clung to Hernando's arm: she feared the worst. Two men in the group avoided looking at her. A third man spoke up: 'I was there. El Futey fell at the battle of Félix. Most of his men died too . . . but above all, women . . . many women. El Tezi and Portocarrero were with El Futey. They did not have enough men to face the Christians, so they disguised the women as soldiers. They fought in the open fields, and then in the houses of Félix. In the end they had to withdraw to a hilltop outside the village, where the marquis's infantry went on attacking them.'

The man fell silent for what to Hernando seemed an eternity. He could feel Fátima's fingernails digging into his arm.

'More than seven hundred of our men and women died. Only a few of us managed to escape to the mountains . . . from where we came here,' he added dejectedly. 'But those who didn't escape . . . I saw women throwing themselves at the horses, knives in hand! Going to a certain death! I saw how many of them flung sand into the Christians' faces when they no longer had the strength to throw stones. They fought as bravely as the men.' He looked directly at Fátima. 'If you can't find him here ... all the survivors were killed. The Marquis of los Vélez doesn't take any men prisoner, nor does he pardon anyone like Mondéjar does. The women and children who did not die were taken as slaves. We saw many bands of Christian soldiers deserting and heading for Murcia, taking long lines of women and children with them.'

They searched all over Ugíjar. Other Moriscos confirmed the story they had heard.

'From Terque?' said a soldier who had heard Fátima asking after her husband. 'Salvador of Terque?' The young woman nodded. 'The rope-maker?' Fátima nodded again, clasping her hands to her breast. 'I'm sorry ... he died. He died fighting bravely alongside El Futey ...'

Hernando caught her in mid-air. She weighed nothing. Almost nothing. She swooned in his arms, and he could feel her tears soaking his face.

'What is all this crying for?' asked Brahim. They were sitting in a circle in the midst of a host of camp fires, eating supper.

'Her husband,' Hernando said quickly. 'They say he was wounded in the mountains,' he lied.

Aisha, who had already heard about the death of the baby's father, said nothing to contradict her son. Nor did Fátima. Yet her obvious grief, and the fact that her husband was supposedly still alive, did not stop Brahim staring at her shamelessly with lust in his eyes.

That night Hernando could not sleep: Fátima's repressed sobs resounded louder in his mind than any of the music or chanting he could hear from the Morisco camp.

'I'm sorry,' he whispered for the hundredth time as he lay by her side in the early hours.

Fátima sobbed an unintelligible reply.

'You loved him very much.' Hernando's words were both a statement and a question.

Fátima allowed a few seconds to go by. 'We were raised together. I'd known him since I was a little girl. He was my father's apprentice, only a few years older than me. Getting married seemed...' She struggled to find the right words. '... seemed completely natural. He had always been there.'

By now her tears had turned into heartrending sobs.

'Now Humam and I are all alone. What are we to do? We don't have anyone else.'

'You have me,' he whispered. Without thinking, he stretched out a hand towards her, but she did not take it.

She said nothing. Hernando could hear her agitated breathing above the sounds of music starting up again from the camp. But before the music became too loud, Fátima murmured: 'Thank you.'

The Marquis of Mondéjar gave the Morisco army camped at Ugíjar a few days' respite. He received the prominent men who came to him to offer their surrender; sent soldiers to attack the caves where the armed Moriscos were hiding; and decided to move on Cádiar before dealing with Ugíjar.

Those days were enough for the Morisco spies, who had been watching everything going on in Granada, to bring news to the village. Curious, Hernando went to join the crowd of men surrounding one of the new arrivals.

'They killed all our brothers being held prisoner in the chancery gaol,' Hernando managed to hear, even though he could not get near the man speaking. The informer fell silent while his audience cursed and shouted insults at the news. 'The Christian soldiers attacked the jail, and the prison officials did nothing. The soldiers killed them like dogs in their cells: they had no chance to defend themselves. More than a hundred of them! Then they confiscated all their estates and possessions. And they were among the wealthiest men in Granada!'

'The Christians are only interested in what they can steal from us!' somebody shouted.

'All they want is more riches!' said another man.

'Both the marquises are facing mutinies in their armies.' Hernando recognized the spy's voice again. More men had come to listen and he found himself encircled by a crowd of Moriscos. 'The moment they get their hands on a slave or any booty their soldiers are deserting . . . Mondéjar has lost many men because of all the spoils he won after crossing the bridge at Tablate and entering the Alpujarra, but they are constantly being replaced by more soldiers who think they can become rich before returning home.'

'What happened to the old people, the women and the children from Juviles?' someone asked.

More than two thousand Moriscos had left their families in the castle there. The rumours that had sprung up after they heard Hernando's news had left them all anxious to learn what had become of them.

'Almost a thousand women and children were sold at auction in the square at Bibarrambla as the spoils of war . . .'

The spy's voice trailed off.

'Speak louder!' several men shouted.

'They were sold as slaves,' the spy said, raising his voice as loud as he could. 'A thousand of them!'

'Only a thousand!' Hernando heard the stifled cry behind him, and began to tremble.

'They put them on display in the square. In rags, and facing public scorn.' A reverential silence descended on the group as the informer's voice faded once more. 'The Christian traders fondled them shamelessly, pretending they wanted to know how healthy they were. The auctioneers cried out the bids, and handed them over while the people of Granada shouted insults, threw stones and spat on them. And all the money raised went into the Christian King's coffers!'

'What about the children?' a voice called out. 'Were they sold as slaves too?'

'They sold boys aged over ten and girls over the age of eleven at a public auction in Bibarrambla. That was the royal decree.'

'What about the younger ones?'

Several people asked the question at once. The spy paused for a moment before replying. The onlookers were pushing, standing on tiptoe, or even climbing on each other's backs to see or hear more easily.

'They were sold as well, but not in public. No one respected the King's decree,' the spy suddenly burst out. 'I saw them. They branded them on the face . . . young children . . . so that everyone could see they were slaves. Then they were quickly carted off to Castile, and even to Italy.'

Hernando saw someone who had climbed on the back of the man in front slide off and fall to the ground. For a long while, nobody dared speak: the grief was almost palpable.

'What about the old people and the invalids in Juviles?' a desperate cry came from somewhere in the crowd. 'There were almost four hundred of them.'

Hernando was all ears: Hamid!

'They were enslaved by Mondéjar's men when they deserted.'

Hamid a slave! Hernando could feel his legs buckling beneath him. He clung to his neighbour for support.

But there was one question nobody dared ask. Over the past few days, Hernando had been assailed by groups of Moriscos, all wanting to hear directly from him the truth about the rumours circulating throughout the camp. They all had wives and children in Juviles, and he was forced to repeat time and again what had happened there. 'But it was pitch black when you fled from the square, wasn't it?' they argued, desperate to deny the possibility that so many women and children had been murdered. 'It was impossible for you to see how many of them were really killed . . .' Hernando always agreed. Although that night he had clambered over hundreds of bodies, hearing and sensing the hateful madness that had taken hold of the Christian soldiers, there was no reason for him to drive these husbands and fathers still further to despair.

'Everyone who was outside the church in Juviles died!' the informer cried. 'All of them! More than a thousand women and children! Not one of them escaped.'

Shortly afterwards, camp fires on the hilltops and mountains told the Moriscos that the Marquis of Mondéjar was marching on Ugíjar with his troops. Aben Humeya was convinced by the other leaders that his father-in-law Miguel de Rojas had advised him to make a stand in Ugíjar because he had made a pact with the Christian commander. In exchange for the King of Granada's head, Miguel de Rojas and his family would go free and be rewarded with the Morisco army's spoils. Hearing this, Aben Humeya summarily executed his father-in-law and most of his family, and repudiated his first wife.

After this, Aben Humeya and his men headed for Paterna del Río on the slopes of the Sierra Nevada. Above the village was nothing but rocks, ravines, mountains and snow. Leaving the other muleteers in the rear, Hernando accompanied the King and his commanders. His mules were laden with gold and silver coins, as well as all kinds of jewels and gold-embroidered clothing. This had been done on the King's orders: Brahim instructed the muleteers to load all the gold and jewels on to his stepson's mules, which were to go in the vanguard. The other mules, carrying the rest of the spoils, brought up the rear as usual.

Occasionally, when the winding path allowed, Hernando would turn his head to try to glimpse the far end of the column of some six thousand people. This was where Aisha, his step-brothers and Fátima and her baby must be, in the group of women. He could not get the image of the girl's black almond eyes out of his mind. Sometimes they were flashing with life; at others they were bathed in tears or downcast in fear.

'Get on!' he shouted at his mules, to rid himself of these sensations.

When they reached Paterna, the King deployed his troops half a league away on a crest that he thought was almost impregnable, and then entered the village with his baggage train and all those unable to fight.

Hernando wanted to avoid meeting Ubaid again, and so as soon as he reached the village he made for a pasture on the outskirts: none of the gardens in the centre was big enough for his team. Nobody tried to stop him. Seeing his own position threatened, Brahim was in despair when Aben Humeya publicly supported his stepson.

'Do as the lad tells you,' he instructed the soldiers guarding the treasure. 'He is in charge of the gold that will bring us victory.'

So Hernando did not even have to justify his decision. While Aben Humeya was installing himself in one of the principal houses, he waited for the last mules to appear, knowing Aisha and Fátima would be with them. He saw them arrive, both weighed down with their sorrows: Aisha because after what the spy had said she was sure that there was no hope her daughters were still alive, Fátima because of her husband and the uncertain future facing her and her son. Aquil and Musa, though, were happily playing at soldiers. The guards accompanied them all to the field with the mules. When they saw Hernando busily tending to his animals, and confident that the Morisco army would repulse the marquis's troops in the natural fortress chosen by Aben Humeya, the guards left and scattered through the village.

It began to snow.

But Aben Humeya was wrong about how impregnable the hillcrest was. Ignoring their own commander's orders, the Christian soldiers rushed to the attack and succeeded in routing the force meant to be defending the village. They charged into Paterna, lusting for blood and plunder: they were sick and tired of the way their captain-general pardoned all the heretics and murderers who laid down their arms.

Chaos reigned in Paterna. The Morisco troops fled. The women and children searched desperately for their men. The freed Christian captives whooped with delight when their saviours arrived, and tried to stop the Muslim women escaping. They were the only ones fighting: apart from the occasional gunshot, the marquis's men launched themselves in search of booty. They found it on the mules that had been abandoned unguarded outside the village church. The fabulous treasure soon led to disputes: the greedy soldiers fought over silks, seed pearls and other riches heaped beside the mules.

In the confusion, none of them seemed to realize there was no gold. There were so many mules that when the soldiers failed to find any of the precious metal, they assumed it must be on another team further off.

With the Sierra Nevada at their backs, and with no houses to block his view, Hernando was the first to see how the Morisco army was fleeing helplessly towards the higher mountains. Half a league from him he saw hundreds of tiny figures dotted in the snow, climbing in complete disarray towards the peaks. Many of the figures fell and slid down ravines and crags; others suddenly stopped moving. It was too far for Hernando to hear the roar of the harquebuses, but he could see their flashes and the dense smoke the Christian weapons created each time they were fired.

'We have to go!' he urged Aisha and Fátima.

Neither woman moved: they were transfixed by the rout of their army.

'Help me!' shouted Hernando.

He didn't have to wait for orders. By the time he had harnessed his team of mules, he saw Aben Humeya galloping as fast as he could out of the far side of the village. Brahim and other riders were spurring their horses on behind him. The soldiers who had been inside Paterna were also on the run. The shots and cries of 'Santiago!' from the advancing Christians were clearly audible.

'What now?' he heard Fátima ask behind him.

'Up this way! We'll head for the pass at La Ragua!' he said, pointing in the opposite direction to the one the King and his followers were taking, hotly pursued by the Christians.

Fátima and Aisha looked where he was indicating. The girl tried to speak, but could only produce a few unintelligible words. She pressed Humam to her breast. Aisha stood open-mouthed. There was no sign of a path, only snow and rocks.

'Come on, Vieja,' Hernando said, grabbing the mule's halter and dragging her to the head of the team. 'Find us a path to the top,' he whispered, slapping her neck.

La Vieja cautiously advanced step by step through the snow. They began their slow climb. By now it was snowing heavily, and the blizzard hid them from the Christians.

12

THE PASS AT La Ragua was situated at more than six thousand feet. It offered a way to cross the Sierra Nevada to Granada without having to skirt the mountain range. Hernando knew the pass well. High up were meadows that offered good pasture in the spring; now, he thought, this must have been where the fleeing Moriscos were headed, since there were few other places for them to hide and regroup. On the northern side of the pass, facing Granada, lay the imposing castle of Calahorra; on this southern side there were no defences.

Hernando also knew of a gorge that lay at the foot of a nearby peak that he used as a reference point. In the past he had gone there to pick the herbs he needed for the potions with which he tended his animals. At the end of summer the ground was covered in a bed of deadly blue flowers: aconite. Everything about them was poisonous, from petals to roots. Extreme care had to be taken if they were to be used for medicinal purposes, and they had been the first thing Brahim had asked him for when the revolt broke out. Since olden times, the Moors had dipped the tips of their arrows in the juice of the plant: anyone hit by one was condemned to die writhing in agony and foaming at the mouth, unless they were immediately treated with quince juice. That summer, however, nobody had foreseen that war would be declared, and so by winter the Moriscos' stocks of aconite were running low.

Now Hernando tried to remember where that field of brilliant blue had been. The snowstorm made it impossible for him to spot it from a distance. He was still at the head of the group, clinging on to La Vieja to avoid missing his step. He kept driving her upwards, making sure she stayed on the path. He continually turned his frost-covered face back to see that the other mules were following. He told his mother and Fátima to grab hold of a mule's tail and to follow the quickly vanishing imprints La Vieja made in the snow. Musa, his younger stepbrother, was walking alongside Aisha; Aquil struggled on his own. The other mules seemed to understand that they should follow La Vieja. They all edged slowly up the mountain. But the sun was setting, and in darkness not even La Vieja would be able to go on.

They needed a refuge. From Paterna they had headed east, avoiding the areas where the Christians were likely to be. Hernando was hoping to find the track that led from Bayárcal up over the pass at La Ragua, but he now realized this would be impossible before night fell. Through the snowstorm, Hernando thought he could spy a rocky outcrop. He led La Vieja up to it.

There were no caves underneath the crag, but even so he thought they could find some shelter from the storm under its overhangs. Stumbling behind the mules, the others appeared. They were hunched up, lips blue with cold, their hands tightly gripping the animals' tails. Fátima was clinging on with one hand; in the other she clutched a bundle to her body.

Hernando lined the mules up against the wind. He cast a quick glance around him: the flint and steel he always carried with him would be no use here. The thick snow made it impossible for him to light a fire, and there were no dry branches or leaves to be seen anyway. Only rocks and snow! Perhaps it would have been better to be captured by the Christians, he thought to himself as he watched the last glow of day fading in the sky.

'How is the baby?' he asked Fátima. She did not reply. She

was rubbing the infant's body through her clothes with both hands. 'Is he moving?' Hernando asked. 'Is he alive?' The question died in his throat.

Still rubbing hard, Fátima nodded. Then she looked out at the storm and the darkening sky. A fearful sigh left her lips.

Why had he made them all flee? Hernando turned to look at his mother: she was hugging both his stepbrothers, trying to warm them. Aquil could not stop his teeth chattering. Musa, who was only four, looked frozen stiff. Why had he forced them to come with him? They were only women and children! Night had fallen. Night . . .

Hernando scooped up handfuls of snow and washed his face, head and neck with them. He used more to wash his hands, then knelt on the wet white blanket and began to pray out loud. He called on the All-merciful, the one they fought and risked their lives for, to help, but he did not reach the end of his prayers. Instead, he clambered to his feet. The gold! The mules were loaded with precious clothes! Dozens of chasubles and other silk vestments embroidered with gold and silver. What use would they be to his people if he and the others died up here? He searched among the bags and in no time had wrapped the women and children in priceless garments. Then he unloaded the animals: their bags would be useful too – some of them were made of leather. So would their harnesses! He heaped all the gold coins into one of the esparto grass bags, flung the rest on the ground, then used the bags and harnesses to make a cover on top of the snow, right next to the wall of rock.

'Huddle as close to the rocks as you can,' he told them. 'Don't lie down on the snow. Keep pressed against the rock wall all night.'

Hernando also wrapped himself up, but only as much as necessary, because he still wanted to be free to move in a way the others no longer could. He had to make sure none of them collapsed on to the snow and got their clothes soaking wet. He pushed the line of mules as close as he could to the rocks.

He tethered them to each other so that they could not move, and shoved them towards the huddled women and children. He threw the last mule's halter against the rock, and then crawled under their bellies until he was inside the improvised shelter too. He struggled back to his feet between Fátima and Aisha. La Vieja, who was closest to them, looked on impassively.

'Vieja,' he said, making room for himself, 'there will be more work for you tomorrow, I promise.' He pulled on the halter he had thrown inside, and held on tight: none of them could move. '*Allahu Akbar!*' He sighed, feeling the warmth from the clothes and the mules.

The storm raged all night, but Hernando managed to doze off to sleep, satisfied that they were so tightly packed between the rocks and the mules that none of them would collapse on to the wet snow.

The next day dawned sunny and quiet. The sun glinted so fiercely off the snow it hurt to look at.

'Mother?' asked Hernando.

Aisha succeeded in making a slit in all the clothes covering her. When he turned towards Fátima, she also uncovered her face and smiled at him.

'What about the boy?' he asked.

'He took some milk a while ago.'

This time it was Hernando's turn to smile. 'And my ... brothers?' He noticed that his mother was pleased he had called them this.

'Don't worry. They're fine.'

The same could not be said of the mules. Crawling back out under them, Hernando found that the two most exposed to the wind had frozen stiff and were covered in frost. They were from the team that Brahim had brought from Cádiar, but even so it was a loss. He remembered the stone he had thrown at one of them, and patted her neck. The frost came off in a myriad glittering crystals.

'It'll take me a while to get you out of there,' he shouted to the others.

In fact it did not take long. He unhitched the mules, and then simply pushed the two icy statues down the slope. They caused a small avalanche as they crashed to the foot of the rocky outcrop. The other animals were all rigid from the cold too, so he harnessed them slowly, waiting patiently for them to put one leg forward, then the other. When it was La Vieja's turn, he rubbed her back for a long time before moving her away from the women. On the previous evening he had not thought to put their food in a safe place, and now he could not find any. Like most of the objects he had thrown off the mules' backs, it was buried in deep snow.

'It looks as though only the baby will be fed today,' he said.

'If his mother does not eat,' Aisha warned him, 'the baby is not likely to get anything either.'

Hernando surveyed them: they were stiff as well, and could move only slowly and painfully. He looked up at the sky.

'There'll be no snow today,' he told them. 'We'll reach the meadows in half a day. Our people will be there, and we'll get something to eat.'

La Vieja soon found the trail to La Ragua pass. They walked along, untroubled, wrapped in their golden cloaks. Hernando had prayed devotedly, with the wind still howling in his ears and, in his mind, the unforgettable memory of Fátima's huge almond eyes when she had stopped rubbing her baby's body and stared out in panic at the night like a defenceless victim looking at her killer. He thanked Allah a thousand times for sparing them from death. He remembered Hamid: how right he had been about prayer! Then he thought of Ubaid. He thought he had seen some of the Morisco fighters escape the Christian army. Shaking his head, he forced himself to forget the muleteer. He harnessed and loaded up the mules, then he sent his stepbrothers to look for any booty that had fallen in the snow: only the gold and silver coins had been kept apart. Musa and Aquil took their mission as a game. In spite of their hunger and the cold, they had fun playing in the snow. At the sound of their laughter Fátima and Hernando exchanged glances. They did nothing more; they did not say anything, or smile, or gesture to each other, but her eyes sent a warm shiver down his spine.

As soon as they reached the main track leading up to La Ragua pass, they came across some Moriscos. Many of them were fleeing in defeat, and did not even look round when they passed the picturesque group that Hernando, the women and children made in their richly embroidered garb. Not all the Moriscos were running away, however: some were carrying provisions, and others were prowling round the slopes. Several came up to Hernando's little band.

'These are the King's spoils,' he explained.

Whenever one of them attempted to confirm this by approaching the bags, Hernando drew his scimitar and warned them off. Some of them immediately ran to tell the King the news.

By the time they reached the meadows of La Ragua, where the remains of the Morisco army had raised a makeshift camp, Aben Humeya and the outlaw leaders were waiting for them. Brahim was amongst them, while behind and on all sides stood a crowd of soldiers, as well as the women and children who had managed to escape with their men.

'I knew you could do it, Vieja. Thank you,' Hernando whispered to the mule when they were only a few hundred yards from the camp.

Despite having to flee so quickly, Aben Humeya was richly dressed. He watched with his usual haughty arrogance as they covered the remaining steps. Nobody came forward to greet Hernando. He and his party walked on, and as they drew near, the Moriscos could see the news was true: the lad was bringing with him all the gold they had plundered. The first cheer went up. The King joined in, and all those present applauded.

When Hernando turned back to look at Aisha and Fátima, they urged him to go on ahead of them.

'This is your moment of triumph, my son,' his mother shouted.

Hernando walked into the camp laughing. It was a nervous laugh he could not control. They were all acclaiming him! The very same ones who had called him the Nazarene. If Hamid could see him now . . . He caressed the scimitar at his waist.

The King offered them one of the precarious shelters that had been built from branches and scraps of cloth. Brahim immediately came to join them. Out of the booty he had saved, the King also gave Hernando ten ducats in solid silver coins, which his stepfather eyed greedily, as well as a turban and a tawny-coloured tunic embroidered with purple flowers and rubies that shone every time Hernando moved inside the shack. Aben Humeya invited him to come to eat in his tent. Hernando tried awkwardly to adjust the tunic in front of Fátima, who was sitting on one of the leather bags. After evening prayer, performed so loudly that the Christians down below must have heard it, Aisha had taken Humam in her arms, and then left the tent with her two sons. She did not say a word, and Hernando did not see the look the two women exchanged before she left: his mother encouraging, the young woman accepting.

'It's too big for me,' he complained, tugging at one of the tunic sleeves.

'It fits perfectly,' the girl lied, standing up and smoothing the tunic across his shoulders. 'Stay still!' she scolded him gently. 'You look like a prince.'

Even through the rich jewelled work on his shoulders Hernando could feel Fátima's hands touching him. He flushed. He could smell her perfume; he could . . . he could touch her too, lift her by the waist. But he did not dare. Her eyes lowered, Fátima fiddled for a few moments longer with the tunic, then she turned round to carefully pick up the turban. It was made of gold and crimson silk, with a crest of plumes, in the midst of which was an inscription in tiny emeralds and pearls.

'What does it say there?' she asked him.

'In death, hope is everlasting,' he read.

Fátima straightened in front of him, stood on tiptoe, and

crowned him with the turban. Hernando could feel the slight pressure of her breasts against his body. He trembled so much he was almost on the point of passing out as her hands slid down until they were around his neck, and she clung to him.

'I've already suffered one death,' she whispered in his ear. 'I would prefer to have hope in life. And you've already saved my life twice.' Fátima's nose brushed his ear. Terrified, Hernando stood stock-still. 'This war ... Perhaps God will allow me to start again ...' she murmured, leaning her head against his chest.

This time Hernando did dare to take her by the waist. She kissed him. At first it was a gentle kiss, as she ran her half-open lips down his face to his mouth. Hernando closed his eyes. When he tasted her savour in his mouth, he grasped Fátima more firmly; her whole body was behind that tongue drilling into him. And she kissed him, kissed him a thousand times as her hands roamed his back, at first on top of the bejewelled tunic, and then underneath it, her hands running up and down his spine.

'Go to the King,' she said suddenly, pulling away from him. 'I'll wait for you.'

I'll wait for you. Hearing that promise, Hernando opened his eyes. The first thing he saw were Fátima's immense eyes staring at him. There was not the slightest trace of shame in them; desire filled the room. He gazed down at her breasts below the golden necklace. Two large wet patches of milk made her erect nipples stand out beneath her shift. Fátima took one of his hands and placed it on her breast.

'I'll wait for you,' she promised a second time.

13

THOSE WHO still believed in the revolt kept arriving at Aben Humeya's camp, but there was also a steady stream away of others who had lost hope and were deserting in order to take up the Marquis of Mondéjar's promise that their lives would be spared and they would be given a safe conduct to return to their homes. The Morisco King's main tent had little of the luxury of his house in Ugíjar, although there was no lack of provisions. Still feeling uncomfortable in his rich garments, and with the scimitar at his waist making the bag of coins jingle, Hernando was warmly received. He handed his sword to a maiden, and was seated between El Gironcillo, who smiled at him, and El Partal. He looked for Brahim among the guests, but could not see him.

'Peace be with the man who protected the treasures of our people,' Aben Humeya said in greeting.

A murmur of approval rippled round the tent. Hernando shrank still further in between the huge leaders of the rebellion.

'Enjoy it, my boy!' roared El Gironcillo, clapping him on the back. 'This feast is in your honour.'

Hernando could still feel the weight of El Gironcillo's hand on his back when the music began. Several young women appeared carrying platters filled with raisins and jars of lemonade, which they flavoured with a paste contained in small bags. They stood the jars on the rugs in front of the circle of seated men. The men drank and ate, watching the dancers perform in the middle of the room. Sometimes they danced on their own; at others, one or other of the men joined in. Soon the clumsy Gironcillo got up to dance with a young girl who snaked around him. He even sang!

'Oh, to dance the *zambra*,' he howled, trying to follow his companion's movements, 'all troubles past and with a lovely Moorish maid . . . inside you, my beloved Alhambra!'

The Alhambra! Hernando remembered its fortress outlined against the Sierra Nevada, colouring Granada red at sunset. He imagined dancing with Fátima in the gardens of the Generalife. They were said to be so wonderful! His thoughts flew to Fátima, her youthful body and the gold ornament between her breasts – the same one worn by the dancer in front of him. And she was stretching out her hand, forcing him to stand up! As she got him to move, he could hear others applauding or shouting encouragement. Everything began to whirl around him. His feet moved nimbly, but he could not stop or control them. The girl was laughing, and moved closer. He could feel her body, as he had felt Fátima's not long before . . .

While they were dancing, one of the women brought more jugs of drink. Placing them on the ground, she took out a paste made from celery and hemp seeds, poured it into the lemonade and stirred it, just as she had done with all the jars she served.

El Gironcillo raised his glass to El Partal and drank deeply.

'Hashish,' he said with a sigh. 'It looks as if we won't be using it today to help us fight against the Christians.' El Partal nodded, also taking a mouthful of lemonade. 'So instead we'll dance in the Alhambra!' he added, raising his glass with the drug dissolved in it.

Hernando did not get the chance to sit down again. The lutes and tambourines fell quiet. The girl, still holding on tightly to him, looked enquiringly towards Aben Humeya. The King understood, and smiled his consent. The lad found himself being dragged out of the tent and into a hut where other women in the King's entourage were sitting. The dancer did not even try to find any privacy, but fell on top of him in front of all the others. Hernando was unable to resist as she stripped off his clothes, then started to undo her own skirts and the thick rolled stockings covering her legs up to her knees. As she was doing so, one of the women cried: 'He's not been gelded!'

The other women all crowded round Hernando. Two of them stretched out their hands towards his erect penis. Still struggling out of her stockings, the dancer narrowed her eyes and warded them off. 'Get out!' she cried, swatting at the others with her free hand. 'You can have your turn later.'

Hernando woke with a parched mouth and thumping headache. Where was he? The first light of day filtering inside the shack brought back vague memories of the night before, the celebrations ... and after that? He tried to move. What was stopping him? Where was he? His head felt as if it was about to explode. What ... ? A pair of plump, soft arms weighed heavily on him. Then he realized that his naked body was pressed against ... He leapt out of the bed made of branches. The woman did not even move. She merely grunted, and carried on sleeping. Who was she? Hernando stared at her enormous breasts and her great belly flopping to one side on the blanket covering the branches. What had he done? A single one of her thighs was thicker than both his legs together. He started to retch, and shivered with cold at the same time. He looked round the room: they were alone together. He searched for his clothes. They were scattered all over the floor. He started pulling his undershirt on to protect himself from the freezing early morning air, his teeth chattering all the while. What had happened? he wondered. As his shirt brushed his groin, he felt a burning pain. He looked down at his penis: it looked raw and red. There were scratch marks on his chest, arms and legs. What about his face? He found a broken piece of mirror and looked at himself: it had scratches on it too, and his neck and cheeks were bruised as if someone had been trying to suck his blood. He tried to think back to the feast, and details gradually began to emerge. The dance ... the dancer. The young girl's face flashed through his mind, intense, dancing next to him . . . and then sitting astride him, riding him, grasping his hands and placing them on her breasts, just as he had done a little while earlier with . . . Then the dancer had bitten her bottom lip, and howled with pleasure. Several other women had thrown themselves on him, plying him with more drink, and . . . Fátima! She had promised to wait for him! He tried to find his new tunic. He could not see it anywhere. He fumbled at his belt – the bag with the silver coins had gone! So had the rich turban . . . and Hamid's sword!

He shook the woman. 'Where is my sword?' The fat woman grumbled in her sleep. Hernando shook her more roughly. 'And my money?'

'Come back to bed with me,' the woman protested, opening her arms. 'You're really strong . . .'

'What about my clothes?'

She seemed to wake up. 'You don't need them. I'll warm you up,' she whispered, parting her thighs lasciviously.

Hernando glanced away from her obese, hairless body. 'You bitch!' he insulted her, looking desperately all round the shack. This was the first time he had ever abused a woman this way. 'Bitch!' he repeated, as he realized with a sinking heart that everything had disappeared.

Heading towards the curtain that served as a door, he found his clothes chafed so painfully he could hardly walk. He hobbled out, keeping his legs as far apart as possible.

Although day had dawned, silence still reigned in the camp. Seeing a guard outside Aben Humeya's tent, Hernando went over to him.

'The dancers robbed me,' he said without a word of greeting.

'I see you also had fun with them,' replied the guard.

'They stole everything,' Hernando insisted. 'My ten ducats, the tunic the King gave me, the turban—'

'Most of our army deserted in the night,' the armed guard interrupted him in a weary voice.

Hernando looked round the camp. 'Why would they take the

sword if they are going to surrender to the Christians?' he asked out loud.

'Your sword?' asked the guard. Hernando nodded. 'Wait.' He disappeared inside the tent and a moment later emerged carrying Hamid's scimitar. 'You took it off when you first arrived last night,' he said, handing it back to Hernando. 'It's difficult to sit and eat wearing it.'

Hernando carefully took it from him. At least he had not lost the sword – but what about Fátima?

Hernando dug his nails into the scimitar. He looked all round the camp; it was almost deserted after the night-time flight of most of the Morisco army. He walked towards the shack where Brahim, Aisha and Fátima were sleeping, but, before reaching it, he suddenly dodged behind one of the empty huts: Fátima was coming out. She was carrying Humam. He saw her raise her head to the cold, clear sky, then quickly ducked behind the wooden hut when she stared round the camp, solemn-faced. What could he say to her? That he had lost everything? That he had been raped by dancers, and had just woken up in the arms of an old hag with no hair on her body? How could he appear before her, his body covered in scratches, his neck and face disfigured by bruises? He could . . . he could lie to her, tell her the King had kept him there all night. He could do that, but what if she wanted to give herself to him as she had promised? How could he show her his flayed penis? His swollen and bitten groin? He had not even dared to look at it closely, but he knew it hurt, and burnt as he walked. How could he explain all that? He watched her clutch Humam close, as though seeking refuge in him. He saw her cradle the baby against her breast, then kiss him gently and sadly before disappearing back inside the hut.

He had failed her! He felt guilty and ashamed, terribly ashamed. Without stopping to think, he decided to get away. He started to run aimlessly, but as he passed by Aben Humeya's tent once more, the guard stopped him.

'The King wants to see you.'

Panting, blind from self-loathing, Hernando stepped inside the tent. Humeya was already dressed, and greeted him ostentatiously, as if nothing had happened.

'The army . . .' Hernando stammered, pointing out towards the camp. 'The men . . .' Aben Humeya came closer, and studied the bruises on the lad's neck. 'They've all fled!' Hernando wailed.

'I know,' the King replied calmly, smiling at the sight of his visitor's face. 'I cannot blame them.' At that moment a tall, muscular Morisco soldier Hernando had seen before came into the tent. He stood silently to one side. 'We are fighting without weapons. We are being cut to pieces throughout the Alpujarra. After Paterna, the Marquis of Mondéjar has taken many other villages, but he has always been magnanimous and pardoned the inhabitants. That's why my men have fled: they want to be spared. And that's why I called you here.' Hernando looked surprised, but Aben Humeya smiled at him again. 'Don't worry, Ibn Hamid, they will be back. Almost two months ago, after my coronation, I sent my younger brother Abdallah to ask the bey of Algiers for help. There is still no news from him. All I have been able to do is send him a letter . . . Words!' Aben Humeya snatched a fist in the air. 'But now we have a fortune in plunder to persuade him. My men are running away, and the promised aid has not arrived. So I want you to leave at once for Adra, with the gold. Al-Hashum here will go with you.' Aben Humeya pointed to the giant soldier standing behind them. 'He will sail to Barbary with the treasure, and offer it to our brothers, the believers in the one true God. You are to return here and keep me informed. The journey will be dangerous, but you must reach the coast and find a ship. Once you have reached Adra, with the gold you have it will not be hard for you to find what you need to cross the strait, or to enlist the support of the local Moriscos. Is everything ready?' he asked the soldier.

'The mule has been loaded up,' replied al-Hashum.

'May the Prophet be your companion and guide,' the King concluded.

Hernando followed al-Hashum out of the tent. They were going to Adra on the coast, which was a long way away. What would Fátima think? She had looked sad, but he had been ordered to go . . . the King had ordered it! At once, he had said. He did not even have time to say goodbye. What about his mother? They walked round the royal tent. On the far side they found Brahim holding one of the mules. Hernando's stepfather looked him up and down curiously, his eyes widening when he saw all the bruises.

'What about the King's gifts?' he growled.

As always when challenged by Brahim, Hernando hesitated. 'I don't need them for the journey,' he said, pretending to check the mule's harness. 'I'm going to say farewell to my mother.'

'We have to leave now,' al-Hashum objected.

Brahim hid a smile. 'You have a mission to fulfil,' he said firmly. 'This is no time for a mother's tears. I'll tell her all about it.'

Against his better judgement, Hernando agreed. He and al-Hashum mounted up, and Brahim watched them ride off. For once he was pleased at the confidence the King was showing in his stepson. He smiled to himself as he remembered Fátima's voluptuous curves.

14

'IS THE earth flat?'

In normal times, their journey would have taken between three and four days, but Hernando and his companion were forced to travel along impassable tracks and across fields, trying to avoid the many bands of Christian soldiers roaming the region. They were laying waste to villages, stealing, killing and raping the women, and then making slaves of them. Usually in groups of around twenty, with no captains or standard-bearers, they were greedy, violent men who abused the name of their Christian god and wreaked bloody vengeance on the Moriscos with the sole aim of enriching themselves.

Hernando was pleased with their slow pace for one reason: it gave him plenty of time to find the herbs he could use to ease the pain in his groin.

They were hiding in some thick bushes, stuck with the mule on a rocky pass, waiting for a gang of Christian thugs to finish their looting. They suddenly saw one of the soldiers split off from the group, dragging a girl no more than ten years old with him. She cried and kicked as he hauled her close to where the two men were crouching. They both dropped their hands to their weapons. Right in front of them, on the far side of the bushes, the soldier knocked the girl to the ground with a blow, and then began to undo his breeches, his blackened teeth showing in a hideous grin. Hernando unsheathed his scimitar, waiting for the man to expose the back of his neck as he bent over his victim, but suddenly felt al-Hashum's hand on his arm. Turning towards him, he saw him shake his head. His face was wet with tears. Hernando obeyed, and slowly sheathed his sword, watching closely as the blade slid back into the scabbard. In order not to give themselves away, they had to stay where they were and witness the scene. The huge, battle-hardened al-Hashum could not look. He knelt and stared fixedly at the ground, sobbing in silence. Hernando found he could not close his eyes. He dug his fingers into the hilt of Hamid's sacred scimitar, clasping it tighter and tighter as the girl's protests diminished until they were little more than an inaudible sobbing.

Her bitter cries merged with the memories of Fátima that had haunted him ever since he had left Aben Humeya's camp. Coward! He accused himself over and over. She had said she had nobody, and he had replied that she could count on him. By now both Fátima and his mother must have heard from Brahim about the mission the King had entrusted him with, but even so . . . What if the Christians had been so determined they had climbed up to the pass and even now were raping Fátima?

He finally relinquished his grip on the scimitar when al-Hashum, wiping the tears from his eyes with a sleeve, motioned with his other hand that they should move on. Hernando's fingers ached.

Al-Hashum seemed to know Adra well. They waited until nightfall out beyond the dry fields and sand dunes that stretched down to the sea. Hernando had discovered during their journey that the Morisco warrior was a man of few words, although he was not in any way rough or arrogant. In fact, he seemed to be kinder and more gentle than Hernando would have believed possible in someone who had lived for so long in the mountains as an outlaw. As they sat on a hill watching the colours of the sea change with the sunset, al-Hashum spoke more than he had done on all the previous days.

'Adra is held by the Christians.' Although he tried to whisper, his harsh, guttural voice made this almost impossible. 'It was here that El Daud was betrayed at the start of the uprising, along with all the people from the Albaicín in Granada who wanted to cross to the Barbary coast to seek support. Just like us now, they needed a caravel, and eventually found one. But the Morisco who acted as go-between – God condemn him to hell! – drilled holes in the vessel, then used wax to block them up. The ship began to founder a short distance from the coast, so all the Christians had to do was wait for El Daud and his men on the beach and seize them.'

'Do you . . . do you know anyone you can trust?' asked Hernando.

'I think so.'

The waters of the sea were turning black in the growing darkness.

'I see you are walking more freely,' al-Hashum suddenly remarked. 'Your potions seemed to have cured your problem.'

Even in the dusk, Hernando had to turn his reddening face away. But the other man persisted: he knew what must have happened to cause the rawness in the lad's groin. He went on to talk about his own wife and children. He had left them in Juviles but, like everyone else, was not sure if they had been inside the church or out in the square.

'Dead or enslaved,' al-Hashum said, his voice by now a true whisper. 'Which is worse?'

They went on talking as night fell. Hernando told him about Fátima and his mother.

They hid in a house belonging to an old couple who had been unable to escape to the mountains when the revolt began, and who looked after a vegetable garden and an orchard on the outskirts of the town. Zahir – that was the man's name – insisted they bring the mule inside the house.

'We don't keep animals,' he said. 'A mule outside would make people suspicious.'

Zahir's wife kept the house spotless, but agreed with her

husband, and so they tied the mule up in what, they were told with pride, was the bedroom of their young sons who had gone off to fight for the one true God.

They stayed in the house for several days without ever once going out. Zahir made discreet enquiries about a ship for them. Hernando and al-Hashum knew at once they could trust their hosts, but could they also trust the men Zahir was dealing with?

'Yes,' Zahir declared without hesitation. 'They are Muslims! They pray with me, and although they have not taken up arms, they collaborate however they can with our young men. And they are all well aware of how important it is to get our gold to Barbary. The news we hear from the Alpujarra is not encouraging. We need help from our Turkish and Berber brothers!'

News! Every night, as they shared the frugal meals the old couple could offer them, they listened anxiously to what Zahir had learnt about the war.

'Village after village has surrendered,' the old man told them one night. 'They say that Ibn Umayya is wandering in the mountains without weapons or food, and accompanied by only a hundred of his closest supporters.'

Just thinking of Fátima and Aisha lost in the ravines of the Sierra Nevada without anyone to protect them made Hernando tremble. Al-Hashum looked grim when he saw how troubled the lad was.

'Why do they surrender?' he growled.

Zahir shook his head helplessly. 'Out of fear,' he said. 'Ibn Umayya has no one with him any more, but the other rebels in the Alpujarra are being decimated. The Marquis of los Vélez has just fought a battle with our brothers at Ohánez. He killed more than a thousand men, and captured two thousand women and children.'

'But Mondéjar pardons everyone,' mused Hernando, imagining what might happen if Fátima became a slave.

'Yes. The two noblemen are behaving very differently. Mondéjar maintains that the "earth is flat". He has written as much to the Marquis of los Vélez, urging him to cease his attacks on the Moriscos and to offer pardon to all those who lay down their arms . . .'

'And so?' al-Hashum wanted to know.

'The Marquis of los Vélez has sworn to hunt down, kill, or enslave all our people. The letter apparently only reached him after the battle of Ohánez. When he returned to the village he found the heads of twenty recently decapitated Christian women lined up on the top step of the stairway to the church. They say his calls for vengeance could be heard on the mountaintops.'

The three men sitting on the floor fell silent for a long moment. So too did Zahir's wife, who was standing nearby.

'You have to take the gold to Barbary!' Hernando exclaimed finally.

Hernando learnt that Aben Humeya was in Mecina Bombáron. The King had secretly descended from the mountains to Válor, his home town and fief, in search of food, respite and comfort. That night, however, he was expected in Mecina Bombáron for a Muslim wedding. Mecina was one of the many locations that had surrendered to the Marquis of Mondéjar. When the killings had begun, all the town's Christians had fled, and so for the time being at least everything was quiet. Always someone willing to enjoy himself, however bad the situation, Aben Humeya did not want to miss this feast.

Alone, leading the mule, and alive to the slightest suspicious sound, Hernando set off for Mecina to inform the King of the results of his mission. He had left Adra as soon as the caravel Zahir had found vanished into the dark waters of the night, and he had seen there were no Christian ships pursuing it, or any obvious signs of holes being patched up with wax. Together with the old man and a couple of fishermen, he prayed on the beach. They beseeched their God to see al-Hashum's mission to a safe conclusion. Then, against Zahir's advice, Hernando set off under a moonlit sky. He was in a hurry to get back;

he wanted to see Fátima and his mother as soon as possible.

He hid from everyone and everything on the way, nibbling now and then at the unleavened bread and meat stew Zahir's wife had given him. He could not stop thinking of Fátima, his mother and the army that was to come and set them free from beyond the coasts of Granada.

What Hernando, Aben Humeya or al-Hashum during his night crossing could not have imagined was that both Uluch Ali, the beylerbey of Algiers, and the Sultan of the Sublime Porte had their own plans. As soon as he had heard the news of the uprising in the Alpujarra, the beylerbey had called on his followers to gather in defence of the Andalusian Moriscos. But when he saw how many men arrived, eager to fight, he decided it would be better to employ them for his own ends, and so embarked on the conquest of Tunis, then being held by Muley Hamida. In compensation, he issued a decree authorizing anyone who so wished to travel to Spain and fight. In addition, he pardoned all those criminals who enlisted for the war in al-Andalus. He also set aside a mosque for the collection of those weapons – and they were numerous – that the brothers in faith of the Moriscos wished to give to the struggle, although at the last minute he decided to sell rather than donate them. Something similar happened with the Sultan in Constantinople. The revolt in the Alpujarra meant that the King of Spain had to fight on another front, and this cleared the way for the Sultan to try to conquer Cyprus. He set about making preparations for this, meanwhile getting in touch with his governor in Algiers and telling him that as a goodwill gesture he should send two hundred Turkish janissaries to Granada.

Approaching Mecina, Hernando could hear the music of lutes and *dulzainas*. As in most of the Alpujarra villages, the clusters of houses clinging to the Sierra Nevada seemed to be built one on top of the other. There were also a few larger houses, including that of Aben Humeya's cousin Aben Aboo, where the King usually sought refuge. By the time Hernando tied up the mule and entered Mecina, night had fallen. The joyful sounds of the music guided his footsteps. He could not help thinking that he would soon be seeing Fátima again. She must still be up in the King's mountain camp: but what could he say to her? What excuses could he give?

He arrived just in time to see the bride, tattooed with henna and dressed in a long shift, being transported to the groom's house seated on the joined hands of two of her relatives. She had her eyes closed, and her feet were kept off the ground all the way. Hernando joined the happy procession. The women were still shouting the chants and ululations reserved for weddings, according to the Muslim law stating that all marriages should be public and open. No one in Mecina could dispute the fact that, after all the stipulated exhortations to the betrothed, this had not been a public, transparent union. Surrounded by a throng of rejoicing people, the bride reached the small front door of her husband's two-storey house. Someone gave her a mallet and a nail, which she hammered into the wood. Then, to cries of joy from everyone around her, she stepped with her right foot into her new home.

After this the bride, accompanied by all the women who could fit into the small house, was taken up to the nuptial bed on the first floor. There she lay down motionless under a white sheet, waiting silently with eyes closed while the women offered her gifts. All of them knew that with the defeat of the Moriscos they would soon see the return of the Christian priests and with them the renewal of the banning of their traditional costumes and rites, and so for one last time they followed their age-old customs, entering the house with their faces covered and only revealing them in the intimacy of the bridal chamber, where no men were allowed.

There were so many people trying to get into the downstairs room with the bridegroom that Hernando had difficulty even reaching the front door.

'I have to see the King,' he said to the back of an old man who was trying to stop him going in.

The man turned and gave him a piercing look with tired eyes. Then he glanced down at the scimitar hanging from his belt. Nobody was armed in Mecina.

'There's no king here,' he scolded him. Despite this, he allowed Hernando in, and told the others in front of him to do the same. 'Remember,' he said, as Hernando pushed past him, 'there is no king here.'

It was as if the old man's message had been passed down the line of waiting men. Hernando was allowed all the way through from the street to the tiny room where the male wedding guests were crowding round the groom. At first, he could not find Aben Humeya. The person he did see was Brahim, who was eating sweetmeats as he laughed and talked to some of the outlaw leaders Hernando knew from the camp. Brahim seemed pleased with himself, he thought when their eyes met. He turned aside and met the gaze of Aben Humeya, who recognized him at once. The monarch was dressed simply, like all the men of Mecina. Hernando went up to him.

'Peace be with you,' the King greeted him. 'What news do you bring me?'

Hernando told him of his journey.

'I'm glad,' Aben Humeya said, cutting him short with a gesture after the lad had confirmed that, God willing, al-Hashum should by then have already disembarked in Barbary. 'Despite your age, you are a loyal servant. You had already demonstrated that. Once again I am in your debt, and will give you your reward. But for now let us enjoy the feast. Come with me.'

The men were all heading for the upper floor, where the women were waiting for them with covered faces. Most of the guests had brought gifts: food, silver coins, kitchenware, lengths of cloth. They gave these to the women who had taken charge of the ceremony, positioned at either side of the wedding bed. Hernando had nothing to offer. Only close relatives could demand to see the bride, still lying supine under the white sheet. The King was also allowed that prerogative, and when he rewarded the bride with a gold coin, the women lifted the sheet for him.

'Now let us eat!' cried Aben Humeya, once the honours had been done.

Because of the restricted space in the newlyweds' home, the celebration was held in the village streets and neighbouring houses. Once the giving of gifts had finished, the bride and groom shut themselves in for the eight days prescribed by law during which their families would take them food. Aben Humeya and Hernando headed for Aben Aboo's house, where a whole lamb was being roasted to the sound of lutes and drums. This was a rich house, with furniture and tapestries, full of the scent of perfume and with many servants. Brahim was among the retinue of trusted followers who went with them.

Before the women retired to another room, Hernando searched for his mother. He did not know whether she had come down to the village with his stepfather, but was anxious to see her again. All the women had their faces covered, however, and many of them were similar in build to Aisha. Brahim was still laughing and talking to a group of men beneath a huge mulberry tree in a corner of the garden. His handsome weather-beaten face seemed to have grown younger over the past few days. Hernando had never seen him looking so contented. He decided to join the group.

'Peace,' he said to them. They were all head and shoulders taller than him, so he hesitated before continuing. Finally he asked: 'Brahim, where is my mother?'

His stepfather stared at him, as if amazed to see him there. 'She's in the mountains,' he replied, making as if to turn back to his conversation. 'Looking after your brothers and Fátima's baby,' he added casually.

Hernando started: had something happened to Fátima? 'Fátima's baby? Why . . . ?' he stammered.

Brahim did not even bother to answer, but one of his companions did so for him.

'The baby who'll soon be your brother,' he said, bursting out laughing and clapping the muleteer on the back.

'Wha . . . what?' the lad managed to stammer. He was trembling so badly it seemed to affect even his voice.

Brahim turned towards him again. Hernando could see a gleam of satisfaction in his eyes.

'Your stepfather', another of the men explained, 'has asked the King for the girl's hand.'

Hernando could not believe his ears. He must have looked so incredulous that the man felt almost obliged to say more. 'It's been confirmed that her husband died at Félix, and since she has no relatives to look after her, your father came to see the King on her behalf. You should be pleased, boy! You're going to have a new mother.'

Hernando's mouth filled with bitter bile. He began to retch uncontrollably, and ran to the far end of the garden, barging into several men standing waiting for the lamb to finish cooking on its spit. He did not manage to be sick, but kept on retching so violently it felt as if someone had kicked him in the stomach. Fátima! His Fátima married to Brahim?

'Is something wrong, Ibn Hamid?'

It was the King, who had come over to him, his face showing his concern. Wiping the bile from the corner of his mouth, Hernando took a deep breath before he spoke. Why not tell him everything?

'Your Majesty has said he was in my debt . . .'

'So I am.'

'Then I need to ask a favour of you,' Hernando added disconsolately.

Even before Hernando had finished his story, Aben Humeya smiled at him. What did he not know about love affairs? Demonstrating yet again his changeable nature, he grasped the lad by the arm and, without thinking twice, led him back to the group of men.

'Brahim!' he shouted. The muleteer turned round. His face fell when he saw the King and his stepson together. 'I have decided not to allow you to marry that girl. Someone to whom our people are greatly indebted wants her for himself: your son. I offer her to him.'

The muleteer clenched his fists, containing the anger that made him tense every muscle in his body. This was the King! The other Moriscos fell silent, staring directly at Hernando.

'And now,' the King added, 'let us all enjoy my cousin Ibn Abbu's hospitality. Eat and drink!'

Hernando stumbled off in Aben Humeya's wake. The King came to a halt a couple of yards further on in order to speak to one of the outlaw leaders. Hernando was breathing so heavily he could hardly hear what they were saying. He did, however, see out of the corner of his eye that Brahim had left Aben Aboo's house with a furious sweep of his hand.

He did not get a glimpse of Fátima. During the feast, the women stayed hidden inside the house. Hernando made sure he drank only clear fresh water, after first carefully checking it contained no hashish paste. His mind was racing. People were already starting to leave, and as the crush diminished, he realized he would soon have to explain himself to her. Aben Humeya had told Brahim that Hernando was claiming her for himself . . . and he had agreed! Did that mean he must marry her? All he had wanted was for her not to marry Brahim! As the night wore on, many of the wedding guests stared at him and whispered to their neighbours; some even pointed at him. Everyone knew already! How could he explain to Fátima? And what about Brahim? How would his stepfather react to losing Fátima to him? The King was on his side, but even so . . .

There were only about ten guests left at Aben Aboo's house, among them Aben Humeya, El Zaguer and El Dalay, the bailiff of Mecina, when a Morisco soldier came running in.

'The Christians have surrounded us!' he announced to the King. 'One detachment has gone to Válor, another has already reached Mecina,' he explained when Aben Humeya pressed him. 'They are heading straight here. I heard their captains give the order.'

Aben Humeya did not need to tell any of his followers what to do. All of them who did not live in Mecina or had not been pardoned by the marquis leapt over the garden walls and disappeared into the night, heading for the hills.

Hernando suddenly found himself alone in the garden with Aben Aboo.

'Run away!' the Morisco urged him, pointing to the wall.

The women still inside the house came rushing out. Their faces were uncovered because of the emergency.

'Fátima!' shouted Hernando.

The girl came to a halt. By the light of a torch, Hernando saw her huge black eyes gleam. At that moment, a group of Christians broke into the garden and collided with the fleeing women. In the precious few seconds of chaos, Hernando ran to Fátima, grabbed her by the arm, and ran with her inside the house. They heard the soldiers shouting in the garden: 'Where is Fernando de Válor and Córdoba, the falsely named King of Granada?'

Those were the last words Hernando heard as he scrambled with Fátima out of a window that gave on to the street.

These were not soldiers. The Marquis of Mondéjar's army had disbanded after it had seized the plunder from a punitive expedition to the Guájaras. Most of the men who left the Christian camp that night to trap Aben Humeya were adventurers fighting for the rich pickings to be had; men with little experience of war and even fewer scruples, whose only objective was to get their hands on as much loot as possible.

Válor was laid waste. When the old men of the village came out to receive the Christians and offer them food, they were killed on the spot. The Christians surged on into the village. The same fate awaited Mecina. The mob, utterly out of control, killed the men, sacked the houses, and took the women and children captive to sell as slaves.

A group of them burst into Aben Aboo's garden in a vain attempt to find Aben Humeya.

'Where is Fernando de Válor?' one of them asked repeatedly, smashing the butt of his harquebus into Aben Aboo's face. Despite the repeated blows, the Morisco refused to say a word.

'You will talk, you accursed heretic!' muttered a man with a bushy beard and blackened teeth. 'Strip him and tie his hands behind his back!'

The men tore off Aben Aboo's clothes and tied him up. Their leader pushed him over to the mulberry tree with his harquebus. He took a slender rope and threw it over a branch. One end dangled above Aben Aboo's head. The man took the rope and made as if to tie it round his neck.

Aben Aboo spat in his face. The man ignored this and swung the rope in front of the other man's face.

'You'll wish you had been hanged,' he told him. He knelt down and tied the end of the rope round the Morisco's scrotum, above the testicles. As the soldier tightened the knot, Aben Aboo stifled a cry of pain. 'You'll end up wishing I had tied it round your filthy gizzard,' he growled, grasping the other end of the rope.

He pulled as hard as he could. As the rope tightened, Aben Aboo tried to stand on tiptoe, but the pain in his scrotum was almost unbearable. When he saw Aben Aboo could not reach any higher without falling over, the corporal handed the rope to one of the men. He tied it round the trunk of the mulberry.

'You will talk, you Muslim dog. You'll talk until you renounce your sect and your Prophet,' the man spat, thrusting his face at him. 'You'll curse your Allah, your god's lapdog, the worst excrement in the world, you worthless—'

Aben Aboo lashed out with his right foot and caught the man squarely in the groin. He doubled up in pain, but in lashing out Aben Aboo lost his balance and toppled over.

His scrotum was ripped off. His testicles flew through the air, spattering everyone under the mulberry tree with blood. Aben Aboo lay writhing on the ground.

'You can bleed to death like the pig you are,' the man muttered, still recovering.

'May Allah grant that Ibn Umayya live even if I die,' Aben Aboo managed to gasp.

After leaving the wedding feast, Brahim had wandered through Mecina in search of hashish and a woman who would help him forget the King's rebuff. He found both, but when he saw the Christian men starting to sack the village, he thought he might be able to turn the chaos to his advantage and gain revenge on Hernando. Avoiding all the lit torches, he ran back to Aben Aboo's house.

He arrived just as the men were leaving, carrying their booty. Brahim sneaked past them and found the King's cousin bleeding to death in the garden.

'Let me die,' Aben Aboo begged.

Brahim did not listen to him. Instead, he helped the wounded man into the house, settled him as best he could on a bed, then left in search of help.

15

Our enemy is too cruel for us to surrender to them, as they are so enraged. Let us hasten therefore and go to meet an honourable death with manly pride, defending our women and children, and doing what we must to save the lives and honour that nature obliges us to defend.

Luis de Mármol, *History of the Rebellion and Punishment of the Moriscos in the Kingdom of Granada*

HERNANDO AND Fátima fled from Mecina. They ran across the countryside through the night, heading for the mountains. They stumbled and fell many times, but only when the noise from the looting became a distant murmur did they stop to catch their breath. Hernando tried to say something to Fátima, but she prevented him.

'"In death, hope is everlasting,"' she said. 'Do you remember saying that?'

High above the ravine, with its towering rocks and thick undergrowth, the moon seemed to be shining directly on their faces.

'I—' Hernando started trying to excuse himself.

'Your stepfather has asked the King for my hand,' the girl cut in, 'and—'

'The King has changed his mind.'

He would have liked to see the moon's reflection shimmer on

Fátima's features, to see her white teeth flash in its amber light, or the gleam of her dark eyes. All he met with, though, was a stony face and a painful silence.

'He gave you in marriage to me instead,' he admitted.

For a few moments they were both silent.

'I am yours then.' Fátima betrayed no emotion as she spoke these words; they cut through the icy air between them. 'You have saved my life several times. Tonight you did so again. You can enjoy me as the Prophet decrees, but—'

'Stop!'

'You can have me, but you will never win my heart.'

'No!'

Turning on his heel, Hernando walked a few steps away. He would have given anything not to hear what she had just said. What could he say to excuse the way he had behaved that night in the camp? Nothing.

'Try to follow my footsteps,' he said eventually, his voice strained. Disconsolately, he renewed the climb up the mountain, keeping his face hidden. 'Otherwise you might fall over the edge.'

In the month that Hernando was away in Adra, Brahim had found shelter in one of the many caves in the mountainside above Válor and Mecina. Aben Humeya and his most faithful followers had done the same.

After Hernando and Fátima had climbed the slopes up to the snow-covered February peaks, it was she who guided them to this cave. Hernando saw the team of mules silhouetted in the moonlight by the cave entrance. He made to go up to them, but Fátima hung back, hesitating to approach.

'Brahim?' He heard the sound of someone's voice before he saw who it was in the cave mouth: Aisha.

'No, this is Fátima,' the girl replied. 'I'm here with Ibn Hamid. He . . . What about Brahim? Is he back?'

'No. He hasn't arrived yet.'

Hearing this, Fátima rushed inside the cave.

'Wait! I'll—' said Hernando, trying to stop her.

She did not even hesitate.

'I'm sorry, Mother,' he said. 'I had to leave. It was the King's orders. Didn't Brahim tell you?'

Almost in spite of herself, his mother hugged him tight. Then, wiping away her tears and shaking her head, she stepped away from him and followed the girl back into the dark cave. Hernando was left outside on his own: he stood there, arms hanging limply by his sides. He looked at the mule team, and went over to them. He felt his way along until he reached La Vieja, who brayed gently and turned her head towards him. He stroked her with all the affection he wished he could have shown his mother.

Brahim did not return for another fortnight. He spent all that time at Aben Aboo's side, waiting for him to recover. During this time, Hernando never once entered the cave. He slept out in the open, and neither Aisha nor Fátima said a word to him, apart from on the morning after his arrival, when his mother came out to give him breakfast alongside the mules.

'You ran away with no explanation.'

Hernando tried to stammer an excuse, but Aisha stopped him with a brusque gesture. 'You ran away, and that gave full rein to your father's appetites, which you are well aware of. You left Fátima to him. Like a coward, you handed her over to your step-father . . . and me as well.'

'I did not run away! The King entrusted me with a mission. Brahim knew all about it, and promised he would tell you!' Hernando managed to say. 'And I've made amends for what I did to Fátima. The King has changed his mind: she will not have to marry Brahim.'

Aisha shook her head. Her mouth was drawn in a tight line. Then her chin began to tremble, and she turned aside to hide the tears welling in her eyes.

Taken aback by his mother's reaction, Hernando stopped speaking.

'You don't know what you're saying,' she wailed. 'You have no idea what the consequences of the King's change of heart will be.'

But Aisha did not cry when Brahim hit her as hard as he could. He struck her outside the cave as soon as he returned. Fátima, the children, and several Moriscos who were sharing out their scant provisions nearby were all witnesses. When Hernando saw his mother collapse to the ground, he drew his scimitar.

'He is my husband!' Aisha screamed as she lay prone.

For a few long moments Brahim and his stepson stared at each other defiantly. In the end, the lad lowered his gaze; the scene had taken him back to his childhood and, despite himself, he felt powerless faced with the utter hatred glinting in his step-father's eyes. He knew Brahim was capable of unleashing all that hate on his innocent mother. Seeing Hernando hesitate, the muleteer knocked him down with a single blow, then threw himself on the boy and went on furiously punching him. Hernando did not fight back: better that than to see his mother beaten.

'Stay away from Fátima!' Brahim muttered, sweating from the punishment he had meted out. 'Or your mother will be the one to feel the weight of my fists. Is that clear? The King may hold you in high regard, you Nazarene dog, but nobody would dare interfere in the way a Morisco treats his wife. I don't want to see you in my house.'

In spite of his other shortcomings, Aben Humeya had remained constant in his affection for the young muleteer. Following the Christian attack on Mecina, the King had been concerned about what had happened to Hernando. He had sent for him, and been happy to learn he had escaped safe and sound. He had smiled at him and asked after Fátima: Hernando had muttered an incomprehensible reply that Aben Humeya had taken to be shyness. He then ordered him to look after the animals in the camp. 'We need your skill with horses,' the King had said. 'I told you the men would be back, didn't I?'

It was true. Over the past fortnight Hernando had seen how the number of horses in the camp had grown. The Moriscos had returned to the mountains to accompany their King, and were swearing to be faithful to him until death.

'The Marquis of Mondéjar has been stripped of his command as captain-general of the kingdom. They have called him back to court,' El Gironcillo explained to Hernando one day as he was shoeing his dappled stallion, which still bore not only his immense weight but that of his harquebus, the longest and heaviest in all the Alpujarra. With the horse's hoof on his thigh, Hernando raised his head towards him. 'The lawyers and clerks in the chancery have won. They are the ones who stole our lands, and now they have been quick to complain to the King about the way the marquis was pardoning our people. They want to wipe us out!'

Hernando waved to El Gironcillo to pass him the horseshoe as quickly as possible. 'Who is in command of the Christian troops now?' the lad asked, before he hammered on the nail fixing the shoe to the hoof.

El Gironcillo was silent for a while, admiring Hernando's prowess. 'Prince John of Austria,' he said when the shoe was in place. 'He's the Emperor's bastard son, the half-brother of King Philip II. He's a haughty, arrogant youth. It's said the Spanish King has ordered the regular troops and the Naples galleys to return to Spain to serve under the Prince, the Duke of Sesa and the Knight Commander of Castile. They are taking this seriously.'

Hernando let go of the dappled stallion and straightened up in front of the Morisco warrior. Despite the winter cold, he was pouring with sweat.

'If things are so serious, why are so many men coming back to the mountains? Wouldn't it be better for them to surrender?'

It was a saddler who had recently arrived in the camp, and whom Aben Humeya had put in charge of looking after the bits, tackle and saddles, who provided the answer. He came towards them, keen to hear what El Gironcillo had to say.

'We already have done,' he called out, still some way from them. They both turned to look at him. 'Some of us did surrender, and where did it get us? They stole from us. They killed the men and made our women and children their slaves. None of the Christians respected the safe conducts the Marquis of Mondéjar promised. Better to die fighting for our cause than to be betrayed and killed by those wretches.'

'The Prince and the fresh troops will take some time to reach Granada,' said El Gironcillo. 'In the meantime, there is no one in command. Mondéjar has been ousted; most of the Marquis of los Vélez's men have deserted, and he does not yet know what his new role will be. There are thousands of wild, leaderless men roaming the Alpujarra, looting, killing and taking prisoner people who only want peace. They want to make money and return home before John of Austria takes charge.'

What had begun four months earlier as a rebellion in defence of Muslim customs, justice and their traditional way of life had now turned into a fresh revolt, a fight for life and freedom. Surrender and submission led only to death and slavery. So from all over the Alpujarra, the Moriscos, with their families and their few possessions, came flooding to the Sierra Nevada to be with their King.

Despite Aisha's constant exhortations to do so, Fátima refused to leave her. Brahim submitted Aisha to daily humiliation, making sure the girl was present on each occasion, as though constantly to remind her she was the one responsible. Seven-year-old Aquil imitated his father, seeking his approval with violent, disdainful behaviour towards his mother. As a consequence, the two women sought solace in each other: Fátima tried to comfort Aisha silently, feeling she was the one to blame. Aisha welcomed her as if she were one of her daughters lost at Juviles, and tried to show by her affection that she did not consider her responsible for her troubles. Neither of them spoke of their grief. Every rough gesture or insult from Brahim brought the two women closer together.

Each evening when Hernando returned after dealing with the horses, he became the anguished witness of Brahim's behaviour. Aisha would not let him intervene, and he could not approach Fátima, who still seemed not to have forgiven him. Yet because he could not bear to be apart from the only two people he loved, Hernando stayed close to the cave, on guard to make sure his stepfather kept his word and did not physically mistreat his mother. Whenever he heard Brahim insulting her, he gripped Hamid's scimitar in impotent rage. Fátima had not said another word to him, and it was Aisha who silently brought him a bowl of food every evening.

As soon as he heard the call to prayer, Hernando joined in devoutly. One night he even found himself calling on the Christian Virgin. Andrés, the Juviles sacristan, had stressed how the Virgin could intercede on his behalf with God, and so he commended himself to her, also conscious of what Hamid had taught him:

'As Muslims, we defend Maryam. We believe in her virginity. Yes,' the old holy man insisted when he saw his pupil's surprised reaction. 'Both the Koran and the Sunna confirm it. Don't listen to anyone who mocks her purity and chastity. Many Muslims do so, but they are forgetting our teachings simply in order to attack the Christians still further, to pour scorn on their beliefs. But they are wrong: Maryam is one of the four models of perfection for women. She did give birth to Isa, the person the Christians call Jesus Christ, without losing her virginity. Even from the cradle, Isa defended her. The Koran teaches us that shortly after his birth Isa spoke in defence of his mother's virginity when his family were insulting her because they did not believe her story.'

Despite his own blind faith in Hamid, at this point Hernando had screwed up his eyes doubtfully. How could they as Moriscos defend the mother of the Christian god?

'Remember,' Hamid went on in order to convince him, 'that when the Prophet finally succeeded in conquering Mecca and made his triumphant entrance into the Kaaba, he commanded that the idols be destroyed: Hubal, the patron of Mecca; Wad, Suwaa, Yagut, Yahuq, Nasr and many others. He also ordered all the wall paintings be covered over, except for the mural showing Maryam and her son. 'And don't forget', Hamid added sagely, 'that Maryam never committed original sin. As the Koran and the Sunna state, she was born pure.'

But had it not been one of the priests of the son of Maryam who had raped his mother when she was a defenceless child? Hernando asked himself that night. Had that not been the start of all his mother's troubles? And his stepfather constantly spat 'Nazarene dog!' at him. Whenever he heard that, Hernando clenched his fists, driving the nails into the palms of his hands. Everyone else heard it too! If he had not enjoyed Aben Humeya's favour, they would all have treated him the same way. He knew it: he could see how the Moriscos glanced at him out of the corner of their eyes, and muttered behind his back. In spite of his pleas for Maryam to intercede, neither the Christian nor the Muslim God showed any sign of offering any help to Aisha, Fátima, or him.

As the days went by Aben Humeya took advantage of his enemy's indecision and the unconditional support of his own people to regroup and, above all, to rearm. He named new governors for the Alpujarra districts and set up a tax system for his kingdom: the tenth part of all fruit and other harvests, and the fifth part of all booty won from the Christians. The sailing season had just begun, and with it came adventurers, soldiers of fortune, and janissaries keen to help their brothers in al-Andalus. Finally the Moriscos were seeing the so-often-promised soldiers from the Sublime Porte!

The King of Granada and Córdoba won two important victories over the Christians, which raised his followers' hopes still higher. The first was at Órgiva, against Prince John and his men; the second was at La Ragua pass, against a hundred of the Marquis of los Vélez's troops.

Following these skirmishes, a period of calm descended on

the Alpujarra. Everything was so quiet that a market grew up in Ugíjar that became as important as the one at Tetuan. So many merchants came and the market was so busy that Aben Humeya decided to set up a customs force to collect taxes on all the transactions.

The two victories also meant there were many more horses for Hernando to look after in the stables, most of them captured from the Christians.

'You should learn to ride,' the King told him one day while he was inspecting the horses in a meadow, surrounded by several of the harquebusiers in the special bodyguard he had created. 'That's the only way to really get to know them. Besides' – Aben Humeya smiled at him – 'my most trusted men ought to be able to ride alongside me.'

Hernando looked at the horses. He had only been on horseback once, when he had been fleeing from Tablate with El Gironcillo, and yet . . . what was it about the King that inspired such confidence? His smile? Hernando tilted his head to one side. His noble bearing, which came from being one of the most prominent councillors in Granada, and now a king? His grace and bravery?

Aben Humeya was still smiling at him. 'Come on,' he pressed him.

The King allowed him to choose his mount. Hernando put a bridle on a bay stallion, which looked to him to be the quietest, most docile animal he had under his care. As soon as he tightened the girths, the reddish tints of its black coat came to life and shone in the bright Sierra Nevada sun. He hesitated before raising a foot to the stirrup; by now both horse and rider were breathing heavily. He turned back to look at the King, who waved for him to mount the horse. Hernando slid his left foot into the stirrup and was swinging his right leg over when all of a sudden the horse neighed and took off at a gallop.

Hernando could not bring his mount under control. Within a few strides he fell off and landed on his back among the rocks and bushes. Aben Humeya came over, but Hernando quickly got to his feet despite the pain and refused the hand the King held out to him. Some of the bodyguards were laughing.

'Your first lesson,' Aben Humeya told him. 'Horses are not stupid mules or donkeys. You can never be sure that a horse will behave the same way with you on his back as he does when you are on the ground.' As he listened to him, Hernando was studying the horse, which stood calmly chewing at some shrubs a few yards away. 'Try again,' the King added. 'There are two ways to ride. The first is using a bridle, as Christians in all countries do, although the Spaniards less than others, perhaps because of what they have learnt from us. Their armour is so big and heavy they are not agile on horseback. When that Devil Iron Head climbs on to a horse, it starts to tremble and urinate out of fear. I've seen it happen. He controls and dominates them through brute strength, just as he does with men. But we Muslims ride differently, like the Berbers in the desert do, with short stirrups and controlling the horse with our legs and knees rather than bridle and spurs. Be strict if need be, but above all be intelligent and sensitive. That is the only way to control animals like these.'

Hernando made as if to catch his first mount again, but Aben Humeya went on: 'Ibn Hamid, you've chosen a mount with a black coat. Horses' colours relate to the four elements: air, fire, water and earth. Dark bays like that one take their colouring from the earth. That's why they are melancholy, and although they might appear to be quiet, they are also bad-tempered and short-sighted. That's why it threw you off.'

Having said this, the King turned away, leaving Hernando on his own with the horses, uncertain as to what elements the other horses' coats corresponded to, or what attributes and faults they might have.

Every day, he returned to the cave at night with all his bones aching. Some days he hobbled along; on others, he was completely lame; more than once he had to take his food with one hand. However, whether from luck or simply because of his youth, he had no broken bones. At least when he put his foot in the stirrup of one of the horses, he managed to forget Aisha and

Fátima, Brahim and all the Moriscos whispering behind his back . . . and that was what he needed.

Occasionally the King himself rode with him and gave him lessons. Being a nobleman, the King was a fine horseman. As they rode through the mountains, something like a friendship grew up between them. The King told him about the jousting contests and bullfights he had taken part in. He also told him the meaning of the other shades of horses' coats: white steeds were from water and were stolid, soft and slow; dark brown horses were from the air, and moved gracefully. They were good-tempered and agile, while chestnuts were fire animals, quick to flare up, impetuous and swift.

'A horse which combines all these colours in its coat, the coronets of its hoofs, or its fetlocks, in the star on its forehead or in any whorls, in its mane or tail – that horse will be the best,' the King explained one morning.

Aben Humeya was riding easily on a light chestnut stallion. By his side, Hernando was struggling once more with the bay, which the King had given him.

At nightfall Hernando would return to his mules outside the cave. Aisha and Fátima would see him go past looking dejected, greeting everyone and no one, and then seek refuge among his animals, as if they were the only reason for him being there. The mules, especially La Vieja, were the only beings he talked to. But the two women noticed that he never forgot his scimitar, which he reached for instinctively as soon as he heard Brahim's voice. Jealous of the favours the King showed the Nazarene, the Moriscos living in the other caves nearby had all sided with the muleteer. Even those who had their doubts did not want a quarrel with the burly stepfather.

Aisha suffered in silence to see her son in this state. Even Fátima could see how downcast Hernando was. For the first few days she had been so angry she treated him with disdain. How often had she thought of the way he had abandoned her during the month he was away? She had waited for him all that first night: Aisha had found a few drops of perfume for her, and as soon as she heard the noise in the King's tent begin to die down, she had sprinkled it between her breasts, fantasizing about the caresses Hernando would give her. But he never appeared! Her desire turned to scorn. She imagined how she would spit at his feet when he eventually reappeared, turn her back on him, shout at him ... even hit him! Then came Brahim's ignoble pursuit of her, his leers and constant insinuations. When she heard how Brahim, having learnt of her husband's death and knowing she had no other family, had asked the King for her hand, she cursed Hernando and heaped insults on him through her tears. On the night that he saved her at Mecina and told her of the King's change of mind, she felt both relieved and offended. While this meant that she would no longer have to marry the hateful Brahim, she could not believe the way Hernando had behaved. Did he and the King think they could decide Fátima and her son's future without even consulting her?

Yet the days went by and he was always there to watch over them. Sometimes he strode back; at others he came limping to the cave because of some fall or other. He seemed resigned to the contempt the two women showed him, and yet was ready to spring to their defence: he had shown that when he had allowed Brahim to beat him without a murmur. The Nazarene, they all called him behind his back. Aisha had been forced to tell her why he was called that, and for the first time since Hernando had returned, she felt a tightening in her throat. Perhaps Hernando thought she felt the same contempt? What exactly was he thinking, all alone with his mules?

One evening, when Aisha was going to take her son his supper, Fátima went up to her and took the bowl. She wanted to be near him. She was so conscious of how badly her hand was trembling she barely noticed the worried look Aisha gave her.

Hernando was standing waiting for her. He could scarcely believe it was Fátima walking towards him.

'Peace be with you, Ibn Hamid,' Fátima began when she reached him. She held out the bowl.

'Filthy sow!' came Brahim's shout from the cave mouth.

The bowl fell from her hands.

Fátima turned and saw by the firelight how Brahim was slapping Aisha. His hand on the hilt of his scimitar, Hernando took a couple of steps towards them, then came to a halt. When Brahim looked up and stared at her, Fátima realized why Aisha had grimaced: she had been trying to warn her. If Fátima went anywhere near Hernando, she would be the one to face the consequences. As he raised his hand to strike his wife again, an expression of evil glee crossed Brahim's face. Fátima ran back to the cave. Brahim watched her rush past him, and laughed out loud.

16

IN APRIL 1569, the regrouped Morisco army and its followers, including women and children, marched towards Ugíjar. Aben Humeya and his most trusted companions were in the lead; Hernando rode proudly among them. At the head of the long column rode a company of harquebusiers, carrying the new russet-coloured banner Aben Humeya had adopted.

The King and his bodyguard were followed by the Morisco cavalry and then the infantry. The Moriscos had learnt from the Christians and had been deployed in formation. They marched in platoons commanded by a captain, each carrying their own standard. Some of these had been sewn during their stay in the caves above Mecina, and were made of white, yellow or crimson cotton or silk, with silver or gold crescent moons in the centre, silk or gold fringes, or tassels adorned with seed pearls. Others marched proudly beneath banners and standards from the days when the Muslims ruled in al-Andalus. Among them were the men of Mecina, with their gold-embroidered taffeta banner boasting a castle with three silver towers in its centre. Still others marched with banners stolen from the Christians, like that of the Holy Sacrament from Ugíjar, in scarlet damask fringed with silk and gold, on top of which the Moriscos had embroidered silver moons.

As usual the baggage train, with the women and children and all those unable to fight, brought up the rear.

Drums and rebecs sounded as they converged on Ugíjar.

Along the way they were greeted enthusiastically by the locals working in the fields as the King had commanded: it was vital for them to continue producing crops. The Christians could bring in supplies from beyond Granada, but the Moriscos had to survive on their own resources. The unexpected truce brought about by the handover to Prince John of Austria, who was still caught up in discussions in the city, had given them the opportunity to sow and harvest a new season's crops.

Hernando sat erect in the saddle, by now completely in control of his bay. He constantly reined his mount in, however, because he had no wish to join the group of horsemen in front of him. Brahim, who had become Aben Aboo's inseparable companion, was one of them. The King's cousin had to ride with several lambskins under him to prevent his scars hurting, but even so he often grimaced with pain. He rode alongside the King, with Brahim right behind them.

Even from the saddle Hernando could not make out the rear of the column, because his view was blocked by the giant Morisco warriors. Aisha and Fátima were far off, with the other women and the mules, which were being looked after by Aquil and a quick-witted young boy called Yusuf, whom Hernando had met up at the caves and asked if he could help his step-brother. There were far too many mules for Aquil to look after on his own.

Ugíjar welcomed them with flags, music and dancing. It was a different town from the one they had fled. Workmen were busy converting the collegiate church back into a mosque. The bells the Moriscos had taken out their wrath on lay smashed at the foot of the bell tower. The triangle in between the three defensive towers had been turned into a vast market that spilled over into the neighbouring streets. The entire place was a mass of colour, smells and noise. Above all, it was full of new people: Berbers, corsairs and Muslim traders from the far side of the strait. Most of them dressed in a similar fashion to the Moriscos, although some wore djellabas, but what truly amazed Hernando was their appearance: some were tall and blond, with milky-white skins; others were red-haired and green-eyed; and there were many freed Negro slaves. They all moved about among the Berbers as though they belonged.

'They're renegade Christians,' El Gironcillo explained when he saw that Hernando was so dumbfounded at the sight of a huge albino that he almost collided with him.

The albino smiled at him in a curious way, as if . . . as if inviting him to dismount and go with him. Confused, Hernando turned towards the outlaw leader.

'You must never trust them,' El Gironcillo warned him when they were out of earshot. 'Their customs are very different from ours: they adore young boys like you. The renegade Christians are the real rulers of Algiers; they are pirates and they look down on us. Tetuan belongs to the Moriscos, and so do Salah, La Mámora and Vélez, but Algiers—'

'Aren't they Turks?' Hernando interrupted him.

'No.'

'What then?'

'In Algiers there are janissaries who live alongside the renegades. They are Turkish soldiers sent by the Sultan.' At this, El Gironcillo stood on his stirrups and peered round the market. 'No, they're not here yet. You'll recognize them as soon as you see them. They take their orders directly from the Sultan, not the beylerbey of Algiers. They have their own leaders, the agas. Forty years ago, Khair ad-Din, the one the Christians call Barbarossa, made his kingdom a vassal of the Sublime Porte, of our Sultan, the one who has promised to help us in our fight against the Christians . . . But make no mistake, you cannot trust the renegades from Algiers, especially since you're such a good-looking lad.' He laughed. 'Never turn your back on them!'

El Gironcillo's laughter brought their conversation to an end. Aben Humeya was dismounting, and looked round for Hernando to come and take the horses. In the tumult of the army's arrival, Hernando tried to spot Fátima and Aisha, but the rearguard had not yet reached the village. First he had to take care of the horses; then he could see what had happened to the women.

Just as he had done in Paterna, Aben Humeya now ordered several of the harquebusiers from his personal guard to accompany Hernando. On the outskirts of the village beyond the teeming streets behind Ugíjar church, he found a suitable two-storey house that had enough land for the King and his lieutenants' horses. The house must have belonged to one of the Christian families murdered during the revolt. There was no direct access from the street, as the property was surrounded by a low wall.

'Clear the house!' one of the guards shouted at the Morisco family who came rushing out to greet them.

They were a middle-aged couple. Like most Morisco matrons, she was quite fat; he was even plumper, and was carrying an ancient gun that he lowered when he saw the soldiers. They were surrounded by a swarm of seven children of all ages.

Hernando could see that the wife was as submissive as all Morisco women were. A child no more than two years old was hiding behind her, clutching at her rolled-up stockings. Perhaps, he thought, perhaps the presence of this family and all their children could create a different atmosphere from the one in the cave.

'Do you know anything about animals?' Hernando asked the man, hoping against hope he would say yes. 'In that case,' he said, after the man had twisted his mouth in a way he chose to interpret as an affirmation, 'you and your family can help me with the King's horses, and we can share the dwelling.'

Despite being slowed up by three children round his feet, Hernando quickly unsaddled the dozen animals in his charge. He did not care about the man's obvious lack of experience: the only thing that mattered to him was to find Aisha and Fátima.

He left the house as quickly as he could. He would feed the animals when he got back. But when he went out through the wrought-iron gate into the earthen street and saw that Aben

Humeya's soldiers were spreading through the whole village and coming up the street, he turned back.

'Close the gate and stand guard behind it,' he ordered the harquebusiers. 'Nobody is to come in. Keep watch on all sides. Remember: these are the King's horses.'

As two of the men began to carry out his orders, a large group of soldiers and their families tried to push their way into the house.

'This place is for the King's horses,' he warned them. The guards slammed the gates shut behind him.

He had to struggle against a flood of people. The village was too small to accommodate all the Moriscos; a mass of soldiers and their families was heading for the outlying houses just as he was trying to reach the centre. He tried to skirt the crowds he ran into, but sometimes found he had to force a way through the crush of people. Where could he find the women? The mules! It would be easy enough to find them, even if—

Hernando collided with a man.

'*Cornuti!*'

He felt himself being pushed violently against another group coming towards him; they in their turn drove him in the opposite direction. The flood of men and women halted. A small space opened up in the middle of the street.

'*Señori . . .*'

Bewildered, Hernando turned to face the man who had pushed him. What language was he speaking? 'I'll kill you!' He understood that plainly enough, and at that moment saw a man with blond curls rushing towards him brandishing a fine dagger with a bejewelled hilt. The stranger loosed off another volley of incomprehensible words. He was not speaking Spanish, Arabic or the *aljamiado* language. To Hernando it sounded as if he was mixing up words from many different tongues.

'Dog!' the man growled.

Hernando understood that too, but he was in a hurry. If Brahim found the two women before he did, he might take them somewhere else. That meant he would lose track of them, because he could not leave the King's horses. He tried to escape and continue on his way, but found his path blocked by the crowd that had gathered to watch the argument. Someone pushed him back into the centre of the circle around the blond stranger. More people thronged to look at what was going on. His opponent was waving the dagger threateningly in small circles in front of him. When Hernando saw this was his only weapon, he unsheathed his scimitar.

'Allah is great!' he cried in Arabic. Grasping the sword in both hands, he held it level with his chest, as if about to strike. He planted his feet firmly on the ground and stiffened his whole body.

The blond stranger stared at his blue eyes.

'*Bello!*' he suddenly said, softly rolling the l's as he spoke.

'Beautiful!' Hernando heard someone say beside the man. He kept staring straight ahead.

One of the Moriscos laughed. Some others whistled.

'*Bellissimo!*' said the blond man, rolling the l's once more. All at once he tucked the dagger back in his belt and started up a loud, incomprehensible conversation with his companion. Hernando was still on the alert, scimitar raised and a defiant look on his face, but how could he attack an unarmed man who was not paying him the slightest attention? The stranger looked his way again. He smiled and winked before turning and forcing his way through the crowd, which hastily opened before him.

'*Belllllo,*' Hernando heard one of the Moriscos repeat amusedly.

He could feel the blood rushing to his cheeks. As the guffaws spread through the crowd he could feel himself growing hot with shame. He sheathed his sword, unable to look anyone in the face.

'Beautiful!' laughed the man he pushed out of the way to escape. As he forced his way through, somebody else pinched his buttocks.

He found the two women with the mules at the entrance to the village, wondering where they should go. The young boys were trying to prevent the team of mules wandering off with one of the streams of people flowing round them. Neither Aisha nor Fátima, nor even Hernando's stepbrothers, could hide their relief at the speed with which he took charge of the situation. Even the mules, starting with La Vieja, seemed pleased to hear his familiar voice when he began to shout and get them into line. No one had any news of Brahim.

When they reached Salah's house, the obese Morisco received them so deferentially he was almost servile. Hernando told himself that one of the guards must have mentioned the esteem he was held in by Aben Humeya.

Salah installed his family on the ground floor, and let the new arrivals take over the upper storey. One of the bedrooms still boasted a big bed with what must once have been a magnificent canopy. He told them he had sold the rest of the furniture, swearing on his life that before he did so he had destroyed all the Christian tapestries and images.

Salah was a sly merchant who sold both Christians and Muslims what they needed. In wartime there was a lot of money about, so why should he, as he often said, break his back trying to make stones grow as the farmers of the Alpujarra did on their inhospitable lands, when he could be selling what others produced?

Night was falling. Fátima and Aisha helped Salah's wife prepare the supper. She did not seem to mind in the least that she had five extra mouths to feed. Yusuf, the boy who had helped with the horses, seemed more than happy to share the comforts the new house offered. Hernando accepted him because he had seen how good he was with the animals. He could not count on much other help: his stepbrothers shunned him and would not go near the mules if he was present, while despite their father's willingness, Salah's children knew nothing about animals.

Fátima brought out some fresh lemonade to the men on the

front porch. She was not wearing a veil, and smiled at Hernando when she handed him his drink. The lad felt a wrench in his stomach. Had she forgiven him? He could also hear his mother talking and laughing in the kitchen. There was still no sign of Brahim. When Hernando relieved the guards, he told one of the soldiers to ask after his stepfather and come back with whatever news he could find.

'You'll find him with Ibn Abbu,' the soldier reported, after asking one of the King's captains for his whereabouts.

Before going back inside the house, Fátima had looked Hernando in the eye for several seconds. And she had smiled at him again!

'A good wife,' Salah commented, breaking the spell. 'Nice and quiet.'

Hernando raised the glass to his mouth. He glanced at the merchant out of the corner of his eye. Although it was a cold night, the man seemed to be in a sweat. Hernando mumbled something unintelligible to him.

'Allah has blessed you with a son. My first two children were daughters,' Salah went on.

Hernando was annoyed at his chatter. He could of course throw him and his family out . . . but then he again heard his mother chatting happily in the kitchen: how long had it been since he had heard her laugh? But he did not want to explain too much to Salah about his own family.

'But then He brought you four boys,' he said.

Salah was about to reply, but at that moment the muezzin's call to prayer silenced the hubbub of the market and stifled his curiosity.

The two men prayed and then had supper. The merchant had a well-stocked larder. He kept the provisions under lock and key together with a wide variety of other goods down in the basement, where the Christian family had kept their oil press. When they had finished eating, Hernando took Yusuf and went to inspect the horses and mules. They were all grazing peacefully, but they had destroyed Salah's wife's vegetable garden, and although she looked beseechingly at her husband, there was nothing either of them could do about it. 'They're the King's horses,' Salah told her helplessly, also turning his head eloquently towards the armed guards.

They're going to need barley and fodder, thought Hernando. In a couple of days they would have completely stripped the garden, but the King had told him the horses should be ready at all times, which meant he could not take the animals to graze in the fields outside the village. He would have to find enough feed for them the next morning. His inspection complete, Hernando laid out blankets on the porch.

'I prefer to sleep out here to be near the animals,' he explained hastily, before Salah could ask him what he was doing.

Yusuf stayed with him, and the two of them talked until they fell fast asleep. The boy listened keenly to everything Hernando had to say. The new guards dozed at their posts. The women and children went to sleep on the two floors of the house: Aisha had the main bedroom. Even though he was outside, for the first time in many nights Hernando slept soundly: Fátima had smiled at him again.

At first light he attended to the animals, then decided to go and see the King to ask for money to buy fodder. The King had again installed himself in the house of Pedro López, the chief administrator for the Alpujarra, which was close to the church. He could not see Hernando because he was receiving the commanders of a company of janissaries who had just arrived from Algiers. These were the two hundred men the Sultan had ordered the beylerbey to send to al-Andalus, to keep their brothers in faith happy, if not to give them a false impression.

Hernando saw them wandering around the huge market-place that Ugíjar had become. As El Gironcillo had said, it was impossible not to notice them. Although the town was full of people – traders, Berbers, soldiers of fortune, Moriscos and Aben Humeya's troops – whenever these Turkish warriors appeared, everyone shrank back in fear. They were not dressed in the caps and cloaks in which Farax (who was now lost somewhere in the mountains) had disguised his Morisco followers when they were trying to encourage the inhabitants of the Granada Albaicín to join the revolt. Instead, they sported big turbans, many of which flopped down to one side, so that their fringes almost brushed the ground. They wore pantaloons, long tunics and workmanlike slippers, and many of them had long, fine moustaches. But what was most impressive about them was the amount of weapons they carried: long-barrelled harquebuses, scimitars and daggers.

They had disembarked on the coast of the Alpujarra under the command of Dalí. He was the janissaries' *ayabachi*, one of the highest positions beneath that of aga, and was chosen democratically by the divan of almost twelve thousand members in Algiers. Dalí had with him two subordinates: Caracax and Hussein, and these were the three men Aben Humeya was busy talking to.

The janissaries had been set up as an élite militia on the Sultan's orders. They were faithful, indomitable soldiers. They were forcibly recruited from Christian children over the age of eight who lived in the extensive European settlements in the Ottoman empire. One was taken from every forty houses, and they were then taught the Muslim faith and trained as soldiers, despite their young years. Once they became fully fledged janissaries they were entitled to be paid for life and enjoyed many privileges. They administered their own justice: no janissary could be held to account or punished even by the bey. They were governed entirely by their aga, who always tried them in secret.

The Algiers janissaries had, however, abandoned the system of forced recruitment of Christian boys in the Ottoman empire. The janissaries originally transferred to Algiers from the empire were gradually replaced by their sons or other Turks, or even renegade Christians, although Arabs and Berbers could never join this élite corps. The janissaries were a privileged caste. They constantly looted the villages of Barbary and Algiers. Secure in their power and privileges, they showed utter contempt for everyone else, and thought nothing of raping children and women. No one could touch a janissary!

The two hundred of them whom the Sultan had ordered the bey of Algiers to dispatch to al-Andalus to appease the Moriscos were there to fight, but that did not mean they gave up any of their privileges. Hernando could see as much while he waited outside the administrator's house for the soldier from Aben Humeya's bodyguard to return with the King's answer.

While he was waiting, in order to satisfy his curiosity and to keep him from staring in fascination at the janissaries lounging outside the building, he asked one of the harquebusiers on guard in the doorway: 'Do you know what's become of Brahim the muleteer? He's my stepfather.'

'He left last night,' the man replied. 'He went with Ibn Abbu and a company of soldiers to Poqueira. The King has appointed his cousin mayor of Poqueira, and Ibn Abbu has made your stepfather his lieutenant.'

'How long will they be in Poqueira?' Hernando asked, unable to keep an eager note out of his voice.

The guard shrugged.

Brahim had left! Hernando turned with a smile towards the market spread out in front of the house. Just at that moment, a street-seller came by carrying a basket of raisins on his back. One of the janissaries grabbed a handful. The seller turned and, without thinking, roughly pushed the man who had stolen his humble produce.

It all happened in an instant. None of the janissaries took the seller to task for his insolence, but several of them grabbed hold of him. One forced his arm out straight, and with a single clean blow from his scimitar the offended janissary chopped his hand off at the wrist. The hand fell into the basket of raisins. The fruit-seller was kicked on his way, while the janissaries resumed their conversation as though nothing had happened. This was the punishment for anybody who dared touch one of the soldiers of the Sultan of the Sublime Porte.

Hernando found it impossible to react. He stood rooted to the spot, mesmerized by the trail of blood the fruit-seller left behind him until he collapsed on the ground a few steps further on. He was so absorbed by the sight that the King's guard had to tap him on the shoulder to attract his attention.

'Follow me,' he told Hernando when the lad finally looked round.

The house was again perfumed with musk, but this time Hernando was not led into Aben Humeya's presence. Instead, the guard took him to a room on the first floor. Two harquebusiers stood outside the carved wooden door. The treasure the King had not sent to Algiers must be stored inside, thought Hernando.

'Are you Ibn Hamid?' he heard someone ask behind him. Hernando turned and found himself facing a richly dressed Morisco. 'Ibn Umayya has told me about you.' The stranger held out his hand. 'I'm Mustafa Calderón. I'm from Ugíjar and a King's councillor.'

After this greeting, Mustafa felt for a bunch of keys at his waist, and opened the door.

'Here you have all the barley you need for your horses,' he said, holding out his hand for Hernando to step inside.

How could the barley be in there? This was not a granary. Hernando was so surprised that he did not get beyond the doorway.

The loud laughter from Mustafa and the three harquebusiers did nothing to lessen Hernando's astonishment: by the light from a small window high on the wall, he saw almost a dozen young boys and girls huddled inside the room. The girls stared at him, terrified, trying to hide behind each other, huddled at the far end of the room.

'The King wants to keep the jewels and money he has left,' the councillor explained, sniffing loudly. 'Gold is easier to transport than the children he has been given as his share of the plunder ... and coins do not eat!' He laughed again. 'Choose the one you want and sell her in the market. With what she fetches, you'll be able to buy all you need, although I'll expect to see you once a month to account for your spending. It's not what I would have done, but it is what the King wants. He has also said that if you are to ride with him, you must buy yourself some proper clothing.'

'How ... how am I going to sell a girl?'

'They'll snatch her from you, my boy,' said Mustafa. 'Christian women are much sought after in Algiers, a city in the power of Turks and renegade Christians who have no wish to marry Muslims. Not even the Turks want to! Listen,' he said, putting a hand on his shoulder, 'a Christian captive can be rescued by those Mercedarian or Trinitarian friars who go to Barbary with lots of money, but they will never free a woman. One of the few laws governing the lives of the corsairs is one which forbids the sale of women. They worship them!'

'But ...' Hernando began to say, noting how the girls were clinging together even more tightly.

'Choose the one you want, now!' Mustafa pressed him. 'We're holding a meeting with the Turks, and I can't waste any more time here.'

How was Hernando going to sell a girl? What did he know about ...?

'I can't ...' he protested, until suddenly he saw the straw-coloured hair of a trembling, filthy little girl right in front of him, whom one of the older girls had pushed roughly out of the group. 'That one!' he shouted without thinking.

'Done!' Mustafa concluded. 'Tie her up and give her to him,' he ordered the guards before hurrying off. 'Remember, I will see you in a month,' he said as he left.

Hernando was no longer listening. He was staring at his captive. It was Isabel, Gonzalico's sister! What could have become of Ubaid? he wondered, remembering how the muleteer had triumphantly held up the boy's heart before flinging it at the girl's feet.

In no time at all he was outside in the street again. Soldiers and janissaries stared at him as he stood there with the rope attached to the little straw-haired girl. Dazzled by the thousand reflections the sun cast all around him, he was afraid to move. How had he not noticed this before? Why did the market place seem like such a new world to him?

'Hey, my lad, where are you going with that beauty?' he heard someone ask slyly.

Hernando did not reply. Why had he accepted Mustafa's offer? What on earth was he going to do with Isabel? Sell her? Memories of the massacre at Cuxurio and Isabel's cries for help mingled with the thousands of colours and smells floating in the air. How could he sell her? Hadn't the young girl already suffered enough? Why was she to blame? But why then had he chosen her? He had not even thought about it. The rope pulled tight, and Hernando turned back to look at the little girl: a janissary was trying to seize hold of her, and she had drawn back fearfully.

He took a step towards the Turk, but the memory of the fruit-seller's severed hand brought him up short. Isabel had started to sob again. Her eyes were open wide, and she was staring straight at him, begging him to help just as she had done in Cuxurio when Ubaid had murdered her brother. Isabel backed into the guardsmen, but could not get through. The janissary began to stroke her golden hair.

'Leave her!' Hernando cried. He dropped the rope and unsheathed his sword.

He did not even have time to raise it. With astonishing rapidity, the janissary drew his own scimitar and in the same movement struck Hernando's weapon, which went flying through the air. The lad shook his hand to relieve the pain, while all the onlookers guffawed.

'Leave the child!' Hernando insisted, despite his reverse.

The janissary turned to look at Hernando, while with one hand he continued caressing Isabel's budding breasts. His white teeth gleamed in a lecherous smile, adding another glinting reflection to the market place. 'I want to see the goods,' he said slowly.

Hernando hesitated for a few moments. 'And I want to see your money,' he stammered. 'Before you inspect the goods.'

As if this was all a game, several of the other janissaries cheered Hernando on.

'Well said!' they laughed.

'Yes, show him your money . . .'

At this instant, the guard who had prevented the girl escaping, and was also the man who had shown Hernando into the King's house, whispered something in the janissary's ear. The Turk listened in silence, and then twisted his mouth in disappointment.

'She's not worth a ducat!' he growled after thinking it over for a few seconds. He pushed Isabel away.

'You'll get more than three hundred for her, my lad,' another janissary put in.

Hernando picked up the rope, and then went over to where Hamid's scimitar was lying, beyond the group who were still chortling at him. He pulled on the rope and set off, making sure he carefully avoided the janissaries.

'That old scimitar will be no use to you unless you learn to hold it tight,' one of the men shouted as he picked it up.

The noise, crowds, colours and smells of the market place came flooding back to Hernando. Sheathing his sword, he stood upright. What was he going to do with the girl? he wondered. Even as he did so, he saw several merchants come rushing towards him.

17

'GO ON. You're free.'

Hernando had managed to ignore the merchants' shouted offers as he crossed the market. 'She's already sold!' he said, tugging on Isabel's rope to keep her away from them. 'Don't touch her!' He also had to run the gauntlet of others who, when they saw the young Christian girl, followed the two of them and made all kinds of propositions, without even knowing what her price was.

When they finally reached the outskirts of the village, he crouched down with her behind a low wall that ran between the road and an olive grove. He untied her.

'Run!' he whispered when he had undone the knot.

Isabel was trembling, and so was he. He was setting free the slave the King had given him to buy fodder for his animals!

'Run away!' he hissed at the girl, but she did not move. Unable to say a word, her eyes showed nothing but terror. 'Go on!'

He pushed her away, but she merely crouched closer to the wall. Hernando stood up and made as if to leave her.

'Where should I go?' she asked in the faintest of voices.

'Well . . .' Hernando waved his hands in the air. Then he took a good look at the mountains in the distance. Here and there he could see the camp fires of the soldiers and Moriscos there was no room for in Ugíjar; most of them were part of Aben Humeya's great army. 'I don't know! I've enough problems of my own.' He sighed. 'I ought to sell you and buy fodder for the King's horses. How am I supposed to feed them if I let you go? Do you want me to sell you?'

Again Isabel said nothing, but looked up at him imploringly. Hernando saw a group of men coming, and ducked down beside her, motioning to her to be quiet. They waited for the men to pass by. What was he going to do? he wondered. How could he feed the horses? What would the King do if he found out?

'Go on! Run away!' he repeated as soon as the men's voices died away in the distance. How could he possibly sell Gonzalico's sister? He had not been able to persuade that stubborn young boy to renounce his faith. He had not even convinced him he only had to lie! He had a vivid memory of the youngster who had slept peacefully by his side, holding his hand, the night before Ubaid had slit his throat and ripped his heart out. 'Get out of here!'

Hernando stood up and walked back towards the village. He did not dare look back, but after a dozen or more steps, he was gripped by curiosity, and turned. She was following him! Barefoot, wretched, tears streaming down her cheeks, Isabel was scurrying along behind him. Her mop of unkempt straw-coloured hair glinted in the noonday sun. He gestured in the opposite direction, but she did not move. He told her to run, but she stood stock-still.

Hernando went back to her. 'I'll sell you!' he said, dragging her off the road to the wall once more. 'If you follow me, I'll sell you. You've seen how everyone wants to buy you, haven't you?'

Isabel was still crying. Hernando waited for her to calm down, but the tears kept flowing.

'You could escape,' he insisted. 'You could wait until nightfall and slip through them.'

'And then what?' Isabel interrupted him, still sobbing. 'Then where would I go?'

Hernando had to admit that the Alpujarra was all in the hands of the Moriscos. From Ugíjar to Órgiva, for more than seven leagues to where the Marquis of Mondéjar had his camp, there were no Christians. Nor were there any between Ugíjar and the Marquis of los Vélez's army in Berja. Everywhere was teeming with Moriscos, who were on the lookout for anyone who moved. Where could a little girl like her go without being captured? And if she was captured . . . If she was captured, they would find out he had set her free. Hernando realized what a blunder he had made, and wearily blew his cheeks out.

To avoid crossing the market place again, he walked round the outskirts of the village until they reached Salah's house. In case they met anyone, Hernando tied the girl up again with the rope. What was he going to do with her? Pretend she was a Muslim? Everybody in Ugíjar had seen her head of dry straw hair! They would be bound to recognize her! How could he explain it? How could a Christian girl live with them? As they walked, they ran into many groups of Moriscos and soldiers who examined her with interest. Eventually, they reached the boundary wall at the back of the house.

'Hide here,' Hernando told Isabel, untying the rope once more. The girl looked round: all she could see were the wall and empty fields. 'Get down in the weeds, they'll cover you. Do as you like, but hide. If they find you . . . you know what will happen to you.' And to me too, Hernando thought to himself. 'I'll come and fetch you, but I don't know when. I don't know why either,' he said, clicking his tongue and shaking his head. 'But you will hear from me.'

He walked along the wall until he came to the main entrance to the house, trying desperately to put Isabel out of his mind. All he saw was that she dropped to the ground as soon as he started to leave her. What was he going to do with her? And even if he found a solution, what about the barley? And the fodder? Where was he going to get hold of food for the animals? They would soon have eaten all the grass around the house. Isabel! What had possessed him to choose her? He could have picked out any of them: the one who had pushed her forward, for example. But would he have been capable of selling her either?

Traditionally, the Moriscos had always helped the Berber corsairs in their raids on the Mediterranean coasts. Many of them had even joined the pirates, especially the Moriscos from Tetuan, but also the ones from Algiers. They were born in al-Andalus, and with the help of family and friends they captured Christians and sold them as slaves in Barbary. Sometimes, if they were paid the ransom, they even agreed to free them on the beaches, before setting off back to their home ports. That was in the coastal lands of the former Nasrid kingdom, not in the high Alpujarra, where the rich Moriscos usually had black Guinea slaves. Then, as Hamid had told him, the Christians banned them from keeping black slaves at all. Hernando had never sold anyone, or helped capture any Christians. How could he sell a young girl, even if she was Christian, knowing what would become of her in the hands of those corsairs or janissaries? As always when he remembered the wise old scholar, he stroked the hilt of his scimitar.

Absorbed in these thoughts, Hernando walked through the iron gates leading to the house. What . . . what was going on? More than a dozen Berber soldiers were standing talking in the yard outside. They were surrounded by harnessed horses and loaded mules. All at once Hernando felt weak and slightly dizzy. His stomach wrenched, and he broke out into a cold sweat.

One of Aben Humeya's Morisco guards came out to meet him. Hernando took an involuntary step backwards. The man looked surprised.

'Ibn Hamid . . .' he began.

Did they already know about Isabel? Was he going to be arrested? Ubaid! He saw the Narila muleteer behind one of the mules.

'What's he doing here?' he asked, raising his voice and pointing to Ubaid.

The harquebusier turned in the direction he was pointing and shrugged. Ubaid scowled.

'Him?' the harquebusier said. 'I've no idea. He came with the corsair captain. That's what I was trying to tell you: he and his men have come to join us.' Hernando was only half listening: his attention was still on Ubaid, who continued glaring at him defiantly. 'The King has allowed him to stable his animals with ours, because there is enough fodder for everyone.'

'Here?' Hernando blurted out.

'So the King says,' replied the guard.

Hernando's knees were knocking. For a brief moment, he was tempted to run away. To run away . . . or to go back to Isabel, tie her up again and sell her once and for all. It couldn't be that difficult.

'But there's another problem,' the harquebusier went on. Hernando closed his eyes: what more could go wrong? 'The Turk says that he and his men are staying here too. There is nowhere else in Ugíjar. He says if he's come here to help us fight, he's not going to sleep out in the open.'

'No,' Hernando tried to object. More people! And Ubaid too! He had a Christian captive hiding in the garden, and not a grain of barley for . . . one, two, three, four more horses, and the same number of mules. 'That's impossible . . .'

'He's already done a deal with the merchant. The corsair and his men are to have the ground floor; Salah and his family will sleep out on the porch.'

'What deal?'

The harquebusier smiled. 'I think it was something along the lines of: if Salah didn't give up the ground floor, he would bite off his nose and ears, then nail them to the mainmast of his ship.'

'The main . . . mast?'

'That's what he said,' the guard replied, shrugging his shoulders again.

Why was Hernando asking? What did he care about Salah's ears or where the corsair might nail them?

'Arrest that man,' he ordered, pointing to Ubaid again. The guard looked puzzled. 'Arrest him!' Hernando insisted. 'He . . . he's not permitted to be with the King's horses,' he said, after trying desperately for a few moments to think of an excuse.

The harquebusier seemed confused at the order, but something in Hernando's voice led him to call over several other guards, and together they went to arrest Ubaid. As they did so, some of the Berber soldiers intercepted them. They were not janissaries. Although similar in dress to the Moriscos of Granada, their skin was much lighter: they must be renegade Christians. The two groups faced each other defiantly. Hidden behind the mules, Ubaid was still staring furiously at Hernando.

'Where is their captain?' asked Hernando when the harquebusier turned towards him to receive further instructions.

The guard pointed towards the house. Hernando found the corsair captain in the dining room, seated on a pile of gaily coloured silk cushions. When he saw him, Hernando had no doubt he would be capable of biting off any ear he chose. He was a stocky man with fierce, angular features. He greeted Hernando with the same accent as the blond man who had threatened him with the dagger and then made fun of him. Another renegade Christian!

Hernando found it impossible to return his greeting. His gaze wandered from the corsair captain's face to one of his burly arms. He was twisting the curls of a young boy's hair with his right hand. The boy was richly dressed and sat on the ground at his feet.

'Does my little boy please you?' he asked when he saw Hernando's astonishment.

'What . . . ?' Hernando realized what was happening. 'No!' The word came out far more strongly than it should have done.

He saw the corsair smile, and also saw how he was looking at him lasciviously. What was the matter with these men? he asked himself in embarrassment. There he was, standing in front of a corsair captain who threatened to tear people's ears off, and yet sat there gently caressing a young boy's hair. At that moment another, slightly older boy came into the room, followed by Salah. The boy was as richly clothed as the first one, in a yellow linen djellaba over a pair of pantaloons and soft slippers of the same colour. His movements were effeminate. He handed a glass of lemonade to the captain, and then sat down close beside him.

'What about this one? Don't you like him either?' the corsair asked, before raising the lemonade to his lips.

Hernando turned to Salah for support, only to find that the merchant's puffy eyes were fixed on the trio in front of them.

'No, I don't,' Hernando eventually replied. 'I don't like either of them.' All three seemed to strip him naked with their gaze. 'You can't stay here,' he said, to put an end to the awkward situation.

'My name is Barrax,' said the corsair.

'Peace be with you, Barrax, but you cannot stay in this house.'

'My ship is called the *Flying Horse*. She is one of the fastest ships in Algiers. You'd love to sail in her.'

'That's as may be, but—'

'What is your name?'

'Hamid ibn Hamid.'

The captain rose slowly to his feet. He was wearing a simple white linen tunic, and was a good head taller than anyone else in the room. Hernando had to stop himself taking a step backwards; Salah did retreat. The corsair smiled again.

'You are a brave lad,' he acknowledged, 'but listen to me, Ibn Hamid. I am staying in this house until your King leaves with his army, and no Morisco dog, however much he enjoys the protection of Ibn Umayya, is going to stop me.'

'But we are expecting my stepfather . . . and Ibn Abbu! Yes!' Hernando said, stumbling in his agitation. 'They are in Poqueira. He is the King's cousin, and is mayor of Poqueira. If they come back, there'll be no room . . .'

'The day that happens the women and children on the top floor will have to leave to make room for the noble and valiant Ibn Abbu, as well as your stepfather.'

'But . . .'

'Don't worry, you can sleep with us, Ibn Hamid.'

With these words, the corsair captain made to leave the room, accompanied by the two small boys. One of them shimmered with gold; the other gleamed blood-red.

'Then the muleteer must not stay here,' Hernando insisted. The captain halted and raised his hands enquiringly. 'I don't want him here,' was all the explanation Hernando gave.

'Who will look after my horses and mules?'

'Don't worry about your animals. We'll take good care of them.'

'Agreed,' said the corsair as if this were a minor detail. All at once he gave a broad smile and added: 'But I consider this a favour towards such a brave young lad, Ibn Hamid. You will be in my debt . . .'

Hernando had no barley, but the animals needed feeding. Before he was forced to leave the house, Ubaid had been demanding the same thing. Through Salah, Hernando learnt that the muleteer had joined up with Barrax in Adra, where he had fled after the Marquis of Mondéjar's troops had taken Paterna. Corsairs, Berbers and Turks were constantly arriving on the coast of al-Andalus. They knew that the Spanish galleys from Naples would arrive at any moment, and that this would make any landing much more difficult. Piracy up and down the coast would also be much harder with the arrival of the Spanish fleet under the Knight Commander of Castile, and as a result many of the corsair captains wanted to make money out of the uprising or from trade with the Moriscos as quickly as possible. Barrax needed horses and mules to transport his possessions, especially the clothing and other personal effects of his young boys, who were the only ones among the corsairs allowed to travel with baggage. He had therefore hired Ubaid, who although he had only one arm had recovered his skill with animals and knew all the trails of the high Alpujarra.

It was also Salah who told Hernando of the muleteer's demand for animal fodder.

'That's my business,' Hernando replied curtly, trying to get rid of him.

When the sweaty trader had left, Hernando wondered yet again how on earth he was going to find supplies for all the animals.

It was noon, and the women were preparing a meal, but with the arrival of Barrax and his men the previous day's relaxed intimacy had vanished. Now Aisha, Fátima and Salah's wife went around the house full of strangers with their heads and faces covered. Although she could no longer smile at him, Fátima tried to let her tender gaze linger on him a few seconds longer than necessary, yet it was not long before both she and Aisha realized there was something wrong.

'What's the matter, my son?' Aisha asked when there was no one else within earshot. Hernando pursed his lips and shook his head. 'Your stepfather has not returned – I heard you telling the corsair captain as much. So what is wrong?' Seeing Hernando avoid her gaze, Aisha added: 'Don't worry about us. It looks as though the corsair is not interested in women . . .'

Hernando did not listen to any more. Of course Barrax was not interested! Wherever he went, Hernando was conscious of the pirate's lewd eyes upon him, whether Barrax was on his own or idly caressing one of his boys. He had stared at him all through the meal, when Hernando was sitting opposite them with Salah. Everyone else ate outside. How could he tell his mother what was going on, if she had not already guessed? And how could he confess that he was keeping a young Christian girl hidden out by the wall in the field, a girl who by now was probably starving, scared out of her wits, and capable of . . . What would Isabel be capable of? What if she left her hiding place and was caught? The King's men would come for him. How could he explain to Aisha that he had no barley for the animals, and that by nightfall, or the next day at the latest, Barrax's men would be demanding what Aben Humeya had promised their captain? How could he tell her he had disobeyed the King and stolen one of his captives? They had cut the Narila muleteer's hand off for stealing a crucifix; what would happen to him for robbing Aben Humeya of a Christian girl who was probably worth three hundred ducats?

'Why are you trembling?' asked his mother, clasping his cheeks in her hands. 'Are you ill?'

'No, Mother. Don't worry. I'll sort everything out.'

'What needs to be sorted out? What—?'

'Don't worry!' he cut her off sharply.

He spent the afternoon looking after the animals. He also tried to approach the part of the wall where he thought Isabel must still be hiding, but did not manage to get close enough to speak to her, even if only over the wall. This was because Yusuf was always by his side, alert, wanting to learn and constantly asking him exactly what he was doing to the horses.

At one point, however, when they were near to where Hernando thought Isabel must be, he showed Yusuf how the horses' muzzles were covered in earth.

'Do you know why?' he asked.

'Because they're trying to eat roots,' the boy replied, surprised that Hernando should be asking him such a simple question.

'Yes, because there's no food!' Hernando said loudly, trying to make his voice carry beyond the wall. 'We'll all have to make do until tomorrow!'

'She's had something to eat,' Yusuf whispered. Hernando nearly jumped out of his skin. 'I heard someone crying and went to see what was going on,' the boy explained. 'I gave her a hunk of bread. Don't worry,' he hastened to add, seeing how worried Hernando looked, 'I won't tell anyone.'

What would happen the next day, though? Hernando could not help thinking. He patted Yusuf affectionately on the cheek, and then looked up at the leaden skies covering the Sierra Nevada.

That evening, prodded by the worried Aisha, Fátima also tried to discover what was wrong with Hernando. She did it in such a gentle way he almost imagined he could see her features beneath the veil covering her face.

He raised his right hand to lift the veil, but just as he was doing so, a sudden noise drove Fátima away.

'Where's the barley?' he heard Salah ask.

The fat merchant had slid silently into the room, which was next to the steps descending to the cellars where Salah kept his treasures. As Fátima tried to edge past him, the merchant stepped in her way and brushed himself against her, obviously enjoying the contact.

Hernando was still standing with his hand held out towards the veil. Fátima's sweet whisper still caressed his ears.

'Leave her alone!' he shouted. 'Why are you so interested in the barley anyway?' he asked bitterly, once he had seen Fátima escape the other man's clutches and disappear upstairs.

'Because there isn't any.' Salah's tiny eyes glittered in the dim glow of a lantern hanging over the top step of the stairs. 'Everyone in the market place is talking about a young Morisco with a scimitar at his belt who was dragging along a pretty young Christian girl he had been given by the King in order to buy fodder.'

'So?'

'The girl isn't here, and you haven't sold her. No one in Ugíjar has bought her from you. I know.' Hernando had not thought of this possibility, and yet all of a sudden he felt relieved. The answer was staring him in the face. As he thought through his plan, the anxiety he had felt all day vanished. Salah was still talking, a triumphant sneer on his lips. 'Thief! What have you done with her? Did you rape and kill her? Have you kept her for yourself? She's worth a lot of money. If you hand her over to me, I won't say a word . . . but if you don't . . .' The merchant was threatening him. Hernando did not flinch. '. . . I'll go and see the King, and you'll be executed.'

'But I have sold her,' Hernando calmly replied. He glared at the fat, sly merchant.

'You're lying.'

'I sold her to the only merchant I know in Ugíjar. I thought that by selling to him I could get a better price, but . . .'

'Who's that . . . ?' Salah started to ask, but fell silent when he saw Hernando feeling for his scimitar.

'But that fat merchant hasn't paid me,' Hernando calmly continued. 'So now I don't have the Christian slave, and I have no money to feed the King's horses either.'

He drew his sword and pressed the point against Salah's belly. The merchant retreated as far as the wall. Hernando grasped the sword hilt tightly in his hand: he had no intention of being disarmed this time.

'Who would believe you?' stammered Salah, realizing the trap Hernando was setting for him. 'It will be . . . it will be your word against mine. You'll never be able to prove you handed her over to me.'

'Your word?' said Hernando, narrowing his eyes. 'No one will ever hear your side of the story!'

As he made to thrust with the sword, Salah fell to his knees. The blade ripped through his clothes and stayed level with his throat.

'No!' Salah begged. Hernando pressed the sharp tip against his Adam's apple. 'I'll do whatever you say, but spare my life! I'll pay you! I'll pay whatever you wish!'

He burst into tears.

'Three hundred ducats,' Hernando conceded.

'Yes, yes. Of course. Three hundred ducats. Whatever you say. Yes.'

The tears dried up as suddenly as they had appeared. Hernando pressed a little harder at his throat. 'If you try to cheat me, you'll pay for it. On my word of honour.' Salah shook his head vigorously. 'Now get up and open your cellars. We're going to get the money.'

They went down the steps, with Salah in front and Hernando holding the sword to the back of his neck. Salah took some time to undo the two locks guarding access to the cellars: his back blocked out the light from the lantern that Hernando was now holding.

'On your knees!' growled Hernando when the door finally creaked open and Salah made as if to enter. 'Walk like a dog.' The merchant obeyed, crawling into the cellar on all fours. Hernando kicked the door shut behind them. Still pressing the sword into the panting Salah's body, he tried to see what was in the room. 'Now, flat on your face, with your arms and legs outstretched! If you make the slightest movement, I'll kill you! Where is there another lantern?'

'In front of you, on the chest,' said Salah, coughing as his words raised dust from the floor.

Hernando found the lantern, lit it, and looked round the room.

'Heretic!' he exclaimed as his eyes grew accustomed to the gloom. 'Who would ever believe your word?' The cellar was filled with a pile of statues of the Virgin, crucifixes, a chalice, mantles, chasubles and even a small altarpiece, all of them heaped alongside old barrels stuffed with foodstuffs, clothing and all kinds of other goods.

'They're worth a lot of money,' the merchant blurted out in his defence.

Hernando said nothing for a few moments, then he reached out and touched a figure of the Virgin and Child that stood near him. This time you did save me, he almost said. If it had not been for those Christian images, one or other of them would have died.

'Where are the ducats?' he asked.

'In a small chest, next to the lantern.'

Hernando found it. 'Sit up,' he ordered. 'Slowly, with your legs out and open wide,' he quickly added when he saw the merchant trying to rise to his feet. 'Count out three hundred ducats and put them in a bag.'

When Salah had finished, Hernando put the bag and the box back where he had found them.

'Are you going to leave them there?' Salah asked, bewildered.

'Yes. I can't imagine a better hiding place for the King's money.'

They shut the door in the same way they had opened it, with Hernando threatening Salah the whole time.

'Give me one of the keys. That one, the big one,' he demanded, when Salah had finished with the locks. When he was clutching it safely in his hand, he went on: 'Now for one last thing. You are to come with me to see the captain of the guards. If you say anything, I'll talk my way out of it. They may or may not believe me, but with everything you've got hidden here you won't live to find out. They'll kill you without a second thought. Do you agree?'

Out in the courtyard, Salah said nothing as Hernando talked to the leader of the harquebusiers. He gave him orders to place one of his men outside the entrance to the cellars at all times.

'The King's money is in there,' he explained. 'The only people who can go in are Salah and me, together. If something should happen to me, you are to break down the door and recover what belongs to the King.

'Pray to the All-merciful', he told Salah once the pair of them were back inside the house, 'that nothing happens to me.'

'I will pray for you,' the merchant said, through gritted teeth.

Early the next morning each of them used their key to open the locks under the watchful gaze of the guard at the top of the stairs. Once they were inside, Salah made to shut the door behind them, but Hernando forced him to keep it half open. He wanted the merchant to be listening out for any noise from the stairs that might mean someone would see his hoard. Hernando took several ducats out of the bag and handed them to Salah.

'Go and buy barley and fodder,' he told him. 'Enough for several days for all the animals. I want it here by the end of the morning. Oh, and I need you to buy me some rich clothing.'

'But—'

'Those are the King's orders. Accept the fact that this is going to cost you more. I also want some black – no, white girl's clothes.' Hernando smiled. 'And a veil. I especially need a veil, and I need it right away. I'm sure you'll be able to find things like that amongst . . . amongst all this,' he said, gesturing towards the piles of goods in the cellar.

Shortly afterwards, Hernando left the cellar dressed in green with a red and silver taffeta tunic. On top of this he wore a gold and purple cloak embroidered with pearls and a cap with a small emerald in the centre. He had Hamid's scimitar at his waist, and was carrying Isabel's clothes. He could sense Salah's look of hatred behind his back. During the night, Hernando had gone over countless plans as to how to get Isabel out of Morisco territory, but none of them had satisfied him, until . . . Well, why not? Hadn't he resolved the problem of the animal feed? He had to follow his instincts. On his way out he ran into Barrax and his little boys. The corsair captain stepped to one side and bowed. Hernando pushed through them, wishing them peace.

'I would fill this cap here with sapphires as blue as your eyes if you would come with me.' The corsair sighed as he passed by.

Shocked, Hernando stumbled, but then recovered his composure. He reached the porch, and asked Yusuf to bring his horse round. Shortly afterwards, the boy reappeared with the bay saddled and bridled.

'I have to do something for the King,' Hernando told Fátima and his mother. The two women could not hide their admiration at his elegant attire.

He mounted his horse, spurred on, and galloped out of the house up to where the Christian girl was hiding.

'Put these on.' Isabel was still crouching where he had left her the day before. She did not move until the horse was almost on top of her. 'Do as I say!' Hernando insisted when he saw her hesitate. 'What are you looking at?' he shouted at a group of soldiers who had come to see what was going on.

Hernando drew his sword and charged the Moriscos. His

golden cloak shimmered around the animal's flanks. The men ran off.

'Hurry up,' Hernando insisted, returning to Isabel.

The girl had nowhere to hide, but knelt down and tried to cover herself as best she could while she took her own clothes off. Hernando turned his back on her, but was worried by how long she was taking. More soldiers could arrive at any moment.

'Are you ready yet?' When there was no reply, he turned towards her, and glimpsed her tiny breasts. 'Hurry up!' Isabel was struggling with clothes that were very different from the ones she was used to. Overcoming his embarrassment, Hernando got off his horse to help. 'The veil! Don't forget to cover your head properly.'

When she was ready, Hernando swung her up on to the horse in front of him, so that he could clasp her round the stomach. He rode off, and although Isabel swayed and rocked, she did not complain. Hernando hesitated between heading for Órgiva or Berja. He decided that although the Devil Iron Head was in Berja, he would be more likely to meet Moriscos on the way to the other village. Aben Aboo and Brahim were roaming around Válor, and the last thing he wanted was to run into his stepfather. He knew the way to Berja: he had passed it on the way to Adra a couple of months earlier. About half a league from the coast he would need to turn off towards the east, and aim for the foothills of the Sierra de Gádor. When he felt he was far enough away from Ugíjar and Aben Humeya's army, Hernando reined in the bay, which was already in a lather.

'Where are you taking me?' Isabel asked.

'To your own people.'

After they had trotted on for a while, she asked a second question. 'Why are you doing this?'

Hernando did not reply. Why was he doing it? For Gonzalico's sake? Because of the warmth of the hand that had held his through the little boy's last night? For the link he had established with Isabel while the two of them were watching Gonzalico being butchered? Or simply because he could not bear to see her fall into the hands of some Berber or renegade Christian? Hernando had never even asked himself the question. Instead, he had reacted as his instincts told him to. But why in fact was he doing this? He was only creating problems for himself. What had the Christians ever done for him that he should be defending one of them?

Isabel repeated her question. He spurred the bay into a canter.

'Why?' the girl asked again. He dug his heels into his mount until it was going at full gallop. He held Isabel tightly round the waist so that she would not fall off. She weighed hardly anything: she was only a little girl. That was why he was doing it, Hernando concluded with satisfaction as the wind whipped round his face. Because she was nothing more than a little girl!

None of the Moriscos they met along the way tried to stop them. Instead, they moved out of the way, staring curiously at this odd pair: a slight female figure in white, head and face covered, and a proud-looking rider dressed in rich clothes who was holding her tight, while his scimitar clinked against the haunches of his mount.

They reached Berja before noon. Every house had its own garden, and the village was protected by several high towers that rose above the roofs. To give his horse a rest over the last stretch, Hernando slowed to a walk. It was then that for the first time he could really feel Isabel's body pressed against him. Her robe was wet with sweat, and her stomach was hard and tense beneath his hands.

When he saw the village of Berja in the distance he put these thoughts out of his mind. People were working in the fields. Some Christian soldiers were resting out in the open; others were collecting fodder for the horses. The noonday sun beat down. The bay, feeling itself reined in and aware of its rider's anxiety, snorted and tossed its head. The red tints in its coat glinted in the sun, just like Hernando's cloak . . . and like the armour of the Marquis of los Vélez and that of his son, Don Diego Fajardo, who at that very moment were standing outside the town gate.

As Hernando swung Isabel down to the ground, a group of soldiers ran towards them, weapons at the ready. He pulled off her veil so that they could see her blond hair. He drew his scimitar and raised it to the back of the girl's neck. The soldiers in the lead came to an abrupt halt some fifty paces away, and the others piled into them.

'Run, child! Get away from him!' one of the soldiers shouted, loading his harquebus.

Isabel did not move.

Hernando sought out the Marquis of los Vélez's eyes. The two men looked at each other for a few seconds, then the Christian commander seemed to understand. He gestured to his soldiers to pull back.

'Peace be with you, Isabel,' Hernando whispered to her as soon as the soldiers had obeyed the marquis's command.

Hernando turned his horse and galloped away, whirling the scimitar through the air and howling loudly in the way the Moriscos always did when they launched themselves at Christian forces.

18

We have had word that we must confront some twenty-two thousand well-armed Moriscos; we are no more than two thousand men ourselves. I alone am in command of two thousand men, and two thousand horse. But what are nine thousand Moriscos against the courageous footsoldiers of our brave army, or nine thousand against you, my distinguished horsemen, who have shown such courage and effort? Besides, there is still the warlike sound of our trumpets whose terrifying noise will strike fear into another ten thousand Moriscos.

Rallying call by the Marquis of los Vélez to his army,
in Ginés Pérez de Hita, *The Civil Wars of Granada*

HAD HIS efforts to save Isabel served any purpose? wondered Hernando a little more than a month later, when he found himself once more outside Berja. Was she still in the village? If so, the Moriscos would capture her again . . . They might even discover she had not been sold.

Aben Humeya had been forced to attack Berja by the Moriscos of Granada's Albaicín, who were demanding the defeat of the bloodthirsty nobleman if they were to join the rebellion. Now was the time to move: the marquis's ranks had been decimated by desertions, but reinforcements, expected from Naples, had arrived on the coast of Andalusia with the royal fleet.

Could there be the slightest doubt that the Muslims would destroy the army of the Devil Iron Head?

The King had given the order to attack by night, and darkness was already falling. The vast Morisco encampment just beyond the town was bustling with activity. Everyone was preparing for battle. This time they had plenty of weapons; they shouted and sang and entrusted themselves to God. Yet even in the thick of the preparations and commotion, many of the men, including Hernando on his mount, as well as the King and his retinue, found themselves closely watching a group of some five hundred soldiers gathered slightly apart from the rest.

These were made up of Turkish mujahidin and Berbers all clad in white surcoats, which they wore to stand out in the darkness, as the Spanish regular soldiers did. Sure of victory, they all wore garlands of flowers on their heads. Hashish flowed freely amongst these soldiers of Allah who had sworn to die for God; they also requested from the King the honour of leading the attack on the fortress.

As soon as Aben Humeya gave the order, Hernando watched them rush blindly towards the town walls. How could they fail? he asked himself again. The shouts and cries of war; the harquebus fire; the rumble of drums and the sound of *dulzainas* swirled round the youth. What did Isabel matter in the face of these martyrs for God? Like almost all the soldiers waiting in the rear, Hernando was chilled to the bone, but shouted triumphantly when the mujahidin overwhelmed the Christians defending the gate. Aben Humeya then gave the order for the main body of the Muslim army to join the attack.

Several outlaws near Hernando roared wildly and spurred their horses on towards Berja. Hernando drew his scimitar and galloped off in a frenzy, shouting like a man possessed.

But it was impossible to fight in the alleyways of Berja. Hernando could not even control his mount: so many Muslim soldiers had poured into the town that they engulfed the Morisco cavalry in the narrow streets. Hernando did not come across a single enemy soldier to run through with his scimitar. He was surrounded by Muslims. The Christians lay in wait, taking up position inside their houses and on the flat roofs, from where they fired non-stop. They did not even need to take aim! Men fell dead or wounded everywhere. The smell of gunpowder and saltpetre wafted through the streets and the smoke from the guns made it all but impossible to see what was happening. Hernando was frightened, very frightened. He grasped in an instant that, like the others on horseback, he stood out above the footsoldiers and made an inviting target for the Christians. At the same time, he was in the line of fire of the harquebus shot and arrows the Moriscos were aiming at the terraces. He dug his spurs into his horse to escape the trap but the animal could not find a way through the throng. He heard the hiss of a lead ball as it whizzed past his head. He clung to the pony's neck, praying. Suddenly he felt a searing pain in his right thigh; an arrow had pierced him close to the knee. The pain was becoming unbearable when the Muslim army was ordered to retreat. His horse was almost toppled over as the fleeing soldiers rushed out of the town. Hernando lost control, but miraculously the horse recovered itself, turned and made its own way out through the gate.

All night long, Aben Humeya ordered wave after wave of attacks. In the Morisco camp, a barber forced Hernando to drink water with hashish. He made him wait while he tended to other casualties before cutting into the flesh on his thigh, ripping out the arrow and skilfully stitching the wound. Hernando fainted.

Towards dawn, Aben Humeya relented and ordered a retreat. Throughout the night, the Marquis of los Vélez, making the best of his strategic position, had driven back every attempt to take the town. Hernando joined the mad gallop of the King's retinue as it pulled back. Unable to rest his right leg in the stirrup, it hung loose, but he gritted his teeth and willed himself not to fall. Behind them they left some fifteen hundred dead.

* * *

'May the Prophet and victory go with you.'

Fátima had bade him farewell with these words as he left for Berja: a farewell fit for a warrior!

The marquis's army did not pursue them – it would have been madness for them to come out into the open – so the battered and disheartened Moriscos made their way back towards the mountains. Hernando let his horse trot in step with the others, and took refuge in the memory of Fátima as a way of forgetting the humiliating defeat and the shooting pain in his leg.

In the days following Isabel's release, and before Aben Humeya's decision to attack Berja, Fátima had grown closer and closer to him. She seemed to have forgotten all her bitterness and fear. Aisha was looking after Humam and her own children, while Brahim, who had only fleetingly visited the house where his family was living to show he was still alive, stayed on in Válor at Aben Aboo's side. Barrax disported himself shamelessly with his young men, while Ubaid made himself scarce in the town, awaiting his commander's call. Salah wandered around with a long face, still regretting the loss of his three hundred ducats and the expensive robes to Hernando, and always keeping a watchful eye on his cellars where the rest of the treasure was stored.

Fátima and Hernando sought each other out and made the most of every encounter. They talked and went for walks together, their shoulders gently touching; whether by day or beneath the stars they recalled all that had happened to them over the previous months. During one such walk, Fátima grew serious and spoke of her husband, the young apprentice whom she had loved more as a brother than a lover.

'I remember him being in our house ever since I was a little girl. My father was very fond of him . . . and so was I.' Fátima looked at Hernando as if she were trying to tell him something. He was silent. 'He was attentive, and tender . . . he was a good husband, and he adored Humam,' she added.

She took a deep breath. Hernando waited for her to say something more. 'When he died, I wept for him. Just as I had wept at my father's death. But' – Fátima looked at him suddenly; her black eyes seemed more intense than ever – 'now I know there are other feelings . . .'

A gentle kiss sealed her words. Then, suddenly overcome by shyness, the two of them made their way back to the house in silence. For a few moments they had forgotten about Brahim and his threats, but as they walked, his angry words echoed in their ears. What would become of Aisha if her husband discovered that Fátima had given herself to Hernando?

On the day the army's departure for Berja was announced, Fátima had brought him fresh lemonade. Hernando was getting the horses ready. It was first thing in the morning and the air was full of the nervous excitement that precedes battle. Laughing, Hernando lifted her on to his horse. He could feel her body quiver as he grasped her waist. When he went to help her back down, Fátima took advantage of the moment to fall back in his arms. Clinging to him, she kissed him on the mouth. Yusuf slipped away but watched them out of the corner of his eye. Hernando returned her kiss passionately, pressing himself against her breasts and hips, wanting her and also feeling her desire. Later on, he was so busy with the preparations for departure that he did not realize that the girl and his mother had both disappeared for the rest of the day.

That same evening, Aisha let them have the canopied bed and went to sleep with the children. She had spent the day hiring clothes and jewellery for Fátima, shutting her ears to any half-hearted protests. She bought some perfume and spent almost the entire evening making her ready. She bathed her and washed her black hair in henna mixed with sweet olive oil until every curl shone with a coppery glint. Then she perfumed her with orange-blossom water. With the same henna powder, she carefully tattooed her hands and feet, tracing small geometric shapes. Fátima let her do it, sometimes with a smile, at other times hiding her eyes. Aisha washed those eyes with an essence made of myrtle berries and antimony, and held her chin steady until the girl's huge black eyes shone clear and bright. She clothed her in a long white silk robe embroidered with pearls and slit at the sides, then bejewelled her with large earrings and bracelets on her ankles and wrists, all of gold. Only when she made to put a necklace on her did the girl gently refuse to let her remove the hand of Fátima at her breast. Aisha stroked the small, outstretched hand and left it in place. She prepared candles and cushions. She filled a basin with fresh water, and set out lemonade, grapes, dried fruit and some honeyed sweets she had bought at the market.

'Try to keep still,' she said when Fátima offered to help. A barely noticeable flicker of sadness crossed the girl's face.

'What is it?' Aisha asked, worried. 'Are you not sure?'

Fatima lowered her gaze. 'Yes, I'm sure,' she said eventually. 'I love him. But what I don't know . . .'

'Tell me.'

Fatima looked up and placed her trust in Aisha. 'Salvador, my husband, liked to take his pleasure with me. And I pleased him as often as he wished me to, but . . .' Aisha waited patiently. 'But I never felt anything. He was like a brother to me! We grew up together in my father's workshop.'

'That won't happen with Hernando,' Aisha assured her. The girl looked enquiringly at her, as though longing to believe her. 'You will feel it yourself! Yes, you will, when desire makes your whole body tremble. Hernando is not your brother.'

After night prayers, Aisha went off to look for her son in the front porch and, offering no explanation, made him go with her to the upper floor. Salah and his family noticed how Aisha made him follow her, while Barrax and the two youths of his retinue saw them pass by the open door of the dining room where they slept. Barrax gave a deep sigh.

'She promised to wait for you,' Aisha told Hernando on the threshold of the bedroom. Hernando tried to say something but could only gesture awkwardly with his hand. 'My son, I will not allow you both to miss out on loving each other through any fault of mine. It would be useless. Go in to her,' she urged, taking him by the wrist and half opening the door. Before he entered, Hernando tried to embrace her, but Aisha stepped back. 'No, my son. It's her you must embrace. She is a fine woman . . . and she will make a fine mother.'

Hernando could not get beyond the threshold. He stood there, entranced. Fátima was standing waiting for him, near the cushions that Aisha had placed around the food.

'Go in!' his mother whispered, giving him a gentle push so that she could close the door.

Once the door was shut, Hernando again stood stock-still. The candlelight flickered playfully over the body he could just make out beneath the long dress; the pearls bordering Fátima's garment sparkled brightly, as did her hair, the gold jewellery, the tattoos on her hands and feet. She seemed to be enveloped by the scent of fresh orange blossom . . .

Fátima came towards him smiling and held out the water basin. Hernando washed his hands nervously after managing to stammer some words of thanks. Then, tenderly, she invited him to sit down. In some alarm, Hernando took his eyes off her breasts outlined beneath the silk, but could scarcely bring himself to look into her enormous dark eyes. He sat down and let her serve him. He ate and drank, unable to conceal his shaking hands or excited breathing.

They finished the raisins. Also the dried fruit and lemonade. Time and again Fátima revealed her body to him through the open sides of her long silk dress but Hernando, as if wanting to avoid the moment, looked away, perturbed. He could not even recall a single thing from his one and only experience of women! He was reaching for another little honey cake when she whispered his name: 'Ibn Hamid.'

He saw her standing proudly in front of him. Fátima slipped off her long dress. The beauty of her body took his breath away; her large, firm breasts rose and fell rhythmically in time with a desire she could no longer hide.

You will feel it yourself, Aisha had said.

'Come,' she whispered again after a few moments during which the two young people's heavy breathing was the only sound.

Hernando moved towards her. Fátima took his hand and guided it to her breasts. Hernando caressed them, gently squeezing a hard nipple. Some breast-milk trickled from it and Fátima gasped. Hernando persisted. A spurt of milk wet his face. They both laughed. Fátima gestured to him and he bowed his head to suck the nectar while she slid her hands along the curve of his back to his taut buttocks. Then she slowly undressed him, running her lips over his entire body, kissing him softly and tenderly. Hernando shuddered when Fátima's lips touched his erect penis. She led him to the bed. As they lay down together, she was determined to find in the inexperienced Hernando the pleasure that had eluded her with her husband. As he moved on top of her, she recalled one of the pieces of advice from the Nefzawi sheik of Tunis, which was handed down from woman to woman. She whispered it in his ear: 'I will not love you unless you bring the bracelets on my ankles up next to my earrings.'

Hernando paused in his thrusts and raised himself up, taking his weight off her. What was she saying? Her ankles to her ears? He looked at her, puzzled, and she smiled slyly as she began to raise her legs. He entered her gently, responding to her commands: 'Slowly, I love you, slowly, make love to me . . .' but when their two bodies were at last one, Fátima let out such a howl that the spell was broken and Hernando's hair stood on end. From then on, she made known her needs through a mixture of whispers and gasps, and Hernando surrendered to the rhythm set by her groans of pleasure. They soon reached orgasm, after which, sated, they lay in silence. Some time later, Hernando opened his eyes and looked at Fátima's face: her lips were pressed tight and her eyes were firmly shut, as if she were trying to preserve the moment.

'I love you,' said Hernando.

Fátima's beautiful black eyes stayed shut, but a smile creased her lips.

'Tell me again,' she whispered.

'I love you.'

The night flew by in kisses, laughter, caresses, playfulness and promises, thousands of them! They made love again and again, and Fátima finally understood each and every one of the ancient laws of pleasure; her body sensitive to the lightest touch, her soul given over to the indulgence of the senses. Hernando followed her on her journey, exploring the infinite realms of sensation that can only find fulfilment in the convulsions and spasms of ecstasy. After each time they swore their undying love for each other, come what may.

The rout at Berja changed nothing in the overall situation. Following the battle, the Marquis of los Vélez withdrew to the coast to await reinforcements. Don John of Austria confined himself to strengthening the Christian outposts at Órgiva, Guadix and Adra, and so Aben Humeya kept control of the Alpujarra. The King of Granada conquered Purchena, where the victory was marked with lavish games. There were dancing contests for couples and for women only, poetry and singing challenges, wrestling, jumping and weight-lifting competitions, stone-throwing and marksmanship, either with harquebuses, crossbows or slingshots, in which the Moriscos of al-Andalus competed with Turks and Berbers for the love of the ladies and for the important prizes the King offered to the winners: horses, gold-embroidered garments, scimitars, laurel crowns and dozens of sovereigns and gold ducats.

While all this was going on, Hernando prolonged his convalescence so as to enjoy his romance with Fátima in Ugíjar. Aisha and Fátima had not followed the army but stayed at home with Salah and his family. Although the King was not in the village, Hernando commanded the bailiff of Ugíjar to place a Morisco on guard at the stairs to the cellar; the remainder of the King's money was there and he might at any moment return to the village in need of it.

Little Yusuf busied himself with the mules still left with the army and from time to time sent word about how things were going. Hernando took full advantage of his stay in the house at Ugíjar. Brahim's absence made for a very calm atmosphere: Aisha took care of him, displaying her affection without qualms, while Fátima attended him diligently. After the night of love seized before he went off to battle, they could only exchange longing looks and fleeting embraces.

As soon as her son returned from the battle at Berja, Aisha raised the matter with both of them. Both women well understood the Muslim rules.

'You ought to get married,' she told them, trying to put out of her mind the consequences such a marriage would have for her.

The look on their faces showed that they both agreed; then, however, Hernando's face fell.

'I have no way of offering her a dowry . . .' he began. Aben Humeya's ducats? he thought, gazing inside the house, but Aisha guessed what he was thinking.

'You would have to seek permission from the King first. It is his money. You must search out a dowry for her because you cannot expect your stepfather, who is your only family, to give anything towards it. You', she said, turning to Fátima, 'are a free woman. Following the death of your husband you have fulfilled the edicts of our law by honouring the four months and ten days of *idda* or mourning. I counted them,' she added before either of them could begin to work it out. 'Of course, you have not fulfilled your obligation to remain in your husband's house during the period of mourning, but with the marquis's army in Terque, it was impossible for you to do so. As regards the dowry,' she said, addressing Hernando, 'you have three months to sort that out. Since you have slept together without being married, a wedding is not possible until she has bled three times, unless . . .' Aisha clicked her tongue. 'If you were with child you would be unable to marry until after the birth, nor would you be able to enjoy your love during this time. Our law forbids it. We would never find a witness willing to attend the wedding of a pregnant woman. Remember, my son: you have three months to secure the dowry.'

To continue to make love would have meant postponing the wedding even further. Fátima's first bleeding calmed them both. The decision, however hard, was a simple one: three months of abstinence.

As for the dowry, Hernando determined to approach the King as soon as his wounded leg had healed. If anyone could help him it was Aben Humeya, the man who had taught him to ride and who had presented him with a horse. Had he not shown him his gratitude in the past? Despite himself, Hernando was concerned what those signs of affection meant. Rumours about the King's decadent lifestyle were spreading throughout the mountains. What Hernando did not know was that time was not on his side.

Unfortunately, the rumours were not unfounded: power and money had made a tyrant of the King. Aben Humeya was consumed with greed and there was not a single dwelling he did not ransack; he lived a debauched existence, doing exactly as he pleased. He surrounded himself with women and took them without scruple. As a descendant of a long line of nobles from Granada, he distrusted Turks and Berbers; he lied, swindled and treated those in his service cruelly. His behaviour had already made public enemies of some of his best captains: El Nacoz in Baza, Maleque in Almuñécar, El Gironcillo in Vélez, Garral in Mojácar, Portocarrero in Almanzora and of course Farax, his rival for the crown.

Almost inevitably, it was a woman who put an end to Aben Humeya's dissolute life. The King was much taken with the widow of Vicente de Rojas, brother of Miguel de Rojas, his father-in-law, whom he had had murdered in Ugíjar before divorcing his first wife. The widow was a great beauty and noted dancer who also played the lute with consummate skill. In accordance with custom, on the death of her husband, his cousin Diego Alguacil of the Rojas clan, a secret enemy of the King, courted her. Aben Humeya kept Diego Alguacil busy, sending him on journeys and missions throughout the Alpujarra, until on his return from one such venture he discovered that the King had raped the widow and was keeping her as a common concubine.

Humiliated, Diego Alguacil hatched a plot to get rid of Aben Humeya, who was then in Laujar de Andarax.

The King could not write, so all the commands he dispatched to his captains throughout the Alpujarra were written and signed in his name by one of Alguacil's nephews. By now, Aben Humeya had freed himself from the troublesome, arrogant Turks and Berbers by sending them off to fight with the army of Aben Aboo, around Órgiva. Through his nephew, Diego Alguacil became aware of a letter on its way from the King to Aben Aboo. He intercepted the messenger, killed him and together with his nephew drafted another letter in which the King ordered Aben Aboo to use his Morisco soldiers to slaughter all the Turks and Berbers in his ranks.

Diego Alguacil himself took this letter to Aben Aboo, who could not contain the anger of Turks such as Hussein, Caracax and Barrax. Aben Aboo, with Brahim by his side, Diego Alguacil, the Turks and the leaders of the corsairs rode quickly towards Laujar de Andarax, where they found Aben Humeya in the Cotón inn.

None of the three hundred Moriscos who made up Aben Humeya's personal bodyguard did anything to prevent Aben Aboo and his followers from entering the inn. Once inside, such was the hatred that Aben Humeya aroused among even his closest followers, that a further select bodyguard of twenty-four men allowed the Turks to break down the King's bedroom door.

Aben Aboo and the Turks and Berbers caught the King in bed with two women, one of whom was the Rojas widow.

Aben Humeya denied the contents of the letter but his fate was already sealed. Aben Aboo and Diego Alguacil tied a rope round his neck and, one on either side, pulled until the King was strangled to death. They immediately divided his women among themselves, not only the two who had been sharing his bed, but also the many others who were part of his retinue. They also shared out his hoard of looted treasure.

Before he died, Fernando de Válor, King of Granada and Córdoba, renounced the revelation of the Prophet and cried out that he was dying in the Christian faith.

19

'I COULD NOT wish for more nor be content with less.' This was the motto that Aben Aboo, the self-proclaimed new King of al-Andalus, had emblazoned on his standard. Just like his predecessor, the new monarch was presented to his people clad in purple, with an unsheathed sword in his right hand and the standard in his left. With the exception of Portocarrero, all the enemy captains who had been with Aben Humeya swore allegiance to the new King, who at once promoted the Turks to the highest ranks of his army. The money and prisoners Aben Humeya had amassed were sent to Algiers to purchase weapons, which Aben Aboo then distributed at low cost to the Moriscos until he had created an army of six thousand harque-busiers. Apart from the division of the spoils, he set in place a monthly stipend of eight ducats for Turks and Berbers and regular provisions for the Moriscos. He nominated new captains and bailiffs amongst whom he divided up the territory of the Alpujarra, and gave orders that the watchtowers be constantly manned, using smoke during the day and fires by night to make known any incident and to prevent the passage of anyone who was not part of the army. The eunuch Aben Aboo was determined to succeed where his dissolute pre-decessor had failed: he would conquer the Christians.

Hernando heard the news of Aben Humeya's execution. His legs trembled and a cold sweat ran down his back when he heard the new King's name: Aben Aboo. Salah, who was also listening to the messenger, narrowed his eyes and mentally weighed up the shift of power.

Hernando went in search of Aisha and Fátima who were in the kitchen preparing a meal with the merchant's wife. 'Let's go!' he shouted to them. 'We have to get out of here!'

Aisha and Fátima stared at him in surprise.

'Ibn Umayya has been murdered,' he explained hastily. 'Ibn Abbu is the new King and with him . . . Brahim! He will come for us. He will come for Fátima! He is the King's lieutenant, his friend, his confidant.'

'Brahim is my husband,' Aisha said quietly, interrupting him. She looked at Fátima and her son and leant back defeated against one of the kitchen walls. 'You two go.'

'But if we do that,' Fátima protested, 'Brahim . . . he'll kill you.'

'Come with us, Mother,' Hernando begged her. Aisha shook her head, tears filling her eyes. 'Mother . . .' he tried once more, stepping closer to her.

'I don't know what Brahim will do: whether he will kill me or not if he does not find you here with me,' murmured Aisha, trying to control the panic in her voice, 'but what I do know is that I will die anyway if you don't escape. I could not bear to see you . . . Flee, I beg you. Go to Seville, or Valencia . . . Go to Aragón. Get away from this madness. I have other children. They are his sons. Perhaps . . . perhaps it won't go beyond a beating. He cannot kill me! I haven't done anything wrong! The law forbids it. He cannot blame me for what you two do . . .'

Hernando tried to embrace her. Aisha's voice became firmer as she straightened up and pushed him away.

'You can't ask me to abandon your brothers. They are younger than you. They need me.'

Hernando shook his head at the thought of how Brahim would unleash his anger on his mother. Aisha looked at Fátima pleadingly. The girl understood Aisha was seeking her support.

'Let's go,' she said resolutely. She pushed Hernando out of the kitchen but before leaving Aisha, she turned round and looked sadly at her. Aisha forced a smile. 'Get everything ready,' Fátima urged Hernando once they were out of the kitchen. 'As fast as you can.' She had to shake him, shocked as he was, his eyes still fixed on Aisha. 'I'll see to Humam.'

Get everything ready? He watched Fátima take the child in her arms. What was there to get ready? How would they get to Aragón? And his mother? What would become of her?

'Didn't you hear her?' Aisha insisted from the threshold of the kitchen. Hernando made as if to return to her side, but Aisha was adamant. 'Flee! Don't you realize? He will kill you first. When you have sons of your own one day you will understand my decision, a mother's decision. Go!'

I could not wish for more nor be content with less. Brahim, elevated to a position of power by the man he had saved from certain death, contemplated that motto and its implications for him.

They captured Hernando in the cellar, together with Salah, as he was trying to take what was left of the three hundred ducats the merchant had been forced to give him. Hernando and Fátima would have more need of it than the unfortunate Aben Humeya. From the cellar they heard the shouts of the soldiers Brahim had sent to break into the house; they did not move a muscle. Then, after some confusion, they heard footsteps clattering down the steps that led to the merchant's treasure trove.

Somebody kicked open the half-closed door. Five men entered the basement, swords drawn. The man who appeared to be in charge began to say something but fell silent when he caught sight of the sacred objects piled up there; behind him, the others peered into the shadows.

Crucifixes, gold-bordered chasubles, a statue of the Virgin, some chalices and other religious objects lay at Aben Aboo's feet. Close by, their hands bound, stood Hernando and Salah, and behind them Fátima and Aisha. Unlike Aben Humeya, the new King did not stand on ceremony and listened to Brahim where they happened to be: in a narrow alleyway in Laujar de Andarax with a retinue of Turks and captains crowding around them. The soldiers accompanying Brahim had noisily dropped the objects seized from the merchant's basement on to the ground in front of the new King.

Before the tinkle of a chalice rolling on the stones had faded, Salah whimpered and tried to excuse himself. Brahim silenced him with a blow from the butt of his harquebus; a trickle of blood spilled from the merchant's mouth. Hernando was looking straight at Aben Aboo, who was much fatter and flabbier than he remembered from the wedding party at Mecina. Women and children were leaning from the windows and balconies of the small two-storeyed whitewashed houses.

'Is this the woman you have talked so much about?' asked the King, pointing at Fátima. Brahim nodded. 'Then she's yours.'

'But I'm going to marry her,' Hernando protested. 'Ibn Umayya . . .' He waited for Brahim to strike him, but it did not happen. They let him speak. 'Ibn Umayya has granted me her hand and we are to marry,' he stammered.

Twenty or more people, including the King, were staring straight at him.

'The law . . . the law says that since she is a widow she has to consent to marry Brahim,' pleaded Hernando.

'And she has done so,' said Aben Aboo cynically. 'I saw her give her consent. We all saw it, did we not?'

All the men around him agreed.

Hernando instinctively turned towards Fátima, but this time Brahim did strike him, and her face became a distant blur.

'Are you doubting the word of your King?' asked Aben Aboo.

Hernando did not reply; there was no answer. Disgusted, the King poked the statue of the Virgin with his foot.

'What is the meaning of all this?' he went on, regarding the matter of Fátima as closed.

Brahim explained about all the objects the soldiers had

found in the cellar of Salah's house. When he had finished, Aben Aboo intertwined the fingers of both hands and rested his forefingers on the tip of his nose. He thought for several moments without taking his eyes off the Christian treasures.

'Your stepfather always said you were a Christian,' he said to Hernando. 'They call you the Nazarene, don't they? I understand now why Ibn Umayya always protected you: the heretical dog died entrusting himself to the god of the papists. As for you . . .' he continued, pointing at Salah. 'Kill them both,' he suddenly barked, as if he was tired of the whole business. 'Put them on a spit in the square and roast their bodies, then leave them to the animals.'

Salah fell to his knees and howled, begging for mercy. Brahim struck him again. Hernando paid no attention whatsoever to the sentence. Fátima! Better to die than to see her in Brahim's hands. What did life matter if Fátima . . . ?

'I will buy the young man!'

The offer stunned Hernando. He lifted his head and, straightening up, found himself facing Barrax, who had stepped in front of him. Many of those present smiled openly.

Aben Aboo thought some more. The Nazarene deserved to die; it was apparent that this was what Brahim wanted, but one of the causes of Aben Humeya's misfortune had been his failure to satisfy the Turks and corsairs. He did not want to make the same mistake.

'Agreed. Speak with Brahim about the price. The Christian is yours.'

Hernando found himself dragged through the alleyways of Laujar in exactly the same way as he had pulled Isabel along. He stumbled behind several of Barrax's men as they took him towards the corsair chief's camp. He lost a shoe but kept going. As he dragged his feet, he also dragged up memories. What would become of Fátima? He shut his eyes in a vain effort to dispel the image of Brahim lying on top of her. What would she do? She couldn't refuse him, but . . . what if she did? He came to a halt until a rough tug on the rope forced him on. He stumbled again. Someone spat the word 'Nazarene' at him loudly. He glanced at the Morisco; he did not recognize him. Nor did he recognize the man a little further on who called him a heretic dog. As they rounded a street corner, several Moriscos mocked him in front of a group of women they were talking to. One of them handed a stone to a child no more than five years old to throw at him. When it struck his hip weakly the whole group cheered the little boy. Hernando put Fátima out of his mind and lunged at the Moriscos. Barrax's man, taken by surprise, lost hold of the rope. Hernando threw himself on the man nearest him. His guffaws of laughter turned into a shriek of panic before he was tumbled to the ground. Hernando tried to punch him but his hands were tied. The man raised his arms to push him away, but in an uncontrollable fit of rage Hernando bit him as hard as he could. Barrax's henchmen hauled him away unceremoniously; Hernando stood up defiantly, his mouth stained with blood, ready to do battle, but not only did the Berbers not harm him, they seemed ready to protect him from the other Moriscos; swords and daggers were drawn as the two groups faced each other.

'If you have any complaint,' one of the Berbers cried, 'take it up with Barrax. This man is his slave.'

At the mention of the corsair leader's name, the Moriscos put away their weapons. Hernando spat at their feet.

From then on, the Berbers lifted him up and carried him as though he were a piece of valuable merchandise. It took four of them to deal with his kicking, howling and biting.

When they reached Barrax's camp they tied him to a tree. Hernando went on shouting, hurling insults at anyone who came near. He fell silent only when Ubaid approached and stood in front of him, rubbing the stump of his right wrist.

'Get away from him,' a soldier ordered. When Hernando had forced Barrax to make Ubaid leave the house in Ugíjar, news of their dispute had spread by word of mouth. 'This lad is untouchable,' the soldier warned him.

Ubaid mouthed the words silently: 'I will kill you.'

'Try it!' Hernando challenged him.

'Get out of here,' the soldier shouted in turn, pushing away the one-handed muleteer.

The wedding party and the bride's dowry; that was the price Brahim agreed with Barrax for the purchase of his stepson. The commander insisted that the deal also included Hamid's scimitar; he had noted the tender way the lad caressed the sword and wanted to make a gift of it to him the moment he submitted to his will, which he surely would. They all did in the end! Thousands of young Christians were living very comfortably in Algiers as the playthings of Turks and Berbers after they had renounced their religion and converted to the true faith.

'Take the sword,' Brahim answered. 'Keep all his clothes. Take everything that belongs to him. I want nothing that might remind me of his existence . . . I have enough with his mother.' Brahim narrowed his eyes and thought for a few moments. His days as a muleteer were over: he was now the King of al-Andalus's lieutenant and had acquired a valuable amount of gold booty. 'I also need a white mule for the bride, the most beautiful white mule in the whole of the Alpujarra. I will exchange my entire pack of mules for that.

'You are getting a bargain,' he insisted, as the corsair hesitated. 'White mules can be found in many villages throughout the Alpujarra. Perhaps even here. I don't have time to bother with such details.'

A couple of days after agreeing the deal with Brahim, Barrax approached the tree where Hernando was tied, showing him a beautiful white mule Ubaid had bought in a nearby village. Barrax had ordered that Hernando be chained and left without food, with only water for sustenance. Hernando refused to speak to his new master.

'Your beloved will ride this when she gives herself to your stepfather,' Barrax said, stroking the mule's neck. His blue eyes sunken and bruised, Hernando stared at the animal.

'Renounce your religion and give yourself to me,' Barrax insisted.

Hernando replied by making the sign of the cross openly in front of him. Profess the faith . . . to profess the faith would be the first step towards succumbing to the corsair. How ridiculous! Old Hamid had had to persuade his neighbours in Juviles that Hernando was a genuine Muslim and now . . . now he had to pretend to be a Christian to avoid falling into the clutches of Barrax. Or was he a Christian? What was he? He was not in any frame of mind to pursue the question: for now it was a matter of defending his Christianity. Barrax frowned at his defiance, and loomed over him, but went on speaking calmly.

'You have lost everything, Ibn Hamid: the King's favour, your beloved and your freedom. I am offering you a new life. Become one of my "sons" and you will flourish in Algiers; I know you will, I can foresee it. You will live well, wanting for nothing, and when your time comes you will be as important a corsair as myself; perhaps more important, yes, probably more important. I will help you. The prince of the corsairs, Khair ad-Din, named his "boy" Hasan Agá captain-general; then Dragut the Indomitable, who was also one of Khair ad-Din's "boys", succeeded him as beylerbey, and after him our great Uluch Ali, who in his time had been one of Dragut's "boys". I myself . . . Don't you understand? You have nothing and I'm offering you everything.'

Hernando made the sign of the cross once more.

'You are my slave, Ibn Hamid. You are regarded as a Christian. Give in, because if you do not you will become a slave in one of my galleys, and will regret your decision. I will wait, but bear in mind that time is passing for you and without your youth . . . I don't want your body, I have as many as I could possibly desire, boys or women; I want you at my side, ready for anything. Think about it, Ibn Hamid. Untie him from the tree!' he suddenly ordered his men, looking straight into Hernando's sunken eyes. 'Shackle his ankles and set him to work. If he is going to eat, at least let him earn his food. You!' he added, addressing Ubaid, well aware of the hatred that existed between him and Hernando, 'you will answer with your life if anything happens to him. I promise you that your death will be much slower and more painful than any you could inflict on him.' And finally: 'Take a good look at this white mule,' he said to Hernando. 'With her your hopes and dreams in al-Andalus are at an end.'

Aisha prepared Fátima in the same inn where Brahim and Aben Aboo were staying; they were in a room that one of the Turkish captains had lent them. Brahim accompanied the two women as far as the door.

'Woman,' he growled to Aisha, while he busily undressed Fátima with his eyes, 'I want her to be the most beautiful bride ever to enter into marriage in al-Andalus. Make her ready. As for you, Fátima, you have no family, and therefore the King has offered to give you away. You are a widow. You must give authority to a *wali* or guardian to give you away. Do you consent to him?'

Fatima remained silent, staring at the floor, fighting against the grief she knew lay in store for her.

'I'll tell you one thing for sure: you will be mine. You can be so as my second wife or as my slave. You must have known what was hidden in the merchant's cellars, and I'm also certain you knew about the Nazarene's Christian practices and said nothing, or perhaps even took part in them yourself . . . in front of your son!' Fátima trembled. 'Speak. Do you give the King the authority to hand you over in marriage?' She nodded without a word. 'Remember what I have told you. If you do not consent to the request for your hand in marriage, or if you object to any of the vows, your son and the Nazarene will die just like the merchant; that is what I have agreed with the corsair commander. If you don't consent, he will hand me back the Nazarene dog, and I will roast him on a spit myself, side by side with your son.'

The thought of Humam and Hernando dying in the same

agonizing manner as Salah made Fátima retch. Brahim had forced them to witness his execution: the merchant had squealed just like the pigs the Christians slaughtered. Several Moriscos held his fat, naked body down on all fours, while another man thrust a spear into his rectum. The onlookers applauded when Salah's screams of panic turned into howls of pain: howls that died away as the spear, driven by a couple of soldiers, bored through his body until the tip appeared out of his mouth. By the time he was hung on the spit ready to rotate above the hot coals, surrounded by a gang of excited children, the merchant was already dead. The stench of burnt flesh engulfed the square at Laujar and its surroundings for a full day, clinging to clothes and seeping into the nearby houses.

Brahim smiled grimly and left the room.

Fátima refused to allow Aisha to wash her.

'What makes you think he will notice?' she said hoarsely, when Aisha insisted on performing the ablutions. 'I don't want to be clean when I enter into this marriage.'

Aisha did not argue: the girl was sacrificing herself for Hernando. She lowered her gaze.

Fátima also asked her not to renew the tattoos she had painted on her feet the night Fátima had given herself to Hernando, and refused to perfume her body with orange-blossom water. Instead, Aisha left the room and found some jasmine oil. Then, with a heavy heart, she adorned the bride with the jewellery Brahim had sent, giving instructions it was to be used only for the wedding and was not part of the dowry. She handed Fátima a necklace, and the girl made as if to tear off the gold amulet hanging around her neck. Aisha stopped her, placing her hand on the precious object.

'Don't give up hope,' she told her, at the same time pressing the golden image against her breast.

For the first time, Fátima burst into tears.

'Hope?' she stammered. 'Only death can offer me any hope . . . an everlasting hope.'

* * *

The engagement took place in the same inn, in a small, cold interior garden, in the presence of the King in his role as *wali*, and of the motley retinue who accompanied him. Dalí, captain-general of the Turks, and Hussein stood as witnesses. Brahim presented himself and, as was the custom, asked for Fátima's hand from Aben Aboo, who acquiesced. Then an old holy man from Laujar recited the marriage vows. As a widow, Fátima had to respond to these herself, and swore that there was no god but God, and that, swearing on the Koran, the answers she gave were truthful: she wished to be wed in honour of and according to the Sunna of the Prophet.

'If you swear in good faith,' the holy man concluded, 'Allah is your witness and He will bestow grace upon you. Likewise, if you do not swear in good faith, may Allah destroy you and not bestow His grace upon you.'

Before the King recited the thirty-sixth sura of the Koran, Fátima raised her eyes to heaven and repeated quietly, 'May Allah destroy us.'

Her tattooed feet were all that could be seen of Fátima as she rode the white mule. Covered from head to foot in a white tunic, she sat side-saddle, led by a black slave. Applauded and encouraged by thousands of Moriscos, she made her way through the village back to the inn. When she arrived, she went straight up to Brahim's bedroom. There, as Muslim tradition ordained, she was silently covered with a white sheet, under which she was to lie with her eyes closed. While the celebrations continued with music and dancing outside in the streets, Fátima could sense the comings and goings of dozens of people in the room. Only once was the light robe that covered her raised up.

'I understand your desire,' she heard Aben Aboo sigh as he raised the sheet more than was necessary to see her face. 'Enjoy her for me, my friend, and may Allah bless you with many children.'

Once the visits had come to an end, Fátima got out of bed, sat on the cushions on the floor and tried to put the forthcoming encounter with Brahim out of her mind. She ignored the shameless, non-stop advice of the gloating women who stayed with her; she refused any food they offered and, as she waited, hearing the music drifting up from the streets, she tried to call up a memory she could seek refuge in . . . but they were singing for her! They were celebrating her marriage to Brahim! The sight of Aisha, seated motionless opposite her next to a brazier, her eyes filled with tears at the thought of her newly enslaved son, afforded her no comfort. She clung to the only consolation she had: prayer. She prayed in silence, like someone condemned to death; she recited every prayer she knew, letting her fears mingle with her prayers. It was a desperate act of faith but her strength grew with each word and invocation.

After midnight, a commotion among the women announced Brahim's arrival in the bedroom. One of them tidied her hair and settled the tunic on her shoulders. Fátima refused to look anywhere near the door through which the women were hurriedly leaving, but gazed instead at the brazier. 'In death, hope is everlasting,' she murmured, closing her eyes, but it was not death that awaited her. What hope could there possibly be? The sound of the key in the lock silenced the songs and music. All Fátima could hear was Brahim's excited breathing. She shuddered.

'Reveal yourself to your husband,' the muleteer ordered.

When Fátima tried to stand up, her legs almost gave way beneath her. She finally managed to get up from the bed, and turned towards Brahim.

'Undress,' he gasped, moving towards her.

Fátima straightened up, trembling, scarcely able to breathe. She could smell the muleteer's putrid breath. Brahim gestured with his greasy, bearded chin towards her tunic. Fátima's fingers struggled clumsily with the knots until it slipped from her shoulders and she stood naked before him. He took pleasure in letting his lascivious eyes roam all over her body: she was not yet fourteen years old. He reached out a calloused hand towards her full breasts; Fátima sobbed and half closed her eyes. Then she became aware that he was stroking her breasts, scraping the delicate skin where Humam's head was meant to rest, before grasping one of her nipples. Silently, her eyes tightly shut, she commended herself to God and to the Prophet, to all the angels. Droplets of milk began to flow from her nipple and trickle down Brahim's fingers. Still squeezing her nipple, Brahim thrust the fingers of his other hand into her vulva, forcing them into her vagina before flinging her on to the cushions and taking her violently.

The music and dancing, the shouts and shrieks from the streets of Laujar rang in Fátima's ears all through an endless night during which Brahim took his pleasure with her time and time again. Fátima bore it all silently. Fátima obeyed silently. Fátima submitted silently. She only wept, for the second and last time that day, when Brahim sucked her breasts.

20

OWARDS THE end of October Aben Aboo, with ten thousand men under his command, attacked Órgiva, the most significant town under Christian control anywhere in the Alpujarra. Following some initial attacks which the soldiers repelled from their fortress, the Morisco King set about wearing them down through hunger and thirst.

Laying siege meant little action, so that boredom spread throughout the Morisco camp. His feet shackled, Hernando followed behind the army with the rest of the non-combatants. He made his way to Órgiva mounted on La Vieja. He had to sit side-saddle like a woman, suffering torments as the bones of the starving mule thrust into him – exactly as Ubaid had intended. Throughout the journey he was a constant object of scorn for the women and youngsters accompanying the army. Only Yusuf, who had followed the mules as though he were part of the agreement between Brahim and the corsair captain, showed him any kindness. Whenever Ubaid was not on the lookout, Yusuf drove away the youngsters who came up to Hernando to mock him. In spite of his discomfort and shame, Hernando tried unsuccessfully to catch sight of Fátima or his mother among the people on the road. He did not come across them until a few days after Aben Aboo's troops had taken up position around the town.

'Humiliate him,' Barrax instructed his two 'sons'. 'Don't mistreat him unless it is absolutely necessary. Humiliate him in front of captains, janissaries and soldiers, but above all in front of that Morisco woman. Strip away all his pride: he's blinded by it. Make him forget he is a man.'

In the army camp, the two boys dressed Hernando in a tunic of fine green silk and baggy trousers adorned with jewels, clothes that belonged to the elder of the two boys. Hernando tried to resist, but the intervention of several Berbers standing idly by rendered his efforts useless. When he tried to tear off the clothes, they tied his hands in front of him. Hands tied, ankles in chains, and clad in green silk, the boys paraded him through the camp, among the tents and huts, past soldiers and women cooking.

They had taken no more than a couple of paces before Hernando threw himself to the ground. The older boy hit him on the back of the head several times with a stick, but this only encouraged Hernando to offer him his face.

'Hit me!' he challenged the boy.

Soldiers, women and children were looking on. The boy raised his stick but just as he was about to strike another blow, his younger companion stopped him.

'Wait,' he said, winking at him.

He was prettily dressed in a scarlet linen djellaba. He knelt beside Hernando and licked his cheek. Hernando went red with fury, and there was a deathly silence until some of the on-lookers began to clap and yell, while others booed. Many women showed their disgust with gestures and insults while the children simply looked on wide-eyed. The older boy began to laugh, his stick now by his side, while his companion slid his tongue from Hernando's cheek to his neck, at the same time feeling with his right hand between Hernando's legs. Hernando twisted away at his touch although, tied up as he was, it was almost impossible for him to evade the groping. He tried to bite the boy but could not do that either. All he heard were shouts and laughter. The older boy came closer to him as well, a smile on his face.

'Enough!' shouted Hernando. 'You win.'

The two boys hauled him to his feet and continued on their way.

Hernando shuffled through the camp as fast as the chains round his ankles would allow. It was not long before they bumped into Aisha and Fátima, their faces hidden beneath veils. Hernando recognized them without having to look at Humam and Musa, who were with them. His stepbrother ran to join the gaggle of youngsters escorting the procession. This was no chance encounter: the boys had gone to Brahim's tent under orders from Barrax.

Ashamed and humiliated, Hernando gazed down at the irons on his ankles. Fátima looked away, while Aisha burst into tears.

'Take a good look!' Standing at the entrance to his tent, Brahim roared so loudly his words were plainly audible above the laughter, murmuring and chatter of the crowd. Hernando raised his head instinctively just as Fátima and his mother obeyed their husband. Their eyes met, although none of them betrayed any emotion. 'This is what all Nazarenes deserve,' laughed Brahim.

'He will try to escape,' Barrax warned the captain of his guard and the boys that same evening, after Hernando had been displayed to the entire army as yet another of the corsair's lovers. 'Perhaps this very night, perhaps tomorrow or within a day or two, but he will certainly try. Don't let him out of your sight, but don't stop him. Let me know.'

Hernando made his attempt after three days. After parading him through the camp once more, the boys took him to the stream where the women washed clothes and made him clean Barrax's clothes. That same night, with no moon in the sky and without caring whether the guards were keeping watch or not, Hernando dragged himself under the mules, hands and feet bound, until he came to a small ravine. He threw himself down the slope without a second thought. He crashed into stones, bushes and branches, but felt no pain. He felt nothing. On elbows and knees, he followed the course of the stream in the dark. He crawled ever more determinedly as the sounds from the camp fell further and further behind. He began to laugh nervously. He was going to make it! Suddenly he bumped into a pair of legs. The corsair commander was standing upright in the middle of the stream.

'I warned you my boat was called the *Flying Horse*,' Barrax said to him calmly. Hernando's head fell like a dead weight on the sand. 'Few Spanish ships have escaped my clutches once I have set my sights on them. You will not succeed either, my boy. Never!'

Aben Aboo defeated the Duke of Sesa's army, which had rushed to the defence of Órgiva. This victory gave the Moriscos control of the Alpujarra, from the mountains to the Mediterranean, as well as strategic positions close to the capital of the kingdom of Granada itself, including Güéjar and many other more remote locations, among them Galera, from where the Christians feared the rebellion might spread all the way to the kingdom of Valencia.

Faced with this danger, King Philip II gave the order to expel all the Moriscos in the Albaicín from the kingdom of Granada, and for the first time since the uprising, he declared all-out war. He gave a free hand to all those who fought under his flag or standard, authorizing them to keep any goods, money, jewellery, cattle or slaves they captured from the enemy. Also, as a way of recruiting more men, he exempted the soldiers from paying the royal share on any of their booty.

In December, months after he had been appointed captain-general, Don John of Austria obtained permission from his stepbrother King Philip II to join the battle himself. The Prince formed two powerful armies to carry out a pincer movement against the Moriscos: one under his command, which would approach from the east by way of the river Almanzora, and the other led by the Duke of Sesa, which would attack from the west through the Alpujarra. The Marquis of los Vélez fought on separately with his scant forces.

In the meantime, weapons and reinforcements for the rebels were continually arriving from Barbary.

The Christians recaptured Güéjar. Don John, with the Neapolitan infantry and almost five hundred horsemen under his command, set out to lay siege to the hilltop fortress of Galera. The first thing he saw were the heads of twenty soldiers and a captain of the Marquis of los Vélez's army skewered on lances on top of the castle keep. Despite all the veteran soldiers' experience and the use of artillery brought especially from Italy, the Prince's army lost so many dead and wounded that in the wake of the Christians' hard-won victory, the Moriscos of Galera paid with their lives. They were executed en masse in the presence of Don John of Austria himself. He then ordered the destruction of the town, which was burnt, razed to the ground, and then sown with salt.

During the siege, the Prince also gave the order to kill women and children regardless of age or condition. In spite of this slaughter, the Christian army left with 4,500 women and children as slaves. They also made off with gold, seed pearls and silk, and riches of all kinds, as well as enough wheat and barley to keep the army supplied for a year.

Aben Aboo did not come to the defence of Galera and the thousands of Moriscos who had sought refuge there. Following the surrender of Órgiva, he attacked Almuñécar and Salobreña, where he was routed. He then scattered his forces throughout the Alpujarra, with orders only to engage the enemy in skirmishes until the promised help from the Sublime Porte arrived. This never materialized, and his miscalculation allowed the Duke of Sesa to enter the Alpujarra and take control of all the land between El Padul and Ugíjar. For his part, Don John of Austria continued putting entire villages to the sword.

Death, the hunger resulting from the Christians' scorched earth tactics, and the cold (the mountains were already covered in snow) all began to take their toll on the spirits of the Moriscos and their allies from across the strait.

*   *   *

Hernando alone took any satisfaction from the rout at Salobreña. When the commander of the fortress, Don Diego Ramírez de Haro, repelled the attack, the Moriscos fled towards the mountains. The women, children and old people who accompanied the army with the baggage trains struggled as best they could to escape, while Aben Aboo, Barrax, Brahim and the rest of the officers and infantry rushed ahead of them, concerned only for their own lives.

Helped by Yusuf, and even though his feet were shackled, Hernando took advantage of the confusion to hop over to La Vieja. Next to the mule he came across another one laden with the clothes, perfumes and other luxuries that Barrax's 'sons' always took with them. People were shouting and scurrying about; no one was looking or showed any interest in him. He could try it. Why not? He saw Aisha and Fátima fleeing from the camp. He also saw the boys in their shimmering tunics running bewildered through the crush in search of their mule. They loved their possessions; he had watched them perfume and adorn themselves the way women did – perhaps even more so. What would they do if they saw all their treasures were at risk?

He signalled Yusuf to keep watch. Just before the boys came running angrily up to them, he untied the straps and saddle-bags and loosened the harness on the mule's chest. Ubaid gave the order to depart and the string of mules set off. Almost at once the saddlebags slipped sideways. All the boys' treasures came cascading out, and they were forced to run after the mule and gather them up from the ground. Ubaid saw what was going on but did not stop; the Morisco army was scattering in front of them. Yusuf was smiling to himself, turning his head this way and that, first towards the boys, then to Hernando.

The commander's lovers struggled to pick up the trail of clothes, scent bottles and ornaments that were scattered all along the road. They managed to grab some things, but lost many others. Standing like bright lanterns in their highly coloured garments, they screamed at Ubaid to wait.

Nobody came to their aid.

Mounted on La Vieja, Hernando took in the scene: an older woman gave one of the boys a shove when she saw him crouching down to gather up a tunic, and the boy fell flat on his face, dropping everything he was carrying. When his friend rushed to help him, shrieking curses, another woman tripped him up. The next woman spat at him and the one behind her kicked him. In the commotion both boys lost their precious slippers, which some youngsters grabbed hold of to play with. As the column advanced, children and women picked up more things from the road. The last time Hernando caught sight of the two boys, they had been left a long way behind, and were standing, barefoot and filthy, crying in the no-man's-land between the rearguard of the Morisco army and the Christian vanguard.

They had run away. At least that was the explanation Ubaid offered Barrax when they arrived at Ugíjar. Hernando and Yusuf listened to the conversation from a few steps away. The corsair captain grasped the muleteer by his tunic and hoisted him up with one arm, bellowing, his face and open mouth dangerously close to the latter's nose.

'They fled,' Hernando confirmed from where he stood. Barrax turned towards him, still keeping hold of the muleteer. 'Does that surprise you?' Hernando added cheekily.

Barrax looked from one to the other several times, before throwing Ubaid into the dirt several yards from him.

Aben Aboo pitched camp near Ugíjar, where he left those he thought would be a hindrance in his new strategy of guerrilla warfare. From there he worked strenuously to bring all the troops scattered throughout the Alpujarra under his control. Barrax and his men returned to the Morisco stronghold after clashing with Don John of Austria at Serón. Initially, the battle favoured the Moriscos; the Christian soldiers were so hungry for plunder that they attacked the town without waiting for orders. Don John disciplined his troops, attacked a second time, and captured the village.

Hernando found himself urgently summoned to Barrax's quarters.

'Heal him,' Barrax ordered as soon as he came into the tent. 'Ubaid tells me you know about potions.'

Hernando looked at the man lying at Barrax's feet: there was a large bloodstain on one side of his grey sweat-soaked undergarment. His breathing was irregular; his body was twisted in pain and his face, framed by a neat black beard, seemed strained. Hernando guessed he must be about twenty-five years old. His eyes strayed to the finely wrought suit of armour piled next to him.

'It's from Milan,' Barrax announced, picking up the helmet and examining it closely. 'Made not far from his birthplace, most likely in the Negroli workshop. A knight like him, who is close to that bastard Christian prince,' he said, throwing the helmet to the floor, 'will bring us a ransom worth more than all the booty we have seized so far. There is no inscription on the armour; find out his name and who this nobleman is.'

'I've only healed mules,' Hernando said by way of excuse.

'In that case, healing a dog will be easy. You have made your decision, Nazarene. I warned you. You have chosen not to renounce your faith. If he dies, you will go with him to the grave; if he lives, you will row as a galley slave in my ship. You have Barrax's word for that.'

With these words he left him alone with the Christian.

The knight had been wounded by Barrax himself on the approach to Serón as he tried to protect the Christian soldiers who were fleeing in all directions. The bodies of hundreds of dead were left on the roads and in the ravines until Don John was able bury them some days later, but the noble prisoner had been thrown on to a horse like a sack and brought to the Morisco camp.

Hernando knelt close to the knight to examine the extent of his wound. What was he going to do? With great care he tried to remove the knight's undershirt; it was padded with layers of cotton to protect him from the rubbing of the armour. He had never before treated a man . . .

'He called you Nazarene.'

The words, spoken with difficulty, startled Hernando as he held the fabric in his hands.

'Do you understand Arabic?' Hernando asked him in Spanish.

'He also said you have not . . . that you haven't renounced your faith.'

The knight was struggling to breathe. He tried to sit up and blood spurted from his wound, soaking Hernando's fingers.

'Be quiet now. Don't move. You have to live,' Hernando said. 'Barrax keeps his word,' he muttered to himself.

'In the name of God and the Blessed Virgin . . .' mouthed the knight, 'by the nails of Jesus Christ, if you are a Christian, get me out of here.'

Was he a Christian?

'You wouldn't be able to take two steps,' said Hernando, dismissing the question he had asked himself. 'Besides, there are thousands of Morisco soldiers camped here. Where would you go? Stay quiet while I take a look at you.'

The wound seemed deep. Could it have affected his lungs? What did he know? Hernando examined the wound again; then did the same with the knight's face. He wasn't spitting blood. So what? What possible significance did it have that he wasn't spitting blood? The only thing he knew with any certainty was that if the knight died, he died too. He had noticed a change in Barrax's attitude; it was very different now from when he had been trying to win him over. Now he spoke to him in exactly the same way he addressed Ubaid or any of his men. Like most of the Berbers and janissaries, the corsair captain was worried about the course the war was taking. And if Hernando didn't die, he would row as a galley slave on the *Flying Horse* for the rest of his life. Who would pay a single maravedí of ransom for a Christian who was really a Muslim? He touched the knight's forehead: it was very hot; the wound must have become infected. Hernando knew this from treating his mules. He had to get rid of the infection and staunch the bleeding. As for any internal wounds . . .

He needed horns. He called Yusuf.

'Tell the commander I need two or three horns, preferably stag horns, a pestle, a bowl and whatever it takes to light a fire—'

'Where are we going to find horns?' the boy interrupted him.

'From the harquebusiers. Many of them keep their gun-powder in them. I'll also need a strip of copper, bandages, fresh water and cloths. Run!'

When Yusuf returned, Hernando started to grind down the end of one of the horns in the pestle.

'Barrax told me to stay with you and help,' said the boy when Hernando turned to him.

'In that case, you see to the horns. You need to grind the tips.'

Yusuf began his work. Hernando undressed the knight, who by now seemed to be only semi-conscious, then cleaned the wound with fresh water. Once Yusuf had finished grinding the ends of the horns, he heated the powder in the pestle and smeared the ashes on the wound. The knight groaned. Hernando covered the wound with the copper strip and wound a bandage round it.

Which God should he entrust himself to from now on?

Fátima had driven Brahim crazy. He did not allow her to leave the hut that he had ordered built for the two of them in the camp. He even neglected his duties to the King in order to be with her. Aisha, her children and Humam took refuge under some branches beside the hut. Fátima showed complete indifference when Brahim went anywhere near her. Enraged by her contempt, the muleteer would beat her until she submitted to him. He forced her to caress him and she did so until Brahim was in ecstasy, but he found only scorn in her big dark almond eyes. She obeyed his commands. She gave herself to him, yet each time the muleteer found only her passive body, the girl won a small revenge, but this was a satisfaction that always faded during the endless days she spent cooped up in the hut.

One night, Brahim appeared with a terrified Humam dangling from his right hand like a heavy sack.

'I will kill him if you don't change the way you behave,' Brahim threatened her.

From that night on, with Humam always near them to remind her what would happen to him should she fail to satisfy her new husband, Fátima was forced to recreate everything she had learnt from her mother and the other Morisco women about the art of love. She tried to remember what had pleased her first husband, and to recall all the chat between the women about how they fulfilled their menfolk's needs. Time and again she feigned the pleasure she had denied Brahim until now. Afterwards, Brahim left her on her own, taking Humam with him. Alone in the hut, she spent most of her time praying and watching Aisha and her son through the cracks in the wall. She wept and stroked the hand of Fátima still hanging round her neck, waiting for the moment when she could suckle her child. This was the only time her husband allowed her to be with him, as he sought to isolate her from everyone, including her son.

Meanwhile, on the opposite side of Aben Aboo's camp from where the Moriscos came and went to skirmish with the Duke of Sesa's soldiers, Hernando was trying to save the Christian's life . . . and his own. For some days, the knight remained semiconscious, fighting the infection. When he was awake he prayed, commending himself to Jesus Christ and the Virgin while Hernando took the chance to give him some broth to drink. On one occasion, he asked Hernando to pray with him, refusing to take any food until he did so. Hernando yielded, and prayed while trying to force some of the broth into the knight's mouth, although most of it ended up trickling through his beard. Another time, when he was completely lucid, the man fixed his gaze on Hernando's blue eyes.

'Those are the eyes of a Christian,' he said, peering down at his tattered clothes. 'Set me free. I will pay you back.'

If I were to do that, where would he go? thought Hernando, glancing at the shadow of the Berber on permanent guard outside the tent.

'What is your name?' he asked.

The nobleman again peered into Hernando's blue eyes. 'I will not bring the dishonour of dying in the tent of a renegade corsair down on my family, nor will I have my Prince worry about my captivity.'

'If you don't say who you are, they will not be able to ransom you.'

'There will be time enough for that if I survive. I am aware I am worth a great deal of money, but if I am to die here I would prefer to do so without my people knowing.'

Hernando read the inscription on one side of the flat hexagonal blade of the noble's hand-and-a-half sword hanging with Hamid's scimitar from the post at the tent entrance. Ever since Barrax had brought in the wounded Christian Hernando had had to sleep in the commander's tent, with a guard outside night and day. On the first evening, the corsair had caught him stealing a glance at the scimitar on the floor in the corner. He had gone across, picked it up, and hung it from the wooden post next to the knight's sword. The Berber on guard watched him in silence.

'If you wish to die,' Barrax warned Hernando, 'all you need do is brandish one of these.'

From that moment on, whenever he came into the tent Barrax would glance across at the post and the guard nearby.

'Do not unsheathe me without reason or sheathe me without honour', read the inscription on the nobleman's sword. Hernando peered at the face of the sleeping knight. What reason did the Spanish have to unsheathe their weapons? They were violating the peace treaty signed by their monarchs at the surrender of Granada. The Moriscos too were subjects of the Christian kings. They had been for years, paying more tithes to their majesties than any Christian did; ridiculed and hated, they had dedicated themselves to working peacefully for the good of their families on harsh, inhospitable land that had been theirs since time immemorial. They were Muslims, plain and simple, but Queen Isabella and King Ferdinand knew that on the day they had pledged peace. What kind of peace was it that they were offering? Following the Alpujarra uprising, Philip II's territory was swamped with Morisco slaves. Merchants bought and sold them for next to nothing all over Spain. Thousands of subjects of the King, forced to become Christians, found themselves enslaved. The same King! It was said that in the Indies, a place also ruled by that King, the natives who were baptized by force could not be made slaves. Why should the Moriscos be any different? Why did the Church not defend both peoples equally, when they were both vassals of the same King? It was said that the natives of the Indies ate human flesh, worshipped idols and believed in their witch doctors, and yet the Spanish monarchs had exempted them from slavery. Muslims on the other hand believed in the same God of Abraham as the Christians, they did not eat human flesh, nor did they worship idols, yet, despite having been baptized and forced to share the same faith, they could be enslaved!

Hernando too was a slave – for being a Christian! What sort of madness was that? To some, he was just a Morisco whom they would kill as they did all those over twelve years of age; to others he was a Christian who would row for the rest of his life in a corsair galley – if they didn't kill him first. And if he swore to uphold the Muslim faith, his own faith, he would become the plaything of a renegade. He, who had been born a Muslim! Or did the Christian blood running through his veins count for something? The knight would be ransomed for a sack of gold coins that would make the corsair wealthy. Barrax would return to Algiers a rich man while the nobleman would go back to the lands he owned to take up the fight against the Moriscos once more, and go on making slaves of them.

21

DECREE IN FAVOUR OF ALL WHO SURRENDER

My Lord the King, aware that the majority of the Moriscos from this kingdom of Granada who rebelled against his laws did so moved not by their own will but were cajoled and compelled, duped and persuaded into the revolt by agitators and trouble-makers, chiefs and leaders who moved among them and continue to do so; which said persons enticed them to rise up for their own ends, so that they might enjoy and help themselves to the property of the common people, and not in order to bestow any benefit on them; and having dispatched men of war to punish them as befitted their sins and crimes, who retook the places they had seized on the Almanzora River, in the Filabres hills and in the Alpujarra, when many of them were killed or taken prisoner, forcing them to wander lost and astray in the mountains, living like savage beasts in the caverns and caves and in the forests, suffering extreme hardship; moved by all this to pity, a virtue befitting his royal status, and wishing to show mercy towards them, considering that they are his subjects and vassals, and moved by his knowledge of the acts of violence, violations of the womenfolk, spillage of blood, robberies and the other great evils that the men of war have committed without excuse, His Majesty has delegated us in his name to treat them with royal clemency and to admit them once more under his royal authority in the following manner:

Assure all those Moriscos who have rebelled against the due

obedience and grace of His Majesty, men and women of whatever status, rank or condition, that if within twenty days from the date of this decree they lay down their arms and place themselves in the hands of His Majesty and Don John of Austria in the King's name, he will spare their lives, and will listen and dispense justice to all those who can prove that acts of violence and oppression forced them to rebel, dealing with them in accordance with his customary mercy; and further promises similar consideration towards all those who besides giving themselves up and surrendering carry out a particular service, such as slitting the throats of or capturing Turks or Moors from Barbary who have joined forces with the rebels, or doing the same with those others of his kingdom who have been captains and generals in the rebellion and who persist in their sedition, refusing to accept the grace and mercy His Majesty sees fit to bestow on them.

Furthermore: all those over fifteen years of age and under fifty who surrender within the allotted time and who hand over to His Majesty's officials an harquebus or crossbow with their ammunition, will have their lives spared and will not be enslaved; in addition to which they will be able to nominate two people among those they have brought with them to be set free, be it a father or mother, children, wife or siblings; none of these shall be slaves either but will enjoy complete freedom and rights. Of those who do not wish to avail themselves of this forgiveness and mercy, no man of fourteen years or more will be allowed into any part of our kingdoms, but will face the punishment of death without mercy or compassion.

This edict issued by Don John of Austria in April 1570 passed from hand to hand throughout the Alpujarra. The Christians translated it into Arabic and made copies, which they distributed amongst informers and merchants. In some instances those who could read discreetly repeated the contents, well away from the outlaws, janissaries or Berbers; on other occasions the edict was proclaimed in the streets. The

Prince also decreed severe penalties for anyone who dared detain, rob or maltreat any Morisco who came forward to surrender, as had happened on previous occasions.

Both sides were facing a crisis: in the Alpujarra, the price of bushels of wheat and barley had increased tenfold, with the result that soldiers and their families were going hungry. Aben Aboo could do nothing to remedy the situation, so that following an exchange of letters with Alonso de Granada Venegas, a man held in esteem by the Moriscos, he formally delegated to El Habaquí the negotiation of the terms of surrender. But the mere fact of entering into negotiations only served to worsen the Moriscos' plight. Three galleys had just arrived from Algiers carrying foodstuffs, weapons and munitions. They began to offload their provisions on the beaches of Dalías, but as soon as they heard that Aben Aboo was negotiating a surrender, they loaded up again and sailed back to Algiers. The same thing happened with seven more galleys that arrived along the coast under the command of Hussein, brother of Caracax, who had come with four hundred janissaries and an assortment of weaponry, but on hearing about the peace negotiations immediately headed back to the corsairs' stronghold.

The situation was even more complicated on the Christian side. On the one hand, the guerrilla warfare adopted by Aben Aboo rendered an outright victory practically impossible. On the other hand, the uprising had already made its impact felt in nearby Seville, where ten thousand Morisco vassals of the Duke of Medina Sidonia and the Duke of Arcos rose up as a result of the outrages they were subjected to. King Philip II succeeded in resolving the matter by ordering the noblemen to go in person and pacify their lands, but fears grew that the uprising might at any moment spread to the kingdoms of Murcia, Valencia or Aragón, where a large number of Moriscos lived.

However, what really drove King Philip to allow Don John of Austria to offer terms of surrender was the actions of the Ottoman Sultan.

In February 1570 the Turks, imitating the corsairs from

Algiers who were concentrating their forces on the conquest of Tunis, attacked Zara in Venetian Dalmatia. In July they took back the island of Cyprus. In March of the same year, Philip II received an envoy from Pope Pius V in Córdoba; he had convened Parliament there in order to be close to the battles in Granada. In the name of Christendom, His Holiness demanded the launch of a new crusade, to which end he proposed to set up a Holy League to fight the threat from the infidels who, according to the Pontiff, were emboldened because Spain was distracted by its internal conflicts. The devout Spanish monarch accepted, but in order to dedicate forces to this enterprise he first had to resolve the problems with the Moriscos in the Alpujarra.

His edict paved the way for the mass surrender of Moriscos, who made their way to Don John of Austria's encampment in El Padul to hand themselves over. But it also led to the desertion of a large part of the Christian army when they realized there was nothing more they could get out of the war. Of the ten thousand men who were with the Duke of Sesa when he entered the Alpujarra, only four thousand remained.

'We're leaving! We're going back to Algiers!' Barrax's order thundered through the ranks of his men. 'Have everything ready for first thing tomorrow morning.' He strode inside his tent. 'Did you hear me?' he shouted at Hernando. 'Get him ready for the journey,' he added, pointing to the knight.

Hernando turned to the nobleman: he was a little better, but . . . 'He will die,' he said without thinking.

Barrax did not answer. He frowned until his eyebrows formed a single black line above his half-closed eyes. Hernando held his breath while the commander stared at him. Then Barrax turned his back and left the tent. As he did so, he stroked his dagger with his right hand, as if to show Hernando the fate that lay ahead of him.

He was condemned, thought Hernando: death awaited him or, at best, life as a galley slave. Sitting on the ground, he peered at the chains round his ankles. He could not run. He could not even walk! He was a slave. He was nothing more than a slave in irons. And Fátima ... He put his head in his hands, tears falling unchecked.

'Men only weep when they lose a mother or their guts are spilled.'

Hernando looked at the knight and took a deep breath to hold back his tears. 'We're both going to die,' he said, wiping his tears on his sleeve.

'We will only die if that is God's will,' the Christian said with a sigh.

Where had he heard the very same sentiment? Gonzalico! The same outlook, the same acceptance. He clicked his tongue. And Islam? Didn't the word itself imply submission?

'But God has made us free to fight,' the knight went on, interrupting his thoughts.

Hernando answered him with a wry grimace. 'One of us wounded and the other in chains?' As Hernando spoke, he gestured to the camp outside, full of noise and men bustling about as they made preparations to leave.

'If you have already resigned yourself to death, at least let me fight for my life,' the Christian replied.

Hernando glanced down at his chains: they were not thick but they were strong; his ankles were raw where they rubbed against the iron.

'What would you do if I let you go?' he asked, still staring down at the shackles.

'Flee and save my life.'

'I doubt you'd be able to walk. You can't even raise yourself off that bed.'

'Yes, I can,' the knight replied, but as he sat up a stab of pain made him wince.

'There are thousands of Muslims out there.' Hernando turned towards him. He caught an unfamiliar glint in the nobleman's gaze. 'They—'

'They will kill me?' The knight beat him to it.

The muezzin's call to prayer interrupted their conversation. Dusk was falling. Preparations for the journey halted, and the faithful prostrated themselves. 'Now,' whispered the knight in the hush before the prayers began, pointing to the rear of the tent behind which the mules were tethered.

Hernando did not pray. He had not done so for some time. The night prayer was the one the Moriscos could perform with a certain freedom, for, ensconced in their houses, they could escape surveillance by the Christians. What would Hamid have advised? What would the old holy man say about setting an enemy Christian free? He turned to the door post at the entrance to the tent. Hamid's scimitar, the sword of the Prophet! Through the gaps in the tent folds he saw how the people in the camp were turning to face Mecca in preparation for prayer. As always, the Berber was on guard at the entrance, close to the swords. Hernando recalled Barrax's threat: *If you wish to die, all you need do is brandish one of these.* To die. *In death, hope is everlasting.* It was as if those almond eyes of Fátima, whose image suddenly filled his mind, were guiding him. What did any of this matter now? Christians, Muslims, wars, victims . . .

'Pretend you're dead,' he ordered the knight, turning towards him. 'Close your eyes and hold your breath.'

'What . . . ?'

'Do as I say!'

The silence was broken as thousands of Muslims started to pray. Hernando listened to the chants for a few moments, then he poked his head through the tent folds.

'Help me!' he pleaded with the guard. 'The Christian is dying.'

The Berber stepped inside the tent, went down on one knee beside the wounded man and touched his face. The instant the guard had his back to him Hernando unsheathed the scimitar; the whisper of the steel made the Berber turn his head. Without a second's hesitation, Hernando whirled the blade and sliced the guard's neck. He fell dead on top of the knight.

The nobleman struggled to push away the body.

'Hand me my sword,' he asked, trying to get to his feet. Hernando stared fascinated at the scimitar's sharp blade; a thin trickle of blood shone all the way down it. 'For God's sake! Give me the sword,' the nobleman implored him. Hernando stared at the Christian: how could a man in his condition wield such a heavy weapon? 'Please,' the knight insisted.

Hernando handed him the sword and crawled to the far end of the tent: the teams of mules were just on the other side. The nobleman followed, bent double, sword in hand. Hernando could tell from the wounded man's slow, stiff movements that he was weak and in pain. Doubts assailed him again. This was suicide! As if sensing his fears, the knight raised his face to him and smiled gratefully. Hernando crouched down, taking up position by the side of the tent and trying to make out something in the shadows. The knight threw caution to the winds; he slashed the side of the tent, slipped through the gap and began to crawl outside. As he came level with him, Hernando saw that the wound was bleeding again and the bandage over the strip of copper looked as though it was dyed red. He followed the knight, also on all fours, his eyes firmly on the ground and on the scimitar he was dragging along, expecting at any moment to run into another guard. But it did not happen, and in a few moments they found themselves bumping into the mules. The murmurs of the prayers from thousands of the faithful mingled with their own rapid breathing. The Christian smiled at him again, openly, as if they were already free men. Now what? Hernando wondered. The knight would not be able to get very far. He was losing blood; they would never even cover the tenth part of a league. The sky was turning red above the mountaintops as the sun dipped beyond the horizon. Dusk in the Sierra Nevada. How often he had gazed at it in . . . Juviles! La Vieja! He fell silent and looked closely at the mules' hooves. How could he not recognize La Vieja? He had treated her feet a thousand times. He quickly located her and signalled to the Christian to follow him.

Reaching the mule, he stroked her knotted, blistered tendons. La Vieja was saddled up for the journey. Hernando got to his feet without stopping to check if anyone was watching, if anyone was on the lookout. They were all still busy with the night prayers. To his left, a few paces away, he could see a rough track leading down to one of the many ravines of the Alpujarra.

'Stand up,' he urged the nobleman. Hernando helped him lie across La Vieja like a bundle. 'Hold on tightly,' he instructed him, guiding his hands to clasp the animal's girth. When he tried to take the sword from him, the Christian refused and used his other hand to cling on.

Pulling the mule towards the ravine, Hernando hobbled along, hindered by the chains on his ankles. He tried desperately to prevent them clinking, and moved forward without looking anywhere in particular, his eyes fixed on the space opening up over the precipice they were approaching. He felt an urge to pray, to join in the familiar mumbling sounds he could hear from the camp, but knew that was impossible. Only when he reached the edge of the ravine did he turn his head: he could still see a thin reddish glow on the tops of the mountains. Nobody had noticed them. For a few seconds he took comfort from the scene: thousands of people prostrated towards the east, in the opposite direction to where they were heading. The Christian hurried him on, so he jumped up on the mule's back, lying crossways next to the knight and like him he grabbed the girth underneath La Vieja's belly.

'Hold on tight,' he warned him again. 'The descent will be dangerous. Go home to Juviles, Vieja! Take us to Juviles!' He patted one of her haunches, gently at first, then harder, until La Vieja overcame her initial reluctance to set off down the steep path. She extended one of her hooves cautiously, then she sat on her haunches to slide down the slope.

What took only a few moments seemed to them an eternity. The mule managed to avoid stones and trees: to the boy's surprise she even managed to jump down some sheer rocks. La Vieja! His Vieja! They almost fell off several times when the animal sat down to slide downhill. They were scratched by brambles and branches, but in the end reached the bed of a stream running down from the Sierra Nevada. The icy water splashed them with freedom. La Vieja came to a halt with the water up to her shanks. She shook her head violently; her big ears tossed proudly, scattering thousands of droplets in all directions, as if she too was aware of the feat she had just achieved. Hernando let himself collapse into the creek and sank his head under the water. He let out a shout under the surface, and a multitude of bubbles caressed his face. They had done it! Meanwhile, the knight too slithered down until he was standing, leaning against the mule; he was still bleeding and yet, even wearing only a simple undergarment, he seemed distinguished, proud, the large heavy sword grasped firmly in his right hand.

Hernando stayed seated in the stream.

'You see?' said the knight. 'God did not want us to die.' Hernando laughed nervously. 'We have to fight, not weep! Your guts aren't hanging out and your mother has not died on you. Jesus Christ and the Blessed Virgin and . . .'

The knight went on talking but Hernando did not listen. His mother? Fátima?

'Come, let's make good our escape,' the nobleman urged at the end of his speech.

Escape? Hernando asked himself. Yes, that was what he wanted. That was why he had taken such a risk, but he had already escaped once before, to Adra. He had left Fátima and his mother on their own then, and did not want to do so again.

'Wait.'

'They'll come after us, just as soon as they realize we've escaped!'

'Wait,' insisted Hernando. 'The darkness will slow them up.'

'What's wrong?' the nobleman interrupted him.

'A few months ago,' Hernando explained, standing up in the stream and gazing down at Hamid's scimitar with a sudden sadness, 'I managed to rescue my mother from Juviles.' Why go into the details? He thought about it before going on, yet he could not avoid it. 'You Christians massacred more than a thousand women and children,' he said accusingly.

'I did not—'

'Be quiet! You all did it. And you made slaves of as many again.'

'And your side—!'

'What does that matter now?' the young Morisco protested. 'I went back to Juviles to rescue my mother. I succeeded. I also rescued Fátima, my . . . the girl who was to be my wife. Afterwards, I saved their lives again. We have lived through some tough times.' Hernando remembered the snowstorm, fleeing from Paterna, the wedding at Mecina, escaping from the Christians . . . What was all that for? 'I am not going to abandon them to their fate now,' he concluded.

He met the Christian's stare. The knight was bleeding heavily but nevertheless seemed strong and resolute. While he had been forced to live as Barrax's slave, Hernando had banished all thoughts of Fátima and Aisha from his mind; he had dismissed all consideration of them, as if they didn't exist, but now . . . freedom! What strange vigour freedom gave a person! Brahim would not surrender to the Christians, he thought suddenly, but if he could manage to flee with Fátima and his mother and give themselves up, perhaps they could forget that nightmare.

'I need your help . . .' the knight began.

'I'll be of little use to you in the dark. All you need is La Vieja. I have to go to try to find my mother . . . and the woman I love. Do you understand? I cannot allow the Christians to kill them or make slaves of them.'

Stirred by his decision, he made again to climb out of the stream, but fell back into the water because of his chains. He had forgotten about them.

'Your determination does you honour,' the knight agreed, helping him up. 'Come over here,' he added, pointing to the riverbank.

'Why?'

'My lad, there is no Moorish iron that can stand up to good Toledan steel,' the Christian replied, directing him to sit down with his legs stretched out and his chained feet on a small boulder.

Hernando watched him grasp the sword in both hands. He would not be able to do it; he was badly wounded. Even in the twilight he could make out the pain on the knight's face as he raised the sword above his head.

'By the nails of Jesus Christ!' the nobleman shouted.

Sparks flew from the chain and the stone when the steel hit the iron, but Hernando thought he saw his feet released. The grating sound of the splintered shackle coincided with a sudden commotion high above them. The soldiers in the camp had discovered their escape. The Christian leant on his sword, now stuck in the ground, as if the blow had drained the last of his strength.

'Get out of here!' Hernando urged him. The knight did not so much as answer. Hernando reached under his armpits and hauled him over to La Vieja. He helped him up as before, until he lay across the mule's back. He undid one of the girths and tied the Christian to the mule. He kept some other straps for himself. 'Trust her,' he said, bending down to whisper in the knight's ear. 'If you find her stopping, order her to head for Juviles.' La Vieja pricked up her ears. 'Remember: to Juviles. To Juviles, Vieja! To Juviles!' He drove the mule forward with a whack on her rump. He watched her set off down the riverbed, but only for a moment: the ravine seemed to be full of flaming torches cautiously edging their way down.

Hernando hid in some bushes while the Berbers Barrax had sent searched here and there without any great zeal. Barrax himself stood at the top of the ravine shouting orders. A couple of soldiers followed the course of the river in the darkness, but soon came back. They were heading home to Algiers the next day, much richer than when they had landed on the coast of al-Andalus; what did they care if Barrax had lost his prisoner?

Hernando waited until half the night had passed before deciding to climb up along the path the Berbers themselves had made. He tied the dangling ends of the chains up above his ankles with the straps he had taken from the mule. The iron links would probably chafe his skin as the shackles had done before, but they would not hurt so much: where before he had been forced to crawl, now they were little more than a nuisance.

As he lay hidden at the foot of the ravine he could hear the hubbub and celebrations in the camp. Like Barrax, many corsairs and Berbers had decided to return to their homeland and were celebrating their last night in the lands of al-Andalus. For their part, the Moriscos were still leaving in droves to surrender to Don John of Austria, and either stole away from the Muslim camp or walked away quite openly. On this occasion, the Christian Prince's decree was fulfilled, and men and women were respected en route. Even little Yusuf had confessed to Hernando earlier that evening that he intended to escape the following morning and give himself up. The boy had got hold of an old crossbow which he planned to take to Don John's camp as the edict stipulated. He was not yet fourteen but wanted to appear more like a soldier. He announced his decision proudly.

Listening to him, Hernando forced himself to smile.

'I . . .' stuttered Yusuf, not daring to look him in the face, 'I . . .'

'Tell me.'

'Do you think it's all right? Can I?'

Now it was Hernando's turn to look away. His voice failed him as he tried to answer, and he had to clear his throat repeatedly. 'You don't have to ask my permission. You . . .' He stopped and cleared his throat again. 'You are free and you don't owe me anything. In any event, it is I who owe you my gratitude.'

'But . . .'

'May Allah protect you, Yusuf. Go in peace.'

Yusuf came over to him with all the solemnity one might

expect from a young boy, hand outstretched, but in the end he threw himself into Hernando's arms. Even now, at the bottom of the ravine, Hernando could feel him breathing heavily against his chest.

He reached the top of the ravine and walked round Barrax's tent into the camp. There was no need for him to take any precautions: the lookout consisted of one solitary Berber whose head was nodding in a vain attempt to stay awake. The rest were sleeping off the celebrations next to the bonfires. How was he going to find Fátima and his mother? He'd have to search the whole camp, but after being paraded there by Barrax's sons, everyone would recognize him. He spotted a turban discarded beside the embers of one of the fires, but he did not know how to put it on. Although the guard was dozing, surely he would notice someone prowling among his companions; everything was still and the glow of the torches lighting the camp were bound to give him away. He looked all around him, until . . . No!

His legs buckled beneath him. He fell to his knees and a cold sweat broke out all over his body. He vomited. He did so again, and a third and fourth time but there was nothing left to throw up and the retching tore at his insides. He looked again towards the entrance to Barrax's tent: on the same post where Barrax had ordered the swords to be hung, Yusuf's severed head was impaled. His nose and ears had been ripped off and nailed in a row: first one ear, then the other and at the end what must have been the boy's nose. Hernando retched again but this time he did not look away. He imagined the vast bulk of the corsair captain on top of Yusuf as he tore off his nose and ears with his teeth. He had threatened to do it so many times! It could only have been because of him. They must have blamed the boy for his escape; La Vieja was missing and Yusuf was the one who looked after the animals. Hernando searched to see if Ubaid's head was also on display but could not see it. The muleteer must have been more astute, and fled straight away. He stared once more at Yusuf's remains, a bitter testimony to the corsair's cruelty. He stood up and unsheathed the scimitar.

Hernando crept along the top of the ravine until he was behind the Berber on guard. 'That old scimitar will be no use to you unless you learn to hold it tight,' he remembered a janissary once telling him. If he failed, he would have Barrax to deal with again. He tightened his grip on the sword hilt and stiffened all his muscles before bringing the curved blade down with all his might on the soldier's neck. He heard only the whistle of the blade through the air and the dull thud as the man fell to the ground, his head almost severed. Hernando made his way through the camp undaunted by the sleeping Berbers. All his muscles were still tense, and his teeth were clenched as he stared fixedly at the entrance to the corsair leader's tent. He lifted the flap and went inside. Barrax was sleeping on the floor on a straw mattress. Hernando waited until his eyes grew used to the light, then tiptoed towards him. He raised the scimitar above his head; his fingers were hurting, the muscles on his arms and back felt as though they were about to split open. There he was! Defenceless! His neck was much thicker than the guard's and Hernando had not managed to decapitate him completely. He went to deliver the blow but something held him back and the sword stayed above his head. Why not? The corsair ought to know who was going to put an end to his life! He owed it to Yusuf! Hernando kicked him in the ribs. The corsair muttered something, shifted and carried on sleeping. Hernando kicked him even harder in the side. A befuddled Barrax sat up; Hernando gave himself a few moments, just long enough for the other man to work out who it was, long enough for him to look up at the scimitar, just long enough for him to look into his eyes. The commander opened his mouth to scream as the scimitar plunged towards his neck. Hernando sliced his head clean off with a single blow.

Hernando then went quickly through the camp dressed in Turkish fashion, wearing the clothes he discovered in the tent: a turban which hid half his face, some long loose trousers and a wide tunic that reached to his ankles; he kept the chains hidden beneath his trousers wrapped in pieces of cloth. In his right hand he carried the commander's head in a sack. He had several daggers tucked in his belt as well as a small harquebus slung from the other shoulder to Hamid's scimitar. He boldly asked various soldiers he ran into where he might find Brahim's tent, and finally found it. He strode inside, without thinking, his scimitar drawn. What did it matter to him that Brahim was his mother's husband? Aisha's prayers would be worth nothing this time. But the tent the soldiers had directed him to was empty: there was nobody inside. He was replacing the scimitar back in its scabbard when a noise behind him forced him to whirl round, drawing the sword once more. His mother stood silently in the doorway.

'What do you want?' Aisha asked.

Hernando uncovered his face.

'My son!' Aisha went towards him, but for the first time Hernando shrugged off her embrace.

'Brahim?' he enquired brusquely. 'And Fátima? Where are they?'

'My son ... you're alive! And ... free?' stammered his mother.

Hernando saw that tears were streaming down her cheeks.

'Mother, where is Fátima?' he asked again, tenderly this time, as he took her in his arms.

'They have fled. They ran off to surrender to the Christians,' Aisha replied between sobs. 'At sunset last night.' Hernando's disappointment was so obvious that Aisha hastened on: 'The King was forced to reprimand your stepfather several times. He missed meetings of the council and even battles to ...' She hesitated. '... to be with Fátima,' she said finally. 'Since the Christians' edict only grants freedom to two others, he chose Fátima and his eldest son, Aquil, although he also took Humam with him, after she begged him to do so. Perhaps a child only a few months old will not count.'

'Fátima ... Fátima has fled with him?'

'She had to obey him, my son. Brahim—'

'And Musa?' he interrupted her. He didn't want to hear any more details.

'In the tent next to this one. In this one, only—'

'Let's get after them!' he urged her.

Dawn was breaking. They came upon a string of mules near the tent, and Hernando decided to take one of them for his mother to ride. The muleteer, an old Morisco, awoke when he became aware of his animals moving, but Hernando threatened him with the scimitar. He did not kill him; instead he made him stay with them for part of the journey, just long enough so that he could not make their escape known; then set him free.

22

IT TOOK Hernando, Aisha and Musa two days to cover the distance to El Padul and Don John of Austria's camp. On the way they joined hundreds of Moriscos who were also on their way to surrender. The Prince demanded that all those journeying through the Alpujarra for this reason should wear a white cross on their right shoulder, so that from far away these long columns looked like a procession of great white crosses woven into the clothes of the men, women and children who walked along dragging their feet, vanquished, exhausted, starving and ill. They left behind them the fleeting illusion that they had salvaged their culture, their land . . . and their God. They all knew what their destiny was: exile to one of the Christian monarch's other kingdoms, far from Granada, the same punishment as that suffered by the Moriscos from the Albaicín and the plains outside the city.

By nightfall they had reached the outskirts of Lanjarón. Some Moriscos came to a halt there as the light began to fade; many others joined them. There were no festivities, no celebrations or dances; a few fires were lit and people made ready to sleep in the open. There was scarcely any food other than the scant provisions each of them had managed to get hold of at the outset. No one called to prayer.

Hernando chewed a hunk of bread, took the mule's halter and said goodbye to his mother.

'Where are you going?'

'There's something I have to do. I'll be back, don't worry,' he said when he saw how concerned she looked.

He was heading for the impregnable castle of Lanjarón, which controlled the surrounding district. It was built on the summit of a rocky crag some six hundred feet high to the south of the village; three of the fortress's four sides overlooked sheer rock faces. Like many other castles in the region, it had been built during the Nasrid period and had been half destroyed following the first revolt in the Alpujarra in 1500, when the Moriscos had risen up against the harsh rule of Cardinal Cisneros: the rebellion which culminated in the betrayal of the peace accords of Granada by the Catholic monarchs. As he made his way out of the Morisco camp, Hernando kept an eye open for any sign of Brahim and Fátima. Despite the fact that they had set off the previous sunset they would not have been able to travel by moonlight alone and would have had to stop off during the first night of their journey, but he could not make them out among the masses of shadows moving sadly about. Perhaps they were further on, already in Tablate, where some of the Moriscos had gone to spend the night.

He covered the distance separating him from the fortress with the help of the faint golden light of the moon. The mule was skilled and moved carefully, searching for firm footholds . . . just like La Vieja. What had become of poor Vieja? Hernando pushed the thought out of his mind, realizing he was giving way to nostalgia. And the knight? Could he still be alive? He would have liked to know who he was, but the Christian had almost passed out after the blow that had freed Hernando from his chains. Still, had it not been for him, with his eagerness to be free, perhaps Hernando would not have fled and would now be rowing as a galley slave on Barrax's *Flying Horse* . . . or dead like Yusuf. Remembering the boy, Hernando was again overwhelmed with anguish. He peered up at the proud silhouette of the castle and sighed. After all these months of hardship and punishment, the Moriscos were surrendering. Again. What was the point of all the deaths and heartache?

Would that castle ever again defend a wronged and oppressed people?

He climbed the path and reached the ruined castle; he dismounted slowly, dejectedly, and waited for his eyes to adjust to the new darkness. He chose the tower that was still standing, on the south side of the fortress, and made his way towards it.

He tried to work out the direction of Mecca and when he believed he had found it he lifted sand from the ground and cleaned himself with it. He raised his blue eyes to heaven: eyes that were different to those which had looked at Hamid's scimitar that first time. Gone now was the childish glint, veiled beneath a look of grief.

'There is no god but God, and Muhammad is the messenger of God.'

He prayed quietly, in a whisper, holding tightly to Hamid's scimitar in its sheath above his head.

How many times had he refused to say that profession of faith to Barrax?

'Hamid, here I am,' he whispered again. He listened to the silence. 'Here I am!' he howled. His cry echoed through the hills and valleys, taking him by surprise. What had become of the holy man? He let a few moments pass by, and drew breath. 'Allah is great!' he shouted at the top of his lungs. The silence of the mountains all around him was his only answer. 'I swore', he added in a trembling voice, 'that no Christian would ever lay his hands on this scimitar.'

After recalling his promise, he buried the sword as deeply as he could at the foot of the tower, tearing his fingers and nails as he dug into the ground with a leather punch he had found in the camp. Then he prayed, sensing that Hamid was there with him, as had so often been the case in Juviles. Finally he used a stone and the punch to hack at the bolts on the shackles until they came loose and revealed his red, raw ankles.

The sun had passed midday by the time Hernando's group reached Don John of Austria's camp. About a quarter of a league away the women began to uncover their heads and faces and to hide the forbidden jewels in their clothes. The Moriscos were met by several companies of soldiers on the flat plain outside El Padul.

'Throw down your weapons!' they shouted, making the Moriscos line up. 'Anyone who raises an harquebus or crossbow or who wields a sword will die in the act.'

At the head of each of the long rows of Moriscos, clerks seated at tables that looked incongruous out in the fields recorded the personal details of every person, as well as of the weapons they handed in. The clerks were in no hurry to carry out their task, and so the wait seemed never-ending. By their side, another army, this one made up of priests, prayed around the Moriscos, urging them to join in their prayers, make the sign of the cross or prostrate themselves before the crucifixes they brandished in their faces. From the lines of waiting people rose the same low garbled muttering that had been heard for years in the churches of the Alpujarra as the Moriscos complied reluctantly with the priests' demands.

'What have you got there?' a soldier with the red cross of Saint Andrew embroidered on his uniform asked Hernando, pointing to the bag he was carrying in his right hand.

'It's not—' Hernando began, opening it and reaching in slowly with his other hand.

'Santiago!' shouted the soldier drawing his sword at what he thought was a suspicious movement.

Several soldiers quickly heeded their companion's call while the other Moriscos moved away from Hernando, Aisha and Musa. They immediately found themselves surrounded by armed men. Hernando kept his hand in the bag.

'I'm not hiding a weapon,' he tried to reassure the soldiers, beginning very slowly to pull out the corsair leader's head. 'This is what is left of Barrax!' he shouted, holding the head aloft by the hair. 'The corsair captain!'

A murmur spread through the ranks of the Moriscos. One of the veteran soldiers ordered a youngster to go and find a corporal or sergeant, while other soldiers and priests crowded round Hernando and his companions. Everyone knew who Barrax was.

'What's your name?' a corporal asked him, forcing his way through the crowd. At the sight of the corsair's head, he smiled.

'Hernando Ruiz!' came a cry from the far side of the circle before Hernando could even answer.

He whirled round in astonishment. That voice . . . Andrés, the sacristan from Juviles!

The sacristan had joined the group together with two priests. He strode over to Aisha and slapped her face as soon as he reached her. Hernando dropped Barrax's head and leapt towards the sacristan, but the corporal stopped him.

'What is happening? What's going on?'

'This woman killed Don Martín, the parish priest of Juviles,' screamed the sacristan, his eyes bloodshot. He made to strike Aisha once more.

Hernando felt his legs give way when he remembered his mother stabbing the priest. He never imagined they would meet anyone from Juviles, much less Andrés. The corporal seized the sacristan's arm and prevented him striking Aisha.

'How dare you?' one of the priests sprang to the sacristan's defence.

The Prince's orders were categorical: nothing was to be done that might provoke an uprising among the Moriscos.

'Don John has promised a pardon to any Moriscos who surrender and no one is going to go against his decision,' the corporal warned him. 'This lad', he added, 'has brought in his weapons and the head of a corsair captain. The only people who cannot enjoy either the Prince's favour or his pardon are the Turks and Berbers.'

'She murdered a man of God!' insisted the other priest, shaking Aisha by the arm.

'It seems they have also killed a bloodthirsty enemy of the King. Is she with you?' he asked Hernando.

'Yes. She's my mother.'

'Of course!' Andrés erupted again, spitting his words at Aisha. 'You couldn't come with your husband, could you? I saw him in one of the lines with another woman. He swore that you were dead! That's why you've had to come with your son and with the corsair trophy to win your freedom.'

'Freedom is granted by the Prince,' said the corporal. 'I forbid you to take any action against this woman,' he warned the priests. 'If you have anything to say or any complaints, address them to Don John of Austria.'

'We will do!' shrieked the first priest. 'Against her and her lying husband.' The corporal shrugged his shoulders. 'Come with us to look for her husband,' the priest urged him.

'I have better things to do,' the corporal excused himself, at the same time lifting Barrax's head off the ground. 'Go with them,' he ordered a couple of his men, 'and make sure they follow the Prince's orders.'

They were going to look for Brahim! Hernando ignored the Moriscos rushing off to follow the sacristan. Nor did he heed the remarks shouted at him as he passed by; news of the corsair captain's head had passed by word of mouth. They were going in search of Brahim . . . and Fátima!

'There he is!' Andrés's roar, as the sacristan pointed to one of the clerk's tables, brought Hernando back to reality just when his stomach was beginning to churn at the thought of Fátima in his stepfather's hands. 'José Ruiz!' barked the sacristan, hurrying towards the desk. The clerk stopped writing in his book and looked up at the group of people coming towards him. 'Didn't you swear that your wife had died?'

Brahim turned pale when he saw his stepson, Aisha and Musa, the two soldiers, some priests and the sacristan from Juviles rushing towards him. Hernando did not see the look of panic on his stepfather's face; his gaze was fixed firmly on Fátima, thin, emaciated, her beautiful, dark, almond-shaped eyes sunk in violet-coloured sockets. The girl, silent, her face blank, watched them approach.

'What is all this noise about?' asked the clerk, halting them with a wave of his hand before they could swoop on his table. He was a gaunt man with a sickly-looking face and sparse beard, and was clearly annoyed by the intrusion. The sacristan threw himself at Brahim, but one of the soldiers blocked his path. 'What's going on?' the clerk asked again.

'This man has lied to me!' fumed Andrés. The clerk nodded resignedly, convinced that all of them lied. 'He swore to me that his wife had died but the fact is that he was trying to hide a priest-killer,' he said accusingly, grabbing Aisha by the arm and pushing her in front of him.

'His wife? According to him,' said the clerk, as if speaking required a great effort, 'this woman is his wife.' He pointed at Fátima.

'Bigamist!' shouted one of the priests.

'Heretic!' yelled the other. 'He must be reported to the Holy Office! The Prince cannot absolve sins, that is something the Church alone can do.'

The clerk dropped his pen on the register and dried his forehead with a handkerchief. After days of work and listening to hundreds of men and women who did not even speak *aljamiado*, problems like this were the last thing he needed.

'Where are the delegates of the Inquisition?' Andrés insisted. He looked around him and urged the soldiers to go and find them.

Hernando saw how Brahim was trembling and growing ever paler. He knew what he was thinking. If they arrested him and discovered that he had two wives, the Inquisition would put him in jail and . . .

'No, she is not my wife,' mumbled Brahim.

'It says here María de Terque, wife of José Ruiz of Juviles,' grumbled the clerk. 'That is what you told me.'

'No! You misunderstood me! Wife of Hernando Ruiz of Juviles.' Brahim nervously added some words in Arabic, gesturing all the while. 'That is what I said. My son Hernando Ruiz, not José Ruiz. María de Terque is my son's wife,' he shouted to everyone present.

Hernando was stunned. Fátima looked up from Humam, whom she was cradling in her arms, oblivious to all that was going on around her.

'You said—' the clerk insisted.

Brahim fired off another volley of words in Arabic. He tried to address himself to the clerk but the latter interrupted him with a dismissive wave of his hand.

'Hand me your book!' ordered Andrés, shaking with anger.

The clerk seized the book with both hands and shook his head. Then he glanced at the growing line of Moriscos waiting to be registered, all of them fascinated by the discussion. 'How do they expect us to do our work if they only know how to speak Castilian badly?' he complained. The last thing he wanted at that point was to find himself embroiled in the work of the Inquisition, even as a witness; he had already had some dreadful encounters with the Holy Office and anyone who appeared before them could find themselves . . . He picked up his pen once more, dipped it in ink and corrected his entry in a loud voice: 'María de Terque, wife of Hernando Ruiz of Juviles. There we are. No further problem. Hand over your weapons,' he added, addressing the new arrival, 'and let me have your details and those of the people with you.'

'But—' the sacristan protested.

'If you have any complaints, direct them to the chancery of Granada,' the clerk cut him short without looking up from the register.

'You cannot—' one of the priests started to object.

'Yes I can!' continued the official, making a note in his register.

Hernando whispered his details and those of his mother and Musa, looking askance towards Fátima. She remained cut off from all the commotion, her eyes fixed on the little one whom she went on gently rocking.

'They are deceiving you!' insisted Andrés.

'No.' This time the clerk confronted the sacristan, tired of his demands. 'Nobody is deceiving me. I recall now that he definitely said Hernando Ruiz, not José Ruiz,' he lied. 'Where do you wish to live until the Prince determines your expulsion?' he asked Hernando.

'In Juviles,' answered Brahim.

'It has to be on the plains, away from the mountains and the coast,' the irritable clerk announced for the umpteenth time that day.

'On the plain of Granada,' Brahim decided.

'But—' the sacristan attempted to intervene again.

'Next,' the clerk went on angrily, waving them away.

'If, as they say, they were married during the uprising, then you should marry them in accordance with the precepts of the Holy Mother Church,' said Juan de Soto.

As soon as they left the clerk's table, Andrés and the two priests had brought their complaint to Don John of Austria's secretary.

'As regards the woman,' the secretary continued, recalling the Prince's smile of satisfaction on seeing Barrax's head, which was still lying at his feet when he went to consult him about the priests' grievance, 'the promised pardon applies to her too.' The three priests tried to argue but Juan de Soto stopped them: 'You will obey. That is the Prince's decision.'

'Don't go anywhere near Fátima or . . .'

Hernando was taken aback by the threat Brahim made when they were only a few paces away from the clerk's table.

He came to a halt. He was no longer a corsair's slave! It was not two days ago that he had given up his freedom and risked his life to save Fátima and his mother. He had killed three men to make it happen! Apart from the turban, which he dropped on the ground, he was still wearing the clothes of a Turk.

'Or what?' he shouted at his stepfather.

Brahim, who was in front of him, stopped and turned to face

his stepson. Hernando confronted the muleteer. Brahim twisted his mouth in a cynical smile. Then he grabbed Aisha's arm and squeezed it tightly. Aisha resisted for a moment but Brahim went on pressing until she could not hide a grimace of pain. Aisha made no attempt to struggle or get away from her husband.

'Mother!' exclaimed Hernando, feeling for the hilt of a scimitar he would never wield again. Aisha avoided looking at her son. 'This dog, this son of a whore abandoned you in Ugíjar!' he shouted.

Brahim clenched Aisha's arm even more tightly. Still she did not look at her son. Fátima reacted for the first time and clasped Humam to her breast as if her life depended on it.

Hernando faced his stepfather. A barely controlled fury blazed from his blue eyes. He was shaking. His pent-up hatred exploded in a howl of rage. Brahim smiled and twisted his first wife's arm so violently she could not avoid groaning with pain.

'You choose, Nazarene. Do you want to watch me break your mother's arm?'

Aisha was sobbing.

'Enough!' shouted Fátima. 'Ibn Hamid, don't . . .'

Hernando took a step back, incredulous at the mute appeal he could see in the girl's face. He took a deep breath to calm his pounding heart.

Eyes narrowed, the young man remembered Hamid's advice. *Use your intelligence*, the holy man had told him. This was no time to let himself be swayed by his emotions. Without another word, Hernando turned and walked away, struggling to contain his yearning for revenge.

23

May 1570

'MERCY, LORD. May your lordship grant us mercy in the name of His Majesty, and pardon our faults which we know have been grave ones.' With these words El Habaquí prostrated himself before Don John of Austria in surrender. 'I lay down these weapons and this banner in the name of Aben Aboo and all those rebels over whom I have authority,' he concluded, as Don Juan de Soto hurled the flag to the ground.

Just before El Habaquí entered the tent, Aben Aboo's coloured standard with its embroidered motif, 'I could not wish for more or be content with less', was handed over to the Christian cavalry and infantry drawn up in ranks in the camp. A loud volley of gunfire accompanied the shouts of the horsemen and soldiers before the priests said prayers.

El Habaquí secured a pardon from the King for the Turks and Berbers, who were free to return to their homelands. Philip II granted this because he was anxious to end the conflict so he could head the Holy League the Pope had proposed, quite aside from the fear that the arrival of spring would allow the Moriscos to provision themselves and renew the rebellion.

Don John of Austria appointed emissaries and dispatched them the length and breadth of the Alpujarra to secure the complete surrender of the Moriscos in the kingdom of

Granada. El Habaquí took charge of all the arrangements necessary to board the Turks and Berbers on ships in the ports the Prince had designated. Philip II provided numerous sailing vessels and galleys for the transport. The final cessation of hostilities was set for the feast day of Saint John, 1570, by which date all Turks and Berbers were to have left the kingdom of Granada.

By 15 June some thirty thousand Moriscos were registered as having surrendered. El Habaquí managed to get almost all the Turks and corsairs embarked for Algiers, but most of the Berbers opted to continue fighting. Seeing this, Aben Aboo changed his mind and retracted his pledge to surrender: he put El Habaquí to death and retreated to the mountains with nearly three thousand men under his command.

> Today witnessed the final exodus and with it the greatest sorrow in the world, because at the time of departure, there was so much rain, wind and snow that many complained all the way, daughters to mothers, husbands to wives, children to widows, and so on. I myself dragged them along suffering badly for two miles: one cannot deny that to witness the depopulation of a kingdom is the most pitiful thing imaginable. In the end, my Lord, the deed is done.
>
> Letter from Don John of Austria to Rui Gómez,
> 5 November 1570

In November 1570 Philip II ordered the expulsion towards the north of all the Moriscos of the kingdom of Granada. Those who had settled in the plain outside the city, including Hernando, Brahim and their families, were handed over to Don Francisco de Zapata de Cisneros, lord of Barajas and chief magistrate of Córdoba, who was to take them to that city from where they would be dispersed throughout the lands of Castile and Galicia.

The plains to the west of Granada had once been made up of many small farmsteads. It was a flat and fertile region thanks to an intricately devised irrigation system that distributed water via channels built in Roman times and perfected by the Muslims. Following the surrender of Granada to the Catholic monarchs, the distribution of the land in orchards and smallholdings was replaced by large farms: big estates owned by noblemen, prominent Christians and religious orders, such as the one belonging to the Carthusians, which used the large tracts of land to cultivate vines.

For six months thousands of displaced Moriscos lived on these plains. They yearned for the rough terrain of the mountains, valleys and ravines of the Alpujarra, so different from these lands which stretched unbroken as far as the eye could see, cultivated and controlled by Christians, and constantly crisscrossed by monks and priests who reproached them for everything they did.

In accordance with the Prince's orders, Hernando and Fátima were married as Christians in the church at El Padul. The day before the ceremony they were both examined on Christian doctrine inside the church, in the presence of Andrés the sacristan and the same priests who had hounded them as soon as they set foot in the town.

Hernando passed the test easily.

'Now you.' One of the priests pointed at Fátima. 'Recite the Lord's Prayer.'

The girl made no response. After a few moments, the two priests and the sacristan became impatient.

Fátima was still consumed with shame. The night before, in full view of Hernando, Aisha and hundreds of Moriscos huddled on the ground trying to sleep, Brahim had forced himself upon her without the least compunction, as if to show everyone he still owned her. Hernando, in a rage, had had to get away from his stepfather's groans of pleasure. He'd gone in search of fresh air, unable to prevent his eyes filling with hot tears of impotence.

'Do you not know the Our Father?' asked Andrés, half closing his eyes.

Hernando prodded her gently with his forearm and Fátima responded. She recited the Our Father and the Hail Mary, her voice quivering, but was unable to get the Creed, the Hail Holy Queen or the Commandments right.

One of the priests ordered her to come to his parish every Friday for three years until she had learnt the catechism properly. He wrote this down on her document. Then, as was required, she and Hernando were obliged to make their confession.

'Is that everything?' blustered the priest when Fátima had finished reciting her sins. Hernando, who was waiting his turn standing next to the confessional, flinched. 'Don John may have ordered your marriage, but the wedding will not take place if you do not make a proper confession and repent of your sins. What about your adultery? You are living in sin! Your Moorish betrothal is worthless. What about the uprising? The insults and blasphemy, the murders and sacrileges you have committed?'

Fátima stammered a few incomprehensible words.

'I cannot absolve you! I see no sign of contrition or repentance, no offer to mend your ways.'

The kneeling girl could not see the look of satisfaction on the priest's face inside the confessional, but Hernando certainly observed the smiles of Andrés and the other priest as they listened to the confession. What are they smiling at? If they didn't marry them . . . the Inquisition! They were living in sin. Not even the Prince could interfere with the Holy Office.

'I confess!' he shouted, sinking to his knees on the ground. 'I confess that I live in sin and I repent. I confess I have witnessed sacrilege in churches . . .'

Fátima began to repeat Hernando's words without thinking.

They both confessed the thousand sins that the priests wanted to hear, they repented and promised to live in Christian virtue ever after. They spent the night in the church as a penance. Hernando prayed aloud with Fátima kneeling beside him, trying to mask her persistent silence.

The following morning, the couple were married in the sole presence of a watchful, threatening Brahim, and a few old Christians from the village who had been summoned to act as witnesses. They were given communion again. Hernando noticed how Brahim shifted uneasily at the formality of the ceremony and let the 'cake' of the host crumble slowly in his mouth. He was marrying Fátima! What did it matter what happened afterwards? Brahim would claim Fátima again and in the Morisco community she would still be his second wife, but there was nothing the muleteer could do at this moment, faced with the solemnity of this sham marriage, but choke back his protests. The priest pronounced them husband and wife and Hernando silently prayed for Allah's help.

The wedding cost them the mule. Hernando was tempted to refuse and argue that the most a wedding should cost was two reales for the priest, a half-real for the sacristan and a modest sum for alms, but he had no money; all he possessed was that mule, and it was not even his. The final restriction placed on the newlyweds before they left the church was that they should not live together or have relations during the following forty days.

The Moriscos lived in the open on the plains outside Granada. They had hardly any fires because they couldn't use any of the wood from the fruit trees that grew all around them. They sold off anything they had managed to conceal in exchange for wheat. Even water, once shared so plentifully among the fields in accordance with strict ancestral rules, had become a scarce commodity. Destitute, hundreds of them lived wherever they could find a piece of waste land; the houses belonging to the Moriscos expelled before their arrival were now occupied by Christians. The Moriscos shared what little they possessed, waiting all the while for notice of their imminent exodus. After the wedding, Brahim claimed Fátima back. Hernando found himself obliged to go with him as they roamed the forbidden orchards in search of food. Brahim tried to make sure that at no time was his stepson alone with Fátima, and when for any reason they were, she always refused to have anything to do with him.

'Don't insist,' his mother counselled Hernando one day. 'She is doing it for Humam, and for me. Brahim could kill the little one if he found out she was talking to you. He has threatened her with it! I'm sorry, my son.'

Hernando took refuge in the communion they had celebrated in the church at El Padul; in that moment when he had felt he truly was Fátima's husband. How ironic! In a Christian church! Perhaps one day . . .

While they awaited the Prince's decision, the Moriscos finally gave way to despair. Disarmed and subjugated, imprisoned on lands that had once been theirs, they finally appreciated the magnitude of their defeat. Where would they be banished? What would they live on? They were constantly assailed by fears for their future in distant, hostile kingdoms ruled by Christians who made no secret of their hatred for the vanquished. If anyone still had faith that Aben Aboo would return, the reports about him were not encouraging: the Knight Commander of Castile and the Duke of Arcos were fighting effectively against the King of al-Andalus's scant forces.

On 1 November, after the weather had turned for the worse and the wretched Moriscos were losing the battle for survival, Don John of Austria finally ordered their expulsion. The Moriscos from the plains of Granada were instructed to assemble near the Royal Hospital in a large clearing outside the walls of the city. The hospital, the old Elvira gate which led to the Albaicín and the Muslim quarter, the convent of La Merced, the mudéjar church of Saint Ildefonsus and many large walled gardens encircled the clearing.

Thousands of Moriscos gathered in front of the hospital, guarded by soldiers of the chief magistrate Don Francisco de Zapata, while they waited for the clerks and scribes to finish registering them all and make careful note of their destinations.

On 5 November, in the middle of a storm, 3,500 bedraggled,

starving and sick Moriscos, the Ruiz family from Juviles among them, left Granada along the road past the Carthusian monastery. For seven days they were escorted along the thirty or more leagues between Granada and Córdoba. The stages of the journey were adapted to suit the comfort of the magistrate and his officials, who only wanted to stop in places where they could spend the night without forgoing food and a bed.

During the first stage of the journey they walked as far as Pinos, nearly three leagues from Granada. Don Francisco de Zapata stayed in the village but the Moriscos had to spend the night outside in the rain, huddled together as best they could. They also shared what little food they had. The local inhabitants were reluctant to feed anyone who had rejected Christianity. At daybreak, they began the climb to Moclín, where a commanding fortress defended the entrance to the plains and the city of Granada. They covered the same distance as on the first day but this time uphill, feeling the cold of the mountains penetrating their rain-soaked clothes until it seeped into their very bones. They could not leave Moriscos on the road, so all the fit men had to help those who were not well or even carry the corpses, as there was not even a single cart for them. During the climb, Hernando, well away from Fátima and Aisha who were walking up ahead, had to carry an old man who was so emaciated he could not stand. He had a hacking cough that turned into a muffled rattle as the day wore on, grating on Hernando's ears. That night, the old man died, along with seventy other Moriscos. The only consolation for the exiles was that after carrying them to the next evening's camp, the lack of coffins meant they could bury them in fresh ground.

In desperation, some people took flight, but the Prince had decreed that any Moriscos who tried to escape were to become the slaves of whichever soldier recaptured them. As a result any man, woman or child who went missing gave rise to a frantic search by the Christians. They branded their new slaves on the forehead or the cheek; their screams of agony echoed through the rows of exiles. Not a single Morisco succeeded in escaping.

After Moclín they headed for Alcalá la Real, three leagues distant along the crest of the mountains. This time, Hernando had to carry a lame woman in place of the old dead man; he needed another youth his own age to help him. The night before he had noticed that Fátima was concerned about little Humam, whose coughing she tried to soothe against her breast.

It was at Alcalá la Real, at the foot of a hill crowned by another fortress inside whose walls an imposing abbey was being built on top of an ancient mosque, that Aisha told her son about Humam's death during that day's march. As with the old man, his coughs had turned into a wheeze and the child began to shiver so badly that Fátima herself also started to shake uncontrollably, unable to contain her grief. They were not allowed to stop. Distraught, Fátima begged the Christians on her knees to help her, to allow them to stop for a little while so that she could find something warm for the child. Her pleas were met with contempt. The soldiers seemed more interested in the possibility that this young mother, beautiful even in grief, might take the reckless decision to flee to find help for her son. Fátima would fetch a good price at the market in Córdoba.

'Nobody helped us,' sobbed Aisha, recalling the looks of pity from the other Moriscos.

They had kept going until, about a league from Alcalá, both mother and son stopped shivering. Aisha had to prise the child's body from his mother's grasp.

As the girl's Christian husband, Hernando appeared before the clerks, who took down the details and registered Humam's death. Fátima did not say a word. At nightfall, Hernando, Brahim, Aisha and Fátima took themselves off from the Morisco settlement and, like many another Muslim family, buried the child under the soldiers' watchful gaze. Aisha washed the body tenderly with cold, clear water from an irrigation channel. She found the hand of Fátima hidden in Humam's clothes and kept it; now was not the time to give it back to his mother. Hernando thought he heard Aisha sing a song he remembered from the cradle. She hummed the tune quietly, the way she used to when she rewarded him with a lullaby. Brahim dug a grave near the spot. Fátima had no tears left. There was no holy man, no prayers, no shroud in which to wrap the little one. Brahim put him straight into the hole in the ground while the little boy's mother, still stricken with grief, did not so much as approach the grave.

After Alcalá la Real, the stages of the journey grew longer. They descended towards the countryside around Jaén. Brahim helped Fátima, who was falling behind. She did not say a word; she seemed barely alive. Hernando felt sick and shuddered every time he saw Fátima's lifeless body clinging to his stepfather. Three days later, they reached Córdoba. Ragged, barefoot, the young and the sick in tow, they were lined up five deep and flanked by companies of pikemen and harquebusiers. They entered the city to the sound of music, with a crowd of city-dwellers looking on. Dressed in all their finery, the soldiers marched in alongside them.

Of the 3,500 Moriscos who had set out from Granada, only 3,000 remained. Five hundred corpses were scattered on the gruesome road.

It was 12 November 1570.

PART TWO

IN THE NAME OF LOVE

I did not know what this was, otherwise I would not have allowed you to touch what was here before; because you are doing something that could have been done anywhere and have undone something that was unique in the world.

Words attributed to the Emperor Charles V in the year 1526 on seeing the Christian cathedral built inside the mosque at Córdoba, work he himself had authorized, putting an end to the arguments between the civic and cathedral authorities regarding the advisability of its construction

24

THEY LEFT the fortress at Calahorra behind them, crossed the Roman bridge over the Guadalquivir and entered Córdoba through the Puente gate, which gave on to the rear façade of the cathedral. In formation, watched over by the soldiers and gawked at by the locals crowded together as they passed, Hernando, like many of the other Moriscos, who recognized in the cathedral the wonderful mosque from the Córdoba of the caliphs, glanced at the temple. Lowly people from the Alpujarra, bound to the land, they had never had a chance to see the mosque, but they all knew of it and even though they were exhausted, their faces were filled with wonder. Just behind that centuries-old wall, beneath the dome, was the mihrab, the holy place from which the Caliph led the prayers. There was some whispering among the exiles, who unwittingly slowed down. A man with a child on his shoulders pointed out the mosque.

'Heretics!' shouted a passer-by when she saw these displays of interest. Immediately, the crowd joined in the harangue as if they wanted to protect the church from profane eyes:

'Blasphemers! Murderers!'

An old man made to throw a stone at them but some soldiers stopped him and urged the line of Moriscos onwards. When they passed by the back of the cathedral, the streets became narrower and the soldiers dispersed the crowd who could then only continue to watch the procession from the balconies of the whitewashed, two-storeyed houses. The Moriscos went along Calle de los Cordoneros, past the Corn Exchange and Calle de la Pescadería; they crossed Calle de la Feria and arrived at the entrance to Calle del Potro. The head of the procession stopped in Plaza del Potro, the city's main commercial area, and the place the chief magistrate Zapata had chosen to keep them in custody.

Plaza del Potro was a small, enclosed square, in the centre of the district of the same name, where they tried in vain to contain the three thousand Moriscos who had survived the exodus, although most of them finished up scattered through the adjoining streets. Few of them could find lodgings, let alone pay for them, in the Potro inn located in the same square, in the Madera inn, the Monjas inn or in any of the many others to be found nearby. The magistrate set up controls to the area and there the Moriscos remained, the responsibility of the civic authorities until King Philip decided on their ultimate fate.

Night fell while most of them sated their thirst from large pitchers. When their turn came and while Brahim gulped down the water, his head under the stream, Hernando surveyed Fátima: her hair, unkempt and filthy, framed a face with scarred cheekbones, her sunken eyes were covered in bruises, and her features were so thin that her bones stuck out. He saw how her hands shook when she joined them in the shape of a bowl and tried to raise them to her lips; the water drained through her fingers before she could get it to her mouth. What would become of her? She would not survive another journey.

Nobody dared to wash; even though the magistrate had shut off the streets, the measure only affected the Moriscos, so that travellers, merchants, cattle dealers and the artisans who lived and worked in the area – saddlers, sword-makers, linen merchants, needle-makers and tanners – moved freely and contemptuously among the throng of exiles, scrutinizing them in the same way as did the many priests who prowled around, or the crowds of idle passers-by who haunted the place daily:

beggars or rogues who made the most of the opportunity to sneer at them.

The Moriscos were exhausted and starving. Suddenly, the Christians showed up with large copper pots of vegetable soup . . . and pigs' innards! The priests made a point of stopping here and there to check that nobody was refusing to eat this food forbidden by their religion.

'Why are you not eating?' one of them enquired, pointing at Fátima. She was sitting on the ground leaning back against a wall of one of the buildings on Calle del Potro. The bowl of food sat untouched between her feet.

Fátima did not so much as look up when she heard the priest. Brahim, engrossed in the bits of entrails floating in his bowl, made no reply. Nor did Aisha.

'She's unwell,' Hernando hurried to explain on her behalf.

'In that case, food will be good for her,' argued the priest and, with a gesture, urged her to eat.

Fátima did not move. Hernando knelt beside her, lifted the ladle and filled it with broth . . . and a bit of pork.

'Please, eat,' he whispered to Fátima.

She opened her mouth and Hernando fed her some soup. Grease ran down the girl's chin before she retched, coughing up the food at the priest's feet. He jumped backwards.

'Moorish bitch!'

The Moriscos near them drew back and formed a circle. Still on his knees, Hernando turned to the priest and crawled towards him.

'She is sick!' he shouted. 'Look!' He scraped the piece of pork off the ground and raised it to his mouth. 'She is . . . she's my wife. It's just that she's sick,' he repeated. 'Look!' He went back to the cauldron, filled the ladle with bits of pork and ate them. 'It's just that she's sick,' he stammered with his mouth full.

The priest spent a good while watching how Hernando chewed and swallowed the pork, and took more, until he seemed satisfied.

'I'll be back,' he said before turning away from them and

facing the Morisco nearest him, 'by which time I trust that she will have improved enough to do justice to the food which the city of Córdoba has so generously shared out among you.'

Opposite Fátima and Hernando, on the other side of the street, there was a little dead-end alley scarcely wide enough for two men, which led from Calle del Potro down to the Guadalquivir. The wooden gate to the alleyway was open just then revealing a row of shops and small premises, some of them only one floor high, on both sides of the street. Standing at the gate to the alleyway, chatting to the clients going in and out of the brothel, the armed bailiff of the Córdoba whorehouse was watching the Moriscos. Behind him, not daring to venture out because of their forbidden clothes and jewellery, which could only be worn inside the brothel, some women leant their heads out; and there in the middle of them all, trying not to rouse the bailiff's suspicions, was a man who was closely watching the young Morisco's entreaties on behalf of the young girl. Did he say that was his wife? There was a hint of a smile, which was lost on his right cheek where the infamous letter 'S' had been branded into his flesh. Hernando! Almost two years had passed since they said goodbye in the castle at Juviles. He had thought of Hernando every day since; he was the son he had never had. Overjoyed to see him alive, he thought with pride that the young lad had grown and, despite his ragged appearance, it was evident he was now a man. What age would he be? Sixteen? Hamid wondered.

'Francisco!' roared the bailiff, noticing him at the gate. 'Get back to work! And you others as well,' he added, shooing the women back inside with his hands.

Hamid gave a start and limped the length of the alley, trying hard to contain his tears. Hernando! He had thought he would never see him again . . . How many more neighbours from Juviles had arrived in that new crowd? He had not seen them but he knew there were several slaves from Juviles in the city; they had been taken prisoner before the amnesty granted by Don John of Austria; all the remaining free Moriscos to be found in Córdoba hailed from the Albaicín or from the countryside around Granada, and had come with the first wave of deportees.

He offered silent thanks to the All-merciful for protecting the boy's life and liberty. But what was happening to his wife? She looked sick; she was shaking convulsively. Hernando must love her given that he leapt blindly to her defence, crawling on his knees to the priest. Hamid stopped outside a little two-storey shop and put his ear to the door. There was no sound inside. He knocked.

'You have to eat.' Hernando dropped to the ground beside Fátima. Brahim looked up from his bowl at once.

'Leave her,' he grunted. 'Don't go near her.'

'Be quiet! Do you want her to die? Would you leave her to die and then kill my mother because I tried to help her?'

Brahim looked at the girl: she sat hunched and trembling uncontrollably.

'You see to her,' he ordered Aisha, who closed her eyes every time she lifted the spoon to her mouth. 'Make sure she doesn't die.'

'You have to feed yourself, Fátima,' Hernando whispered into her ear. She did not reply or look at him, but just went on shuddering. 'I know how much you miss Humam, but not eating won't bring him back to life. We all miss him . . .'

'Leave it to me,' Aisha said, standing in front of him. Hernando raised his blue eyes, his face full of anxiety. 'Leave it to me,' she repeated tenderly.

Aisha did not manage to get a response out of Fátima either. She tried to make her swallow the soup, herself eating the bits of pork in case any priest came back, but no sooner had she forced some soup or vegetable into the girl's mouth than she brought it up again. Squatting beside them, Hernando watched his mother struggling to feed Fátima. He held his breath when she succeeded and despaired, hitting the ground with his knuckles, when he saw how the girl's body rejected the food.

'They say there's a hospital on the square,' a Morisco woman told him; she was watching the scene with concern.

Hernando looked at her enquiringly, and the woman pointed to Plaza del Potro. He raced across it, but soon had to come to a halt. There was a crowd in front of what must have been the entrance to the hospital: a porch enclosed by a semicircular double arch. Despite this, he ran forward and pushed himself through, ignoring the protests.

'I've already told you', he heard the chaplain say, 'that the fourteen hospital beds are occupied and over half of them have two people to a bed. Apart from that, admission to the hospital requires the order of the doctor or the surgeon and at the moment neither of them is here.'

Hearing this, some of the crowd turned away and left the porch; others stood their ground, showing their injuries, coughing, or raising their arms imploringly. A child was in its death throes at the chaplain's feet while the father wept inconsolably. What could *he* achieve? thought Hernando as he saw the chaplain shaking his head stubbornly. The image of Fátima shivering and vomiting drove him on, and for the second time that night he sank to his knees before a priest.

'In the name of God and the Blessed Virgin . . .' he implored, his hands clasped level with the chaplain's stomach. Then he recalled the Christian nobleman's words of entreaty in Barrax's tent. '. . . by the nails of Jesus Christ, help me!'

The priest stood stunned for a moment, then he bent forward to try to pull Hernando to his feet. This was the first Morisco who had prayed to Jesus Christ! Hernando stayed on his knees.

'Help me', he repeated as the priest took him by the hands and struggled to raise him up. 'Where can I find this surgeon? Tell me. My wife is very sick . . .'

The chaplain let go of his hands brusquely. 'I'm sorry, my boy.' The man shook his head. 'The Charity Hospital only admits men.'

Hernando could not bear to hear how, after their long

journey, the rest of the Moriscos broke out in prayers to the Holy Trinity.

The hours went by, and it was already completely dark. The Moriscos tried to sleep on the ground, some on top of others. Hernando paced from side to side, without straying far from Fátima, stifling his sobs at the sight of the girl still shaking uncontrollably. Brahim was sleeping against a wall, with Musa and Aquil curled up by his side. Aisha was stroking Fátima's hair, keeping vigil over her as if . . . as if awaiting her death.

It was already well into morning when the sound of the alleyway gate opening startled Hernando. First he saw a young fair-haired girl coming directly towards him – what was that woman up to? – and then, limping along behind her . . .

'Hamid!'

The holy man put his finger to his lips and hobbled towards him.

Hernando threw himself into his arms. At that moment he realized just how much he had missed his friendly, familiar face, the face of the person who had been his greatest comfort during his miserable childhood.

'Let's go! There's no time to lose,' Hamid urged him, clasping him tightly in return. 'That one, his wife, that girl' – he indicated Fátima to the girl who had come with him –'help her up. Let's go.'

'What . . . what are you going to do?' asked Hernando, unable to look away from the letter branded on the holy man's cheek.

Aisha got to her feet, and she was the one who helped the fair-headed girl lift Fátima under the arms.

'To try to save your wife,' Hamid answered as the two women made their way across the street, dragging Fátima along between them. 'You must not go through the gate, Aisha,' he added. 'I'll take charge of the girl.'

Hernando remained paralysed. His wife? She was his wife as far as Christians were concerned, but to Hamid . . . and Brahim? What would Brahim say when he discovered that

Fátima was not there? The fact that it was Hamid who was helping the girl might just take the edge off his anger.

'She is not my—'

Aisha, now free of Fátima, grabbed his forearm and indicated to him to keep quiet. Hamid did not hear him: his only concern was that no one should see them.

'Tomorrow', he said before shutting the brothel door, 'I will come out to buy things. We'll speak then, but bear in mind that I am only a slave here; I'll choose the moment . . . And call me Francisco, the name the Christians gave me.'

25

ON 30 NOVEMBER 1570, by order of King Philip II, the three thousand Moriscos who had come from the plains of Granada with the chief magistrate Zapata left for their final destinations: Mérida, Cáceres and Plasencia amongst other places. This restored relative calm to Córdoba as a whole and the usual frenetic business activity to Plaza del Potro. First thing in the morning, from beyond the Martos mill on the banks of the Guadalquivir, Hernando saw them cross the Roman bridge in columns, just as he had done three weeks earlier in the opposite direction.

At the sight of that column of men, women and children, silent and resigned to their fate, the bundle of stinking, bloody hides he was carrying on his shoulders became really heavy, much more so than had been the case going along the road outside the city walls, as the city council stipulated, from the slaughterhouse to Calle Badanas down by the river, where Vicente Segura's tannery stood. For a few moments Hernando slowed down as he watched the long lines of deportees. He could feel the blood of the beasts running down his back until it soaked his legs, and the pungent stench of freshly flayed skin and flesh that the authorities refused to allow in their streets seemed only to reinforce the sense he had of the suffering of the Moriscos forced to leave. What would become of them all? What would they do? A woman walked past, frowning at him; Hernando responded and set off; his master did not allow delays, therefore he could not let himself linger.

That was the deal Hamid had obtained for them through the prostitute Ana María who took charge of Fátima, hid her and looked after her on the second floor in the brothel. Hernando smiled when he thought of Fátima; she had eluded death.

When the order came to dispatch the Moriscos, the council officials took an interest in them once more. They took all their names again, and divided them up according to their destinations. At this point, Fátima had to leave the brothel and Hernando could see for himself that the news brought to them from day to day by the holy man was accurate: even though her face was lined with sadness, she had put on weight and looked healthier.

None of them had had a chance to meet Ana María.

'She's a good girl,' Hamid remarked one morning.

'A prostitute?' Hernando let slip.

'Yes,' said the holy man gravely. 'They are usually good people. Most of them are girls from ordinary homes without means whose families hand them over as children to well-to-do households where they work as maids. The usual arrangement is that as soon as they are old enough these wealthy families are supposed to give them a modest dowry so that they can make a decent marriage. But in many, many instances the agreement is not fulfilled: when the time comes, they accuse them of stealing or of having slept with the man of the house or his sons – something by the way that they are often forced to do . . . far too often,' he moaned. 'Then they are thrown out penniless and with the stigma of being thieves or whores.' Hamid pursed his lips and let a moment or two pass. 'It's always the same story. Most of them end up in brothels.'

Hamid had been made a slave following the arrival of the Christians in Juviles. The pardon granted by the Marquis of Mondéjar counted for little. In the chaos that began with the slaughter of women and children in the church square, a number of soldiers seized the men who were ensconced in the village houses and deserted with the meagre booty of those Moriscos who had not been able to flee with the Muslim army. Before they even reached Granada, Hamid, branded, lame and filthy, was sold without haggling and for very little money to one of the many merchants who followed the army. From there he was carted off to Córdoba and purchased by the landlord of the brothel; what better slave for a place full of women than a man who was lame and frail?

'We'll buy your freedom!' Hernando exclaimed indignantly when he heard the story.

Hamid responded with a resigned smile. 'I couldn't escape from Juviles with our brothers. What happened to the sword?' he asked, suddenly remembering it.

'Buried at the castle of Lanjarón, beside—'

Hamid signalled him to keep quiet. 'He who is called to find it will do so.'

Hernando thought about this before insisting once more: 'And your freedom?'

'What would I do as a free man, lad? All I know is how to farm fields. Who is going to take on a cripple to do that? Nor can I expect alms from the faithful. Here in Córdoba, if I were to devote myself as a holy man to what I have done throughout my life, freedom would only mean death—'

'Freedom? Does that mean that you intend to continue with your work as a holy man?' Hernando interrupted him.

Hamid hushed him, glancing out of the corner of his eye to see if anyone was listening to them. 'We'll talk about it later,' he whispered. 'I fear we will have plenty of time.'

'You know about herbs,' the boy persisted. 'You could devote yourself to that.'

'I am neither a doctor nor a surgeon. Anything I might do with herbs would be regarded as witchcraft. Witchcraft . . .' he repeated to himself.

He had had to persuade young Ana María that his knowledge was not witchcraft, although in the end the girl still did not seem convinced. One day, shortly after arriving at the brothel, he came upon her crying disconsolately in her room when he went to fetch her some clean bed linen. To begin with, she stubbornly refused to answer his questions; Hamid was the landlord's property and what guarantee did she have that he wouldn't tell him? Hamid read that distrust in her eyes and kept at her until, little by little, she opened up to the holy man and confessed. Chancre! A small lesion had appeared in her vagina. It was painless and almost invisible, but a sure sign that in no time she would develop syphilis. The doctor sent every fortnight by the authorities to check on the prostitutes' health and hygiene had just visited the brothel and had not noticed anything, but he would surely do so the next time. The girl started to weep again.

'He'll send me to the Lámpara hospital,' she sobbed, 'and there . . . there I will die among the syphilis cases.'

Hernando had heard talk about the nearby hospital. Córdobans all feared going into any of the many hospitals in the city. 'Only the poorest go to hospital,' was a common expression, but the Lámpara, an asylum for women afflicted with incurable venereal diseases, was a name spoken with dread among the prostitutes. Heavily guarded by the authorities as a health precaution, going in there was sure to mean a slow and painful death.

'I could . . .' Hamid began to say, 'I know . . .'

Ana María turned to him and begged him with her green eyes.

'There is an old Muslim cure that might . . .' He had never treated anyone for chancre in the Alpujarra! What if it did not work? By now, though, the girl was on her knees, clinging tightly to his legs.

'May God grant her a cure!' Hamid prayed silently that same night when he washed Ana María's vulva with honey and afterwards sprinkled over the wound ashes that he took from a small reed tube full of a mixture made from barley flour, honey and salt.

'May God grant it!' he prayed night after night as he repeated the treatment. The next time the official doctor called, the lesion had disappeared. Was that tiny fistula really the start of syphilis? wondered Hamid, while a grateful Ana María wept for joy in his arms. It was the Prophet's remedy, he concluded: a remedy fit to cure chancre and syphilis. Had he not commended himself to God each time he treated her?

'Tell no one about this, I beg you,' Hamid asked, pushing her away from him. 'If they knew ... if the landlord or the Inquisition heard what has happened here, they would put me on trial as a sorcerer ... and you as someone bewitched ...' he added, to make doubly sure. 'What are you doing, my girl?' he asked in surprise when he saw Ana María was taking off her bodice.

'All I have is my body,' she answered, as she opened her blouse and showed him her young breasts.

Hamid could not look away from those smooth, white breasts and the large dark areolae around her nipples. How many years had it been since he last enjoyed a woman?

'Your friendship is enough for me,' he excused himself, flustered. 'Cover yourself, I beseech you.'

From that day on, Hamid enjoyed a respect bordering on reverence from all the women in the brothel; even the landlord altered his manner. What had Ana María told him? The old man preferred not to know.

'I have arranged it so that you can all stay in Córdoba,' Hamid announced to Hernando one morning. The holy man took a breath before going on: 'You are all the family I have ... Ibn Hamid,' he said in a low voice, drawing close to Hernando's ear. The young man shuddered. 'And I would like to have you near me, in this city. Besides, your wife would not survive another exodus.'

'She's not my wife,' Hernando admitted at last.

Hamid looked at him questioningly and Hernando told him the story. The old man understood why Brahim had been so furious with him that first morning they met. He had thought it was due to the fact that Fátima had been taken to a brothel and he'd told Brahim bluntly: 'No man will be with her. Trust me.' The muleteer had wanted to argue, but Hamid had turned away. It was Aisha who had once again stood up to her husband. 'They are making her better, Brahim. She'll be of little use to you dead.'

Ana María knew one of the judges in Córdoba: a man who was smitten by her and who regularly frequented the brothel. The judges were called upon to act as a counterbalance to the councillors in the government of the city. Unlike the latter, who were all noblemen, the judges were men of the people, chosen by their fellow citizens to represent them on the council. With the passage of time, however, the office became hereditary, able to be passed on, and the various monarchs either used it as a reward for services rendered or sold it as a way of acquiring substantial profits. The election in the parish church took on the air of a ritual pantomime and the judges, lacking the nobles' titles and riches, tried to put themselves on a par with them and the councillors. The judge who visited Ana María seized on the girl's request as an opportunity to demonstrate his power beyond the bed, and in a show of vanity accepted the task of ensuring that these Moriscos could stay on in Córdoba.

'They are relatives of the lame Morisco,' Ana María explained in a honeyed voice, referring to Hamid. The judge lay sated beside her in bed. 'One of the women is sick. She can't travel. Will you be . . . ? Will you be able . . . ?' she asked innocently, ingratiatingly, leading him on, fully aware that the judge would reply with something along the lines of 'How could you doubt it?' as indeed he did. Ana María caressed his flabby chest. 'If you can do it,' she whispered, 'we'll have the best sheets in the brothel,' she added with a mischievous wink.

Permission to stay in Córdoba required that the menfolk had jobs. The judge managed to get Brahim set up in one of the many farms on the outskirts of the city.

'Muleteer?' scoffed the judge when Ana María told him how Brahim made his living. 'Does he have any mules?' The girl shook her head. 'Then how does he propose to work as a muleteer?'

As regards Hernando, there was no room for discussion: he was sent to work as a labourer in Vicente Segura's tannery.

And that was where he was on that 30 November 1570, carrying hides to Calle Badanas along the banks of the Guadalquivir, his gaze fixed on the last Moriscos who were at that moment passing the Calahorra fortress and leaving behind them the Roman bridge that was the entry point to the city of the caliphs.

Calle Badanas began at the church of San Nicolás de la Ajerquía down by the river and then, following a jagged line, came out at the Potro church very near the square. Most of the tanneries were located in this district because that was where they had access to the plentiful waters of the Guadalquivir; the air the tanners breathed was acrid and stinging as a result of the different processes the hides were subjected to before they were transformed into fabulous cordovans, embossed leather, soles, shoes, belts, harnesses or any other object made of leather. Hernando went into Vicente Segura's tannery through the rear door, the one looking out on to the river, and offloaded the hides in a corner of the large courtyard, as he had done for the three days he had been working there. One of the foremen, a bald, strong Christian, came across to check the condition of the hides without so much as greeting Hernando, who was once more engrossed in the bustle inside the courtyard that took up all the space between the river and Calle Badanas. Tanners, apprentices, and a couple of slaves who did nothing except fetch fresh water from the river, were all toiling without a break. Some rendered the hides: that was the first job to be done as soon as a skin was brought into the tanner. This involved putting the hide in a shallow tub of fresh water until it was softened, for as many days as it took depending on the type of hide and its condition. Some of the pelts, already rendered or in the process of being cured, were stretched on tables with the flesh part exposed, ready for the workers to scrape them clean with sharp knives, taking off the flesh, blood and any dirt that might have stuck to them.

Once the hides were cured, it was time for the hair to be removed. This process involved steeping them in a mixture of water and lime with the flesh side facing downwards. The liming process depended on the type of hide and what it was to be used for. Hernando noticed that some of the apprentices were cleaning the hides of fur and then airing them on sticks, the amount of time determined by the season of the year, before steeping them again and repeating the process a few days later. The liming could last between two and three months, according to whether it was winter or summer. All the hides were cured and limed; then when the master tanner felt the hide was ready, the procedures varied according to whether it was to be made into soles, shoes, belts, cordovans or embossed leather. The tanning of the hides took place in tanning vats, holes in the ground covered with stone or brick, in which the hides were immersed in water mixed with bark from the cork oak tree, which was plentiful in Córdoba; the master tanner oversaw the tanning process carefully. Hernando watched the master and the foreman, who was standing in one of the vats, naked from the waist down, trampling on kid goat skins destined to be black cordovans, and constantly turning them over and washing them with water and sumach. That part of the job would last eight hours, during which time the workmen never stopped treading, turning and soaking the skins.

'What are you staring at? You're not here to waste time!' Hernando jumped. The bald worker he had given the hides to was waiting, holding out what seemed to be the one in the worst condition of all. 'This is for your pit,' he said, pointing to it. 'Go to the dung heap as you did on the other days.'

Hernando did not want to look near the far end of the courtyard, where in a remote and hidden corner a deep pit had been dug. A column of hot, stinking air from the rotting manure rose out of the hole into the cold of the November day. When he stepped down into it, as he had had to do on the two previous days, that column of smoke would come alive, clinging to his every move and enveloping him in heat, stench and murk. The master had decided to use manure and not lime on any of the hides that were flawed, such as the one the other worker had just given him. The process was much shorter than the usual two months; above all, it was much cheaper. The resulting hides, which were of inferior quality because manure did not achieve the same effect as lime, were used to make soles for shoes.

Hernando crossed the courtyard, passing the tubs, the tanning vats, the long tables where they were working on the hides with sharp knives or blunt ones as necessary, and the poles on which the hides were hung. He passed an apprentice in one of the tubs, and dragged himself reluctantly towards the dung heap. Several of the young apprentices smiled at each other: there was no more thankless task and the Morisco's arrival meant they were freed from the dung heap. Vicente, who was near the tanning vat where they were tramping the cordovan, saw what was going on and let out a roar. The smiles vanished and workers and apprentices got on with their jobs, ignoring Hernando, who was already at the edge of the pit. The manure covering the hides was bubbling.

On the first day he had almost fainted. He could hardly breathe; he gasped for air but the burning smell invaded his lungs, suffocating him. He'd had to get to the edge of the pit and lean out with his chin at ground level to search for air. He nearly threw up, but the worker in charge that day shouted at him not to vomit over the hides, so he shut his mouth and stifled his retching.

Hernando looked at the manure and removed his shoes. He took off his clothes and jumped into the pit. Where was the Sierra Nevada now? Its clear, pure air? Its freshness? Where were the trees and the ravines with their thousands of streams running down from the snow-capped peaks? He held his breath. He had learnt this was the only way to endure the job. He had to lift the hides to let them breathe, so that they would not heat up any more than was necessary. He poked around in the manure where the hides were piled up until he found the first of them. He shook it and managed to get it out of the pit before it was impossible for him to hold his breath any longer. Then, at ground level again, he took another deep breath. The first hide was the easiest to lift. The deeper he delved into the pit, the higher the manure was piled up, making it harder and harder to lift the rest of them. He spent over two hours hauling them up, holding his breath, his hair and body covered in stinking filth. When he had finished, one of the workers came over and checked the state of the hides. He pulled out a pair of them, huge ox hides that he felt were already treated, then told Hernando to let the rest breathe and to use a spade to clear all the manure out of the pit. At the end of the day, he was to pile them all back into it: a layer of manure and a hide, another layer of manure, another hide and so on until they were all covered, so that the next day he could haul them up again.

26

IN THAT year of 1570, the population of Córdoba was somewhere in the region of fifty thousand people. As with all such
cities, beyond the walls the countryside stretched un-
interrupted since it was forbidden to build dwellings outside
the walls that might block open access to the perimeter road or
that might threaten the city itself. The river Guadalquivir
ceased to be navigable from here, and meandered capriciously
if impressively. To the north of the city was the Sierra Morena
and to the south, on the far side of the river, stretched farmland,
the rich 'bread basket'. In the tenth century, Córdoba secured
independence from the East and Abderraman III set himself up
as Caliph of the West, successor to and vicar of Muhammad,
prince of the believers and defender of the law of Allah. From
then on, Córdoba became the most important city in Europe,
cultural heir to the great capitals of the East, with more than a
thousand mosques, thousands of dwellings and businesses, and
some three hundred public baths. It was in Córdoba that the
sciences, arts and letters flourished. Three centuries later,
the city was conquered for Christianity by the holy king
Don Fernando III, after a six-month siege laid from La
Ajerquía on La Medina, the two parts into which the city was
divided.

The Christians did not work on a Sunday so, on the first holy
day they spent in the city, Hernando escaped from the grim
two-storey house on an alleyway leading to Calle de Mucho

Trigo, where seven Morisco families, including his own, were cooped up.

'Some houses have fourteen or sixteen families in them,' Hamid had pointed out when he suggested that house to them. 'The King', he explained when they looked at him in disbelief, 'decreed that the Moriscos share living quarters with old Christians so that the latter could keep an eye on them, but the city authorities decided not to obey this order because they thought no Christians would be willing to live with us. They therefore gave instructions that we live in our own houses as long as these are always located between two Christian-occupied dwellings. Besides,' he added, clucking his tongue, 'all the houses here are owned either by the Church or the nobility, who make good money by renting them out, not something they could do if we lived with the Christians. There must be at least four thousand of us Moriscos newly arrived in the city. It was not difficult for the councillors to reach their decision: they pay miserly wages but make a lot of money out of us, first they exploit us, then they steal our meagre income in the rent we pay for their houses.'

As they were last to arrive, they had to share their living space with a young married couple who had just had a son, something that seemed to awaken fresh feelings of grief in Fátima. She confined herself to following instructions, which Aisha gave her all the time. Once she had carried them out, she retreated into silence, breaking it only to mumble some prayer or other. She looked up from time to time when she heard the little one cry. On the few occasions that he was in the house Hernando tried to work out what those black eyes, always dull now, were trying to say, but all he could read in them was a profound anguish.

Aisha too stole some sad glances at the newborn baby. When the authorities were registering them all, they had seized Aquil and Musa as they had all the exiled children and handed them over to pious Córdoba families who were charged with educating them and converting them to Christianity. Aisha and

Brahim, for once as powerless as his wife, found themselves obliged to watch as their children were taken away from their family in floods of tears and handed over to strangers. The muleteer's face flushed with a savage fury: they were his boys! The only source of pride he had left!

However, it was not Fátima or the prospect of having to share the living quarters with the young married couple and their baby boy for a long time that drove Hernando to get up before sunrise that Sunday and slip out secretly. That night, with everyone crowded into the same room, Brahim had sought out Aisha for the first time in many months and she gave herself to him as his first wife. Hernando, hunched and tense on his straw mattress, listened to his mother's sighs and moans at his side. There was no room to do anything else! In the half-light, his eyes shut tight, it pained him to notice how she sought to give Brahim pleasure, devoting herself to him as Muslim women were taught to do: seeking closeness to God through the act of love.

He did not want to see his mother. He did not want to see Brahim. He did not want to see Fátima!

His distress did not ease even after he had fled the room and begun to walk through the streets of Córdoba beneath the sun that was beginning to brighten them. First he thought he would head for the mosque, so that he could get a closer look at the building that rose above all the others in the city and which he had seen so often when he crossed the Roman bridge, returning to the tannery laden with manure. There was no other mosque left in the city of the caliphs as King Fernando had ordered churches to be built on top of them. Fourteen or so were built at the expense of Muslim places of worship. The rest were razed to the ground. Although it was no longer the mosque of the caliphs, it was said that you could yet see lattices above the entrance doors, and the arabesques on the long rows of red ochre columns crowned with double horseshoe arches that were unique in all the world. It was also said that if you listened hard enough, you could still hear echoes of the faithful at prayer.

Hernando abandoned the idea, remembering the insults the Christians had thrown when he arrived in Córdoba and the distrust with which people looked at him as he approached the mosque, laden with manure, after crossing the Roman bridge. Even children seemed to defend the church from heretics! So he walked aimlessly through the streets of La Ajerquía and La Medina and realized that the whole of Córdoba was one huge shrine to Christianity. In addition to the fourteen churches built by the Spanish King, which made up the city's parishes, another one had been added, together with close to forty small hospitals and sanctuaries, each with its corresponding church. Between the churches and hospitals were great tracts of land with glorious monasteries occupied by religious orders: San Pablo, San Francisco, La Merced, San Augustín and La Trinidad. There were also impressive nunneries like Santa Cruz, adjacent to Calle de Mucho Trigo where Hernando lived, and Santa Marta, plus many others that had been built since the Reconquest. All of them were hidden from prying eyes by dint of long, high, whitewashed walls with no openings other than at the entrance gates.

Every street corner in Córdoba displayed paintings or sculptures of Ecce Homos, Blessed Virgins, saints or Christ figures, some of them life size, as well as countless altars, which the old Christians always kept lit with candles, the sole nighttime lights in the city. Tiny hermitages, chapels and houses of penitents were scattered throughout the city, as were monks or religious brothers who continually asked for alms to the singsong of rosaries sung in the streets.

How were they going to survive as Muslims in that huge sanctuary? thought Hernando as he stood staring at the façade of the church of Santa Marina, near the slaughterhouse, outside the cemetery which surrounded the church on three sides. This was where his footsteps had taken him, to the north of the city.

Juviles! The sierra! he cried out inside his mind. Standing there in the first rays of sunshine, he felt dirty, reeking of rotten manure.

'Don't even think about washing yourself,' Hamid had warned him. 'That's one of the things the Christians look out for; they think it's a sign of heresy.'

'But—'

'Bear in mind that they don't do it,' the holy man interrupted. 'Sometimes they wash their feet, but most of them only have a bath once a year, on their saint's day. The linings of their shirts are nests of lice and fleas. I should know: remember that one of my tasks is to change the sheets at the brothel.'

Reluctantly Hernando had followed his advice and refrained from washing so that the stench was stuck to his skin; it happened with all the Moriscos . . . and with all the Christians. Sniffing himself, he looked at the burial places of the parishioners there at the doors of the church; noblemen and the wealthy who could afford it managed to secure a tomb inside a church or a convent or in the cathedral, but the shopkeepers and artisans lay buried there, in the middle of the streets of Córdoba, while the poor were buried on the outskirts.

On Sunday he had to attend mass accompanied by Fátima, his lawful wife in the eyes of the Christians, who on Fridays went to the church for her catechism classes as she had promised to do on the day of their wedding. He returned to San Nicolás de la Ajerquía walking down next to the San Andrés stream. If Córdoba had more than enough of anything, besides Christian devotion, it was water, just as in the Sierra Nevada, but unlike the crystal-clear water of the ravines in the Alpujarra, the water here overflowed in the squares or ran polluted down to the river. Where Hernando was walking now, along the San Andrés stream, ran the waters that gathered up the waste from the abattoir and from the entire neighbourhood on its banks. Why was it so important to the Christians to keep the dyes off the streets when they allowed the passage of such putrid waters? he complained to himself, carefully crossing one of the planks which the council had ordered placed like bridges between the houses on either side of the stream. So deep was the bed of that stinking stream, which was lower even than the foundations of the buildings, that the Córdoba people had christened it 'the cliff'.

The church of San Nicolás had been built where Calle Badanas met the river. Its interior took Hernando by surprise when he joined Fátima and the rest of the Moriscos to take part in the religious service. When he passed it returning from the slaughterhouse he had noticed the low front of the church, which was no more than five yards high. This made it look very different from the rest of the churches built by King Fernando, which were much bigger and taller. Like the others, it had been built on top of a mosque, but San Nicolás retained the rows of columns complete with arches that were typical of places of Muslim worship, as the cathedral did. That fleeting sensation vanished, however, as soon as the sacristan began to take the roll call of the Moriscos. Some two hundred of them were registered in the parish but, unlike in Juviles, here they were in a minority among the two thousand or more old Christians who were gathered in the church, most of them artisans, merchants and workers – the nobility lived in other parishes – in addition to a significant number of slaves owned by the artisans.

Men and women heard mass separately. There were none of the outbursts and threats they were used to from the priest in Juviles; here, the mass was for the Christians. The ceremony cost the Moriscos a maravedí a head. Afterwards, they went outside, and while they were waiting for the women, a well-dressed man approached them. Without thinking, Hernando glanced at the lace collar of his shirt, expecting to see a louse or a flea jump.

'You're the new Moriscos from the Mucho Trigo alleyway, aren't you?' he asked Hernando and Brahim arrogantly, without offering his hand. When they agreed, the new arrival turned to Hamid, staring contemptuously at him, his eyes lingering on his scarred face. 'What are you doing with them?'

'We're from the same village, your excellency,' Hamid answered meekly.

The man seemed to make a mental note of that information.

'I am Pedro Valdés, justice of Córdoba,' he went on. 'I don't know if your neighbours have spoken of me to you, but be aware that it is my duty to visit you every fortnight to check your circumstances and ensure you are living in accordance with Christian precepts. I trust you will not cause me any problems.' At that moment, Aisha and Fátima approached, but halted a few steps away from the group. 'Your wives?' he asked. He took it for granted that they were and, without waiting for a reply, turned his attention to Fátima, who looked tiny beside Aisha. 'This one is gaunt and thin,' he said, pointing to her as if she were an animal. 'Is she ill? If so, I will need to have her admitted to a hospital.' Hernando and Brahim alike hesitated and looked to Hamid for help. 'Do you need a slave to answer for you?' the justice chided them. 'Is she sick or not?'

'No . . . your excellency,' stammered Hernando. 'The journey . . . the journey was hard for her but she's on the mend.'

'Just as well. The city hospitals are short of empty beds. Take her for a walk through the city. The sunshine and fresh air will do her good. Enjoy the feast of Our Lord and be thankful for it. Sunday is a day of joy: the day on which Our Lord rose from the dead and ascended into heaven. Take her for a walk,' he said again, making as if to leave them. But: 'Are you the slave from the brothel?' he asked Hamid before turning away.

The holy man said yes and the justice made another mental note. Then he headed towards a group of rich merchants and their wives who were waiting for him a little further off.

'Home!' shouted Brahim as soon as the justice and his companions had disappeared.

Aisha and Fátima were already following behind him when Hamid intervened: 'Sometimes they make surprise visits, Brahim. The justices, priests and the marshal amuse themselves with their friends by turning up at our houses. A few glasses of wine and—'

'Does that mean you agree my wife should be paraded

through the city displaying herself to all the Christians with this . . .' He spat, without looking at Hernando. '. . . with the Nazarene?'

'No,' declared Hamid, 'it's not about showing herself to Christians. But nor do I agree that we should attend mass, or say their prayers, or eat their "cake", and yet we do these things. We must live as they wish us to. It is only in this way, without causing trouble, by deceiving them, that we will be able to reclaim our beliefs.'

Brahim mulled over this for a moment or two. 'Never with the Nazarene,' he said, his mind made up.

'To Christian eyes she is his wife.'

'What is it you are trying to justify, Hamid?'

'Call me Francisco,' the holy man corrected him. 'I'm not trying to justify anything, José.' Hamid strained to pronounce Brahim's Christian name. 'It's how things are. I didn't make them that way. Don't go looking for trouble for your people; we are all answerable for what the rest do. You insist that our laws regarding your two wives are honoured and we respect you, but you refuse to accept what is good for our brothers and you seek confrontations with the Christians. Hernando,' he added, addressing him directly, 'remember that according to our law, she is not your wife; behave like the relative of hers that you are. Go for a walk. Carry out the justice's order.'

'But—' Brahim started to complain.

'I don't want any difficulties if the justice appears at your door, José. We have enough problems already. Go,' he insisted to Hernando and Fátima.

Fátima followed him as she might have followed anyone who had tugged on the crumpled dress she was wearing. This time with the silent, abashed young woman by his side, Hernando made his way through the streets of Córdoba again, trying to keep in step with her much slower pace.

'I too miss the little one,' he said to her a few streets further on, after discounting dozens of comments that were going round in his head. Fátima made no reply. How long was this going to last? he groaned to himself. 'You are young!' he burst out, at his wits' end. 'You can have more children!'

He realized his mistake at once. Fátima's only response was to walk even more slowly.

'I'm sorry,' said Hernando. 'I'm sorry for everything. I regret having been born a Muslim; I regret the uprising and the war; I regret not having been able to see what was going to happen; I regret dreaming in hope like thousands of our brothers; I regret our desire for freedom; I regret . . .'

Hernando suddenly fell silent. His wandering had brought them to La Medina, in the parish of Santa María on the far side of the cathedral. This was an intricate network of narrow streets and blind alleys similar to many Muslim cities. A group of people was running towards them: they were fighting to get down the narrow alleyway, shouting and screaming. Some of them stopped to look nervously and fleetingly behind them before racing on again.

'A bull!' he heard a woman shout as she ran by.

'Coming our way!' yelled a man.

A bull? How could there be a bull in this narrow Córdoba street? There was no time to think beyond that. Hernando and Fátima had not moved, and saw how five horsemen in full regalia were riding full tilt towards them. They were pulling a huge bull tethered to their saddles by ropes tied to its horns and around its neck. The horses' rumps smacked against the walls, but the horsemen skilfully turned their mounts around. The bull fought back, bellowing loudly. The horsemen in front pulled it forward when it tried to turn back; those behind pulled on their ropes when it seemed as though the beast was about to charge into the riders in front. The street was filled with the noise of the bull bellowing, the horses neighing, their hoofs clattering on the ground, and the shouts of the riders.

'Run!' he shouted, grabbing Fátima by the arm.

But he left her behind. Hernando stopped and turned as soon as he realized that Fátima's arm was slipping out of his grasp. The first two horsemen were less than fifteen yards away.

They were tugging blindly on the bull, oblivious to what was going on in front of them. For a split second Hernando thought he saw Fátima with her back to him, standing with her head held high in a way she had not done for a long time, resolute, her fists pressed to her sides: she was seeking out death! He jumped on top of her just as the first horseman was about to trample her. The rider had not even attempted to stop. The couple crashed against the wall of a house; he tried to protect Fátima, lying over her body. Another of the horses jumped over them; the bull tried to gore them but, luckily, missed them and gouged the wall above their heads. The last horseman, who was galloping alongside, also overtook them but this time Hernando felt the horse trample his calf.

More people ran past following the horses, but they paid no attention to the two of them, who lay completely still as the din turned into an echo at the far end of the street. Hernando could feel Fátima's body shaking as she struggled to get her breath back. When he stood up, he also felt a sharp pain in his left leg.

'Are you all right?' he asked the girl, as he tried painfully to help her.

'Why do you always have to save my life?' she spat at him once she was on her feet opposite him. She was trembling, but her eyes . . . it was as if having looked death in the face, her dark eyes had become alive again. Hernando stretched his arms out to grasp her by the shoulders, but she shook herself free. 'Why—?' Fátima began to shout.

'Because I love you,' he interrupted her, also raising his voice, his arms still outstretched. 'Yes. Because I love you with all my soul,' he said in a low, quivering voice.

Fátima stared at him. After a few moments a tear slid down her cheek. All at once she began to weep openly in a way she had stopped herself doing since the night of her wedding to Brahim.

She clung to Hernando and cried herself out, while he gently rocked her in the narrow Córdoba street.

A little further away, where the alley joined two other streets to form a small uneven square, a noblewoman dressed in black looked down from the balcony of a small palace, her lady-in-waiting a step behind her, while five young horsemen wooed her by freeing the bull of its ropes and then killing it. Taking cover in the side streets, the common people cheered and clapped.

27

Christmas, 1571

THE CITY council had declared three days' public holiday to celebrate the resounding victory of Don John of Austria over the Turks at the head of the Holy League fleet at the battle of Lepanto. Religious fervour intensified with the Christian forces' triumph over the Muslims and together with the pagan celebrations, the city was teeming with processions and Te Deums of thanksgiving. It was not the best time for the Moriscos to be abroad on the streets of Córdoba joining in the rejoicing and popular fervour. Besides, word had reached them a few months earlier of the final rout of the King of al-Andalus. Aben Aboo was betrayed and killed by El Seniz; his body, filled with salt, was taken to Granada where his head, stuck in an iron cage, still hung above the arch of the Rastro gate, on the road out to the Alpujarra.

Nevertheless, Hernando attended the celebrations in Plaza de la Corredera with Hamid. A wooden castle had been built in the middle of this great Córdoban square in which a battle between Moors and Christians would be re-enacted. Before the performance wine flowed freely from a pelican's beak, with the result that alcohol was soon having its effect on the crowds, who fought with each other to get to the strange fountain. The city council announced a contest for which they put up a prize of eleven lengths of velvet, damask and silver cloth: two for the winners of horse races; four for the best-dressed men; three more for the best infantry companies formed by the guilds; and two for the women from the bawdy house who stood out most!

'It's hard to understand these people,' said Hernando to Hamid while Ana María strutted flirtatiously in front of a large audience who cheered her on shamelessly. 'They give prizes to the women they sleep with in front of their wives and daughters.'

'All the women know their husbands frequent the brothel,' Hamid argued, although he himself could not take his eyes off the way the beautiful Ana María was swaying her hips in front of them. Hernando did the same, although he was more concerned with the efforts of the bailiffs to prevent some already drunken men from jumping on the girl. 'Christians don't seek pleasure from their wives,' the holy man added softly, turning to the boy as a voluptuous black-haired woman took Ana María's place. 'It's a sin. Touching and caressing is sinful. Any position other than lying in bed is a sin. One cannot seek sensuality—'

'A sin!' Hernando broke in, with a smile.

'Exactly.' Hamid signalled him to keep his voice down. 'That's why their wives tolerate them looking for sensuality and pleasure from prostitutes. The whores don't plague them with the problems of bastards and inheritance claims which the concubines and courtesans can pose for them. And their Church supports it.'

'Hypocrites.'

'Several rooms in the brothel are owned by the cathedral chapter,' said Hamid before they both left the contest and walked through the crowd out of Plaza de la Corredera.

'Yes,' said a thoughtful Hernando a few moments later, 'but these women who are so chaste with their husbands then seek pleasure with other men . . .'

Puzzled, Hamid stared at him. He responded with a simple grin, which he quickly wiped from his face when he sensed the holy man's disapproval.

* * *

Over a year had passed since Fátima had thrown herself into his arms after seeking death in front of a bull and runaway horses.

'I am still Brahim's second wife,' the girl cried after kissing Hernando in the street and exchanging promises of love.

'That marriage counts for nothing here!' argued Hernando without thinking.

Fátima looked troubled, and Hernando hesitated. How could he have said . . . ?

'It's our law,' Fátima went on. 'If we renounce that . . . renounce our beliefs . . . Much as it pains me, I must respect my marriage to Brahim: in the eyes of our people he is my husband. I can't allow myself to forget that, however much I would like to. Much as I detest him . . .'

'No. I didn't mean . . .'

'We would be nothing. That's what the Christians want: to torment us until we disappear. They think we are cursed. Nobody wants us here: ordinary people hate us and the nobles exploit us. Many of our people have died in defence of the true faith: my husband, my child. No Christian lifted a finger to help a sick, defenceless child! Damn them! Damn all of them! You buried him yourself . . .' Fátima's voice faltered and became a sob. Hernando pulled her towards him and embraced her. 'We must fulfil our obligations,' she wept.

'We'll find a way,' Hernando tried to comfort her.

'We would be nothing without our laws,' she insisted.

'Please don't cry.'

'It is our religion! The true faith! Damn them!'

'We'll work it out.'

'Christian dogs!' Before she could finish saying it, Hernando buried her face in his shoulder so that her words would not carry.

'I will die for the Prophet if necessary, peace and blessings be upon Him,' she said.

'I will die with you,' he whispered to her.

A little way off in the small square the onlookers cheered

when the spear was plunged into the bull's neck, fatally wounding it.

The young lady watching from her palace balcony applauded politely.

I will die for the Prophet! The determination in that promise was the very same that Hernando had heard from the mouth of Gonzalico before he was slaughtered. What could have become of Ubaid? he wondered. At nightfall he left Fátima in the house on Calle de Mucho Trigo. Brahim and Aisha seemed relaxed and he made his escape again after grabbing a piece of stale rye bread, although not until Fátima gave him permission to go with a barely noticeable tilt of her chin. That Sunday, after the scare with the bull, they had gone down to the river, passing in front of the mosque where, among the priests and chaplains, they clasped hands, their fingers intertwined. On the banks of the Guadalquivir, opposite the water wheel of the Albolafia and the mills dotted along it, they let the hours slip by. Hernando did not have any money. He earned two miserly reales a month, less than a servant girl who also got bed and board, money he handed over to his mother straight away to put with Brahim's wages to pay the rent and for food. The two of them had nothing to eat all day apart from two cold, greasy fritters which a Morisco street-seller gave them for free when he saw how much they savoured the smell he left in his wake.

It was time for vespers and, as convention dictated during the winter months, the doors of the houses of the devout Christians were closed. This rule did not apply, however, in the Potro district where people crowded together: merchants, dealers, travellers, soldiers and adventurers, beggars, vagabonds or ordinary neighbours drank in the guest houses and inns, chatted freely with each other, went in and out of the bawdy house, and quarrelled or closed business deals no matter what time it was. Hernando headed for the brothel but did not manage to spot Hamid in the alleyway: only the brothel doors, open on to Calle del Potro. He wandered aimlessly through the district. *We'll find a way*, he had told Fátima, but how? Only Brahim could renounce her, but he would never do that if it meant that he, the Nazarene, could consecrate his love. Meanwhile, what would become of her? Fátima forced herself not to put on weight and to seem as unattractive as possible to her husband but Brahim still looked at her with lust in his eyes.

'You, lad!' Lost in his thoughts, Hernando paid no attention. 'Hey! You!'

Hernando felt a hand grab his shoulder; he turned round and found himself facing a small, thin man, even smaller perhaps than he was. To begin with he did not recognize him in the dim light from the inns and guest houses, but when the man displayed teeth that were as black as the night around them he remembered: he was one of the muleteers who plied their trade next to the Calahorra tower where he went to get the manure for the tannery. They had occasionally exchanged a greeting when Hernando was busy with the animals.

'Do you want to earn a couple of pennies?' the dealer asked.

'What do I have to do?' enquired Hernando, indicating that he was interested in doing whatever it was.

'Come with me.'

They went down Calle Badanas to the river. The man did not say a word, even to introduce himself. Hernando followed him in silence. Two pennies was a pittance, but even so it was worth two days' work in the tannery. When they reached the river-bank, the man peered nervously first one way then the other. There was no moon and it was almost completely dark.

'Can you row?' he asked Hernando, uncovering a small, dilapidated boat hidden on the bank.

'No,' admitted the Morisco, 'but I can—'

'No matter. Climb in,' the muleteer ordered, pushing the tiny craft into the water. 'I'll row. You concentrate on bailing out the water.'

Bailing out the water? Hernando hesitated just as he was about to jump into the boat.

'Get in carefully,' the dealer warned him, 'it can't handle much movement.'

'I . . .' He didn't know how to swim!

'What were you expecting? One of His Majesty's galleys?'

The boy peered down at the dark waters of the Guadalquivir. They were flowing calmly by.

'Where are we going?' he asked. He hadn't moved from the bank.

'Holy Mother of God! To Seville, if that's all right with you. We'll make a stop there and then go on to Barbary to visit a brothel I like to frequent on Sundays. Shut up and do what I tell you!'

Stepping into the boat, Hernando tried to convince himself that the river really did seem calm. As soon as he put his foot on the bottom, his shoes filled with water.

'How many women are there in this brothel you mentioned?' he asked ironically, once he was seated on what must have once been one of the two benches in the boat. The muleteer was now rowing towards the far bank.

'Enough for the two of us,' laughed the man. 'Start bailing out. You'll find a ladle on your right.' Hernando groped for it and began to bail out water as soon as he found it. The man rowed carefully, trying not to make any splash when he dipped the oars into the water, and all the while keeping an eye on the Roman bridge and the soldiers standing guard there. 'They say there are women from all races and places in the brothels,' he whispered. 'Many of them Christian captives. Very beautiful and skilled in the art of love . . .'

Dreaming of the women in that imaginary brothel, they reached the far bank. They were immediately joined by another man whose features Hernando could not even begin to make out in the darkness. It only took a few moments for the muleteer and the other man to exchange a purse of money and load a keg on to the boat. Not a word was spoken before they whispered farewell. As the muleteer climbed back on board, the boat sank dangerously low in the water. He turned it round and faced Hernando.

'Now you'll have to bail water for real,' he announced. 'If you don't . . . Can you swim?'

They did not say a word to each other until they were in midstream. Hernando could see the water seeping in with much more force. The ladle was not enough! He felt his stomach clench, especially when he realized the man was rowing more urgently, forgetting all precautions, his oar stroke getting shorter and shorter because of the water and the weight in the boat.

'Keep bailing!' the muleteer shouted.

'Keep rowing!' Hernando urged him in return.

Somehow or other they made it back to the bank they had started from. Hernando was soaked and the boat flooded, taking on water through all its dried-out, rotten joints.

The man told him to help with the barrel, which they offloaded. Then they set about hiding the boat.

'There's many a voyage left in her yet,' said the muleteer as they hauled it up. 'The *Weary Virgin*, she's called,' he muttered after giving it a mighty tug.

'The *Weary Virgin*?' Hernando repeated, watching as water cascaded from the hull and the boat became gradually lighter.

' "Virgin" so that Our Lady won't get annoyed if we have to place our trust in her: you never know.' The man pulled harder, until he managed to shift the boat a couple of paces higher up the bank. ' "Weary": well, you've seen her, she always limps back,' he said, laughing as he straightened up. 'What's your name?' he added, covering the boat with branches. Hernando answered, and the man introduced himself as Juan. 'Now we have to—'

'And my money?' Hernando interrupted him.

'Later. We'll wait here until the early hours when everyone is in bed and we can move the barrel discreetly.'

They waited until the voices in the Potro inn died away. Numb from cold, Hernando kept jumping up and hitting his sides with his arms to try to warm up.

Juan told him the barrel was full of wine. 'A good mouthful wouldn't do you any harm,' he said, seeing Hernando trembling, 'but we can't broach it.'

He explained that wine from other places was not allowed into Córdoba and that the taxes on it were very high. The innkeeper would do well out of this barrel . . . and they would too.

'Two pennies?' joked Hernando.

'That's not enough? Don't be pushy, my lad. You strike me as clever and brave. You'll earn more if you learn and make an effort.'

The innkeeper appeared when even the Potro district was asleep. Juan and he greeted each other; they were both the same height, one thin and the other fat. They threw a cloak over the barrel in an effort to disguise its shape and set off. The innkeeper led the way while the other two carted the wine. When they got to the inn on Calle del Potro, they took the barrel to a secret basement. Once the job was done, Hernando ran to warm himself beside the hot coals that were left in the fireplace on the ground floor and Juan handed over the two copper coins . . . and a tankard of wine.

'It'll cheer you up,' he encouraged Hernando, seeing the reluctance in his face.

Hernando was about to take a sip when he recalled what Fátima had said: *We must fulfil our obligations! We would be nothing without our laws!*

'No, thank you,' he said, handing back the glass.

'Drink, Moor!' shouted the innkeeper, who was clearing one of the tables. 'Wine is a gift from God.'

Hernando looked at Juan, who answered by raising his eyebrows.

'This wine is not exactly a gift from your god,' replied Hernando, 'we brought it.'

'Heretic!' The innkeeper stopped scrubbing the table and headed for him, puffing and blowing.

'I told you he was brave, León,' Juan butted in, pushing his hand into the man's chest to prevent him reaching Hernando, 'although I take back clever,' he added, turning to the lad.

'Does my having a drink matter so much to you?' asked Hernando.

'In my inn, yes,' bellowed the innkeeper, still struggling with Juan.

'In that case,' said Hernando, raising the glass in a toast, 'I'll do it for you.'

If they force you to drink wine, then drink it, but do not make a vice of it, he said to himself, taking a long swig.

He left the inn at dawn: a few Christians were coming out of mass. After the first one, he drank several more toasts with Juan and León. The innkeeper, honour satisfied, offered him the scant remains of the guests' dinner, which they reheated on the coals. Hernando headed straight for the tannery. He felt tipsy, but had discovered a nugget of information that might perhaps be of some use to him: when they heard he worked at Vicente Segura's tannery, Juan and the innkeeper had exchanged smiles and increasingly obscene jokes about the tanner's wife.

'Make good use of what you know,' Juan advised him. 'Don't be as rash as you were with León.'

Hernando turned a corner on Calle Badanas, and suddenly quickened his pace. Was that . . . ? Yes. It was Fátima. She was waiting a little beyond the tannery gate the apprentices and workers used.

'What are you doing here?' Hernando asked her. 'What about Brahim? How come he has allowed you—?'

'He's at work,' she interrupted him. 'Your mother won't tell him anything. What happened?' she wanted to know. 'You didn't come home to sleep. Some of the men in the house wanted to report you to the authorities straight away.'

'Here.' Hernando handed her the two copper coins. 'This is what I've been doing. Hide them. They are for us.'

And why not? it occurred to him. Perhaps he could buy

Fátima's freedom from Brahim. If he came by enough money . . .

'How did you get it? Have you been drinking?' Fátima frowned.

'No. Yes. Well . . .'

'You're going to be late, Moor.' The bald, stocky foreman who chose the hides shouted the curt warning from the road to the tannery.

Why should I be so cautious? thought Hernando. He felt capable of anything! Besides, he might never have as good an opportunity again: on his own with the worker who, according to his smuggling companions, was dallying with the master tanner's wife.

'I am speaking to my wife,' he fired back haughtily as the foreman continued on his way.

The man stopped dead and turned round. Fátima cringed and pressed herself against the wall.

'So what? Does that mean you can be late?' he roared.

'Some people waste more work time calling on the boss's wife when he's away from the tannery.' The look of embarrassment on the man's face confirmed his night-time companions had been right. The foreman gesticulated without saying a word. Then he hesitated.

'You play for high stakes, lad,' he managed to say.

'I, and many like me: an entire people! We once staked even more than that . . . and we lost. I don't much care what the outcome of the game is now.'

'And her?' the other man added, pointing at Fátima. 'Doesn't she matter to you either?'

'We look out for one another.' Hernando reached out to Fátima's astonished face and stroked her cheek. 'If anything happens to me, the tanner will find out . . .' Hernando and the worker's eyes locked. 'But then again, perhaps they were just rumours not worthy of attention? Why cast doubt on the honour of a master tanner of high standing in Córdoba and on his wife's good name?'

The other man thought for a few moments: honour and reputation, the most precious possessions any Spaniard could have. Many a one had lost his life over a simple affair of honour! And the master tanner . . .

'People like to gossip,' he said at length. 'But get a move on. Best not to be late.'

The foreman made to walk off, but Hernando called: 'Hey!'

The man stopped.

'Where are your manners? Aren't you going to say goodbye to my wife?'

The foreman hesitated, anger etched on his face, and yet he gave way a second time.

'Madam . . .' he mumbled, staring at Fátima.

'Why humiliate him so much?' she reproached Hernando once the man had disappeared through the tannery gate.

Hernando looked into her black, almond-shaped eyes. 'I will lay them all at your feet,' he promised, and immediately raised a finger to the girl's lips to silence her protests.

28

I<small>T WAS NOT</small> difficult for Hernando to grasp the spirit of Córdoba, beyond the churches and priests, the masses and religious processions, the rosaries or the nuns and friars begging for alms on the streets. In fact, devout Córdobans honoured their religious obligations and gave generously to women from the lower orders, to hospitals or convents, as well as meeting the demand for religious bequests in their wills or rescuing captives from the hands of the Berbers. But once their duty to the Church was fulfilled, their interests and way of life diverged further and further from the religious principles that ought to have driven them. Despite the efforts of the Council of Trent, any priest who did not possess a concubine in his house made use of a slave. It was not regarded as a sin to make a slave pregnant. It was, so Hernando heard, like bringing a horse to a donkey to beget a mule; when it came down to it, so the argument went, the offspring took on the social class of the mother and was born a slave. Efforts by Church authorities to stop confessors extracting sexual favours from women resulted in the need to keep confessor and penitent apart by means of a screen in the confessional. Yet the authorities themselves were hardly a good example of chastity and modesty. The riches and favours that went with their positions were much coveted by the second sons of the noble families, and the dean of the cathedral himself, Don Juan Fernández de Córdoba, a man of distinguished lineage, had lost count of the number of children he had scattered throughout the city.

Civil society was no different. It was as though beneath the purity that was supposed to rule married life there lay hidden a world of licentiousness where scandals happened time after time with bloody consequences for those caught in the act of adultery. Nuns were cloistered mainly for financial reasons by their fathers and brothers – it was less of a drain on family money to hand a daughter over to the Church than give her enough of a dowry to attract a husband of the same social class – and since these young women lacked any religious vocation they competed with the clerics to be seduced by the philanderers who relished the challenge of acquiring such a precious trophy; it was one of the greatest successes they could boast about.

For Hernando and the other Moriscos who had used their hoes to make the stony lands of the kingdom of Granada fertile, Córdoba society seemed lazy and corrupt. Work was despised; workers were denied access to public office. Artisans did just enough to earn a living, while an army of gentlemen, the lowest rung of the nobility, generally without means, would rather die of hunger than humiliate themselves by undertaking gainful employment: honour, the exaggerated sense of honour that imbued all Christians whatever their social class, made it impossible!

Hernando had first-hand experience of this a few days before the celebrations for the victory at Lepanto. He could have apologized, as he tried to do at the outset; do an about-turn and let the matter go; but something inside him would not let him. One evening he was walking along the narrow Calle de Armas, near the Consolación hermitage, where there was an orphanage with its hatch for abandoning unwanted children, when a young gentleman approaching from the opposite direction stumbled as he was passing and almost fell. He had a haughty manner, and was wearing a black cloak with a sword at his belt and a hat adorned with trimmings. Hernando could not help smiling as he tried to help him. Far from thanking him, the young man ostentatiously shook off Hernando's hand and growled: 'What are you laughing at?' as he recovered his footing.

'Forgive me . . .'

'What are you looking at?' The young man made as if to reach for his sword.

Who was he to ask him that? After his stumble, the gentleman was trying to rearrange the packing of sawdust he used to pad out his breeches. Ungrateful wretch! What if he were to teach the fop a lesson?

'I was just wondering . . . what is your name?' Hernando stammered deliberately, lowering his eyes.

'Who are you, you stinking dullard, to be interested in my name?'

'It's that . . .' Hernando's mind raced. The arrogant fool! How could he teach him a lesson? The pointed velvet shoes he could not take his eyes off suggested that this particular gentleman must have some money to his name. He noted the fancy breeches and the lining of his cloak, obviously sewn with great care by some maidservant. 'It's just that . . .'

'Speak!'

'It seems . . . I think . . . I suspect I heard you talked about the other night in the tavern in the Corredera . . .' He let the words hang in the air.

'Go on!'

'I wouldn't like to make a mistake, excellency. What I heard . . . No, I cannot. Forgive my presumption but I must know your name.'

The young man thought for a moment or two. So did Hernando. What sort of a mess was he getting himself into?

'Don Nicolás Ramírez de Barros,' the young man declared earnestly, 'a nobleman by ancestry.'

'Yes, yes,' confirmed Hernando, 'it was your excellency they were talking about: Don Nicolás Ramírez. I remember now.'

'What were they saying?'

'There were two men . . .' Hernando paused, and was about to go on when the gentleman got in ahead of him.

'Who were they?'

'Two men, well dressed. They were talking about your excellency. Definitely! I heard what they were saying.' He pretended not to dare continue. What could he tell him? There was no going back now.

'What were they saying?'

What could they have said? Hernando asked himself desperately. A nobleman by ancestry! The dandy had boasted about that.

'That your ancestry wasn't pure,' Hernando said bluntly.

The young man tightened his grip on his sword. Hernando finally dared look up at his face: it was flustered, furious.

'In the name of Saint James, patron saint of Spain,' the nobleman muttered, 'my bloodline is pure back as far as the Romans. I can trace my family name back to Quintus Varus! Tell me: who has dared to suggest such an insult?'

He felt Don Nicolás's onion breath on his face.

'No . . . I don't know,' he stuttered, not needing to pretend this time. Had he gone too far? The young man was shaking with rage. 'I don't know them. As your excellency will understand, I don't get involved with such people.'

'Would you recognize them?' How could Hernando recognize two men he had just invented? He could say that since it was night he did not see them clearly enough. 'Would you recognize them?' the gentleman insisted, shaking him violently by the shoulders.

'Of course,' said Hernando, retreating away from him.

'Come with me to the Corredera!'

'No.'

Don Nicolás gave a start. 'What do you mean, no?' He stepped towards Hernando, who backed away.

'I can't. They're expecting me at the . . .' What was the workplace furthest from the Potro district? 'They're expecting me at the pottery. Your problems are no concern of mine. All I'm interested in is supporting my family. If I don't turn up at work, the boss won't pay me. I have a wife and children I'm trying to bring up in the Christian faith . . .'

That did it! Hernando congratulated himself on seeing the gentleman slowly fishing around in his stockings until he found a purse. For Fátima! thought Hernando. 'One of them is ill and I think another—'

'Shut up! How much does your boss pay you?' Don Nicolás asked, counting out the coins in the purse.

'Four reales,' Hernando lied.

'Take two,' the other man offered.

'I can't. My children . . .'

'Three.'

'I'm sorry, your excellency.'

The gentleman pressed a four-real coin into his hand.

'Let's go!' he ordered.

To get from the Consolación hermitage to the Corredera was only a matter of crossing Plaza de las Cañas, a few short paces that the gentleman covered purposefully. His hand on the hilt of his sword, he cursed and swore vengeance on those who allowed his family name to be sullied. Hernando went in front, pushed on from time to time by Don Nicolás. And now what? he thought. How was he going to get out of the trap he had set for himself? But he clutched the coin in his hand. Four reales! Money he could put towards buying Fátima's freedom.

'What if they're not there this evening?' he suggested as the gentleman urged him forward with a shove.

'Pray that that will not be the case,' was Don Nicolás's only reply.

They reached the great Córdoban square from the south. Hernando tried to get his bearings in the vast open space. There were three inns on the square: La Romana, on the side where they had just arrived, and two others on their right, on the eastern end of the square – the Los Leones inn and the Carbón inn, close to the hospital of Nuestra Señora de los Ángeles. There was still enough daylight. People were going in and out of the inns and the great square was a hive of activity.

'Well?' asked the gentleman.

Hernando grunted. What if he ran off? As if he had read his thoughts, Don Nicolás grabbed his arm and dragged him to La Romana inn. They unceremoniously pushed a customer standing in the doorway out of their way and entered the establishment. The gentleman shook Hernando roughly, demanding an answer.

'No. They're not here,' said the lad. Several of the customers peered in his direction as he surveyed the interior of the inn.

He made the same claim in Los Leones. Of course they weren't! he thought as they went into the Carbón inn. Why should they be? But then, his four reales . . . What would the gentleman decide to do? He would never let matters rest like this. His honour and his family name were at stake! He would make him wait all night and then . . . He had paid him what he thought was the equivalent of a month's wages!

A loud guffaw interrupted Hernando's thoughts. At one of the tables, a bearded man clad in the uniform of a regular soldier raised a glass of wine and was carousing with two other men at his table. He was clearly drunk.

'That's him.' Hernando pointed, ready to make his escape as soon as Don Nicolás was distracted.

But the gentleman pressed even harder on his arm as if readying himself for the fight.

'You!' Don Nicolás shouted from the doorway.

All chatter in the room suddenly stopped. Laughter was cut short. A couple of customers quickly rose from the nearest table and moved away, knocking over their chairs. Hernando felt his legs start to shake.

'How dare you sully the family name of Varus?' the gentleman shouted again.

The soldier lumbered up out of his seat, gulping down the rest of his wine, which dribbled into his beard. He reached for the inlaid hilt of his sword.

'Who might you be, sir, to raise your voice to me?' he roared. 'To a lieutenant in the Sicilian regiment of His Majesty's army, a noble from Vizcaya!' When he heard this, Hernando shuddered. Another nobleman! 'If you are a true gentleman, which I very much doubt, you are a disgrace to your ancestors.'

'Are you questioning my ancestry?' shouted Don Nicolás.

'I told you so,' Hernando tried to whisper in his ear. 'That's what I heard, that he questioned . . .' But Don Nicolás paid him no attention, and all at once Hernando's arm was free.

'You sully your own family name!' the lieutenant bellowed.

'I demand redress,' screamed Don Nicolás.

'You shall have it!'

Both gentlemen drew their swords. The people still at their tables got up to clear the space and the two men faced each other.

Hernando remained stunned for a few moments. They were going to fight a duel! He opened his sweaty hand and looked at the four-real coin. He tossed it into the air a couple of times, catching it in his palm, and then walked out of the inn. Idiots! he thought, as he heard the metallic clash of their blades making their first contact.

On the way back to Calle de Mucho Trigo Hernando felt troubled, very different from what he had expected after the successful outcome of his risky wager: two noblemen were gambling with their lives without either of them even being aware of what his adversary really intended. And all because of a misunderstanding! On the way, when it was already dark, he ran into a procession of blind people walking tied together in single file. They were reciting the rosary and begging for alms as they did three nights a week, roaming the streets of Córdoba beyond the Hospital for the Blind on Calle Alfaros. A man who was praying and tending the candles on an image of the Virgin at the front of a building dropped a coin in the tin that the first of the blind men shook rhythmically. Hernando stepped out of their way and held on tightly to his four-real coin. Christians!

He had made a good deal of money since finding out about

the goings on between the tannery foreman and the boss's wife. He had thought it over for several nights: he could write and count and surely those skills could land him a better-paid job than his work in the manure pit, for which he was paid less than a servant; and yet he chose to stay where he was. His job at the tannery kept him far away and hidden from the rest of the workers, who hardly ever came near the place, so that he could enjoy a certain freedom, sanctioned by the foreman, which he would not have had in any other job.

From then on, he made several excursions to the far bank of the Guadalquivir in the *Weary Virgin*, which somehow kept surviving the journeys. Hernando and Juan struck up a friendship and their night-time chats about the women in the Berber brothel, beyond the port of Seville, degenerated into good-humoured exchanges of jibes and lewd remarks.

'How are you going to mount three women at a time if you haven't the strength to row a boat?' Hernando mocked him, bailing furiously when the *Virgin* slowed down and threatened to fill with water from the Guadalquivir on their return journeys.

The friendship also brought Hernando more than the two coins the mule dealer had paid him that first time: he soon received a share of the profits from the wine smuggling. The Potro inn and its atmosphere, full of adventurers, scoundrels and rogues, became his real home. He went on working in the tannery; he needed the respectability that the job gave him in the eyes of the bailiff or the priest from San Nicolás church when they came calling to check that they were turning into good Christians, but his real life was in the Potro.

While the boys from the San Lorenzo or the Santa María districts carried the hides for him from the slaughterhouse, Hernando headed for the Calahorra to plot and plan with Juan and the other dealers. He always smiled to himself when he remembered how he had managed to rid himself of such a thankless task. The first few times, as he was walking back outside the city walls, he had noticed how boys from different neighbourhoods threw stones at each other on the perimeter road and the land around it. The fights had left several dead and quite a few wounded among those careless enough to wander through the area, so that eventually the town council decided to put a stop to them, but the youngsters paid no attention to the orders and the stones went on flying. The first time Hernando found himself caught up in one of these battles involving dozens of stone-throwers, he protected himself with the hides until the fighting eased off. On other days he saw them practising for the next battle. Who could beat a stone-thrower from the Alpujarra? he thought. The wager was a penny. The target was a stick: if they lost, they carried the hides to the tannery; if they won, they got the penny. Hernando lost some money but won most of the bets and while the boys fulfilled their part of the bargain, he went to the Campo de la Verdad where he pretended to gather manure by crawling under the mules. Inevitably, some horse dealer would point to the filthy, foul-smelling Morisco, drag him out by the hair and put him on a palfrey to convince the buyer the horse was tame and had no bad habits. Hernando would collapse on to the saddle like a sack, apparently terrified as if he had never been on a horse before, while the dealer extolled the virtues of an animal capable of putting up with such an inexperienced rider. If the deal was closed, Hernando got his money.

One evening, he helped a man climb the wall of a nunnery in Santa Cruz, waiting on the other side to throw him the return rope while first he listened to the pair giggling and then their passionate moans. But not all his outings were so successful. On one occasion, he joined a group of beggars from outside the city who had no licence to beg in Córdoba. Begging was rigorously controlled in the city and only those authorized by the parish priest were allowed to do it. Once the beggars proved they had made their confession and received communion, they were given a special permit, which they wore around their neck. This allowed them to seek alms within the parish boundaries. One of the illegal beggars had a rare talent for holding his breath until he seemed moribund: his face took on a deathly pallor that convinced everyone who looked at him. They chose Plaza de la Paja, where they sold the buckwheat straw for mattresses, and the beggar collapsed and died, causing a great commotion among the passers-by. Hernando and some other cronies approached the body, weeping and begging for alms in order to give him a Christian burial; many of the bystanders were moved by this display, and gave generously. As chance would have it, though, a priest passing through Córdoba had witnessed the same ruse in Toledo, so he went up to the corpse and, much to the indignation of the grieving crowd, began to kick the beggar. At the third kick in the kidneys, the dead man revived. Hernando and his accomplices found themselves forced to flee from the anger of the people they had tricked.

He also worked for the owners of the illegal gaming houses where cards and dice were played. He met a lad a few years older than him by the name of Palomero, whose job was to entice potential customers. Palomero had a special talent for spotting which stranger was looking for a gaming den where he could wager his money and as soon as he saw one he would run after him and cajole him to go to the one run by the Marshal, who paid him. Hernando often helped him, above all preventing the rest of the touts who plied their trade in Plaza del Potro from getting to the gambler Palomero had discovered. He would trip them up, shove them or use any other trick he could think of to keep them away.

'Thief!' it occurred to him to shout one night at a young man he could not block and who was heading towards the gambler Palomero was negotiating with.

A guard appeared out of nowhere and threw himself on the young man, but this was no use at all to Palomero since the gambler disappeared in the uproar.

As was bound to happen, Hernando got caught up in lots of brawls, and took many a thump, something that earned him Palomero's sincere friendship and a bit more money than had been agreed. The two lads chatted, laughed and ate together and Hernando was continually astounded at the faces Palomero could pull.

'Now?' he would ask Hernando.

'No.'

'What about now?' he would press after a few moments.

'No.'

Palomero said he had worked out the trick the Marshal used to fleece not the innocents, the naive people who came to his gaming house, but the swindlers or card sharps themselves, however expert they might be.

'He can move the lobe of his right ear while everything else stays completely still,' he said in amazement. 'No other muscle in his face moves, not even the rest of his ear! He plays with an accomplice who as soon as he recognizes the signal knows what cards the Marshal has and places his wager. Am I doing it now?'

Hernando burst out laughing at his friend's contorted face.

'No. I'm sorry.'

For the most part, with the exception of occasional fiascos like the fake corpse, things were going well for Hernando. So much so that he had already had a word with Juan about making the first payment for a mule: not quite the mule he would have wanted but all he could afford with his money; the dealer gave him a good price. He thought about trading the mule with Brahim in exchange for Fátima. His stepfather would not refuse no matter how much he hated Hernando. It was some time now since he had made any demands of his second wife. Fátima continued her fast, which did not require any great effort given the general shortage of food, so she did not put on any weight and remained painfully thin and listless, not something that held any attraction for Brahim who was always tired from his unaccustomed arduous work in the fields. Aisha played her part in keeping the girl free from worry and satisfied her husband whenever he was up to it. However, ever since Hernando had saved her from the bull in the alleyway, Fátima's dark eyes sparkled day and night. Hernando had to convince her of his plan.

'He'll definitely agree!' he tried to encourage her. 'Don't you see how he gets up at dawn and how he comes back to the house after a day's work in the fields? He's wasting away day by day. Brahim is a man of the road; he's never been a farmer, least of all considering the pittance they pay him. He needs open space. He'll wash his hands of you. I'm certain of it.'

It was true. Not even Aisha's by now obvious pregnancy lightened the muleteer's downcast mood, which only added to his usual bad temper and irritability.

'He hates you to death,' pleaded Fátima, aware that in the past few days Brahim had started to look at her lustfully again. When he passed her in the house, he blocked her way and fondled her breasts. The girl, however, chose not to relay her fears to the hopeful Hernando. It was not the only thing she kept from him these days, she thought sadly.

'But he loves himself more,' said Hernando. 'When I was in my mother's womb, he accepted me in exchange for a mule. Why wouldn't he do the same now, when things are far more difficult for him?'

With the four reales he had just got from Don Nicolás he could give Juan the first payment on a mule, he thought as he turned on to the narrow street leading to the tumbledown house they were all crowded into. A young man stationed on the corner motioned to him to be quiet. What was he doing there? He had seen him in the house; he slept with his family in one of the rooms on the top floor . . . What was his name? Hernando went up to him but the boy put a finger to his lips and signalled him to go on.

From the door itself, he became aware of a festive atmosphere that was both unusual and out of place. Drawn by the sound of a Morisco song sung in whispers, he crossed the entrance and headed towards the inside courtyard of the building, which was typical of many houses in Córdoba. The Christians turned these courtyards into gardens festooned with flowers of every colour and scent around the ever-present fountain. In the houses rented by the Moriscos, they were used for everything other than decoration or self-indulgence. Clothes were hung out to dry; they performed their ablutions, washed themselves, worked silk, cooked and even slept there: no flowers could have survived in the midst of all that activity. As Hernando came in, he saw that everyone from the house was gathered in the courtyard or in the rooms on the ground floor. He spotted several new faces. He also caught sight of Hamid. Some people were whispering to each other; others, their eyes shut as if they wished to flee from this huge Córdoban prison, were humming the song he had heard when he came in. In one corner of the courtyard, a man, perhaps facing towards Mecca, was praying. Now he understood the lookout on the corner of the street: gatherings of Moriscos were forbidden, especially to pray, but . . .

'If you are discovered,' he reproached Hamid, who had immediately hobbled over to him, 'there'll be no way out. The alleyway doesn't have an exit and the Christians could always gain access through—'

'Why do you exclude yourself from our gathering, Ibn Hamid?' the holy man interrupted him.

Hernando was stunned by Hamid's harsh tone. 'I . . . No, I'm sorry. You're right. I meant to say if they discover *us*.' Hamid nodded, accepting the apology. 'What are . . . what is being celebrated? We're taking a big risk. What are you doing here?'

'My master has given me leave for a while. I couldn't waste this day of all days.'

Hernando was not aware of the Christian calendar, much less the Muslim one. Was it some religious feast day?

'I'm sorry, Hamid, but I don't know what day this is. What are we celebrating?' he asked vaguely, looking around at the people. Suddenly, he saw Fátima, with a piece of jewellery in the shape of a golden hand gleaming round her neck. What had become of that hand? Where had she kept it hidden? Fátima looked back at him as if she had sensed eyes on her from a distance. Hernando was about to smile at her but she turned away and lowered her head. What was going on? He looked for Brahim and picked him out near Fátima. He could not get close to the girl in the courtyard to ask her why she had spurned him like that. 'What are we celebrating?' he asked the holy man again, this time in a barely audible voice.

'Today we have rescued our first brother in faith from slavery,' Hamid replied solemnly. 'Him,' he added, pointing to a man whose cheek bore a letter branded by fire.

Hernando glanced at the Morisco who was standing with a woman and receiving good wishes from all those present. How could such a rescue be so important that Fátima . . . ? What was going on?

'The woman beside him is his wife,' Hamid continued. 'She discovered that he was living as a slave in a house belonging to a Córdoba merchant and . . .' He paused.

'And?' Hernando asked, without giving it much thought. What was happening to Fátima? He tried once more to catch her attention, but it was clear she was avoiding him.

'She called upon the community.'

'Good.'

'On her brothers.'

'Aha,' murmured Hernando.

'Everyone gave towards the cost of the ransom. Every Morisco in Córdoba! I too gave some money I had managed to lay my hands on.'

Hernando was surprised again, and looked enquiringly at Hamid.

'Fátima', the holy man acknowledged, 'has been one of the most generous.'

Hernando shook his head as if he wanted to rid himself of the words he had just heard. He felt suddenly so exhausted that the nobleman's four-real coin almost slipped through his fingers. Fátima! One of those who had given the most!

'That money . . .' he stammered, 'that money was to buy her freedom and . . .'

'Yours?' added Hamid.

'Yes,' Hernando answered firmly, pulling himself together. 'Mine. Our freedom!'

He looked for Fátima again and found her standing head erect at the other side of the courtyard. This time she held his gaze, certain that Hamid had told him the fate of their money. Fátima had explained to the holy man why they were saving the money and admitted she could not tell Hernando about it. As Hernando watched her a strange feeling crept through him: she was proud and content, the sparkle in her eyes competing with the gleaming brilliance the lights picked out on the gold jewel adorning her neck.

'Why?' Hernando asked from a distance.

It was Hamid who answered him. 'Because you have abandoned your people, Ibn Hamid,' he reproached him from behind. Hernando did not move. 'While the rest of us were organizing ourselves, trying to pray in secret, keeping alive our beliefs, or helping those of our people who needed it, you devoted yourself to running around Córdoba like a wastrel.'

Hamid waited a few moments. Hernando was rooted to the spot, bewitched by those black, almond-shaped eyes. 'It pains me to see my son among the lowest order of those who rule and govern us.' He noticed that Hernando's shoulders trembled slightly.

'You taught me,' Hernando replied without turning round, 'you taught me that there is a still lower one: the twelfth order, that of women. Is that why Fátima had to forsake her freedom?'

'She trusts in God's mercy. You ought to do likewise. Your bondage, yours and Fátima's, is not the bondage of men, which can be bought and sold. Your bondage is to our laws, to our beliefs and only our God can decide on that. When Fátima gave me the money and explained what it was for, what you were struggling to achieve, I told her to place her trust in God, not to give up hope. She assured me it would only take one phrase to convince you . . .'

Hernando turned to face the man who had taught him

everything. He knew it. He knew which phrase it was, but only by hearing it again did he fully understand its significance: the story that lay behind it, all the sorrows and joys he had shared with Fátima. Hamid half closed his eyes before whispering it: 'In death, hope is everlasting.'

29

'ISOWN ME! If not, kill me! Force yourself on me if that's what you want ... but you will never again have my consent. I swear to God I'll die before I give myself to you again!'

Brahim's rage when Fátima rejected his approach was plain even in the room's half-light. They could see him trembling. Aisha, crouching in a corner, listened to Fátima's words, torn between fear of how Brahim would respond and pride at the girl's strength. The young couple with the child on the mattress at the far side of the room clasped each other's hands and held their breath. Hernando was not there. Brahim stammered something unintelligible. He struck the air repeatedly with his fist and went on snarling and cursing. Fátima held her ground, although she was terrified that one of those blows would strike her face. But it did not happen.

'You will never be free, however much money the Nazarene raises,' Brahim roared. 'Do you understand, woman?' In the face of his fury, Fátima made no answer. 'What did you imagine? I am your husband!' For a moment Fátima thought he was going to take her there and then, in front of everybody, but Brahim looked around him and held back. 'You're nothing more than a bag of skin and bones. Nobody would want to sleep with you!' he added with a gesture of contempt before making his way towards Aisha.

Her knees buckled and Fátima fell to the floor, surprised she had managed to stand up to his threats for as long as she had. It was some time before she stopped shaking and began to breathe normally. She had thought a thousand times of the day when, despite how painfully thin and undesirable she looked, Brahim would try to force himself on her. And so it had turned out. Time had worked in her favour, as had the fact that she had handed over all the money they had saved towards the ransom for the first Morisco. The Muslim community had seen this as the first sign that despite being defeated they were still a people united in faith, and it had convinced her once and for all: why should she have to give herself to a man she abhorred? Had she not just given up all possibility of her freedom, her hopes and her future, for the sake of the followers of the Prophet? The community was grateful to her and to Hernando, who gave way in the end. After listening to Hamid's words, he had looked at her across the courtyard again; she had raised her eyes to the heavens and he followed suit. Then he forgave her with a simple nod of approval. The whole of Córdoba knew about their generosity. Brahim asked where the money had come from and Hamid told him straight out. Fátima felt safer; she knew she could rely on the support of the community – and Brahim was aware of this too. Furthermore, her little Humam was no longer there for him to use as a threat to secure her favours. She thought a lot about that: perhaps ... perhaps God and the Prophet had decided to free the child from what would have been a terrible burden throughout his life. She owed it to herself and her dead son! As for the possibility that Brahim would treat Aisha badly, as he had done in the Alpujarra, what was a Muslim without sons? Musa and Aquil had not been seen again; nothing was known of them, although they were all on the alert for any news. A number of Moriscos made representations to the town council complaining that the children who had been taken from them were treated like slaves by the families they were placed with, but the Christians took no notice, as they took little notice of the royal decree that forbade Morisco children under the age of eleven being enslaved. Like all the

Christian kingdoms, Córdoba had an abundance of children, who were used by their masters as servants or workers until they reached the age of twenty. Aisha was safe enough, Fátima decided: while she was with child and probably while she was nursing the baby, Brahim would not treat her badly, since that would endanger this new, much wanted child.

That night, while she tried to recover her composure, Brahim confirmed her conclusions, and did not vent his anger on his first wife as he had done in the Alpujarra. Fátima wept silently, secure in the knowledge that only a few feet away from where she had collapsed, Aisha too was weeping secretly, wordlessly comforting her in the way the two women had learnt to communicate with one another up in the mountains.

At the same time as this was going on, Hernando was entering the door of a small, dilapidated house on Calle de los Moriscos in the Santa Marina parish. Ever since Fátima had handed over their money as part of the ransom for the first Morisco slave and Hamid had questioned his attitude, Hernando had changed. And he felt all the better for it. Why not trust in God? If Fátima and Hamid did so . . . Besides, she had promised that Brahim would not lay a hand on her and he believed her. God, how he believed her! 'I'll kill myself first,' she had assured him. Encouraged by her promise, Hernando put at the disposal of his brothers in faith the ease with which he could move throughout the city, his many contacts, his intelligence and his craftiness. The community received it all with fondness and gratitude. Fátima shared these feelings too, much more so than on those occasions when he had handed over a coin towards the purchase of the mule which he intended to use as barter for her. Then she had taken the money and hidden it, almost out of a sense of duty, but showing her unhappiness, as if she was unsure that this was the right approach. He had put her value as that of an old mule! Hernando chided himself now when he saw her smile and those black almond eyes of hers open wide when she learnt of the latest service Hernando had provided for one of their brothers. There was much to do, Hamid had assured him during the long conversation they had had after the celebration for the first ransom paid.

Because, despite everything, Córdoba was a magnet for Moriscos. It was the city of the caliphs, the city that had scaled the heights of Muslim culture and religion in the West, while living conditions there were no worse than those the Moriscos endured in any other Spanish city or town. In all of them pressure from the Christians was suffocating; if possible, this was even more true in the villages, where the Moriscos suffered the hatred of the old Christians at close quarters. And everywhere without exception they were exploited by the authorities or the Christian lords. For this reason, two years after their deportation, a steady stream of illegal immigrants still kept arriving in Córdoba, drawn both by its past glory and its current prosperity.

The Moriscos were forbidden by royal decree from leaving their places of residence without carrying the relevant permit issued by the local authorities. This contained a detailed physical description of the person, where he was going, why, and how much time he was permitted to be absent from the town where he was registered. Dozens of Moriscos found some excuse to get their hands on the permit and arrived in Córdoba, but when their permits elapsed they found themselves in the city without proper papers.

In agreement with Hamid and two elders from the Albaicín in Granada who had become leaders of the community, Hernando busied himself with these recent arrivals. Once their permits had expired, they had two options: marry a Morisco woman previously registered in Córdoba, or allow the authorities to arrest them and go to jail for three or four weeks. The council knew that the influx of newcomers was good for the city, supplying cheap labour and more rent for house owners. In both cases, whether through marriage or by serving the jail sentence, the Moriscos were then given the relevant permit according the holder the status of Córdoba resident.

Hernando knew about all the Moriscos who hid in the houses of their co-religionists when the permits allowing them to roam freely through the city had expired. He played the part of matchmaker, as on that night when he went into the small building in Calle de los Moriscos to announce that he had found a wife for a good wool carder from Mérida, a skill that was much in demand in Córdoba among the weavers' guild.

But not all those without the proper documents were wool carders, nor were all the Morisco women of Córdoba willing to enter into marriage, and so most of the men ended up in prison, where Hernando had to be extremely careful.

The royal prison was nothing more than a business leased to a governor. The authorities' only responsibility was to provide a place in which to detain convicts with the corresponding shackles and chains. The prisoners had to buy their own food or have it brought in from outside; their beds were rented in accordance with the tariffs the King had allotted to the offences committed. Cost varied depending on whether one, two or three people shared the same mattress. Those who were able to, paid. The poor and destitute lived in the prison on public charity, but such charity was hardly going to be extended to the heretical new Christians who had carried out so many atrocities during the uprising.

Hernando had to determine when was the best time for a Morisco to be arrested according to what was available in the prison. He made sure that the governor was paid appropriately, and that the community provided food for the prisoner. He had not stopped his night-time forays in the Potro district, but now he was after information rather than money. When was a bailiff planning to search the Morisco houses that he was responsible for? What was the news from the prison? Who was the best bailiff to arrest a Morisco and where? Who owned Morisco slaves and how much had they cost him? How long would it take the city council to grant residence to some person or other? Any information was worthwhile, and when the opportunity arose he would spend some of the scarce funds the elders gave him to buy someone's goodwill or to persuade a servant drinking wine in a tavern to tell him the name and origin of this or that slave living in his house.

Freeing the slaves taken prisoner during the war in the Alpujarra had become the community's main objective. However, the Christians, who had bought these men and women at much lower prices than if they had been Negroes, mulattos or white people of whatever origin, soon discovered their co-religionists' interest in them, and hugely increased the cost of the ransom. Every Córdoban Christian who owned Morisco slaves became a small-scale trader determined to reap profits. This was especially true of the men, since the women were rarely put up for sale as the children of slaves inherited their mother's status. Getting a Morisco woman pregnant therefore guaranteed a good return within a relatively short time.

Hernando hesitated over whether to continue his trips in the *Weary Virgin*. Juan pressed him to keep working with him. What harm could it do him to make some good and easy money? 'The boy who goes with me now', Juan complained with a knowing wink, 'doesn't like to chat about the women in the Berber brothel.' He even offered more money, but one day when Hernando was walking towards Plaza del Salvador along Calle Marmolejos, he saw a sight that led him to dismiss any idea of continuing his night-time outings on the boat. All along Calle Marmolejos, up against the wall of the San Pablo convent, was a series of stone benches where the corpses of people who had died in the countryside and been brought to the city by the Brothers of Mercy were displayed. Hernando got used to looking at the corpses, trying to judge by their clothes or complexion (although neither was much different from their Spanish counterparts) whether he was dealing with a Morisco or not. If it seemed he was, Hernando would let the elders know so that they could enquire in other communities if anyone had lost a relative. But the benches were not only used to display corpses. They were used for many other things: bread and any other confiscated goods were sold there; jobless workers put themselves forward for hire; illegal traders or swindlers were held up to public scorn; and, above all, wine from outside the region was poured away. On this particular day, on a stone bench next to one on which the body of a woman was beginning to decompose, a customs officer and a bailiff were standing alongside a large wine-keg, surrounded by a swarm of youngsters ready to throw themselves to the ground to drink the wine as soon as the first blow of the official's axe split it open. Unlike other goods, confiscated wine was not resold. Hernando could not help looking at the barrel. He recognized it at once: he had transported many similar ones on the *Weary Virgin*. With his stomach in knots, he hurried on, leaving behind the sound of splintering wood and the whoops of delight from the youngsters as they hurled themselves on the wine. That night he did not find León in his Potro inn.

'They arrested him,' Juan explained a few days later, in the midst of his mules in the Campo de la Verdad. 'The customs people discovered where he hid the barrels, although given how they made straight for the spot, it seems likely someone informed on him.'

30

MANURE WAS a valued commodity in the Córdoba of kitchen gardens and a thousand flower-filled courtyards. Hernando went on working in the tannery for the two miserly reales a month they paid him. This enabled him to demonstrate to the authorities that he had a steady job, but at the same time, thanks to the protection he enjoyed from the foreman who was dallying with the boss's wife, he could continue with his other activities. But he was so busy that he could not collect enough manure for steeping the hides in, and although the foreman made excuses for him, the shortage of manure had become untenable.

At dawn on the first Sunday in March fifteen fighting bulls from the pastures outside Córdoba, accompanied by some cows, came thundering across the Roman bridge into the city. Cowhands on horseback drove them on with the long poles they had run the bulls with from the countryside. Despite the early hour, at the far end of the bridge the fun-loving people of Córdoba awaited their arrival. From there, the bulls were sent along the bank of the Guadalquivir to Calle Arhonas, then up that to Calle del Toril and into Plaza de la Corredera, where the bulls would be corralled until evening.

The day before, the foreman had warned Hernando: 'We

need manure. Tomorrow there is to be a bullfight with fifteen bulls. You'll find plenty of it along the route they take and in the squares near the Corredera where the noblemen's horses will be.'

'Working on a Sunday is not allowed.'

'Maybe so, but if you don't work tomorrow be sure you'll not work on Monday either. The tanner has already warned me. Yes,' he added quickly, seeing the threatening look on Hernando's face, 'I won't have a job either. If that's what you want, we'll both lose our jobs.'

'The noblemen's servants won't let me.'

'I know them. I'll be there. They'll allow you to collect manure. Take it from the bulls first.'

So there was Hernando positioned at the end of the Roman bridge in the midst of the throng. He was carrying a large, woven grass basket and sheltered behind a fence the town council had built to force the bulls to turn and continue their run along the riverbank. The locals spilled out on either side, so that in the event of any trouble their only way out was to jump into the river. At the narrow entrance to Calle Arhonas another barricade had been put in place to make the bulls take that street. From there, anywhere where the bulls ran along the adjoining streets of La Ajerquía was protected by large wooden planks, and Calle del Toril was blocked off, with only one exit: Plaza de la Corredera.

Hernando saw how nervous everyone became when they heard the rumble of the bulls and cowhands in the Campo de la Verdad.

He heard shouts of: 'Here they come! They're on the way!'

The thunderous noise of the animals crossing the ancient stone bridge mingled with the shrieks of the crowd. Some men jumped over the fences and began to run in front of the herd; others made ready darts to throw at the bulls or old capes to distract them from their path. Hernando watched the big fighting bulls pass in front of him, following the cows: they bellowed, galloping blindly in a group ahead of the cowhands.

There was a sharp, sloping turn from the bridge to the river-bank so that several bulls collided heavily with the wooden fence. One of them fell, sliding along the ground and was trampled on by the ones coming behind. A young man tried to wave a cape at it, but the bull jumped up with astonishing agility and gored his thigh, tossing him over its head. Hernando saw how two other men running in front were also gored, but when the bulls turned round to finish them off they were forced to continue their stampede by the cowhands' prods.

The shouts, chases, dust and deafening noise lasted only a few moments before bulls, people and horses disappeared round the corner of Calle Arhonas. Hernando forgot all about the manure he was supposed to collect and stood mesmerized by the people left behind after the bull run had passed: the man with the cape was bleeding profusely from the groin, clinging to a girl who was shouting in despair; men, women and children were trying to climb out of the river where they had jumped as the bulls roared by; and there was a trail of the wounded, some on foot, limping and moaning, others laid out on the bank of the Guadalquivir. By the time he remembered his task, several old women and children had already rushed forward to scoop up the manure trampled into the road. He looked at his empty basket and shook his head. He was not going to get a single dropping there. He came out from behind the fence and approached the wounded man, who was already surrounded by a large group of women, to see if he could help him in some way.

'Clear off, Muslim!' an old woman dressed in black spat at him.

'That young man will die, if he's not already dead,' Hernando finished saying to Hamid after high mass. They were standing beyond the cemetery with Fátima and a pregnant Aisha; Brahim was chatting to some other Moriscos a little way off.

'Yes. Many do die . . .'

'What pleasure do they get out of it?'

'The fight, the struggle between man and beast,' Hamid answered. Grimacing, Hernando spread his palms in a gesture of incomprehension. 'We did it ourselves too,' the holy man pointed out. 'There were famous bullfights in the court at Granada. The Zegrí family, the Gazules, the Venegas, the Gomeles, the Azarques and many other noblemen distinguished themselves at the time by fighting and killing bulls. What's more, no Muslim holy man ever dared ban those festivals, and yet the Pope of Rome forbade Christians to take part on pain of excommunication. Any Christian who dies in a bullfight does so in a state of mortal sin and any priests who attend are defrocked.'

Hernando remembered then the army of priests who ran out of the houses on Calle Ribera once the bulls had passed, trying to save the souls of the injured with holy oils and prayers.

'In that case, why do they fight bulls? Are they not so religious after all?'

Hamid smiled. 'Spain loves its bulls. The aristocracy love bulls. The people love bulls. It must be the only topic, apart from the question of money, that puts King Philip's Christian faith at odds with Pope Pius V.'

The Muslim noblemen Hamid had mentioned were only part of the nobility of Córdoba. There were also the Aguayos, the Hoces, the Bocanegras and, of course, the members of the distinguished house of Fernández de Córdoba and its no less illustrious branch, the Aguilar family. Córdoba was nothing if not aristocratic! Many noble families had won titles and royal favours during the Reconquest, and whenever there was a fiesta for bulls, they tried to outdo each other in displays of luxury and ostentation.

After the noonday meal and before the bullfight began, in each palace the lords' teams of assistants formed up. These teams consisted of servants richly clad in matching costumes. There might be as many as thirty, forty or sixty servants to each noble, but only two of them fulfilled the function of footmen: they were the ones who would accompany the lord into the square. The people of Córdoba positioned themselves in front of the palace of the Fernández de Córdoba family on the Bailío hill, outside the palace of the Marquis of Carpio on Calle Cabezas, or around the many other palaces and family mansions, to view and applaud the noblemen as they came out on horseback, accompanied by their families and escorted by their teams of servants laden with food, wine and seats for their betters.

The Plaza de la Corredera had been made ready for fighting the bulls that burst on to it one by one through the arch and passageway leading to Calle del Toril in its east façade. In the north wall, the longest on this unevenly shaped square, barriers had been put up in front of the porches of the houses that looked on to the square, and their balconies, adorned with tapestries and shawls, were rented by the town council to noblemen and rich merchants who competed with each other in the lavishness of their dress. Among them, mingling discreetly and in defiance of the papal edict, were priests and members of the cathedral chapter. On the south side, against a white wall which the town council had ordered built in order to close off the square, rose wooden platforms on which could be found the chief magistrate as representative of the King and the governor of the bullring, together with other nobles and gentlemen. Dotted around the rest of the square there were more fences, behind which members of the public could protect themselves from the bulls.

From Plaza de las Cañas, where the servants were installed with spare horses for the bullfighters and those of their families, Hernando heard the roar of the crowd as the opening parade got under way. Each nobleman was accompanied by the two footmen carrying their lances, and they were all dressed in Moorish costume, their garments adjusted to allow them freedom of movement. Their hats and cloaks hung from their left shoulders, and they all wore swords. Every nobleman was dressed in the colours that matched his team's livery, and rode in Moorish fashion with short stirrups. The foreman from the tannery kept his word and was waiting for Hernando in Plaza de las Cañas. Thanks to him, Hernando succeeded in getting past the bailiffs, who were preventing the public from mixing with the gentlemen's servants. Hernando had his large grass basket with him, but he could see he was not the only one who had come to collect manure.

That March evening, eight horsemen were lined up to fight the bulls. The chief magistrate solemnly handed the bailiff the key to the square to signify that the fiesta could begin. Four of the horsemen left the arena while the remaining four took up position. The horses pawed the ground, snorting and sweating. Silence fell in the Corredera as the bailiff opened the barrier closing off Calle del Toril, and then all at once there was a loud cheer as a huge black bull, prodded by the assistants, ran bellowing into the square. The bull plunged round the square at full gallop, battering against the stockades whenever people shouted at it, slapped the planks or launched darts at it. After the initial rush, the bull slowed to a trot, and more than a hundred people leapt into the ring and goaded it with capes; the most daring went right up to it, swerving wildly to one side when it turned to face them. Some did not manage to get out of the way in time and were gored, trampled underfoot or hurled into the air. While the crowd enjoyed itself, the four noblemen stayed in position, reining in their horses, judging the beast's mettle and whether it was worth doing battle with.

At a set moment, Don Diego López de Haro, a gentleman of the house of Carpio, who was decked out in green livery, called to the bull to attract its attention. One of his footmen ran towards the people pestering the bull and forced them back. The space between the bull and the horseman was cleared and the nobleman shouted again: 'Bull!'

The enormous beast turned to face the horseman and they eyed each other from a distance. In almost complete silence, the entire square waited for the imminent charge. At that moment, the second footman rushed up to Don Diego with a lance hewn from ash. It was short and thick with a sharp iron point; about three handspans from the tip cuts had been made in the wood, which were covered in wax. This was so that it would snap easily when plunged into the bull. In case their help was needed, the three other horsemen edged closer, careful not to distract the bull. The nobleman's horse bucked nervously until it was sideways on to the animal. The square was immediately filled with whistles and shouts of protest: the encounter had to be head-on, face to face, without any tricks contrary to the rules of horsemanship.

But Don Diego did not need any censure. He was already spurring his horse to line it up facing the bull. The footman stayed beside his lord's right stirrup with the lance held up so that all he had to do was grab it as soon as the bull charged.

Don Diego taunted the bull again, while at the same time waving the green cape on his shoulder in the air. The glittering green fluttering in the rider's hands caught the bull's attention.

'Bull! Come on, bull!'

He did not have to wait long for the charge. A vast black blur hurled itself at horse and rider. Don Diego firmly gripped the lance his footman was holding up, pressing his elbow tight to his body. The footman escaped just as the animal met the horse. Don Diego struck the bull on its withers with the lance. It sank in a few inches before snapping, halting the beast's vicious lunge. The crack of the splintering wood was the signal for the square to break out in cheers, but although it was fatally wounded, with blood gushing from its side, the bull made an effort to attack the horse again. By now, however, Don Diego had unsheathed his heavy two-handed sword and dealt the animal a well-aimed blow to the forehead, splitting its skull. The huge black beast keeled over dead.

While the horseman galloped round the square, patting his horse's neck, saluting the crowd and receiving their applause and the honours of his victory, people threw themselves on the animal's corpse, fighting each other to grab the tail, testicles or whatever part they could cut off before the fiesta began again.

These were the 'offal sellers' who afterwards sold the leftovers, especially the valuable bull's tail, to the innkeepers of the Corredera.

Hearing the shouts and sudden silences from Plaza de las Cañas, Hernando tried to imagine how the bullfight was progressing. He had never seen one before, and the closest he had been to a bull was when he had jumped on top of Fátima to save her from one. What would be happening in the square? As he wondered he fought for the manure with the others who were trying to collect it. 'You mustn't let us down this evening,' the foreman had warned him. 'At the very least you've got to fill the basket. It will do for the top layer of the pit.'

Hernando had one advantage over the others who were after the manure: he was not frightened of horses and was able to take advantage of this. Collecting manure from a street once the horses had already gone by was different from collecting it just as the animal dropped it. The horses were nervous near the square; they knew what was happening. This was not the first time they had faced the bulls, in the city or the countryside, and they were rearing and whinnying with obvious anxiety. His rivals were not used to dealing with thoroughbreds belonging to noblemen, some of which were bad-tempered, and all of which were highly strung. As soon as Hernando saw that one of them was dropping dung and that someone was running to collect it, he would rush out and deliberately startle the horse. His rivals would usually back off in fear from the steed's threatening legs, and Hernando would pounce on the manure. The noblemen's servants who acted as grooms and who alternated between Plaza de las Cañas and the Corredera, depending on whether their lord was there or not, found this contest highly amusing, and would alert Hernando when one of the horses began dropping.

By the time the square was cheering the arrival of the seventh bull, he had filled the large grass basket. He was not permitted to enter the tannery on a Sunday so he sent word to the foreman who came looking for the manure.

'We'll have time to fill another one,' the man said as he took the basket.

Hernando snorted angrily when the foreman turned his back and headed for the tannery. He took advantage of the moment to slip through the servants until he reached the entrance gate for the horsemen beside the white wall on the south side of the square. He found himself alongside a young groom with whom he had exchanged smiles during the tussles over the horse droppings. Until now, the fiesta had proceeded without incident: each nobleman displaying his bullfighting craft with more or less skill for the enjoyment of the people. Hernando managed to lean on the fence that served as a gate just as a large red bull launched itself at a horseman mounted on a horse similar to the one Aben Humeya had once presented to him. For a moment or two, Hernando felt that tough horse between his legs again, and imagined he was a Muslim nobleman high in the Alpujarra, free in the mountains, eager for victory . . . The din ringing throughout the square brought him back to reality. The horseman had made a mistake with the lance, which had slipped and pierced the bull's rump, where the wound was not fatal. Instantly, another nobleman came to the rescue and pranced about on his horse to distract the bull and get it away from the first horseman so it didn't attack him. Once the horseman had steadied himself, the second lance was enough to wound the bull fatally. The eighth bull, a nut-brown beast, did no more than trot round the square threatening to gore and then running away from the people who taunted it. One of the noblemen shouted at it and the bull raced four or five yards before stopping in front of the horseman and backing off. People began to whistle.

'What's happening?' Hernando asked the young servant.

'It's too tame,' he answered without taking his eyes off the bullring. 'The horsemen won't fight it,' he added.

And so it turned out. The four noblemen in the Corredera at that moment withdrew solemnly, making those at the gate clear a path. The gangway was shut again; and by the time Hernando had taken up his position once more, he saw that the square had filled with people and even dogs, who were chasing and taunting the animal. One of the many capes they threw at its head got snared in the bull's horns, blinding it. This was the cue for several men to jump on its back and set about stabbing it. Others set about its legs to slit its tendons. One of the men succeeded in severing the main tendon of the animal's left leg with a scythe and the bull fell. From there they went on stabbing until it was dead.

They had still not finished cutting off its tail when the next bull entered the square; a smaller one but very agile, full of movement, dark coloured with a white nose.

'Out of the way, idiot!'

Hernando was so absorbed by the bull that he did not realize the groom and the others had moved away from the fence. He obeyed the order and cleared a path for a fat nobleman whose tunic looked as if it was about to burst over his stomach. Two sullen footmen followed in his wake, while behind them rode three more nobles who joked as they pointed at the fat horseman ahead of them.

'The Count of Espiel,' the young servant whispered, as if, despite the racket and the distance separating them, the count could hear him. 'He has no idea how to fight bulls but he insists time and again on coming out to the square.'

'Why?' Hernando asked in the same whisper.

'Pride? Honour?' was all the young man said by way of reply.

No sooner had he set foot in the square than the footman who was not carrying the lances began to shout at the crowd to stop pestering the bull and let the confrontation with his lord take place. They grudgingly gave up on the entertainment the other nobles had let them enjoy, and even avoided whistling when the Count of Espiel called the bull and turned his horse quickly to the left to be better able to deal with the charge. Hernando saw that the other noblemen were no longer smiling. One of them, clad in purple, was shaking his head. Despite the fact the horse was in a good position for taking on the bull, the count missed and struck the animal on the snout with the point of the lance when it jumped up before reaching the horse. The lance was knocked from his hand. The count swore and, unable to stop the charge, missed a precious opportunity to get the horse out of the bull's path.

He sank his spurs in the horse's flanks but the bull had already hurled itself at it and, in full flight, gored the horse's stomach with its two impressive horns. The count was thrown and rolled on the ground while his horse remained hoisted on the spirited bull's horns. After a few strides the bull raised its head, pitching the horse into the air and slitting its belly as if it were nothing more than an old piece of cloth. The horse's dying neighs reached the furthest spectators in the Corredera. The bull lowered its head; the horse fell to the ground and the bull went on tormenting its victim, goring it time and again, dragging it round the square, determined to destroy it and oblivious to the riders trying to distract it. The beast pushed the horse over to the fence where Hernando was standing. Blood spattered him when the bull tossed the horse again; the animal's intestines and organs flew through the air.

Before Hernando realized it, the Count of Espiel had positioned himself in front of the bull and the dead horse, sword in hand.

'Bull!' he roared, grasping his weapon in both hands high above his head. The bull heard the call and raised its blood-soaked head to the nobleman, at which point he landed a tremendous blow on the nape of its neck. The fine Toledo steel sliced halfway through the mound of flesh and the bull toppled over beside the horse.

This was a count, a Spanish grandee! To begin with, the cheering was restrained, and came only from the nobles, his equals, but when the Count of Espiel raised his blood-spattered sword as a sign of victory, cheers rang out all round the Corredera.

'A horse!' the count shouted to one of his footmen while he proudly received the people's acclaim.

Hernando and the others had to make way again as the footman ran towards Plaza de la Paja in search of another horse.

'What for?' Hernando asked the servant.

'Noblemen have to leave the square on horseback,' he answered. 'They can't do so on foot. If his horse dies, they fetch him another one. It's not the first time it's happened with the count,' he went on to say just as the count's footman was coming back, leading a tall chestnut stallion by the bridle.

'My horse!' the count demanded from the bullring.

Hernando and the servant helped to open the gangway fully to let the new mount through but as soon as it set eyes on the first horse and the bull dead in front of it, and smelt the blood from the huge pool that encircled them, it reared up and broke free among the crowd. A servant tried to grab it again but the animal was in a frenzy. It whinnied frantically and reared again, its hooves flailing in the air close by the servants' heads, and immediately afterwards kicked out wildly. Two men were knocked flying by kicks to the chest and stomach, while another suffered a similar fate when the horse butted him fiercely. The count kept shouting for his horse but there was little space in the gangway and the crowd of servants trying to deal with the stallion only enraged it still further. Some of the other horsemen fighting the bulls approached the entrance to the square but did not seem inclined to help; one of them even smiled when he heard the Count of Espiel's exasperated shouts.

At this point, the stallion rose up on its hind legs and pawed the air just where Hernando and his companion were standing. Hernando jerked out of the way, seeing in his mind's eye the image of the horse's bloodshot eyes popping out of their sockets, the same colour of blood that burst from his companion's face when the stallion's hoof struck him full on the forehead. It would smash them to pieces! The animal was pawing the ground ready to rear up again when Hernando jumped on its head. He covered its eyes with his body, then grabbed hold of one of its ears and bit it as hard as he could, while he wrenched at the other one. He felt the horse's painful whinny in his stomach, and when the animal lowered its head under his weight, Hernando twisted its neck sharply and viciously until he'd hauled it to the ground.

With Hernando lying on its head and still biting its ear, the horse tried to stagger to its feet, but failed because it could not bend its neck. It struggled as hard as it could for a few moments but gradually gave up.

'Keep still!' he heard someone shout at the servants who had come running.

He stopped biting the animal's ear but kept the other one twisted in his hand. All he could think to do was quietly recite some suras with his lips close to the horse's ear in an effort to calm it down. He stayed that way for a few long moments, without looking at anything or anybody, reciting suras while the horse began to breathe normally again.

'I'm going to cover its face with a cloak, lad.' It was the same voice that had ordered the servants to stay still. Hernando could only see some silver spurs. 'I'll slip it between your body and the horse's head. Don't let it get up.'

Hernando clung on, making room for the man with the silver spurs to spread the cloak. As he was doing so, Hernando also heard him complain quietly: 'Pompous ass! He doesn't deserve to own such horses.' Hernando pulled his stomach in, watching the man slide the cloak between his belly and the horse's head. 'Idiot grandee!' the man muttered as he finished the task. 'Now,' he told Hernando, 'you must let him up bit by bit. First he'll turn his neck to lift his head and then he'll stretch his front legs to give him some purchase.' Hernando already knew this. 'That's when you must finish wrapping the cloak under his jaw so that he can't get free. Can you do it? Can you handle it?'

'Yes.'

'Now,' the man said.

Exhausted, the stallion got to its feet much more slowly than Hernando had been anticipating, so he had no difficulty knotting the cloak under the jaw as the man with the spurs had said. Once on its feet, the horse stood quietly, its face hooded. Hernando stroked its neck and whispered to calm it. One of the count's servants went to take the horse by the bridle but a hand stopped him.

'Incompetent fools!' Hernando turned towards that familiar voice. Don Diego López de Haro, a councillor of Córdoba, master of the King's horse to Philip II, was standing next to him. 'You'll only enrage the poor horse again,' he said to the servant. 'You don't even know how to recognize a good horse, like your—' He fell silent and shook his head. 'You're only fit to deal with asses and donkeys! Lad, you lead it to the count.' Hernando noticed how Don Diego spat out that last word.

What he did not see was the way the nobleman half closed his eyes and rested his chin in his right hand, interested to see what Hernando would do when he entered the square: the stallion would smell the blood again. And it did. The horse tried to pull back, but Hernando tugged at the bridle and gave the animal a sharp kick in the stomach. The stallion quivered, but obeyed and stepped into the Corredera. Hernando had already gone past the corpses of the horse and the bull, with Don Diego nodding in satisfaction at his back, when the Count of Espiel shouted at him from where he was still waiting: 'How dare you kick my horse? It is worth more than your life!'

The two footmen attending the nobleman in the square ran towards Hernando. One snatched the bridle out of his hand, while the other tried to grab hold of his arm.

'Seize him!' the Count of Espiel ordered.

After their long wait, the crowd began to shout again. No sooner had Hernando felt the footman touch his arm than he roused the stallion, which whirled round and sent the footmen flying with its rump. Hernando took advantage of the con-fusion to make his escape. He leapt over the carcass of the bull and started to run towards Plaza de la Paja. As he passed by Don Diego, the nobleman waved at the servants he had been talking to as he watched how Hernando got on in the square. The foot-men ran after him. When he saw that two footmen were chasing the lad, one of the bailiffs who was keeping an eye on Plaza de la Paja threw himself on Hernando and managed to hold on to him. A little further back, several of the Count of Espiel's servants were also trying to catch up with him.

'What—?' began the bailiff.

'Let him go!' one of the footmen ordered, snatching his prey out of the bailiff's hands.

'Seize them!' the other footman added, pointing to the Count of Espiel's servants. 'They want to kill him!'

That simple accusation was enough for the bailiffs to confront the count's men, and enough also for Hernando and the footmen to make themselves scarce on the way to Potro.

Meanwhile, the Count of Espiel rode his horse proudly round the Corredera, to the cheers of the public.

'Get those carcasses out of here.' Pointing at the dead bull and horse, Don Diego ordered all the servants watching the scene from the gate. 'Otherwise,' he said with quiet irony to two horsemen near him, 'that idiot will be incapable of leaving the square and we'll be here until nightfall.'

31

A FEW DAYS before the Sunday of the bullfights, Fátima and Jalil, whose Christian name was Benito and who, together with Hamid, was one of the elders of the Morisco community in Córdoba, were heading for the prison, each of them carrying food they had managed to collect for the prisoners, as they had been doing regularly. They were talking about Hernando and his work for the community.

'He's a good man,' said Jalil, 'young, healthy and strong. He should get married and have a family.'

Fátima said nothing. She lowered her gaze and slowed her steps.

'There is a chance to sort out your difficulty,' said Jalil, who was well aware of the situation.

She stopped and asked the elder, 'What do you mean?'

'Has Aisha had her baby?' Jalil asked her, indicating that she should keep walking. They circled the mosque until they came to the Perdón gate where Calle de la Cárcel began. Fátima saw how the elder was looking out of the corner of his eye at the symbol of Muslim domination of the West while she quickened her step to catch up with him.

'Yes,' she answered. 'A beautiful boy.' She said it sadly. Córdoba had taken Humam from her; Córdoba had given Aisha a new son.

Jalil believed he understood her. 'You are still young and, despite appearances, you are strong. You prove it day by day.

Trust in God.' Jalil said nothing for a while, but as they entered Calle de la Cárcel, he spoke again. 'When you married Brahim, was he poor?'

'No. He was the deputy of Ibn Abbu, the King of al-Andalus, and had everything he could ask for. He rode the streets of Láujar on the finest white mule . . .'

She fell silent at once when they came face to face with two women dressed in black who were accompanied by servants and followed by some pages who were holding aloft the trains of their dresses to prevent them getting dirty. There was not enough room in the narrow street for so many people to pass by and the two Moriscos wisely stepped aside. The two women did not even notice them, but Fátima and Jalil both noticed the children acting as pages: they were probably Moriscos, children stolen from their mothers in order to convert them to Christianity. The elder sighed and the two of them stood silently for a few moments while the women and their train went down the street.

'It was the best white mule in the Alpujarra,' she whispered once the group had turned towards the cathedral.

Jalil nodded as if that revelation was interesting. He came to a halt a few steps from the prison gate, where relatives of the prisoners were crowding round.

'The money your husband makes . . . I mean, who supports you?'

'I don't know,' she admitted. 'All of them. Brahim and Hernando both hand over their wages to Aisha to manage—'

'Hernando's as well?' Jalil interrupted her.

'Of course! Although it might not amount to much, we couldn't live without it. Brahim does nothing but complain about it.'

'And now, with a new child, I imagine it will be even more difficult.'

'It seems that's the only thing on his mind: his new son, a "man child" who has brought the smile back to his face!' Fátima wondered if in fact she had ever seen him smile openly, aside from that cynical curl of the lip he customarily adopted. Certainly not, she concluded. 'But if he's not with the boy,' she went on, 'all he does is moan about the miserable wages they pay him in the fields.'

Jalil nodded. 'A husband', he then explained, 'must look after his wife. He must provide food and drink for her, dress her, give her shoes to wear . . .' At this point the elder looked down at Fátima's feet, at her leather clogs, which were torn and had holes in them, the soles almost completely worn away. 'He must provide an appropriate dwelling. If he does not do all this, his wife can ask to be rid of him.' The girl shut her eyes and dug her nails into the piece of hard bread she was bringing to the prison. 'Our laws state that only if a wife married her husband in the full knowledge that he was poor does she lose the right to seek a divorce if he cannot provide for her.'

'How can I ask for a divorce?' the girl burst out hopefully.

'You would have to go to the *alcall*, and if he thinks you are right, he will grant Brahim somewhere between eight days and two months to improve his situation. If he succeeds, he will be able to return to you, but if the waiting period stipulated by the *alcall* has lapsed and he is still unable to provide for you properly, you will be able to marry someone else and Brahim will have no further rights over you.'

'Who is the *alcall*?'

The elder hesitated. 'We . . . we do not have one. I imagine it could be me, or Hamid, or Karim,' he added, referring to the third elder who made up the council.

'If we don't have an *alcall*, Brahim could refuse to comply.'

'No.' The elder was emphatic. 'Having two wives is in keeping with our laws. He cannot invoke those laws when they work to his advantage and deny them when they work against him. The community will be on your side, it will follow our customs and our laws. Brahim will not be able to dispute anything, neither with us nor with the Christians. Aren't you officially married to Hernando?'

Fátima was pensive. What about Aisha? What would happen

to Aisha if she were to seek a divorce? Faced with the girl's silence, Jalil urged her to carry on towards the prison. Hernando had done a good job and one of the gatekeepers took the food for the Morisco prisoners. A stream of people were constantly going in and out of the building but they themselves did not go in; they did not want to arouse any ill will towards their own people who were prisoners. Fátima handed over the hard bread, some onions and a piece of cheese before setting off once more down the street. At the moment, she thought, Brahim seems contented with his new son. But how long would that last? Although . . . he had other children as well! And what if he had more with her? What if he forced himself on her? It was his right. He could . . .

'I want a divorce, Jalil,' she said at once.

The elder was in agreement. They found themselves once more in front of the Perdón gate of Córdoba's mosque.

'In there,' he said, stopping and pointing towards the temple. 'That's where you should make your claim before the *alcall* or the *cadi*. I ask you, Fátima de Terque,' he added with great formality, 'why do you seek a divorce?'

'Because my husband, Brahim of Juviles, is unable to provide for me as he should.'

After talking to Don Diego López de Haro's footmen in Plaza del Potro, and after checking that the Count of Espiel's servants were no longer chasing them, Hernando went to look for Hamid. The brothel was closed on Sundays and the holy man came out into Calle del Potro without a problem. The whole of Christian Córdoba, including the brothel landlord, as well as most of the Moriscos, were in the square to watch the bull run.

'They want me to work in Córdoba's royal stables,' Hernando said after greeting him, 'with the King's horses. There are hundreds of them. They breed them and break them in and they need people who understand horses.' Then he told him about the business with the count's stallion. 'Apparently that's what made Don Diego notice me.'

'I heard something about it,' said the holy man. 'Some six or seven years ago, King Philip gave instruction that a new breed of horse was to be created. The slow, heavy warhorses are no longer any use to the Christians. Spain is at peace. Of course, Spain wages wars in far-off lands but not here, and ever since the King's father, the Emperor Charles, adopted the ways of the court of Burgundy, the nobles have needed horses to show themselves off on their excursions, at their festivals, their jousting contests or at their bullfights. I understand that what they are trying to create is the perfect courtly horse. And the King chose Córdoba to put his plan into practice. They are building some magnificent stables near the fortress, where the Inquisition is based. Some Morisco builders are working on it. I congratulate you,' Hamid said finally.

'I'm not sure.' The look on Hernando's face reflected his doubts. 'I'm fine here. I can do what I want and can move freely around the city. Despite the wages . . .' He thought about the salary of twenty reales a month plus a dwelling that Don Diego's footmen were offering him. 'If I say yes, I wouldn't be able to look after the Moriscos arriving in the city.'

'Take the job, my son,' Hamid urged. Hernando was about to object but the old man went on: 'It's vital that we get well-paid, responsible jobs. Someone else can carry out the work you are doing now and don't think for a moment that you will have nothing to do for the community. We must organize ourselves. Little by little we're getting there. When our brothers begin to work as artisans or merchants and leave the fields behind, they acquire money for our cause. Any one of them is infinitely more valuable than those idle Christians. Make the most of it. Work hard and, above all, keep up the learning we worked on in the Alpujarra: read, write. All over Spain men are making themselves ready. We – I – will be gone one day and someone must carry on after us. We must not allow our beliefs to be forgotten!' Hamid grasped Hernando by the shoulders impulsively in the middle of the empty street. The contact and his obvious passion sent a shiver down the boy's spine. 'We cannot let them conquer us again and we cannot let our children forget the religion of their ancestors!' Hamid's voice broke. Hernando looked him in the eyes; they were moist. 'There is no god but God, and Muhammad is the messenger of God,' Hamid intoned, as if it were a victory chant.

A tear . . . a single tear ran down the holy man's cheek.

'Know', Hernando added, reciting the Morisco profession of faith, 'that all people must understand there is only one God in His kingdom. He created everything that exists in the world, the high and the low, the throne and the footstool, the heavens and the earth . . .'

When Hernando had finished, the two men embraced.

'My son,' Hamid mumbled, his face buried in the boy's shoulder.

Hernando held him tightly in his arms.

'There is a problem,' Hernando complained after a few moments. 'They have offered me a dwelling. Fátima . . . As far as the Christians are concerned, she is my wife, she's registered as such, which means she would have to come and live with me, and that's impossible. I don't know if I can turn down the lodging or if I have to live in it.'

'Perhaps you won't have to turn anything down.' Hamid drew away from him. 'A few days ago, Fátima asked for a divorce from Brahim.'

'She didn't say anything to me!'

'We are dealing with it in council. We asked her not to tell you; we asked her not to say anything to anybody until we began the hearing and informed Brahim.'

'Can she . . . Will she be able to divorce him?' stammered Hernando.

'If what she claims is correct, and it is, then yes. This very day, when everyone was at the bullfights, we met and agreed to start the process. If the decision goes in favour of Fátima, and Brahim does not come up with enough money to provide for her within two months, she will be a free woman.'

* * *

That night, Hamid and the two other elders on the Muslim council presented themselves at Brahim's house in Calle de Mucho Trigo. The holy man had asked Hernando to make sure he was out that evening, and to find somewhere else to sleep, which he had no difficulty doing.

For her part, Fátima knew that the council was meeting that Sunday to deal with her request for divorce. Jalil had told her so.

That afternoon, when Brahim and the rest of the household went to see the bullfight, Fátima stayed with Aisha and the baby. They had baptized him with the name Gaspar, the same as one of the godparents, two old Christians whom the parish priest of San Nicolás had chosen for that role as was required in the case of baptisms of Morisco children. Neither Aisha nor Brahim had a preference for any particular Christian name and went along with the priest's suggestion: the child would be called Gaspar.

The baptism cost them three maravedís for the priest, a cake for the sacristan and some eggs as a gift for the godparents, as well as the white linen stole the baby wore, which was left for the church. Brahim had to ask for a loan to cover these expenses. Before the baptism, the priest checked that Gaspar was not circumcised, just as the midwife who had attended the delivery had done. No one, though, checked how, when they got home, Aisha washed the newborn's little head time and time again to clean off the holy oils. They had decided to give him the Muslim name of Shamir. The ceremony had taken place one night, a few days before the Christian baptism, with the baby held pointing in the direction of Mecca after he had been washed from head to foot, dressed in clean clothes, and the gold hand of Fátima placed around his neck while prayers were recited in his ears.

On that Sunday evening in March, the two women were sitting in the courtyard of the house.

'What's wrong?' Aisha finally asked her, breaking the silence.

Fátima had asked her to let her have Shamir and she spent a long while rocking him, singing softly, looking at him and caressing him, so completely absorbed in the baby that she said nothing to Aisha. At first Aisha thought the young girl was missing Humam and so she respected her silence and her grief, but as time passed and the girl did not even look at her, she felt there was something more to it.

Fátima did not answer her question. She pressed her lips to stifle a slight shiver, which Aisha immediately noticed.

'Tell me, child,' she persisted.

'I have asked for a divorce from Brahim,' she admitted.

Aisha took a deep breath.

For the first time since Fátima had taken Shamir in her arms, the two women looked at each other. It was Aisha who allowed tears to flow first. Fátima was not long in joining her and they both wept looking at each other.

'Finally . . .' Aisha made an effort to overcome the weeping. 'Finally you will be able to escape. You should have done so a long time ago, when Ibn Umayya died.'

'What will happen?'

'What will happen is that you will find happiness at last.'

'I mean . . .'

'I know what you mean, dear one. Don't worry.'

'But—'

Aisha reached out her arm and very gently put her fingers on the girl's lips. 'I am happy, Fátima. I am happy for you both. God has put me to the test and after all the misfortunes I've suffered He has rewarded me with the birth of Shamir. You have suffered as well and you deserve to be happy again. We must not doubt the will of God. Enjoy the blessings He has decided to grant you.'

But what would Brahim say? Fátima asked herself, unable to contain a shiver of fear when she thought about the muleteer's violent nature.

Brahim let fly with a thousand curses when Jalil, accompanied by Hamid and Karim, informed him of his second wife's petition for divorce. Fátima and Aisha sheltered one another, staying as close to each other as they could in a corner of the room. Then, as if it had just occurred to him, Brahim called into question the council's authority.

'Who are you to make a decision about my wife?' he bellowed.

'We are the leaders of the community,' answered Jalil.

'Says who?'

'As far as you're concerned' – this time it was the other elder, Karim, or Mateo by his Christian name, who intervened, gesturing towards the door – 'for now, they do.'

As if in answer to a prearranged signal, three sturdy young Moriscos appeared and stood behind the elders. Merely sizing up the strength of one of them was enough for Brahim.

'It does not have to be like this, Brahim,' said Hamid in an attempt to calm things down. 'You know that to all intents and purposes we are the leaders of our community. Nobody has elected us but neither have we set ourselves up in this position; we have not sought to be such. You will respect the learned. You will obey the elders. Those are the commandments.'

'What is it you want?'

'Your second wife', Jalil explained, 'has complained to us that you do not provide for her in an appropriate fashion—'

'And who can do so in this city?' Brahim interrupted, shouting. 'If I had my mules . . . They rob us! They pay us a pittance . . .'

'Brahim' – Hamid spoke again, evenly – 'think about the consequences of your words before you say anything. In the light of Fátima's petition, we are bound to instigate a hearing and that is what we have done. That is why we are here, to give you a chance to present whatever you think is relevant, to call on witnesses if you so wish, and then to reach a decision in accordance with our laws.'

'You? I know perfectly well what decision you will reach. You've already done it once, do you remember? In the church at Juviles. You'll always take the side of the Nazarene!'

'I will not take part. No judge can do so if he is in possession of facts before the hearing. Rest easy on that score.'

Jalil decided to intervene to put a stop to any possible personal disputes. 'Brahim of Juviles, your second wife, Fátima, has complained that you are unable to provide for her. What have you to say to that?'

'To you?' spat Brahim. 'To an old man from the Albaicín in Granada? It was probably you and others like you, cowards the whole lot of you, who decided not to join the uprising. You betrayed your brothers in the Alpujarra—'

'I am asking about your wife,' Jalil insisted.

'Do you have a wife, old man? Can you provide for her? Can anyone provide for a wife in this city?'

'Does that mean you cannot provide for her?' Karim interjected.

'I mean', drawled Brahim, 'that nobody can do so in Córdoba.'

'Is that the extent of your plea to this hearing?' asked Jalil.

'Yes. You all know it, you're all aware of our situation. Why put on this pantomime?'

Jalil and Karim conferred quietly. In the corner, Aisha reached for Fátima's hand and squeezed it tight.

'Brahim of Juviles,' Jalil pronounced, 'we recognize the hardships afflicting our people. We suffer them as you do and we realize the difficulties facing one and all, not just in providing for their wives but in feeding and dressing their children. We would not accept a wife's petition based on such reasons. It is true that I cannot provide for my wife either, not as I was able to do in Granada. However, there is not a single believer in Córdoba who has two wives as you do. If, as you say, nobody can provide for a wife in this city, how can you claim to do so for a second wife? We grant you a period of two months to prove to this council that you are in a position to care adequately for both of your wives. Once that period of time has elapsed, if you cannot comply and she insists, Fátima will be taken away from you.'

Brahim listened to the verdict without moving a muscle. Only his narrowed eyes gave any indication of the anger that was gnawing away at him. Then Karim spoke. Hamid had made a request of the two elders. 'I know him well,' he'd said, referring to Brahim. 'He could kill her rather than hand her over,' he'd assured them.

'Out of consideration for your son and given the scant resources at your disposal, we do not demand of you, as normally required by law, that you support your second wife during the *idda*. We free you from that responsibility for the sake of the child. But, in the meantime, Fátima will live under our protection.'

'You dog!' muttered Brahim, confronting Hamid.

The three young Moriscos immediately moved between him and the holy man.

'Come with us, Fátima,' Jalil urged her.

Aisha prised apart her and Fátima's tightly entwined fingers. Both their hands were clammy. Fátima reached out to touch her companion one last time, and then walked towards the elders.

32

A T DAWN, Hernando arrived at the royal stables, a new building beside the fortress of the Christian monarchs, seat of the Córdoba Inquisition. Since arriving in Córdoba, Hernando, like the rest of the Moriscos, had stayed clear of that district, San Bartolomé, situated between the mosque and the episcopal palace, the Guadalquivir and the western edge of the city wall. It was not just that the Inquisition and its prison were to be found there, or the episcopal palace, with its constant comings and goings of priests and those involved in the Inquisition, but that, unlike the rest of Córdoba's neighbourhoods, not a single free Morisco was registered in San Bartolomé. Its inhabitants were different from the rest of the city: this was a parish that had been added to the plan of the city devised after the Reconquest and that, by royal decree, was populated with stout, sturdy men required to be skilled archers in time of war: a kind of city militia always ready to defend the city walls. These qualities epitomized the privileged people from San Bartolomé, who considered themselves above the rest of the inhabitants. They even married amongst their kind, and had many running battles with the rest of the parishes. Few Moriscos wanted to get involved with inquisitors, priests or such proud and haughty people.

That night, Hernando was able to shelter in the house of the wool carder who had found himself a wife. He was treated to a fine dinner, which they all enjoyed in an atmosphere of some nostalgia, with salted spicy lamb, pepper and dried coriander, all fried in oil as was the way in the Granada they all yearned for. Before they had finished eating, Karim, who also lived on Calle de los Moriscos, called at the wool carder's house and joined the gathering after leaving Fátima in his wife's care. Hernando and she were not allowed to see each other during the two months that had been granted to Brahim.

What were two months? Hernando again thought to himself as he made his way to the stables. His happiness would be complete . . . if it weren't for his mother. When they were outside the house saying goodbye, Hernando asked after Aisha, and Karim told him his mother was facing up to the situation with great strength of mind, that he should not worry: the community was behind them.

'Prosper, my boy,' the elder encouraged him. 'Hamid told me about Don Diego and the horses. We need people like you. Work hard! Study! We'll look after all the rest.'

Karim disappeared into the cool darkness of that March evening with the words, 'We have faith in you,' which disrupted the fantasies about Fátima that Hernando let himself indulge in endlessly that night. *We have faith in you!* When Hamid had said that to him, it was as if he were addressing the child from Juviles, but hearing it from the lips of that unknown elder from the Albaicín . . . They had faith in him! For what? What more was required of him?

He crossed the Campo Real, scattered with litter as usual, and glanced to his left where the majestic fortress stood tall. The Inquisition! A shiver ran down his spine on seeing the four towers, each one different, which rose up from the corners of the fortress with its high, crenellated walls. The long façade of the royal stables began right there, at the end of the fortress. Hernando could smell the horses inside, hear the shouts of the grooms and the neighing of the animals. He stopped at the broad entrance door, next to the ancient wall, near the Belén tower.

The stable was open, and those sounds and smells he had

picked up on the other side of the façade hit him when he stopped at the threshold of the open door. Nobody was guarding the entrance and, after waiting for a moment or two, Hernando took a few steps forward. To his left a great nave-like building stretched ahead of him, with a broad central corridor on both sides of which, between pillars, were stalls full of horses. The pillars supported a long straight sequence of low vaults, which led the visitor on past one arch, then another and another . . .

Youngsters were working with the horses in the stalls.

Standing still at the entrance to the body of the building, in the middle of the corridor, Hernando clicked his tongue to stop the first two horses on his right, tethered to a ring on the wall, from biting their necks.

'They do it all the time,' said someone behind him. Hernando turned quickly when the man who had spoken followed suit and clicked his tongue more forcefully. 'Are you looking for someone?' he asked.

He was a middle-aged man, tall and sinewy, dark-skinned and well dressed, with leather buskins above the knee fastened with straps along the calf, his shoes and fitted white breeches free of frills or embellishments. After looking him up and down, the man smiled at him. He was smiling at him! How many times had anyone done that in Córdoba? Hernando smiled back.

'Yes,' he answered. 'I'm looking for the groom of Don Diego . . . López?'

'López de Haro,' the man came to his aid. 'Who are you?'

'Hernando is my name.'

'Hernando what?'

'Ruiz. Hernando Ruiz.'

'Well, Hernando Ruiz. Don Diego has many grooms. Which of them are you looking for?'

Hernando shrugged his shoulders. 'Yesterday, at the bullfight—'

'I remember now!' the man interrupted him. 'It was you who

led the Count of Espiel's stallion into the square, wasn't it? I knew you looked familiar,' he added while Hernando agreed. 'I see they didn't catch you, but you should not have helped the count. That man should have had to leave the square on foot and in disgrace; what sort of victory is it when the bull kills a horse because of his stupidity? It was a fine animal,' he muttered. 'In fact, the King should forbid him from getting on a horse, at least in front of a bull . . . or a woman. Good, now I know who you're after. Come with me.'

They left the building with the stalls and went out to a huge central courtyard. There, three horsemen were breaking in horses, two of them mounted on magnificent examples while the third, whom Hernando recognized as Don Diego's groom, was on foot and making a two-year-old colt run in circles around him as far as the head halter the animal was wearing on top of the bit and bridle would allow; the loose stirrups were knocking against its flanks, getting it worked up.

'That's him, isn't it?' The man pointed. Hernando nodded. 'He's called José Velasco. By the way, I'm Rodrigo García.'

Hernando hesitated before shaking Rodrigo's proffered hand. He was not used to Christians offering to shake hands. 'I . . . I am a Morisco,' he announced so that Rodrigo would not be deceived.

'I know,' the other man answered. 'José told me this morning. But here we are all horsemen, trainers, grooms, farriers, bit-makers, whatever. Here, horses are our religion. But be very careful repeating that in front of any priest or inquisitor.'

Hernando noticed that Rodrigo stretched his hand out to him openly as he said these words.

After a while, when the colt's flanks were sweating, José Velasco made it stop, tied up the halter he used to make it run round and led it to a mounting block. He climbed up on this and, helped by a groom who was restraining the colt, mounted it carefully. The other two horsemen stopped their exercises. The young horse stood still and expectant, tensed, its ears drooping, feeling Velasco's weight.

'It's the first time,' Rodrigo whispered to Hernando, as if raising his voice might cause a mishap. Velasco held a long switch crossed over the colt's neck, with the reins and the halter gripped in both hands; he held the reins loosely as if not wanting to disturb the colt with the bit he was chewing at; the halter though was tight to the ring that hung beneath the animal's lower lip. He waited for a moment to see if the colt reacted, but there was no sign and it stayed nervously still, forcing him to encourage it gently. First he clicked his tongue; then, getting no response, he slowly dragged the heels of his spurless boots until they grazed its flanks. At that point, the colt took off like a shot, bucking. Velasco took on the challenge and in the end the colt stopped again, of its own accord, with the rider doing nothing more than holding on.

'That's it,' said Rodrigo. 'He's learnt some manners.'

So it proved. The next time, the colt came out tense, but did not buck. Velasco guided it by means of the halter and at the last moment, without hitting it, he let it see the whip on one side of its head to make it turn the other way, talking to it all the while and patting its neck.

The nearly one hundred Spanish horses quartered in Córdoba's royal stables constituted the select specimens, the flawless ones. They had been chosen from the almost six hundred breeding mares that made up King Philip II's stock and were spread throughout several pastures around Córdoba. Just as Hamid had explained, in 1567 the King had ordered that a new breed of horses be established, to which end he arranged for the purchase of the twelve hundred finest mares in his territories; but it was impossible to find so many mothers of the required quality, so the brood mares came to half that number. Moreover, he instructed that taxes from the salt mines be directed to the enterprise, to include the building of the royal stud in Córdoba and the hire or purchase of pastures needed to accommodate the mares. He put Don Diego López de Haro in charge of the project. The new royal stable master and director of the breed was a Córdoba councillor from the house of Priego.

The new breed of horse had to have a small head, slightly arched with a lean forehead; dark eyes, alert and haughty; quick, lively ears; wide nostrils; flexible, arched neck, thick at the join with the trunk and smoothly linked to the nape, with a little fat where the abundant and thick mane started; and likewise with the tail. It had to be self-assured with a short manageable back, prominent croup and wide, round hindquarters.

But the most important characteristic of a Spanish horse had to be its way of moving, its airs above the ground: elevated, graceful and elegant, as if it did not want to place any of its feet on the burning soil of Andalusia but, after doing so, would hold them in the air, suspended, dancing for as long as possible, fluttering its front legs on the trot or gallop, as if the distance to be covered was of no importance; showing itself off proudly, parading its beauty before the world.

For six years, as the man in charge of the breeding, Don Diego López de Haro sought each and every one of these qualities in the colts born in the pastures of Córdoba, to breed another generation and produce ever more perfect descendants. Animals lacking the desired qualities were sold as rejects, so that in the stables of Córdoba were found the purest, the most perfect, which were named by royal decree the Spanish Thoroughbred.

José Velasco charged Hernando with the care, cleaning, and above all the training of the colts to eat from the trough. During that month of March, spring arrived and with it the time to cover the mares. The royal stable master selected the one-year-old colts to be brought in from the pastures to replace the broken-in horses that were bound for Madrid and the royal stables of the Escorial to be presented to King Philip. No horse of the Spanish breed that Don Diego considered to be among the finest was ever sold; they were all for the King, for his stables or for him to present as gifts to other monarchs, noblemen or leaders of the Church.

The colts arrived wild from the pastures. As Hernando was told during the days leading up to the animals' arrival, there was a great deal of work to do, so that by the time they were two-year-olds the horses were used to the saddle and had been mounted for the first time. He and the others had to get them accustomed to human contact, to letting themselves be touched, groomed, tacked up and looked after. They also had to learn to live in stables, permanently tied to the wall-rings in the stalls, living with other horses beside them. They had to learn to eat and drink from the trough; to obey the halter and be led; and to accept the bits or the weight of the saddle necessary to mount them. All this was unfamiliar to the young horses, who until then had lived freely with their mothers.

If at some point Hernando had dreamt of mounting one of those splendid horses, his dreams vanished as soon as they outlined what his duties would be. Nonetheless, he did fulfil another dream: on the second floor of the royal stud, above the stables, was a series of rooms for use by the stable hands. He was allotted a large dwelling with two rooms, completely independent apart from sharing a kitchen with two other families. In all his nineteen years he had never had so much space to himself! Not in Juviles, much less in Córdoba. Hernando wandered through those two rooms time and again. The furniture consisted of a table with four chairs, a good bed with sheets and a blanket, a small chest of drawers with a wash-basin (he could wash himself!) and even a large clothes chest. What would he put in there? he wondered, before going to the window that overlooked the stable courtyard. When he had shown him his living quarters, the stable administrator had turned round just as Hernando was opening the chest.

'What about your wife?' he asked him as if it was she to whom he should have been showing the place. 'It says in your papers that you are married.'

Hernando had an answer ready for that question. 'She's looking after a sick relative,' he answered firmly. 'She can't leave him for the moment.'

'In any case,' the administrator cautioned him, 'you should get yourselves registered in the San Bartolomé parish without delay. I don't imagine your wife will have any difficulty leaving the invalid long enough to get that done.'

Would there be some problem? The question assailed Hernando once more as he stood at the window watching how Rodrigo was working a dapple-grey horse, persisting in an exercise that the animal could not get right; the horseman's long, silver spurs glinted in the March sun when Rodrigo stuck them in the dapple-grey's flanks. Fátima was still not his wife. Karim had been adamant: the two months granted to Brahim had to pass, during which time Hernando was not allowed to go near her. And what if Brahim found enough money to retrieve Fátima?

The punishment Rodrigo meted out with the spurs when the horse got the exercise wrong again bit into Hernando's flesh as much as into the rebellious animal's flanks. What if Brahim managed it?

Night had fallen and he could not now return to Córdoba. What excuse was he going to give at the gate? thought Brahim. Crouching among the thickets on the road that led from the Roman tavern to the city through the Seville gate, he watched several merchants pass, all of them armed, travelling in groups for protection. He had got hold of a dagger; a Morisco who worked with him in the countryside had lent it to him after he had pestered him time and again.

'Be careful,' the man had warned him, 'if they catch you with it they'll arrest you and I'll lose my dagger.'

Brahim was well aware of that. It was fairly straightforward to bring a hidden weapon into Córdoba mingled with the crowd of people coming back from work in the fields, but to return at night, alone and armed, was nothing other than reckless. In any case, the dagger was not much use to him. Brahim brandished it determinedly at any hint of footsteps and horses. I'll jump on them the next chance I get, he vowed to himself after letting one party of merchants after another get away while he hid in the bushes. But when that new party showed up on the road, the hand he was grasping the dagger with became drenched with sweat, and the legs that were supposed to run towards them refused to do so. How was he going to take on several men armed with swords? Cursing himself, he listened as the sound of their laughter and joking faded into the distance. The next ones, he tried to convince himself. The next lot won't escape me.

He had almost made up his mind when two women and a number of children passed by him, hurrying on their way to Córdoba with a basket of vegetables, but neither of them displayed a miserable bracelet, not even an iron one, on either their wrists or their ankles. What was he going to do with a basket of vegetables?

Darkness descended, and the road, despite being right in front of him, disappeared from sight. No other merchant dared take that route as the shadows lengthened, and the road became silent, leaving him to regret his cowardice still more.

More than half of the two-month term the elders had granted him to prove he could provide for Fátima had passed, and Brahim had not acquired a single coin beyond what they paid him in the fields. In addition, part of his daily wages since then had to be used to pay off the loan for Shamir's baptism. It was impossible to make money working, but equally impossible to steal it.

The Nazarene would keep Fátima. Not even that possibility, which tormented his conscience without respite, infused him with the courage to risk his life against a handful of Christians, however lightly armed they were.

Brahim knew about Hernando. Aisha had seen it as her duty to tell him about his son, and seeing that her husband did not react violently but bottled it up inside himself, panic overcame her as she finally grasped the magnitude of what was happening: Brahim would lose Fátima; Brahim would be insulted and humiliated in front of the community . . . Him! The muleteer from Juviles, Aben Aboo's deputy! On the other hand, that stepson of his, whom he had taken in exchange for a mule and whom he had always despised, was flourishing. He had a well-paid job and, most important of all, would snatch his precious Fátima from him.

Two horsemen racing along the road at full gallop startled him.

'Noblemen!' spat Brahim.

'Ask the Sierra Morena bandits for money,' the dagger man advised him the next day, after Brahim handed it back and admitted his incompetence. 'They always need people in the cities or in the fields, brothers who can supply them with information about when convoys are about to set off and about the comings and goings of people or what the Holy Brotherhood is up to. They need spies and collaborators. I got the dagger from them.'

'How can I find the bandits?' Brahim asked. 'The Sierra Morena is vast.'

'It'll be a case of them coming across you if you venture into the Sierra Morena,' the man replied, 'but be careful the Holy Brotherhood don't get to you first.'

The Holy Brotherhood was a municipal militia made up of two captains and platoons of soldiers, usually a dozen, who kept watch for crimes committed outside the town centres: in the countryside, in the mountains and in villages with fewer than fifty inhabitants that were beyond the reach of all municipal administration. Their justice was usually summary and cruel, and at that time they were hunting for Morisco brigands who kept terrorizing good Christians, ruffians like El Sobahet, a ruthless Valencian outlaw who led one of the bands that held sway in the Sierra Morena, to the north of Córdoba. These were mostly made up of desperate slaves, fugitives from some lord's estate, where vigilance was more lax than in the city, who, owing to the brand on their faces, could not hide in the cities and so opted to do so in the mountains.

The bandits were his only hope, thought Brahim.

At dawn the next day, after passing the church and the cemetery of Santa Marina and leaving behind on their left the Malmuerta tower, which served as a prison for noblemen, Brahim, Aisha and little Shamir left Córdoba through the Colodro gate, heading north towards the Sierra Morena.

He had instructed Aisha to get ready to leave with him and the child. He told her she should bring food and warm clothing. So emphatic was his tone that the woman did not dare ask questions. They went through the Colodro gate in the midst of a swarm of people off to work in the fields or at the slaughterhouse, and then headed in the direction of Adamuz, above Montoro, on the Camino de Las Ventas, the route that linked Córdoba with Toledo across the Sierra Morena. Not far from Montoro they came across four Christians with their throats slit and their tongues cut out; the outlaws must be patrolling the area.

There were several inns on the Camino de Las Ventas for travellers making the journey, so Brahim was careful to take paths away from the main route, even going across country, but their first encounter with the Holy Brotherhood came before they reached Alcolea. Tied to a post sunk in the ground was the decomposing, arrow-pierced body of a man, food for the scavengers and a warning to the local inhabitants: this was the death sentence the Brotherhood imposed on delinquents who dared commit a crime outside the cities. Brahim remembered the precautions he had been advised to take, and forced Aisha to abandon the path they were on and head straight into the sierra, even though it was off the beaten track and they were using it to try to get round the foothills of the Sierra Morena. Among cork oak trees and ravines, his muleteer's instincts enabled him to get his bearings easily and find those little, unknown tracks that only goatherds or people who knew the mountain inside out used.

He and Aisha, who was walking silently behind him with the child on her back, took all day to cover the distance separating

Córdoba from Adamuz, a small village owned by the lord of Carpio; they camped on the outskirts, among the trees, hidden from travellers and from the Brotherhood.

'Why are we fleeing from Córdoba?' Aisha dared to ask her husband as she handed him a piece of stale bread. 'Where are we going?'

'We are not fleeing,' her husband replied brusquely.

The conversation finished there, and Aisha turned her attention to the child. They spent the night in the open air without lighting a fire and fighting off sleep, petrified by the howling of wolves, the grunts of the wild boars, or any sound that might indicate the presence of a bear. Aisha shielded Shamir with her body. Brahim, however, seemed happy; he looked at the moon and let his gaze drift among the shadows, greatly enjoying what had been his way of life before the deportation.

At dawn, in fact, it was the bandits who came upon them. The brigands lay in wait along the Camino de Las Ventas, on the lookout for any traveller coming from Madrid, Ciudad Real or Toledo who had not been prudent enough to travel in company or with protection. They had already noticed them the day before, keeping watch as they always did for any movement that might indicate the arrival of the troops from the Brotherhood, but they had not taken much notice of them: a man and a woman with a child, who were travelling on foot and without baggage, staying off the main roads, were of little interest to them. Despite this, it suited them to know what the three of them were doing in the mountains.

'Who are you and what are you after?'

Brahim and Aisha, who were sitting eating breakfast, had not even heard them approach. Suddenly, two fugitive slaves, their faces branded by red-hot irons and armed with swords and daggers, stood in front of them. Aisha clasped the child to her breast; Brahim made a move to get up but one of the slaves gestured him not to.

'My name is Brahim of Juviles, muleteer of the Alpujarra.'

The bandit nodded that he knew the place. 'My son and my wife,' he added. 'I want to see El Sobahet.'

Aisha turned to look at her husband. What was Brahim after? An immense foreboding overcame her, tightening her stomach. Shamir responded to his mother's distress and burst out crying.

'What do you want to see El Sobahet for?' asked the second bandit.

'That's my business.'

Immediately, the two escaped slaves reached for their swords.

'In the mountains, everything is our business,' one of them replied. 'It doesn't look as though you're in a position to make demands.'

'I want to offer him my services,' Brahim admitted.

'Burdened with a woman and child?' laughed one of the slaves.

Shamir wailed.

'Shut him up, woman!' Brahim ordered his wife.

'Come with us,' the slaves conceded, after exchanging glances and shrugging their shoulders.

They made their way right into the heart of the mountains. Aisha stumbled behind the men, trying to soothe Shamir. Brahim had said he wanted to offer himself to the bandit. It was obvious that Brahim was looking for money to claim back Fátima, but why was he bringing them along? Why did he need little Shamir? She trembled. Her legs gave way and she fell on her knees to the ground with the child clutched to her breast, but she got up and forced herself to keep going. None of the men turned towards her . . . and Shamir would not stop crying.

They came to a small clearing that had been used as a camp by the bandits. There were no tents or shacks; only blankets scattered on the ground and the embers of a bonfire in the centre of the clearing. Leaning against a tree, El Sobahet, tall with bushy eyebrows and an unkempt black beard, was listening to the two slaves who had accompanied Brahim and Aisha. He scrutinized Brahim from where he was, and then ordered him to step forward.

Nearly half a dozen bandits, all branded and in rags, were breaking camp: some of them kept an eye on the new arrivals; others looked at Aisha with undisguised desire.

'Say whatever you have to say quickly,' the outlaw chief warned Brahim before the latter had even reached him. 'As soon as the men we're missing return, we're off. What makes you think I might be interested in your services?'

'Because I need money,' Brahim answered honestly.

El Sobahet grinned cynically. 'All Moriscos need money.'

'But how many of them escape from Córdoba, go deep into the Sierra Morena and reach you?'

The bandit weighed Brahim's words. Aisha tried to listen to the conversation from a few paces off. By now the child had settled.

'The Christians would pay good money to capture me and my men. Who's going to guarantee me that you're not a spy?'

'There you have my wife and my boy child,' argued Brahim pointing towards Aisha. 'I place their lives in your hands.'

'What could you do for us?' El Sobahet asked, satisfied by the answer.

'I'm a muleteer by trade. I took part in the uprising and was deputy to Ibn Abbu in the Alpujarra. I know mule trains; I only have to see them, to glance at their tack and trappings to work out what they are carrying and what their shortcomings are. I can travel with a pack of mules through any place, however dangerous it might be, by day or night.'

'We already have a muleteer with us: my second-in-command, my confidant,' El Sobahet interrupted him. Brahim turned to look at the slaves. 'No. It's none of them. We're waiting for him. And we've already thought about using mules to help us but we move quickly; they would only slow us up.'

'With good animals I can move as fast as any of your outlaws and through places no man would ever reach. You should have them, they would swell your profits.'

'No.' The bandit's no was accompanied by a wave of the

hand. 'I'm not interested . . .' he began to say as if to put an end to the conversation.

'Just let me show you!' Brahim persisted. 'What risk would you be taking?'

'Putting our loot in your hands, muleteer. That's the risk we'd be taking. What would happen if you fell behind with your laden mules? We'd have to wait for you and risk our lives . . . or trust you.'

'I won't let you down.'

'I've heard that promise too many times,' El Sobahet said with a frown.

'I could act as a spy?'

'I already have spies in Córdoba and in the towns around it. I know about every convoy that moves on the Ventas road. If you want to join my band, I'll test you, as I do with everybody. It's the best I can offer you.' At that moment, another group of bandits appeared through the trees. 'Let's go!' shouted El Sobahet. 'I'm thinking about what you said, muleteer, and you can come if you want. But only you, without your wife or child.'

'Bitch! What's that whore doing here?' The roar rang out in the midst of the bustle of men getting ready to leave. El Sobahet gave a start. Brahim turned to where Aisha was.

Ubaid! Aisha stood paralysed in front of the muleteer from Narila who had just arrived back at the camp. In the sudden silence that followed his insults, Ubaid turned to look at Brahim, as if after having come across his wife, he sensed his presence. The two muleteers stared at each other.

'All I need is the Nazarene to make my best dreams come true,' smiled the one-handed muleteer. Brahim trembled and turned towards the bandit chief for help. 'This is the man I've told you about so often.' El Sobahet's expression hardened. 'It was he who cut off my hand.'

'He's yours, my friend. Him and his family,' muttered El Sobahet, pointing to Aisha and the child, 'but be quick about it. We have to get on the road.'

'What a shame the Nazarene is missing! Cut off his hand,'

Ubaid ordered. 'Cut it off! His hand and his son's. So that generations to come will always know why they call Ubaid of Narila the One-handed.'

Before Ubaid finished speaking, two men seized Brahim. Aisha screamed and shielded Shamir just as other bandits tried to snatch him away. The child started wailing again and while Aisha defended her child, lying on top of him on the ground, the men who were struggling with Brahim forced him to his knees. Brahim was shouting, hurling insults and trying to defend himself. The two men stretched out his arm and held it tight before a third bandit sliced the wrist with a scimitar. Brahim, staring wide-eyed at the horrific sight of his chopped-off hand, was immediately dragged to the embers of the fire, where they held the stump to cauterize the wound. Brahim's screams, Aisha's groans and the baby's weeping all mingled together in a single lament when the bandits managed to wrestle the child from his mother's arms.

Aisha leapt after them until she fell at Ubaid's legs.

'I am the Nazarene's mother!' she shouted on her knees, grabbing the bandit's tunic in both hands. 'The child will die. What will hurt Hernando more? Kill me! I give my life for his, but spare my little one, what is he to blame for?' she sobbed. 'What blame . . . ?' she tried to say again before she fell, overcome by uncontrollable weeping.

Ubaid did not try to push the woman away, and this made the outlaws carrying the child stop. The man from Narila hesitated.

'All right,' he agreed. 'Let the child go and kill her. You,' he added, addressing Brahim as he writhed in agony on the ground, 'you will take her head to the Nazarene. And tell him that I have finished here, in Córdoba, what I should have finished in the Alpujarra.'

Aisha let go of Ubaid's tunic and he strode away, leaving the woman alone on her knees. He designated one of the bandits, a branded slave, to execute her. The man approached her with his sword unsheathed.

'There is no god but God, and Muhammad is the messenger of God,' Aisha recited with her eyes closed, surrendering herself to death.

On hearing this profession of faith, the slave halted. He lowered his head. Ubaid raised the fingers of his left hand to the bridge of his nose; El Sobahet observed the scene. The bandit's sword hung in the air for a few moments. Even Shamir was silent. Then the man looked to his companions for support. They were not murderers! Among their number were a silversmith from Granada, three dyers, a shopkeeper . . . they had been forced to become bandits to escape unjust slavery and ignominious treatment. Fight and kill Christians? Yes. Christians had robbed them of their freedom and their beliefs. They were the ones who had enslaved their wives and daughters. But killing a Muslim woman . . .

Before the bandit laid down his sword, El Sobahet and Ubaid exchanged glances. It was not possible to ask that of his men, the bandit chief seemed to say to his deputy, nor should he do it himself; she was a Muslim. Then Ubaid intervened: 'Take your child and your husband and go. You are free. I, Ubaid, grant you your life, the very thing I will take away from your other son.'

Aisha opened her eyes without looking at anybody. She stood up slowly, trembling, and went to the man holding Shamir; he offered him to her without a word. Then she went to where Brahim was sprawled near the embers. She looked at him with contempt and spat at him. 'Dog,' she insulted him.

She left the clearing in the woods in tears, without knowing where to head for.

'Show her where the Ventas road is,' El Sobahet ordered one of the bandits when he saw her heading in the wrong direction, towards the rugged mountains.

33

HERNANDO HANDED a fine three-year-old over to Rodrigo. It was a proud skewbald, with large brown patches on its white coat. Once the colts had been broken in and allowed themselves to be ridden in the riding school at the royal stables, they had to get used to the countryside, to bulls and other animals, to learn to cross rivers and jump obstacles, to gallop along roads but to pull up short with a single tug on the reins. They also had to get to know life in the city: to stay quietly at the blacksmith's and not to react to the blows of the hammer on the anvil; to move among people without being affected by children darting about or the many animals that ran loose in the streets of Córdoba – dogs, hens, and of course the many dark, hairy, black-tailed pigs with pointed ears and snouts often concealing an impressive row of sharp teeth; not to shy at the sound of music and fiestas, as well as all other kinds of unexpected noise. What would happen to these horses, or more especially to their trainers, if the King or any of his family or favourites fell off because their mount was startled by the sound of fifes and drums during a military parade, or the cheering of a crowd at the sight of their lord?

The new colts had not yet been brought in from pasture, and so Hernando did not have any specific tasks in the stables. Every morning Rodrigo mounted the skewbald, while Hernando walked alongside with a long, flexible rod in his hand, as the two of them set off into the city to expose the spirited colt to all kinds of new experiences.

'I've seen you working in the stables and I'm pleased with what you're doing,' said the rider as he put a foot into the stirrup. 'But at the moment you're no different from the other grooms. I want to see if you really do have that special talent that Don Diego thought he spotted in you. Let's ride through Córdoba and show this colt the streets. It's bound to be frightened. When that happens, if you think there is nothing more I can do and that to use my spurs or your rod would be counter-productive, I want you to step in and control it as you see fit. Do you understand?'

Hernando nodded, and Rodrigo mounted the horse. How was he supposed to know when and how to intervene?

'If the colt throws me, which often happens on these first outings,' Rodrigo went on, settling in the saddle, 'your concern is the horse. Whatever happens – if I crash against a wall, or the horse kicks an old woman or destroys a market stall – you must get control of it, make sure it doesn't gallop off through the city, and above all see that it comes to no harm. And remember one thing: by royal order, nobody – I repeat: nobody – not the chief magistrate, nor the bailiffs, nor the officials, nor even the city councillors has any authority or jurisdiction over the horses and staff of the royal stables. Your mission is to protect this animal. If anything happens to me, you are to bring it back safe and sound to the stables, whatever happens and whatever anyone says to you.'

Hernando followed Rodrigo to the stable door, still wondering exactly what was expected of him, but like the horse he had no time to reflect on this much further. As soon as the colt took its first step outside the building and pricked up its ears, bewildered by all the people walking in the Campo Real and by the unknown buildings all round it, Rodrigo spurred it on firmly. The colt leapt forward, and Hernando had to run in order not to fall behind. From then on they spent a hectic morning: the rider forced his mount to gallop down narrow alleyways through throngs of passers-by. He looked for places and situations that were most likely to disturb the animal, while

Hernando struggled to keep up. They rode along Calle de los Caldereros in the cathedral district, where the colt had to withstand the noise of hammering on copper cauldrons. Then they went to the tannery, with all the hustle and bustle there; they paused at the wool carding and dyers' workshops, as well as those of the silversmiths and needle-makers. They passed through Plaza de la Corredera and the markets several times, and went as far as the slaughterhouse and the pottery district. Rodrigo's experience and skill made Hernando's presence almost unnecessary.

In fact he was only called upon on one occasion. Rodrigo pushed his mount close to one of the many pigs that wandered loose on the streets. The huge hog snapped at the horse, squealing and showing its teeth. Terrified, the horse turned and reared, catching its rider unawares. But before it could bolt away from the pig, Hernando whipped it across the haunches, forcing it to stay where it was until its rider regained control. Apart from this incident, all he had to do was to keep the rod close behind the horse and to click his tongue whenever, despite the spurs and its rider's encouragement, it was scared by a noise or sudden movement and did not want to go on.

By the end of the morning, both the colt and Hernando returned to the stables sweating and out of breath.

'Well done, lad,' Rodrigo congratulated him as he jumped to the ground. 'We'll continue tomorrow.'

Hernando led the colt into the stalls and handed it over to a groom. As he was about to leave the stables, a blacksmith who was inspecting the shoes on another horse, someone he had seen several times already, shouted to him.

'Come and help me. Hold this up!' he said. The dark-skinned man passed him one of the colt's rear hooves. When Hernando held it up on his thigh with his back to the horse, the smith started to scrape all the dirt off the shoe. 'I have a message for you,' he whispered, still scraping. 'Your mother's been put in prison.' Hernando almost dropped the horse's hoof. The animal stirred nervously. 'Keep hold!' the smith said, this time in a loud voice.

'How . . . how do you know? What's happened?' he asked, his mouth almost pressed against the smith's ear.

'The elders gave me the message.' From the respectful way he spoke of them, Hernando could tell he was a brother in faith. 'The Inquisition arrested her on the Camino de Las Ventas as she was coming back to Córdoba with her baby in her arms. She had no permit to be outside the city, and has been condemned to sixty days in jail.'

'What was she doing there?'

'Your stepfather has disappeared. Your mother told the Inquisition official that her husband had forced her to leave Córdoba, but that she had given him the slip and was on her way back.' Aisha of course had been careful not to tell the men, and then the official, that they had gone to meet the Muslim outlaws. 'They told me to tell you not to worry, that she is safe, and that they have found a blanket for her and clothing for the baby, and that they are taking them food.'

'How is she?'

'She's well. Both of them are well.'

'And my . . . Did you hear anything about Fátima?' If Brahim had decided to flee from Córdoba, Hernando reasoned, he might have taken Fátima with him. Or had she given herself up?

'She is still living with Karim,' the smith replied. He seemed to know the whole story.

Still apparently concentrating on the smith's efforts to clean the horseshoe, Hernando could not help wondering what exactly this meant: Brahim had fled, leaving Fátima in Córdoba! How much time had to elapse before the *idda* was completed? Two or three weeks?

'Who are you?' he asked when the smith finished his work and indicated that he could put the hoof down.

'My name is Jerónimo Carvajal,' the man said, straightening up.

'Where are you from? When—?'

'Not here.' Jerónimo quelled the lad's curiosity. He paused and rubbed his kidneys, waving his hand as though in pain.

'This work will be the death of me. Follow me,' he said, gathering up his tools and heading for the stable exit.

They passed by the entrance to the building, on the right of which stood a small room that served as the administration office for the stables. There they found the assistant head groom and a clerk who was scribbling in some ledgers.

'Ramón,' the smith said firmly to the groom from the doorway, 'I need some things. I'm taking the new lad with me.'

Ramón, who was standing beside the clerk, merely waved his hand in agreement without even looking up from what the other man was writing. Jerónimo and Hernando went out into the street.

'I am from Oran. My true name is Abbas,' Jerónimo told him once they had left the stables behind. 'I came to Spain to work in the stables of one of the noblemen who defended the city ten years ago. After that, Don Diego took me on in the royal stables.'

They walked beyond the bishop's palace and came to the rear wall of the mosque. Hernando took a good look at Abbas. His African origins were plain to see: his skin was considerably darker than that of the Spanish Moriscos, who were often indistinguishable from the Christians; he was slightly taller than Hernando and had the powerful chest and arms of someone used to hammering on the anvil and to shoeing horses. He had a thick mop of jet-black hair, dark eyes and well-defined features spoilt only by a bulbous nose, which looked as if it had been broken at some point in the past.

'What are we going to buy?' Hernando asked.

'Nothing, although when we get back say we've been looking for things but that I could not find what I wanted.'

By now they had reached the corner of the street with the Sol tavern in it, which flanked the mosque down to the Perdón gate.

'Well then, could we . . .?' Hernando suggested, pointing to the street on their right.

'The prison?' Abbas queried.

'Yes. I'd like to see my mother. I know the governor,' he added, seeing the other's man's hesitation. 'There won't be any problem. I have to speak to her.'

Abbas finally accepted the idea, and they turned down Calle del Sol.

'And I have to talk to you,' he said as they were walking up towards the Perdón gate, leaving on their left the remains of Moorish culture in the shape of magnificent doorways and arabesques sculpted in the stone of the mosque. 'I can understand you want to visit your mother, but don't spend too long there.'

'What do you want to talk about?'

'Afterwards,' the smith replied.

Hernando mixed with the stream of people going in and out of the prison until he finally found the gatekeeper. Abbas stayed outside. Around an interior courtyard flanked with arcades, there were two floors that contained the cells, the governor's quarters and other offices, as well as a small tavern. Hernando greeted the gatekeeper and asked after the fat, slovenly governor, who soon appeared when he heard that the Morisco was there.

A stench of excrement accompanied his arrival. Hernando backed off in horror as the governor held out a right hand smeared with faeces and soaked with urine.

'Someone else trying to hide in the latrines?' Hernando said by way of greeting, after gingerly taking the prison governor's hand.

'Yes,' the other man said. 'He's been condemned to the galleys. This is the third time he's rolled around in shit to try to stop us getting hold of him.' Hernando could not help but smile, in spite of the warm dampness of the hand clutching his. This was a common ruse employed by prisoners about to be taken out to serve their punishment: they would hide in the latrines and roll in the filth left by the other prisoners. None of the guards wanted to have to go in and arrest them, but three times was probably too much, and the governor himself had been called on to get the condemned man out to the galleys. 'I was told we wouldn't be seeing you here again,' said the governor, finally withdrawing his hand.

'I'm here on a personal matter.' Hernando noted how the prisoner governor's eyes suddenly shone with interest. 'The Inquisition has sent a woman and child here.' The governor appeared to be thinking this over. 'Her name is Aisha: María Ruiz.'

'I'm not sure . . .' the governor began, shamelessly rubbing his thumb and forefinger together to show he expected the usual bribe.

'Governor,' Hernando protested, 'that woman is my mother.'

'Your mother? And what was your mother doing on the Camino de Las Ventas?'

'I see you remember her. That's what I'd like to know: what was she doing there? And don't worry, I'll see you're looked after.'

'Wait here.'

He walked off towards one of the cells hidden behind the arcades. Hernando saw two guards appear, grumbling and cursing the whole time and filthy from excrement and urine, flanking the prisoner condemned to the galleys. His face caked in dirt, the prisoner was smiling at the bad-tempered guards, while from the cells came shouts of farewell. Everyone quickly stepped aside in disgust as he came near. Hernando watched the trio until they had gone out of the prison, and when he turned back towards the courtyard, he found Aisha standing there. She was on her own, as she had left Shamir with another female prisoner.

'Mother?'

'Hernando,' Aisha muttered when she saw who it was.

'Where can we be alone for a while?' Hernando asked the governor.

He let them have a small windowless room next to the gatehouse, which was used as a store.

'What were you doing—?' Hernando began the moment the governor had shut the door behind him.

'Hold me,' Aisha cried.

He stared at his mother standing there with her arms raised, as if she did not dare take a step towards him. She had never asked him to hold her! He briefly remembered how, in Juviles, she had suppressed any show of affection if there was even the slightest chance she might be found out, and now . . . He threw himself into her arms and hugged her tight. Aisha cradled him and began to croon a lullaby, although she could not help her voice choking with sobs.

'What were you doing on the Las Ventas road, Mother?' he eventually asked, his own voice unsteady with emotion.

Aisha told him about the flight into the mountains, and their meeting with the outlaws and Ubaid. She told him how his stepfather's hand had been chopped off, and her own life been spared.

'I spat on him and insulted him,' she concluded hesitantly, still unable to accept the fact that she had abandoned her husband in the Sierra Morena after his hand had been cut off.

Hernando was tempted to laugh or shout out loud. Dog! he thought. At last his mother had rebelled! Yet something told him to keep quiet.

'He brought it on himself,' was all he eventually said.

Aisha hesitated again before nodding her head slightly. 'Ubaid wants to kill you,' she warned her son. 'He's dangerous. He's become one of the outlaw chief's right-hand men.'

'Don't worry about that, Mother,' Hernando cut her short, although he was perturbed. 'He will never come down to Córdoba to find me or anyone else. Just think of yourself and the boy. How are they treating you here?'

'Nobody bothers us . . . and we eat.'

As they walked away together Abbas respected his companion's silence. It had been a long farewell: Aisha was sobbing and seemed to want to keep Hernando with her for ever, and he . . .

he did not want to leave her there either. However, when Aisha noticed her son's chin trembling and his breathing becoming agitated, she forced him to go before he too could burst into tears. Hernando found the governor and promised him money and anything else he wanted if he would treat his mother well and keep an eye on her. He left the prison looking back time and again at the cell his mother had disappeared into.

'What did you want to talk about earlier?' he asked Abbas once he felt calmer.

'Is your mother all right?' his companion wanted to know. Hernando nodded. 'Has she been whipped?'

'No . . . not that I know of.'

'In that case they have given her a light punishment. They would have condemned a man to death if he had gone to Granada, to the galleys for life if he had gone ten leagues out of Valencia, Aragón or Navarre, plus a good whipping, or four years in the galleys if he had been found anywhere else outside his place of residence.'

Hernando thought about it: he had hugged his mother tight, and she had not complained. They must not have flogged her . . . or had they?

'Later you can tell me everything that happened, especially to your stepfather,' said Abbas. 'We need to know.'

'*We* need to?'

'Yes. All of us. People are watching us. Someone who flees . . . affects the whole community. They will investigate all his family.'

'Nobody will say a word.'

They were wandering around the medina, an intricate network of narrow, twisting lanes, surrounded by areas of wasteland with countless more alleyways leading off it.

'Make no mistake, Hernando. That's the first thing you must learn: there are traitors amongst us, believers who act as spies for the Christians.'

Hernando halted and frowned at him.

'Yes,' Abbas insisted. 'Spies. The council of elders has chosen you—'

'One moment. Who are you really? How do you know so much?'

Abbas gave a sigh. Both men started walking again.

'They took advantage of the fact that I work in the royal stables for me to warn you as quickly as possible about what had happened to your mother, but they also have a proposal for you.' At this point he fell silent, but seeing that Hernando said nothing, he went on, 'All the Muslim districts of Spain are getting organized. They all have religious leaders and holy men who are working in secret. Valencia, Aragón, Catalonia, Toledo, Castile . . . in all those regions communities of true believers have been established: in some of them there is even someone they call their king! All the other towns where the Granadan Moriscos have been deported are organizing themselves, either joining the groups of Moriscos who were already there, or, as in Córdoba where there was almost no one left, setting up their organization once more.'

'But I—'

'Quiet. The first thing you need to remember is to trust no one. Not only are there spies, but there are many more of our brothers who, without wishing to, will give way under torture from the Inquisition. We can discuss anything you wish, and I'll try to answer all the questions you want to ask, but swear to me that if you do not accept our proposal you will never tell anyone anything about what we have said.'

Their walk had brought them to Calle del Reloj, so called because here stood a low tower with the town clock on it. The two men stood for a moment watching a group of small boys throwing stones up at the clock face. 'Do you swear?' Abbas insisted. A Jesuit priest came out, shouting and waving his arms, trying to stop the boys.

'Yes,' Hernando promised, watching the little urchins scattering in front of the priest. 'But how do I know I can trust you?'

Abbas smiled. 'You learn quickly! Do you trust Hamid, the

slave who works in the brothel?'

'More than I do myself!' Hernando replied.

So the two of them turned their steps towards the brothel. Hamid was busy and could not come out, but made a sign of approval from the doorway that Hernando immediately understood: the blacksmith could be trusted.

That night, shut in his room and after checking more than once that the door was properly barred from the inside, Hernando sat on the floor and slid his fingers under the cover of a threadbare copy of the Koran written in *aljamiado*. Then he opened the holy book and leafed through its pages.

'I am not in a position to speak of your virtues or defects,' Abbas had told him that morning, 'but you do have something that is very important for the needs of our brothers in faith: you know how to read and write, which is something most of us cannot do.'

Books written in Arabic or that contained references to Islam were strictly forbidden. Anyone found in possession of one ended up in the dungeons of the Inquisition. Abbas, who lived with his family above the royal stables, seemed relieved when he could secretly pass the Koran on to Hernando.

'There are many more books spread among our people,' he said. 'Translations, and the works of the great scholar Iyad on the miracles and virtues of the Prophet, but also simple verse manuscripts or prophecies in Arabic or *aljamiado*. They are kept hidden as best we can in order to preserve our laws and beliefs. Each one of them is a real treasure. Cardinal Cisneros, the man who convinced the Catholic monarchs to go back on the peace treaties they had signed with the Muslims, burnt more than eighty thousand copies of our writings in Granada. You must cherish this divine work for what it is: the treasure of our people.'

The treasure of our people! Hernando had once more been made the keeper of the true believers' riches.

He had to read and learn. To write. To pass on the knowledge and keep the spirit of the Muslims alive. He had accepted Abbas's proposal without thinking twice about it: the smith then invited him into a tavern, and to his surprise ordered two glasses of wine. They drank them in full view of all the other customers.

'You have to be more Christian than the Christians, while at the same time being a better Muslim than any of us,' Abbas whispered in his ear.

Hernando raised his glass and nodded.

'Allah is great,' he mouthed silently when Abbas raised his own glass for the toast.

From his room in the silence of the night he could hear the noises of the hundred horses kept in the stables. Some were pawing the ground nervously, others whinnied or snorted. He could also smell them, but how different that smell was from the rotten manure in the tannery! It was a strong, penetrating smell, but it was healthy. The manure from the royal stables was regularly cleaned out and taken to the kitchen gardens the Inquisition owned, which meant it never rotted under the horses' hooves.

Hernando closed the Koran. For want of any better hiding place, he put it into the bottom of the clothes chest. He would find a safer place for it, but for now it would be the only thing the chest contained until Fátima came to join him. Perhaps she would fill it with her possessions and clothes – even those of a child! He closed the chest and locked it. Fátima! He was sure he would have accepted the proposal anyway, but when Abbas had told him she was with them, he had no doubts.

'It is our women who teach the children,' the smith had explained. 'They are responsible for their education, and they are all glad and proud to do it. It is also a way to avoid any betrayals to the Inquisition. It's almost unheard of for a child to denounce their mother. You cannot and should not meet with any women to explain doctrine to them: a woman must do that. Nobody suspects a woman meeting other women.'

34

THE TWO-MONTH *idda* came to an end in the middle of a week, but Karim asked Hernando not to go in search of Fátima until after high mass on Sunday. They were not yet married according to the law of Muhammad, and the wedding ceremony, which was to be performed in secret, presented Hernando with a problem: he had no money for the presentation, and without a dowry the ceremony could not be held. Most of his wages had gone to pay the prison governor, and what little he had left barely covered the expenses. He had no gold ring as the law required! How had he not thought of that?

'A cheap ring will do,' Hamid said, trying to reassure him.

'I don't even have enough for that,' replied Hernando, thinking of the expensive silversmiths in the city.

'Iron. It can be made of iron if need be.'

That Sunday Hernando walked from San Bartolomé church to Calle de los Moriscos in Santa Marina. He crossed the whole city of Córdoba at a leisurely pace, allowing Karim and Fátima to take their time. As he walked, his fingers caressed the magnificent iron ring Abbas had made for him from a scrap of metal. Although his massive hands were very different from the delicate ones of the jewellers, he had even managed to engrave a decorative pattern on it.

When Hernando reached their street, he was warmly greeted by two young Moriscos who were pretending to be talking but were in fact keeping an eye open for any visiting priest or bailiff.

A third young man who appeared out of nowhere accompanied him to Karim's house, a small, ancient one-storey dwelling with a garden behind it. Like everyone else, Karim had to share it with several other families. The front of the house, though, had been whitewashed by the women, as had most of the humble houses in Calle de los Moriscos. Like the Morisco houses of Granada, all the rooms inside were kept spotlessly clean.

Jalil, Karim and Hamid headed the small number of guests there to greet Hernando: just enough to make the wedding ceremony a public affair, as required under Muslim law. This was one of the few customs they could maintain in Córdoba. Hamid embraced him, but Hernando could not help thinking about his mother: the second time he had gone to visit Aisha in prison, she had begged him not to come again. 'You have a good job with the Christians,' she said, 'and I'll be out of here soon. You shouldn't be seen here, visiting a Morisco woman who has broken the law; besides, they could link you to Brahim, who's disappeared.' But how much Hernando wished his mother had been there that day!

Hamid stepped back, took him by the shoulders, and forced him to turn and look at Fátima, who had just appeared. She was dressed in a borrowed long white tunic, which contrasted sharply with her dark skin, the gleam in her huge black eyes, and her long curly black hair that the women had decorated with brightly coloured tiny flowers. Karim's wife had given her a delicate white shawl that covered her beautiful locks. Fátima displayed all the splendour of her seventeen years. At the base of her neck, just where Hernando could detect her beating pulse, she wore the forbidden piece of golden jewellery.

He offered her his hand, and she took it with the same resolution she had shown in all her actions until now. Understanding this, Hernando grasped hers firmly in response. They sought out each other's eyes and stared into them. Nobody interrupted them; nobody dared even move. Hernando wanted to say that he loved her, but with an almost imperceptible gesture she restrained him, as if she wanted to prolong this moment and enjoy their victory. It was so hard-won! For a few seconds, they both remembered all they had suffered: the forced marriage and how Fátima had been obliged to give herself to Brahim . . .

'I love you,' said Hernando, although he could guess what thoughts were going through his future wife's mind.

Fátima pressed her lips together. She also could guess what he was thinking. Hernando had become a slave out of love for her!

'And I love you, Ibn Hamid.'

They smiled at each other. Seeing this, Karim's wife urged them to hurry up. It was dangerous to take too long over the ceremony.

Hamid pronounced the vows. He seemed to have aged all of a sudden; at times his voice quavered and he repeatedly had to clear his throat in order to keep going. When she was given the rough iron ring, all semblance of composure or serenity deserted Fátima. Her hands trembled as she found the finger it would fit, and then she managed a nervous smile. There was no music or dancing, not even a wedding feast. All they did was pray in whispers facing the kiblah, after which the married pair left Calle de los Moriscos like any other couple. Fátima had taken the flowers out of her hair and changed the white tunic for her normal clothes. Her head was still covered by the white shawl, and she was carrying a small bundle. How much of that chest there still was to fill! thought Hernando when he felt how light her bundle was.

They hid the hand of Fátima inside the Koran, which they covered with the white shawl, carefully folded by Fátima. As was the custom, they put a small bag of almonds under the mattress. Then for the umpteenth time Fátima roamed through the two rooms, peering here and there, fantasizing over her future with Hernando. Finally she came to a halt with her back to him, next to the washbasin. She gently dipped her fingertips into it, touching the surface of the clean water. But she asked him to leave her on her own until nightfall.

'I'd like to make myself ready for you.'

Although he could not see her face properly, the sensual tone of her voice told him all he wanted to hear.

Containing his anxiety, he went down to the stables, which on Sundays were deserted. The only person there was a stable lad, who was lounging about in the yard outside. Hernando went into the stalls and absent-mindedly patted the colts' haunches and hindquarters. How would Fátima be getting ready for him? She no longer had the white tunic with slits up the sides in which she had received him that first night they had made love, in Ugíjar. It wasn't in her bundle! He shuddered at the memory of her hard, full breasts outlined against the light, how they had provoked him when he caught glimpses of them swaying as she served him, caressed him . . .

He had no time to get out of the way. One of the wild colts recently brought in from pasture kicked out as he went by and caught him on the calf. Hernando felt a sharp pain, and clutched his leg; luckily the colt had not been shod, and gradually the pain subsided. Stupid! Hernando reproached himself for being so careless. Why was he patting horses that were not yet used to human contact? The colt was called Saeta, and its fiery nature had already suggested it would give him more problems than all the others. Hernando went up to it, and Sacta strained at the halter attaching it to the wall. This time keeping careful watch on the colt's legs, which could kick again at any moment, Hernando stood beside the colt. He waited quietly for it to calm down. At first he said nothing, but began to whisper to it once Saeta had stopped struggling and shifting nervously in the small space it was confined to. Hernando spoke gently for a long while, just as he used to do with La Vieja in the mountains. He made no attempt to get closer or to put a hand on its neck to pat it. Saeta did not look at him, but its ears twitched with each change in his tone of voice. This went on for some time. The colt did not soften, but remained obstinate, tense, staring forward and not making the slightest attempt to turn its head to lick him or nudge him in any way.

'You'll give way,' Hernando said when he decided now was not the moment to try to go any further, 'and the day that happens you'll surrender completely, more than any of the others,' he muttered, still wary of the colt's hooves as he left the stall.

'I'm sure that's what will happen.'

Startled, Hernando whirled round when he heard these words. Don Diego López de Haro and José Velasco were watching him. The nobleman was dressed in his finest: slashed breeches in various shades of green, with velvet stockings and shoes; a tight-fitting black sleeveless doublet, with frills at the neck and wrists; a cape and a sword at his waist. José his servant was standing beside him, and the stable lad a few steps behind. How long had they been observing him? Had he said anything wrong when he was talking to the colt? He tried to remember ... he had spoken to it in Arabic! 'Did the kick hurt?' Don Diego asked, pointing to his leg. So they had seen Saeta kicking him – they had been listening from the very start!

'No, your excellency,' he stammered.

Don Diego came over and laid a friendly hand on the lad's shoulder. But this contact unnerved Hernando: he had even recited some suras!

'Do you know why he's called Saeta?' The stable master did not wait for his answer. 'Because he is as rapid and swift as an arrow. He's also agile and proud, and prances so high with all four legs it's as if he wants his knees and hocks to touch the sky. I have high hopes for that colt. Take care of him. Take good care of him. Where did you learn about horses?'

Hernando hesitated. Should he tell him?

'In the Sierra Nevada,' he said, trying to avoid the question.

Don Diego tilted his head to one side, as if waiting for some further explanation.

'In the mountains only the brigands had horses,' he said when none was forthcoming.

'I was . . . I was with Aben Humeya,' Hernando was forced to admit. 'I looked after his horses.'

Don Diego nodded. His right hand was still resting on Hernando's shoulder. 'Don Fernando de Válor y de Córdoba,' he mused. 'They say he died proclaiming his Christianity. Don John ordered the exhumation of his body in the mountains so that it could be given Christian burial in Guadix.' The nobleman thought for a few moments. 'Leave now,' he told him. 'Today is Sunday, you can continue tomorrow.'

Hernando looked towards the windows: the sun was beginning to set. Fátima! He bowed clumsily and rushed out of the stables.

Don Diego however stood staring at Saeta. 'I've seen lots of men react violently when a colt kicks them or defends itself,' he commented to his servant without turning towards him. 'They mistreat them and punish them, and only reinforce their bad habits. This lad on the other hand was gentle with him. Take care of that lad, José. He knows what he's doing.'

Hernando ran up the steps leading to his rooms and hammered on the door.

'You'll have to wait,' said Fátima from inside.

'Night is falling,' he heard himself saying in the most naive way.

'You still have to wait,' she replied firmly.

He paced up and down the corridor outside the rooms until he was tired of doing so. What was he doing? Time was passing. Should he knock again? He hesitated. In the end he decided to sit down on the floor outside the door. What if someone saw him? What would he say? What if one of the other employees living on the top floor . . . ? What if Don Diego himself . . . ? But he was downstairs, in the stables. What had he heard of the words he had whispered to the colt? It was forbidden to speak in Arabic. He knew the Moriscos had presented a petition to the city council in which they explained how difficult it was for them not to use the only language they knew. They were calling for a postponement in the application of the royal ordinance to give time for those who did not know Spanish to learn it. Their petition was refused, and so speaking in Arabic was still punishable by fines or imprisonment. What punishment was there for reciting the Koran in Arabic? But Don Diego had not said a word. Could it be true that in the stables, horses were the only religion?

Several timid taps on the door brought him out of his daydream. What did they mean?

He heard the tapping again. Fátima was knocking from inside the room.

Hernando stood up and pushed at the door. It was not barred.

He stood there, paralysed.

'Close it!' cried Fátima in the faintest of voices, though there was a smile on her lips.

He obeyed awkwardly.

Fátima did not have her slit tunic, so she received him naked. The light from the setting sun and a flickering candle behind her played over her figure. Her breasts seemed to have been painted with henna in a geometric design that rose like a flame to lick the fingers of the hand of Fátima that was once more hanging from her neck. She had also painted her eyes, outlining them in long lines that accentuated their almond shape. A delicious perfume of orange blossom enveloped Hernando as he gazed at his bride's slender but voluptuous body. The two of them said nothing, and the silence was broken only by their excited breathing.

'Come,' she said.

Hernando stepped over to her. When Fátima made no attempt to move, he traced the outline of her breasts with his fingertips. Then, still standing next to her, he fondled her erect nipples. She sighed. When he made to cup one of her breasts in his hand, she stopped him and led him over to the washbasin. There she began gently to undress him and wash his body.

Hernando spoke his first stumbling words, then gave in to

the shivers of delight that ran through his body when one of Fátima's breasts brushed against him, or as her wet hands ran sensually over his torso, his shoulders, his arms, his abdomen, his groin . . .

As her hands ran over him, Fátima whispered softly to him: 'I love you; I want you; make me yours; take me; take me to paradise . . .'

When she had finished, she flung her arms round his neck.

'You're the most beautiful woman on earth,' said Hernando. 'I've waited so long for this . . .'

Fátima did not let him continue. She raised both her legs and wrapped them round his waist. She was clinging on to him, and started to delicately move until she found his erect penis. They began to pant together as Fátima slid down and he penetrated her, thrusting into her body's deepest recesses. Supporting her with his arms clutched tightly round her back, Hernando's muscles began to glisten with sweat. She arched her back and swayed to and fro in search of pleasure. It was she who set the rhythm: she listened closely to his breathing, sighs and unintelligible whispers, stopped occasionally to bite his earlobes and neck, telling him to slow down and promising him everything, before starting her measured dance on his penis once more. In the end, they reached orgasm at the same time.

Hernando howled with pleasure; Fátima was swept away in an ecstasy that was even louder than her husband's.

'Bed, take me to the bed,' she begged him when he made as if to lift her off him. 'Like this. Carry me like this!' She clung to him even more tightly. 'The two of us together,' she demanded. 'I love you.' She tugged playfully at his hair as he carried her over to the nuptial bed. 'Don't withdraw. Love me. Stay inside me . . .'

Still clinging to each other, they fell on to the bed. They kissed and caressed until Fátima could feel desire stirring in him once more. They made love again passionately, as if it were the first time. Then she got up and made lemonade, and brought it to the bed with some dried fruit. While Hernando was eating, she licked him all over his body, moving like a cat until he joined in the game and tried to reach her with his tongue as she flitted from side to side.

That night the two of them explored time and again the ancient paths of love and pleasure.

35

Feast of the Immaculate Conception, 8 December 1573

THEY HAD been married for seven months. Aisha had served her sixty-day sentence and was released. Hernando obtained permission from the administrator for Aisha and little Shamir to share their rooms above the stables. Fátima was five months pregnant; Saeta had finally surrendered to his tender care. He had not spoken to the horse in Arabic again. On their wedding night, as they lay in bed, covered with sweat, he had explained to Fátima what had happened with the colt and Don Diego.

'A Christian will always be a Christian,' she replied, in a tone very different from the one she had used throughout the night, suspicious of his insistence that the only religion in the stables was horses. 'Damn them! Don't trust them, my love: with horses or without them, they hate us and always will.'

Then Fátima reached once more for her husband's body.

Hernando worked from dawn to dusk. Twice a day he had to exercise the colts in the yard. The horses were lunged at the end of a long rope, a flexible stick coated with honey in their mouth. The thickness of the stick was gradually increased until it reached that of a lance, so that the horses became accustomed to the iron bit they would one day have to use. Sacks of sand were laid across their backs, to get them used to the weight of a rider. In the stables they groomed the horses, rubbing a cloth all over their bodies and cleaning heads, eyes, ears and feet. They scraped their hoofs in readiness for the moment when they would be shod. Saeta was the first to accept the work in the yard with a sack of sand on his back and a thick stick in his mouth. On top of all this, one of the riders often asked Hernando to accompany him travelling around the city, as he had done with Rodrigo.

Hernando loved his work and the colts were the picture of health and good behaviour. He surprised the grooms with suggestions for some foodstuffs to complement the hay and oats the colts usually ate. The spirited Saeta should eat a paste of boiled broad beans or chickpeas with bran and a handful of salt during the night; a timid colt should complement its food with wheat or rye, also boiled the previous night until it formed a paste to which bran, salt, and in this case oil should also be added. Although the grooms were at first very sceptical about these recommendations, Don Diego decided that as they could in no way harm the colts he would follow the Morisco's advice. The results were obvious and immediate. Without losing his spirit, Saeta quietened down, and the timid colts became contented and more courageous. Riders, stable lads, blacksmiths, and harness-makers began to respect Hernando. Even the administrator quickly granted him everything he asked for, such as the request that Aisha assist in the silk spinning.

That 8 December of 1573, day of the Immaculate Conception of the Blessed Virgin Mary, the inquisitors had plans to celebrate an auto-da-fé in Córdoba cathedral. Hernando and Fátima watched anxiously how the news was welcomed by the inhabitants of the city, including the grooms at the stables. The same had happened for two years now, as the auto-da-fé was celebrated on the same date. The celebration the previous year had reached the heights of popular fervour and morbid curiosity. After a lengthy trial that had included the use of torture, sentence was passed on seven witches, among them the famous sorceress of Montilla, Leonor Rodríguez, known as 'La Camacha'. After publicly renouncing her crimes, she was sentenced to receive one hundred lashes in Córdoba and another hundred in Montilla. She was also banished from Montilla for ten years. For the first two of these she would be forced to work in a hospital in Córdoba. On the days before the auto-da-fé it seemed as though even the animals in the street were gripped by religious fervour, so the Moriscos tried to go about their neighbourhoods unnoticed. La Camacha confessed to having learnt her black arts from a Morisco woman of Granada!

This year neither Hernando nor Fátima was able to stay out of the way of the Inquisition. The previous night, Abbas had paid them a visit.

'Tomorrow we should go to the mosque to attend the auto-da-fé,' he announced brusquely after greeting them.

Hernando and Fátima exchanged glances.

'You think so?' asked Hernando. 'Why on earth . . . ?'

'Several Moriscos have been condemned.'

In spite of his African origin, Abbas got on well with the inquisitors. He himself followed the instructions he had given Hernando, so that he appeared to his ruthless neighbours in the fortress as more Christian than the Christians, and it was not unusual for him to be held up as an example of the conversion of someone born into the sect of Muhammad. In the same way, his trade allowed him to win the trust and gratitude of the miserly inquisitors and members of the Holy Office. The iron-work on an unhinged door, an iron railing that had given way, a broken ornament, even the bars on the tiny dungeon windows: all these little repairs were entrusted to the skilful blacksmith, who said he did them out of piety, and wanted no other reward.

'Even so,' Hernando insisted, 'what reason could there be for us to witness the auto-da-fé?'

'In the first place, our devotion and respect for the Holy Inquisition,' replied the blacksmith with a wry grimace. 'They should see us there. Secondly, I want you to meet someone; and thirdly, and most importantly, to learn the exact reasons why our brothers are being tried, and what penalties are imposed on them. We should inform Algiers of how the Muslims in Spain are treated by the Inquisition.'

Fátima and Hernando reacted sharply.

'Why is that?' asked Hernando.

Abbas signalled to him to listen closely. 'For every Morisco punished here, the Turks will punish the Christians held captive in the ancient bathhouses of Algiers. That's how it is,' he insisted, when he saw Hernando's surprised reaction, 'and the Christians know it. Not that the Inquisition stops punishing what they consider heresy, but it is a good way of applying pressure that perhaps can influence them when they decide how severe a sentence should be. I know. I have heard them talk about it. The news comes and goes. We send it to Algiers and from there it returns in the mouths of the rescued Christians or the Mercedarian monks when they come back from ransoming captives. That has always been the way. Before the time of the Catholic monarchs, corsairs captured in Spain were stoned to death or hanged. There would be an immediate response on the other side of the strait: the corsairs would execute a Christian in reprisal. Eventually the two groups came to a tacit agreement: a life sentence in the galleys for both sides. A similar thing happens with the Inquisition. Before the arrival of the deported Moriscos from Granada, there were none of us here in Córdoba. Now it is up to us to organize a system they have been employing for many years in the other kingdoms.'

'How do we get this information to Algiers?'

'More than four thousand Morisco muleteers cross Spain every day! Believers are constantly embarking for Barbary. Despite the fact that the Moriscos are prohibited from going near the coast, it is not hard to do so: the Christians aren't very vigilant. Through the muleteers, news about the Inquisition's sentences reaches the outlaws in the mountains and the slaves and escapees who meet up with them to flee to Barbary. They then pass it on.'

'Is Ubaid with them?' Hernando blurted out, recalling his mother's account of what had happened in the mountains.

Abbas frowned. 'You mean the one-handed muleteer?'

'Yes. That man has sworn to kill me.'

Taken aback, Fátima shot her husband a questioning look. Hernando had not wanted to tell her about the events on the Camino de Las Ventas. He and his mother had only said that Brahim had fled and that Aisha had managed to escape.

Hernando took Fátima's hand and nodded.

'What is Ubaid doing in Córdoba? When did you hear about him?' she insisted, knowing full well the dangerous threat that man represented.

'The outlaws are very useful to us,' Abbas interrupted her, 'but we are even more useful to them. Without the help they get from the Moriscos in the countryside and the places where they have to hide, they wouldn't be able to survive. Why has he sworn to kill you?'

Hernando told him the story, including the threats the muleteer from Narila had made against Brahim and himself. However, he kept quiet about the fact that he had hidden the silver crucifix that led to Ubaid losing his hand.

'Now I understand!' Abbas said. 'That's why he chopped off your stepfather's hand. We could not understand why he had reacted so violently towards a brother in faith. I also understand Hamid's mistrust of El Sobahet and Ubaid.'

Fátima took all this in, and fixed her black eyes accusingly on Hernando's face.

'We thought it better for you not to know,' he admitted, squeezing his wife's hand more tightly. 'But how do you know all this?' he added, turning to the blacksmith.

'I've already told you we are in permanent contact.' Abbas lifted his hand to his chin and rubbed it repeatedly. 'I will try to sort this matter out. We will demand that he leaves you alone. I promise.'

'If you know so much about the outlaws,' Fátima interrupted him, concern showing on her face, 'what has become of Brahim?'

'He has recovered,' Abbas replied. 'I heard he joined a group of men hoping to cross to Barbary.'

And so it had been. What nobody knew, not even the men whom Brahim had joined up with in his escape, was that the agony of his severed limb seemed to disappear when Brahim took a last look at the lands of Córdoba spread out at the feet of the Sierra Morena. The constant, tremendous stabs of pain he felt in his arm faded in face of the rage engulfing him at that moment. He was giving up the only thing in his wretched life among the Christians that he wanted: Fátima. From the distance, he imagined the wife the elders had robbed him of in the arms of the Nazarene, giving herself to him, offering her body to him. Perhaps she already had the bastard's seed in her belly . . . 'I swear I will return for you!' muttered Brahim, looking down on the plain.

It was a little after three on a cold but bright day. Hernando hesitated as he was about to go through the Perdón gate of the Córdoba mosque. Fátima noticed at once, but Abbas was a couple of steps ahead. Soon though the crowd behind pushed them inside, as the bells rang out from the ancient Muslim minaret, transformed into a bell tower.

Hernando had been living in Córdoba for three years and had passed by the mosque dozens of times. Sometimes all he did was keep his eyes on the ground, at others he looked out of the corner of his eye at the fortress-like walls surrounding the place of prayer of the caliphs of the West and of the thousands of faithful who made Córdoba the beacon radiating the true faith to the Christian world. He had never dared to go inside. In the cathedral there were more than two hundred priests, even excluding the members of the chapter, who officiated at the more than thirty daily masses held in the many chapels.

Abbas returned to join them once they got past the domed vestibule that opened out behind the great pointed arch of the door. Hernando and Fátima were spat out by the throng of people flooding into the orchard garden of the great cloister in front of the cathedral, planted with orange trees, cypresses, palms and olives. The blacksmith seemed to read the young man's thoughts, pursed his lips and gestured encouragingly for him to continue. Dressed in the white shawl she had worn on her wedding day, Fátima clutched his arm.

The cloister garden took the form of a wide enclosed rectangle, surrounded on three sides by rows of columned arches, whose proportions coincided with the northern façade of the cathedral. In spite of the cool of the trees and the fountains, the three Moriscos shrank from the sight of the hundreds of penitential garments hanging from the cloister walls, a clear and permanent warning that the Inquisition kept watch and punished heresy. In Muslim times, the faithful purified themselves and performed their ablutions in four washrooms, two for women and two for men, that the Caliph al-Hakam had built outside the mosque in front of the east and west façades. They would then enter the prayer room through the nineteen doors that opened into it, which the Christians had bricked up. For this reason they were now obliged to go in through the doorway of the Bendiciones arch, where, in days gone by, the banners of the troops who went to fight against the Muslims had been blessed. Once inside, they waited for their eyes to adjust to the light from the lamps that hung from the ceiling, only nine yards high. Even though he had often seen it, Abbas could not help but share the awe that brought Fátima and Hernando to a standstill in the midst of the torrent of people, some of whom dodged around them while others shoved past. In front of them, calling them to prayer, they saw a forest of close to a thousand columns in rows, joined by double arches one on top of another, with red brickwork alternating with ochre stone.

For a few moments the two of them stood still, breathing in the strong smell of incense. Hernando was absorbed in the contemplation of the variety of Visigoth or Roman capitals where the columns joined the arches. Fátima was in the middle of the two men.

'There is no god but God, and Muhammad is the messenger of God,' she whispered as if impelled by some magical external force.

'Are you mad?' Abbas rebuked her, looking round to see if anyone might have heard her.

'Yes,' Fátima replied out loud, as she advanced, intoxicated, towards the inside of the mosque, stroking her prominent belly.

Abbas glanced at Hernando, imploring him to stop his wife doing anything stupid.

'Please be quiet, for our son's sake,' he begged her, catching up with her and putting his hand on her swelling stomach. Fátima seemed to come out of her trance. 'I once swore to you that one day I would lay the Christians at your feet. Today I swear to you that one day we will pray to the one God in this sacred place.' She half closed her eyes. That commitment did not seem to be enough. 'I swear it before Allah,' added Hernando, in a low voice.

'Ibn Hamid,' she answered, still without thinking. People continued flowing past them, chatting excitedly about the auto-da-fé they were going to watch. 'Always remember the oath you have just sworn, and keep it, come what may.'

Abbas breathed a sigh of relief when he saw Fátima take hold of her husband's arm again.

They could not get much further into the mosque. Thousands of people were already surrounding the area where they were building the new Renaissance cathedral. This was in the form of a cross, supported on great pillars and Gothic buttresses, constructed in the heart of the Muslim place of prayer: the central nave that led to the mihrab. The new cathedral rose through the centre of the mosque's roof to emerge imposingly above it, and so reach the proportions the Christians insisted on for their temples. This magnificent building, begun many years earlier and still ongoing, was destined to replace the small, primitive church also built inside the mosque, on the site of the kiblah, in the extension made by Abderraman II. The erection of the new chancel had been rejected by the Córdoba council, some of whose members feared that its construction would overshadow their own chapels and altars. Against the wishes of the cathedral chapter, the councillors and judiciary of Córdoba passed an ordinance by which any worker volunteering to work on the building would be sentenced to death. The Emperor Charles V put an end to the argument by authorizing the construction of the new cathedral.

They had to wait for the arrival of all the faithful, many of whom had to be content with staying in the cloister's garden, as well as of the tribunal of the Holy Office, the members of the church and municipal councils, and above all that of the accused, who were led in to murmurs, laughter and comments from the spectators. This gave Hernando time to examine the interior of the great building, which could accommodate thousands of people. Independent of the garden, the floor plan of the mosque was almost quadrangular. In the centre were the beginnings of the new cathedral, which was still surrounded by hundreds of double arches of red and ochre columns. The remaining space between the last line of columns and the walls of the mosque contained numerous chapels, placed there by the nobles and the Christian prebends and dedicated to their saints and martyrs. Altars, statues of Christ, paintings and religious images, like those found across the length and breadth of the streets of the whole city, were displayed to popular fervour as a sign of the power of the noble houses that had paid for them and endowed them with bequests and legacies. Hernando could make out the coats of arms and heraldic symbols of the nobles, knights and princes of the church. They were sculpted out of the stonework itself, on walls, arches and columns; carved into the wrought iron of a great many of the railings that enclosed the chapels of the perimeter; on the gravestones, almost all at floor level; on the altarpieces and paintings of the chapels and anywhere else that could be found: locks, lamps, door handles, chests, chairs ... They also appeared on the shields and helmets of the Spanish, German, Polish or Bohemian knights that hung all around in thanks for the victories won in the name of Christianity.

Muslim among Christians, thought Hernando, as he heard the sound of the organ music and the canticles of the choir heralding the arrival of the bishop, the Inquisitor of Córdoba and the chief magistrate. They came in followed by their respective entourages, and then the accused. Like this building, he added to himself, stroking one of the columns. The Christian faith was evident in all the chapels clustered all around the temple yet the space opening out from these chapels, with its thousand columns and red and ochre arches, was a song of praise to the magnificence of Allah; then in the centre, Christian once more, rose the new chancel and the choir.

Hernando raised his eyes to the roof of the cathedral. The Christians tried to get closer to God in their buildings, raising them as high as their technical resources allowed; with solid foundations and slender heights. At the same time, the mosque of Córdoba was a miracle of Muslim architecture, the result of a daring exercise in construction, the power of God descending over His believers. The higher of the two arches resting on the columns was twice as thick as the arch beneath. Contrary to the Christian construction, in the mosque the solid foundation, the weight, was supported by the slender columns, in evident and public defiance of the laws of gravity. The power of God was placed on high, the weakness of the believers who prayed in the mosque, at the bottom.

Why had the Christians not destroyed all traces of that religion they hated so much, as they had with the rest of the city's mosques? Hernando wondered, his eyes still on the double arches over the columns. The chapter of Córdoba cathedral, together with its nobles, was among the richest in Spain and did not lack the piety to undertake such a project. They could have planned the construction of a great cathedral like those of Granada or Seville, and yet they had allowed the Muslim memory to remain in those columns, in the low ceilings, in the layout of the aisles . . . in the spirit of the mosque! The magical union that, regardless of who is here, you feel inside this building, sighed Hernando.

None of them got to see the auto-da-fé, which was celebrated on a platform next to the old chancel. Only the rows of people closest to the security cordon mounted by the justices and bailiffs around the protagonists were able to watch the event. However, they heard the short public reading of the charges and sentences. No justifications were given; mention was made only of the sins committed by the forty-three accused from the kingdom of Córdoba and their punishment. Twenty-nine of them were Moriscos, over whom the tribunal exercised its jurisdiction. The Christians listened to the verdicts in silence, then cheered or booed when they heard the sentences.

Two hundred lashes for a Christian from Santa Cruz de Mudela, for maintaining that the assurance that God would come to judge the living and the dead, as affirmed by the Creed, was false. 'He has already come once!' the accused maintained. 'Why should He come back?' Various other floggings were handed down to other Christians for having stated publicly that it was not a sin to have carnal relations or to live together outside marriage. Two hundred lashes and three years in the galleys for a man from Andújar for bigamy; a fine for a weaver from Aguilar de la Frontera for declaring that hell only existed for Moors and bandits ('Why should Christians go to hell when there are Moors?'); a fine and exposure to public scorn bound and gagged for another man for saying that it was not a sin to pay to sleep with a woman. There were lesser sentences of fines and the wearing of penitential garments for several men and women for blasphemy and casting doubt on the effectiveness of excommunication, or for uttering rude, scandalous or heretical words. Two Frenchmen who were followers of the sect of Luther had their properties confiscated and were given lashes and lifetime sentences on the galleys. Three people from Alcalá la Real who had renounced Catholicism in Algiers after being captured by corsairs were sentenced to having their effigies burnt at the stake.

'Elvira Bolat,' the clerk of the court called out. 'New Christian from Terque.'

'Elvira!' gasped Fátima. A man and a woman in front of them turned round in surprise, looking first at her and then towards Hernando. Fátima tried to explain: 'She was my friend before—'

Abbas crossed himself ostentatiously.

'Fátima,' Hernando interrupted her, crossing himself like the blacksmith, 'you must renounce this kind of childhood friendship. They will bring you no good. Pray for her,' he added, squeezing her arm. 'Pray for the intervention of the Virgin Mary so that Our Lord will guide her on the right path.' The man who had turned round nodded in agreement with the reprimand, and he and his wife went back to listening to the sentences.

A fine, penitential garments, and one hundred lashes. Fifty in Córdoba and fifty more in Écija, where Elvira lived, for 'Moorish activities'. Similar fates, plus an order to attend catechism classes in their parishes and either one or two hundred lashes, according to gender, befell the rest of the Morisco defendants. All were reconciled with the Church after admitting their offences and heresies.

The next accused was a slave, recently captured trying to flee to Barbary, who had remained faithful to the sect of Muhammad. To be burnt at the stake. The crowd burst into cheers and applause. Now they were guaranteed their spectacle! The burning of the three inanimate effigies of the apostates from Alcalá held captive in Algiers did not satisfy anyone. The unrepentant slave, whose insistence denied him the opportunity of being garrotted first, would be burnt alive. This appealed to the crowd.

'We pronounce and declare it thus.'

The members of the tribunal brought an end to the

auto-da-fé and the accused were handed over to the secular arm of the Church, which was to carry out the sentences imposed. Before they even heard the final words, many people were already running towards the site of the burnings, in the fields of Marrubial, on the eastern outskirts of the city.

The noise of the departing crowd allowed Hernando to speak to Abbas freely. He was horrified at the way men and women of all ages were rushing to get out, laughing and shouting.

'One less Moor!' he heard one of them say.

A chorus of guffaws greeted the words.

'Do we also have to watch how they burn one of our own?' Hernando asked.

'No, because they are waiting for us in the library,' replied the blacksmith coldly, 'but we ought to.' Hernando suddenly realized his mistake. 'He will die proclaiming the true religion in front of thousands of zealous Christians, all baying for blood and revenge. Think of how all the believers condemned today will feel proud of this. The women will use the cold as an excuse to ask for penitential garments for their young children to wear so that they can accompany them. We will show them all that we have not forgotten our God, that the faith is still alive among the believers.' Fátima listened, her eyes half closed and with both hands over her belly. Hernando started to apologize, but Abbas wouldn't allow him to. 'Not long ago, we were informed that several days after the celebration of an auto-da-fé in Valencia, the executioner who carried out the sentences visited the small mountain village of Gestalgar to charge our brothers for the costs of his monstrous work. One of them refused to pay because he had not been lashed. They confirmed the mistake and the man received the one hundred lashes in front of his family and neighbours. Only then, with his back red raw, did he pay the executioner. He could have just paid and saved himself from the lashes, but he preferred to suffer the sentence like his brothers. That is how our people are!' The blacksmith paused for a moment. He cast his gaze over the forest of columns and arches as if those witnesses to the power of the Muslims could confirm his assertion. 'Let's go,' he concluded.

They left the mosque among the stragglers and those who for one reason or another were unable to attend the burning. None of the authorities now remained inside the mosque. They circled the transept of the cathedral that was under construction, whose arms had been adapted to the dimensions of the original Muslim naves. They left behind the three small Renaissance chapels situated behind the high altar. The chancel was already finished, but the elliptical dome destined to cover it was yet to be built, and a temporary cover was supported on scaffolding. They headed for the cathedral's south-eastern corner, where the magnificent cathedral library occupied an ancient chapel. It contained hundreds of documents and books: some were manuscripts more than eight hundred years old. Although the library was enclosed by a magnificent wrought-iron railing, the door was open.

'Is your wife capable of waiting here for us without doing anything stupid?' said Abbas, who had already reached the railing.

Fátima moved to confront the blacksmith, but Hernando stopped her with a simple gesture.

'Yes,' he replied.

'Does she understand that the lives of many men and women depend on our discretion?'

'Yes, she does,' Hernando confirmed again, as Fátima nodded ashamedly.

'Let's go in then.'

The two men passed through the railings that led to the library and stopped. Inside, on shelves, were hundreds of bound volumes, rolls of parchment and some reading tables. Around two of them sat a circle of five priests. When the blacksmith realized that a meeting was taking place he tried to withdraw, but one of the priests noticed their presence and called them over. Big as he was, Abbas bent his head, raised his hands to his chest and entwined his fingers in a sign of prayer. Hernando did likewise, and both approached the group.

'What do you want?' the priest who had called to them

asked irritably before they had even reached the group.

'I know him, Don Salvador,' said the oldest priest among them. He was short, bald and fat but with a gentle voice that belied his appearance. 'He is a good Christian and collaborates with the Inquisition.'

'Good day, Don Julián,' Abbas greeted him.

Hernando murmured a greeting.

'Good day, Jerónimo,' replied the priest. 'What brings you here?'

One of the priests went to a shelf to get a book. The others, apart from Don Salvador who was still glaring at them, looked on apparently uninterested until Jerónimo's words caught their attention.

'Some time ago . . .' Abbas cleared his throat a couple of times. 'Some time ago, when the Moriscos from Granada arrived, you asked that if I found a good Christian among them who knew how to write Arabic well, then I should bring him to you. My friend here's name is Hernando,' added the blacksmith, taking his companion's arm and pushing him forwards.

Write in Arabic! Hernando felt even the eyes of the crucified Christ presiding over the library upon him. Had Abbas gone mad? Hamid had shown him the rudiments of reading and writing in the universal language that united all the believers, but from that to being presented in the cathedral library as an expert . . . Something compelled him to turn towards the entrance, where Fátima was listening behind the railing. The girl encouraged him with an imperceptible movement of her lips.

'Good, good . . .' Don Julián began.

'Isn't he too young to know how to write Arabic?' Don Salvador interrupted.

Hernando sensed Abbas stir uneasily. Perhaps he had not thought about the consequences of what he had said? He could sense the hostility dripping from Don Salvador's words.

'You are right, Father,' Hernando answered meekly, turning

towards him. 'I think my friend places too much value on my limited knowledge.'

Don Salvador raised his head to meet the Morisco's blue eyes. He hesitated for a moment. 'Even if it is limited, where did you acquire it?' he queried, in a tone of voice possibly slightly less harsh than that which he had used previously.

'In the Alpujarra. In the parish of Juviles. Don Martín, God rest his soul, taught me all I know.'

Under no circumstances was he going to mention Hamid, and as for poor Don Martín . . . the image of his mother stabbing him flashed into his memory. What would the members of the Córdoba cathedral chapter know about the parish priest of a little village lost in the mountains of Granada?

'And how is it that a Christian priest knew Arabic?' the youngest priest wanted to know.

Don Julián was going to answer, but Don Salvador spoke first. They all seemed to respect him.

'It is perfectly possible,' he confirmed. 'Many years ago now the King ruled that it was advisable for the preachers to know Arabic in order to convert the heretics. Many of them know no Spanish and are not even capable of expressing themselves in *aljamiado*, especially in Granada and Valencia. We need to know Arabic to be able to contradict their polemic writings, to know what it is that they think. Well, lad, show us what you know, little as it may be. Father,' he added to Don Julián, 'fetch me the most recent polemical manuscript that has fallen into our hands.'

Don Julián hesitated, but Don Salvador urged him to go, waving the fingers of his outstretched right hand. Hernando felt a shiver go down his spine. Avoiding eye contact with Abbas, he looked towards Fátima, who winked at him from the other side of the railing. How could she wink at him in a moment like this? What was she trying to tell him? His wife encouraged him with a movement of her chin and a smile, and then he understood her. Why not? What did those priests know about Arabic? Were they not looking for him to be their translator?

He took the ragged piece of paper that Don Julián held out to him and studied it. It was written in a cultured Arabic. To judge by the language, it came from much further away than al-Andalus, and was different, as Hamid had repeated over and over again, from the dialect established in Spain over the course of centuries. What was the text about?

'It is signed as being from Tunis,' he announced confidently, quickly trying to get the gist of the text. 'It is about the Holy Trinity,' he added as he read the characters. 'It says the following, more or less: In the name of he who judges with truth,' he extemporized, pretending that he was reading, 'of he who is understanding, of the Compassionate One, the All-merciful, of the Creator—'

'Yes, yes, all right,' Don Salvador interrupted him, waving his arms angrily, 'forget those blasphemies. What does it say about the dogma of the Trinity?'

Hernando tried to decipher the writing. He was well aware what the dispute between Muslims and Christians was: there is only one God, so how can Christians maintain that three Gods, father, son and holy spirit, exist in one? He could have spoken about that polemic without needing to work out the exact content of the text, but . . . He crossed himself solemnly and then made the sign of the cross and laid the piece of paper down on the desk.

'Father, do you truly want me to repeat in this holy place' – he gestured towards the cathedral – 'what is written on this paper? Many people were condemned this morning for much less.'

'You're right,' conceded Don Salvador. 'Don Julián,' he added, turning to him, 'prepare me a report on the contents of these documents.' Hernando heard Abbas breathe a sigh of relief. 'Where do you work?' the priest asked him.

'In the royal stables.'

'Don Julián, speak with the royal stable master, Don Diego López de Haro, and arrange it so that this young boy can teach us Arabic and assist with the books and documents alongside his work with the King's horses. Convey to him that both the bishop and the cathedral chapter would greatly appreciate it.'

'I will do so, Father.'

'You may leave.' Don Salvador dismissed Hernando and Abbas.

Fátima smiled at her husband as he crossed the library railing.

'Well done!' she whispered.

'Silence!' urged Abbas.

They headed towards the San Miguel gate at the far west of the mosque. Hernando and Fátima followed the blacksmith the length of the south wall. They passed in front of the chapel of Don Alonso Fernández de Montemayor, a governor of the border provinces in the time of King Henry II. Abbas stopped.

'This chapel, dedicated to Saint Peter' – he knelt reverently before it, inviting Hernando and Fátima to do the same – 'is built in the entrance to the mihrab of al-Hakam II.' The three of them remained kneeling there for several moments a little beyond the magnificent lobular arches so different from the horseshoe-shaped ones in the rest of the mosque. Inside the entrance had stood the *maqsura*, the area reserved for the Caliph and his court. 'Back there' – Abbas indicated with his chin – 'in what is now the chapel sacristy, is the mihrab, where the King prohibited the burial of any Christian.' Unlike most of these burials, which were inlaid in the floor, the remains of Don Alonso, the King's lieutenant, were displayed in a large, plain white marble sarcophagus. 'Here, yes,' the blacksmith whispered to Fátima, 'here you can pray.'

'Allah is great,' she murmured, keeping her head down as she stood up.

Each of them, in their own way, tried to picture what al-Hakam's famous mihrab must have looked like, although now it had been desecrated and converted into a simple and common sacristy of the chapel of Saint Peter. There, in the mihrab, their people had once read the Koran. The copy of the Koran kept in the treasury was brought to the mihrab every

Friday, and placed on a lectern of green aloe studded with gold. It had been handwritten by the Prince of the Believers, Usman ibn Affan, and was decorated with gold, pearls and jacinths, and was so heavy it had to be carried by two men. In the entrance, as in the mihrab itself, the Caliph further demonstrated the magnificence of Moorish culture in Córdoba by merging various architectural styles until he achieved a combination of incomparable beauty. The niche where the Koran was guarded was reached by passing beneath a carved octagonal dome. It was in the Armenian style and its arches did not meet in the centre but crossed along the walls. Byzantium was also there, with its veined or white marbles, and above all in the coloured mosaics made from stone brought by artisans who had come specially from the capital of the Eastern empire. Inscriptions from the Koran in Byzantine gold and marble. Arabesques. Elements from the Greco-Romans and the Christians, whose masters also contributed to the construction, had made the site of the chapel of Saint Peter one of the most beautiful places in the world.

The three of them prayed in silence for a few moments and, deep in thought, left the mosque through the San Miguel gate. They came out into Calle de los Arquillos, where the episcopal palace was built on top of the ancient palace of the caliphs of Córdoba. They crossed under one of the three arches of the bridge that passed above the street and linked the ancient palace with the cathedral. They went on towards the stables. As they got beyond the fortress of the Christian monarchs, Hernando decided to tackle the issue that was worrying him.

'I can't translate those documents,' he admitted. 'They are written in classical Arabic. How am I going to teach classical Arabic to this priest?'

Abbas walked on a few more paces without answering. Doubts were crowding his mind. Fátima had seemed reckless and unaware of what she was doing; and yet, he reminded himself, everyone relied on her. Besides, he acknowledged, was it not he himself who had just shown her the hidden site of the mihrab, urging her to pray? Did they not all feel the same deep down?

'On the contrary,' said the smith, when they were near the door of the stables. 'It is Don Julián who will teach you classical Arabic, the Arabic of our divine book.'

Hernando stopped in his tracks, surprise written on his face.

'Yes,' Abbas nodded, 'Don Julián is one of our brothers, and the most knowledgeable of all the Muslims in Córdoba.'

36

AT AROUND the same time as Aisha was being released following her arrest in the Sierra Morena, Brahim left El Sobahet's band of outlaws together with two fugitive slaves. The gob of spittle his wife had launched at him before leaving the camp only added to the intense pain in his arm. Shortly after Aisha had disappeared amongst the trees, the outlaws were on the move, and Brahim had dragged himself after them. He could not stay in the mountains alone, or return defeated and with a hand missing to Córdoba. So he followed them, always at a distance, like a beaten dog. El Sobahet did nothing to stop him. Ubaid laughed at him and threw him his leftovers. When Brahim heard that two of the men were going to try and escape to Barbary, he joined them and together they headed for the Valencian coast. For several long days they stole food and sought assistance in the houses of Moriscos, always careful to avoid the bands of the Holy Brotherhood who patrolled those ancient and now neglected Roman roads. They headed eastwards towards Albacete, from where they took the road to Xátiva. From there they could reach the coastal villages of the kingdom of Valencia between Cullera and Gandía, all inhabited almost exclusively by Moriscos.

Despite the efforts of successive viceroys of Valencia, there was a constant flow of Moriscos to Barbary from this coast. They were helped by the corsairs who came to plunder the kingdom. The Spanish would not leave the new, forcibly baptized Christians in peace, but neither would they let them escape. Not only would the nobles and landowners lose cheap labour but the Church was committed to saving their souls. The Duke of Gandía, Francis Borgia, the Jesuit Superior General, championed the cause. His view was that 'we must save all these souls that might otherwise be lost'. But the Moriscos were already planning on saving their souls – by heading for the lands where Muhammad was worshipped. Their Valencian brothers helped everyone who had decided to leave kingdoms that had been theirs for centuries and cross to Barbary.

Brahim and his companions, together with half a dozen more Moriscos, achieved this goal when one September dawn nearly fifty corsairs travelled along the coast to plunder the outskirts of Cullera. The corsairs employed their usual tactic: under the cover of night three small galleys dropped anchor beyond the mouth of the river Júcar. They disembarked there, some way from the place they intended to attack. The following day, at dawn, they headed on foot towards their objective. Unless they were attacking as part of a large fleet, the corsairs relied on surprise and speed for their raids. Any looting needed to be done speedily before the alarm was raised and the city under attack and the surrounding area responded. The corsairs did not want a pitched battle. Their galleys would come to pick them and their plunder up at some prearranged spot on the coast.

On that September night, a scouting party of corsairs went inland to meet the local Moriscos and gather intelligence to help their looting; the new Christians were banned from going near the coast under threat of a three-year sentence in the galleys. It was then that Brahim, the two slaves and some other Moriscos joined up with the expedition. Two men who knew the area accompanied them to show the corsairs the route to Cullera.

'Give me a sword, and I'll go with you,' Brahim asked a man who seemed to be the leader. They were on the beach where the corsairs were hiding until daybreak. The galleys remained well off shore in order not to be sighted.

'Morisco and one-handed?' the corsair growled. 'Stay out of the way!'

Brahim gritted his teeth and headed for the group of Moriscos sitting silently on the sand, far away from the corsairs.

'What are you looking at?' Brahim cursed one of the slaves who had escaped from Ubaid's band, lashing out with a kick that caught him in the face. Still raging, Brahim remained standing until one of the corsairs rudely ordered him to sit down like the rest and stay quiet.

At dawn, the corsairs swooped on the outskirts of Cullera. They took the peasants who had come to work their lands by surprise, and seized nineteen captives. Instead of chasing after the many others who had fled in terror, the corsairs returned quickly to the point where they had arranged to meet the galleys, on this occasion close to Cullera. Neither the forces inside the city nor those nearby had the opportunity to counter-attack. Before they had even realized what had happened, corsairs, captives and runaway Moriscos were already aboard their ships, heading for the open seas.

However, once they were out of range of the shore, the three galleys turned back towards the coast and hoisted the flag of truce. The ships were already sufficiently laden with plunder from other incursions, and the sailing season was coming to a close. The Valencians knew what the white flag meant: the corsair captains were willing to negotiate there and then the ransom of their captives. The Christians accepted the truce and began the negotiations, with small boats ferrying back and forth. By the end of the morning fifteen men had been released. The other four would journey on to the slave markets of Algiers.

During two peaceful days of return voyage, the galleys had to work hard to make progress in a calm sea. Brahim could see the contempt of the corsair crew, made up of Turks and renegade Christians, for the Moriscos; it was exactly the same as they had suffered during the uprising in the Alpujarra. Nobody wanted anything to do with them. They fed them as if they were dogs, and did not even use them to row across the Mediterranean. Why did they agree to carry them then? He recalled how delighted the Valencian Moriscos had been to see the corsairs. The mere thought of the damage the corsairs would inflict on the Christians was satisfaction enough for them, especially as it kept alive the hope of future assistance from the Sublime Porte. Brahim watched the slaves rowing hard to the commands of the galley overseer. The fleeing Moriscos had been divided into groups so they could be accommodated in the limited space left between the sides of the galley and the rowing benches. Brahim turned his attention to the captain of his ship, who was standing in the prow. His long blond hair, typical of the renegade Christians of the Adriatic, fell over his shoulders, swaying gently to the rhythm marked out by the rowers. Brahim spat into the sea. Helping them escape was merely a business transaction: the corsairs only agreed to transport the worthless human cargo to obtain the locals' favour.

The flotilla of galleys made port in Algiers. To the sound of kettledrums, officials, holy men and assorted individuals ran to receive them. As soon as Brahim glimpsed the city's huge, imposing walls he decided he was not going to spend any length of time there. That nest of corsairs could only be hostile to the Moriscos of al-Andalus. For a couple of days he drifted about the streets. He stayed away from the Moriscos who, as in Spain, came to sell themselves as cheap labour to the owners of the numerous market gardens and orchards surrounding the city, or even in the vast wheat-fields of the Yiyelli plains. Finally in the souk he came across a caravan that was leaving for Fez and tried to join it. He promised to work as hard as anyone in return for leftover food. He was ravenous! All he'd had to eat were scraps discarded by the Algerians, and he'd had to fight for those with men stronger than he was, who had two arms.

'I am a mule-driver,' said Brahim when he saw how the man in charge of the caravan, an Arab from the desert in Bedouin dress, looked at the stump of his arm and shook his head. Brahim wanted to show his worth with animals, even with only one hand. He hesitated as he remembered the problems that Ubaid had faced managing the mules in the Alpujarra, but in the end he made for a large group of resting camels that were lying down, their four legs tucked under them. It was the first time he had ever seen a camel, and even with their legs bent in that complicated position their humps were higher than any of the mules Brahim had handled.

To the caravan leader's puzzlement and the camel's complete indifference, Brahim made to stroke the animal's head. He tried to get the camel to its feet, tugging its halter with his left hand. The camel did not even turn its head. As he used to do with his mules when they refused to move forwards, Brahim pulled the halter from side to side to trick it into setting off moving to the side. However, this animal remained stubbornly impassive. Brahim noticed that a small group of people had gathered around the Arab and were watching the scene, smiling. One of them pointed at him, and urged another camel-driver to come and see the spectacle. What was all the hurry? Brahim wondered. He felt a burning embarrassment and yanked sharply at the camel's halter to get it on its feet. He was about to give another yank when the animal lashed out and bit him in the stomach. Brahim leapt back, tripped and fell to the ground right in the middle of the camels' pile of dung. The onlookers burst out laughing. That was why! They knew the camel was going to bite him. He got to his knees, keeping his back to the group of camel-drivers. The laughter stopped, except for a shrill childish giggle that continued to echo around the camp.

As Brahim rose to his feet, he resisted turning to face the source of that laughter, which was both innocent and irritating. Finally he looked round and was confronted with a boy of about eight, dressed from head to toe in embroidered green silk, like a little prince. At his side stood a bejewelled man armed with a scimitar, its shining scabbard inlaid with numerous precious stones. The man was dressed as richly as the boy. Behind them three women were wearing black full-sleeved tunics, covered in black or blue cloaks fastened with silver pins. Their faces were covered by veils with a slit for their eyes, and their wrists and ankles were adorned with thick silver rings. Brahim looked straight at the boy. He was hungry! Very hungry. Staying in the city would mean dying of starvation or being killed at the hands of some janissary or corsair. That was the only fate ahead of him – either that, or a return to work in the fields. With only one hand he could not even enlist as an oarsman or sell himself as a galley slave.

He saw how the man with the scimitar rested an affectionate hand on the boy's shoulder. The boy had stopped laughing now, and it was then that an idea occurred to Brahim. He winked at the child and stepped forward. He placed his bare foot on one of the many droppings that seemed to be scattered everywhere, and let himself slip, exaggerating a heavy fall on his backside. The peals of childish laughter burst out again and from the corner of his eye Brahim saw the man's lips twist in a smile. On the ground, Brahim waved his arms and made ridiculous gestures as he thought what more he could do to win over the boy and his father. He had never acted the fool, but he needed to now. He had to leave that city where everyone looked down at him, just as they had in Córdoba! He had not made such a long journey only to end up a vulgar peasant again, no matter how many mosques he could attend to bemoan his fate! Encouraged by the child's laughter, he feigned tripping up again and again as he tried to get back to his feet. He approached another resting camel and jumped on to its hump, letting himself fall like a sack straight over the other side. The child's laugh was joined by others he did not recognize but which he assumed came from the camel-drivers. He tried to climb on again with the same result. He finished up by walking around the camel, examining it carefully and lifting up its tail, as if he was trying to discover where it hid its secrets.

When Brahim heard the first guffaw of the man with the scimitar, he went up to them and bowed. The child's huge brown eyes were moist with tears. The man nodded and handed him a gold coin, minted there in Algiers. Only then did Brahim notice the pain that gripped his whole body, especially his stomach where the camel had bitten him.

The rich merchant, Umar ibn Sawan, allowed Brahim to travel with them as his son's jester. Umar had almost fifty camels laden with expensive merchandise, guarded by a small army he had hired. They set off on a journey across central Barbary, from Algiers to Tlemcen, and from there to the magnificent and rich city of Fez, built among the hills and peaks in the centre of the Moroccan realm. On the journey Brahim realized why the camel had bitten him; their drivers treated them affectionately and extremely gently. All they used to make the camels get up or lie down was a thin stick that they brushed against their knees and neck. Instead of whipping them on faster during the long days, they sang to them when tiredness started to take hold. To the Alpujarra muleteer's amazement, the animals responded by trying harder and taking more determined strides. Umar and his son, Yusuf, travelled on horseback. They rode Arabian desert horses; their steeds were small and lean from their diet of camel milk twice a day, but, Brahim discovered, the father's horse was worth a fortune. It had beaten an ostrich in a race in the Numidian deserts, where the merchant had acquired it. Umar's three wives travelled concealed in wickerwork cages covered with beautiful tapestries that swayed to and fro with the movement of the camels transporting them.

Using part of the money the merchant had rewarded him with, Brahim had bought a pair of old shoes and a turban before he joined the train. He travelled on foot with the camels, drivers, slaves, servants and soldiers, amongst whom he was the butt of endless jokes and an object of ridicule and derision. The members of the caravan constantly pushed him around. The muleteer feigned grotesque falls, so that at any given moment they could make fun of him. He responded to their taunts with smiles and comic gestures. He discovered that if he walked on all fours, protecting his stump with the cloth of his turban and feeling a stab of pain every time it touched the ground, he could make the travellers laugh out loud. They also laughed when, for absolutely no reason, he started to run in circles around a camel or a person, shrieking like an idiot. Little Yusuf laughed too from atop his horse; he travelled apart from the procession and always accompanied by his father.

They're all fools! thought Brahim whenever they stopped to rest. Could they not see the rage in his eyes? Every time Brahim made them laugh, an uncontrollable burning sensation started in the pit of his stomach and spread through his entire body. Surely it was impossible for them not to notice the fire burning in his eyes? He walked among the camels and looked out of the corner of his eye at the two horse riders, seeing how they chatted and galloped up and down the caravan, continually giving orders that the men carried out with humble obedience. He also looked at the luxurious tapestries that covered the cages where the three women sat. At night, after having spent a good while entertaining little Yusuf, he would look enviously at the big tents where the merchant and his family lived. They were overflowing with comfortable fabrics, cushions, all kinds of furniture, and copper or iron pots and pans: the tents were far more luxurious than any of the dwellings Brahim had ever known. When Umar, Yusuf and his women retired for the night, Brahim lay down on the ground outside.

When they were a day's journey from Tlemcen, Brahim came to the conclusion that he had to escape. They had crossed mountains and deserts, and among the caravan the talk was of the next desert awaiting them after they had passed the city. This was the Angad desert, where bands of Arabs attacked caravans travelling the route between Tlemcen and Fez. *Arabs.* He was among Arabs now: the kingdoms of Tlemcen, Morocco and Fez. He was tired of humiliation, beatings and ridicule! He was sick of deserts and camels that moved to the sound of stupid songs!

The soldiers guarding the tents took him for a crazy fool, as did the slaves and the majority of those who made up the caravan. For some time now they had stopped watching his movements or what he did while he slept beside the tent. Therefore the night they camped a few leagues from Tlemcen, Brahim had no trouble in crawling under one of the side flaps and sneaking into Umar's tent. Father and son were fast asleep. He listened to their regular breathing, waiting for his eyes to adjust to the faint glimmer from the bonfire outside the tent, around which the three guards were sleeping. He studied the interior, the silks and tapestries, the merchant and his son's rich clothes – and, next to Umar, a small metal chest set with precious stones. Almost crawling, so that no shadow could be seen from the outside, he moved over to Umar and grabbed the chest. He had to put it down in order to hang the merchant's magnificent dagger at his own waist. He picked up the chest with his one hand and left as he had entered. He crawled out of the tent and realized that he had just taken a terrible gamble: escape or death. If they found him . . . He hid the little chest inside his turban, tied it securely to his belt and walked nervously between the camels and the sleeping people. He advanced very slowly to minimize the clinking noise coming from inside the chest, which was audible in spite of the cloth he had wrapped round it. He reached the place where they stored the merchandise the camels carried, which was also under guard. Brahim looked around him for one of the fires that had been lit during the night. Spotting one, he headed towards it. He took off his shoe and placed a glowing ember inside it, then went back to the piles of merchandise and, hiding a few feet away, waited for the patrol of guards to go past. He threw both ember and shoe towards the pile. They landed on some bundles of what seemed to be rich lengths of silk. Without checking the result of his throw, Brahim headed for where Umar and his son's horses were sleeping.

He stroked the horses to calm them and get them used to his presence. These animals he knew. Several men were asleep nearby. When he thought the horses would accept his handling without getting upset and waking their grooms, he silently untied them, and bridled Umar's horse, the one that had beaten the ostrich. He crouched down and waited. Someone would soon raise the alarm. Time passed slowly and nothing happened. Brahim could already imagine Umar's scimitar against his neck, in swift retribution for the theft he had just committed, when the first shout rang out, followed by many more. A dense cloud of smoke was rising into the dark night from the pile of merchandise. The men jumped to their feet and to Brahim's surprise a spectacular roaring blaze erupted. Chaos seized the camp. For a few moments he was captivated by the sight of the tongue of intense red fire licking at the sky.

'What are you doing with the horses?' shouted the groom who looked after them, making for the animals instead of heading towards the fire.

Brahim came to his senses. He pulled a grotesque face, trying to hoodwink the lad. When the youngster stared at him, puzzled by his reaction, Brahim drew the dagger and sank it into his chest. That would be the last act of foolery of his life, Brahim vowed to himself, as with one jump he mounted the horse bareback, wearing only one shoe.

As people ran hither and thither trying to put out the fire, Brahim set off at full gallop northwards. Yusuf's horse galloped at his side, heading for home. Horses and rider were soon lost in the night.

After several days' riding from Tlemcen, Brahim reached Tetuan towards the end of October 1574. He avoided all paths, navigating by instinct and his experience as a muleteer, always heading north. He hid from the slightest sign of movement, and did not allow himself to become overconfident, even though he was certain by now that Umar would not pursue him through these hostile lands. The two horses were very valuable, and the chest revealed a second fortune of precious stones and all kinds of different gold coins.

Tetuan was a small city set at the foot of Dersa mountain, in the valley of the river Martil. It was only six miles from the Mediterranean and nearly eighteen from the Strait of Gibraltar, at a strategic point for naval traffic. The city was fertile, enjoying an abundant supply of water from the Hauz and Rif mountains. The walled old town had been rebuilt and re-populated by the Muslims who had fled when Granada was surrendered to the Catholic monarchs, and the majority of its inhabitants were Moriscos.

Brahim broke his vow to never again play the fool. After hiding his horses and money in the mountains, he entered the city by the Bab Mqabar gate next to the cemetery, dressed like a crazy beggar, and with only a few coins hidden in his clothing. In the city he found he could breathe in the spirit of Andalusia. The way the people spoke and dressed, the layout of the streets that could have been the Albaicín in Granada or any small Alpujarra village, instantly convinced him this was where he should live. He persuaded a scruffy urchin, with huge round bright eyes and bald patches on his scalp from scabies, to act as his guide round the city. To the surprise of both the boy and the merchants in the market, he bought new clothes and everything necessary to look distinguished when he presented himself in this new place. He also bought clothes for Nasi, as the little ragamuffin was called. He could not enter Tetuan looking destitute if he was travelling with two magnificent horses and a chest full of gold.

After that he went back with the astonished boy to where he had hidden the horses. He washed himself in a stream and made Nasi do the same. He dressed in his new clothes and threw a blanket over the horse to use as a saddle. He loaded Yusuf's horse with the baggage so that Nasi, his head covered with a turban, could travel behind him as if he was his servant. As soon as he heard the offer of a meal a day, the boy happily agreed to this arrangement.

'If you say a word about who I am, I'll cut your throat,' Brahim threatened him, flashing the dagger blade.

Nasi did not seem bothered by the sight of the knife, but his response sounded sincere: 'I swear to Allah.'

They rented a good, one-storey house with a garden at the rear.

In the last quarter of the sixteenth century, when Brahim established himself in the city, the business of piracy changed completely. From the Tetuan port of Martil numerous ships, generally small galleys, set sail to attack the Spanish coasts, rivalling those from Barbary's other corsair cities: Algiers, Tunis, Sargel, Vélez, Larache or Salé. But the arrival of large French, English or Dutch galleons in the Mediterranean caused the ship-owners in Algiers to replace their light, narrow galliots and galleys with large deep-hulled sailing ships armed with rows of cannon that could keep pace with those new vessels and defeat them. Thus the Algerian corsairs' influence reached the most remote areas of the Mediterranean, and even the Atlantic: England, France, Portugal and as far as Ireland.

The plundering of the Spanish coast in lightning raids did not cease completely, but became a secondary activity for the great corsair cities. This was the situation Brahim found when he established himself in Tetuan and used his new-found wealth to become a ship-owner. He fitted out three galleys, each with twelve benches of rowers, and imposed one condition that the ship's captains readily accepted: Brahim would personally accompany the expeditions because, although he knew nothing of sailing, who better to direct the attacks than a muleteer who knew every inch of the Granada, Málaga and Almería coasts?

In March 1575, at the start of the sailing season, and at the head of a band of thirty Moriscos, the former Alpujarra mule-driver landed on the coast of Almería, close to Mojácar. Not one guard in the nine defensive towers spread along seven leagues of coast between Vera and Mojácar itself sighted the ships or sounded the alarm.

'The defences are either unmanned or in ruins,' the captain sailing with Brahim commented. 'Some towers don't even have a guard, or it is just an old man who prefers to spend his time in his vegetable garden rather than do the job King Philip pays him for.'

And so it proved. Even though the corsairs still often raided the Spanish coast, the defence system of watchtowers stretching all along the coastline, with guards and runners who were meant to alert the cities and troops, had fallen into decline from a lack of financial resources, and was now practically useless.

On this occasion, nobody prevented Brahim from taking part in the looting of some farms near Mojácar. Almost fifty men, Moriscos and freed galley slaves, landed on the coasts of al-Andalus, whilst the others stayed with the ships. The majority split into groups and scattered in search of booty. Brahim paused for a moment and watched them running inland. Spain! He breathed deeply and his chest swelled with pride. He had returned to Spain and those were his men! He paid them! He had a small army at his service.

'What you waiting for?' the captain urged him. 'We don't have much time!'

On the far side of the beach they came across some peasants working their land. Brahim saw them flee, with the corsairs close behind them. They caught up with two of them.

'Over there!' Brahim shouted, pointing to his left. 'There are some houses.'

He remembered them from the days when he had travelled as a muleteer in the area.

The Berbers ran to where the former muleteer pointed. By the time they reached the small group of humble dwellings, their inhabitants had also run off, alerted by the shouts of those who had fled the fields.

Brahim kicked the door of one of the houses down. It was pointless, but the violence made him feel powerful, invincible. Yet there was nothing worth stealing in the home of a miserable peasant family.

After a while all the corsairs met up again on the beach. They had suffered no casualties, and had not even had to fight.

They had discovered only a little money, some trinkets and a lot of clothing of little value, but they did have fifteen captives. Standing out among them were three young, healthy and voluptuous women from Galicia who would fetch a good price on the Tetuan slave market. They were among those brought down to repopulate the kingdom of Granada after the expulsion of its own people.

As the men boarded behind him, a sweating, flushed Brahim fixed his eyes once more on the lands of al-Andalus. In the distance rose the Sierra Nevada, with its peaks, its rivers, its forests . . .

'I have returned, bastard Nazarene!' he shouted. 'Fátima, I am here! I swear to Allah that one day I will take back what is mine!'

37

HERNANDO SPURRED Corretón on and the cold air of the Córdoba meadows caught him full in the face. The resounding echo of hooves on damp earth could not drown out the curses of José Velasco and Rodrigo García, who were galloping behind him, trying to catch up. He had challenged them right there in the meadow, surrounded by mares and foals: 'Corretón can beat any of your horses.' The two veteran horse-breakers were incredulous, but jokingly accepted the challenge.

'The last one to reach that plantation of cork oaks', said Hernando, pointing to the edge of the meadow where the trees marked the boundary of the field where the mares were kept, 'buys a round of wine.'

He leant forward in the saddle over Corretón's extended neck, keeping the reins loose but maintaining a light contact with the horse's mouth, and feeling in his legs the frantic rhythm of his mount's swift, impulsive strides. Hernando continued to spur the horse on, increasing the gap on his pursuers. It was a great day for all Moriscos. Before they had left for the pasture the news had spread through Córdoba as all the church bells began to toll. Don John of Austria had died of typhus at Namur. At that time governor of the Low Countries, the scourge of the Alpujarra had ended his days in a simple hut.

Few horses galloped like Corretón, and Hernando shouted at the top of his lungs. *For the women and children of Galera, whose execution the Christian Prince had ordered!*

Less than a quarter of a league from the trees, first Rodrigo and then José overtook him, throwing up a shower of mud and pebbles. Hernando slowed down until he reached the two riders waiting for him. They were already in the wood, cantering slowly so that their mounts could recover.

'We'll drink to you!' Rodrigo boasted.

José smiled and mimed raising a glass to his lips.

'He's much younger than your horses,' the Morisco defended himself.

'You should have thought of that before you started bragging,' Don Diego's groom retorted. 'Are you going to try and get out of it?'

'You know I am not! I chose the wrong distance.'

Rodrigo drew near and slapped him on the shoulder. 'Well, that will cost you money.'

The horses began to breathe more easily. They had begun their ride back to the city when Rodrigo attracted their attention to something. 'Look!' he exclaimed, pointing towards the undergrowth.

The rump and hindquarters of a mare were sticking out from beneath some bushes. They approached and dismounted. José and Rodrigo went to examine the body of the mare, whilst Hernando stayed with the horses.

'It's one of the oldest mares,' José said from beside the animal. They returned to where Hernando was waiting and mounted up. 'But she bore good foals,' he added, like an epitaph. 'We'll go back to Córdoba,' he told the Morisco, 'you go and find the keeper of the brood mares, and tell him he has a corpse here. Come back with him, and when he has skinned the mare, take the hide to show the administrator. He will remove the mare's details from the books. Be quick about it, before some wild creature gets to work on the carcass and the King's brand vanishes!'

If the mare's body was attacked by scavengers and the brand of a crowned R disappeared, it would be impossible to prove the death to the administrator and the keepers of the brood mares would be in trouble.

Hernando carried the dead mare's hide thrown over the front of his saddle, with its brand clearly visible. It smelt like the ones he used to carry from the slaughterhouse to the tannery more than seven years ago. How his life had changed in that time! Finding the keeper of the brood mares, returning to the wood and skinning the body had taken most of the rest of the day. By the time he had finished the sun was already going down, its rays flickering around the silhouette of Córdoba. It was possible to make out the cathedral emerging from the middle of the mosque, the fortress, the tower of Calahorra and the bell towers of the churches, all illuminated by a reddish glow above the house roofs. As they rode at a walk through the countryside the silence was almost complete. Corretón stepped softly as if aware of the spell. Hernando sighed. The horse's ears flicked back in surprise, and the rider patted its neck.

Nearly a year and a half earlier a young horse-breaker had suffered an accident in the pastures. The bull he was running had brought down the horse and gored the man in the groin.

Alonso, the injured man, was taken to the royal stables. He was bleeding profusely, but the horn did not seem to have affected any vital organs. Nevertheless, when the surgeon arrived at the stables and examined Alonso's groin, he diagnosed that he would need to operate on his penile gland. Alonso would not let them come near him until a public scribe came to testify that his penis had not been circumcised prior to the operation. It was Hernando who had to run and find the man. He feared Alonso might bleed to death in the time it took for the official to respond, but nobody seemed disturbed by that possibility. Everyone present, even the surgeon, accepted

Alonso's demand as logical. Not to appear Jewish or Muslim was more important than life itself! To Hernando's surprise, the scribe reacted promptly. As soon as he heard him, he handed Hernando his papers and instruments to carry, and ran to the stables. The scribe followed the surgeon's fingers and explanations with great interest, and despite all the blood and torn flesh was able to personally confirm that Alonso was not previously missing his foreskin. He certified how, during the operation, according to the surgeon, it had been necessary for medical reasons to remove the rider's foreskin. He handed the document to the patient, who clutched it as if it contained his life . . . or his honour.

'I don't think Alonso will be able to ride again any time soon,' Don Diego commented to his groom after he had witnessed the public document. 'Can you ride?' he immediately asked Hernando, who was still standing next to the scribe.

'Yes . . .' Hernando stammered. This was the opportunity he had so much longed for.

Don Diego put his response to the test by mounting him on a four-year-old horse ready to be sent to the King. As soon as Hernando felt the power of a horse between his legs, every single piece of advice from Aben Humeya rang through his head. Upright, sit up straight; proud, above all proud; light-handed; the control is in your legs; use force only if necessary; dance! Dance with your horse! Feel it as part of yourself! And so he danced with the horse. He asked it to move in the ways that, over hundreds of days, he had observed the expert riders obtain from their mounts as they worked them in the yard or in the covered school the King had ordered built to protect the animals from the extremes of summer and winter weather. Hernando himself was surprised by how the horse responded to his legs and hands. He was captivated by the manners of this beautifully trained thoroughbred of the new Spanish breed.

'He has the same instinct, the same gift in the saddle as he does on the ground with the colts,' Don Diego commented to

José and Rodrigo as they studied the performance of rider and horse. 'Teach him. Teach him all you know.'

And the horse-trainers did teach him. So too did Don Julián in the library of Córdoba cathedral, which the chapter had decided to move that year. From Don Julián, Hernando acquired a deep understanding of the sacred language, and he gradually came to master classical Arabic. He went to the mosque in the evening when his work at the stables was finished, and the comings and goings of priests and worshippers had diminished. He was there before compline and sometimes even afterwards, when they were about to close the cathedral doors. Don Julián was the last of the priests that first the Mudéjars and later the Moriscos managed to introduce surreptitiously into the great mosque.

'Since King Fernando conquered Córdoba and the mosque fell into Christian hands,' Don Julián's gentle voice explained to Hernando as the two of them sat alone at a table in the library bent over documents by lamp light, 'there has almost always been a Muslim here disguised in the habit of a priest. Our function has been to silently pray in this holy place, as well as to find out what the Church is thinking, what it is intending to do so that we can warn all our brothers about it. This can only be done if we are inside their churches and councils.'

'You're not wanting me to be ordained as a priest!' exclaimed Hernando.

'No, of course not. Unfortunately, it is now almost impossible to infiltrate new Muslims into Christian religious orders. The attestations of pure blood, and the demand for information before any position on the cathedral chapter can be attained, have become stricter over time.'

Hernando knew about the attestations of pure blood. This was an administrative process by which a person had to prove that there was no converted Muslim or Jew among their ancestors. Pure blood had become an essential prerequisite not only to join the clergy, but also to be appointed to any public office in Spain.

'This cathedral's statute of pure blood', Don Julián went on, 'was approved in August 1530, although it was not ratified by papal bull until more than twenty years later. During the intervening years it was put into practice by order of Emperor Charles. At the time I passed this test, years ago now' – the old priest shook his head as if the memory saddened him – 'an attestation was twelve pages long and the information was quite superficial. Today they can reach two hundred and fifty pages, or more, and include detailed investigations of parents, grandparents and other ancestors; where they lived, their work, their way of life . . . In short, I doubt very much that when I'm gone, if they don't find me out before then, we will be able to carry on this deception. We should therefore strengthen those means of protection that are not dependent on us having a presence within the churches.

'Only in Granada is it any different,' the priest went on to explain. 'There the archbishop appears reluctant to apply the attestations of pure blood. Granada is still populated by great families descended from the Muslim nobility, who integrated with the Christian hierarchy in the times of the Catholic monarchs. There are even priests, Jesuits and monks descended from Moriscos. It is genuinely difficult to enforce the statutes of pure blood in that kingdom . . . But it will happen; they will be applied to them as well.'

During the five years he had spent working with Don Julián, Hernando had come to know what the priest meant by 'means of protection'. They operated through the Morisco council. This was made up of the three elders of the community: Jalil, Karim and Hamid, together with Don Julián, Abbas and himself. For the six to meet was extremely difficult for Hamid, given his status as a slave, but was also highly dangerous, especially for the cleric. Because of this Hernando acted as messenger between them all when there was a crisis that required a collective decision. Given that he needed to go to the cathedral at night, he obtained a special document from the stable scribe that allowed him a freedom of movement seldom given to the other Moriscos of Córdoba.

This happened almost as soon as he had started work in the library. In 1573, the Muslim community heard that an uprising was being planned in Aragón. Word came via the outlaws and the muleteers who travelled from place to place. The Moriscos of that realm had made contact with the French Huguenots, promising them military and economic aid if they invaded Aragón. As the news spread, many men from Córdoba and its region showed their willingness to go to Aragón to take up arms against the Christians. The council decided to calm these desires, and begged all the faithful in Córdoba to wait and not make any hasty decisions. Two years later, the Frenchman who had acted as intermediary between the Huguenots and Moriscos was detained by the Inquisition and confessed under torture. The Count of Sástago, viceroy of Aragón, also ordered the inquisitors to arrest and torture Moriscos chosen at random from towns across the kingdom, to uncover the details of their plans.

In December 1576 events repeated themselves. Copies circulated of a letter from the Sultan of the Sublime Porte, which announced the arrival of three Muslim fleets that would land simultaneously in Barcelona, Denia and Cartagena. In May of the following year, the Inquisition got hold of a letter from the governor-general of Algiers. It warned the Spanish Moriscos that the fleet would not arrive until August and its landing would coincide with an invasion from France. It urged the Moriscos to capture the mountains when this happened. However, by October 1578 nothing had been heard of fleets or landings.

'Our brothers in faith are only concerned with their own interests,' Karim affirmed. It was Sunday after mass and un-usually all of them except Don Julián had managed to meet in Jalil's house. They were sitting on mats on the floor whilst the youngsters kept a lookout in Calle de los Moriscos for the arrival of any justices or priests. Hamid and Jalil lowered their gaze at Karim's assertion. Abbas started to object, but Karim stopped him. 'No, Abbas, it's true. In the Alpujarra uprising all they did was send corsairs and renegades, whilst the troops they had promised us attacked Tunis and the Sultan invaded Cyprus. Not long ago the Algerians occupied Tunis and Bizerte and have succeeded in expelling the Spanish from La Goulette, and as for the Sultan—'

'It has been some time now since the Sultan came to an agreement with King Philip that the Turkish fleet would not attack Mediterranean ports,' Hernando butted in. The three elders looked at him in surprise, and Abbas gave a snort of incredulity. 'He who all of you will know' – not even in private did they want to name Don Julián, as they were the only five people in Córdoba who knew the priest's real allegiance – 'has heard of this situation. These are secret agreements. The King does not want to send a formal ambassador but has dispatched a Milanese nobleman to negotiate peace. He is so anxious to keep the negotiations secret that the noble goes about Constantinople dressed as a slave. King Philip does not want either the French interfering in his negotiations or the Christian world considering him a traitor for agreeing to make peace with the heretics, but that is how it is. The Turks are directing their efforts towards Persia, with whom they are at war, and therefore they are as interested as the Christians in these peace agreements.'

'That means . . .' Karim started to say.

'That all the promises of liberation made to our people are once again false,' Hamid concluded.

As Hernando listened to the holy scholar his stomach clenched. It had been an effort for Hamid to speak. His words were harsh, cutting and cold, but after speaking he seemed empty. He appeared to age suddenly, growing almost visibly older before Hernando's eyes.

For several moments silence reigned in the large room, as each one considered the reality of the situation.

'They must not know this!' exclaimed Karim. 'The community must not know what's going on.'

'What good would it do them?' said Hernando.

'We can't take away their hope,' Jalil added. Hernando saw Hamid nod in agreement. 'That's all we have left. The people speak of Turks, Algerians and corsairs with their eyes glowing. What could we do without their help? Rise up again?' Jalil punched the air violently with one hand. 'We don't have weapons, and the Christians control our every movement. We were defeated in the mountains, when we were armed and enthusiastic and on our own rugged territory; this time they will annihilate us! If we deny our people the hope that help from the Sublime Porte represents, they will sink into despair and throw themselves into the arms of the Christians and their religion. That is what the Christians want, but we must keep the dream alive. All our prophecies announce it: We Muslims will rule again in al-Andalus!'

Hernando had no choice but to agree.

'God, He who grants power, He who humbles the mighty,' said Hernando, his eyes meeting Hamid's, 'will protect us.'

Hernando and Hamid gazed intently at one another; the others respected that moment of communion.

'God', whispered the holy man in a sing-song voice, as he had done in the Alpujarra, 'leads whomsoever He wishes astray, and guides whomsoever He wants. May your soul, O Muhammad, not waver in the face of affliction. God knows what He is doing.'

Several moments passed by in silence.

'So then we continue to accept the promises of help that reach us on behalf of the Turks.' It was Jalil who broke the spell cast by Hamid's words. 'We shall pretend to receive them with hope, but at the same time will try to ensure our brothers do not get swept up in imaginary plans.'

They considered the session closed, and Abbas helped Hamid to his feet. As a precaution they were in the habit of leaving their meeting places separately, allowing some time to elapse between each departure. Hamid limped to the door of the house.

'Lean on me,' said Hernando, offering him his arm.

'We shouldn't . . .'

'A son always has a duty to his father. It's the law.'

Hamid relented. Forcing a smile, he leant on the arm offered him. The brand marking him out as a slave was blurred by the myriad lines scored in his face.

'It fades over time, doesn't it?' he said when they were in the street, conscious that Hernando was casting sidelong glances at the degrading mark.

'Yes,' Hernando acknowledged.

'Not even slavery can defeat death.'

'But you can still clearly see the outline of the letter,' Hernando tried to encourage him as they said goodbye with a brief nod of the head to one of the watching youngsters who continued pretending to play in Calle de los Moriscos.

Hamid walked slowly, trying to hide the pain caused by his bad leg. The sky seemed grey and heavy. They passed the back of the Church of Santa Marina and walked down Calle Aceituno and Calle Arhonas to reach the Potro district. By going this way they avoided the crowded cobbled streets near Calle de Feria, where the people of Córdoba took their Sunday strolls. Besides, thought Hernando, in La Ajerquía they were less likely to run into any young nobles who might have decided to woo some girl by running a bull under her window. Hamid would not have been able to get out of the way. However, the walk was not at all pleasant. In this year of 1578 drought had again devastated Córdoba, as it had the year before. Even now in October the lack of rain caused the cesspits to give off a strong, foul smell because there were no drains. Added to this was the stench from the many dumps where the population deposited their rubbish.

'How's your family?' asked Hamid.

'Well,' replied Hernando. In five years of marriage he and Fátima had had two children. 'Francisco' – the eldest was called Francisco in honour of Hamid, but had no Muslim name for fear that the children might start to use it – 'is growing strong and healthy, and Inés is beautiful. She looks more like her mother every day; she has her eyes.'

'If she also grows like her in character,' the holy man went on, in acknowledgement of Fátima's work, 'she will be a great woman. And Aisha, has she got over—?'

'No,' cut in Hernando, 'she hasn't got over it.'

They had talked about Aisha on other occasions. When she came out of prison and took stock of her new situation after Brahim's flight, she also accepted that, given the circumstances, she could never again have a man by her side. Hernando explained to her how under Morisco law after a period of four years with no word of her husband, she had the right to ask the council to grant her a divorce.

'I'd also have to ask the bishop,' she retorted. 'Any new marriage would not be valid in the eyes of the Christians. Brahim is declared a fugitive. It's what I said when I was arrested, without thinking of the consequences it could have for me in the future. The bishop will never allow me to marry again . . . and I will never subject myself to his judgement. Nor do I need to marry again.'

Determined that Shamir should not know the truth about his father, Aisha had prepared a story she would tell him when the child was old enough to ask. It was a story in which he was the son of a hero, killed in the Alpujarra during the Morisco uprising; a story in which she remained faithful to her husband's memory. From that moment onwards, Aisha threw herself into recovering her family, the children the Christians had stolen from her as soon as she had arrived in Córdoba. She spoke of it with her first-born.

'You are the head of the family now,' she told him. 'You earn a good wage and we have two rooms at our disposal, something that the great majority of Moriscos don't have. Now you work in the cathedral' – unlike Fátima, his mother did not know the whole truth about what he did in the library – 'so nobody could complain that your brothers would not be instructed in the Christian faith. They are your brothers. They are my children! I want them with me, like you and Shamir!'

And they were the children of that animal Brahim! thought

Hernando. However, he kept quiet. The tears that ran down his mother's cheeks, and the sight of her trembling, clenched hands awaiting his decision, were enough to make him promise he would do everything possible to find and free them. Musa would then be about thirteen or fourteen and Aquil about seventeen. He let Fátima know he was going to do what his mother asked, but did not discuss it with her or give her the chance to argue. He explained it all to Don Julián and obtained a recommendation signed by Don Salvador, who turned out to be the cathedral precentor, in charge of the hymn books that were chained to the benches, mending them when necessary or ordering new ones. Don Salvador examined him on his knowledge of the Arabic language, and over time, sometimes indirectly and at others openly, he also sought to verify the assertion that Abbas made when he presented Hernando as a good Christian. Hernando demonstrated his beliefs and knowledge with both firmness and humility, always seeking Don Salvador's advice and explanations, and the cathedral precentor was satisfied. With the help of the priests, Hernando managed to get the municipal council to tell him which families his brothers had been given to for their conversion. However, when everything was ready for them to be returned, the potter and the baker, the devout Christians who had taken charge of them, declared that the children had fled. By way of proof they produced the reports they had filed with the council at the time.

In reality, as Hamid explained, they had sold them, as was the case with many other Morisco children. In spite of being below the age stipulated by King Philip, children from every Spanish kingdom had been enslaved. Hamid told Hernando that some, when they reached adulthood, went to court and demanded their freedom, but it was a lengthy and costly process. Many others did not even try or were unaware of the fact they could do so. In the case of Aisha's sons, not knowing where they had been taken or to whom they had been sold, there was little that could be done to help them.

Aisha found the news unbearable and sank into a despair

that with the passing of time degenerated into an empty, meaningless life devoid of all hope. In Córdoba they had stolen two of her sons and in Juviles they had murdered her two daughters. Not even the presence of Shamir could draw her out of her depression.

'She hasn't got over it,' said Hernando, and Hamid squeezed his arm in consolation.

They passed in front of a large mural on the wall of a building that depicted a crucified Christ. Several people were praying; others lit candles at the foot of the mural, and a man asking for alms for the altar approached them. Hernando gave him a penny and crossed himself as he murmured what the man took to be a prayer. Why would God, as good and compassionate as they told him He was, allow four of his half-brothers and -sisters to have come to such an end? Why had they stolen the freedom and the way of life of an entire people? He watched how Hamid copied him and crossed himself as well, and they continued on their way.

Reaching the intersection of Calle Arhonas with Calle de Mucho Trigo and Calle del Potro, where five streets met, they turned and walked in silence towards the brothel.

'And you,' Hernando dared to ask a few steps from the door of the brothel, 'how are you feeling?'

'Good, good,' muttered Hamid.

'What's wrong?' Hernando insisted. He stopped and squeezed the wasted hand resting on his arm, to show he did not believe him.

'I'm getting old, my lad. That's all.'

'Francisco!' The shriek made Hernando jump. He looked towards the door of the brothel and saw before him a large, thickset woman with greasy hair. She was sweating and her sleeves were rolled up above her elbows. 'Where were you?' the woman continued shouting, in spite of the fact they were only a few steps from her. 'There's a lot to do. Come in!'

Hamid went to go in, but Hernando held him back.

'Who is she?' he asked.

'Get in now, Moor!' the woman insisted.

'No one . . .' Hernando tightened his grip on the hand he was still holding. 'She's the new slave who looks after the women,' Hamid conceded.

'Meaning?'

'I have to go in, my son. Peace be with you.' Hamid extricated himself from Hernando's grasp and limped to the brothel without looking back. The woman was waiting for him, arms akimbo.

Hernando watched him enter the brothel slowly and awkwardly. He frowned and clenched his fists, remembering the grimaces of pain he had seen etched on Hamid's features.

When the holy man passed by the woman, she shoved him in the back. 'Get a move on, old man!' she shouted.

Hamid stumbled and almost fell to the floor.

Hernando felt sick. His stomach churning, he stood motionless until the gate to the brothel alley closed behind the woman. Then he heard more shouts and curses. A new slave: that meant Hamid was no longer useful to them!

Several men on their way down Calle del Potro bumped into him as they went past.

What would become of Hamid? he wondered as he wandered on. How long had he been in that situation? How could he not have realized, not have understood the significance of the pain and resignation shown by his . . . father? Had he been so blinded by his own happiness that he could no longer see the suffering of others?

'Ungrateful wretch!' His exclamation surprised one of the innkeepers in Plaza del Potro, where Hernando had walked without meaning to. The man studied the new arrival for a few moments, weighing him up; well dressed in his riding boots, yet another of the eccentric characters who hung around the area. 'You wretch!' Hernando reproached himself again. The innkeeper scowled.

'A glass of wine?' he offered. 'It will cure your troubles.'

Hernando turned to the man. What troubles? He had never

been happier! Fátima adored him and he adored her in return. They talked and laughed, made love at every opportunity and worked for the community, both of them. They wanted for nothing and felt they led full lives, satisfied and proud. They could see their children were growing up strong and healthy, happy and loving. Whereas Hamid . . . A glass of wine? Why not?

Hernando drained his glass, and the innkeeper filled it a second time.

'The old Moor of the brothel?' the innkeeper asked when Hernando, his mind slightly befuddled by the two glasses of wine, enquired about him.

Hernando nodded sadly. 'Yes, the old Moor.'

'He's for sale. The landlord has been trying to get rid of him for some time, to save on the leftovers that he has to feed him. Every night he offers him to everyone who passes through the Potro.'

Hamid had been up for sale for some time! Why hadn't he said anything? Why had he allowed his son to sleep peacefully at nights alongside his wife, giving thanks to God for everything he had, when those same nights the landlord was trying to sell him?

'Nobody wants to buy him.' The innkeeper burst out laughing as he filled the wine glass again. 'He is good for nothing!'

Hernando put down the glass he had raised unconsciously to his lips, and refused to drink another drop. What was the man saying? He was talking about a holy scholar! 'Children, Hamid taught me . . .' How often had he begun a conversation with them using that very phrase? They were only little, but he enjoyed telling them things. In those moments Fátima took his hand and squeezed it with great tenderness, and Aisha let her memories drift towards that small mountain village in the Alpujarra. The children watched him wide-eyed, hanging on his every word. Maybe they were too young to understand what he was trying to communicate, but Hamid was always there with them. He was with them in their most intimate moments, in those of the greatest happiness; the family all together, healthy, without hunger, all their needs satisfied. And he was good for nothing? How could Hernando not have realized? Again he reproached himself. How could he have been so blind?

'Why?' The innkeeper interrupted his thoughts. 'Why are you interested in that old cripple?'

Hernando looked the man straight in the eye. He took out a coin and left it on the counter. He shook his head and got up to leave, but . . .

'How much is the landlord asking for the slave?'

The man shrugged his shoulders. 'A pittance,' he answered, with a lazy wave of his hand.

'He asked . . . no, he insisted we should not tell you about it,' Abbas explained to him.

After speaking with the innkeeper, Hernando had gone straight to the stables. As soon as he passed through the gate he headed for the forge.

'Why?' he almost shouted. Abbas asked him to lower his voice. 'Why?' he repeated more calmly. 'The community frees slaves whenever it can. I myself contribute. Why not him? I heard they are asking a pittance. Did you know that? A pittance for a man who is a saint!'

'Because he doesn't want it. He wants young people to be freed. And this pittance they have quoted you would be if the bailiff sold him to another Christian. If they found out we were trying to liberate him, the price would not be the same. You know full well what happens: for every one of our brothers we pay far higher than the asking price.'

'So what if it costs money? He has dedicated his whole life to working for us. If anyone deserves to be freed, it is Hamid.'

'I agree with you,' Abbas conceded, 'but we have to respect his decision,' he added before Hernando could start arguing, 'and that is why money hasn't been spent on him.'

'But . . .'

'Hamid knows what he's doing. You've said it yourself, he's a saint.'

Hernando left the forge without saying goodbye. He was not going to allow it! Some Christians, especially pious women, liberated their slaves if they were no longer useful. The brothel landlord was not one of them. That man would hold on to Hamid until somebody offered money for him, however little that was. The traffic in human beings was one of the most thriving and profitable businesses in Córdoba, and not only for the professional dealers, but for anyone who had a slave. Everyone traded in slaves and obtained rich rewards. But although he was lame, old and in pain, the person who acquired Hamid would surely not do so to keep him idle. They would force him to work in order to recover their investment, and possibly somewhere far away from Córdoba. No matter how much he insisted, the holy man did not deserve such a fate at the end of his days. Hernando himself did not deserve it either, he acknowledged in his innermost thoughts as he went to his rooms on the top floor. He needed Hamid! He needed to see him and talk to him, even though it was only once in a while. He needed his advice, and above all he needed to know he was always there to give it. He needed to enjoy in Hamid the father he had not had in his childhood.

He talked to Fátima and she listened carefully. When he had finished, she smiled and stroked his cheek.

'Free him,' she whispered. 'Whatever it costs. You're earning good money now. We'll be all right.'

So he was, Hernando told himself as he crossed the Roman bridge towards the tower of Calahorra, absent-mindedly showing his special document to the bailiffs who controlled the traffic on the bridge. They had increased his salary to three ducats a month plus ten bushels of good wheat each year, although this was less than the Christian horse-breakers earned. Even Abbas, as a blacksmith, received a more generous salary. Fátima saved every bit of spare money, as if their prosperity could end at the most unexpected moment.

On holidays, the Campo de la Verdad filled with the inhabitants of Córdoba strolling along the banks of the river. They gazed at the line of three windmills standing on the Guadalquivir down river from the Roman bridge. Or they sought the peace of the meadows opening out on the other side of the outlying suburbs. Given the influx of people, and in spite of it being Sunday, the horse and mule dealers had their animals on sale in case any of the citizens felt like buying.

Juan the muleteer walked with a stoop, which made him appear much shorter than he actually was. He smiled, showing gums that were missing many of the black teeth he had had when Hernando had first known him.

'The great Morisco horseman!' the mule dealer greeted him. Hernando was stunned. 'You're surprised?' Juan added, slapping him affectionately on the back. 'I know about you. In fact, a lot of people know about you.'

That possibility had never occurred to Hernando. What else would people know about him?

'It's unusual for a Morisco lad to end up riding the King's horses . . . and working in the cathedral. Some of the dealers you did business with use your name to attract buyers,' explained Juan, winking at him. '"This horse was broken by Hernando, the Morisco rider of the royal stables!" they boast when people take an interest. I thought of saying that you had also ridden my mules, but I don't know if it would work.'

They both laughed.

'How are things, Juan?'

'The *Weary Virgin* finally succumbed,' he said in his ear, taking his arm in a friendly fashion. 'She sank slowly and solemnly, as befitted a lady, but luckily she did so close to the shore and we could recover the barrels.'

'You continued smuggling after—?'

'Look, what a mule!' Juan pointed one out, ignoring the question. Hernando examined the animal. It looked like a good beast: clean legs with good bones and a strong body. What defect could it hide? 'Perhaps the royal stable wants to buy a good mule?' joked the dealer.

'Do you want to earn a couple of pennies?' Hernando asked, remembering the proposal the mule dealer had once made him.

Hesitating, Juan raised his hand to his chin and once again revealed his wasted gums. 'I'm getting old,' he said. 'I can't run any more . . .'

'Can't you enjoy women either? What about that bordello in Barbary?'

'You insult me, lad. Any self-respecting Spaniard would pay to end his days on top of a good female.'

Hernando would pay for the mule dealer's pleasure. That was the deal they agreed over a jug of wine in a tavern near the cathedral. Juan was willing to collaborate, especially when Hernando explained why he was interested in the brothel's crippled slave.

'He's my father,' he said.

'In that case, I'll do it for free,' Juan said, 'but you deserve to pay for insulting my virility. There shouldn't be even a whisper of doubt about that,' he said sarcastically.

'How do I know you haven't tricked me and that in reality you've done nothing more than sleep like a baby in one of those women's laps? I'll not be there,' Hernando answered, prolonging the joke.

'My lad, if you hang about in Plaza del Potro near the fountain, even from a distance, above the noise you'll hear the cries of pleasure . . .'

'There are many women in the brothel, and many rooms. What if it's not yours?'

'My name, boy, you'll hear how she screams my name.'

Hernando remembered him rowing back in the *Weary Virgin*, the skiff flooding with water and each stroke shorter and harder. He was short and thin even in those days, and yet they always reached the shore! He nodded, as if acknowledging Juan's virility, before he went on.

'The landlord mustn't suspect you're interested in ... the slave. He wants to sell him and he'll let him go for any price. Of course, he mustn't find either that there are Moriscos behind the operation. And my father ... my father shouldn't know anything either.' The muleteer frowned. 'He doesn't want us to waste our money on an old man,' he explained, 'but I can't allow it. Do you understand?'

'Yes. I understand. Leave it to me.' Juan raised his wine glass. 'To the good times!' he toasted.

At nightfall the following Monday, Juan the muleteer entered the brothel. He showed them a bag with several gold crowns in it that Hernando had given him, bragging that today he had done the best deal of his life. The landlord congratulated him on his good fortune and laughed with him as he sang the praises of the women working in the rooms open along both sides of the alleyway. Some of the women were displaying themselves in the doorways, until the muleteer decided on a plump, dark-haired young girl. He disappeared with her inside the small one-storey house. There was just one room and the bed was pushed up against a couple of chairs and a sideboard with a washbasin on it.

For his part, Hernando made his excuses to Don Julián and returned to drift around among the people who always filled Plaza del Potro. He felt slightly nostalgic as he heard the shouting and merriment, the wagers and even when he saw the usual brawls.

For the past year or more there had been more people than ever in the square and the surrounding streets. The usual vagabonds, gamblers, adventurers, soldiers without their officers or officers without their men, as well as all kinds of lowlifes, were drawn there, as if summoned by a beacon. The poor despairing wretches who spent the night in the city on their journey along the Camino de Las Ventas to the rich, sumptuous court in Madrid, where they hoped to obtain some sinecure or other; those heading for Seville hoping to embark for the Indies in search of their fortune; the vast number of undesirables that the viceroy of Valencia had unceremoniously expelled from his lands and who emigrated to Catalonia or Aragón, to Seville (where few more would now be able to survive) or to Córdoba: all of them flocked to Plaza del Potro.

And he, Hernando, had put himself in the hands of one of these characters.

'Do you trust the muleteer?' Fátima had asked as she gave him the fifteen ducats in gold coins, carefully hoarded in a bag next to the Koran in the large chest.

Did he? It had been several years since he had had any dealings with Juan.

'Yes,' he said, persuaded by the memories flooding into his mind. He trusted that scoundrel more than any of the Christians in Córdoba. Together they had lived through danger and uncertainty and many a close call. That bond was hard to break.

Juan enjoyed the pleasure that Ángela, the young dark-haired girl, gave him. Once satisfied he intentionally knocked a jug of wine over the bed sheets.

'Change them!' he bellowed, pretending to be drunk.

'Haven't you had enough?' said the girl, surprised.

'Girl, I'll tell you when to stop. Aren't I the one paying?'

Ángela threw on a cloak and went to the door. 'Tomasa!' she shouted, revealing a voice far harsher than the one she used with the clients. 'Clean sheets!'

Hernando had explained to Juan about Tomasa, but what he had not told him was that Tomasa was a head taller than him and possibly double his weight. When that huge woman appeared in the doorway with the clean bedding, Juan was intimidated; he felt ridiculous clad only in his threadbare pants.

He had planned to threaten her until she called for Hernando's father, whom he needed to be there for the second part of his plan. However, at the first sight of those strong forearms and the rolled-up sleeves, Juan had second thoughts. A slap in the face from Tomasa would hurt more than the kick of a mule.

The woman bent over to take off the dirty sheets and presented him with an enormous backside. It was now or never! If she finished making the bed . . .

For Hernando!

He clenched the few teeth he had left, reached out with both hands and dug his fingers into her buttocks.

'Two women!' he shouted as he did so. 'Santiago!' he howled as he clutched the woman's hard backside.

Ángela burst out laughing. Tomasa turned and made to slap the muleteer, but Juan was ready for her and dodged out of the way. Then he leapt on top of her and buried his face in her huge breasts. He clung on like a tick, gripping Tomasa with his arms and legs although he could not wrap them completely around her immense frame. Ángela was still laughing, and Tomasa struggled in vain to free herself of the creature stuck to her body, its mouth searching between her breasts. Juan found one of her nipples and bit it.

The bite made Tomasa even more furious. She pushed him with such force that the muleteer slammed back against the wall. Tomasa tried to fasten together her ruined bodice that had been almost ripped apart by Juan's brutal search for her nipple.

'B . . . beautiful!' exclaimed Juan, gasping for air as his breath had been knocked out of him.

Several women had gathered in the doorway, their laughter adding to Ángela's. Red in the face, Tomasa looked from Juan to the women.

The muleteer made what he feared would be his last move in life, and went for Tomasa again, lustfully licking his top lip. She waited with knitted brow, trying to push up even further sleeves already about to burst their seams.

'Enough! I knew this would happen sooner or later with a woman attending to the girls,' came a voice from the door. Juan could not stifle the sigh of relief he let out on seeing the brothel landlord. 'Out!' the man shouted at Tomasa. 'Tell Francisco to come and make the bed.'

Alerted by the racket, Hamid was not slow to arrive. The other women had already gone when the old man limped into the room. Only Ángela was still there.

'A Moor?' shouted the muleteer, confronting Hamid. 'How can you send a Moor to touch the sheets I'm going to lie on?' he added, turning to Ángela. 'Go and fetch the landlord.'

The girl obeyed and ran in search of him. Now came the hardest part, thought the muleteer. He only had fifteen ducats to buy the slave. He had not wanted to wipe the smile from Hernando's face or the shine from his blue eyes as he entrusted him with the money that surely constituted his entire fortune, but Juan knew that slaves over fifty years old fetched thirty-two ducats in the market, despite how little work could be expected from men of that age. Hernando had told him the landlord was only asking a pittance, but how much was that going to be?

After the violent reception he had received from the muleteer, Hamid was surprised to see how the man was now quietly thinking, standing in front of him as if he didn't exist. Hamid tried to get round to make the bed, but Juan stopped him.

'Don't do anything,' he ordered. What did it matter now if the slave started to suspect what was going to happen and who was behind it all? 'Stay where you are and keep quiet, understand?'

'Why should I—?' Hamid started to ask, but just then Ángela and the landlord returned to the room.

'A Moor?' Juan shouted again. 'You've sent me a Moor!' The muleteer jabbed Hamid in the chest with his finger. 'And to top it all he has insulted me. He called me a Christian dog and a worshipper of idols!'

Hamid's characteristic composure deserted him and he threw up his hands. 'I didn't . . .' he tried to defend himself.

Juan slapped him. 'Nobody calls me a Christian dog!'

'Leave him alone,' urged the landlord, stepping between them.

'Whip him!' demanded Juan. 'I want to see you punish him. Whip him right now!'

How can I whip him? the landlord asked himself. Poor Francisco would not survive more than three lashes.

'No,' he objected.

'In that case I shall go to the Inquisition,' Juan threatened. 'You have in your establishment a Moor who insults Christians and who blasphemes,' he went on, starting to collect his clothes. 'The Inquisition will punish him as he deserves!'

Hamid remained quiet behind the landlord, who watched as Juan dressed, grumbling under his breath all the while. If the muleteer denounced him to the Inquisition, Francisco would not survive two weeks in its prisons. He would never live to see the next auto-da-fé, and he would never recover a single penny for him.

'Please,' he begged Juan. 'Don't denounce him. He has never behaved like this before.'

'I wouldn't if you punished him. You are his owner. If this heretic slave was mine I—'

'I'll sell him to you!' said the landlord, jumping at the chance.

'Why would I want him? He is old . . . and crippled . . . and foul-mouthed. What use is he to me?'

'He has insulted you.' The landlord tried to provoke him. 'What satisfaction will you get if it is the Inquisition who punishes him? He will confess like all these cowards do, he will repent and they will simply sentence him to wear penitential garments. You can see how old he is.'

Juan pretended to be thinking this over.

'If he was mine,' he muttered to himself, 'he would be cleaning up mule shit all day . . .'

'Fifteen ducats,' offered the bailiff.

'You're mad!'

Five ducats. Juan got Hamid for five ducats, and at this price he also got them to throw in the services of Ángela. He decided not to wait until the next morning. With two clients of the brothel as witnesses he paid with the gold coins he carried in his bag and left the brothel with Hamid at his heels. Nevertheless he arranged to meet with the landlord at daybreak to sign the corresponding contract of sale.

Hernando was listening intently to the story of the five-year siege and subsequent capture of the city of Haarlem. A disabled soldier from the Flanders infantry regiment who had taken part in the campaign, and whom a pleased crowd was happy to buy drinks, related the tale between mouthfuls of wine. The almost blind soldier was seated at a table outside the inn, proudly wearing the rags in which he had fought under the command of Don Fadrique of Toledo, son of the Duke of Alba. He described the hardships of the siege of the fortified city, during which the infantry suffered many casualties, and told how the nobleman had considered abandoning the effort. Then Don Fadrique received a message from his father.

'The Duke of Alba said', the veteran recounted in a ringing voice, 'that if he left the field without conquering the stronghold, he would not recognize him as a son. However, if he died in the siege, then he himself, although he was on his sick-bed, would personally replace him.' The circle around the soldier was an oasis of silence amid the din that reverberated around the rest of Plaza del Potro. 'He added that should they both fail, then his mother would leave Spain to fight and finish what her husband and son had neither the courage nor the endurance to do.'

Murmurs of approval and some applause rose from the audience around the veteran. He took advantage of it to down the remaining wine in his glass. He listened for the sound of it being filled again, and then threw himself into relating the final and bloody taking of the city. Hernando felt somebody pass behind and knock into him.

He turned and saw Hamid, who was limping, head down, behind the muleteer. In his hand he carried a bundle no bigger than the one Fátima had brought to her marriage. Juan had done it! A shiver ran through Hernando's body as he watched them head slowly towards the top of the square.

'On his father's orders,' the soldier exclaimed at that moment, 'Don Fadrique executed more than two thousand five hundred Walloons, French and English . . .'

'Heretics!'

'Lutherans!'

These insults to the resistance of the citizens of Haarlem did not distract Hernando. His attention was on what he recognized as the scraping of the worn-out shoe that Hamid dragged along the pavement, that strange rhythm that had accompanied his childhood. Hernando raised his fingers to his eyes to wipe away the tears. The two figures continued moving away from him, indifferent to the people and the noise, to the arguments and laughter, to the whole world! A small muleteer, stooping and toothless, a rogue and trickster. An elderly man, lame and tired of life, wise and saintly. Hernando fought to control the flood of emotions that threatened to overwhelm him. He clenched his fists and shook his arms imperceptibly. Restraining himself, he could feel the tension in every muscle as he watched how slowly the holy man was crossing the square.

He saw them reach Calle de los Silleros and then Calle de los Toqueros. Then they turned and went round the charity hospital. Hernando scanned the crowd, certain that, like him, everyone must have been aware of that magic couple who had disappeared down the Calle de Armas. But they had not. Nobody else seemed to have paid the slightest attention, and his closest neighbours continued listening to the tales of the disabled soldier.

'They owed us more than twenty months' pay, and they stopped us from plundering the city! All the money the city paid to prevent the pillage went to the King!' the blind man shouted, thumping the table and spilling his glass of wine. His passion roused, he sought to justify the mutiny led by the infantry soldiers after the taking of Haarlem. 'As a punishment they did not pay the sick and wounded like me any of the money they owed us!'

What did he care about this blind man and his fate in that other religious war the Catholic King Philip had supported? thought Hernando as he crossed the square, forcing himself not to run.

They were waiting for him a short distance away in Calle de Armas, both men dimly lit by the glow cast from candles at the feet of a life-sized statue of the Virgin Mary behind a beautiful grille. The street seemed deserted. Juan saw him approach but Hamid didn't; he still had his head down in defeat.

Hernando stopped in front of him and took his hands. Words failed him. Without lifting his eyes from the floor the holy man studied the hands that held his. His eyes moved to the boots that Hernando had worn since his appointment as a rider in the royal stables. That very morning Hamid had walked next to him.

'Hamid ibn Hamid,' he whispered, at last lifting his face.

'You are free,' Hernando said, struggling to get the words out. Before the scholar could respond, he threw himself into his arms and burst out sobbing.

The next morning, in the presence of the public scribe, and with Hamid already under Fátima's care in the stables, Juan and the landlord signed the contract of sale of the brothel slave named Francisco. As if he was dealing with an animal, the landlord did not sell him as healthy, but detailed each and every physical defect that Hamid possessed, both obvious and hidden. For his part, Juan renounced all right to complain about the slave's present or future faults. With this, buyer and seller accepted the deal in front of two witnesses, and the scribe signed the corresponding document.

A little later, in front of another scribe and another two witnesses, so that the landlord would not find out about it, Juan dictated the letter of manumission in favour of his slave Francisco. He granted him his freedom and renounced any powers that the law gave him over his freed slave.

As they left the scribe's house, Hernando kissed the letter of manumission. He wanted to reward his friend with a gold crown, but the muleteer refused it.

'My lad,' he said, 'we were wrong to fantasize about the women of Barbary. None of them can have buttocks like the ones I got to feel yesterday, even though I did not manage to get any further. You were right,' he added, placing a hand on Hernando's shoulder. 'I have grown old.'

'No . . .' Hernando tried to contradict him.

'You know where to find me,' the muleteer said by way of goodbye.

Hernando watched him go. As Juan moved off, Hernando thought he was walking slightly more erect than the day before.

38

ROSES, WALLFLOWERS, lemon- and orange-tree blossom: thousands of flowers! During those spring nights, the small courtyard of the new house where Hernando lived with his family gave off a heady mix of scents. The courtyard was paved with flagstones, inlaid with pebbles forming a star. At its centre was a plain stone fountain, which permanently spouted crystal-clear water. Despite the fact that Córdoba had problems with waste water and its network of sewers, which caused frequent typhoid outbreaks and all kinds of endemic stomach illnesses, especially in the poorer districts of La Ajerquía, it also possessed thirty-nine springs and numerous wells that made good use of the endless supply of precious mountain water. The old city centre, with its intricate layout of streets and alleyways, had the best water distribution. And it was here, in Calle de los Barberos, that Hernando rented a small house belonging to the cathedral chapter. Over the centuries the Church had acquired many houses in the city.

The house and courtyard had all the typical features of the Roman *domus*. Roman houses had inspired the first dwellings in the city, and were later taken by the Muslims as the model for their own houses: an oasis with flowers and water; paradises hidden from the outside. Boxed in between two similar buildings, the rectangular courtyard was closed in on one side by a blank wall, which constituted the party wall with the adjacent house. Along the three remaining sides ran corridors that gave access to the rooms, the central courtyard being surrounded by a covered colonnade. Wooden beams supported a first-floor gallery with wooden railings. This was covered by a roof of small tiles alternately curving either upwards or downwards, which acted as gutters to collect rainwater. Access to the dwelling was by a cool hallway almost as big as a room, the lower half lined with coloured tiles. This entrance was closed to the street by a wooden door and to the central courtyard by a wrought-iron gate. The kitchen, a living room, the latrine and another tiny room occupied the ground floor. On the floor above were four more rooms, reached by the open gallery.

The idea of moving to their own house had been on Hernando's mind ever since his salary was increased and Hamid had arrived. The old scholar ended up accepting both his freedom and the protection Hernando offered him as a natural consequence of the bond that they both considered as strong as any family relationship. However, unlike Aisha, who had insisted on going to work in the silk industry, Hamid shut himself away in the rooms above the stables where he prayed, thought and read the Koran. He made good use of the privacy offered by a place where horses were the only religion. He also took on the education of the three children, Hernando's two and Shamir, Aisha's son, as his personal responsibility.

But even though all those arguments were enough in themselves for Hernando to consider it was time to look for a new house, there was another even more pressing and selfish reason that drove him to pursue the idea. The couple were trying for another child. They wanted one, but their intimacy was compromised by the close presence of their family. They made love, yes, but hidden beneath the sheets, with their movements restricted and their gasps of pleasure stifled. Both hated not being able to enjoy each other freely. Inhibited by the presence of the old holy man, Fátima avoided using the essences and perfumes that had made their love-making so delicious. There was no foreplay, no touching, no stroking, kissing or licking. The thousand positions they had come to enjoy uninhibited were now restricted to what they could manage concealed under the sheets. There was no sign of a pregnancy.

'My vagina can't milk your penis,' moaned Fátima one day. 'I can't relax. I need to be able to hold you tightly inside me, gripping and squeezing, until I draw out every drop of life that you can give me.'

This was the most pressing reason to find a new house. Aisha, Fátima, Hernando and the children established themselves on the first floor. Hamid took the remaining room on the ground floor, so at last Fátima could relax.

The continuation of the straight Calle de los Barberos, where there was a shrine to Our Lady of Sorrows, was named after the Muslim leader Almanzor because it was the site of one of his palaces. From the house it was easy to see the cathedral's entrance tower, the former minaret that rose proudly above the rooftops. Using that as a reference point and a superficial consultation of the stars from the courtyard, Hamid calculated the precise direction of the kiblah and made a slight incision in the wall of his room, towards which he directed his prayers.

The money Hernando earned from the stables allowed them to live comfortably, but that particular house would not have been an option were it not for the reduced rent they obtained, thanks to Don Julián's intervention before the cathedral chapter. This was how the priest thanked Hernando for his self-less effort in making copies of the Koran, the benefits of which went straight to the cause.

'If the Arabic language is lost then so are its laws,' Don Julián reminded him one day in the privacy of the library.

That maxim, already invoked in the war in the Alpujarra, was seen as a priority by the diverse communities of Moriscos spread across all the Spanish realms. The Moriscos defied the Christians' insistence that they abandon the use of Arabic in their daily lives, and their efforts to make them do so were generally in vain. The nobles of those realms, interested only in keeping the Moriscos working for them for next to nothing, were lax about the use of the Arabic language in their lands. However, the municipalities, the Church and the Inquisition, by royal order, made this maxim their own, converting it into one of their banners. The Morisco communities fought back. They secretly promoted madrasas or Koranic schools, but above all they provided the Muslims with prohibited and sacrilegious copies of the divine book, for which a network of copiers was created all over Spain.

'I've finally found some,' Don Julián said one night, laying a sheet of brand-new paper on the table where Hernando worked. They were alone in the library. It was late: the office of compline had ended several hours earlier, and the cathedral had been cleared of the odd assortment of characters who populated it during the day. Among them were the criminal elements who sought sanctuary in the holy place and spent the nights in the cloisters of the entrance garden, safe from the action of common justice, because the bailiffs could not enter the church to arrest them. Hernando recalled the many colourful scenes he had witnessed, and smiled to himself when he heard the gatekeepers running about trying to get some dogs, and that night even a pig, out of the holy precincts.

Before picking it up, Hernando stroked the sheet with his fingertips. It was coarse, with an excessively satin finish. The surface was uneven and there was no watermark to prove its origin.

'I've plenty more sheets,' said the priest with a triumphant smile as Hernando carefully weighed the sheet in his hand. It was noticeably longer and wider than the usual ones. 'Don't be surprised,' the priest added, seeing his student's reaction. 'It's made by hand, in secret, in the houses of Moriscos from Xátiva.'

Xátiva was one of the largest towns in the kingdom of Valencia. A quarter of the residents were Moriscos or new Christians but, as in many parts of that Mediterranean realm, the town was surrounded by small villages where almost all the inhabitants were Moriscos. Thanks to Muslim advances in its manufacture, they had been making paper in Xátiva for more than four centuries. The Christian monarchs granted privileges to the Xátiva Morisco authorities and protected the industry, with the result that many Moriscos worked making paper in their own homes, using old cloth and garments as raw material. These domestic industries now surreptitiously supplied the Morisco community with paper, although of poor quality. Buying paper in sufficient quantities for making copies of books was highly complicated and always suspect.

Although printing had been invented over a century earlier, manuscripts were still widely copied by hand. The publishing of printed books was still in the hands of a very few individuals. Ordinary people, the great majority of whom were illiterate, had neither access to reading matter nor interest in its publication. The great lords who did possess sufficient capital to set up a printing business refused to compromise their honour by spending money on commercial activities unworthy of their status. By the 1580s there was just one portable printing press in Córdoba, used almost as a hobby by the only printer. This meant the trade in paper was almost non-existent. The cathedral chapter ordered its religious books from printers in other cities, such as Seville.

'How did you get hold of it?' asked Hernando.

'Through Karim.'

'And the customs house on the bridge?'

Don Julián winked. 'It's simple enough, though expensive, to hide sheets of paper under the saddles of mules or horses.'

Hernando nodded and again stroked the rough sheet of paper with his fingertips. The priest insisted he charge for his work, but Hernando invested all the money in projects like the liberation of Morisco slaves. Not for anything in the world would he have wanted to become rich by propagating his faith.

So it was that when his training was complete Hernando began to reproduce Korans. He used classical Arabic but with the calligraphy of the copyists, speed and clarity taking precedence over aesthetics. Between the lines of Arabic, he wrote the translation of the suras in *aljamiado*, so that all the readers would be able to understand them. They hid the sheets of paper amongst the numerous parchments in the cathedral library. Thanks to Karim, the copies they made were distributed throughout the realm of Córdoba, where they had a great need for these religious texts because, unlike the Morisco communities of Valencia, Catalonia and Aragón, their exodus meant they had none available.

While Hernando dedicated himself to the forbidden transcription of the revealed book, Fátima took on the verbal transmission of her people's culture to the Morisco women. This enabled them to do the same with their children and husbands.

With the patient help of Hernando and Hamid, who lovingly examined and corrected her, she had learnt by heart some of the suras of the Koran, precepts of the Sunna and the best-known Morisco prophecies. Fátima went shopping every day, her hair covered with her precious embroidered white shawl. Afterwards she amused herself with what appeared to be nothing more than innocent meetings of small groups of women of leisure getting together to gossip in one of their houses over a glass of lemonade.

Sometimes she left home at the same time as Hernando, and the two of them enjoyed a prolonged goodbye before going their separate ways. It became a kind of game: one of them would always turn to watch proudly how the other went to fulfil the duty imposed on them by God for which their people were so grateful. Sometimes both did, and they would catch each other's eye. Smiling, they would then encourage each other on their way with almost imperceptible hand gestures.

'It is our responsibility to transmit our people's laws to the children,' Fátima encouraged the other women. 'The priests want them to forget, and we can't allow that. The men work and return home exhausted when their children are already asleep. Besides, a child will never denounce their mother to the Christians.'

She recited some of the teachings of the Koran over and again to small groups of women, who repeated them softly. Afterwards she added the interpretation Hamid had given her.

Day after day, Fátima repeated her teachings to different audiences. Always, after having dealt with some Koranic precept, the women begged her to recite a *gufur* or *jofor*. These were the prophecies made expressly for their people, for the Muslims of al-Andalus, and they trusted them implicitly. They foretold the return of their customs, their culture and their laws. Their victory!

'The Turks will march with their armies to Rome, and the Christians will not escape, except for those who return to the law of the Prophet; the rest will be captured or killed,' she repeated. 'Do you all understand? This day has already arrived: the Christians have defeated us. Why?'

'Because we have forsaken our God,' an old woman, familiar with the prophecy, answered despondently on one occasion.

'Yes,' agreed Fátima. 'Because Córdoba has become a place of vice and sin. Because all of al-Andalus has succumbed to the arrogance of heresy.'

At this, many of the women lowered their gaze in shame. Wasn't it true? Hadn't they been lax in the performance of their obligations? All the Moriscos felt guilty and accepted the punishment: the Christian occupation of their lands, slavery and disgrace.

'But don't despair,' Fátima tried to encourage them. 'According to the divine book, the prophecy goes on. Fortunately, have you not seen the Christians triumph throughout the earth, only to be defeated within a few days of their victory? This is God's judgement; both before and after it was the believers who were jubilant in victory. He is the one who helps His servants, and God's promise will not fail one jot.'

One by one they looked up at Fátima again, the light of hope in their eyes.

'We must fight!' she exhorted them. 'We can't resign ourselves to misfortune! God awaits us. The prophecies will be fulfilled!'

One spring evening Hernando was returning home wearily. During the day he had helped prepare more than forty horses for a journey to the port of Cartagena, where a ship was waiting to transport them to Genoa and then on to Austria. King Philip had decided to present these superb specimens to his nephew the Emperor, and to the archdukes, the Dukes of Savoy and Mantua. As the King had ordered, first of all they selected the horses to be sent to Madrid for him and the Prince. Then they selected the steeds to be offered as a gift. Don Diego López de Haro had spent all day at the stables. He chose and rejected animals, hesitated and changed his mind. He let the riders, including Hernando, advise him as to which were the best horses for the monarch.

'Will they ensure the bloodline is preserved?' Hernando had asked as he watched a magnificent five-year-old dappled-grey stallion going through its paces with elegant ease. The animal was being set apart by the groom for dispatch to Austria.

'Yes, of course,' Don Diego had replied without turning round, his attention focused on the stallion. 'There are great riders and horse experts in that court. I'm sure that from these stallions they'll breed stock that will become the pride of Vienna.'

Will they really, though? Hernando was wondering when he was surprised to see his front door was closed. At that time of day in May it was usually left open to the wrought-iron gate that opened on to the patio. Could something have happened? He banged hard again and again on the wooden door. His wife's smile as she opened it reassured him.

'Why . . . ?' he started to ask as she quickly barred the door behind them.

Fátima raised a finger to her lips, asking him to be quiet. Then she accompanied him to the courtyard. Hamid had broken the strict rule about where the children should be educated. Hernando had insisted their lessons take place in the bedrooms, so that nobody would be able to hear them speaking Arabic. But Hamid had taken them to the yard instead. Sitting on simple mats beneath the colonnade arches, the children were paying close attention to the scholar as he tried to teach them mathematics.

Hernando was about to complain to his wife but, once again, she had her finger across her lips and he resigned himself to keeping quiet.

'Hamid has said', she explained, 'that water is the source of life. The children won't be able to learn inside a room whilst they hear running water outside. To learn easily they need the scent of the flowers and contact with nature to delight their senses.'

Hernando sighed and as he turned once more he found three smiling children watching him. Hamid looked at him out of the corner of one eye, like a big child.

'And he's right,' Hernando conceded. 'We can't deprive them of paradise.' He took Fátima by the hand and they went over to teacher and students. Day by day, Hamid was recovering, and this act of defiance . . . Deep down, Hernando was pleased.

He greeted his children and Shamir in Arabic. When they heard him, the children themselves urged him to lower his voice. He sat down in the space remaining on Francisco's mat and turned to Hamid.

'Peace,' Hernando greeted him.

'Peace be with you, Ibn Hamid,' replied the old man.

Hernando stayed silent until Aisha and Fátima had prepared the evening meal. He listened to Hamid's explanations and watched the children's progress. Shamir reminded him of Brahim: surly, intelligent, but unlike his father he had a generous heart. He showed this in the way he cared for the younger ones. Francisco was the elder of Hernando's children.

Hernando had to scold him several times for chewing on his tongue as he drew numbers with a stick on a reusable tablet of tar-covered leaves. He was an intelligent, kind boy, but always predictable. His blue eyes, inherited from his father, and his spontaneity clearly signalled his every move, and when he committed any mischief they reflected his sense of guilt. Francisco was incapable of lying; he had no idea how to conceal the truth.

Hernando touched the tip of Francisco's tongue when it stuck out once more when faced with a difficult sum, and saw how quickly it darted back in, like a snake's. Then he turned his attention to Inés. He was conscious that Hamid did the same, as if he could read Hernando's thoughts. She was the image of her mother . . . beautiful! The girl was totally absorbed in writing numbers, and her huge black eyes appeared about to bore straight through the tablet. Inés took an interest in every-thing, and questioned everything. She thought carefully about the answers she was given and, sometimes straight away, some-times after a couple of days, would often raise a further doubt about the same question. Her reasoning was not as agile or immediate as the boys', but unlike theirs was always logical. With every gesture, every movement, Inés lit up their world.

Hernando nodded his head in satisfaction, and his eyes met Hamid's. Yes, they were in paradise. With the door to the street closed to outside interference, they could hear the murmur of the water flowing in the fountain. They breathed the intense aroma of the flowers, splendid in the twilight hours as the sun was setting and the cool of evening revived the plants and aroused the senses. Yet it was the same, they said silently to each other, the exact same thing that for years the scholar had done with the Morisco boy inside a squalid shack lost in the foothills of the Sierra Nevada.

As if not wanting to disturb the children's concentration, Hamid looked at Hernando without a word, acknowledging the worth of his first student. Just as he was now doing with his children, he had imparted his knowledge to Hernando in secret. It had been a long road: being orphaned, a war, slavery at the hands of a corsair and deportation to unknown lands where he found nothing but hatred and misfortune. Poverty and hard work in the tannery; the mistakes and then the return to the community's fold; good fortune in the stables until he had become a leading figure among his companions, and now . . . Both men gazed simultaneously at the three children, and a shiver of satisfaction ran down Hernando's spine: his children!

At that moment Aisha called them to eat.

Hernando helped the old scholar to his feet. Hamid accepted his assistance and leant on him as they crossed the courtyard. They were alone now, the children having scampered across in four rapid strides.

'Do you remember the water in the mountains?' asked the holy man as they paused for a few moments by the little fountain.

'I dream of it.'

'I'd like to return to Granada,' whispered Hamid. 'To end my days among those peaks . . .'

'There is a sacred sword hidden there that someone, some day, will have to raise again in the name of the one God. That day the spirit of our people, and especially yours, Hamid, will be reborn in the mountains.'

If Hamid instilled the truth in the children, it was Hernando who strove to teach them the essential Christian doctrine so that they could testify to their conversions on Sundays in the cathedral, or during the obligatory visits from the priest of Santa María. The parish justice and his superintendent had abandoned their checks, perhaps because of Hernando's position in the hierarchy of the royal stable and his special authority. However, Don Álvaro, the cathedral deacon in charge of the parish, always impeccably dressed in his black habit and biretta, continued with his weekly visits as if he was dealing with any other new Christian, although everyone suspected he was more interested in the good wine and Aisha's delicious sweetmeats than in verifying that the family were true Catholics. He was the guest of honour during his long visits. Don Álvaro settled himself comfortably in a chair under the colonnade and examined the children while he ate and drank. Week after week he listened doggedly to how they recited the prayers and doctrines they had been taught, as if afraid they had forgotten them. It was a farce played out in front of a family terrified lest one of the children let slip a phrase or expression in Arabic. As soon as he had the chance, Hernando took the initiative and sat with the priest to distract him and chat about other matters, mostly about the situation of the other heretical movement that threatened the Spanish empire and in which he was genuinely interested: Lutheranism.

Hamid, for his part, always feigned some indisposition and shut himself away in his little room as soon as Don Álvaro came through the courtyard gate. Hernando was convinced that Hamid went to pray, as a kind of challenge to the presence of the priest.

'It's an act of charity,' explained Hernando in response to Don Álvaro's interest in the invisible Hamid who, according to the parish records, was listed as living in the house. 'He's an old man from our village in the Alpujarra, and as a good Christian I couldn't allow him to die in the street. He suffers from bouts of fever; would you care to meet him?'

The priest took a mouthful of wine, looked around the pleasant garden and, to Hernando's relief, shook his head. Why would he want to go anywhere near an old man who suffered from fevers?

So, after Don Álvaro had checked yet again that the children remembered their catechism, the conversations under the colonnade went on between himself and Hernando, while from the far side of the courtyard Aisha or Fátima ensured they did not run out of wine or sweetmeats. A Spanish version of Calvin's *Institutes* edited in England had recently come into the hands of Hernando and Don Julián. Many Protestant books published in Spanish in England, Holland or Zeeland passed clandestinely through the realms of Philip II. The King and the Inquisition fought with all their might to keep the Catholic faith pure and untainted, free from any heretical influence, to the extent that for twenty years the monarch had prohibited Spanish students from attending foreign universities. An exception was made, of course, for the papal institutions in Rome and Bologna.

Many Moriscos looked favourably on the Protestant doctrines, especially the Aragonese because of their geographical contact with France and Béarn, where they fled to convert to Christianity while at the same time renouncing Catholicism.

The Protestants' attacks on the Pope and the abuses of the clergy, on the selling of papal bulls and indulgences, their condemnation of the use of images as objects of worship or devotion, their support for the right of any believer to interpret the sacred texts independent of any ecclesiastical authority and dislike of the rigid vision of predestination: all of these points were common ground between two minority religions fighting to withstand the attacks of the Catholic Church.

Hernando discussed the matter with both Don Julián and Hamid. They all regretted these coincidences between Muslims and those who were still Christians, whatever sympathy they might feel towards this tendency.

'After all,' argued the priest, 'the Protestants aim to be reconciled with the scriptures within Christianity, whereas the converted Moriscos are not seeking reforms: they want to destroy it. The coincidences between the Lutheran doctrines and the Muslim faith found in some of the believers' own polemic writings will do nothing but weaken our true objective.'

As soon as Don Álvaro left the house, after having railed against the Lutherans and their attacks on the Catholic clergy's way of life, Hamid would come indignantly out of his room and pour what remained of the wine down the drain.

'That costs money,' Hernando scolded him, but had to force himself to hide a smile as he allowed the old man his revenge.

Azirat was the horse's name, and it represented one of the greatest changes in Hernando's life. Since the time of the Emperor Charles V, the monarchy had been continually bankrupt. Five years earlier, the kingdom had stopped repaying its debts. Not even the immense fortunes in silver and gold that arrived from the New World could cover the expenses of the Spanish armies, to which were added the colossal costs of the luxurious Burgundian court, whose protocol the Emperor had adopted. Nor did Spain reap full benefit from her considerable raw materials. The prized wool of the Spanish merino sheep was sold unprocessed to foreign traders, who converted it into woollen cloth that was then resold in Spain for ten or twenty times the purchase price. The same happened with iron, silk and many other raw materials. Gold, for wars or trade, left Spain by the ton. The interest that the King and his bankers paid exceeded 40 per cent, and the income from papal bulls and indulgences sold to finance both Rome and Spain was insufficient. Hidalgos, the clergy and many cities were exempt from paying taxes, so the whole weight fell on the countryside, on the workers and artisans, which made them poorer still and prevented the development of trade. It was a vicious circle that was hard to break.

In 1580 the economic situation became even worse, in the wake of the death in Alcazarquivir of King Sebastian of Portugal during a vain attempt to conquer Morocco. His uncle, King Philip of Spain, claimed the right of succession to the Portuguese throne. The populace refused to crown him, and so he prepared to invade the neighbouring kingdom with an army under the command of the old Duke of Alba, who was then aged seventy-two. Besides Brazil, Portugal dominated the trade route with the East Indies and controlled the African coast, from Tangiers to Mogadishu: the entire edge of the continent.

By annexing Portugal, Spain would become the largest empire in history.

All those enormous expenses also affected the royal stables. Despite Philip II continuing to give himself, his favourites, and the foreign courts magnificent examples of the new breed, they suffered from a lack of funds that Don Diego López de Haro was constantly demanding from the Board of Works and Forests, who were responsible for providing them.

So it was that part of the salary owing to riders and stable-hands was met through giving them colts rejected by the stables, on condition that if the King was interested in them when they were fully grown, they could be exchanged for others. This rarely happened because so many horses were born each year and employees were quick to sell the rejected horses for money. The sale of only eight horses from the King's stable brought in enough to buy thirty good warhorses for the army stationed in the square at Oran!

But Hernando was not willing to sell Azirat, the horse he had been given in part-payment of his wages. His way of life was austere and his needs few. When they had branded the colts out in the pasture and entered their details in the register, they'd called him Andarín, the Dancer, for the elegance of his movements. Yet he had been born with a shining coat of burning red that would never appeal to courtly tastes; his chestnut coat was not admitted in the new breed.

Andarín, whose fiery colour suggested rage, energy and speed, captivated Hernando from the second he first saw him.

'I'm going to call him Azirat,' he told Abbas. He did not pronounce the Spanish z, but used the cedilla and emphasized the t: *açiratt*.

Abbas frowned as Hernando nodded. The Assirat bridge, the bridge at the entrance to heaven, was as long and slender as a single hair and extended over hell. The blessed would cross it in a flash whilst the rest would fall into the fire.

'Changing the original name of a horse not only brings bad

luck,' said the blacksmith, 'but in some cases it is even punishable by death. Foreigners who do so can be sentenced to death.'

'I'm not a foreigner and this horse would be capable of crossing that long and delicate hair,' Hernando retorted, ignoring his friend's warning. 'He would be able to cross it without falling off or snapping it. It's as if he doesn't touch the ground. He floats on air!'

By now twenty-six, Hernando was head of a family clan and one of the most highly regarded and influential members of the Morisco community. Dedicated to helping others, he lived permanently surrounded by people. Azirat offered him moments of freedom the like of which he had never enjoyed before. So, whenever he had the chance, he saddled the horse and rode out to the countryside in search of solitude. Sometimes they walked in the pastures, Hernando calm and thoughtful; at others he would allow Azirat to show off his speed and power. On occasion he looked for the pastures where they grazed bulls and ran them. He was careful not to injure them but only toy with those dangerous horns, which never quite managed to gore Azirat's haunches as he pranced agilely before the bulls, taunting them with his luxuriant tail. They could never resist lowering their heads and charging at the long tail hairs waving in front of them.

Hernando never headed north, towards the Sierra Morena, where Ubaid and the outlaws were camped. Abbas had assured him that the muleteer of Narila would not trouble him. They had sent him a message demanding as much, but Hernando was not convinced.

On Sundays Francisco and Shamir, who had grown up as brothers, rode with him. Whenever it was safe to do so, he let them hold the reins. When Hernando rode on his own, he sought out lonely places in order not to show off excessively in front of the Christians, but with the children he did not go into the countryside, limiting their rides to the outskirts of Córdoba. On one such day, at dusk, he crossed the Roman bridge with the proud, smiling children. Francisco sat astride Azirat in front of him and Shamir behind.

'Look, Father!' Francisco pointed as they left the Calahorra tower behind and reached the Campo de la Verdad. 'There's Juan the muleteer.'

From afar, Juan greeted them with a weary gesture. Every Sunday they passed by there, Hernando saw him looking ever older. He no longer had even the few teeth with which he had managed to bite the brothel woman's nipple.

'Dismount, boys,' Juan told the children firmly once they had reached him. Hernando was surprised, but the mule dealer gestured him to be quiet. 'Go and look at the mules. Damián tells me they've missed you since you last came to stroke them.'

Damián was a mischievous lad Juan had been forced to take on to help him. Francisco and Shamir ran towards the string of mules and the two men remained facing each other. Juan moved his lips over his gums, preparing to speak.

'There's a man, one of your new Christians, asking around, investigating . . .' Hernando waited as the mule dealer checked that nobody was listening. '. . . about the smuggling of sheets of paper.'

'Who is he?'

'I don't know. He hasn't approached me. But I heard he asked one of the mule-drivers.'

'Are you sure?'

'Lad, I know about everything that enters and leaves Córdoba illegally. There's little more I can do now apart from listening to gossip and take my cut here and there.'

Hernando put his hand in his purse and gave Juan some coins. This time he accepted them.

'Aren't things going well?' Hernando asked.

'The master's eyes fatten the horse,' Juan began to quote the old saying, gesturing contemptuously towards Damián, 'but lads and lackeys wear it out and ruin it,' he finished. 'The same applies to mules, but I've run out of options. As for trafficking in smuggled goods . . . right now I couldn't even lift one of the *Weary Virgin*'s oars!'

'If you need anything, you can count on me.'

'You'd do better to worry about yourself, my boy. That Morisco, and I suppose the Inquisition as well, are after all of you who use the paper.'

'All of you? How dare you suggest—?'

'I may be old and weak, but I'm not stupid. Neither the Church nor the scribes need to smuggle in such quantities of paper. Rumour has it that the paper is of poor quality and comes from Valencia. The mule-driver the Morisco questioned was from there, so it's not the sort hidalgos use to write with, nor a publisher for printing his books.'

Hernando puffed out his cheeks. 'Can't we find out who this Morisco is?'

'If the Valencian mule-driver returns some day . . . but I doubt he will, knowing that someone is asking awkward questions. If you could find him there, in his own land . . . but don't waste a second,' the mule dealer advised him.

'Boys!' shouted Hernando, putting his left foot in the stirrup and swinging his right leg easily over the horse's back. 'We're going.' He lifted them on to the horse one at a time. 'If you hear anything else . . .' he added to Juan. The mule dealer nodded with a smile that showed his gums. 'Azirat isn't well,' he told Francisco when he complained about cutting short their ride. He felt the pressure of Shamir's hands on his ribs, as if he didn't believe the excuse given to his little brother. 'You don't want him to get worse, do you?' Hernando insisted, trying to calm Francisco.

In the stables, while the children helped the stable lad unbridle the horse, Hernando warned Abbas of what had happened. Then he ran to Calle de los Barberos.

'I don't want to see a single sheet of paper in this house!' he ordered Fátima, his mother and Hamid – especially Hamid, pointing his finger at him. They met in one of the upstairs rooms away from the children, and he heatedly explained what

Juan had told him. The old scholar tried to argue, but Hernando would not let him: 'Hamid, not even one, understand? We can't put ourselves at risk, not us, not them,' he added, gesturing towards the courtyard, where they could hear the children's laughter. 'Nor any of the rest of us.'

Fátima was the one who protested: 'What about the Koran?' They still kept the copy that Abbas had given them.

Hernando thought for a moment. 'Burn it.' All three stared at him in astonishment. 'Burn it!' he insisted. 'God will not hold it against us. We work for Him and it would be little use to Him if we were arrested.'

'Why don't you hide it somewhere else?' Aisha suggested.

'Burn it! And clear up the ashes. From now on – from the moment you have burnt everything,' Hernando corrected himself, 'I want the front door left open. Suspend the children's classes until we see what is going on. And you, Fátima, hide the necklace where no one can find it. And I don't want any marks in the walls pointing to Mecca.'

'I can't remove them,' Hamid complained.

'Then make more, lots more, in all directions. I'm sure you'll always remember which is the right one. I have to go to the mosque, but we also have to warn Karim and Jalil, especially Karim.' He studied the three of them. Could he trust them to obey his instructions? Would they try to hide the Koran they had spent so many nights reading? 'Come,' he said to Fátima, holding out his hand for her to take.

They left the room and leant on the gallery railing. The children were playing by the fountain below. They were laughing, running around and trying to catch one another and throwing water. The couple stood watching them in silence, until Inés sensed their presence and lifted her face to them, revealing the same black almond eyes as her mother. Francisco and Shamir did the same. As if they understood the significance of the moment, the three children held their parents' gaze. Ascending like the scent of the flowers intermingled with the coolness of the courtyard, a current of life and joy, of innocence, flowed from them to the upstairs gallery. Hernando squeezed Fátima's hand as his mother, standing behind him, laid hers on her eldest son's shoulder.

'We've suffered hunger and great deprivation before reaching here,' said Hernando, breaking the spell. 'We mustn't fail now.' Suddenly he pulled himself together. Of course he should trust them! 'Get on with putting the house in order,' he commanded, turning to Fátima and Aisha. 'Father,' he added, turning to Hamid, 'I trust you.'

He arrived at the cathedral before vespers had finished. Organ music and the chants of the novices who studied with the Jesuits filled the building, flowing between the mosque's thousand columns. The full cathedral chapter took part in the singing. All its members were obliged to attend every service, and their seats in the choir were arranged in order of hierarchy. Hernando was struck by the smell of incense: coming after the fresh scent of the plants and flowers in his courtyard, that sickly sweet air reminded him of why he was there. He joined the congregation taking part in the service. When it was over he spoke to an attendant, asking him to find Don Julián and let him know that Hernando was waiting.

He waited in front of the iron grille to the library, which was undergoing some rebuilding work. After the death of Bishop Brother Bernardo de Fresneda and with the position unfilled, the cathedral chapter had decided to convert the library into a new and sumptuous sacrarium, in the style of the Sistine Chapel, as the one in the Chapel of the Last Supper was no longer large enough. Part of the library was moved to the bishop's palace; the rest would coexist with the building works until a new one was built next to the San Miguel gate.

'Good,' said the priest, trying to calm Hernando after listening to his passionate explanation. 'Tomorrow morning I will order them to move our books and papers to the bishop's palace.'

'To the bishop's palace?' Hernando was astonished.

'Where better?' smiled Don Julián. 'It's his private library.

There are hundreds of books and manuscripts and I am the one in charge of them. Don't worry about it, I'll hide them carefully. No matter how many books Brother Martín tries to read, he will never get to ours. Besides, in this way, when the situation calms down we will be able to continue with our work.'

Could I also, thought Hernando, take advantage of Don Julián's ruse and hide my Koran in Brother Martín of Córdoba's library?

'It's possible I still have a Koran and some lunar calendars in my house . . .'

'If you bring them to me before prime—' Don Julián broke off to return the greeting of two passing deacons. Hernando bowed his head and murmured some words. 'If you bring them to me,' Don Julián repeated when the priests were out of earshot, 'I will deal with them.'

Hernando scrutinized the old priest. His composure: was it real or merely a façade? Don Julián guessed his thoughts.

'Nerves will only lead us to make mistakes,' he said. 'We have to overcome this difficulty and continue with our work. Did you ever think this would be easy?'

'Yes . . .' Hernando admitted hesitantly after a few moments. It had certainly seemed so lately. At the beginning, when he had gone to the cathedral, he had noticed how his muscles tensed and he jumped at the slightest noise, but then, little by little . . .

'We must never become overconfident. We should always be on the alert. We have to find this spy before he finds us. Karim will know the Valencian mule-driver. We have to find him and discover who it was that questioned him.'

Karim had been responsible for everything. The others had tried to convince him he should let them help, but the old man refused, and they had to admit that he was right. 'One person running the risk is enough,' he maintained. Karim took it upon himself to acquire the paper and deal with the Valencian Moriscos and mule-drivers. He made sure the paper reached Hernando and Don Julián, and it was he who received the books and documents when they were copied. After binding them with the help of a press that he kept in his house, he distributed them around Córdoba. With the exception of the sporadic meetings they held, which would prove little or nothing, no one would be able to link the other members of the Morisco council with the production and sale of copies of the Koran.

They left the cathedral by the San Miguel gate. It was already almost completely dark as they headed up Calle del Palacio. Like almost all the Córdoba clergy, Don Julián also lived in the parish of Santa María, in Calle de los Deanes, just round the corner from Hernando. At the junction of Deanes with Manriques, where there was a small square, they were accosted by a brawny-looking man. Hernando's hand went to the knife that he carried at his waist, but a familiar voice stopped his movements.

'Calm down! It's me, Abbas.' They recognized the blacksmith. He did not beat about the bush. 'Members of the Inquisition have just arrested Karim,' he told them. 'They've searched his house and found a couple of copies of the Koran and other parchments. They've been seized, together with the press, the knives and the other equipment he used to bind them with.'

39

His name was Cristóbal Escandalet and he had emigrated from Mérida to Córdoba a few years previously, together with his wife and three young children. He was a *buñolero* by profession. The delicious *buñuelos* were Morisco fritters made of a flour mixture and deep-fried in oil. He wandered the city offering many different varieties of his wares; light round *buñuelos de viento*, the dense *buñuelos de jeringuilla*, elongated and compact *buñuelos* soaked in honey. Hamid found the house where he lived, crowded in with four other families in the poor district of San Lorenzo in the extreme west of the city, close to the Plasencia gate.

Hamid had been following him for a couple of days. He studied the way he talked and how he interacted with people. Cristóbal had great charm, and used it to win over potential customers and then hoodwink them; he treated old and new Christians alike. He was about thirty, of average height, lean and wiry. He always moved slowly, laden down with the equipment for frying the *buñuelos*. Hamid noted the shiny new frying pan. The pastry bag for forming the *buñuelos* was also new.

The price for betraying Karim! he thought to himself. He watched from a short distance away how Cristóbal proclaimed the excellence of his pastries. It was market day and he was in front of the cross of the Rastro, where the Calle de la Feria met the banks of the river Guadalquivir.

A woman passer-by turned round and Hamid held her gaze coldly until she went on her way. Then the holy man returned his attention to the *buñolero*, to his sinewy arms and his thick strong neck. His throat had to be cut and he, Hamid, had to do it! Only he could do it! That was the sentence for a Muslim who had broken his law. For Cristóbal there was no possibility of repentance: he had betrayed his brothers in faith. As soon as the traitor's name was known the death sentence had been pronounced, but how could a weak, unarmed old man carry it out?

The Córdoban Morisco community was rocked by the news of Karim's arrest and confinement in the Inquisition's prison within the Christian monarch's fortress. For days there was no other topic of conversation, and some speculated as to the traitor's identity. A dark shadow fell over the entire community. Karim was a respected old man and many knew of his activities: those who watched the house during the council's meetings; those who bought copies of the Koran, the prophecies, the lunar calendars or the polemical writings; those who used their travels to work in the countryside to carry books out of Córdoba and distribute them to other Morisco communities in the kingdom. Suspicion ran rife and there were many who had to defend their innocence from sidelong looks or direct accusations. The council members, not wanting to spread even more mistrust, decided not to make public the news that it was indeed a Morisco who had questioned the Valencian mule-driver. However, they were also unable to take any steps to discover his identity. Karim was inaccessible in the Inquisition jail, and his wife was old and shattered by the events, which had come as a complete shock to her. She could tell Abbas nothing when the blacksmith finally managed to see her after the Inquisition's officers had completed the inventory of Karim's few belongings for requisitioning by the Holy Office.

Denunciation was by far the most disgraceful and abominable of all the crimes a Morisco could commit. Since the time of Emperor Charles V, the role of the Spanish Inquisition had been acknowledged by royal decree and supported by papal bulls. Both the King and the Church were conscious of the inherent difficulties in the so-called conversion of an entire people who had been forcibly baptized. They could not deny that there weren't enough suitably qualified priests prepared to carry the task through to a satisfactory conclusion. Given this situation, the Church was also acutely aware of the extremely high numbers of relapses, all of whom should clearly end up being burnt at the stake. However, the numbers would be so high as to render the punishment both meaningless and ineffective as a deterrent to others. So it was that for a century the Church had tried to accommodate Moriscos who would simply confess and repent, although in private and without the knowledge of their brothers. The Church was even prepared to extend forgiveness to habitual offenders, offering rewards such as not confiscating their belongings.

However, there was a condition attached to these confessions: the individual also had to denounce other members of their community who practised heresy. None of these offers of clemency were successful. The members of the Morisco community did not betray each other.

On the other hand the people hated the Moriscos. Their industriousness contrasted starkly with the attitude of the Christian artisans, who tried to emulate the nobles and gentlemen in their aversion to any form of work. The people were infuriated to see how the Moriscos, once they had overcome the upheaval of their deportation, prospered once more; little by little, ducat by ducat. The populace also made numerous complaints to the royal councils because of the Moriscos' fertility. Despite producing such large families they were not called upon to serve in the royal armies, unlike the peasants and Spanish townspeople, whose numbers were decimated year after year.

As Hernando had thought, Fátima and Hamid had not consigned the Koran and the other documents to the fire; they had hidden them beneath the flagstones in the courtyard.

'Fools,' he chastised them after finally getting the truth out of them. 'The Inquisition's officials would easily have found them.'

Hernando burnt everything except the Koran. He spent the night awake, terrified of hearing the echo of official footsteps heading for his door. Before dawn he concealed the divine book in his robe and headed for the cathedral, following Don Julián's instruction that he arrive before prime.

Hernando walked down Calle de los Barberos and Deanes and reached the Perdón gate. It was cold, but he carried his robe folded over his right arm, with the Koran pressed against his body. He shivered. With the cold? Only after passing beneath the great arch of the Perdón gate did he realize that the shivers were not caused by the cold. What was he doing? He hadn't even thought about it. He had just picked up the book to take to Don Julián as if it were perfectly normal and now here he was, in the cathedral garden with a Koran under his arm, surrounded by priests heading for morning prayers. Apart from the bishop, who used the ancient bridge that joined the cathedral to his palace, the rest passed through the Perdón gate; the other council dignitaries, identifiable by their rich robes, and more than a hundred canons and chaplains together with organists and musicians, choirboys, altar boys, wardens, sacristans, guards . . . Suddenly he found himself immersed in a steady flow of priests and all manner of cathedral workers. Some chatted but most were half asleep, walking in sullen silence. He shuddered. He was in one of the holiest places in all Andalusia with a Koran under his arm! He came to a halt, forcing three choirboys to make their way round him. He pressed the book to his body and, feigning an indifference that he in no way felt, checked it was still covered by the robe. He watched how the stream of men in black habits and birettas converged on the gate of the Bendiciones arch, and passed through into the cathedral itself. Then he made up his mind, and turned to get out of there. He would hide the Koran on some other—

'Eh!' Hernando heard the shout behind him and trusted it

was not directed at him. 'You!' He looked ahead and quickened his pace. 'Stop!' A sudden cold sweat broke out and ran down his back. The Bendiciones arch was only . . . 'Halt!'

Two gatekeepers blocked his way.

'Didn't you hear the inquisitor calling you?' Hernando stammered an excuse and looked to the other side of the gate, towards the street. He could run. He tried to decide: escape? But they would have recognized him and before he could get to Fátima and the children . . . 'Don't you understand?' shouted the other gatekeeper.

Hernando turned towards the garden. A tall, thin priest was waiting there. He knew that one of the canon seats on the cathedral chapter was reserved for a representative of the Inquisition. He hesitated again. He felt the gatekeepers' breath down the back of his neck and yet . . . the canon was alone; no members of the Inquisition or bailiffs were with him.

He calmed himself and took a deep breath. 'Father.' He inclined his head in greeting, walking back to the inquisitor. 'Forgive me, but I could never imagine that Your Grace would address me, a simple—'

The inquisitor interrupted him, offering his limp hand for Hernando to make the appropriate genuflection. Instinctively he went to take it, but the book under his right arm . . . he took hold of it over the robe with his left and clutched it to his chest as he sank down almost to his knees to ensure that nothing was seen. The inquisitor urged him to get up. Hernando folded the robe over his arm to prevent even the presence of a book being detected. The priest looked him up and down. Hernando pressed the Koran to his chest. The divine revelation was contained there! It should be this book inside the mosque, guarded in the mihrab, and not all those Christian priests with their chants and their statues! There was a warm glow where he held the book, next to his heart, and it spread like a wave through his entire body. Hernando stood up straight and tensed his muscles. By the time the inquisitor finished his inspection, Hernando felt strong again, trusting in God and His word.

'Yesterday,' the inquisitor snarled, 'we arrested a heretic who copied, bound and distributed documents both defamatory and contrary to the doctrine of the Holy Mother Church. He will not be allowed a period of grace for his spontaneous confession. Given the gravity of the case and the need to arrest his possible accomplices before they can flee, we have begun the interrogation in the tribunal headquarters this very day. The books are written in an Arabic that our usual translator cannot fully understand. The council has given me excellent references about you, and you are therefore to present yourself here at the hour of terce to witness the questioning and act as translator of those documents.'

Hernando's heart sank. His courage evaporated the second he imagined himself standing in front of Karim, witnessing his interrogation and possibly his torture . . . while he translated what he himself had written!

'I . . .' he stammered, trying to excuse himself, 'I have to work in the stables . . .'

'The persecution of heresy and the defence of Christianity take precedence over any work!' the inquisitor snapped.

The sound of voices singing the canticles inside the cathedral reached them in the garden. The priest turned back to look at the gate of the Bendiciones arch and glided silently into the building.

'At mid-morning prayers, remember,' he insisted before leaving Hernando alone.

Hernando covered the short distance to his house with his mind blank, trying not to think, murmuring suras and hugging the Koran to his chest.

The fortress, ancient residence of the Catholic monarchs and now the seat of the inquisitional tribunal, had been built by King Alfonso XI on the ruins of part of the caliph's palace. However, for a long time, all the monies collected by the tribunal for the conservation of the site were diverted to cover the inquisitors' personal expenses. Consequently, the facilities had fallen into a steady decline. What should have been bedrooms, halls, offices and archives were now home to chickens, pigeons, stables and even linen laundries whose wares were sold openly by the inquisitors' servants in the doorway on Campo Real. The hygiene levels in the fortress, with animals and dirt, insalubrious jails and two ponds of putrid stagnant water bordering on the river Guadalquivir, lent credence to the saying that everyone who lived in the fortress was ill until they died.

At terce Hernando presented himself as ordered at the door on Campo Real, beneath the Vela tower.

'You'll have to go round,' one of the linen-sellers told him rudely. 'Cross the cemetery and enter by the Palo gate, in the Vela tower next to the river.'

The Palo gate opened on to a walled courtyard, with poplars and oranges, overlooking the Guadalquivir. Two gatekeepers questioned him as if he was on trial until one, with an abrupt gesture, pointed to a small doorway in the southern façade. As soon as he went through the door and left the trees of the patio behind, Hernando felt the unhealthy damp of the place cling to his body. He entered a gloomy corridor that led to the tribunal hall. To his left were the cells, intricately arranged to make the best use of space within the ancient fortress. He knew they were crammed full of prisoners, but the stark silence was such that his footsteps echoed along the corridor.

The tribunal hall was rectangular with high vaulted ceilings. On one side several inquisitors were already seated behind desks, among them the one who had spoken to him in the cathedral garden, together with the prosecutor of the Holy Office and the notary. They swore him to secrecy about what he heard in the 'hall of secrets' and sat him down at a table lower than the others, next to the notary. Set out before them were three badly stitched copies of the Koran and some other loose papers.

Karim had been responsible for stitching the pages of the Koran together before distribution. With the murmur of the inquisitors' conversation in the background, Hernando recognized each copy of the divine book. As he fixed his gaze on them he could recall the exact moment he had written each one: he almost did not need to copy them any more. The difficulties faced, the mistakes made, the quills he had to cut and in what sura he did so, the lack of ink, Don Julián's remarks and comments, the worry and anxiety at any strange and unexpected noise . . . The dreams and the hopes of a people were represented in every character he had managed to write on those overly satiny and poor quality sheets of paper, brought with such difficulty from Xátiva.

At the sight of Karim entering the tribunal hall, Hernando shrank into the hard wooden chair. The old man looked dirty and unkempt, weak and shrunken. What would he think? That he was the informer? When Karim's gaze landed on him it took no more than a second to convince him that nothing was further from the old man's mind.

'I forgive you!' declared Karim to no one in particular when he reached the centre of the hall, interrupting the start of the notary's reading.

The inquisitors were annoyed.

'What have you to forgive, heretic?' one exclaimed.

Hernando ignored the curses that followed. Those words were directed to him. *I forgive you!* Karim had avoided looking at anyone when he said them and had spoken in the singular. *I forgive you!* Hernando's resolve had weakened when he saw Karim enter, but now he pulled himself together. He had felt strong that morning with the Koran pressed against his chest, only to be plunged into despair when he learnt that he would have to witness Karim's trial. Fátima, Aisha and a downcast Hamid had bombarded him with questions, none of which he could answer. And now Karim forgave him, promising to take full responsibility on himself.

All morning Karim responded to the inevitable questions.

'All Christians!' he stated in answer to a question as to whether he had any known enemies. 'Those who broke the peace treaty signed by your monarchs; those who insult us, ill-treat us and hate us; those who steal our papers so that we are arrested; those who prevent us from upholding our laws . . .'

Hernando, his voice shaking, translated a section from the books. To the evident satisfaction of the inquisitor, Karim had admitted they were his. The old man confessed how he had obtained the paper and the ink and how he himself had written them. He and he alone was responsible for everything!

'You can burn me,' he challenged, his forefinger stabbing at all those present. 'I will never reconcile myself with your Church.'

Hernando fought to hold back his tears, aware of his trembling lips.

'Heretic dog!' burst out one of the inquisitors. 'Do you take us for fools? We know for a fact that an old man like you is not capable of doing all this alone. We want to know who has helped you and who has the rest of the books.'

'I have told you there is no one else,' Karim responded.

Hernando watched him standing alone in the centre of the large hall, confronting the tribunal: a great spirit in a small body. In truth there was no one else. Hernando thought how indeed no one else was needed for the defence of the Prophet and the only God.

'Yes there is,' the reedy voice of the cathedral canon asserted, sharp but serene. 'And you will tell us their names.' His last words hung in the air until the inquisitor himself ordered proceedings suspended until the following day.

Hernando did not go to the stables that afternoon. After the justices had taken Karim away, and the inquisitors had left their desks, he tried to get himself excused from attending the following day's session: he had now translated a part of the documents and the Korans were, in any case, interlined with *aljamiado*.

'That is the reason you need to be here,' countered the canon. 'We don't know if these interlineal translations are correct or if they are just another strategy designed to confuse us. You will stay with us for the entire trial.'

He dismissed Hernando with a disdainful wave of the hand.

Hernando took no meals and refused all food. He did not even speak. He shut himself away in his room and, facing the kiblah, prayed for the rest of the day and into the night, until he was exhausted.

Nobody interrupted or bothered him; the women kept the children silent.

At mid-morning on the following day, Hernando was not taken to the hall of secrets. From the corridor leading to the tribunal they instead descended a stairway to some windowless vaults. The inquisitors were already present. They were whispering among themselves, standing in a circle around many and varied instruments of torture: there were ropes hanging from the ceiling, a rack, and a hundred and one cruel iron contrivances for lacerating, immobilizing or dismembering the accused.

The stench inside the large room was warm and cloying, and it soon became unbearable. Hernando stifled the urge to retch at the sight of all those macabre implements.

'Sit there and wait,' the canon ordered, pointing to a nearby table, where the Korans and the court clerk's files were already laid out. The clerk himself was chatting with inquisitors, the doctor and the torturer.

'He is too old,' Hernando overheard one of the inquisitors comment. 'We should go carefully.'

'Don't worry,' replied the torturer, a bald, well-built man. 'I will take care of him,' he added, with more than a touch of irony.

Some of those present smiled.

Hernando forced himself to look away from the group of men, and wished he could close his ears as well. He looked at the files on the table. 'Mateo Hernández, new Christian, Moor', appeared on the first page, written in the neat calligraphy of the Inquisition clerk. There followed details of date, place, the grounds on which the trial was brought, the account of the inquisitors present until, on the last line of that first page, he read:

> Córdoba, the twenty-third of January in the year of Our Lord Fifteen hundred and eighty, before Juan de la Portilla, Inquisitor of the Tribunal of Córdoba, in the Hall of the Holy Office, for the purpose of reporting an act of heresy, there appeared the individual who gave his name as

The line ended there. Hernando looked up at the inquisitors. They were still chatting, waiting for the accused to be brought in. The twenty-third of January! More than a month ago. Who had appeared before the inquisitor over a month ago and made the denunciation that had led to the trial? It could only be . . . Suddenly the room fell silent as Karim was brought in by two guards. As soon as the inquisitors turned their attention to the accused, Hernando turned over the page. One glance was enough: Cristóbal Escandalet. His fists clenched, Hernando resisted the urge to check if anyone had noticed, and waited for the clerk to sit down beside him.

'Cristóbal Escandalet,' muttered Hernando as if he wanted to burn the name into his memory. He was the traitor!

Karim again denied that anyone had helped him. His confident tone of voice drew Hernando's gaze. It contrasted sharply with Karim's exhausted, dejected appearance, especially when they pulled off his shirt to reveal a scrawny, hairless torso.

'Begin the interrogation,' ordered Don Juan de la Portilla, standing with the other inquisitors. The clerk flourished his quill over the paper.

They laid the accused face down on the rack, his arms behind his back, and tied his thumbs together with a cord that connected to a stronger rope. It ran up to a winch suspended from the ceiling and back down again. Karim again refused to answer the inquisitor's questions and the torturer began to pull on the end of the rope.

If anyone was hoping he would scream, they were disappointed. The old man pressed his face against the rack and only emitted some muffled grunts. Hernando felt sick. Karim's groans were punctuated by the inquisitor's persistent questions.

'Who else is with you?' he shouted time and again, becoming increasingly irate as Karim's silence persisted.

When the torturer shook his head, and the inquisitors ceased their efforts and freed the old man from the rack, his thumbs were bent back, wrenched from their joints. Karim's face was flushed, his breathing came in agonized gulps, his tired eyes watered, and trickles of blood ran from his lower lip. He could not have stood if it were not for the torturer holding him upright. The doctor approached Karim and examined his thumbs, manipulating them roughly. Hernando saw his friend's face contort with the agony that until then he had kept concealed.

'He is all right,' the physician announced. However, he turned to Portilla and spoke into his ear. As he did so Hernando saw the clerk write: 'The accused is in good health.'

'The session is suspended until tomorrow,' the inquisitor declared as soon as the doctor moved away from him.

'You must eat,' whispered Fátima, entering the room where Hernando had stayed praying since arriving home. 'It's after midnight.'

'Karim doesn't,' he replied.

Fátima approached her husband, who was kneeling on his heels with his body uncovered. His arms and chest were scratched, bleeding in places as a result of the force with which he had washed, scrubbing at himself as if he wanted to tear off his skin and rid himself of the stench of the dungeon, which in spite of his efforts continued to cling to his body.

'It's cold. You should wrap up.'

'Leave me, woman!' Fátima obeyed and left the bowl of food and some water in a corner. 'Tell Hamid to come,' he added without looking at her.

The old scholar did not delay.

'Peace . . .' Hamid fell silent when he saw Hernando, who did not even turn towards him. 'You shouldn't punish yourself,' he murmured.

'The traitor is called Cristóbal Escandalet,' was Hernando's only response. 'Tell Abbas. He will know what to do.'

He would have liked to kill the man himself with his bare hands, strangle him slowly and watch his dying eyes, to cause him as much pain as Karim had suffered. But since he was at the behest of the Inquisition he decided it was better for Abbas to deal with the dog, and the sooner the better.

'The punishment for one who betrays our people is clear. Abbas will know exactly what he has to do. What worries me . . .' Hamid left the words hanging in the air. He waited for a reaction from Hernando, but he merely continued his preparations for prayer. 'What worries me', the old scholar insisted, 'is if you know what you have to do.'

'What do you mean?' asked Hernando, after a few moments of confusion.

'Karim is sacrificing himself for us—'

'He is protecting me,' Hernando interrupted. He kept his back to Hamid.

'Don't be arrogant, Ibn Hamid. He is protecting all of us. You . . . you are but one weapon more in our fight. Karim is also protecting your wife, and the mothers to whom she teaches the revealed word, and the mothers when they teach it to their children, and the little ones who learn in secret, warned that they mustn't speak of it outside their homes. He is protecting us all.'

Hamid saw Hernando shiver slightly.

'My life is in his hands,' Hernando said eventually, turning his head towards the holy man, who feared that his pupil was on the verge of collapse.

Hamid approached Hernando and with some difficulty knelt down beside him.

'It may be you are right,' conceded Hernando. 'In fact it's certain! He protects us all, but you can't even begin to imagine the terror that grips me when I see such a weak, worn body, broken by torture, subjected to interrogation. How much can an old man like him stand? I'm scared, Hamid, yes. I shake. I can't control my hands or my knees. I fear the pain will drive him mad and in the end he will denounce me.'

The old scholar gave the hint of a sad smile.

'Strength does not reside in our body, Ibn Hamid. Strength is in our spirit. Trust in Karim's! He will not betray you. To do so would mean betraying his people.'

Their eyes met.

'Have you prayed yet?' the holy man suddenly asked, breaking the spell. Hernando thought he heard in those words an echo from Hamid's old house in Juviles. He pressed his lips together, knowing what came next: 'The night prayer is the only one we can perform with any degree of safety. The Christians are asleep.' With a lump in his throat from the nostalgia that flooded over him, Hernando was about to answer that he always did so, but Hamid stopped him. 'We have fought many battles since then, haven't we, my son?'

However, Hamid did not give Abbas the message. The blacksmith was young and strong. Karim would die, either during the torture or burnt as a heretic. Jalil, like Karim, was too old. Don Julián was also elderly, and as he always had to act clandestinely, there was no possibility of his moving among the Moriscos. But Hamid himself . . . He knew that his life would soon be over. Abbas should not take the risk. How could he, Hamid, kill that treacherous dog? These thoughts ran through Hamid's mind yet again as he watched the man nonchalantly selling his *buñuelos* at the centre of the Rastro.

After two days of constant torture, Karim's arms had been completely dislocated on the rack, yet the old man continued to be as stubborn in his silence as Hernando in his fasting and prayer. Fátima and Aisha were worried and even the children sensed that something terrible was drawing near.

'Does he drink the water you leave him?' Hamid asked Fátima.

'Yes,' she replied.

'In that case, he will survive.'

Hamid watched the *buñolero* move his wares over to an area where a large group of people had gathered. His eyes followed him until he saw him stop next to a knife-seller. The *buñolero* shouted out his wares, squeezing *buñuelos de jeringuilla* from the pastry bag. They formed circles in the frying pan and sizzled in the boiling oil until he cut them up for sale to the public. Knives! Even if Hamid managed to make off with one of them, the distance between Cristóbal and the knife-seller was too great for him to be able to take the *buñolero* by surprise and stab him. The cries of the knife-seller would certainly put him on his guard. Besides, he had to cut off his head! How . . . ?

Suddenly, Hamid set his jaw. 'Allah is great,' he muttered through clenched teeth as he limped towards the *buñolero*.

Cristóbal saw Hamid heading purposefully towards him, his eyes fixed firmly on his own. He stopped calling out his *buñuelos* and frowned, but when the holy man drew level with him he smiled. It was just an old cripple!

'Do you want one, Grandfather?' Hamid shook his head. 'What then . . . ?' enquired Cristóbal.

In that instant Hamid grabbed the frying pan with both hands. The hiss of burning skin and flesh as the red-hot pan scalded his fingers could be heard by all around. The old man did not even blink. Some of the crowd just managed to leap out of the way as Hamid hurled the boiling oil at Cristóbal's face. The *buñolero* howled and threw up his hands, before falling to the ground writhing in agony. Still holding the frying pan, and with the smell of burnt flesh filling the air, the old scholar headed for the knife-seller's stand. People stood aside to let him through and the knife-seller, seeing a madman still capable of throwing the remains of the oil at him, was quick to get out of his way. Hamid threw down the frying pan, grabbed the largest knife from the display, and returned to the screaming *buñolero*.

Most of the crowd watched from a distance in stunned silence; one man ran to fetch the guards.

Hamid knelt down next to Cristóbal, who was kicking and howling, lying on his back with his hands covering his face. Hamid slashed at Cristóbal's forearms, and the sudden new pain forced the *buñolero* to uncover his throat. The old man drew the knife across the informer's neck. The cut was deep and accurate, delivered with all the strength of an insulted and betrayed community. A stream of blood spurted out, and Hamid stood up covered in it, with the huge knife still in his hands. In front of him stood a guard, his sword held ready.

'Christian dogs!' Hamid shouted defiantly, finally venting all the resentment he had kept repressed throughout his entire life.

The guard plunged his sword into Hamid's stomach.

The Alpujarra, the white peaks of the Sierra Nevada, the rivers and gullies, the diminutive terraces of fertile land won terrace by terrace from the mountain, the work in the fields and the night-time prayers . . . all of these appeared clearly in Hamid's mind. He felt no pain at all. Hernando, his son! Aisha, Fátima, the little ones . . . Nor did he feel any pain when the guard pulled the sword out of his body. Hamid watched his blood gushing out: the same blood had been spilt by the thousands of Muslims who had decided to defend their law.

The guard remained standing over him, convinced that the old man would fall to the ground at any moment. People stood round in silence.

'There is no god but God, and Muhammad is the messenger of God,' intoned Hamid.

They must not capture him. They must not find out who he was. He would not put his family in danger for anything. He raised the knife and limped towards the river, which ran past the end of the Rastro. People hurriedly got out of his way, while the guard gave chase. He had to destroy himself! He left a trail of blood behind him, but no one tried to stop him. Everyone held still, as if entranced by the aura of the old man calmly heading for the riverbank.

'No!' shouted the guard, realizing Hamid's intention too late, just as the holy man let himself fall into the Guadalquivir and disappeared beneath its waters.

Hernando could not take any more pain. He had just returned from the fortress, where the torture of Karim had become senseless cruelty. The old man continued in his stubborn determination not to disclose the identity of his accomplices, and even the torturer had turned to the inquisitors and gestured that he thought it was pointless to insist.

'Continue!' shouted Portilla, silencing his doubts.

Hernando was forced to witness all the barbarity. Hamid's words had confirmed him in his faith, in the spirit that moved the Moriscos to fight for their laws and customs, and he tried to go to the fortress in this positive frame of mind. However, once in the dungeons, when they tortured Karim and demanded the names of his accomplices, fear gripped him once more. It was his name that Karim was so tenaciously keeping to himself! Only two paces away from him, Karim was being savagely tortured. Hernando could smell his blood and his urine; he gazed at the convulsions of his muscles, contorted with the intense pain; listened to his muted cries, worse than the most terrible screams, and his gasps and sobs when they stopped to rest. Sometimes he felt proud of Karim's victory over the inquisitors, defending his people and his law; but at others he felt an appalling sense of guilt ... And at times a cold sweat merged with the stench of the dungeon at the mere thought that Karim could give in and point a finger: 'Him! It's him you seek!' Petrified, Hernando huddled in the chair. His stomach clenched as he imagined how the guards and inquisitors would leap upon him. He could be next, and nobody would reproach a man, whoever he was, for breaking down under such a weight of torment and giving them what they wanted. Hernando was awash with pride, guilt and panic. His emotions tossed him hither and thither like a rag-doll, wave after wave enveloping him after a simple question, another tug on the rope, a stifled cry ...

Hernando had just returned home when a young boy sent by Jalil told him what had happened to Hamid. Fátima and Aisha curled up on the floor next to the wall and wept, embracing the children.

He could not stand more pain!

'The dead *buñolero* . . .' asked Hernando, his voice hoarse. 'Was he called Cristóbal Escandalet?'

'Yes,' the boy replied.

Hernando shook his head. Perhaps Hamid had not told Abbas after all?

'That man was a spy and a traitor,' he declared, turning again to the young Morisco. 'He was the one who denounced Karim to the Inquisition. Let all our brothers know why our finest scholar took such action! He judged this man, passed sentence upon him, and then he himself carried it out. Let the *buñolero*'s family know this too!'

Once in his room, Hernando wept profusely, ready to give himself over once more to prayer and fasting. Now who would use the little ground-floor room? Now who would kneel down on the floor and pray before the mark of the kiblah on the wall? Hamid had shown him that mark, as proud and innocent as a child who has done something good and awaits approval. Hamid, from whom he had learnt everything, from whom he had taken his name: Hamid ibn Hamid, the son of Hamid!

A tear clouded Hernando's vision, distancing him from reality. Then a spine-chilling cry rang out in the night across the whole district of Santa María: 'Father!'

The guards dragged Karim in by his armpits. His head was lolling to one side and his feet, destroyed by torture, dragged behind him along the floor, as if the person who had joined them by the ankles to be presented to the Inquisition had made some ghastly mistake.

The guards tried to stand Karim up to face Portilla. The torturer grabbed what little grey hair Karim had left, and yanked his head up. The inquisitor clicked his tongue and flicked his hand in frustration.

Hernando saw the old man's battered eyes looking far beyond the walls of the dungeon; possibly seeing death, possibly paradise. Who deserved paradise more than that true believer? Karim's dry lips began to move.

'Silence!' cried the inquisitor.

Karim's mumbling sounded like a distant echo in the large room. He was raving in Arabic.

'What's he saying?' yelled the inquisitor at Hernando.

The Morisco listened carefully, aware that Portilla was watching him.

'He is calling to his wife.' Hernando thought he understood. He was about to repeat the name: Amina. 'Ana,' he lied. 'She seems to be called Ana.'

Karim went on murmuring.

'All this talk just to call to his wife?' said the inquisitor suspiciously.

'He is remembering a poem,' Hernando explained. He seemed to be listening to one of the ancient ones, one of those that appeared carved on the walls of the Alhambra in Granada. 'It describes the wife . . . the wife who presents herself to her husband, beautifully adorned to tempt him . . .'

'Ask him about his accomplices. Possibly now . . .'

'Who were your accomplices?' Hernando obeyed, speaking Spanish, unable to raise his head.

'In Arabic, imbecile!'

'Who . . . ?' He began translating, then suddenly paused. No one in the dungeon apart from Karim could understand him. 'God's justice has been done,' he announced in Arabic. 'He who betrayed our people has had his throat cut according to our law. Hamid of Juviles has taken care of it. You will meet the saintly scholar in paradise.'

Portilla turned his eyes to the Morisco, surprised by the length of his discourse. At that moment an almost imperceptible gleam appeared in the old man's eyes, and his lips contracted into a grimace that could have been a smile. Then he died.

'His effigy will be burnt at the next auto-da-fé,' pronounced the inquisitor when the doctor, after examining Karim, certified what everyone already knew. 'What did you say to him?' he asked Hernando.

'That he had to be a good Christian,' Hernando stated unblinkingly, sure of himself. 'That he had to confess what you wanted to know and be reconciled with the Church to receive the forgiveness of Our Lord and the eternal salvation of his soul . . .'

Portilla raised his fingers to his lips and rubbed them. 'That is good,' he finally conceded.

40

ON 15 APRIL 1581 the Portuguese parliament meeting in the city of Tomar declared Philip II of Spain as King of Portugal, unifying the Iberian peninsula under the same crown. King Philip 'the Prudent' gained control of all the territories and trade with the New World, which the Treaty of Tordesillas had divided between Spain and Portugal.

It was also in Portugal where the possibility of a mass extermination of Spanish Moriscos was first considered. A meeting of the King, the Count of Chinchón and the aged Duke of Alba (restored to health but with a character even old age could not mellow) studied the possibility of loading all the Moriscos on to ships bound for Barbary. Once out at sea the ships would be scuppered, drowning all those on board.

Fortunately, or possibly because the armada was otherwise occupied, this planned genocide was not carried out.

In August of the same year, the King took another decision, also from Portugal, which was to directly affect Hernando. That summer the drought wreaked havoc in the Córdoba countryside. There was not enough grass in the pastures for the mares to eat, and not enough money to feed them costly grain, which was in any case needed for the people. Even the Bishop of Córdoba had found himself forced to purchase imported wheat. As a result the King wrote to the stable master Don Diego López de Haro and the Count of Olivares advising them that the stud should be moved to pastures in the royal territory of Lomo del Grullo in Seville. These lands were under the count's jurisdiction and the horses would be able to graze there.

Over a year had passed since Karim's death at the hands of the Inquisition's torturer and Hamid had disappeared into the waters of the Guadalquivir after avenging the betrayal of the Morisco community. Hernando spent this period in constant penance. Every time he remembered the torture chamber of the Christian monarchs' fortress and Karim's obstinate silence, he was overwhelmed by a sense of guilt which he believed only fasting and prayer could appease.

'He would have died anyway,' Fátima tried to convince Hernando, worried by her husband's appearance. He was thin and haggard, the intense blue of his eyes dulled by dark shadows. 'Even if he had confessed he would never have reconciled himself with the Church. They would have executed him just the same.'

'Maybe yes,' replied Hernando doubtfully, 'and maybe no. We can't know. The only certainty, the only thing I know for sure because I lived it minute by minute, is that for keeping my name secret he died a cruel and agonizing death.'

'Everyone's name, Hernando! Karim kept secret the names of everyone who still believes in the one God, not just yours. You can't take all the responsibility on yourself.'

But the Morisco rejected his wife's words.

'Give him time, daughter,' Aisha advised a weeping Fátima.

Don Diego announced to Hernando that he must travel to Seville with the stud and stay there until it returned to Córdoba. Fátima and Aisha were pleased, hoping the journey and the time in Seville would take Hernando's mind off his guilt and rouse him from the despair into which he had sunk. He appeared unable to find solace, not even in his daily rides on Azirat.

At the beginning of September, nearly four hundred mares, the yearlings and the spring foals set out for the rich pastures of the low Guadalquivir wetlands. Lomo del Grullo was thirty leagues from Córdoba, following the road to Écija, Carmona and then Seville. From there, once over the river, they had to head for Villamanrique, a town next to the royal game preserve. Under normal circumstances the journey could be done in four or five days, but Hernando and the other riders accompanying the horses soon realized it could well take them twice as long. Don Diego hired additional hands to help the keepers of the brood mares, who were walking with the animals and trying to keep together a substantial herd unused to travelling long distances. For the large flocks of sheep that moved between winter and summer pastures along the nearby drovers' road, the Cañada Real de la Mesta, such travels were nothing new. Added to the contingent of men and horses, a group of Córdoba nobles eager to please the King had also come along, as if they were on a pilgrimage. Their presence did nothing but hinder the work of keepers and riders.

Hernando, as Fátima and Aisha had rightly predicted, managed to forget his worries. He concentrated on galloping Azirat up and down, rounding up mares or foals that strayed from the herd. He joined the rest in keeping the animals knotted even closer together whenever the way became narrow or difficult. The fiery red of Azirat's coat stood out wherever he worked, and his agility, his caracoles and spirited jumps aroused admiration among all the travellers.

'And that horse?' an obese noble, settled into rather than mounted on a large leather saddle embossed with silver, asked two others who were accompanying him. They were some distance away from the herd in order to avoid the dust cloud whipped up on the dry road.

Hernando had just frustrated a colt's escape, pursuing, over-taking and wheeling around in front of it. Azirat reared straight up on his hind legs, hanging motionless in the air, forcing the unruly renegade to return.

'Given the colour of its coat it must be a reject from the royal stables,' speculated one of those questioned. 'A real shame,' he pronounced, impressed by both the horse and rider. 'It'll be one of the horses Diego gave to the workers in part-payment of their wages.'

'And the rider?' enquired the first noble.

'A Morisco,' the third man clarified. 'I've heard Diego speak of him. He has great faith in his abilities and there can be no doubt that . . .'

'A Morisco . . .' repeated the obese noble to himself, paying no attention to further explanations.

The three men now watched how Hernando galloped flat out to the head of the herd. As the Morisco passed by him the Count of Espiel stood up in the silver stirrups of his luxurious saddle and frowned. 'Where have I seen that face before?'

The King's orders allowed them to requisition help from the officials and inhabitants of all the villages on their route. Nevertheless, before the end of each day the riders still had to find a suitable place to gather and feed that quantity of live-stock and obtain grain or straw if the chosen grazing was insufficient. At the same time the nobles searched out the comforts of the nearest village.

At night, after caring for Azirat, Hernando collapsed exhausted. He dined on soup prepared by the cook in a cauldron over an open camp fire and chatted a while with the other men. It was only when he took his turn on watch in those open pastures, as unfamiliar to the men as to the livestock, that he recalled the events that had marked the past year.

It was during those moments of silence on watch, mounted on Azirat, that Hernando came to forgive himself. Astride his horse, as he listened to an animal's snort breaking the silence or as he gently rounded up one that tried sleepily to move away from the herd, the Morisco regained his peace of mind. How different were those hours from the tumultuous time with five hundred animals on the move! The neighs and whinnies, the kicks and bites; the immense dust cloud that rose in their wake rendering everything invisible but for a few feet ahead. At night he could contemplate the vast, clear and starry sky, also very different from the one he could see from his house in Córdoba, boxed in between so many other buildings. Alone in the countryside he began to feel as he had in the Alpujarra. Hamid! The old scholar had devoted himself to them. Seeking contact with another living creature, he patted Azirat's neck as the memory of the holy man made his throat tighten. He also thought of Karim. This time though he let the painful scenes he had lived through in the Inquisition's dungeons play out one after another in his mind, without seeking refuge in prayer or fasting to escape the images. Time and again he relived the old man's pain, feeling it in his flesh, seeing it and suffering it. It hurt as if he were there in the chamber where they had tortured Karim . . . and him. Little by little, the images of Karim's bloody face, his stifled howls of pain as he struggled not to give in to his tormentors or allow them any satisfaction, and his body, more broken every day, appeared before Hernando with such intensity that he shrank back on the saddle. There in the vastness of Andalusia, alone in the night and unable to escape from all those memories, he began to learn to live with his pain and face up to himself.

Hernando peered up at the sky, at the moon whose beams outlined the shapes all around him, and suddenly saw a shooting star fall, and then another . . . and another, as if the two old men were watching him and speaking to him from paradise.

Brahim also saw the same shooting stars, but his interpretation was decidedly different from Hernando's. Seven years had passed since he had armed his first pirate ship. After four seasons personally commanding the attacks on the coast of Spain, and several occasions when the militias had almost arrested him, he decided to assign his place in the boats to Nasi, now a young man who was as strong and cruel as his master. Brahim would concentrate on investing his money, running the business with an iron hand, and reaping the considerable rewards this gave him.

Together with Nasi he moved to a small palace in the city of Tetuan, where he lived surrounded by luxury and women. In order to cement a convenient alliance he had remarried. She was the daughter of another of the city's leaders, and she bore him two daughters. When he was arranging the marriage, Brahim was very careful to avoid telling the bride's family that she was no more than his second wife; that his first was detained in Spain and, sooner or later, would return to him to occupy her rightful place.

As the former Alpujarra muleteer gained riches, prestige and respect, his humiliating departure from Córdoba ate away at him more and more. The stump of his right arm served as a permanent reminder, especially during the balmy nights of the North African summer when he was woken, drenched in sweat, by stabs of pain from his missing hand. Then the time until dawn passed in fitful sleep. The greater his power, the greater his desperation. What use were slaves if he was unable to forget the slavery he himself had been condemned to in Córdoba? What good were his fabulous riches when he had been robbed of the woman he desired for being unable to support her? Every time he punished one of his men for stealing and sentenced him to have his hand cut off, he saw himself in the Sierra Morena held down by a gang of outlaws thrusting out his arm to the scimitar: it was his own hand being severed.

Comfort and prosperity, together with the lack of any other worries, led Brahim to become obsessed with his past. There was no Christian captive or fugitive Morisco he did not question about the situation in Córdoba; about an outlaw in the Sierra Morena known as the One-handed One; about Hernando, a Morisco from Juviles who lived in Córdoba and was called the Nazarene; and about Aisha or Fátima. Especially about Fátima, whose black almond eyes remained bright in both the muleteer's memory and his increasingly unhealthy obsession. The interest of the rich corsair, who rewarded any news with great generosity, spread quickly from mouth to mouth. There were few men on his boats who, one way or another, failed to seek out such information to offer on their return from incursions. This was how Brahim came to find out El Sobahet had died and Ubaid had taken his place.

'Do you two know Córdoba?' Brahim asked brusquely in *aljamiado*, cutting across the polite greetings of the two Capuchin monks who had arrived on a mission to rescue slaves. What did he care about formalities?

The shaven-headed monks, dressed in their habits and with crosses on their chests, were surprised and looked quizzically at one another. They were standing before their host in the magnificent reception hall of Brahim's palace in the medina. Brahim, with the young Nasi by his side, spoke from where he lay among dozens of silk cushions.

'Yes, your excellency,' answered Brother Silvestre. 'I spent several years in the convent in Córdoba.'

Brahim could not conceal his delight. He smiled and indicated to the monks that they sit down with him, eagerly patting the cushions on either side of him. Whilst the corsair called for a slave to attend to them, Brother Enrique exchanged a conspiratorial look with his companion: they had to make the most of the great Tetuan corsair's warm reception and win his favour, together with a lower price for the souls they had come to rescue.

Together with other redeeming orders, the Capuchin monks concerned themselves with the rescue of Tetuan slaves. The Carmelites did likewise with those of Algiers. With this aim in mind, Brother Silvestre and Brother Enrique had just visited the Sidi al-Mandri fortress, residence of the governor and obligatory stage in any rescue mission. Firstly, after paying taxes on disembarking and facing the insults and spittle of any onlookers, the friars had to free the slaves belonging to the local governor. The governor invariably broke the conditions stipulated in the complex agreement that gave the monks permission and safe conduct for their rescue mission. He would insist on a higher price and demand a greater number of his own slaves be freed. In view of this, to find themselves with such an amenable sheikh, who invited them to sit and offered food and drink, which an army of black slaves was already serving, was a situation they intended to take full advantage of. They had money, plenty of money. It came directly from the captives' families, from the alms demanded constantly in all the Spanish kingdoms, and above all from the offerings and bequests pious Christians made in their wills. Almost 70 per cent of Spanish testaments bequeathed sums for the rescue of souls. However, all the money in the world was not enough to free the thousands of Christians crammed into Tetuan's underground caverns. The city was built on limestone, and there were immense natural subterranean galleries beside the fortress. They ran under the entire city and it was there that thousands of Christian captives were imprisoned.

The monks had been in those dungeons and the stench and morbid atmosphere had almost knocked them unconscious. Thousands of men were crowded together underground, filthy, naked and ill. There was neither natural light nor air. The only ventilation came from shafts with metal grilles that ran directly up to the city streets. There the Christians awaited rescue or death; in irons, chained and collared, or with their feet secured between long iron bars holding them immobile.

'Tell me, tell me,' Brahim urged. At his words the memory of the savage conditions in which their compatriots were held prisoner overcame the monks once more.

Brother Silvestre knew of Hernando, the Morisco employed by Don Diego in the royal stables and who, on Sundays, rode around Córdoba on a magnificent chestnut horse with two children astride the saddle. The monk had been told he provided services to the cathedral chapter, although he knew nothing of his family circumstances. And yes, of course he knew of the bloodthirsty outlaw whom everyone called the One-handed One – the monk had to make a conscious effort to avert his gaze from Brahim's stump – who after El Sobahet's death had become an outlaw chief in the heights of the Sierra Morena. Neither of the two dared ask why the corsair was so interested in these people. Between mouthfuls of lemonade, dates and sweetmeats, they spoke of Córdoba before they broached the subject of the rescue of the slaves they had come to liberate. To the monks' despair, Brahim left these negotiations in the hands of Nasi.

Little by little, Brahim was piecing together the information he longed for. The corsairs' audacity took them far into Christian territories, to villages some distance away from the coast, but Córdoba, at over thirty leagues by main roads, was too far away for him to run the risk of going there. Besides, what would they do once they were inside the ancient seat of the caliphs?

Now Brahim contemplated those same shooting stars in which Hernando, in a field near Carmona, tried to see a celestial message from his dead loved ones. The corsair had succeeded in finding a way to resolve the problems that stood in the way of his revenge. The solution had arrived in the form of the young and beautiful Doña Catalina and little Daniel, the wife and son of Don José de Guzmán, Marquis of Casabermeja, a rich landowner originally from Málaga. Brahim's men had taken them prisoner, together with their small escort, during an incursion on the outskirts of Marbella.

Doña Catalina and her son Daniel were an extremely valuable catch. The corsair immediately accommodated them in his palace and attended to their every need until the marquis's negotiators arrived. Nobles did not wait for a rescue mission to accumulate funds and the difficult permits needed from the governor of Tetuan and King Philip; the King was highly resistant to the flight of capital to his Muslim enemies although in the end he always found himself forced to capitulate. As soon as noble or illustrious families received news of where their relatives were held (something the corsairs themselves ensured) they entered directly into hasty negotiations to agree terms for their rescue.

Doña Catalina and her son were from such a family, and Brahim did not have to wait long for the visit of Samuel, a prestigious Jewish merchant from Tetuan. The muleteer had already had numerous business dealings with him over the sale of merchandise captured from the Christian boats.

'I don't want money,' Brahim said as soon as the Jew opened negotiations. 'I want the marquis to take responsibility for the return of my family and secure my revenge against two Moriscos from the Alpujarra.'

The last of the shooting stars traced a parabola through the clear night sky, and Brahim smiled as he recalled Samuel's look of surprise when he heard the conditions for the release of Doña Catalina and her son.

'If he doesn't do this, Samuel,' he concluded, 'I will put mother and son to death.'

Brahim was looking up at the sky from the balcony of the large room where he had lodged, in the roadside inn at Montón de la Tierra. It was the last of those on the Camino de Las Ventas from Toledo, and only one league from Córdoba. It was almost eight years since he had passed by there with Aisha and Shamir on his way to find El Sobahet, to propose the deal that had resulted in the loss of his right hand. 'Ubaid!' he muttered. He stroked the hilt of the scimitar hung at his waist. He had learnt to use the weapon with his left hand. In his pocket he carried a document signed by the marquis's secretary, which guaranteed him freedom to travel across Andalusia. One of the noble's men was stationed outside his door, to ensure he was not disturbed while he awaited events. From the balcony he also observed the ground floor of the inn. It was a square courtyard lit by large torches fixed to the walls, around which were arranged the dining room, barn, rooms belonging to the innkeeper and his family, and the stables. Several soldiers from the small army recruited by the marquis hung around in the courtyard, waiting like him. He had handed the innkeeper plenty of money to buy his silence and close the inn to any other travellers.

He gazed again at the sheltering sky and tried to feel something of the calm it spread. He had spent years dreaming of this day. He leant against the wooden rail, his left fist beating rhythmically on it. A couple of soldiers looked up at the balcony.

Four days ago, before he landed on the Málaga coast, Nasi had tried one last time to dissuade him.

'Why do you need to go to Córdoba? The marquis can bring them all to you, including Ubaid. He could hand him over here, chained like a dog. Don't take any risks.'

'I want to be there from the start,' replied Brahim.

The marquis could not understand it either. He was a proud young man, as haughty as his bearing implied. The nobleman had demanded guarantees that once he had completed his side of the bargain, the corsair would fulfil his. To the marquis's surprise the guarantee was presented in the person of Brahim himself.

'If I don't return, Christian,' Brahim threatened, 'you cannot even begin to imagine how your wife and child will suffer before they die.'

He had spoken to Nasi to this effect.

'If I don't return, my wife and daughters will inherit as the law requires,' he added as he said farewell to his young assistant, 'but the business will be yours.'

He knew that if anything went wrong, his life was at stake, but he needed to be there, to see the expressions on the faces of Fátima and the Nazarene, of Aisha, of Ubaid; his revenge would be worth little if those moments were denied him.

Early that morning seven of the Marquis of Casabermeja's men headed for the Almodóvar gate in the western stretch of the wall surrounding Córdoba. The men were of proven loyalty to the noble and totally reliable. During the previous day they had checked out their information about the location of Hernando's house. They did not manage to catch sight of him, but a pair of neighbours, old Christians always happy to slander Moriscos, confirmed that the man who lived there worked as a rider in the royal stables. They also paid a tidy sum to the guard who granted entry through the Almodóvar gate. That morning the large gate was left ajar. The marquis and two footmen, their faces covered, together with seven more soldiers entered Córdoba, leaving two men hidden outside to wait with horses for everyone. The ten men silently descended the deserted Calle de Almanzor until they reached Los Barberos, where one of the men took up position. The marquis, his face hidden in the folds of his hooded cloak, crossed himself before the shrine to Our Lady of Sorrows on the façade of the last house in the Calle de Almanzor. Then he ordered his men to extinguish the candles burning beneath the painting, which gave the only light in the street. Whilst the footmen obeyed, the rest continued to the house, whose strong wooden door was firmly shut. One of his men carried on to the intersection of the Calle de los Barberos with San Bartolomé, from where he whistled to signal there was no sign of danger. Nobody was out walking in that part of Córdoba at those hours, and only an occasional noise disturbed the stillness.

'Forward,' ordered the noble, heedless of the fact that he could be heard.

By the light of the moon that strove to reach down into the narrow alleyways of Muslim Córdoba, one of his men removed his cloak. Lifted up by two companions, he climbed with remarkable agility to a balcony on the second floor. Once there, he threw down a rope for the two men waiting below.

The marquis remained concealed in his cloak. As soon as his men saw their three companions crowded together on the small balcony of Hernando's house, they grasped their swords in readiness for the attack.

'Now!' shouted the marquis.

The sound of two hefty kicks to the wooden shutter covering the window echoed around the streets. As the first shout could be heard from inside the house, the men on the balcony launched themselves at the battered shutter. Smashing it to pieces, they burst into Fátima's bedroom. The men waiting below shifted nervously outside the closed door. The marquis stayed impassive, not even turning his head. There was a confusion of shouts and footsteps as men and women ran through the house. Children's cries and the sound of flowerpots crashing to the floor preceded the opening of the door. The men outside, their swords held high, pushed each other to get through into the entrance hall.

The neighbouring houses began to show signs of life. Lantern light shone from a nearby balcony.

'In the name of the One-handed One of the Sierra Morena,' shouted a man stationed in the alleyway, 'turn off the lights and stay in your houses!'

'In the name of Ubaid, Morisco outlaw, close your doors and windows if you don't want to get hurt!' ordered the other as he ran up and down the street.

The Marquis of Casabermeja still waited calmly in front of the house. Soon afterwards Aisha and Fátima, barefoot and dressed only in their simple loose-fitting nightgowns, were dragged out. Other men held aloft the three crying children.

'There's nobody else, excellency,' one man informed him. 'The Morisco is not there.'

'What do you want?' screamed Fátima.

The man gripping Fátima's arm slapped her in the face. Aisha was also dealt several blows to stop her from shouting too. A terrified Fátima just had time to cast a last look towards her home before the sobs of her children made her turn to them. They were being carried on the shoulders of two men. Another man was dragging Shamir, who was unsuccessfully trying to kick himself free. Inés, Francisco . . . What would happen to them? Again she struggled uselessly in the strong arms of her kidnapper. When she finally gave up, defeated, she let out a hoarse shout of rage and pain which the man smothered with his heavy hand. 'Ibn Hamid!' Fátima then murmured to herself, her face flooded with tears. '*Ibn Hamid . . .*'

'Let's go,' ordered the noble.

They retraced their steps back to the nearby Almodóvar gate, dragging the two women under their arms. The children were carried by the same men who had taken them from the house.

Within a few moments they were on the horses. The women were tossed over the mounts' withers like a couple of sacks, while other riders kept a firm grip on the children. Meanwhile, in Calle de los Barberos, the neighbours milled around in front of the open doors of Hernando's house, unsure whether to enter or not. The marquis and his men set off at a gallop in the direction of the Montón de la Tierra inn.

The kidnap of that family was only one part of the agreement made with Samuel the Jew, remembered the marquis; he also had to deliver to Brahim's feet the outlaw of the Sierra Morena known as the One-handed One. The fact he had not found Hernando also worried him as he raced towards the inn.

Storming a Morisco house in Córdoba was a relatively easy endeavour for the Marquis of Casabermeja. He only needed to count on having loyal and prepared men and let some gold sovereigns fall here and there. Nobody was going to worry themselves about some Moorish dogs. The outlaw was a different matter. The marquis needed to find Ubaid's band in the Sierra Morena, get close to him and then defeat his men so that he could take him prisoner. The pursuit had begun a few days earlier, and it was only when the marquis received word that his men had made contact with the One-handed One that he informed Brahim, who then risked entering Córdoba. Everything had to happen at the same time; the corsair had no wish to spend more days on Spanish soil than were absolutely necessary, and the Marquis of Casabermeja did not want to run the risk of them being arrested.

To capture the outlaw the marquis had enlisted an army of Valencian bandits captained by a noble of lesser rank and fewer economic resources, whose lands adjoined the estates he was lord of in the kingdom of Valencia. He was not the only hidalgo who resorted to dealings with bandits. There were veritable armies under the command of nobles and lords. Protected by their privileges, these nobles used the hired criminals for simple looting expeditions, or for settling disputes in their favour without having to resort to the always slow and costly legal system.

The administrator of the marquis's Valencian lands enjoyed good relations with the Baron of Solans, who maintained a small army of almost fifty men. They led an idle life in a dilapidated castle and willingly accepted the sum offered by the administrator for routing a band of Moriscos. Except for the One-handed One, who was to be handed over alive in the Montón de la Tierra inn, all the rest were to die. The marquis had no desire for witnesses. The Baron of Solans tricked the Sierra Morena outlaws by sending Ubaid a message proposing that, owing to his knowledge of the mountains, they ought to join forces. If they did, together they could tackle more ambitious expeditions around the rich city of Toledo. When both groups finally met in the mountains, it was an unequal fight. Fifty experienced, well-armed criminals against Ubaid and little more than a dozen fugitive Morisco slaves.

Brahim heard men in the courtyard burst into a flurry of activity and ran to the balcony. He reached it in time to see them opening the inn gates to admit a group of riders. He gripped the wooden railing tightly with his left hand. Amidst the shadows and the flickering flames of the large torches he made out the forms of two women, whom the men let fall from their horses as soon as the gates closed behind them.

Aisha and Fátima tried to stand. Aisha leant against a horse, only to fall again when it stepped restlessly to one side. Fátima crawled and stumbled several times before she managed to lift her face to the riders, searching for the children, whose sobs reached her clearly in spite of all the noise. From above, Brahim could make out the children, but . . . Leaning over the rail, he narrowed his eyes.

'And the Nazarene?' he shouted from the balcony. 'Where's that son of a bitch?'

Aisha's hands flew to her face and she collapsed between a horse's legs. She gave a single scream, which rang out above the clattering hooves, the animals' snorting and the riders' orders. Fátima staggered to her feet trembling. Every muscle in her body tensed as she turned her head slowly, as if wanting to give herself time to identify the voice that had just forced its way into her hearing. Finally she raised her huge black eyes towards the balcony. They stared at each other. Brahim smiled. Instinctively Fátima tried to cover her breasts; she felt naked beneath the simple nightgown. Some of the riders had dismounted and one near Fátima guffawed loudly.

'Cover yourself, bitch!' yelled the corsair. 'And the rest of you' – he looked towards the men who appeared to have only just noticed the women's state of undress – 'get your filthy eyes off my wife!' Fátima felt tears welling in her eyes: '*My wife!*' he had shouted. *My wife!* 'Where's the Nazarene, marquis?'

The noble was the only one of the men still mounted and still obscured by his cloak. The glare of the torches picked out the folds of his hood. He did not respond, but one of his lackeys spoke for him.

'There was nobody else in the house.'

'That wasn't the deal,' roared the corsair.

For a few moments there was no sound apart from the children's sobs.

'In that case, there is no deal,' the noble said defiantly, his voice steady.

Brahim remained silent in the face of the challenge. He watched Fátima hugging herself, downcast and afraid, and a shiver of pleasure ran down his spine. Then he turned to the noble: if he reneged on the deal, he would die.

'What about the One-handed One?' he asked, implying he conceded the lack of Hernando.

As if it had been planned, at that exact moment there were a couple of knocks on the old, dry wood of the hostelry door. They echoed round the courtyard. The administrator's instructions had been were clear: 'Be ready with the outlaw. Hide yourselves close by the inn, and when you see my lord enter, bring him.'

First to enter was Ubaid, between two of the baron's henchmen. He came into the courtyard dragging his feet, his arms tied together above his stump. The Valencian noble, old now but solid and tough, looked for the Marquis of Casabermeja. Without a moment's hesitation he approached the cloaked mounted figure.

'Here you have him, marquis,' he said, reaching behind him to grab Ubaid by the hair and force him to kneel at the horse's feet.

'I am grateful to you all, sir,' Casabermeja replied.

As the marquis was speaking, one of his servants stepped up. He handed a bag to the baron, who untied it, opened it and began to count out the gold sovereigns that formed the rest of the agreed payment.

'I am the one who is grateful, excellency,' said the Valencian, satisfied with the reward. 'I trust that when you next visit your estates in Valencia, we can meet and go hunting.'

'You will all be invited to share my table, baron.' The marquis accompanied his words with a nod of his head.

'I am highly honoured,' the baron said by way of farewell. He indicated to the two men accompanying him to move towards the door.

'Godspeed,' the marquis wished him.

The baron responded to these words with an approximation of the bow etiquette demanded of someone taking their leave of a person of higher rank, and headed for the door. Before he had reached it, the marquis turned his attention back towards the balcony where Brahim had been a few moments earlier. The corsair had already come down to the courtyard in order to throw over Fátima, without uttering a word, a lice-ridden blanket he had found in his room. Puffing and short of breath, he then turned towards the muleteer of Narila.

'Don't go near him,' ordered the same servant who had paid the baron, his hand dropping to his sword. Several of the men with him immediately unsheathed their weapons, responding to the unspoken command.

'What . . . ?' Brahim started to complain.

'We haven't heard you agree to the new arrangement yet,' the lackey said.

'I agree,' the corsair growled, pushing the man forcibly out of his way.

Trying to retain his dignity, Ubaid had remained kneeling at the feet of the marquis's horse. When he heard Brahim's voice he turned his head just enough to receive a kick in the mouth.

'Dog! Filthy pig! Bastard son of a whore!'

Aisha and Fátima, who was wrapped up in the coarse, filthy blanket Brahim had thrown over her, tried to make out what was happening amidst the dancing shadows projected by the fire of the torches, the men and the horses: Ubaid!

Brahim had imagined a thousand different ways to gloat over the slow, cruel death he planned for the muleteer of Narila. But the contemptuous sneer on Ubaid's bloody mouth as he looked up at him enraged him so much he forgot all the tortures he had dreamt of. Shaking with fury, he drew his scimitar and dealt a savage blow to the outlaw's body. The blade pierced Ubaid but did not kill him. The others in the courtyard leapt out of the madman's way, with only the marquis staying calmly in his place. Shouting unintelligible insults Brahim showed no mercy to Ubaid, who was curled up in a ball on the ground. He struck out again and again with his scimitar at his legs, chest, arms and head.

'He's already dead,' said the marquis from his horse, at a moment when Brahim paused for breath. 'He's dead!' he shouted when he saw the corsair preparing to deal another blow.

Brahim stopped. Panting, his whole body trembling, he lowered the scimitar and stood quietly beside Ubaid's mangled body. Without looking at anyone he knelt down, and with the stump of his right hand turned over the mass of flesh, searching for what had been Ubaid's back. Many of the men in the yard, including the marquis, hardened as they were to the horrors of war, could not bear to look as Brahim dropped his scimitar and drew a dagger with which he cut open the outlaw's side, searching for his heart. Brahim rummaged around inside the body until, still kneeling, he plucked it out and stood staring at it. It almost seemed to be still beating when he spat on it and threw it to the ground.

'We will leave at dawn,' said Brahim, turning to the marquis. He had stood up, covered in blood.

The noble just nodded. Then Brahim headed towards Fátima and grabbed her by the arm. He still had one part of his dreams left to fulfil. However, first he pushed her over to Aisha.

'Woman!' Aisha lifted her face. 'Tell your son the Nazarene I'll be waiting for him in Tetuan. If he wants his children back he'll have to come and find them in Barbary.'

As the corsair gave an about-turn, pulling Fátima with him, Aisha and her companion exchanged glances. Fátima's denial was almost imperceptible. 'Don't do it! Don't tell him!' she pleaded with her eyes.

Until the sky began to lighten nobody disturbed Brahim, who had locked himself away with Fátima in the upstairs room of the inn.

41

AISHA LEFT the Montón de la Tierra inn at dawn, when she had seen Brahim and the marquis's men disappear into the distance. Ubaid's body was left behind, buried near the inn by the marquis's servants to erase all traces of their presence there. Aisha had spent the night huddled in a corner with Shamir and her grandchildren, fighting back the tears as she tried to console them. She knew she was about to lose another son. What did God have in store for him?

Before departing, Brahim had come down from his room looking satisfied and pleased with himself. Fátima followed a few steps behind, walking painfully and covered from head to foot by the blanket. Only her eyes were visible, through a gap she held half closed with her hands.

The marquis's men prepared the horses and the noise and bustle of departure filled the courtyard.

'You're Shamir, aren't you?' Brahim asked, going up to his son. Aisha sensed a hint of tenderness in her husband. Eyes downcast, the boy allowed the corsair to touch his head. The little one had no idea who the man was; Aisha and Fátima had always told him that his father had died in the Alpujarra. 'Do you know who I am?'

Shamir shook his head, and Brahim's eyes bored into Aisha.

'Woman,' he muttered, 'you're lucky I need you to deliver the message I gave you yesterday. If it wasn't for that I'd kill you right now.'

Then he lifted Shamir's chin until the boy's eyes were fixed on him.

'Listen to me carefully, boy: I'm your father and you're my only son.' Hearing these words, a curious Francisco came over to Shamir. 'Get away!' Brahim spat at him, shoving him with his stump and knocking him to the ground.

'Don't hit him!' Shamir cried, wrenching himself away from the hand holding his chin and launching himself at his father. Brahim burst out laughing and put up with the blows the boy dealt his stomach. He let Shamir carry on until he grew tired of the boy and slapped him away. Shamir fell beside Francisco.

'I admire your spirit,' cackled Brahim. 'But,' he added as if about to spit at Francisco, 'if you persist in defending the Nazarene's son you'll suffer the same fate. As for that one,' he said, gesturing towards Inés, 'she can be a slave for my two daughters. And the day the Nazarene turns up in Tetuan . . .'

Aisha walked wearily along the road to Córdoba. When she recalled the phrase Brahim had left hanging in the air: 'the day the Nazarene turns up in Tetuan . . .' she felt the same chill that had run through her body in the courtyard of the inn. Fátima had shuddered too beneath the blanket, and the two women had exchanged what they realized would be their last look. Aisha had again sensed her companion was trying to say to her: 'Don't tell him! He'll kill him!'

He'll kill him! With that certainty fixed firmly in her mind Aisha entered Córdoba through the Colodro gate. Unlike the last time she had made this journey, with Shamir in her arms, after being forced to follow Brahim to the mountains, this time she managed to escape the attention of the city guards. She slipped through the gate like a soul in torment, her feet bloody and dressed only in her nightshirt. She reached Calle de los Barberos, where the sight of both front door and iron gate flung wide open brought her to her senses. In spite of the fact that it was daytime, a shutter abruptly closed at a balcony window. One of her neighbours two houses down was about to step out into the street, but drew back inside. Aisha entered the house and realized why: her Christian neighbours had spent the night looting it. There was nothing left inside, not even the flower-pots! Aisha looked towards the fountain: at least they had not been able to steal the water gushing there. Then she turned her attention to the place where, underneath a flagstone, they hid their savings. The flagstone was raised. She looked at the next one, still in its place. Hernando had been right. A sad smile formed on her lips as she remembered her son's words.

'We'll hide the money under this one.' Then he had laid the stone flag in such a way that even the dullest observer would clearly see it had been disturbed. It was under the neighbour-ing stone that he had hidden the Koran and the hand of Fátima. 'If anyone comes to rob us,' Hernando had said, 'they'll find the money and I can't imagine they'll think to look for any further treasure, our real treasure.'

Hernando, though, had been thinking of the Inquisition or the Córdoba authorities, not of his neighbours.

'What's happened, Aisha? Where are Fátima and the children?'

Aisha turned to find Abbas standing by the open wrought-iron gate.

'I . . .' she stammered opening her hands. 'I don't know.'

'People say that last night, Ubaid and his men—'

Aisha could not listen to any more. *Don't tell him! He'll kill him!* Fátima's silent plea stole once more into her mind. Besides, Hernando was all she had left. Yet another son had been stolen from her. She had nothing apart from the smiling boy with blue eyes who used to seek out her affection under the cover of darkness in Juviles, hidden from prying eyes. During the night at the inn she had listened to what the marquis's men had to say about Brahim. They all knew why they were there. Aisha had learnt how he had become one of the most im-portant corsairs in Tetuan, living in what the men described as an enormous fortress, and he kept a veritable army under his command. He would never allow Hernando near Fátima again!

'They've killed them all,' she sobbed to Abbas. 'Ubaid and his men have killed them!' she screamed. 'My Shamir, Fátima and Francisco . . . Little Inés!'

Aisha fell to the floor, weeping inconsolably. She did not need to feign either her tears or the pain that gripped her. In fact, perhaps . . . perhaps they would have been better off dead than in Brahim's clutches. She howled at the sky as she thought of Shamir. What would become of her little one? And Fátima? What further hardships did God have in store for her?

Abbas did not go to comfort her. His strength failed him, and he had to cling on to the gate to remain standing. He gasped for breath. He had promised on behalf of all the Moriscos that Hernando would not be troubled by the bandit. Not only that: he had promised to take care of Hernando's family while he was away in Seville. Before he left Hernando had begged him to do this. Abbas had answered him almost contemptuously. 'What could possibly happen?' he clearly remembered telling him.

Consumed by grief, Aisha and Abbas were accompanied only by the constant murmur of the water that rose and fell in the fountain of a beautiful Córdoba courtyard, now in ruins.

Abbas followed the same road as the mares towards the royal preserve of Lomo del Grullo: a day's journey to Écija with a stop in the Valcargado inn; another to Carmona, stopping in Fuentes; a third to Seville, resting in the Loysa inn, and then from Seville to Villamanrique. He forced himself to walk. He put one foot in front of the other and each sad and painful step took him ever closer to a destiny he had no desire to meet. What was he going to say to Hernando? How could he possibly tell him his wife and children had been murdered by Ubaid? How to confess he had not kept his promise?

He had tried to make contact with the One-handed One whilst he waited for the royal stables to grant him permission to leave for Lomo del Grullo. He wanted to know why; he even wanted to come face to face with him so he could kill him. However, none of the contacts through which he usually reached the outlaw could help him: Ubaid and his band had simply disappeared. Perhaps they had gone deep into the mountains and would return some day, but nobody seemed to have heard anything about Ubaid. But why had he killed Fátima and the children?

'Why did he do it?' Don Diego, handing Abbas the safe conduct that would enable him to travel to Seville, was also surprised. 'Isn't he Morisco too?'

'He and Hernando had problems in the Alpujarra,' said Abbas by way of explanation.

'Severe enough to warrant killing a woman and three defenceless children?' replied the noble, waving the document he carried in his hand. 'Holy Virgin!'

Abbas could only shrug his shoulders. Don Diego was right, and, given that Aisha refused to talk about it, he had not even been able to find the bodies to give them a decent burial. In response to questions as to where the slaughter had occurred, Aisha's only answer had been 'somewhere in the mountains'. Whenever the blacksmith tried to glean more specific details that might shed some light on the exact location, Aisha broke down in tears and always ended up sobbing the same words: 'Go and find my son, I beg you.'

Now Abbas was doing just that, step by step under the Andalusian sun. With stomach clenched, the taste of bile permanently in his mouth and tears pricking at his eyes, he thought about how to tell a good friend that his wife and two children had been savagely murdered deep in the mountains of the Sierra Morena.

All the careful phrases he had come up with vanished from his mind at the mere sight of Hernando, who left the horses and jumped down lithely from Azirat to run towards him. Hernando was tanned by the sun and his blue eyes were more brilliant than ever. A wide, sincere smile revealed his white teeth.

Abbas's eyes misted over, and the horses became just a shapeless blur. However, he sensed that Hernando stopped abruptly a few paces short of where he stood. Hernando's presence merged into the thousand dark stains of the mares behind him, and his words seemed distant, as if carried on the wind from some faraway place.

'What's happened?'

'Ubaid . . .' whispered Abbas.

'What about Ubaid?' Hernando's blue eyes, now reflecting a growing unease, seemed to bore straight through him. 'Has something happened? My family . . . are they all right? Speak!'

'He's killed them,' the blacksmith managed to utter, 'all of them but your mother.'

Hernando stood dumbstruck. For several moments he stayed motionless, as if his mind refused to accept what he had just heard. Then very slowly he lifted his hands to his face and howled at the sky. 'Fátima! The children!

'You son of a whore!' he suddenly shouted at Abbas. He punched the blacksmith, who fell to the ground. Then he leapt on him. 'Dog! You promised me they would be safe! I asked you to watch over them, to take care of them!'

Abbas did not move as Hernando punched him, unwilling even to protect himself from the beating.

The last thing the blacksmith was aware of before losing consciousness was how the other men pulled Hernando off him. He no longer heard the curses and insults Hernando was still shouting at him.

Before reaching Seville, Azirat refused to continue galloping at the same speed he had kept up since leaving Lomo del Grullo. Hernando dug his spurs into the horse's flanks once more, as he had been doing over the almost seven leagues covered at a flat-out gallop. But the animal was incapable of carrying on and despite the spurs his gallop became ever slower and more laboured until finally he could not go on.

'Come on!' cried Hernando, spurring him and urging him on with his body. Azirat staggered. 'Gallop,' Hernando sobbed, tugging furiously at the reins. The animal sank down on the road. 'God! No!'

Hernando jumped from the saddle. Azirat was covered in lather; his flanks were bloody, his nostrils dilated with the effort to breathe. Hernando placed his hand over Azirat's heart: it seemed about to burst.

'What have I done? Are you going to die too?'

Dead! The madness of the gallop in which he had tried to seek refuge vanished at the sight of the broken animal. Pain coursed through Hernando once more. Weeping, he pulled on the reins to get Azirat to his feet, and forced him to walk. The animal swayed as if drunk. There was a stream nearby, but Hernando did not lead the horse to it until he saw some signs of recovery. When they reached it, he did not allow him to drink: he offered some water in his cupped hands, but Azirat could not even lick. Hernando took off the saddle and bridle. Using his tunic as a sponge he rubbed him all over with cool water. In Hernando's imagination the blood on Azirat's flanks, caused by the cutting of the spurs, merged with Ubaid's brutality. He rubbed the animal down again and again, and then forced the horse to walk, all the time offering him water from his hands. After a couple of hours, Azirat extended his neck to drink directly from the stream. Hernando covered his face with his hands and abandoned himself to grief.

They spent the night out in the open, next to the stream. Azirat nibbled at the grass, while Hernando cried inconsolably as images of Fátima, Francisco and Inés danced before him. As he heard their voices and their innocent laughter he beat the ground until his knuckles bled; he howled with pain as he smelt them once more and thought he felt the warmth and tenderness of their bodies beside his. At the same time, he tried to banish the unimaginable scenes of their deaths at the hands of Ubaid, whom he also saw in his mind's eye standing triumphant with the still-beating heart of Gonzalico in his hands.

Hernando made the next day's journey on foot. Those who

crossed his path were unsure if it was the man pulling the horse or the horse that was dragging the wreckage of a man holding on to its reins. It was only as dawn broke on the third day that he dared mount up again. Although Azirat showed some signs of recovering, Hernando kept him at a walk for the next two days, until they finally crossed the Roman bridge and passed the Calahorra tower.

Hernando had no more success than Abbas when it came to obtaining information from his mother.

'Why do you want to know?' she ended up shouting on the night of her son's arrival in Córdoba, once the countless visits of condolence had finished and they were alone. 'I saw it! I saw how they all died! Do you want me to tell you about it? I managed to escape or perhaps . . . perhaps they didn't want to kill me. Then I spent the whole night wandering in the mountains until I found a way back to Córdoba. I've already told you all that.' At this Aisha had collapsed defeated into a chair. She had found herself forced to lie a thousand times throughout the day; so often that she had considered telling him the truth. At every question their visitors asked, at every expression of regret, at every silence, she could see the tremendous pain in his face. But no! She mustn't! Hernando would run straight to Tetuan. She knew it; she was certain. And she would lose the only son she had left.

'Why do I want to know?' muttered Hernando, pacing the gallery with his hands clenched. 'I need to know, Mother! I need to bury them! I need to find the son of a whore who killed them and . . . !'

Sensing the blind rage in her son's voice, Aisha raised her head. She had never seen him like this. Not even . . . not even in the Alpujarra! She was about to say something, but kept quiet. She was terrified by the sight of Hernando, staring into the distance, scratching viciously at the back of his hand.

'I swear I'll kill him,' her son finished his sentence, as he gouged deep bloody furrows on his hand.

* * *

'Ubaid!'

The howl shattered the peaceful silence of the August morning and rang out across the mountains.

'Ubaid!' Hernando shouted again from the highest point of one of the Sierra Morena peaks, out over the dense forests spread at his feet. He stood upright in the stirrups as if trying to rise higher than the mountains all around him, making himself visible to anyone who might be hidden in the vegetation. The only answer was the scurrying and flapping of surprised animals. 'Vile dog!' he continued. 'Come to me! I'll kill you! I'll cut off your other hand – I'll tear you apart and scatter your remains to the scavengers!'

His shouts were lost in the vastness of the Sierra Morena. Silence returned. Hernando collapsed back down into the saddle. How was he going to find the One-handed One in those mountain ranges? It had to be the outlaw who responded to his challenge! He unsheathed his sword and raised it to the sky.

'Vile pig!' he howled again. 'Murderer!'

Hernando had left Córdoba astride Azirat after he had made all the necessary arrangements. He had said goodbye to his mother after one final attempt to persuade her to give him some information, the slightest detail with which to begin his search. She had still not said a word.

'Where are you going?' Aisha asked him.

'Mother, to do what every man who calls himself a man should do: take revenge on Ubaid and find the bodies of my family.'

'But . . .'

Hernando left her with the words still in her mouth. After that, he headed to Jalil's house, where the old man promised him he would have what he needed: a good sword, a dagger and an harquebus; they would be handed to him secretly on the Camino de Las Ventas.

'May Allah go with you, Hernando.' The old man bade

him a solemn farewell, standing as straight as his body allowed.

Hernando went to the stables to see the administrator. For a few moments, as the Morisco explained the reasons for his absence, the man behind the desk studied him: his face was wan, and the dark rings round his eyes were evidence of a sleepless night spent sobbing, lashing out at furniture and walls, crying out for revenge.

'Go,' muttered the administrator, 'and find the man who murdered your family.'

That first day, after waiting in vain for Ubaid to respond, Hernando urged Azirat down the mountain. Until the sun set he rode through reedbeds, crossed streams and climbed hills from where he again issued his challenge. He asked at inns and questioned people he met on the road: nobody knew anything as to the whereabouts of the outlaws. They had not been active for some time.

On returning to Córdoba Hernando hid the weapons in a thicket so he could cross the Colodro bridge without problems. He left Azirat in the stables. Before going home he visited the stone benches outside the convent of San Pablo, to check if the Brothers of Mercy had been more fortunate and had discovered his family's bodies. His emotions were in a turmoil as he pushed his way through the curious onlookers to get a closer look at the decomposing bodies: on the one hand he prayed to be able to find and bury them, on the other, he did not want it to be here, surrounded by Christians, stolen goods and guards, jokes and laughter.

'I'll find him! I swear I will, even if I have to cross all Spain!'

This was all he said to his mother when she let him into the house again. Then he shut himself in his bedroom, torturing himself with Fátima's still lingering scent.

The next day Hernando made ready to leave even before first light. He wanted to take full advantage of the daylight hours! Again, he returned to Córdoba empty-handed. The next day he did the same, and the one after, and the one after that.

Every day Aisha watched him return a little more crushed.

She wept, her own sobs accompanying those she heard coming from her son's room in the still of the night. She again considered telling him the truth, even if it was only to see him smile again, but she did not do so. Fátima's pleading look and the fear of being left alone, of sending her only remaining son to a certain death, prevented her. She herself had already lost five children. Surely Hernando would survive the same misfortune? Children died in their hundreds before reaching puberty, and as for Fátima, he would surely find another wife. But also . . . also she was afraid; she was afraid of ending up alone.

Hernando continued to roam the mountains, every day more haggard than the one before. By now he did not even speak or cry out for revenge. At night the only sound was the murmur of his constant prayers.

'He'll get through it,' Aisha told herself every day. 'He has a good job,' she repeated, trying to convince herself, 'and he's well respected. He's the best horse-breaker in the King's stables! Abbas says so; everybody agrees. There are dozens of healthy young girls prepared to marry a man like him. He'll be happy again.'

But when nearly twenty days had gone by, Aisha realized that her son was going to devote his life to the search. He was never going to give up. Should she tell him the truth? Aisha was overcome by a tremendous sense of anxiety. Her whole body shook: not only had she deceived him, but she had allowed him to torture himself all this time. How would Hernando respond? He was a man, a deranged man. If he did not beat her, at the very least he would hate her, just as he hated the person he thought had killed his family. What could she do? She imagined Hernando screaming abuse at her, and the beatings from Brahim seemed mild by comparison. He was her son – the only one she had left! She could not confront him!

The following morning, after Hernando dragged himself off on yet another search for the outlaw, Aisha left Córdoba by the same Colodro gate. She walked head bowed, carrying a small bundle. The late August sun still beat fiercely down. As she had on that fateful morning, she travelled the league between the city and the Montón de la Tierra inn. When it came into view, she was almost paralysed by the pain gripping her and thought she would be unable to go on. What if her plan did not work out? She would kill herself, she resolved.

After Brahim had killed the outlaw and shut himself away with Fátima in the upstairs room, she remembered how the Marquis of Casabermeja's four men had left the inn to bury the body. She struggled to put her husband's lecherous expression out of her mind; she strove to forget the words he had hurled at her as he passed by, dragging Fátima. *Woman! Tell your son the Nazarene I'll be waiting for him in Tetuan. If he wants his children back he'll have to come and find them in Barbary.* The marquis's men: they were what interested her and she tried to concentrate. Fátima's pleading look, begging her not to do it, to tell Hernando nothing, came flooding back into her mind with unusual clarity.

Aisha stopped, squatted down by the roadside, buried her face in her hands and broke down in tears. Hernando! Shamir! Fátima and the children!

After a while she managed to recover. This was her last chance.

The marquis's men, she whispered to herself.

They had not taken long to return to the inn and she seemed to remember they had not been carrying spades or tools. The outlaw's body could not be far away. She ran her gaze over the inn's surroundings. Where would they have buried him? Whilst she tried to relive the scene, she lifted her eyes to the burning sun as if it could help her. Where . . .?

'You're sure nobody will find it?' She heard the words of the marquis's footman when the gravediggers returned echoing in her ears, as if they were saying them right there and then. At the time she had not paid any attention. 'You all know his excellency wants this body to disappear; no one must know it wasn't the outlaw . . .'

'Don't worry,' one of the soldiers replied offhandedly. 'Where we've left it . . .'

Left it! They had said 'left'! Soldiers didn't like to work; why exert themselves? Aisha walked round the inn, paying careful attention to the undergrowth and stubble. No, it could not be there. She looked at trees and their roots, remembering the ones in the Alpujarra that formed hollows large enough to accommodate a man on horseback. She kicked at several mounds of dry earth, and even dug with a little spade she carried in her bundle in what could have been suitable burial mounds. The sun had passed its midday zenith and was blazing down; Aisha was sweating as she searched. Finally she came across a dry and unused irrigation channel. She followed its route and her eyes fell on the spot where it joined another. The way was blocked with stones. She did not hesitate. She hurried over, and only had to remove a few rocks and poke around in the earth below until all of a sudden the putrid smell of the body hit her. The outlaw!

Aisha wiped away the sweat running down her face, straightened up and gazed about her. In the afternoon heat, after the midday meal, nothing moved. She continued digging up the body until Ubaid appeared. It was definitely him: his heart, torn out by Brahim, had been placed on his stomach. She stared at it for some time. Then she took Fátima's delicately embroidered white shawl out of the bundle, kissed it sadly and dirtied it with dry earth. She had found it behind a flowerpot the day after the kidnap, overlooked in her Christian neighbours' pillaging. She had kept it for Hernando, but not wanting to upset him had not managed to give it to him yet. She knelt down by Ubaid's remains and tied the shawl round his neck. She got up and turned to look around her. Only the buzzing of insects swarming all over the outlaw's body disturbed the silence. She still had to carry out the most important part of her plan. The Camino de Las Ventas was close by. Gripping the body under the armpits, she started to pull it from behind. She decided to head along the channel leading to the road. The outlaw's heart fell on to the ground. Aisha took a long time: she had to stop and rest after every few steps and check that nobody was in the vicinity, but at last she did it. With a final effort she dragged the body to the roadside. When she let go of it, she felt tremendous stabs of pain in every muscle. A tear rolled down her cheek as she looked at the white shawl tied to the outlaw's neck. She went and hid behind some trees a short distance away, waiting for someone to find the body. As the heat diminished, Aisha saw a party of merchants come to a halt beside Ubaid's body. She slid out from among the trees and made her way back to Córdoba.

'They say the body of Ubaid, the One-handed One of the Sierra Morena, has been found on the Camino de Las Ventas, near the Montón de la Tierra inn,' Aisha remarked to one of the guards at the Colodro gate. 'Do you know anything about it?'

The man did not deign to reply to a Morisco woman, but Aisha's features twisted into a sad smile when she saw him sprint off to find his sergeant. Moments later, a group of soldiers set off at a gallop towards the inn.

Hernando was surprised to see a press of people gathered around the Colodro gate. He even thought twice about going in that way, but what did he care now what happened to him? He'd spent another unsuccessful day hurling shouts, threats and insults into the void between the mountain peaks. He had even had to flee when he ran into a hunting party's mastiffs chasing a bear. He spurred Azirat on towards the crowd; as he drew closer he could make out a large number of guards and soldiers amongst them, as well as richly attired nobles; he even thought he recognized the chief magistrate walking up and down.

To get through the gate he decided to keep to one side of the main body of people and make his way through the curious onlookers who were standing around at a distance. From his vantage point on the horse he could see over the heads of the crowd. It was then that he saw the man's body. It was tied to a stake driven into the ground; the manner by which the Holy Brotherhood executed criminals captured outside the city. A shiver ran down his spine. That body . . . it had only one hand. He didn't need to get any closer, only sharpen his gaze and even just smell the air around him. Ubaid!

He paid no attention to the people who were arguing whether it was or was not the feared outlaw of the Sierra Morena. He pulled on Azirat's reins and approached the stake, unable to take his eyes off the Narila muleteer's corpse.

'Where do you think you're going on that horse?' A soldier stopped Hernando as he rode blindly forwards, forcing men and women to leap out of his way.

Hernando jumped down and handed the reins to the soldier, who took them, perplexed. Hernando pushed his way past nobles and merchants until he stood squarely in front of Ubaid's body. The Brotherhood, even though he was dead and they were unsure of his identity, had shot him full of arrows.

Suddenly people made room for him. Don Diego López de Haro was there, and gestured to them to stand aside.

'Is it the outlaw?' he asked, coming up to Hernando. 'You knew him. Is this the man who killed your wife and children?'

Hernando nodded without a word.

A murmur ran down the lines of people.

'He'll commit no further crimes now,' the Brotherhood's leader asserted.

Hernando stayed silent, his eyes fixed on Fatimá's shawl around the outlaw's neck.

'Go home, lad,' the royal stable master advised him. 'Get some rest.'

'The shawl,' Hernando managed to stammer. 'It was . . . it was my wife's.'

It was the Brotherhood captain himself who went up to Ubaid and carefully untied the garment. He gave it to Hernando.

In spite of the dirt, Hernando could sense how soft the material was. He fell to his knees, buried his face in the shawl, and wept. But these tears were unlike the many he had shed until then; they were liberating. Ubaid was dead, although it had not been at his hands, and he blessed whoever had put an end to the murderer's miserable life.

Hidden in the crowd, Aisha saw Hernando, but did not find the peace she sought. He was holding the shawl firmly in one hand as he took Azirat's reins from the guard with the other. Aisha had seen him arrive; with every step her son took towards the stake she had felt a sharp stab of pain in the depths of her being. She tried to picture what was going on beside the body, and as if God had transmitted it to her, she broke down in tears at the exact moment when Hernando began stroking the shawl.

'I'll take care of you, son,' she sobbed, as she watched him pass through the Colodro gate on foot, leading his horse.

From that day on Hernando let her do it. His previous obsession gave way to melancholy and sadness. Why search for his family's bodies after so many days? If they had been left in the mountains they would already have been devoured by wild animals. He had seen what happened during his rides in those woods: nothing was rejected; thousands of creatures were lying in wait, ready to pounce on the slightest mistake, the most insignificant chance for food. Even so, Hernando kept visiting the benches outside the convent of San Pablo.

A few days after Ubaid's body was found, Hernando received word from Don Diego requesting he return to his job: the mares were in Seville, but there were still colts in the stables.

Aisha thought she sensed a change of attitude in her son when he returned home after attending to the animals and hope was reborn in her. But she could not have foreseen how wrong she was.

42

'YOU ARE to hand your horse over to the Count of Espiel,' Don Diego López ordered Hernando as soon as he arrived at the stables one morning. 'The King has given him the horse.' Hernando jerked his head away as if trying to distance himself from the words, but nevertheless he had to hear the stable master out.

'But . . . I . . . Azirat . . .' His attempts at protest amounted to nothing more than nonsensical hand gestures.

'I know you've worked this animal and I also know, in spite of his colour, he is one of the finest these stables have produced. I'll allow you to choose another, even one that isn't a reject, so long as it isn't one destined for the King—'

'I want this one! I want Azirat. He's mine!'

He immediately regretted his words. Don Diego tensed, frowned and paused for a few seconds before answering.

'He's not yours, nor will he ever be, and it matters little what you do or you might want. You knew the agreement when you chose to receive a horse as part-payment of your wages: it would always be at the King's disposal. The count has succeeded in getting King Philip to honour him with this horse. He has apparently asked for it specifically. The King's wishes have to be fulfilled.'

'He'll destroy him! He doesn't know how to ride or to run bulls!'

Don Diego was aware of that. Hernando himself had heard

him say it, had seen him making fun of the fat Count of Espiel, who always lounged in the saddle as if in an armchair . . .

'It's not your place to judge how well a nobleman does or doesn't ride,' the royal stable master answered him sharply. 'He has more honour in one of his boots and has rendered greater service to these realms than your entire community could ever offer. Watch your tongue.'

The Morisco let his arms drop to his sides and he stood crestfallen before the horse. 'Can I . . . ?' he stammered. What did he want? What did he want to ask? 'Could I ride him one last time?' Don Diego hesitated. 'Perhaps . . . I may not deserve this favour, but I'd like to feel him beneath me one more time, excellency. It's only one last ride. Sir, you're a great rider. Sir, you know of my many and grievous recent misfortunes . . .'

Changing the original name of a horse brings bad luck. How right Abbas had been, warning him of that! thought Hernando as he tightened the girth. The memory of the blacksmith troubled him. After what had happened in Lomo del Grullo they saw each other in the stables, but did not speak; they did not even greet each other. Hernando was unable to forgive him. He jumped on to Azirat, who shied nervously as his rider flung himself hard down in the saddle: he had Abbas in mind and was gripped by anger. Azirat knew it! Thanks to that sixth sense animals have, he knew something bad had happened; he could sense it at the first contact with his rider. He chewed incessantly on the bit, as if trying to communicate with his rider through his constant, unaccustomed fretting on the reins.

Hernando patted Azirat's neck and the horse responded by tossing his head and snorting, all under the watchful gaze of Don Diego, who was still standing in the large open square in front of the stables. He pressed the fingers of one hand over his mouth, with his thumb under his chin. Possibly he was reconsidering his decision. Hernando did not give him the chance to change his mind, and sped out of the stables, giving the stable master a quick nod as he passed.

Now they were taking Azirat from him! What sin could he have committed? Why did God punish him so? In little over a year he had lost nearly all his loved ones: Hamid, Karim, Fátima and the children . . . As the Morisco lifted the sleeve of his tunic to his eyes, Azirat stepped out freely. Now it was his horse! Abbas, another of his friends . . . he had broken his promises!

Now the Count of Espiel had managed to make the King give him Azirat. It had not been hard for the noble. From Seville, where he left the herd of royal mares to head for the salt marshes, he had sent his secretary to Portugal with a petition to the King, requesting of him the favour of presenting Espiel with the chestnut horse that caracoled and galloped so magnificently on the journey from Córdoba to Seville. The King was happy to grant the aristocrat's request, particularly as all he wanted was a reject from his stables. Hernando remembered his first meeting with Espiel, when the noble had challenged a bull so clumsily that in the subsequent charge his horse had inevitably been gored. He had seen him run bulls on other occasions, always with similarly unfortunate results for his mount. Azirat felt his rider's legs shaking and shied nervously. Hernando had also attended the tournament in the Plaza de la Corredera, where nobles engaged in various forms of mock warfare to the sound of kettledrums and trumpets. The other nobles displayed great valour in the simulated combat; using leather shields they deftly blocked and parried the theoretically inoffensive cane spears. The count on the other hand had problems from the very start of the display, as he soon let down the team of which he had been drawn to be part. He couldn't throw his spear far enough without getting closer to the opposing side than the rules of chivalry and courtesy allowed, and the crowd were swift to boo his team.

Why would the count have chosen Azirat if he was nothing more than a reject? Because of him? Because of what happened in that first bullfight? The count was a cruel and vengeful man. Hernando had heard as much from the same mouth that had admonished him that very morning, when he called the Count of Espiel's riding ability into question. It had been about eight years earlier.

'Have you heard the latest about the Count of Espiel?' Don Diego had asked a group of nobles riding with him to try out the King's horses. Hernando and the stable hands were accompanying them.

'Tell us,' one of the nobles urged him, smiling in anticipation.

'Well, it turns out that a couple of weeks ago the doctor confined him to bed because of a recurrent fever. He was bored as he couldn't ride or hunt, so he devised a way of doing it from his bed . . .'

'Shooting arrows at the birds through the window?' joked another noble.

'Ha!' exclaimed Don Diego, unable to keep the grin from his lips. 'Every servant who does something wrong – and the count's servants do a lot wrong! – has a cushion tied to their backside. Then the count makes them run and jump about the room until he, armed with his arrows in bed, manages to shoot them in the arse.'

The group of riders burst out laughing. Even Hernando smiled, imagining the fat, sweaty count in his nightshirt, trying excitedly to aim his crossbow at a servant jumping over chairs and furniture with a cushion tied to his behind. However, he quickly wiped the smile off his face when his eyes met those of José Velasco who, as Don Diego's servant, fidgeted anxiously in the saddle.

'They say,' blurted out Don Diego between guffaws, 'they say he has become the strictest steward in his own house, and he constantly . . .' The stable master had to stop talking until he managed to compose himself, clutching his stomach. '. . . asks about the slaves' and servants' work and any possible mistakes they may have made, so that they can be released into his bedroom like hares.'

'And the countess?' one of them managed to say between hoots of laughter.

'Huh! She's beside herself!' Don Diego was again bent

double. 'She's changed the poor wretches' silk cushions for harder cotton ones, so that she doesn't end up without servants . . . or furnishings.'

Howls of merriment broke out afresh among the riders.

And that is the man who is going to ride my horse! thought Hernando, the nobles' laughter still ringing in his ears after all this time.

He urged Azirat on with a simple click of his tongue, and the horse began to gallop. It was a magnificent autumn day. He could escape! He could gallop until he reached . . . where? What about his mother? Now they only had each other. He had galloped steadily for half a league, heading nowhere in particular, when he felt Azirat tense: to his right was a pasture where fighting bulls grazed. As he had done so often in the past, the horse seemed to want to play with them.

Hernando did not think twice. He shortened the reins, lowered his heels and gripped with his knees to give himself a securer seat in the saddle. He entered the pasture and for a good while he once again was in heaven. He shouted and laughed, caracoling in front of the bulls' horns, even managing to touch them briefly as he swerved from side to side. Azirat was agile and fast, gentle on the bit, responsive as never before to his legs and movements. He was the best! Despite his red colouring, he was the finest horse out of the hundreds that had passed through the King's stables. And this magnificent specimen was going to fall into the hands of the worst and most arrogant rider in all Andalusia!

Then Azirat pulled up, facing an immense wicked-looking black bull. The two weighed each other up from a distance, the bull snorting defiantly and the horse pawing the ground.

Hernando imagined he could hear the crowd in the Plaza de la Corredera whistling at and booing the Count of Espiel.

The horse tossed his head and pawed the ground again, as if he himself was challenging his adversary. Hernando did not know what was going on; he could feel Azirat's rapid breathing against his legs.

Suddenly the bull charged furiously. Hernando pulled on the reins and pressed Azirat's flanks, ready to turn his mount aside. The horse did not respond. In a flash the booing still echoing in Hernando's head turned into applause and wild cheering. When he could see the black bull's furious eyes, Hernando let the reins drop, leaving the horse to choose its own destiny. Azirat reared up on his back legs and offered his chest to the bull's horns.

The blow was mortal. Hernando was thrown several feet from Azirat's back. Instead of venting its rage on the fallen horse, the bull trotted off proudly. Perhaps it did so because of the law governing the life of animals, honouring one of their own who had chosen not to run away from a challenge.

Later José Velasco, whom Don Diego had ordered to follow and keep a discreet eye on the Morisco, would swear to anyone who cared to listen that it was the horse that had deliberately delivered itself to a certain death. It had confronted numerous bulls throughout the autumn morning and had outwitted them all with an elegance and artistry the like of which he had never seen before.

However, José Velasco's affirmation, dismissed as a fantasy by all those who took the trouble to listen, was not sufficient for Hernando to avoid the arrest and imprisonment that Don Diego, in accordance with the authority vested in him, immediately ordered. The Morisco had begged him to grant his wish, and now Don Diego's good faith had been thrown back in his face. To the stable master's disappointment was added his concern about the Count of Espiel's predictable and undoubtedly violent response to the death of his horse.

Hernando was literally carried, battered and bruised, from the pasture by José Velasco. 'You've had the chance to prosper and you've wasted it,' Don Diego told him in front of the stable hands, Abbas among them. 'I can't do anything for you. It's up to the law and the Count of Espiel, owner of the horse you've killed before its time, to decide what to do with you.'

But Hernando was not listening, and did not react to Don Diego's words. Instead, he was lost in the magic of the moment when Azirat had exercised his free will and chosen his own destiny. He had never ridden a horse that had done anything like it!

'Take him to jail,' the stable master ordered his men. 'I, Don Diego López de Haro, master of the horse to His Majesty Philip II, so order it.'

Hernando turned his head towards the noble. Jail! Could Azirat have foreseen that? Perhaps he should have died too, he thought as he walked along the Campo Real, passing in front of the Christian monarchs' fortress, home to the Inquisition. He was escorted by José Velasco and two other men. He had nothing to live for. Only his mother, he thought sadly. They headed for the street with the jail in it; Hernando limped along with José gripping his arm. José was still confused by what he had witnessed in the pasture and the rational explanations offered by those who had heard his account and refused to believe it. But he'd seen it! José and Hernando looked at each other and exchanged a rueful, collusive grimace. They went under the cathedral bridge and walked up Calle de los Arquillos in silence, the mosque to their right. People looked curiously at the little procession as it went by.

Only God could have guided Azirat's steps, the same as He did with all true believers, Hernando concluded. But if he himself had escaped unharmed, what was the purpose behind the horse's sacrifice? For him to end up in jail at the behest of the man for whose cause Azirat had given his life? 'The devil will never enter a tent where an Arab horse resides,' wrote the Prophet, elevating the noble beasts to defenders of the believers. What was God trying to tell him through Azirat? The doubt caused Hernando to stop walking. José Velasco tugged at his arm. What divine message could be contained in the events of that morning? he continued to wonder.

'Keep moving!' one of the men ordered, shoving him in the back.

It felt like one of the hardest blows he had ever received. Surely Azirat could not want him to end up imprisoned? But how could he save himself from jail? He would not be able to run more than a few steps, and the men were armed whereas he . . .

'Get on with it!' A second shove nearly threw him to the ground.

José Velasco let go of his arm and looked at him oddly. 'Hernando, don't make it any harder,' he implored.

The Deanes gate, which gave on to the mosque garden, was only a few feet away. The Morisco stared at it.

'Don't try . . .' the guard tried to warn him.

But despite the pain he felt in his entire body, Hernando was already running towards the mosque.

He made it through Deanes gate just as the three men leapt on him. They all fell inside the cathedral's orange garden. Hernando fought and kicked to get them off him, but his muscles no longer responded. Surrounded by the people who happened to be in the garden, José Velasco managed to immobilize him. The other two, who were back on their feet by now, seized him by the wrists and ankles to carry him out of the garden, as if they were transporting a bale of hay.

'Shout it!' said one of the onlookers.

Shout what . . . ? thought Hernando.

'Say it!' another man urged him.

What did he have to say?

Don Diego's men had already lifted him off the ground, and he hung there like a dead animal.

'Sanctuary!' he heard a woman's voice shout.

'Sanctuary!' the Morisco cried out, suddenly remembering how often he had heard this plea when he had been working in the cathedral. 'I claim sanctuary!'

The men carrying him came to a halt just inside the Deanes gate. They hesitated for a moment, but then immediately rushed to get him out of the cathedral boundary.

'What are you doing?' A priest blocked their path. 'Didn't you hear this man claim sanctuary? Release him under pain of immediate excommunication!' Hernando felt the pressure ease on his hands and feet.

'This man—' José Velasco tried to explain.

'It is sacrilege to violate the immunity and right of asylum of a holy place,' insisted the priest, interrupting him abruptly.

The groom gestured to the men with him and they released Hernando, who fell at everyone's feet.

'You won't be a fugitive in the cathedral for long,' José Velasco spat, already fearful of the punishment his master would impose for having allowed the detainee to escape. 'They'll throw you out of here within thirty days.'

'That is for the ecclesiastical judge to decide,' the priest said. José and his men, who both looked as worried as he did, scowled but said nothing. 'And you,' he added to Hernando, 'go and find the vicar to inform him under what circumstances you are claiming this right.'

43

WHILST HERNANDO tried painfully to get to his feet, some of the onlookers applauded the priest's intervention. If he had been in pain before, after fighting with José and his companions and the tremendous blow to the kidneys when he fell to the ground, he was now almost unable to move. A man with curly fair hair and blue eyes like his own came to help him.

'Silence!' shouted the priest. 'Anyone causing a commotion loses the right to asylum and will be thrown out of the temple.'

The cheering stopped immediately, but the crowd continued to jeer at and make fun of the men from the royal stables who had been forced to concede to the demand for asylum as soon as the priest was far enough away not to hear – or at least they did when they judged he would not make the effort to return and admonish them. This turned out to be the case, as although the priest shook his head wearily at the sound of laughter breaking out behind him amidst the large group of delinquents and unfortunates who took refuge in the cathedral to escape secular justice, he did not even turn round.

'I'm Pérez,' said the fair-haired man who had helped Hernando to his feet, holding out his hand.

'But we call him "the Diver",' butted in another man who joined them, shirtless despite the October cold.

'Hernando,' he introduced himself.

'Pedro,' said the bare-chested man in turn.

'Let's go and see the vicar,' the Diver suggested.

'You don't need to come with me,' the Morisco said.

'Don't worry about it,' insisted the fair-haired man, already heading for the cathedral interior, 'we've nothing to do here; they don't even let us play cards. We can't even cheer, as you've seen for yourself.' Hernando tried to catch him up but staggered with the pain. Pérez waited for him and they entered the building together. 'He quarrelled with the vicar,' the man explained, gesturing towards Pedro who had stayed behind in the garden. 'It seems he had a problem with a very valuable necklace,' he continued as they strolled between the columns of the ancient mosque, 'but he doesn't want to tell us the details; apparently he doesn't want to explain himself to the vicar either.'

As Hernando well knew, the sacristy was built on to the south wall of the cathedral next to the treasury. It was in a chapel between the mihrab and the library, where building work was still going on to convert it into a larger sacrarium. Halting in the doorway, Pérez humbly asked permission to enter. He was surprised to see Don Juan, the vicar, receive the new fugitive with a smile.

'The Count of Espiel is a bad enemy to have,' Don Juan said after he had heard Hernando's explanation. Pérez listened carefully to the story whilst the vicar made notes. 'I'll pass this information to the vicar-general, and see what he decides regarding your situation. I hope to be able to tell you something soon . . . and I'm sorry about your family,' he added as the two fugitives left the vestry.

'How does he know you?' his companion asked as soon as they were outside the door. 'Is he your friend? How—?'

'Let's go to the library,' Hernando interrupted him.

Don Julián was busy with the library's remaining volumes. The new library, next to the San Miguel gate, was smaller and the majority of the books and scrolls ended up in the archbishop's personal library, which was also where the Korans and Arabic prophecies were hidden.

'May I?' asked Hernando from the metal grille that now

separated scaffolding and workers from the rest of the mosque.

'You know the librarian too?' whispered the surprised Diver on seeing Don Julián smile as he welcomed the Morisco; a smile that had been tinged with sadness since the disappearance of Fátima and the children.

They walked among the mosque's thousand columns with the Diver behind them. Hernando had to repeat the same story he had just finished telling the vicar.

'The Count of Espiel!' sighed Don Julián, agreeing with the vicar's gloomy predictions. 'In any case, the vicar-general will be on your side: the Espiels were one of the noble families who were most vehemently opposed to the construction of the new cathedral, until it was authorized by Emperor Charles V. The new works meant the Espiels lost their chapel, so, in defiance of the cathedral chapter, they financed another church, where they managed to secure patronage for their chapel. Since then relations between the count and the bishop have been somewhat strained.'

'How will it help me to have the vicar-general on my side?'

'As ecclesiastical judge he is the one who has to decide if your asylum complies with canonical and chapter rules. You aren't a murderer or a highway robber and, from what you've told me, your offence could in principle qualify for ecclesiastical asylum. But there's another more important issue: the right of asylum isn't indefinite; if it were, churches would become home to delinquents. Here in Córdoba it is restricted to a maximum of thirty days. This allows the fugitive time to negotiate in mitigation of their offence. Knowing the Count of Espiel, you won't be able to do that.' Hernando nodded sadly. 'The count won't give an inch. He won't even agree to a sentence that doesn't involve corporal punishment, which is one of the most common ways of bringing asylum to an end: the Church demands a formal promise from the secular courts that they will treat the offender leniently and, if an agreement is signed, they hand him over. This is where the vicar-general has the greatest influence, because if this agreement isn't forthcoming, he can extend the period of asylum indefinitely.'

'What would the count achieve by not coming to an agreement with the Church? He won't be able to remove me from the cathedral or receive any compensation for my . . . crime?'

'The majority of Christians', said Don Julián, 'don't dare contravene the right to sanctuary. The simple threat of immediate excommunication of anyone who threatens to violate sanctuary is enough to frighten their pious consciences.' Hernando's hand went instinctively to his kidneys. He immediately recalled the speed with which José Velasco and his men had let him go at the mere mention of excommunication. 'But the Count of Espiel, like many other illustrious individuals,' the priest went on, 'can hire people to act on his behalf and by doing so avoid excommunication. Trust no one. As soon as he finds out you're a fugitive here his men will be posted on the gates to prevent you receiving food or visits; in short, to make life impossible for you. Don't trust anyone who approaches you in the garden, not even in here. They could kidnap you and hide you in a dungeon on one of the count's estates.'

'This means, if I'm not kidnapped,' murmured Hernando, 'I'll have to spend my whole life here?'

Don Julián paused. He turned towards the Diver and gestured authoritatively for him to move away.

'This means', whispered Don Julián after checking Pérez was two columns away from them, 'that perhaps the time has come for you to flee to Barbary.'

'And my mother?' was all Hernando could think to ask.

'She can go with you.' The two men stared at each other. How much they had shared, all their work and hopes! 'I'll start preparing the journey,' added Don Julián when Hernando let several moments go by without opposing the idea.

'If you can sort out this escape, bear in mind I first have to go via the Alpujarra, the castle at Lanjarón . . .'

'The sword?'

'Yes,' he confirmed, his gaze lost in the forest of columns. 'The sword of Muhammad.'

'It will be dangerous, but I imagine it could be possible,' said the priest. 'In spite of the ban and the new deportations they've carried out in Granada, there are many Moriscos who return there.' Don Julián smiled. 'The magical effect of those red sunsets! Good. From Granada you could go to the coast of Málaga or Almería and board a Morisco vessel from Vélez, Tetuan, Larache or Salé.'

When night had fallen Hernando left the cathedral and went out into the garden. He had Don Julián's promise to deal with everything, the escape as much as speaking to the vicar-general on his behalf. He found Aisha waiting for him; Don Julián had ordered she be informed.

'We'll escape to Barbary,' he announced in a whisper, putting an end to any further explanations as to what had happened. In the semi-darkness he could not see how the expression on his mother's face changed.

'I'm too old now for adventures,' Aisha apologized.

'I'm twenty-seven years old, Mother. You had me when you were fourteen. You're not that old! First we'll go to Granada and from there, or from Málaga, it won't be hard for us to cross by boat to Tetuan.'

'But—'

'There's nothing else we can do, Mother, unless you want me to end up in the count's hands. It won't be easy for us either,' he concluded. He knew Don Julián was right. 'We'll have to wait for the days to pass and the Count of Espiel's men to get tired and stop watching me so closely. You need to be ready.'

Despite the shock of the news and her haste, Aisha had thought to bring some food: bread, lamb and fruit. There was water in abundance in the garden's well. The service of compline had just finished when Aisha at last said goodbye to her son. The gatekeepers closed all the cathedral gates and everyone who had taken refuge in the cathedral precincts, or just prowled around inside, settled down for the night in the large garden. Some left, while the fugitives or refugees gathered together in spots they had fought to win from each other. Apart from the area occupied by the Perdón gate, the bell tower and a closed section set aside for the archdeacon's council, the three cloisters surrounding the garden were at the fugitives' disposal. There they sought shelter during the cold nights.

'Was it your mother?'

Hernando turned to find himself with the Diver, who, because of the new resident's obvious contacts with the ecclesiastical hierarchy, had decided to include Hernando in his group, on the off chance he might be of some use to them.

'Yes.'

'Come with us. We have some wine.'

Hernando accepted and accompanied by the Diver turned to cross the garden from the Perdón gate, where he had said farewell to his mother, to the cloister on the south wall. He saw Aisha pass beneath the great arch. In spite of the plan he had just proposed to escape to Barbary, she seemed sad. Where did that sadness come from? he wondered.

'Diver?' he queried a few steps further on, finally voicing what he had been wondering about all day.

'Yes. That's what I am,' smiled the fair-haired man. 'A diver. I work— I worked', he corrected himself, 'for a Basque captain who held the royal concession for the salvage of sunken ships and treasure along the Spanish coasts. We fell out over some gold coins I found a long way from the shipwreck we were salvaging in Cádiz,' he said, clicking his tongue. 'I fled, and when they were about to catch me I managed to take refuge in here.'

Despite Pérez's explanations, as he stopped in front of the Morisco to enlighten him with words and gestures, by the time they reached the cloister Hernando still had not fully grasped the workings of that fabled bronze contraption thanks to which divers were able to salvage sunken treasures.

'Don't worry,' said a man who would later introduce himself

as Luis. He had sharp features and a broken nose, and his head was covered by a red scarf tied behind his neck. 'None of us understands it either. It's most likely a lie.'

Pérez let fly a kick, which the other man laughingly sidestepped.

By the light of the large torches hanging in the arches of the garden cloisters another six men were sitting on the floor, gathered around a small wineskin and food supplied by their friends or relatives.

'Welcome to the children's cloister,' a man with straight fair hair greeted him, making a space beside him.

Hernando looked along the cloister, where all he could see were similar groups. 'Children?' he asked with surprise as he sat down.

Juan, the man with straight hair, was a surgeon who had tried to supplement his earnings by some unorthodox practices. He had sought sanctuary after being denounced by some widows, whom he had relieved of their health problems – and their purses. He explained: 'Several years ago this cloister was set aside for the shelter of Córdoba's foundlings. They slept in cots on this very spot,' he added with an expansive gesture, 'until one night a herd of pigs devoured a few infants. Then the dean of the cathedral, who was very devout, paid for a foundling hospital and returned the cloister to the fugitives. That's why they call it the children's cloister.'

Hernando couldn't help but remember Francisco and Inés. How much his life had changed in so little time! And now, Azirat, his arrest . . . Suddenly he was aware of the six men staring at him intently.

'Drink some wine,' advised Pedro, who was still half naked despite the cold of the night.

Hernando refused the wineskin Pedro offered. By the flickering flames of the torches the penitential garments hung on all the walls of the cloistered garden seemed to tremble in the night. There were hundreds of them, recalling all those punished by the Inquisition, giving the place a macabre feel.

'Give it to me!' The man beside him, who was called Mesa, dark-skinned and with oriental features, took the skin out of his hands and poured wine straight down his throat, swallowing compulsively. The mouthfuls of wine were usually carefully measured, but on this occasion nobody stopped Mesa from almost finishing it.

'There's a rumour going round they're going to hand him over to the law,' a man they called Galo whispered to Hernando in Mesa's defence. 'We don't know why, but the priests hate him. In fact he only stole a permit so that he could work. He'll be the first of this lot they expel.'

'One day or another they'll do the same to us all. They'll throw us out. Let's enjoy it while we can.' The man who spoke was also called Juan, like the surgeon, and was a gunsmith recently arrived from the Indies. He had run into difficulties linked to the mysterious disappearance of a consignment of harquebuses.

'No—' Pérez started to object.

'Which one of you is Hernando?'

The shout echoed across the garden. The silhouette of a man with his arms akimbo was outlined in the firelight beside the Santa Catalina gate, where the children's cloister began.

'Quiet! Keep calm!' ordered the surgeon when Hernando made to stand up.

'Where's the son of a whore they call Hernando?' the man shouted again from the gateway.

'What's all this racket?' asked Pérez, getting to his feet. Everyone knew the Diver. 'The priests will come if you keep shouting. What's the story with this Hernando?'

'The story is that the cathedral is surrounded by the Count of Espiel's men searching for this man. The story is they've threatened me that if the rest of us try to leave they'll arrest us and hand us over to the law, unless we hand this Morisco over to them first.'

The fact was that the majority of the fugitives ventured out into the Córdoba night, even though it jeopardized their right to asylum. The Potro was close by and waiting there were cards, dice and wagers; wine, fights and women. The guards and agents of justice could not mount a permanent watch round the cathedral; besides, slowly but surely, even though it was only after an agreement had been reached about more favourable treatment, the offenders were handed over to the city authorities. They were reluctant therefore to lose any sleep over a hapless bunch who sooner or later would fall into their hands anyway. But if on the one hand the count was paying for the surveillance, and on the other the fugitives were prevented from enjoying their nights outside, the matter became complicated.

Several fugitives from the other cloisters approached the Santa Catalina gate; in the children's cloister to the north some others got to their feet.

'It's true. I've seen armed soldiers patrolling the streets,' one declared.

'It seems you're in a worse position than me,' said Mesa, grimacing after another mouthful of wine, 'and you haven't even been in here a day.'

Hernando hesitated, shifting about restlessly.

'Keep calm! Stay calm!' muttered the Diver.

'Who's this Hernando?' asked someone from the south cloister.

'We have to hand him over to the count's soldiers!' shouted another.

In the darkness, many of the fugitives crossed the garden in the direction of Santa Catalina gate.

'Fools!' This time it was Luis who shouted at them all. 'What does it matter to you all who he is? I'm Hernando!'

'Me too!' added the surgeon at once, realizing his companion's intention.

'I'm also called Hernando,' declared the Diver. 'If we give in, today it will be this Hernando, but tomorrow it could be any one of us. You,' he added, pointing to the nearest man, 'or you.

There's someone after us all. Perhaps they don't have the count's money to hire an army of soldiers, but if they find out we kick out our own ... Besides, it's sacrilege to violate sanctuary, whoever does it. If we hand him over, tomorrow it will be the bishop who throws all of us out! And His Grace would be more than happy if he could get rid of us all.'

'Maybe you'll get lucky,' Mesa said to Hernando, as all those present were seized by a moment of doubt. They were the only two of the group still sitting down in between their companions' legs.

'But we can't get out,' someone insisted. The muttering which followed his words was interrupted by some curses.

'Hand him over! The bishop won't even find out.'

'Or maybe he will,' added Mesa somewhat sarcastically, turning to take the wineskin.

'No, we can't give him up,' Luis declared, addressing all the others. 'Those who want to go out should do so in large groups and through several gates at once – make them have to split up if they want to catch you. The count's soldiers won't want to risk their lives if you let them check that this man isn't in your group. They'll get nothing out of it; no one's going to pay them for one of us. Show them your daggers and fists.'

'Any one of us can take on three of them!' someone exclaimed proudly.

This time the murmur among the fugitives was one of approval, and a group assembled next to the gate, weapons in hand. Others peered out and confirmed that the count's soldiers indeed seemed wary of seeing several armed men leaving the cathedral precincts together. Once they had made certain that the Morisco was not among them, the fugitives were allowed to continue on their way. Word spread quickly and a new group hurried off in the direction of the Deanes gate.

'It looks as though you've got away with it this time,' smiled Mesa when the others were sitting down again.

'I thank all of you—' Hernando began to say.

'Tomorrow', the surgeon interrupted him, 'you can speak to the librarian on Mesa's behalf.'

The Morisco looked at the permit thief. His almond-shaped eyes, glassy with the wine, stared searchingly at him.

'Fate is fickle,' joked Hernando.

In spite of the fact that these scoundrels guaranteed his safety, Hernando did not get any sleep that night, but was constantly on the alert for anyone passing by him. He was still in danger and knew full well that a couple of gold crowns would be more than enough for many of those taking refuge there to smuggle him out of the cathedral. They came and went, arguing or joking, and for all the risk of sacrilege or excommunication they would be perfectly prepared to betray him. There was only one thought that could calm his torment and he clung to it, trying to not think of his dead family or his life in ruins: Barbary!

The peal of bells announcing the service of lauds brought all the groups of fugitives in the garden to their feet. Hernando stretched, ready to join them before the flood of priests, musicians, singers and other cathedral employees began to overwhelm the area. He stopped, however, when he saw his night-time companions still lying idle.

'Aren't you getting up?' he asked the surgeon, who lay next to him.

'We know a better way to start the day, and it's not at the command of the bells. Wait and you'll see. One coin says yes!' he exclaimed.

'I agree,' the Diver accepted the bet.

'Two says he won't manage it!' bet Luis.

'I'll take that wager!' Mesa cried.

'Look,' said the surgeon, pointing at a man standing in front of them. He was three or four paces away, between some orange trees in the middle of one of the pathways that ran from the cloister into the garden.

Hernando watched him: he was bald, he had his eyes half

closed and his mouth in a tight smile, as if wanting to hide his lips, although a tooth stuck out between them; he was standing like a statue, with a flat marble floor tile balanced on his head.

'What's he doing?'

'Palacio? Wait and you'll see.'

Along with the people, some stray pigs and packs of dogs had also invaded the garden. They chased after the priests, in hot pursuit of the lingering scent of breakfast on their hands, or poised to lick the flagstones where the fugitives had eaten. Hernando noticed how some of the dogs put their tails between their legs and started running at the mere sight of Palacio.

'Why—?'

'Quiet!' interrupted the Diver. 'There's always one that doesn't know him and rises to the bait.'

He started watching again precisely at the moment when a dirty hound with a kinked tail sniffed the man's shoes and ragged red breeches. The dog turned round and round looking for the perfect spot and when it finally cocked its leg ready to urinate over Palacio's leg, the man calculated the trajectory and tilted his head. The tile slid off, its full weight landing on the animal's back. Rudely interrupted in the act it ran off, howling with pain. Still motionless, as if to salute his audience Palacio smiled broadly, uncovering his protruding tooth.*

'Bravo!' shouted Mesa and the surgeon, as they held out their hands for their winnings.

'He always does this?' asked Hernando.

'Every day! Regular as the bells,' answered the Diver. 'Despite the fact on some occasions he has been forced to run from the dog's owner, if it has one. We give odds of ten to one on the dog's owner appearing,' he added with a laugh.

* * *

* With my admiration and thanks to the master of the novel, Miguel de Cervantes, from whom I have borrowed the 'Madman of Córdoba', a character from the second part of *Don Quixote*. (Author's note.)

That night Hernando did not sleep in the garden.

'Only yesterday at nightfall, probably at the same moment as he was sending his men to keep watch on the streets around the cathedral, the count requested an audience with the bishop,' Don Julián explained after lauds, when he had heard the Morisco's account of the previous night's events. 'I've been told he was beside himself with anger. I don't think the bishop agreed to receive him, which means the Count of Espiel will do everything in his power to seize you. If he has to send a raiding party to kidnap you, he'll do it. I'm sure of it.'

'It was just a horse to him, Don Julián! A reject from the King's stables! Why go to all this trouble?'

'You're wrong: it's not just a horse, it's his honour! A Morisco has sullied his name and trespassed on his rights; for a noble there is no greater insult.'

Honour! Hernando remembered how, years ago, the knight who claimed descent from the Roman Quintus Varus had gone as far as to risk his life when he merely suspected someone had dared cast aspersions on his lineage. Then he recalled how he had made money from the gullible gentleman, and how he had run to hand it to Fátima. His Fátima . . . !

'As you well know,' continued Don Julián, interrupting his thoughts, 'as well as being the librarian I'm also chaplain of the San Bernabé chapel, one of the three small chapels behind the main altar. Tonight I'll get you a set of keys to its grille. While the gatekeepers are closing the cathedral and moving people out, you can hide in a cupboard there. I'll empty it out during the day. Let a reasonable amount of time elapse, then come out. Find yourself some other place to sleep, but be careful to stay hidden. Even with the temple closed there are guards, especially in the treasury.'

'You shouldn't take such risks. If they find me . . .'

'I'm old now, and there's still much you can do for us, even if it's from Barbary. God knows, you have suffered many setbacks, but the hope of our people rests on you and those like you.'

The priest tried to convince Hernando that the other

fugitives would not be concerned about his nocturnal absences. Hernando had not forgotten his promise to intercede on behalf of Mesa, the permit thief. The priest listened sadly and wearily promised to do what he could for him. Meanwhile, the Count of Espiel increased the vigilance in the streets. His henchmen stripped Aisha of the food she was bringing in, despite the fact this was also considered sacrilege and grounds for excommunication. It was this that finally convinced Hernando of the need to shelter inside the mosque at night. Don Julián, with the help of Abbas, who begged the priest to keep Hernando ignorant of his intervention, tried to find a way for him to escape to Barbary. Aware that this was the Morisco's only chance, the count also turned his attention in this direction: his spies, with plenty of money and few scruples, paid off or intimidated all those involved in such dealings.

Hernando found it relatively easy to avoid the gatekeepers who were chivvying out anyone still inside the cathedral grounds after vespers. Yet he couldn't prevent his heart beating frantically, or his hands sweating. He was trembling so much that the bunch of keys he was carrying started to jingle. To him it sounded like a loud clang and he looked anxiously from side to side. Don Julián had oiled the lock and hinges of the excessively tall metal grille at the entrance to the small San Bernabé chapel.

'Come on, out of the cathedral!' he heard the gatekeepers demand, their voices raised but not shouting, as he shut the grille behind him. To his left the cupboard mentioned by Don Julián was concealed behind a magnificent tapestry.

However, Hernando stood captivated by the reflections cast on the chapel's white marble interior by the light from the oil lamps hung from the roof of the cathedral and the thousand flickering candles of the chapels and altars. He had passed by that chapel countless times but now, his fingers stroking the marble altar and altarpieces that completely covered the wall, he noticed how very different it was from all the rest. San Bernabé's chapel was a gem of the Roman style so difficult to introduce in lands so intensely Catholic as those ruled by King Philip. The different scenes on the altarpieces had been sculpted by a French master in white marble, and contrasted strongly with the profusion of colours, gilt mouldings and dark or apocalyptic images which adorned the rest of the cathedral.

Hernando took a deep breath, trying to saturate himself with the serenity and beauty that reigned in the chapel. Then he heard the gatekeepers return from closing the cathedral's entrance gates. They began to check the grilles on each chapel. Hearing their laughter and banter, he jumped for the tapestry, and managed to get inside the cupboard just as the gatekeepers peered into San Bernabé's chapel.

That night he did not leave his hiding place. Exhausted after many nights filled with painful nightmares, he curled up on the floor and let sleep overtake him. He was awoken by the noise that broke out in the cathedral at dawn, and had no difficulty slipping out of the little cupboard: the office of prime was under way at the main altar and choir, at the far side of all the new building work. Not wanting to be caught with the keys he hid them beneath the lowest bar of the grille, tied on with a rusty piece of wire.

Hernando did not leave the cupboard in the nights that followed either. He was frightened of being discovered, and so slept half sitting, hugging his legs to him, or standing up. Sometimes he just wept: for Fátima and his children, Hamid and all those he had lost. He had the whole long, tedious day to recover his strength. Each evening he bade a speedy farewell to his companions of the first night, and paid no heed to their curiosity. From a distance one morning he looked on as Mesa, the permit thief, was removed once and for all and handed over to civil justice. The guards were waiting in the street outside the Perdón gate. Aisha had appealed to the faithful brothers of the community to take Hernando food, and each day one of the many Moriscos came to the garden with supplies. Aisha also had to seek refuge among the Moriscos when the cathedral chapter unceremoniously evicted her from the courtyard house of Calle de los Barberos for not paying the rent.

'To recover the back rent they've taken everything our brothers gave us,' she sobbed. 'The straw mattresses, the saucepans . . .'

But Hernando had stopped listening to her: he felt that the last thread tying him to his previous life had broken; the house where he had found a happiness apparently forbidden to followers of the only faith was no longer his.

'And the Koran?' he suddenly interrupted, saying the word out loud. Astonished, Aisha glanced rapidly all round her in case anyone had heard.

'I gave it to Jalil when they warned me of the eviction.' Aisha paused for a few moments. 'What I didn't hand over was this.'

With these words she discreetly slipped the hand of Fátima, the small gold necklace his wife had worn, into her son's fingers. Hernando stroked the pendant; the gold seemed tremendously cold to the touch.

That night, hidden in the cupboard in San Bernabé's chapel, and with tears in his eyes, he kissed the hand of Fátima a thousand times. His wife's scent filled his senses and her words echoed in his ears, the words Fátima had pronounced right there, in the house of the believers: *Ibn Hamid, always remember the oath you have just sworn, and keep it, come what may.*

He swore to Allah that one day they would again pray to the One God in that sacred place. He squeezed the gold necklace in his hand. *Keep it, come what may*, Fátima had solemnly insisted. He kissed the necklace one more time and tasted the salty tears which soaked his hand and the gold. He had sworn to Allah! He had also sworn to put the Christians at her feet . . . and now Fátima was dead. He had to keep his oath!

He left his refuge and came out into the faint light of lamps and candles. He tried to work out how much time had gone by but inside the cupboard he lost all sense of it. *Come what may!* he repeated in his mind again and again. The cathedral was silent, except for a murmur of voices coming from the sacristy of the Punto, in the south wall. That was where all the implements for celebrating ordinary masses were kept, together with the cathedral's treasure and relics. The main sacristy was on the right, followed by the sacrarium, in the chapel of the Lord's Supper. Next to that, in the chapel dedicated to Saint Peter, stood the wonderful mihrab built by al-Hakam II, now defiled and converted into yet another ordinary sacristy.

His heart in his mouth, Hernando passed around the high altar and the choir stalls, built in the centre of the cathedral. His attention was fixed on the entrance to the Punto sacristy, from where he could hear the guards' voices. He reached the back of the Villaviciosa chapel, in the same nave as the mihrab. He skirted the chapel until he came to a halt with his back against its south wall, just in front of the believers' holiest place, only nine columns away.

Today I swear to you that one day we will pray to the one God in this sacred place. The oath he had made to Fátima echoed in his ears. *Come what may!* she had demanded of him. Suddenly, in the shelter of the forest of columns erected in homage to Allah, he felt strangely calm. The murmuring of the guards became the chanting of thousands of believers. For centuries they had prayed in unison in this very place. A shiver ran down his spine.

He had nothing to purify himself with; neither clean water nor sand. He took off his shoes, raised hands wet with tears to his face and rubbed. Then he did the same with his arms, rubbing them up to the elbow. After running his hands over his head, he lowered them to his feet and continued rubbing as high as his ankles.

Then, oblivious to everything around him, he knelt and prayed.

Every day, hidden from the others' eyes, he took care to purify himself properly before the cathedral gates were closed, using water from the garden well among the orange trees. At night he repeated his prayers, trying to reach Fátima and the children through them.

Sometimes the guards emerged from the Punto sacristy to patrol the cathedral, but as though warned by God Hernando always noticed in time. He pressed his back to the wall of the Villaviciosa chapel and did not move, hardly daring to breathe as the guards passed through the building chatting unconcernedly.

His companions of the first night disappeared one by one. Only Palacio continued every morning to try to hit the unhappy dogs drawn to the smell of his breeches and shoes.

Whilst the ecclesiastical judge deliberated on his asylum and Don Julián unsuccessfully tried to overcome the problems the Count of Espiel's constant vigilance and tricks posed for his escape, Hernando lived only for the moments when he knelt facing the kiblah. In a place so defiled by the Christians, he could still feel the vibrations of the true faith.

Night after night the cathedral belonged to him. It was his mosque! His and all the true believers'; no one could take it from them.

'Make way!'

Behind three mace-bearers, more than half a dozen armed men, attired in red uniforms bordered with gold and coloured slashed breeches, burst through the Perdón gate into the garden. It was the morning of All Saints' Day, the first day of winter.

The Bishop of Córdoba himself, richly attired and surrounded by a large number of cathedral chapter members, waited at the gate of the Bendiciones arch.

'Today, before the solemn mass,' Don Julián had commented to Hernando that morning when he saw how busy the cathedral was, 'the Duke of Monterreal, Don Alfonso de Córdoba, who has just returned from Portugal, plans to attend to honour his dead.' The Morisco shrugged his shoulders. 'I agree,' conceded the priest, 'it matters little to you, but I advise you not to stay inside the building during his visit. The duke is one of the Spanish grandees. A descendant of the Great

Captain, he belongs to the house of Fernández de Córdoba and his men do not like people hanging around him. Making an enemy of another Spanish grandee is the last thing you need!'

'Stand aside!' shouted one of the duke's men, violently shoving an old woman who stumbled in her escape.

'Son of a whore!' Hernando blurted out. He tried to catch the woman, but could not prevent her sprawling to the ground. As he bent to help her he noticed it had gone very quiet around him and several of those who were beside him stepped back. Still bending down, Hernando turned his head.

'What did you say?' the man hissed, coming to a halt.

Hernando, still trying to help the old woman to her feet, held his gaze.

'It wasn't him,' he heard the woman declare. 'I let it slip, excellency.'

Hernando shook with rage to see the cynical smile with which the man received the old woman's words. Although safe from the Count of Espiel, he was a prisoner dependent on the aid of his brothers. Each day he received whatever food they could provide for him, as if he was a beggar. Day after day he listened to his sobbing mother's tales of woe, and now a weak, elderly woman had to speak out in his defence.

'Son of a whore!' he muttered again when the servant, apparently satisfied, made to continue on his way. 'I said son of a whore,' he repeated, straightening up and letting go of the woman.

The footman turned sharply and reached for his dagger. Those who still had not moved away from Hernando now did so as quickly as they could, and several of the lackey's companions retraced their steps to see what was going on. The duke's party was just entering the garden through the Perdón gate.

'Put up your weapon!' a priest watching the scene scolded the servant. 'You are in a holy place!'

'What's going on here?' one of the duke's company asked. The servant held his dagger to Hernando's chest. The other two men held him immobile.

The duke himself, preceded by a servant carrying a long rapier held point upwards, and hidden between the chancellor, chamberlain, secretary and chaplain, was obliged to stop. Out of the corner of his eye Hernando could just make out the aristocrat's luxurious robes. Behind the duke several richly dressed women were also waiting.

'This man has insulted one of your excellency's servants,' a bailiff from the nobleman's court answered.

'Put your dagger away,' the duke's chaplain ordered the servant, coming up to the group. He waved his arms around in the air to push the cords of his green hat out of his eyes. 'Is this true?' he enquired, turning to Hernando.

'It's true and I claim sanctuary,' replied the Morisco proudly. At the end of the day what difference did it make, one nobleman or two?

'You cannot claim sanctuary,' the chaplain stated calmly. 'Those who commit a crime in a holy place lose the right to asylum.'

Hernando went weak and felt his knees buckle. The servants who had him by the armpits pulled him upright.

'Take him to the bishop,' ordered the bailiff as the chaplain turned his back on them to rejoin the main party, which had set off again. 'His Grace will order this delinquent's expulsion.'

If they removed him from the cathedral, he would be sentenced first by the duke but after that by the Count of Espiel. What would become of him – and his mother? Barbary! They had to escape to Barbary. That was what Don Julián was preparing for. All he could do now was to beg for mercy! He let himself fall as if he had fainted and as soon as the servants bent down to get a better grip on him, he broke free and set off at a run towards the man he believed to be the duke.

'Mercy!' he begged, kneeling in the duke's path and throwing himself down to kiss his velvet shoes. 'In the name of God and the Blessed Virgin!' Several men leapt on Hernando, pulled him to his feet and dragged him out of the duke's way. The nobleman did not even have to break his stride. 'By the nails of Jesus

Christ!' Hernando shouted, kicking and struggling between the lackeys.

By the nails of Jesus Christ!

When he heard these words a look of surprise appeared on the duke's face. For the first time he bothered to look at the commoner who was being such a nuisance. Hernando raised his head and his eyes met the duke's.

'Be still! Release him!' Don Alfonso ordered his men.

His party all came to a halt. Some at the back craned their necks to see what was happening. The members of the chapter started to approach him, and even the bishop narrowed his eyes to see what was happening.

'I said release him!' the nobleman insisted.

Ragged and filthy, Hernando stood before the imposing Duke of Monterreal. They looked at one another in astonishment. There was no need for questions or confirmation. In the same instant the memories of nobleman and Morisco returned to the tent of Barrax, the corsair captain, on the outskirts of Ugíjar; where Aben Aboo had made his camp after the defeat at Serón.

'What of La Vieja?' Hernando suddenly asked.

One of the bailiffs considered the question an impertinence, and made to slap him, but without taking his eyes from Hernando, Don Alfonso stopped him with an authoritative gesture.

'She did her duty, just as you said she would.' The chancellor and the secretary, severe and sober men, jumped visibly to see their master treat such a ragged person so kindly. Other members of the party exchanged whispers. 'She carried me close to Juviles, where I met with the Prince's soldiers on the road. Unfortunately I don't know what happened to her after that. I was almost unconscious; they took me from there to Granada and then on to Seville, in order to treat me.'

'I knew La Vieja wouldn't let me down,' said Hernando.

They both smiled.

The murmuring among the crowd grew louder.

'Did you find your wife and mother?' asked the nobleman in his turn, ignoring all the others around them.

'Yes.' Hernando's answer was almost a sigh. Yes, he had found Fátima, but now he had lost her for ever . . .

The duke's words interrupted his thoughts: 'Know one and all,' he proclaimed, raising his voice, 'I owe my life to this man they call the Nazarene, and from this day on he enjoys my favour, my friendship and my eternal gratitude.'

PART THREE

IN THE NAME OF FAITH

... Since men have called me 'God', and 'Son of God', my Father, in order that I be not mocked of the demons on the day of judgement, has willed that I be mocked of men in this world by the death of Judas, making all men to believe that I died upon the cross. And this mocking shall continue until the advent of Muhammad, the messenger of God, who, when he shall come, shall reveal this deception to those who believe in God's law.

Gospel of Barnabas

44

Hernando watched the process of painting and re-modelling the cathedral library to convert it, once empty of books, into the chapel of the sacrarium. The place held a powerful attraction for him and he went there regularly. Apart from horse riding and shutting himself away to read in the great library of the Duke of Monterreal's palace, his new home, he had little else to do. The duke had resolved his problems with the Count of Espiel by means of some agreement of which Hernando never learnt the details. As was the way of Spanish noblemen, he forbade Hernando to work, assigning him a monthly sum so generous Hernando did not even know how to spend it. It would have been an insult to the House of Don Alfonso de Córdoba for someone enjoying his protection to be reduced to any form of remunerative work!

However, and despite the esteem in which he was held by the duke, Hernando remained excluded from the other social activities with which those gentlemen of leisure amused themselves. The duke had his own duties and obligations at Court, as well as those imposed by his extensive, rich possessions, which obliged him to be absent from Córdoba for long periods. Although Hernando had saved the duke's life, he was still a

Morisco, tolerated only with great difficulty by haughty Córdoba society.

If this was the case with the Christians, a similar thing also happened with his brothers in faith. The news that he had freed the duke in the war in the Alpujarra, and the favours this action now brought him were on the lips of the whole community. Hoping his fellow Muslims would understand in the end and not place undue importance on something that happened so long ago, Hernando accepted the noble's protection. But when he tried to explain himself, the story spread round all Córdoba, and the Moriscos began to refer to him contemptuously by the name he hated so, which had pursued him since infancy: the Nazarene.

'They don't want your money any more. They don't wish to feel obliged to a Christian,' Aisha informed him one day when he tried to hand her a substantial sum to help rescue slaves.

As well as the money destined for this endeavour, Hernando gave his mother enough to carry on comfortably sharing a house with several Morisco families. He went to look for Abbas, the only one of the former members of the council who had survived the outbreak of the plague that had devastated the city two years previously. Nearly ten thousand people, a fifth of the city's population, had died, among them Jalil and the good Don Julián. Hernando found Abbas alone in the forge at the royal stables.

'Why won't any of you accept my help?' he asked after muttering an almost unintelligible greeting. Their friendship had never recovered from Hernando's violent reaction to the news of Fátima and the children's deaths. 'Fátima and I were the first to contribute towards the liberation of Morisco slaves, and we did far more than others in the community, remember?'

For a few moments Abbas turned his attention away from the tools he was working with on a table. 'Our people don't want handouts from the Nazarene,' he answered curtly, before turning back to his work.

'You more than anyone should know I'm not a Christian. All

the duke and I did was join forces to escape from a renegade corsair who—'

'I don't want to hear your explanations,' Abbas interrupted him, without stopping work. 'We all know many things that aren't true, and yet . . . all the Moriscos swore loyalty to their King, that's why they are here suffering this humiliation, because they lost the war. You also swore loyalty to the cause and yet you helped a Christian. If you were able to break that oath, why are you such a harsh judge of those who have been unable to keep their promises?'

With these words, the blacksmith straightened up in front of him. He was an imposing figure. Why do you continue to judge me? his eyes asked. There was nothing I could do to prevent your wife's death, they seemed to want to say to him.

Hernando remained silent. He rested his gaze on the anvil where the horseshoes were shaped. It was not the same: Abbas had promised to take care of his family; Abbas had assured him Ubaid would not trouble them. Abbas . . . he had failed! And Fátima, Francisco, Inés and Shamir were dead. His family! How could forgiveness exist for such a thing?

'I hurt no one,' replied Hernando.

'Oh, no? You gave back life and freedom to a Spanish grandee. How can you guarantee you truly didn't hurt anyone? The outcome of wars depends on them, on each and every one of them: on their fathers and brothers, on the agreements they can reach if one of their family is taken prisoner. This holy city', continued Abbas, raising his voice, 'let itself be reconquered by the Christians because a single nobleman, just one, Don Lorenzo Suárez Gallinato, convinced King Abenhut he was stationed with a large army in Écija, only seven leagues from here! And that he should go to assist Valencia instead of coming to the aid of Córdoba.' Abbas snorted; Hernando did not know what to say. 'A single noble changed the destiny of the Muslim capital of the West! Do you still say you hurt no one?'

They did not even say goodbye.

* * *

Abbas's reproach ate away at Hernando for several days. Time and again he tried to convince himself that the corsair Barrax only wanted Don Alfonso in order to obtain a ransom for him. His freedom could not have influenced the outcome of the war in the Alpujarra! He repeated this to himself insistently, but the blacksmith's words kept coming back into his mind at the most inopportune moments. That was why he liked to visit the cathedral's sacrarium chapel, the old library that held so many memories for him. There he found peace, whilst he watched how Cesare Arbasia, the Italian master contracted by the cathedral chapter, painted and decorated the chapel from floor to ceiling, including the walls and the double arches. Little by little the ochre and red-toned background was being covered with angels and coats of arms. The artist's hand reached every corner; even the capitals of the columns were covered by a layer of gilt.

'The great master Leonardo da Vinci said believers prefer to see an image of God than to read a document talking about God,' he explained in Italian on one of Hernando's visits. 'This chapel will be identical to the Sistine of Saint Peter's in Rome.'

'Who is Leonardo da Vinci?'

'My master.'

Hernando and Cesare Arbasia, a serious, highly strung and intelligent man of about forty-five, had struck up a friendship. The painter couldn't fail to notice the Morisco, always dressed impeccably in the Spanish manner of the duke's court, sitting in the chapel watching him work for hours on end. The third time he saw him they began to talk. They got along well with each other.

'Images don't matter very much to you, do they?' Arbasia had asked him one day. 'Obviously you don't look at them with devotion, but I've never seen you look at them even with curiosity. You're more interested in the painting process.'

It was true. What most attracted Hernando was the fresco technique the Italian used to paint the chapel of the sacrarium:

it was so different from what he was used to with the leather embossers and painters of Córdoba.

The Italian master plastered the part of the wall he wished to paint with a mixture of a particular thickness made with coarse sand and lime. Afterwards he scrupulously smoothed and then polished it with marble sand and more lime. It could only be painted on whilst still fresh and damp. On occasion, when the painter saw the plaster was going to dry out before he could finish, the shouts and curses in his mother tongue echoed round the entire cathedral.

For some moments the two men silently observed each other. The Italian knew Hernando was a new Christian but sensed he continued to profess the faith of Muhammad. The Morisco was not worried about admitting it to him. He was sure Arbasia was also hiding something. He behaved as a Christian, painted God, the Virgin, the martyrs of Córdoba and angels; he worked for the cathedral; but something in his manner and his words set him apart from the pious Spaniards.

'I prefer reading,' admitted the Morisco. 'I'll never find God in simple images.'

'Not all images are so simple; many of them reflect things that books hide.'

That enigmatic declaration was the last thing the master said to him that day.

The Duke of Monterreal's palace was in the upper part of the district of Santo Domingo. The main section dated from the fourteenth century, the period when the city of Córdoba was reconquered, and an ancient minaret that rose from one corner recalled the splendour of the caliphs. The house consisted of two floors with very high ceilings, to which several buildings had been added until they formed a veritable maze. There were two large gardens and ten internal courtyards, which linked the different buildings. Altogether, the palace occupied an immense area of land. Displayed in the interior were the riches befitting a noble: a profusion of large pieces of furniture, sculptures, embossed leatherwork and tapestries (although these were gradually being replaced by oil paintings); silver and gold dinner services and cutlery. Leather and embroidered silk appeared everywhere. The palace had every convenience: multiple bedrooms and latrines, kitchen, storerooms and larders, chapel, library, accounts office, stables and vast halls for parties and receptions.

In 1584 Hernando was thirty years old and the duke thirtynine. Don Alfonso had a sixteen-year-old son from his first marriage. From his second, eight years ago to Doña Lucía, a Spanish noblewoman, he had two daughters aged six and four, as well as two-year-old Benjamín. Fernando, the first-born son, had been sent to the court in Madrid, but Doña Lucía and her three offspring lived in the Córdoba palace. Living with them were eleven relatives of varying ages, hidalgos without fortune from one or other branch of the family, whom Don Alfonso de Córdoba, as head of the family, took in and maintained.

As well as these proud and arrogant knights, akin to the one who had once paid Hernando four reales to tell him who had questioned his lineage, other more distant relatives inhabited this diverse court. They were withdrawn and silent, like Don Esteban, an infantry sergeant with the use of only one arm, who was one of the *pobres vergonzantes*, 'proud poor', whom Don Alfonso brought into his home.

The 'proud poor' were a special category of beggars. They were men and women with nothing to fall back on, whose honour prevented them from working as well as from begging, and who were accepted by decent Spanish society. How could honourable men and women be expected to beg for money? Brotherhoods were established to attend to their needs. If investigations into their origins and circumstances showed them to be genuinely needy, the brotherhoods themselves went from house to house asking for money on their behalf. The fruits of these missions were then handed over in private. During one of his sojourns in the city, Don Alfonso de Córdoba presided over the brotherhood, and thus discovered the existence of his distant relative; the very next day he offered him his hospitality.

Hernando returned to the palace after spending the afternoon with Arbasia. He slowly covered the distance between the cathedral and the Santo Domingo district, stopping occasionally for no other reason than to waste time, as if he wanted to put off the moment of crossing the palace's threshold. Only on the rare and infrequent occasions when the duke arrived in Córdoba, and asked him to sit at his side, did he feel at ease in the beautiful and tranquil mansion. In contrast, when Don Alfonso was away, Hernando was subjected to many subtle humiliations. He had often considered the possibility of leaving the palace, but found himself incapable of taking any decision. The deaths of Fátima and his children had shrivelled his heart and diminished his willpower, leaving him without the strength to face up to life. He spent many nights unable to sleep, clinging to his memories; and many more plunged into nightmares where Ubaid murdered his family time and again, and he could do nothing to prevent it. Then, little by little, these terrible images that haunted his dreams began to make way for other, happier memories, which filled his mind as he slept: Fátima in her white shawl, smiling; Inés, serious, waiting for him in the doorway of their house; and Francisco, totally absorbed in writing the numbers dictated by Hamid's dear voice. Hernando took refuge in these visions, but this meant he found the days interminable, and all he did was wait for them to end. Night reunited him with his loved ones once more, albeit in dreams. The rest mattered little to him: apparently his place was neither with Christians nor Moriscos. He did not know how to do anything except ride a horse. His work in the royal stables had ended after the terrible incident with Azirat: he had no friends left there now. What future awaited him if he left the palace? A return to the tannery? Facing daily the contempt of his brothers in faith? On one occasion, convinced a job would help him out of his melancholy state, he had dared to suggest to Don

Alfonso the possibility of his working as a horse-breaker. The answer he received was unequivocal:

'Surely you do not want people to think I am not generous towards the man who saved my life?' They were in the duke's office. Don Alfonso was reading a document while a large group of people waited in the anteroom. 'Are you trying to tell me you are lacking something here?' he added, his eyes not leaving the paper. 'Are you not well treated?'

How could he tell the duke that his own wife was the first to humiliate him? Hernando knew that Don Alfonso de Córdoba's gratitude was sincere, and could not detect a single jot of deceit in him, but Doña Lucía . . .

'Well?' insisted the noble from behind his desk.

'It was just a foolish notion,' Hernando excused himself.

Come what may, he would never return to the tannery, he told himself yet again as he reached the palace gates that day. The doorkeeper made him wait just a second too long before opening the door. He received Hernando in silence, without the bow with which he greeted the other gentlemen. The Morisco handed him his cape.

'God be with you,' he said anyway, as the man took it without even looking at him.

Knowing full well the doorkeeper was watching him from behind, Hernando suppressed a sigh and walked into the immense palace: from that moment, until he could take refuge in the solitude of the library, he would have to face a barrage of petty insults. The evening meal was soon to be served and Hernando saw several servants moving silently and hurriedly about the palace. More than a hundred people attended the duke and duchess, their family and all those who swarmed around them.

Hernando had had to learn to distinguish between them all. At the top of the list came the chaplain, the chamberlain, the valet and lady-in-waiting. These were followed by the head steward and the head groom, the clerk and the treasurer. Behind these came the victualler, the cellarer, the steward, the keeper of the silverware; the purchaser, the dispenser, the administrator, and the scribe. Then there were the children's governesses and teachers. Finally the rest of the servants, tens of them: mostly male; some free, others slaves, among which were several Moriscos. Last of all were half a dozen page boys.

Doña Lucía had insisted that Hernando be instructed in courtly manners, primarily those of the table, which was one of the most important ceremonies at which gentlemen had to distinguish themselves. The duchess had taken this decision following Hernando's first meal at the long table where she and the duke, the chaplain and the eleven hidalgos sat. That day, the pages and footmen served a first course of capons and pigeons, mutton, kid and suckling pigs. Then the usual stew Christians ate, cooked with chicken, mutton, beef and vegetables all seasoned with a stock of pork fat. After that were the white-meat delicacies: slow-cooked chicken breasts in a sauce of sugar, milk and rice flour, and to finish, pastry cakes and fruit. Sitting at the duke's right hand, Hernando found himself confronted with silver forks, knives and spoons, all neatly arranged; plates and cups, crystal goblets and glasses, salt cellars, napkins, and a bowl of water the page brought him. As the hidalgos and the chaplain looked on with amusement, Hernando was about to lift the bowl to his lips when he was embarrassed to see the duke wink at him before proceeding to wash his hands in it.

Doña Lucía had no intention of tolerating such a lack of manners at her table. When they finished eating, the Morisco was called to a private room where the duke and duchess awaited him. Don Alfonso was sitting in an armchair, his eyes downcast and looking rather uncomfortable, as if he had found himself obliged to yield to his wife's demands. In marked contrast to the duke, Doña Lucía was waiting standing up, her expression haughty, dressed all in black except for the delicate white lace edging her neckline. Hernando could not help but compare her with Muslim women, who were always demure and retiring when meeting strangers. Unlike them, but in common with all noble Christian women, Doña Lucía showed no such reserve, although, like any respectable lady, she tried to conceal her charms: she bound her breasts after flattening them with strips of lead, and tried to make her complexion as pale as possible, even going to the length of swallowing bits of clay.

'Hernando, we can't . . .' she began. The duke cleared his throat, so that Doña Lucía sighed and softened her tone. 'Hernando, it would greatly please the duke and me if you were to receive instruction in etiquette.'

They assigned him to the oldest of the relatives living in the palace, a cousin of the duke by the name of Sancho, a foppish hidalgo. He took on the task with some reluctance, and for almost a year taught Hernando how to use the cutlery, how to conduct himself in public and how to dress. He even insisted on trying to correct the pronunciation of Hernando's *aljamiado*, which, in common with that of all the Moriscos, suffered from certain phonetic defects, among them the tendency to convert the s's into x's and vice versa.

Hernando bore Don Sancho's daily lessons stoically. He was so depressed at that point that he did not even register the humiliation of being treated like a child; he simply obeyed unthinkingly, until one day the hidalgo airily suggested he learn to dance, as if this might please him.

'You should learn the steps,' Don Sancho announced, prancing round the room where they studied. '*Floretas, saltos, encajes, campanelas,*' he recited, skipping around clumsily and tracing a circle with one foot, '*cabriolas.*' At this, Hernando turned on his heel and left the room in silence. '*Cuatropeados,*' he heard the hidalgo calling from the room, '*giradas . . .*'

From that day on, Doña Lucía considered that the Morisco was fit to live alongside them. She knew he was hardly likely to find himself in a situation where he'd have to demonstrate his talents in the art of dance, and considered his instruction finished. Yet, despite his new airs and graces, the snubs he suffered in the palace whenever Don Alfonso was not present showed no signs of abating.

The night of that Friday when Hernando had confessed to Arbasia he could not find God in his images, the palace dined on fresh fish caught in the Guadalquivir. On the days of abstinence the fourteen guests' conversations were distinctly more sober and serious than when they dined on meats and pork fat. It was well known that many, the priest among them, subsequently visited the kitchen for bread, ham and blood sausage. During the dinner, Hernando paid no attention to the conversation between the hidalgos, the chaplain or Doña Lucía, who presided majestically over the long table. They in turn took no notice of him.

He longed to go the library, where he took refuge every night amongst the nearly three hundred books Don Alfonso had collected. As soon as the duchess decreed that dinner was over, he did exactly that. Fortunately for him, he had been excluded from the interminable nightly gatherings where they read books out loud or sang. He crossed several rooms and two courtyards before reaching what they called the library courtyard, behind which was the great reading room. He had spent several days immersed in reading *The Araucaniad,* whose first part had been published fifteen years previously, but that night he had no intention of continuing with this interesting book. Arbasia's words that afternoon, when he had quoted Leonardo da Vinci and spoken of seeking God in images, had made him think of an exhange he had once had with Don Julián in the silence of that same chapel.

'Read, because your God is magnanimous. It is He who has taught man to use the quill.'

'What do these verses mean?' Hernando asked him.

'They assert that calligraphy is a divine link between the believers and God. We must honour the revealed word. Through calligraphy we can visualize the Revelation of the divine word. All the great calligraphers have striven to embellish the Word. The faithful must be able to find the Revelation written in their places of prayer so that they always remember it and have it in front of their eyes, and the more beautiful it is the better.'

During the days when they both copied Korans, Don Julián talked to him about the different types of calligraphy, principally Kufic, chosen by the Ummayads of Córdoba to consecrate the mosque, or the Nasrid script used in the Alhambra in Granada. But whilst they took pleasure in discussing the strokes or the magnificent effects some calligraphers achieved using several colours, they did not look for beauty in their own writings; the more copies of the Koran they could offer the community the better, and speed was not compatible with perfection.

That night, after entering the library and turning up the lamps, Hernando had only one thing on his mind: to take quill pen and paper, and surrender himself to God, just as Arbasia did through his paintings. He could already visualize the first sura of the Koran neatly scripted in the Arabic of Andalusia: the vertical strokes of the rectilinear letters, which then lengthened into fluid curves; the superscript characters in black, red or green. Would there be coloured ink in the library? Neither the secretary nor Don Alfonso's scribe used it in their writings. In that case, he would have to buy it. Where could he find some?

Thinking this, Hernando sat down at a desk, surrounded by books stacked on delicately carved shelves of fine woods. As he expected, there was no coloured ink. Hernando examined the quills, inks and sheets of paper. He should practise first, he decided. He inked one of the quills and carefully, taking pleasure in the stroke, drew a large letter. The *alif*, the first letter of the Arabic alphabet, was described in ancient times as being long and sensuously curved like the human body. He drew the head with its brow, the chest and the back, the stomach . . .

A burst of laughter in the courtyard made him jump. He shuddered. What was he doing? His palms were sweating so much he nearly knocked the inkwell over; he grabbed the paper and quickly folded it to hide it under his shirt. With his heart pounding in his chest, he listened as the laughter and footsteps moved away to the far end of the courtyard. He hadn't been thinking, he reproached himself while he felt his heartbeats return to normal. He could not dedicate himself to Arabic calligraphy in a Christian duke's library, where one of the hidalgos or a servant could enter at any moment! But nor could he shut himself away in his bedchamber, he thought after considering the possibility. He had spent two years going regularly to the library after dinner, whilst the others read or sang until Doña Lucía retired to her apartments, leaving them free to go in search of Córdoba's night-time pleasures. They would be suspicious of a change in his habits. Besides, where was he going to keep the writing implements and paper? The servants, and perhaps not only them, went through his belongings – he had noticed it from the beginning – even what he kept in the large chest under lock and key; someone had made a copy of the key, he deduced when for the third time he realized they had searched his things. From his first day in the palace he had kept the golden hand of Fátima, his only treasure, hidden in the fold of a coloured tapestry depicting the scene of a wild boar hunt in the mountains; it was safe there. But to hide quills, inks and paper . . . it was impossible!

Where could he write without the risk of being discovered? Hernando ran his gaze over the large library: it was a rectangular room with a door at either end. Between the bookshelves and the barred windows looking out on to the gallery and courtyard were a large table and chairs, with lamps for reading, and three separate desks. There were no hiding places. He noticed a third door at the back of the room, squeezed between the bookcases, which gave access to the ancient minaret set against a corner of the palace. He had occasionally wandered inside the minaret, but all he found there was nostalgia, as he imagined the muezzin calling the faithful to prayer. It was a simple, narrow square tower, with a central pillar around which steps spiralled upwards. He had to find a place to write, even if it meant altering his habits or doing so outside the palace in another house. Why not? He pulled the crumpled paper out from his shirt and contemplated the *alif*. The character seemed different from everything he had written until then; it was infused with a devotion that his previous attempts had lacked. He made to tear up the paper, but changed his mind: this was the first thing he had written in which he tried to represent God, in the same way as Arbasia did with his holy images.

Where could he conceal his work? He got up and, taking a lamp, walked around the library, discounting possible hiding places. Finally he found himself at the foot of the minaret stairs. It did not look as if anybody went there often; the stairs were full of fine sand from the crumbling old stone blocks. That tower had not been repaired in centuries, possibly because of what it represented for the Christians. He started to ascend, holding on to the central pillar. Some of the stones moved. What if he could hide his papers beneath one? He touched them carefully, trying to find a suitable one. Suddenly, halfway up, one of the stones gave way. Hernando brought the light closer: it had not been a single stone, but a couple of them next to each other had shifted, exposing an almost imperceptible crevice. What was it? He pushed firmly and displaced the stones: a small secret door appeared, which opened on to a tiny hollow inside the pillar itself.

He brought the light up to it; the lantern shook in his hand as he came across a casket: the only thing that could fit into such a tiny space. It was made of an embossed leather and iron-work in a style very different from that of the chests found in the palace, most of which were in the Mudéjar style, inlaid with bone, ebony and boxwood, or made in Córdoba and adorned with embossed leather. He pulled the casket out and, bringing the lamp nearer, knelt on the stairs to examine it: the leather was well crafted, and amidst several plant motifs, he made out an *alif* similar to the one he had just traced. It could not be anything but an *alif*!

He brought it as close to the light as he could and swept the dust from the leather. He coughed. Then he lifted the flame of the lamp to the characters he had just cleaned, running his fingertips over the worn letters as he read them: '*Muham . . . ibn*

Abi Amir. Al-Mansur!' he murmured reverently. He could read little more. A shiver ran down his spine. It was a small Muslim chest from the time of the great leader Almanzor! What was it doing hidden there? He sat down on the floor. If only he could open it!

He inspected the lock fixing the two iron strips across the middle of the casket. How could he get it open? As his fingers played with the fastening, the aged, rotten stitching gave way with a faint noise. The strip of iron came gently off the leather and Hernando found himself with the lock in his hand. After a few moments' hesitation he knelt down once more and reverently opened the lid.

He shone the light inside and found several books written in Arabic.

45

CESARE ARBASIA lived alone in a house near the cathedral, beside the market square. The night he invited Hernando to dine he had the courtesy to avoid pork fat together with radishes, turnips and carrots, which the Moriscos considered food for pigs and consequently hated.

'What I haven't managed to achieve', confessed the painter before dinner, whilst the two drank lemonade in the gallery overlooking a pristine courtyard, 'is for the meat to have been sacrificed in accordance with your laws.'

'We have not been able to allow ourselves those foods for a long time now. We live protected by the *taqiya*, a dispensation that permits believers to conceal their faith when under threat, persecution or compulsion. God will understand. Only very occasionally, in isolated farmhouses lost in the countryside, can some of our brothers slaughter animals according to our customs.'

Both men exchanged silent glances, breathing the perfume of flowers in the spring night. Hernando took the opportunity to take a sip of lemonade and allow the scent to transport him with the memory of another similar courtyard and the laughter of his children as they played with the water. That very morning he had seen the final face Arbasia had painted in the fresco of the Last Supper that embellished the chapel of the sacrarium. The painting appeared on the triangular gable at the entrance, above the niche destined to house the body of Christ, the most sacred spot. Hernando could not take his eyes off the figure who sat on the Lord's left, embraced by Him: it looked like . . . it looked like a woman!

'I have to talk to you,' he said, his eyes fixed on the female figure.

'Wait. Not here,' the painter had answered, following the Morisco's gaze and sensing his confusion.

That was when he invited him to dine at his house for the first time.

With the ever-present murmur of water in the fountain, they chatted a while until the master decided to take the initiative: 'What did you want to talk to me about? The painting?'

'I understood only the twelve apostles were present at the Last Supper. Why have you painted a woman being embraced by Jesus Christ?'

'It is Saint John.'

'But . . .'

'It's Saint John, Hernando, don't argue.'

'All right,' Hernando agreed. 'Listen to me then, because there is something I want to tell you. About a month ago in the ancient minaret by the duke's palace I found copies in Arabic of several books, together with a note from a scribe of the court of the caliphs. In the two years I have spent in the duke's house I have read much about al-Mansur, whom the Christians call Almanzor. He was the military leader of Caliph Hisham II, and the greatest general in the history of Muslim Córdoba. He attacked as far north as Barcelona and even Santiago de Compostela, where he allowed his horse to drink water from inside the cathedral. He had the bells from there carried by Christians to Córdoba, where they were melted down and turned into lamps for the mosque. Many years later, King Fernando "the Saint" avenged that insult.'

Arbasia listened carefully, sipping lemonade.

'But Almanzor was also a religious fanatic, which led him to commit vile crimes against culture and science. Hisham's father, al-Hakam II, was one of the most learned caliphs of

Córdoba. He was determined to gather together all of mankind's knowledge in the city. He sent emissaries to the far corners of the globe with instructions to bring back all the books and scientific treatises they found. He built up a library of more than four hundred thousand volumes. Can you imagine? Four hundred thousand volumes! More books than in the library of Alexandria or in the one now to be found in papal Rome.'

Hernando paused to take a drink and check the effect of his words on the artist who nodded slightly, as if trying to imagine such a treasure trove of knowledge.

'Well,' Hernando went on, 'Almanzor decreed that apart from those relating to medicine and mathematics, all the books that deviated from or were not related to the revealed word must be burnt: books of astrology, poetry, music, logic, philosophy . . . of all the known arts and sciences! Thousands of books, each unique and full of wisdom not to be found elseswhere, burnt in Córdoba! Almanzor himself threw them on to the pyre.'

'What barbarity! What madness!' whispered the master.

'In the letter I found in the chest, the scribe explained everything I've told you about the burning as well as the attempt on his part to save the content of some of the books for posterity. Unlike Almanzor, he believed they deserved to survive, even if only in the form of copies that he made in great haste, without fine calligraphy or corrections or even lines.'

'Four hundred thousand volumes!' Arbasia lamented with a sigh.

'Yes,' agreed Hernando. 'It seems the library's catalogue alone took up forty-four volumes of fifty pages each.'

The two men paused for thought, until Arbasia indicated that his guest should continue.

'Every night since then I have devoted myself to reading some of these copies, hiding them inside large Christian tomes. They are magnificent poems and treatises on geography; and one about calligraphy, although the copyist's speed did the material little favour.'

Arbasia spread his palms questioningly, as if what he had heard so far did not explain Hernando's urgent need to speak with him.

'Wait,' urged Hernando. 'One of these books is the copy of a Christian gospel; a gospel attributed to the apostle Barnabas.'

On hearing that name, the painter sat straight up in his seat.

'On the title page the scribe criticizes the Muslim doctors and scholars appointed by Almanzor for being so inflexible when choosing what books should be destroyed. They hadn't hesitated when they came across a Christian gospel, but he considered the text of Barnabas, despite having been written by a disciple of Christ and being older than the Koran, actually did nothing but support Muslim doctrine. He ended by saying he thought Barnabas's teachings were so important that, besides making the copy, he would try to save the original from burning by hiding it somewhere in Córdoba. But obviously in his writing he doesn't state if he managed to do so or not.'

'What does this gospel say?'

'In general terms, it maintains that Christ was not the son of God, but a human being, another prophet.' Hernando thought he saw in Arbasia an almost imperceptible gesture of approval. 'It also states that he was not crucified, that Judas took his place on the cross; it denies he is the Messiah and heralds the arrival of the true Prophet, Muhammad, and the future Revelation. It also asserts the need for ablutions and circumcision. We are dealing with a text written by someone who lived at the time of Jesus, who knew him and saw his deeds, but, contrary to the rest of the gospels, it confirms the beliefs of our people.'

Silence reigned between the two men. There was only a little lemonade left and a servant appeared at the other end of the courtyard with a new jug, but Arbasia gestured for him to leave.

'It is well known that the popes have manipulated the doctrine of the gospels,' added Hernando.

He waited for a reaction from Arbasia to his last words, but the painter remained strangely impassive.

'Why are you telling me this?' he asked finally, in an abrupt tone. 'Why the urgency to speak with me? What makes you think—?'

'Today,' Hernando interrupted him, 'in front of your painting, I have seen in the Jesus Christ you painted a normal man, a human being, who is embracing a . . . who lovingly embraces another person; he is kind; smiling even. It is not the Jesus Christ, the Son of God, absolute and all-powerful, suffering and wounded, bloody, that can be seen in each and every corner of the cathedral.'

Arbasia did not answer; he stroked his chin and remained thoughtful.

'You are Muslim,' he said at last. 'I am Christian . . .'

'But—'

The master begged him to stay silent. 'It is hard to know who possesses the truth . . . You? Us? The Jews? Or now the Lutherans? They have split away from the official doctrine of the Church; are they right? Many other Christians do not accept the official doctrine either.' Arbasia fell silent for a moment. 'The fact is we all believe in a single God, who is always the same: the God of Abraham. The Muslims invaded these lands because other Christians, the Arians, today considered heretics, called for them; but the Spaniards were Arians. There were Arians in the north of Africa as well, and it took the Spaniards a long time to realize the Arabs who had come to their aid were actually Muslims. Do you see? Arianism, which was but a form of Christianity, was very similar to Islam. For them Islam was a religion akin to their own: both denied the divinity of Jesus Christ. That was the reason why all these realms were conquered in only three years. Do you think it would have been possible to conquer all Hispania in only so short a time if it had not been because those who lived in these lands embraced the new beliefs without abandoning their own faith? It is a single God, Hernando, that of Abraham. From that starting point, we all interpret things in our own way. It's best not to investigate too closely. The Inquisition . . .'

'But if the Christians themselves, those who knew Jesus

Christ, maintain he was not the son of God . . .' Hernando tried to insist.

'It is we men who separate ourselves from one another, who interpret, who choose. God remains the same; I don't think anyone denies that. Let's eat,' Arbasia said, getting suddenly to his feet. 'The mutton should be ready now.'

During the meal, Arbasia shied away from any discussion of his paintings in the chapel of the sacrarium or the gospel of Barnabas. He steered the conversation towards trivialities. Hernando did not demur.

'May fortune and knowledge go with you,' he bade farewell to the Morisco from the doorway of his house.

What should he do with that gospel? Hernando wondered, when he was back in the palace. Abbas, according to what Aisha said during their frequent meetings, had surrounded himself with violent and reckless men driven by malice and hatred towards the Christians. No means now existed to furnish the Muslim community with the revealed word; the new council had voted overwhelmingly to fight, and rumours about uprisings and attempts at insurrection spread from mouth to mouth through the city of Córdoba, which exacerbated the animosity between Christians and Moriscos. The last attempt at an uprising had taken place a year before, and provoked the immediate reaction of the Council of State, which requested a detailed report from the Inquisition. It had been a conspiracy between the Turks and the Huguenot King of Navarre, Henry III, a bitter enemy of Philip II, to invade Spain with inside help from the Moriscos.

'They are uneducated men,' declared Aisha, referring to the new members of the council. 'From what I've heard none of them can read or write.'

Hernando knew he would not be well received by Abbas and his followers. What would they do with the copy of the gospel? They would probably do the same as Almanzor had done in his day: for all it supported the Koranic doctrines, they would condemn the book as heresy because it had been written by a

Christian. Besides, in spite of its antiquity, it was still only a copy, and they were sure not to trust him. Could the scribe have saved the original from the fire?

Hernando sighed: if anything was certain it was that violence would not improve his people's situation. They would always be crushed by a superior force, as had already happened in the past. Any rebellion would just provide the Christians with an excuse to give free rein to their profound hatred of the Moriscos. Could there be another way for them all to live together in peace?

A week after the dinner with Arbasia, Hernando was called to the presence of the duke, who had stopped off in Córdoba en route from Madrid to Seville. The request was delivered to him in the palace stables, just as he was about to set off on a ride on Volador, the magnificent grey the duke had given him, branded with the 'R' of the new breed created by Philip II. Come what may that horse was his, Don Alfonso assured him, aware of what had happened with Azirat. To prove it, he handed Hernando a document of ownership issued by his secretary and signed in the Duke of Monterreal's own hand.

He returned Volador to the stable boy and set off behind the young page who had delivered the duke's summons.

They had to cross five courtyards, all full of flowers, all with a fountain at the centre, before they reached the antechamber where a large group of people were waiting to be received by the aristocrat. As soon as they had heard of the nobleman's arrival, many had hurried to request an audience. On the visitors' benches along the walls of the room sat several priests, a councillor from Córdoba, two magistrates, others whom Hernando did not know, and three of the hidalgos who lived in the palace. On another bench sat the servants, busy attending to the visitors whilst they were waiting. The page who had accompanied Hernando sat down on a low stool beside the bench as soon as the head steward took charge of the Morisco.

Hernando could sense the looks full of hatred from the other visitors as he crossed the chamber: he was being received before all of them. Unlike those who waited dressed in their finest attire, he was wearing riding clothes: knee-length boots, simple breeches, shirt and a close-fitting doublet. The guard outside the entrance to the duke's office knocked softly on the door when he saw Hernando and the steward approach, and then showed them in without delay.

'Hernando!' The duke got up from behind his desk to receive him as if he were a good friend.

Secretary and scribe both frowned.

'Don Alfonso,' the Morisco greeted him, accepting with a smile the hand held out towards him.

Hernando and the duke moved over to a couple of leather chairs at the other end of the office, some distance away from the secretary and the scribe. The duke asked Hernando about his life, and Hernando answered his many questions. Time passed and people continued to wait outside, but that did not seem to bother the nobleman, who was now talking at length about the volumes he had in his library, this topic of conversation having arisen by chance.

'I would like to have as much time as you do to devote to reading,' he said. 'Enjoy it, because shortly you will not be able to do so.' The duke caught Hernando's look of surprise. 'Don't worry, you'll be able to take all the books you wish with you. Silvestre,' he called to his secretary, 'bring me the document. Now you'll see what it's all about,' he added once the document was in his hands. 'As you know, I have the honour of being a member of His Majesty's Council of State. Actually what I am going to tell you is a problem that concerns the treasury, but its officials are so useless at obtaining the resources the King needs that His Majesty can do nothing but rant at them when they deny him money. The Alpujarra . . .' Don Alfonso came out with it then, handing him the document. 'Didn't you say you wanted work?' He smiled. 'Almost all the territory of the Alpujarra belongs to the Crown, and His Majesty is furious because it does not yield as much as it should. This is in spite of him having granted the new settlers exemptions from the payment of taxes as well as other benefits. The revenues are not what they should be, His Majesty told me, and he is very angry about it. It occurred to me that perhaps you, who know the area, would be able to investigate so that His Majesty could compare your reports with those of the tribunal of the people of Granada and the treasury. The King accepted this proposal willingly. He would like to teach the members of the council a lesson.'

The Alpujarra! The word filled Hernando's mind. Don Alfonso was proposing he travel to the Alpujarra! He shifted uncomfortably in his armchair, fingered the document Silvestre had handed to him and looked at the sour-faced secretary who was still standing behind the duke. He was tempted to break the document's wax seal, but Don Alfonso had more to tell him.

'After the expulsion of the new Christians from the Alpujarra, the King sent agents to Galicia, Asturias, Burgos and León to find settlers who could come and repopulate the territory. They assigned houses and lands to the new inhabitants, and as I have told you they granted them concessions regarding the payment of taxes, as well as supplying them with seeds and animals in order to help them cultivate the land. His Majesty is aware the repopulation was not complete, and that many areas are still empty, but even so, the lands do not yield what they should. Your task will be to travel through the area as my personal envoy – never that of the King, is that understood? His Majesty does not wish the chief sheriff of the Alpujarra or the attorney general to think he does not trust them.'

'So . . . ?' asked Hernando.

'Another of the benefits granted to these people is to have a stallion cover their mares without the need for royal consent. The stock of horses should therefore have increased considerably during the past few years. As explained in this document, your task is to find good brood mares for my stables. You know about horses. Most likely you will not find any that are acceptable to you. I don't think any animals of quality exist in the

Alpujarra, but should you consider one is indeed of merit,' he smiled, 'do not hesitate to buy it.'

Hernando thought for a few moments: the Alpujarra, his land! Despite everything he suddenly broke out in a cold sweat.

'There will still be Christians there who lived through the war. How will they receive a new Christian . . .?'

'Nobody would dare lay a hand on an envoy of the Duke of Monterreal!' Don Alfonso's voice grew harsh. However, the uncertainty reflected on Hernando's face obliged him to restate his assertion. 'You were Christian. You knew how to pray. You did so with me, remember? We prayed to the Virgin together. You also do so now. Presumably you have friends who could testify to your status if someone were to call it into question?'

Hernando saw Silvestre stiffen and draw closer to Don Alfonso in order to hear his response. What Christian friends did he have in Juviles? Andrés the sacristan? He would hate him for what his mother had done to the priest. Who else? He could not remember anyone, but he daren't admit this to the duke: he could not reveal how his liberation had only been a matter of chance.

'You do have some, don't you?' Silvestre asked from behind the duke's chair.

Don Alfonso allowed his secretary to intervene, then insisted: 'I have promised the King this investigation would be carried out.'

'Yes . . . yes,' Hernando hesitated, 'I have.'

'Who are they? What are their names?' the secretary burst out.

Hernando's eyes met Silvestre's. The secretary's eyes bored into him: he seemed to know the truth. It was as if he had anxiously been waiting for this moment: the moment when the true faith of the man who received so many favours from his master, who had even been given one of the new breed of horses, would be revealed!

'Who?' Silvestre repeated when Hernando made no reply.

'The Marquis of los Vélez!' Hernando said, raising his voice.

Don Alfonso sat upright in his chair. Silvestre took a step backwards.

'Don Luis Fajardo?' said the duke in surprise. 'What on earth could you have to do with Don Luis?'

'The same as I had with you, sir,' explained Hernando. 'I also saved the life of a little Christian girl called Isabel. I handed her over to the marquis and his son Don Diego at the gates of Berja. I saved several people,' he lied as he glanced defiantly at Silvestre, whose face had turned pale. The duke listened carefully. 'But in order to do this I had to appear Morisco, otherwise it would have been impossible for me to do so. Some came to know the truth about me, but most of them did not. Isabel certainly knew me, and as she was just a child I took her to where the Los Vélez family were. You could ask them about it.'

'You are speaking of the second Marquis of los Vélez, the Devil Iron Head who fought in the Alpujarra. He died soon afterwards,' the duke informed him. 'The current marquis, the fourth, is also called Luis.' Hernando sighed. 'Don't worry,' Don Alfonso encouraged him, as though he had understood the reason for his sigh. 'We can confirm your story. His son Diego, a knight of the order of Santiago who accompanied him at Berja, is still alive and is a distant relative of mine.' The duke paused for a few moments. 'I admire you for what you did in that accursed war,' he said. 'And I am certain that all those who live in this house share this sentiment, is that not so, Silvestre?'

Don Alfonso did not even turn towards his secretary, but the imperious tone of his words was enough for Silvestre to understand his master was not going to tolerate any more whisperings or suspicions about his Morisco friend.

'Of course, excellency,' he replied.

'Well, make contact with Don Diego Fajardo de Córdoba and enquire about that Christian girl. I believe you, Hernando,' he explained, turning towards him. 'I do not need to verify your story, but when you ride through the Alpujarra I want you to be received as what you are: a Christian who risked his life for other Christians. The interests of the King would be endangered if any of the old Christians living there are even slightly suspicious of you.'

The duke clearly felt their audience was at an end. It had taken up much more time than other important matters, which he dealt with rapidly.

'Let's continue with the petitioners,' Don Alfonso ordered. At that moment, a page appeared from nowhere (or so it seemed to Hernando) and set off at a run to notify the steward. 'That will not be necessary,' the duke said, halting the boy's headlong charge.

The boy stopped in surprise and glanced enquiringly at the secretary. Silvestre signalled that he should return to a small stool situated in a dark, hidden corner, where another young page was also sitting. Breaking protocol, the duke himself accompanied Hernando to the door, opened it and, to the astonishment of the people waiting outside, who always had to respond to the calls of pages with their instructions and messages, he embraced Hernando and bade him farewell with a kiss on either cheek.

While confirmation from the Marquis of los Vélez's son still had not arrived, the rumour of the help Hernando had given to Isabel and an indeterminate number of Christians during the uprising – a number that grew steadily as the story passed from mouth to mouth – spread through both the Christian and the Morisco communities. The duke's Morisco slaves made sure to bring it to the attention of Abbas and the other members of the council, who found in it the proof of all those accusations voiced against the traitor.

'How is it possible?' shouted Aisha on one of the occasions when he went to visit her. They were walking along the bank of the Guadalquivir towards the windmill at Martos, close to the tanneries from where years ago he had boarded the *Weary Virgin*. The city council had decided to make that area a place of recreation for the people of Córdoba. Aisha didn't care if anyone overheard them: her voice was full of outrage, but tinged with sadness too. 'You deceived us all! Your people! Hamid!'

'It was just a girl, Mother. They wanted to sell her as a slave! Don't believe the gossip . . .'

'A girl like your sisters! Do you remember them? The Christians slaughtered them in the square at Juviles together with more than a thousand women. More than a thousand, Hernando! And those that weren't murdered ended up sold at auction in the Plaza de Bibarrambla in Granada. Thousands and thousands of our brothers were executed or enslaved. Hamid himself! Do you remember?'

'How could I not remember—?'

'And Aquil and Musa,' his mother interrupted him, gesticulating wildly, 'what about them? They were stolen from us as soon as we arrived in this accursed city. They were sold as slaves, despite being only children. No Christian came to their defence! They were children just as much as that . . . that Isabel of whom you speak.' They walked on a fair way in silence.

'I don't understand,' moaned Aisha wearily. By now they were close to the windmill that jutted out into the river where it could use the current to grind the grain. 'Your story with the nobleman was hard enough for me to take, but now . . . you betrayed your people!' Aisha turned towards her son; her face showed a determination he had seldom seen in her before. 'Maybe you are the head of the family – of a family that now does not exist – and maybe you are all I have left in this world, but even so, I don't want to see you again. I want nothing to do with you.'

'Mother . . .' stammered Hernando.

Aisha turned her back and set off towards the Santiago neighbourhood.

46

HERNANDO RECALLED each and every one of those hours and minutes fourteen years ago when, wretched and beaten, he had covered that same road heading towards Córdoba, together with thousands of other Moriscos. Once again he felt the weight of the old ones he had helped carry, and heard the echoing lament of mothers, children and the sick.

Abruptly he gave the order to halt for the night in the abbey of Alcalá la Real, still under construction.

'We could continue a little further,' complained Don Sancho. 'In spring the days are longer.'

'I know,' answered Hernando, sitting very straight astride Volador. 'But we will stop here.'

Don Sancho, the hidalgo appointed by the duke to accompany Hernando on the journey, pulled a face at the commanding tone of the instructions. Not so long ago this had been his pupil. The four armed servants who accompanied them, and guarded the line of mules loaded with their belongings, exchanged knowing looks. This was simply a further demonstration of the authority the Morisco had displayed many times over the previous days. Yet Hernando would have preferred to travel alone.

The group settled into the abbey. The sun began to set and the Morisco asked for Volador to be saddled up again. At a steady walk, watched by the people of the town, he descended the hill alone. Fortress and abbey were above him, the extensive cultivated lands at his feet and the Sierra Nevada in the distance. He soon left the town behind and found himself in open countryside. He spurred Volador on. The horse bucked with delight, as if in thanks to his rider for demanding a gallop after the long, slow and tedious days of being restricted by the mules' slow pace.

It was not hard for Hernando to identify the patch of flat ground where they had spent the night during their exodus to Córdoba, but finding the irrigation channel where Aisha had washed Humam after wrenching his body from Fatimá's arms was a different matter. It could not be far from the camp. He rode around the fields paying careful attention to the channels watering them. They had not marked the little one's grave; they had buried him in virgin soil, wrapped only in Fátima's melancholy silence and Aisha's monotone chanting.

He thought he recognized the place, close to a rivulet of water that still flowed as it had then. It was a debt he owed, he thought to himself. He owed it to Fátima and her children, whom he had not even been able to bury; he owed it to himself. The grave of that dead child was all that remained of his wife, and of his children who, like Humam, had been born of Fátima. Hernando dismounted in front of a small burial mound of stones that the passage of time had not managed to conceal. He was certain the body of Fátima's son lay beneath this earth. He looked quickly all round him. There was no one in sight; the only sound was the horse's breathing at his back. Tethering Volador to some bushes he headed for the irrigation channel, where he washed slowly and carefully. He contemplated the glittering reds of the setting sun, took off his cloak and knelt on it. But when he began the prayers a lump formed in his throat and he broke down in tears. Sobbing, he tried to chant the suras until the ashen colour of the sky indicated it was time for the night prayer to draw to an end.

Then he got to his feet, searched in his clothes and took out a letter written with saffron ink: the 'letter of the dead', which pleads for the deceased at the hour when their actions are weighed in the divine scales.

He dug down with his hands where he imagined the child's head must be and buried the letter.

'We couldn't give you this letter when you died,' he whispered as he covered it with earth. 'God will understand. Permit me to include within it prayers for your mother and the brother and sister you never had the chance to meet.'

Like all the villages they had passed through on the road from Lanjarón (before whose ruined fortress Hernando could not help but think of the sword of Muhammad buried at the foot of its tower), Ugíjar, the capital of the Alpujarra, appeared almost deserted. The Galicians and Castilians brought down to replace the expelled Moriscos were not numerous enough to fully repopulate the area, and almost a quarter of the villages were abandoned. The feeling of freedom he experienced as he went through the valley, with the peaks of the Sierra Nevada to his left and the Contraviesa to his right, was marred by the sight of the houses boarded up and in ruins.

But despite the all-pervading air of neglect in the village, Hernando was filled with nostalgic joy at the sight of every tree, every animal, every stream and every rock along the way. His eyes roamed constantly over the landscape, and memories crowded into his mind. Don Sancho and the servants did not stop grumbling, making no attempt to conceal their revulsion at the poverty of the lands and houses.

Almost two months had passed by after the duke had spoken to Hernando about his mission before the moment of departure arrived. During this time, Hernando spoke with Juan Marco, the master weaver in whose workshop Aisha was employed. They knew each other. On occasion he had gone to the workshop and talked with him; he was an arrogant weaver of velvets, satins and damasks who considered himself above those in his own guild who dealt in other types of cloth: silk workers, veil-makers, spinners, and even those 'lesser' weavers, the taffeta workers. The master weaver made no secret of his desire to sell his wares at the Duke of Monterreal's house.

'Increase her daily rate,' Hernando urged him one evening. He had waited, hidden in a corner close to the workshop, until his mother's figure disappeared down the street. Ever since their argument Aisha had refused to accept any help from her son.

'Why should I?' the weaver retorted. 'Like many other women from Granada, your mother knows the product, but she has never done any weaving. The regulations stop me from giving her any work beyond that of assisting—'

'Increase it anyway. It won't cost you anything,' said Hernando, slipping three gold sovereigns into the man's hand.

'That's easy for you to say! You don't know what these women are like; if I increase the wage of one of them, the others will be on me like a pack of wolves.'

Hernando sighed. The weaver was playing hard to get.

'Nobody needs to know; just her. If you do this, I'll suggest to the duke he take an interest in what you produce,' said Hernando, looking the man straight in the eye.

Hernando's promise, together with the gold sovereigns, convinced the weaver, who nevertheless still had a final question on his lips:

'All right, but . . . why?'

'That's no concern of yours,' Hernando snapped. 'Just keep your side of the bargain.'

Once this problem was resolved, there remained one more. How few preparations he had to make before a journey! Hernando thought, after knocking one night at the door of Arbasia's house. Yes, both were important, but there were still only two things he had to do. The servant who opened the door made him wait in the semi-darkness of the entrance hallway. The last time he had needed to travel he had just left the house in Fátima's hands and asked Abbas to look after his family . . .

'To what do I owe your visit, Hernando? It's late,' a tired-looking Arbasia interrupted his thoughts.

'Forgive me, master, but I must leave on a journey and in all of Córdoba I think there is only one person I can trust.'

He held out a roll of leather. Hidden inside was the copy of the gospel of Barnabas. Arbasia guessed as much and made no move to take it.

'You're putting me in a difficult position,' he explained. 'What would happen if the Inquisition found this document in my keeping?'

Hernando kept his arm outstretched. 'You enjoy the favour of the bishop and the council. Nobody will trouble you.'

'Why don't you hide it where you found it? It lay un-discovered there for years.'

'That's not the point. Certainly, there are plenty of places where I could hide it. The only thing I want is for this valuable document not to be lost again if anything should happen to me. I'm sure you'll know what to do with it should that situation arise.'

'And your community?'

'I don't trust them,' admitted Hernando.

'Nor they you, apparently. I've heard rumours . . .'

'I don't know what to do, César. I risked my life fighting for our laws and our religion. A man told me I should appear more Christian than the Christians, and now this same man rejects me as a Muslim. The entire community looks down on me. They think I'm a traitor; even my own mother!' Hernando took a deep breath before continuing. 'And that isn't all: from what I've heard, my brothers see violence as the only way to break free of oppression.'

Arbasia took the gospel. 'Don't seek your brothers' approval,' the painter advised him. 'That is no more than pride. Seek only that of your God. Continue fighting for what you believe in, but always remember that the only way is that of the Word, of mutual understanding, never that of the sword.' Arbasia remained silent for a few moments before bidding him farewell: 'Peace, Hernando.'

'Thank you, master. Peace be with you also.'

* * *

In Ugíjar the chief sheriff of all the Alpujarra had been advised of his arrival. Just as Hernando had taken certain measures before leaving, so the duke too had ordered his secretary to send word ahead to the highest-ranking official of the Alpujarra capital. He also asked him, using information the Los Vélez family had provided him with, to look for that girl, now a woman, by the name of Isabel.

Hernando and his companions arrived at the main square. The church had been restored. Mounted on Volador, Hernando gazed around the place. How much had happened to him in and around that square! He remembered it packed to bursting with the men of Aben Humeya's army. The market, the janissaries and the Turks whom he had met for the first time here. Fátima, Isabel, Ubaid, Salah the merchant, the arrival of Barrax and his 'sons' . . .

'Welcome!'

Hernando was so absorbed in his memories he had not even noticed the arrival of a small group led by the sheriff, a short, rough-looking man, with hair as black as his suit, who was accompanied by two bailiffs. Following Don Sancho's lead, Hernando dismounted. The sheriff headed purposefully towards the hidalgo, who gestured curtly that he should approach the other rider.

'In the name of the governor of Granada,' he added, now standing in front of the Morisco, 'I welcome you all.'

'Thank you,' said Hernando, and shook the sheriff's solemnly offered hand.

'The Duke of Monterreal alerted us to your arrival. We have prepared lodgings for you all.'

Several onlookers came closer to the group. Hernando fidgeted, uncomfortable with the reception. Believing he should follow the sheriff to the house made ready for them he took a step forwards, but the man continued speaking.

'Sir, I must also welcome you in the name of His Excellency Don Ponce de Hervás, judge of the royal chancery of Granada.'

Hernando spread his palms to show this meant nothing to him. 'He is the husband of Doña Isabel,' explained the sheriff, 'the girl you valiantly saved from slavery at the hands of the heretics. The judge, his wife and all his family wish to thank you personally, and through my humble person they beg you, once you have completed the mission that brings you to the Alpujarra, to go to Granada, where you will be honoured in the house of his excellency.'

Hernando let slip a smile. The girl was alive. Right here in this square, he had tugged the rope binding her, trying to avoid the merchants and reject the offers he received. 'You'll get more than three hundred ducats for her!' he remembered one of the janissaries at the doors of Aben Humeya's house yelling at him.

'What shall I tell him?' asked the sheriff.

'Tell who?' asked Hernando, coming back to the present.

'The judge. He is awaiting a reply to his invitation. What answer do I give him?'

'Tell him yes . . . I'll go to his house.'

The duke had been right: the mares born in the Alpujarra were not of good quality. They were small, clumsy and stiff-necked. Their large heads appeared excessively heavy. Hernando travelled on his own through towns and villages asking about horses; Don Sancho and the servants were quite happy to let him do so. He rode Volador, who in himself aroused the admiration of the poor people who came up trying to sell him one of their horses. Nobody recognized him as one of the Moriscos who had rebelled fourteen years before. Dressed in Spanish-style clothes that were so rich they made him feel awkward, his blue eyes and his complexion, paler even than that of many of the inhabitants of the Alpujarra, prevented them having the slightest suspicion about him. Feeling himself to be a traitor to his people, he remembered Don Sancho's lessons and tried to speak as he had been taught, without using the characteristic Morisco accent. All of this allowed him to move around freely. He visited Juviles. Several villages in the district were abandoned, and no more than forty people now lived in the village where he had spent his early years.

Conflicting emotions filled Hernando at the sight of the houses, the church and its adjoining square as he followed the village mayor to the place where he kept four horses that might possibly be of interest to him. As they were crossing the square, Hernando closed his eyes and immediately heard the noise of the harquebuses and the cries of the women; he breathed in the smell of gunpowder, blood and fear. A thousand women had died in that square! He breathed deeply, trying to recover his composure . . . That night he had seen Fátima for the first time; that night his half-sisters had died. That night he had become a hero to his mother, the same woman who now shunned him . . .

The man continued walking towards the edge of the village, in the direction of what had been his old home, and Hernando immediately realized the horses were kept where he once had stabled his mules. He walked beside the mayor, leading Volador, and as they drew near the sound of his hooves mingled in Hernando's mind with the slow plodding of La Vieja as she returned on her own to the village to announce the imminent arrival of the mule train. He could not help recalling the absolute terror he used to feel, knowing he would have to go and meet his stepfather. Brahim . . . what could have become of him? How he hoped he was dead!

He examined the mayor's four horses, pretending more interest than he felt, and took the chance to look around. Thrown into a corner he discovered the anvil where he had mended his mules' shoes, and several other objects that also took him back to his childhood. The house was uninhabited, serving only as a storeroom and, according to the mayor, used by himself and his wife to breed silk worms.

'The rooms on the top floor were already prepared for the breeding of cocoons, with rows of canes fixed to the walls,' he explained as if this had saved him a lot of work. 'All I had to do was to make use of the heretics' labour!' He laughed.

The mayor was upset, however, by Hernando's refusal to buy the only mare he possessed.

'You will find none better in all the mountains,' he blurted out, spitting on the ground.

'I'm sorry,' replied Hernando. 'I don't think it's what the duke wants for his stables.'

At the mere mention of the duke, the man shifted about nervously, as if he had insulted the noble by spitting.

Lazy, careless and good for nothing: that was the impression Hernando formed of the new settlers in the lands that had once belonged to his people. He left the mayor with his nags and his cocoons, and climbed the mountain slopes. All the small terraces hard won from the mountain over the years were left uncultivated now and overrun with weeds: the terrace he had worked, Hamid's, and those of many other hard-working Moriscos who had made the stony ground fertile by toiling with pick and hoe. The low stone walls supporting the terraces on the mountain slopes had collapsed in many places, so that earth fell freely down on to the ones below. The canals that irrigated fields and vegetable plots were neglected and broken, allowing the water, source of all life, to escape.

Incompetent at cultivation and incapable of farming livestock, concluded Hernando. Each one of the new settlers had three times as much land as the Moriscos and yet they were dying of hunger. The villagers tried to excuse their idleness.

'All these lands belong to the King,' a thickset man from Galicia surrounded by other villagers explained to Hernando, when he stopped at an inn. 'Therefore they are directly controlled by the governor of Granada, including the high pastures, where during the summer the vegetation, scrub and coarse grass provide grazing for the livestock. Since the pastures are communal, many important people from the city, friends of the governor, send their flocks to graze in the Alpujarra. They allow their animals to ruin crops and mulberry trees. And when they move them from one pasture to another they use armed men who choose the best ones and just take them, even if they aren't theirs.'

'They rob us, excellency,' shouted another man, hot and bothered, 'and the sheriff of Ugíjar does nothing to protect us.'

But Hernando was not listening to him. He was remembering with nostalgia how as a boy he had to round up the flocks after they had been scattered to escape paying the tithe.

'Will your excellency do something?' insisted the Galician, making as if to grab Hernando by the arm, until an old man at his side stopped him abruptly.

'I've only come to buy horses,' Hernando answered him sharply. What did these Christians know about robberies and the violations of people's rights? As they badgered him for help, full of expectation, all he could think of was the impunity with which the Moriscos were mistreated. These people knew nothing about that. They did not even pay duties: they were exempt. Work! he was on the verge of exhorting them.

In spite of the fact he was now certain why the royal income was so meagre, and still more certain that he would find no mares worthy of Don Alfonso's stables, Hernando decided to prolong his stay in the Alpujarra. The irritation Don Sancho and the servants showed at having to live in a small house lacking in comforts in a desolate village was reward enough. The uncouth sheriff and the abbot of Ugíjar, together with some of the six canons, were the only people with whom the knight deigned to converse, and then only briefly. Hernando usually left Ugíjar on horseback at dawn after mass. He liked to pass by the house of Salah the merchant, now inhabited by a Christian family, and go round all the places he had come to know during the uprising. He studied commerce in the region and spoke with people to discover the real reasons for the stagnation of activity in the area, where many Moriscos had once been able to feed themselves and raise their families. On occasion he sought shelter for the night in some house and slept far from Ugíjar. He climbed up to the castle of Lanjarón but did not dare dig up the sword of Muhammad. What was he going to do with it? Alone at its resting place he knelt and prayed.

But Don Sancho gradually became so bored that one day he insisted on accompanying Hernando on his excursions.

'Are you sure?' the Morisco asked him. 'Don't forget the areas through which I pass are extremely rugged . . .'

'Are you doubting my horsemanship?'

They set off one morning at dawn; the knight had dressed as if for a royal hunt. Hernando had heard of some horses that grazed around the pass at La Ragua, and he set off for Válor in order to climb up into the mountains from there. Now it was his turn to teach the duke's cousin a thing or two.

'I know what your mission is all about,' the knight advised him, shouting at the top of his voice from the other side of a stream that Volador had easily jumped. Don Sancho urged on his horse, which also cleared it. Hernando had to admit the knight could handle himself in the saddle with an agility that belied his age. 'And I don't believe this trip is necessary to find out why the King doesn't obtain sufficient income—'

'Do you know the lands, and what is cultivated where?' Hernando asked him. Don Sancho shook his head. 'Then could it be that are you scared?'

The knight frowned and clicked his tongue for his horse to move on.

It was a magnificent day at the end of May, sunny and cool. They continued upwards, Don Sancho following Hernando. They negotiated gullies, descended ravines and overcame all manner of obstacles. Both riders were now utterly focused on their mounts and the ground where they walked, in silent competition; the only sounds were the animals' snorts and the words of encouragement they both used to urge their horses on. Suddenly Hernando came to an almost sheer mountain slope where he could just make out a goat track. He did not think twice. He raised himself up in the stirrups and with one hand gripped the horse's mane, almost at Volador's forehead, and then spurred him hard. The horse began the ascent and Hernando, pulling on his mane and holding the reins with his other hand, pressed close to Volador's neck. The horse was almost looking at the sky.

Volador ascended in small leaps without pausing for an instant, incapable of moving normally up that sheer cliff face. The stones of the track skittered away into the void, and halfway up, when Volador lost his footing and slid a short way back down, sitting on his haunches and whinnying, Hernando realized the grave risk he ran: if he did not stay upright, if Volador stepped off the track even one inch, they would inevitably roll down the mountainside.

'Hup!' he shouted, digging his spurs into the animal's rump. 'Come on!'

Volador reared and leapt upwards once more. Hernando almost flew off backwards.

'You're going to kill yourself!' shouted Don Sancho from the foot of the precipice.

'*Allahu Akbar*!' Hernando howled into Volador's ear, trying to make himself heard above the sound of falling stones, the horse's hooves slipping on the ground and its snorts. He kept his body flat along the animal's neck, his head almost between its ears. 'Allah is great!' he repeated with every leap the horse completed.

Volador almost had to climb over the lip of the gorge, where his front legs could no longer help drive him upwards. Hernando leapt from the saddle and ran to the horse's head, pulling on the reins to help him up and over. Covered in sweat, horse and rider found themselves quaking and fighting for breath on a small expanse of flat land, filled with flowers.

Kneeling, Hernando peered over into the void.

'Now it's my turn!' Don Sancho shouted, seeing the Morisco's head appear over the edge of the precipice. He could not be bested by the Morisco! 'Santiago!'

'No!' Hernando cried out. The knight stopped just before launching himself up the track. Hernando struggled to his feet. 'It's madness,' he shouted down.

Don Sancho made his horse take a few steps back so that he could see the Morisco.

'I am an hidalgo . . .' Don Sancho began to declaim.

He'll kill himself, thought Hernando. And he would be responsible. He had encouraged the old man!

'In the name of God and the Blessed Virgin, a Spanish knight is capable of climbing the same as a—'

'You, my lord, are,' Hernando interrupted him before he could finish. 'Your horse, no!'

The knight thought for a second and contemplated the climb. His mount shifted uneasily beneath him. He looked up to the top, gently stroked his horse and then reluctantly backed off, yielding to Hernando's advice.

'You ride extremely well,' acknowledged Hernando after coming down from the plateau where he had found himself and meeting up with Don Sancho again. Volador was sweating and bore the bloody marks of Hernando's spurs.

'I know,' snapped the knight, trying to hide his relief at not having to follow the Morisco's lead.

'Let's go back to Ugíjar,' Hernando suggested, proud to feel superior to the hidalgo.

That same night, Hernando announced they would leave for Granada the next morning.

'Apparently,' Don Sancho told him during the journey, 'Doña Isabel was taken in by the Marquis of los Vélez.'

The two were riding at a walk in front of the servants and mules, with the horses' reins loose.

'How do you know that?'

'From the senior abbot of Ugíjar. He explained to me – several times, by the way – while you were wandering about in the mountains.' Hernando raised his eyebrows as if he did not understand. 'Yes, yes,' Don Sancho muttered. 'Doña Isabel entered the marquis's house as a companion for his daughters; they grew up together and she became so dear to them that the Devil Iron Head's successor offered a substantial dowry for her marriage. She married a lawyer who prospered thanks to the help of the Los Vélez family. Thanks to another Fajardo de Córdoba, a judge in Seville, he became a judge in one of the chambers of the Granada chancery.'

'Is that important?'

Don Sancho let out a low whistle before answering. 'The chancery of Granada, along with that of Valladolid, is the most important tribunal of the realm of Castile. In Aragón there are others. The only higher authority is the council of Castile, which rules on behalf of His Majesty, and then only on specific matters. So yes, it is important. Don Ponce de Hervás is a judge in one of the civil chambers. All the lawsuits in Andalusia end up before him or one of his colleagues. This brings him a lot of power . . . and money.'

'He's well paid?'

'Don't be naive. Do you know what the Duke of Alba used to say about justice in this country?' Hernando turned in the saddle towards Don Sancho. 'That there is no case whatsoever, be it civil or criminal, that isn't sold like meat in the butcher's, and that the majority of the councillors sell them daily to whoever wants to buy them. Never bring a lawsuit against a powerful individual.'

'Is that what the duke says as well?'

'That is a piece of advice from me to you.'

Since they did not want to arrive at their host's at an unsociable hour, they spent the night in Padul, a little more than three leagues from Granada. Hernando surprised Don Sancho by insisting on going to the church before leaving the following morning. This was where he had married Fátima, according to the edict of Prince John of Austria. A false marriage, only valid in the eyes of the Christians, but for him it had signified a ray of hope. Fátima . . . The church, empty at this time of day, seemed to him a cold place, as frozen as his soul. He closed his eyes, knelt down and pretended to pray, but from his lips came only: 'In death, hope is everlasting!' That phrase pursued him: it seemed to have sealed his fate from the very day he pronounced it for her. Why, God? Why Fátima . . . ? He had to dry his tears before standing up and to Don Sancho's surprise he maintained a stubborn silence until they arrived at the city of the Alhambra.

They entered it at mid-morning through the Rastro gate. They crossed the river Darro through an area where they sold all kinds of wood. A skull in a rusty iron cage hanging from the arch of the city gateway greeted Hernando like a bad omen. Some peasants and merchants who were trying to pass through the gate complained out loud when he stopped to read the inscription displayed above the cage:

THIS IS THE HEAD OF THAT GREAT DOG ABEN
ABOO, WHOSE DEATH PUT AN END TO THE WAR

'Did you know him?' asked Don Sancho in a whisper, while more annoyed people had to steer their mules and horses to either side to get around the riders.

Aben Aboo? That castrated dog had sold him as a slave to Barrax and given Fátima to Brahim in marriage. Hernando spat.

'I see you do,' declared the hidalgo, urging his horse on after Hernando, who had hastened to pass through the gate beneath the skull of the King of al-Andalus.

Following the course of the Darro through the city, they reached the wide and bustling Plaza Nueva. Here the river disappeared, to emerge once more on the other side of the Santa Ana church. To their right stretched the road leading uphill to the Alhambra, presiding over Granada; to their left stood a large palace that was nearing completion.

'How do we find out where Don Ponce lives?' Hernando asked the hidalgo.

'I don't think it will prove too difficult.' Don Sancho addressed an armed guard positioned in front of the palace under construction. 'We are looking for the residence of Don Ponce de Hervás,' he said peremptorily from his horse. The guard, recognizing a nobleman, responded.

'At this moment, his excellency is inside here.' The man pointed towards the building where he stood guard. 'This is the new chancery building, but he lives in a villa in the Albaicín. Would you like me to send word to him?'

'We have no wish to disturb him,' Don Sancho replied. 'We only want to reach his house.'

The guard glanced round the square and called to two lads who were playing there. 'Do you two know the house of the judge Don Ponce de Hervás?' he shouted at them.

Hernando, Don Sancho and the servants with the mules accompanied the children deep into the labyrinth of narrow streets that constituted the Albaicín of Granada, rising up the other slope of the valley formed by the river Darro, facing the Alhambra. Many of the little houses belonging to Moriscos appeared shut up and abandoned and, as in Córdoba, where there had once been a mosque there now appeared a church, a convent or one of Granada's many hospitals. They ascended a long uphill road, narrow and winding, and descended another much shorter and steeper one that came to a dead end at the large double doors of a house. Leaving the horses and mules to the servants, Hernando handed a penny to the youngsters, while Don Sancho grasped the lion's head knocker and rapped on the wooden door.

They were received by a liveried doorkeeper. His expression visibly altered when he heard Hernando's name, and he ran to inform his mistress, leaving them in the gardens that spread out behind the doorway. Hernando and Don Sancho leant against one of the many brick balustrades enclosing long and narrow gardens and vegetable plots that descended the hillside below the house in a series of terraces. The grounds ran down to the boundary with the next villa or one of the humble Morisco houses that jostled together in the Albaicín. Both men stared straight ahead, intoxicated by the view: amidst the scent of flowers and fruit trees, with the murmur of water from numerous fountains, the Alhambra rose magnificent and splendid on the far side of the Darro valley.

It seemed as if they could almost reach out and touch it.

'Hernando . . .'

The voice behind him sounded shy and faltering.

Hernando took a long time to turn round. What would that little girl with straw-coloured hair and fearful brown eyes be like now? It was her blond hair that he first noticed: pulled up into a bun, it contrasted with the black dress of a beautiful woman whose eyes, despite being clouded by tears, were alive and shining.

'Peace be with you, Isabel.'

The woman tightened her lips and nodded, remembering Hernando's farewell in Berja, before her saviour had galloped off, howling and brandishing the scimitar above his head. Isabel was holding a baby in her arms and next to her stood two other children, one clutching at her skirt and the other a little older, about six, standing calmly by her side. She pushed the oldest in the back for him to step forwards.

'My son Gonzalico,' she presented him, as the little one shyly held out his right hand.

Hernando did not take it, but crouched down in front of him.

'Has your mother told you about your uncle Gonzalico?' The boy nodded. 'He was a very, very brave boy.' Hernando felt a lump coming to his throat and coughed a little before continuing. 'Are you as brave as him?'

The boy turned to look at his mother, who nodded with a smile.

'Yes, he is,' she said.

'One day we'll go for a horse ride, would you like that? I have a horse that comes from King Philip's stables, the finest in Andalusia.'

The little boy's eyes opened wide. His brother let go of his mother's skirt and came closer.

'This is Ponce,' said Isabel.

'What's its name?' asked Gonzalico.

'The horse? Volador. Would you two like to ride him?'

Both boys nodded.

Hernando ruffled their hair and straightened up.

'My companion, Don Sancho.' He indicated the hidalgo, who took a step forwards to bow down before Isabel's outstretched hand.

Hernando watched Isabel as she answered Don Sancho's polite questions. The terrified little creature of years ago had turned into a beautiful woman. He surveyed her for a while as she smiled and shifted gracefully, aware she was being watched. When the hidalgo took a step back and Isabel turned her gaze towards him, her brown eyes conveyed a thousand memories. Hernando shuddered and, as if seeking to free himself from those sensations, urged her to tell him about all that had happened to her during the intervening years.

47

DON PONCE DE Hervás, an austere and reserved man, thanked Hernando with a warmth that surprised even the house's servants. He was a small, plump man with undistinguished features and a round face. He always dressed in black and was a head shorter than his wife, whom he clearly adored. He honoured his visitor with a simple bedchamber on the villa's second floor next to the couple's own rooms, with access to a balcony overlooking the gardens and the Alhambra. Don Sancho was lodged on the same floor near to the children's rooms, on the opposite side of a long corridor full of nooks and crannies that crossed the mansion.

Hernando's presence did not change Don Ponce's habits. He threw himself into his work as if that was the only way he could maintain his standing alongside Isabel, a Spanish grandee's protégée, who with a mere movement of her hand, a smile or a word, eclipsed the little judge. Don Sancho, for his part, requested his host's permission to disappear off into Granada to spend time with relatives and acquaintances. Hernando was left to spend his days in the house and gardens with Isabel and her children.

During the first days of his stay Hernando had the judge's permission to use his own study on the ground floor, so he could write to the duke informing him of the results of his enquiries.

'It would be possible to establish a raw silk market in Ugíjar,' he proposed, after warning of the indolent character of the people and the problems he had found on his travels in the Alpujarra.

> If this were done, the villagers would not have to sell their silks at a loss in Granada, as it seems they are currently forced to do. They would save the costs of the journey to the city and it would not affect the numerous textile mills in Granada as their supplies of silk come from many other places besides the Alpujarra.

Childish laughter distracted him from his work. Hernando got up from the judge's simple carved wooden desk and went to the double-fronted door, half open to admit the breeze from the main garden. This was a long stretch of narrow land along one side of the house. In the centre and occupying the entire length of the garden was a pool fed by numerous fountains set at intervals along its sides. The garden was covered with vines supported on arching overhead frames, which at that time in spring were growing vigorously. They made a cool, agreeable tunnel that ended in an arbour. Stone benches were placed at the foot of the growing vines, so that visitors could pause and enjoy the many jets of water spraying upwards into the air before tumbling down into the pool.

Hernando leant against one side of the door. Isabel was sitting on a bench with a piece of embroidery on her lap. She was smiling at her children's antics as they tried to escape their governess's watchful care. A ray of sunshine filtered through the vines, illuminating her figure in the tunnel's leafy shade. Hernando gazed at her. As usual, she was wearing a black dress: her straw-coloured hair, the same as had attracted his attention years earlier and saved her from slavery, emphasized her soft, lovely features: full lips, a long neck beneath tied-back hair, and ample breasts struggling against the rigid confines of the dress, a narrow waist and wide hips; the voluptuous body of a young mother of three children. When Isabel stretched out her hand to warn Gonzalico not to go so close to the pool, the sun glinted off it. Hernando followed the movement of that white and delicate hand and was entranced. Then he looked at the child, who was again running away from the governess, paying no heed to his mother. He turned to Isabel once more, as a strange tingling sensation ran down his spine: her brown eyes were fixed on him. His breathing quickened as he saw how Isabel's breasts trembled beneath the corset binding them. What was going on? Troubled, he held her gaze for several moments longer, convinced she would soon turn her attention to the children or her embroidery, but she did not waver. Hernando began to feel the tingling descending to his groin, and abruptly abandoned the garden, looked for one of the servants and ordered him to saddle Volador.

A week later Don Ponce and his wife organized a celebration in their guest's honour. During those seven days Hernando spent the mornings working with his back to the doors, trying to concentrate on the report for the duke and ignore the laughter that seemed to call to him from the garden.

> Set up an annual duty-free fair for the people of the Alpujarra to be able to sell their wares . . . Give them access to a port . . . Plant mulberry trees and vines . . . Give the villagers the right to sell the lands awarded them . . . Organize justice in the area . . .

Suppressing the instinct prompting him to turn towards the garden to see Isabel, he developed each and every one of the ideas that occurred to him for promoting trade in the area and helping increase the royal income. But the fact was he worked slowly; he felt tired. He did not sleep well. At night every noise he heard from Doña Isabel's bedchamber echoed in his room. Without wanting to, without being able to prevent it, he found himself pricking up his ears, listening intently and holding his breath to hear the murmurs from the other side of the wall. He thought he heard the rustle of the sheets and the creaking of the canopied wooden bed whenever Isabel turned over. It had to be her; at no moment in his sleepless night could he believe that any of those sounds came from the judge. Sometimes he thought of Fátima and his stomach clenched, as it had the first time he had visited the brothel after her death, but he soon found himself concentrating on the adjoining room again. However, by daylight he did all he could to avoid Isabel, torn between embarrassment and discomfort.

On the morning of the celebration Hernando managed to put the final touches to his report. In a separate letter he informed the duke of his stay in the house of Don Ponce de Hervás and his wife Isabel. As he did not have a seal, he asked the judge to seal it with his own. According to Don Ponce an expedition was about to leave for Madrid, so Hernando took advantage of this fact and dispatched one of the servants with his assignment.

The celebration was planned for that evening. The judge had paid for new outfits for Hernando and Don Sancho so that they would not look out of place in the lavish event he was planning. Standing as requested by Don Ponce at the villa's entrance, the hidalgo and Hernando waited to be presented to the guests. Don Sancho could not hide his nervousness.

'You should have learnt to dance,' he told Hernando, admiring himself.

'*Campanela!*' Hernando mocked him, giving a little jump in the air.

'The art of the dance—' the hidalgo began to respond.

Some restrained applause interrupted his words. 'You know how to dance as well?' he heard a woman's voice say.

Hernando spun round. Isabel stopped clapping and headed towards them, proud and erect. She walked slowly on shoes with a high cork sole adorned with silver inlays, which could be glimpsed beneath her skirt. Isabel had exchanged her habitual black for a dress of dark green satin, slit vertically to reveal underskirts in different shades of the same colour. The bodice, edged with a high lace collar that rose to her ears, was shaped like an inverted cone, whose point lay over the hooped skirt belling out from her waist. The cone concealed a corset that compressed her breasts perhaps more than usual, hiding the natural fullness Hernando had been aware of on other days. Her prominent cheekbones were coloured with rouge. Her eyes shone, outlined with a mixture of kohl dissolved in alcohol. A magnificent pearl necklace provided the finishing touch.

Realizing his scrutiny transgressed the bounds of politeness, Don Sancho scolded himself and looked away from her. He rested his hand on Hernando's forearm, trying gently to warn him, but did not even succeed in getting him to close his mouth. Hernando just stood gaping in wonder at the woman walking towards them.

'Do you know how to dance?' repeated Isabel, by now at his side.

'No . . .' he stammered, enveloped in the waft of perfume accompanying that dazzling figure.

'He didn't want to learn,' the hidalgo said quickly, trying to break the spell, conscious of the sidelong glances of some of the liveried servants awaiting the other guests.

Isabel answered Don Sancho with a slight nod of her head and a faint smile. Her face was only inches away from Hernando's.

'It is a shame,' whispered the woman. 'I am certain many ladies would be pleased to have you dance with them tonight.'

There was a heavy, almost palpable silence, which Don Sancho suddenly broke.

'Don Ponce!' exclaimed the hidalgo. A flustered Isabel turned round. 'I thought I had seen him,' Don Sancho apologized, in response to the questioning look she thew him when she could not see her husband anywhere.

'Please excuse me,' said Isabel, hiding her embarrassment by speaking quite sharply. 'I still have matters to attend to before the guests arrive.'

'What are you doing looking at a lady in that way?' Don Sancho reprimanded Hernando in a whisper when

Isabel had moved away from them. 'She is the judge's wife!'

Hernando could do no more than spread his hands wide. What *was* he doing? he asked himself. He had no idea. He only knew that for the first time in years he had felt bewitched.

Hernando and Don Sancho, together with the judge and Isabel, endured the hand-kissing and introductions to nearly a hundred people, all of them delighted to accept the invitation of the rich and important Granada judge: colleagues of Don Ponce, cathedral canons, inquisitors, priests and friars, the governor of Granada and several city councillors, knights of a variety of orders, nobles, hidalgos and scribes. Hernando received as many congratulations and displays of gratitude as there were people passing by him. Don Sancho stayed at his side, trying in vain to participate in the conversations, until the Morisco, conscious of his desperation, tried to give him an opportunity: 'I present to you Don Sancho de Córdoba, cousin of the Duke of Monterreal,' he said to the person who'd just been announced to him as the parish priest of the church of San José.

The priest greeted the noble with a nod of his head, and there ended his interest in him. 'I consider myself fortunate', he declared, speaking to Hernando, 'to meet the man who saved Doña Isabel from martyrdom at the hands of the heretics. I know of your heroic feat with Don Alfonso de Córdoba and many other Christians.' Hernando tried to hide his surprise. Since his arrival in Granada rumours had been circulating about many exploits beyond the only two acts that could legitimately be attributed to him. 'Doña Isabel', continued the priest, waving discreetly at her, 'is one of my most pious parishioners – it could be said the most pious of all – and we are truly grateful that you saved her soul for the Lord.'

Hernando looked across at his hostess, who accepted the compliment modestly.

'I have spoken with some of the cathedral canons,' the priest went on, 'and there is a certain matter we would like to propose to you. I am sure the dean, who I believe will be sharing your table, will speak to you of it.'

These words preoccupied Hernando as he greeted the rest of the eminent individuals entering the house. What 'matter' was he referring to? What could the members of the cathedral chapter possibly want with him?

It was not long before he found out. Hernando was indeed invited to occupy a place of honour at the large top table placed in one of the main garden's vine-covered colonnades. He was seated between Don Ponce and the city governor. Opposite him were Juan de Fonseca, dean of the cathedral, and two titled councillors of Granada, a marquis and a count. The rest of the guests were seated in order of precedence. There was an identical table in the colonnade on the other side of the pool, where Hernando could distinguish Don Sancho talking animatedly with his fellow diners. As well as these two tables there were many more set out across the terraced gardens and vegetable plots that spread down the hillside. Some were for the men, most of them dressed strictly in black according to Tridentine norms. At others were the women, vying with each other in ostentation and beauty. In the arbour at the end of the main garden was a group of musicians playing a sackbut, a cornet and an oboe, two flutes, a tambour and a vihuela; the music enlivening the cool, clear and starry night.

While they were enjoying the first course of stuffed partridges and capons, Hernando had to satisfy the curiosity of Don Ponce's guests. He was bombarded with questions about the captivity and escape of Don Alfonso de Córdoba, and one or two of a more cautious, polite nature about the judge's wife.

'I gather', intervened one of the councillors as he nibbled on a partridge wing, 'that besides the duke and Doña Isabel you helped many more Christians.'

The question hung in the air just as the vihuela struck up a song, and one of the musicians began to sing. Hernando listened to the instrument's melancholic strum, so similar to that of the lutes played at Morisco celebrations.

'Do you remember who they were?' asked the governor, turning towards him.

'Yes, but not in every case,' he lied. He had prepared the answer when he heard the rumours about his supposed help of more Christians.

The councillor stopped picking at the wing, and there was an uncomfortable silence.

'Who?' the cathedral dean pressed him.

'I would prefer not to say.' At that, even Don Ponce stopped munching on a capon breast and looked at him. Why not? his eyes seemed to ask. Hernando cleared his throat before explaining: 'Some of them had to leave family and friends behind. I saw them weep as they fled; love and terror clashing in their consciences as they fought to survive. There was one who, when he was free and safe in hiding, chose instead to return and be executed alongside his children.' Several of the listening diners nodded solemnly, their lips pursed, some with their eyes closed. 'I ought not to reveal their identities,' Hernando insisted. 'It would serve no purpose now. Wars . . . wars cause men to forget their principles and act according to their instincts.'

His words gave rise to more nods of agreement and a silence that allowed them to hear the vihuela's final lament, lingering in the night until the diners recovered their spirits.

'You do well to say nothing,' Dean Fonseca agreed. 'Humility is a great virtue in people, and the fear of death or torture pardonable in those who yielded. However, I trust your silence does not extend to the heretics who shed so much Christian blood and committed so many acts of sacrilege and desecration.' Hernando fixed his blue eyes on the dean. 'The Archbishop of Granada is carrying out an investigation into the martyrs of the Alpujarra. We have information and declarations from the thousands of widows who lost husbands and children in the slaughter. However, we believe the knowledge of someone like you, a good Christian who experienced the tragedy from the position of the Moriscos, as one of them, could be an invaluable source of information. We need you to help us in the study of the martyrs. What happened? When? Where? How? Who ordered it and who carried it out?'

'But . . .' Hernando stammered.

'Granada has to verify these martyrs with Rome,' the governor interrupted him. 'We have spent almost a hundred years, from the very moment the city was reconquered by the Catholic monarchs, searching for the remains of its patron Saint Caecilius, but all efforts have been in vain. This city needs to be on the same footing as the other Christian centres in the Spanish realms: Santiago, Toledo, Tarragona . . . Granada was the last city seized from the Moors. It lacks Christian antecedents, like the apostle Saint James or Saint Ildefonsus. It is precisely those valiant Christians who make their cities great. Without saints, without martyrs, without Christian history, a city is nothing.'

'You know I live in Córdoba,' was the only excuse Hernando could think of when he found the eyes of all the other diners upon him.

'That is no problem whatsoever,' the dean was quick to point out, as if by so doing he was closing the door on any other objection. 'You will be able to continue doing so. The archbishop will provide you with documents and sufficient money for your trips.'

'I knew you would not fail such a just and holy cause,' Don Ponce declared, patting Hernando on the shoulder. 'As soon as I discovered the church in Granada was interested in your participation, I wrote to the Duke of Monterreal asking his permission, but I knew it would not be necessary.'

Someone raised a glass of wine, and immediately the guests closest to Hernando drank a toast to him.

The dinner ended and the musicians moved inside the mansion to the main hall, which had been cleared of all furniture. Some of the guests dispersed in groups around the garden or the large terrace that extended out from the hall, rising above the bed of the river Darro. The Alhambra was opposite them and the Albaicín at their feet. Other guests prepared for the dance. Hernando saw Don Sancho lingering in the hall waiting for the music to start, and envied his happiness and lack of cares. That assignment from the archbishopric was all he needed! Even his mother had turned her back on him, and now he had to work for the Church . . . denouncing his brothers!

He listened to the music and watched how men and women danced, in circles or in rows, in pairs or in groups, drawing near to one another, smiling, flirting even, everyone leaping at the same moment; as the hidalgo had done in Don Alfonso's palace. He recognized Isabel in her green dress and high cork-soled shoes, which glittered when her skirt lifted off the floor. The height of her shoes did not prevent her from dancing elegantly. On several occasions he thought he caught her glancing at him out of the corner of her eye.

As the dance wore on, Hernando found himself obliged to greet the many guests who approached him and to answer their questions, although his mind was elsewhere.

His entire life had been the same, he thought, whilst a woman dressed in blue talked to him; he let her words flow over him without paying attention. He had spent his whole life caught between Christians and Muslims. The son of a priest who had raped a Morisco girl, as a child they had wanted to kill him in Juviles church for being Christian; later Aben Humeya had honoured him as the saviour of their brothers' treasure, yet he had ended up falling into slavery accused of being a Christian, a time when he had to refuse to renounce a religion that was not his own so as not to become one of Barrax's 'sons'. In the cathedral of Córdoba itself, he had worked as a Christian for the cathedral chapter, copying the revealed word a thousand and one times. At the same time, the Inquisition had forced him to witness, as a good Christian who collaborated with the Holy Office, the torture and death of Karim. And now, just as he had found the strange, surprising gospel of Barnabas, the Church had reappeared yet again, imposing a new collaboration on him. And yet he knew who his God was, the one, the merciful ... What would the good Hamid think of him if he could see him now?

'I am sorry, I do not know how to dance,' he blurted out in response to the questioning gaze of the lady in blue, who was still at his side and seemed to be waiting for an answer.

He had not heard her question. Perhaps that was not the appropriate response, he concluded when he saw the woman's offended expression. She turned her back on him without bidding him farewell.

The dance continued until well into the night. Don Sancho reappeared sweating on the terrace when at Don Ponce's insistence the music stopped. The dance was over.

'As a finale to the celebrations,' shouted the judge from the small platform where the musicians had been playing, 'I invite you all to witness the firework display we have prepared in honour of our guest. Please would you all move to the terraces and gardens.'

Don Ponce looked for his wife and then went to Hernando. 'Please join us,' he requested.

They were in the front row, next to the balustrade that enclosed the terrace of the main hall. Isabel was behind Hernando and Dean Fonseca. At a signal from someone in the gardens, part of the Alhambra walls erupted in an intense yellow flame. The people crowded behind them gasped in delight as balls of fire shot up into the starry sky, and they all pressed closer to the balustrade to get a better view of the display. Streaks of light shot across the night sky, as Hernando felt the warmth of Isabel's body. The thunderous explosions of gunpowder and Isabel's warm, rapid breathing in his ear mingled inside his head. Isabel did not move or seek to avoid the contact. The guests were absorbed in the fireworks; nobody noticed the gesture but Hernando felt a hand brush against his own. He turned his head. Isabel gave him the hint of a shy smile. He gently squeezed her hand. Amidst the tumultuous throng of guests on the terrace, their fingers stroked and intertwined. They pressed their bodies up against one another, until a string of firecrackers brought the firework display to an end and everyone broke out into cheers and applause.

Soon afterwards the guests began to leave. This time Hernando had no doubt: amidst the hustle and bustle of good-byes, when his eyes fixed on Isabel, she held his gaze.

48

'WHAT HAPPENED in Juviles?'
The cathedral chapter clerk was quick to ask this question once the formal introductions had been completed. He was ready to write down everything Hernando said in the small room next to the archive.

Early in the morning after the celebrations, while the rest of the house was still asleep – except for the judge, whom nothing or nobody could keep from his duties – Hernando had been obliged to answer the dean's summons. He mounted Volador and, accompanied by a servant, crossed the Albaicín to Calle de San Juan. He went past the San Gregorio hermitage and from there into Calle de la Cárcel, which gave on to the cathedral. As in Córdoba, this was still being built: work on the chancel was complete, and the towers were being raised; however, unlike in Córdoba, the building in Granada was not on top of the old mosque, but alongside it. The large mosque and its minaret had been converted into the sacristy, which included several chapels and ecclesiastical offices. Hernando passed under the low ceilings of the Muslims' place of prayer, staring up at the white stone columns ending in arches that supported the wooden roof beams and divided the mosque into five naves. From there a priest accompanied him to the chapter clerk's office.

What should he say about Juviles? he wondered while the man, quill poised to write, waited for his reply. That his mother had stabbed the parish priest to death?

'It is hard and truly painful for me', said Hernando, trying to avoid the question, 'to tell you about Juviles and the horror I was forced to witness there. My memories of it are very confused.' The clerk raised his eyes and frowned. 'Perhaps ... perhaps it would be more practical if you allowed me to think it over, gather my thoughts, and then write them down and send them to you.'

'Do you know how to write?' asked the clerk, surprised.

'Yes. In fact, it was the Juviles sacristan, Andrés, who taught me.'

What had become of Andrés? he wondered. He had heard nothing more of him since arriving in Córdoba.

'I am sorry to have to tell you that he died recently,' said the clerk, as if reading his mind. 'We learnt he had gone to live in Córdoba, and searched for him so that he could testify, but to no avail.'

Hernando sighed with relief, but then started to shift uneasily on the hard, battered chair on which he was sitting at the clerk's desk. Why not put an end to this farce? He was a Muslim! He believed in the one true God and in Muhammad's prophetic mission. As he was thinking this over, the clerk closed the bundle of papers on his table.

'I have a lot to do,' he said. 'You would save me valuable time if you told us what you have to say in writing.'

Time and effort, Hernando said to himself when the man stood up and shook his hand.

The sun was shining brightly, and Granada was bustling with activity. Hernando climbed back on Volador and considered dismissing the servant so that he could wander through the city. He could explore the silk-weavers' quarter or find an inn where he could try and make sense of everything that was happening to him. The previous evening, when the house and garden had emptied of guests, he had prayed, thinking of Isabel. He remembered the warmth of her body and the touch of her hand. Why had she felt for his hand? The servant was awaiting his orders impatiently. And on top of that, Juviles. All of a sudden, Hernando tugged on his horse's reins. He recalled the Christians in the village, naked and with their hands tied behind their backs, waiting in a line to be killed in a field, while the Moriscos, his mother among them, finished off the priest and his assistant. Many of those men had survived thanks to El Zaguer's clemency, when he went against Barrax's orders. What might they have said? They must all have witnessed Aisha's cruelty, and her cries to heaven invoking Allah, the bloody dagger still in her hand after she had wreaked her vengeance. Had they linked her to him? Hernando's mother had murdered Don Martín! Probably not, he reassured himself. The most they would have done was connect Aisha with Brahim, the village muleteer, rather than with a fourteen-year-old boy, although there was still the possibility . . .

'Let's go back to the house,' he told the servant, spurring his horse on without waiting for him.

Hernando found Don Sancho having breakfast on his own. 'Good morning,' he greeted him.

'I see you're up early,' the hidalgo replied. Sitting at the table, Hernando explained the dean's summons and his prompt appearance in front of the clerk. Don Sancho listened while he ate. 'Well, I have another summons for you. Last night I dined with Don Pedro de Granada Venegas,' he said. Hernando frowned. What more did the Christians want from him? 'Every so often,' Don Sancho went on, 'Don Pedro invites people to his house. This time he would like us to come.'

'I am very busy,' Hernando said. 'You go.'

'The invitation is for both of us. In fact, I think it is you that Don Pedro wants to meet,' the hidalgo admitted. 'These are important people,' he insisted. 'Don Pedro is the lord of Campotéjar and chief magistrate of the Generalife. His circumstances are somewhat similar to yours: his family are Muslims who converted to Christianity. Perhaps that is why he wants to meet you. His grandfather, a descendant of the Moorish princes, played a prominent role in the reconquest of Granada, and after that supported the Emperor. His father, Don Alonso, collaborated with King Philip II in the Alpujarra war so whole-heartedly it almost ruined him. To compensate for his losses the King has awarded him a modest pension of four hundred ducats. Many interesting people go to his gatherings. You cannot snub a Granada noble who is related to the grandest Spanish families: my cousin Don Alfonso would be insulted if he found out.'

'If you're threatening me with your cousin's displeasure, you must really want me to go,' Hernando replied sarcastically. 'We'll talk about it another time, Don Sancho,' he said, putting an end to their conversation by standing up.

'But—'

'Some other time, Don Sancho, some other time . . .' he insisted, already on his feet.

Hernando hesitated whether to leave the gardens or not, and in the end decided to take refuge in his bedroom. Isabel, Juviles, the cathedral chapter, and now this invitation to the house of a renegade Muslim noble who had collaborated with the Christians in the Alpujarra war. Everything had gone crazy! He needed to forget, to seek calm, and the best way to do that was to shut himself in and pray for the rest of the morning. He went past the door to Isabel's bedroom just as her chambermaid was leaving the room after helping her to dress. The girl greeted him, and Hernando turned his head to respond. Through the half-open door he could see Isabel smoothing down the skirt of her black dress. The maid took a few moments to close the door, long enough for Isabel, who was leaning over in the centre of the room with the sunlight streaming in through the large window giving on to the balcony, to raise her head and fix her eyes on him.

'Good morning,' Hernando stammered to neither of the two women in particular. He could feel a hot flush spreading through his body.

The maid's lips sketched a discreet smile as she bowed her head. Isabel had no chance to answer before the door shut completely. Hernando found he was breathing heavily when he reached his room, recalling the sensation of Isabel's body pressed against his. Still flustered, he gazed around the room: the magnificent four-poster bed that had already been made; the inlaid clothes chest; the tapestries with biblical scenes all round the walls; the table with a washbasin to wash in, and the carefully folded linen towels next to it. And in the far wall the door leading to the same balcony that ran outside the judge's bedroom and that of his wife, overlooking the Alhambra.

The Alhambra! 'Unhappy he who lost such a thing.' Staring out at the fortress, Hernando recalled the phrase that the Emperor Charles was said to have uttered. Someone had explained to the King how Aisha, mother of Boabdil, the last Muslim King of Granada, condemned him for weeping as he abandoned the city to the Catholic monarchs: 'You are right to cry like a woman for what you did not have the courage to defend like a man.'

'The King's mother was right to say what she did,' it was said the Emperor replied, 'because if I had been him, I would have preferred this Alhambra to be my tomb than to live without my kingdom in the Alpujarra.'

Fascinated by the palace's red outline, Hernando was startled to see that Isabel had left her room and was leaning languidly over the low stone balustrade of the balcony on the second floor of the house, also contemplating the wonderful Nasrid fortress. Still inside his own room, Hernando gazed at Isabel's blond hair gathered up in a net, her slender neck, and the voluptuous curves of her body.

Hernando took two steps out on to the balcony. When she heard the noise, Isabel turned towards him; her eyes were shining.

'It's hard to choose between two such beautiful sights,' said Hernando, gesturing towards her and the Alhambra.

She straightened up, turned, and came towards him, hardly knowing where to look. They were so close they almost breathed as one. She reached out and brushed the fingers of his hand.

'But you can only possess one of them,' she whispered.

'Isabel,' sighed Hernando.

'I have dreamt a thousand nights about that day we rode together,' she said, moving his hand down towards her stomach. 'A thousand nights I've shivered just as I did that day when your hand touched me.'

Isabel kissed him. A long, warm, sweet kiss that Hernando received with his eyes tight closed. When she drew her head back, Hernando pulled her into his room. He made sure that the door to the corridor was barred, and did the same with the one that gave on to the balcony.

They kissed again in the centre of the room. Hernando slid his hands down her back, struggling with the hooped skirt that prevented him feeling her body. Despite her passionate kisses and excited breathing, Isabel did not move her hands from his waist to hold him. Hernando tried to undo the fastenings of the bodice of her dress, but was too clumsy.

Isabel moved away from him and turned so that it would be easier for him to undo it.

As Hernando struggled with the hooks with trembling fingers, Isabel undid the detachable sleeves and threw them on the floor. Hernando finally managed to undo the fastenings of the top half of her bodice, which fell forward and freed her breasts from the pressure of the corset. He untied the laces round her waist, and Isabel finally stepped out of her uncomfortable skirts. Feeling for her breasts beneath her shift, Hernando removed her bodice. He started to kiss her neck. Isabel tried to pull back, but he squeezed her all the more tightly. Whispering in her ear, he slid his hand down towards her thighs; the hem of her voluminous chemise was gathered beneath her groin and buttocks, covering her most intimate parts. He clumsily untied the knots.

'No . . .' Isabel protested when she felt Hernando's fingers probing the moistness between her legs. He paused, and she escaped from his grasp. Flushed and trembling, she murmured, 'No,' a second time.

Was he rushing her? Hernando wondered.

She stretched her hands out to his chest. To his surprise she did not start to undo his doublet, but instead kissed him, and then turned away towards the bed. She lay on it still in her shift, her legs bent and slightly apart.

Hernando stood at the foot of the bed, watching her breasts rise and fall in time with her rapid breathing.

'Take me,' she said, opening her legs a little further.

'Take me'? Was that all? She was still dressed! He had not even seen her naked, or been able to caress or play with her until she was aroused, to get to know her body. He went over to the bed and lay alongside her. He made to lift the chemise to get a glimpse of the dark triangle veiled underneath, but Isabel sat up and caught hold of his hand.

'Take me,' she repeated, after kissing him passionately once more.

Hernando got to his feet and began to take his clothes off. She might not be able to . . . but he was. He continued until he was stark naked at the foot of the bed, his penis erect. Isabel turned her head, staring into space. She sighed as she opened her legs a little further. The chemise fell back to the top of her thighs.

Hernando looked at her. It was obvious she wanted him: she was sighing and moving nervously in the bed, waiting for him to enter her, and yet . . . this was the only position she knew! Sin! It was a sin to take pleasure in making love. An image suddenly flashed through his mind: Fátima, naked, tattooed with henna and covered in oil, moving until she found the most pleasurable position for both of them, writhing between his legs, directing his caresses without any sense of shame. Fátima! He heard Isabel groan and returned to reality. Christians! he said to himself, before plunging on top of her despite the barrier of the shift between them.

Isabel could not free herself from her prejudices as

Hernando started to move slowly, rhythmically on top of her. She clasped him round his back, but still looked away, as if scared of meeting his eye. And her hands did not claw at him.

'Enjoy it,' he whispered in her ear.

Isabel bit her lips and closed her eyes. Hernando moved gently to and fro, trying to understand her stifled groans.

'Free yourself!' he urged her, as the light from the window enveloped their bodies.

'Push,' he begged her. 'Feel me. Feel yourself. Feel your body. Let yourself go, my love. Enjoy it, for God's sake!' Hernando reached his climax still urging her to take pleasure in their love-making. He lay panting on her. He wondered whether Isabel would enjoy it more a second time. Would she . . . ? The answer came when she wriggled from beneath him, as though to show she wanted to get away. Hernando rested his body on his hands, kissing her once more. There was no answering passion in her kiss. He got up off the bed and she did the same, still not look-ing at him.

'There's no reason for you to be ashamed,' he said, trying to reassure her and reaching out to cup her chin. Isabel would have none of it, and ran out barefoot on to the balcony and back into her room.

Hernando clicked his tongue, then bent to pick up his clothes, strewn all round the foot of the bed. He had no doubt at all that Isabel desired him, he reflected as he put his shirt on, but feelings of guilt, sin and shame had overwhelmed her. 'Woman is a fruit that only offers her perfume when rubbed in the hand,' he remembered Fátima explaining to him in her soft voice, repeating the lessons she had learnt from the Muslim books about love. 'Woman is like a basil plant, or like amber, which only gives off its scent when warmed. If you fail to arouse a woman with caresses and kisses, sucking her lips and drink-ing from her mouth, biting the inside of her thighs and squeezing her breasts, you will not find what you want in her bed: pleasure. Nor will her affection for you last if she does not reach ecstasy, if, when the moment comes, her vagina does not grip your penis.' How shocking pious Christian women would find these lessons in love!

On the far side of the strait separating Spain from Barbary, stretched out in the semi-darkness of the palace Brahim had built for her in the centre of Tetuan, Fátima found it impossible to sleep. By her side she could hear the breathing of the man she most hated in the world. She could feel the touch of his skin, and could not prevent a shudder of horror running through her. As on every other night, Brahim had satisfied his desire with her; as on every other night, Fátima had pressed herself to him so that he could rub the stump of his arm between her breasts, easing the pain he still felt there. As on every other night, the groans from the Christians held captive in the underground jails of the city were like echoes of the thousand unanswered questions swirling round her brain. What could have become of Ibn Hamid? Why had he not come in search of her? Was he still alive?

Throughout the three years she had been in Brahim's power, she had never lost hope that the man she loved would come and rescue her. As time went by, however, she realized that Aisha must have respected her silent plea. What could she have said to her son to prevent him coming to find her? It could only have been one thing: that they were all dead. If not that . . . if she had said anything else, Ibn Hamid would have followed her and fought to win them back. She was certain of that! But even if Aisha had assured him that his family was dead, why had he not sought to take revenge on Brahim? In the still of the night, she heard once more the cries of the Marquis of Casabermeja's men as they abducted her: *In the name of Ubaid, Morisco outlaw, close your doors and windows if you don't want to get hurt!* Everyone in Córdoba must think it was Ubaid who had killed them, and if Aisha had said nothing . . . Ibn Hamid would not know anything about what had happened. That must be it! If not, he would have moved heaven and earth to avenge them. She was sure of it . . . Revenge! The same sentiment that, over a period of months when she finally became convinced Hernando was not coming to rescue her, she had managed to stifle in Brahim.

'He's nothing but a coward,' Brahim had said repeatedly. 'If he doesn't come to Tetuan to rescue his family, I'll send a party to kill him.'

Fátima was careful to avoid telling him that she thought Hernando was not going to come, that she herself had made a silent plea to Aisha not to tell him what had happened.

'If you abandon your plans to kill him, I will give myself to you,' she said one night after he had mounted her as though she were an animal. 'You'll be able to enjoy me like a real wife. I will give myself completely. If you don't, I'll kill myself.'

'What about your children?' Brahim threatened her.

'They will be left in God's hands,' she murmured.

The corsair thought her proposal over. Eventually: 'Very well,' he said.

'Swear it by Allah,' Fátima demanded.

'I swear by God Almighty,' he said, already thinking of what he was going to gain.

'Brahim,' said Fátima, frowning and speaking sternly to him, 'you must not try to deceive me. If you break our pact, I'll be able to tell from your smile, your state of mind.'

From that moment on, Fátima had kept her side of the bargain. Night after night, she led Brahim to ecstasy. She bore him two more daughters, and the corsair no longer visited his second wife, who was relegated to a separate wing of the palace. Shamir and Francisco – who had been renamed Abdul – were both circumcised as soon as they reached Tetuan. They were preparing to go to sea some day soon under the orders of Nasi, who was daily assuming more responsibilities in the acts of piracy as if he were Brahim's true successor. Brahim himself grew fat, and was only concerned with counting and recounting the profits from the raids on Spain, as well as his many other business ventures. It was easy for Nasi, the flea-bitten waif that the corsair had taken on when he first arrived in Tetuan, to take the place that should by right have gone to the eldest son: Shamir refused to recognize Brahim as the father he had never had. At first, he was so terrified, and missed the mother he had left behind so much, that he refused to show him any affection, and sought refuge in Fátima and Francisco. Aisha had told him his father had been killed in the Alpujarra! Brahim felt slighted, and responded with his habitual brutality. He would snatch the boy out of Fátima's arms, and beat and insult him when he tried to escape his grasp. Francisco, also mistreated by Brahim, became his inseparable companion in misfortune. Nasi took advantage of the situation, and made sure the corsair saw how faithful and loyal he was, constantly and slyly reminding him of all they had been through together. Little Inés, meanwhile, who had been given the name of Maryam, met the fate Brahim had foretold in the Montón de la Tierra inn: she became his second wife's maid. She stayed a servant until Fátima had her and Brahim's first daughter, following a night of passion, she managed to convince him that there could be no one better than Maryam, her half-sister, to look after the newborn baby Nushaima.

Brahim's snores, mixed with the cries from the dungeons, interrupted Fátima's thoughts. She fought against her urge to move, to get up from the bed, to shift Brahim's stump off her body. She was a prisoner . . . a prisoner in a golden jail.

She saw herself as nothing more than another slave, one of the many who served in the luxurious palace Brahim had built. It was in the style of an Andalusian house round a central courtyard, and stood in the market, near the public baths, the fortress and the Sidi al-Mandari mosque, constructed by the exile from Granada who had refounded the city. Fátima had never before lived with slaves: men and women who were willing to satisfy every demand their masters made of them. She saw their total lack of expression, as if they had been robbed of their souls and all feeling. When she looked at them, she saw herself reflected in their faces: obedient and submissive.

The new palace the corsair leader had built for himself and

his family was situated in al-Metamar Street, on top of the vast network of subterranean caves on Mount Dersa, where Tetuan stood. The caves were used as dungeons for thousands of Christian prisoners. During the day, when Fátima went out with her slaves to one of the city's three gates to buy fresh food from the farmers who brought their produce there from the fields outside, she often saw the captives straining under the whip, shackled together and dressed in coarse woollen tunics. There were four thousand Christians forced to do whatever was required of them in the city.

Surrounded by all these subjugated slaves and captives, Fátima soon understood that walking round the streets would bring her no respite. Tetuan was like an Andalusian city, but there was no Christian influence in its buildings whatsoever. The houses were the clearest examples of the sacredness of the family home: to the streets they were situated on, they presented blind walls with no windows, balconies or openings. The laws of inheritance meant the buildings were divided and subdivided until they became chaotic jumbles, while the streets were no more than the external projection of these private properties. This meant that the city's public spaces were filled with shops and stalls that sprang up utterly randomly. Some of these overhung the streets; others protruded into them or blocked them completely as a result of an agreement between neighbours – usually family members. The city authorities had no control over it at all.

Fátima was not only a slave in her palace; outside it there was nowhere in this corsair stronghold that gave her any respite from her predicament, even for a few brief moments. God seemed to have forsaken her. It was only in the squares, where three or more streets met, that she found if not spiritual relief, then at least some entertainment, thanks to the performers who sang or told legends to the sound of a lute, or sold people pieces of paper inscribed with elaborate lettering they claimed would ward off all ills. She was also amused by the snake charmers, who had snakes wrapped round their necks or arms at the same time as they made monkeys dance ridiculous jigs for coins thrown by the public. Fátima herself occasionally rewarded them with one. At night though there was no escape, as she lay there with Brahim's stump between her breasts, her ears filled with the cries and groans of the thousands of Christians incarcerated beneath the palace, sounds that rose clearly up through the holes in the rocks that were the only ventilation for the underground dungeons that stretched beneath almost the entire city. One day I will be free, Fátima told herself. One day we will be together again, Ibn Hamid.

49

FACED WITH Don Sancho's insistence, Hernando finally gave in and agreed to go to the Casa de los Tiros, where the Granada Venegas family held their gatherings. At dusk one June day the two men mounted their horses and rode down from the Albaicín to the Realejo, the former Jewish quarter the Catholic monarchs had taken possession of after they had conquered Granada and expelled the Jews. The district was on the left bank of the river Darro, beneath the Alhambra. The Casa de los Tiros was situated in front of the Franciscan monastery and church, together with other palaces and noble houses built on the land of the demolished Jewry.

During their ride, Hernando was hardly listening to the contented hidalgo's conversation. In the days preceding this visit he had tried to fulfil the promise he had made to the cathedral chapter clerk to write his version of what had happened in Juviles during the Alpujarra uprising. He had found, though, that not only did he lack the words to excuse the monstrous outrages his brothers in faith had perpetrated, but that whenever he tried to concentrate, his mind wandered to Isabel and to the memories he had of the day when his mother had butchered Don Martín.

I don't want to see them die, he recalled saying to Hamid when they saw the long line of naked, bound Christians being led out into the field. *Why do we have to kill them?*

I don't like it either, the holy man had replied, *but we have to . . . They forced us to become Christians under threat of expulsion,*

and that is another form of dying, to be sent far from your home-
land and your family. They have refused to recognize the one true
God; they have not taken advantage of the opportunity they were
given. They have chosen to die.

How was he supposed to make sense of Hamid's words in a
report for the archbishop? As for Isabel, she seemed to have
recovered from the sense of shame that made her flee the bedroom after their only meeting, and went around the house and
garden with no apparent qualms. And yet whenever their eyes
met, Hernando could not be sure: sometimes she kept looking
at him for an instant longer than necessary, at others she
quickly looked down. The person who did not look away was
Isabel's chambermaid, who even allowed herself to grin
cheekily at him: she must have been the one who picked up her
mistress's clothes.

The morning of the day he was to go to the Granada Venegas'
gathering he again met Isabel on the balcony. Their mutual
desire was plain from the uncomfortable silence between them.
Despite the passion he felt, Hernando had no wish to repeat an
experience that had only satisfied his instincts, without giving
them the pleasure he had hoped for.

'You need to learn to enjoy your body,' he whispered to her,
watching her shudder as he spoke the words.

Isabel blushed, but said nothing, and allowed herself to be
taken a second time into Hernando's room.

Hernando had wanted to tell her it was possible to find God
through pleasure, but in the end he simply tried to give her as
much satisfaction as possible, endeavouring not to frighten her
when she went stiff and tried to stifle her groans. Isabel allowed
him to caress her breasts, but would not bare them, and stood
with her back to him, biting her lower lip when she felt him
squeezing her erect nipples. Afterwards, she was gone like a soul
snatched by the devil, leaving her clothes on the floor as she had
done before.

'We've arrived,' said the hidalgo, startling Hernando out of
his daydreams.

Hernando found himself outside a square tower with battlements. There were two balconies on the front, and five full-length sculptures of figures from antiquity. Behind the square tower was a substantial building, with many large rooms on several floors arranged around a courtyard of six columns with Nasrid capitals, and a garden at the far end. After they had left their horses with servants, the two men entered the palace, and were led up a narrow stairway to a large hall on the second floor.

'This hall is known as the Golden Stable,' Don Sancho whispered as the servant pushed open a pair of doors with laurel-crowned busts carved on them.

As soon as he entered the room, Hernando understood its name. The hall was illuminated by golden reflections from the magnificent coffered ceiling, painted in green and gold and full of sculpted male figures.

'Welcome.' Don Pedro de Granada came across to them from a group of men he was talking to. He held out his hand to Hernando. 'We were presented at the celebration the chief magistrate Don Ponce held in your honour, but could only exchange a brief greeting on that occasion. You are most welcome in my house.'

Hernando took the noble's hand, which seemed to be gripping his longer than necessary. He was able to survey him close to – a thin man, with a broad, clear forehead, a carefully trimmed dark beard and an intelligent gleam in his eyes – and tried hard not to let the prejudices he had brought to their meeting show: Don Pedro and his ancestors had renounced the true religion and collaborated with the Christians.

After greeting the hidalgo, the lord of Campotéjar presented them to the others: Luis Barahona de Soto, a physician and poet; Joan de Faría, a lawyer and chancery official; Gonzalo Mateo de Berrío, also a poet; and several other people. Hernando felt ill at ease. Why had he allowed Don Sancho to persuade him to come? What did he have to talk about with all these strangers? In one of the corners of the room stood two men, each with a glass of wine in their hand. Don Pedro led him over to meet them.

'Don Miguel de Luna, physician and translator,' he said, introducing the first of them.

Hernando greeted him.

'Don Alonso del Castillo,' said their host, referring to the other elegantly dressed man. 'He is also a physician, and the official translator from Arabic for the Granada Inquisition, and now for King Philip II.'

Don Alonso held out his hand, not taking his eyes off Hernando's face. Hernando held his gaze and shook his hand.

'I wanted to meet you.' Hernando was startled. The translator was not only speaking to him in Arabic, but was increasing the pressure on his hand. 'I have heard of your exploits in the Alpujarra.'

'One should not attach too much importance to them,' replied Hernando in Spanish. More praise for setting Christians free! 'This is Don Sancho, from Córdoba,' he said, freeing his hand and gesturing towards the hidalgo.

'Cousin of Don Alfonso de Córdoba, the Duke of Monterreal,' Don Sancho boasted, as he had done with everyone else to whom he had been presented.

'Don Sancho,' Pedro de Granada butted in. 'I don't think I've introduced you to the marquis yet.' The hidalgo puffed himself up at the mere mention of the title. 'Come with me.'

When Hernando made to follow the two men, Castillo laid his hand on his forearm and held him back. Miguel de Luna stepped in front of him as well, so that the three men formed a small group in the corner of the Golden Stable.

'I have also heard', the translator went on, this time in Spanish, 'that you are collaborating with the bishop over the Christians martyred in the Alpujarra.'

'That's right.'

'And that you used to work in the royal stables at Córdoba,' added Miguel de Luna.

Hernando frowned. 'That is also correct,' he said brusquely.

'In Córdoba,' the former said, ignoring Hernando's tone and still holding him by the arm, 'you helped in the cathedral as a translator—'

'Gentlemen,' Hernando said, cutting him short and freeing his arm, 'did you invite me here to subject me to an interrogation?'

Neither of them reacted.

'There's someone who worked in the library of Córdoba cathedral . . .' Don Alonso went on, taking Hernando gently by the arm once more, as though to prevent him escaping, '. . . Don Julián.'

Hernando looked askance at them, and again broke free of the pressure on his arm. For a few moments the three men stared at each other in silence, trying to judge what each was thinking. Miguel de Luna was the first to speak.

'We have heard of Don Julián, the librarian in the Córdoba cathedral chapter.'

Hernando hesitated, and fidgeted restlessly. Elsewhere in the hall, groups of people were standing talking animatedly, or sitting in luxurious armchairs near low tables crammed with wines and sweetmeats.

'Listen,' Castillo said. 'Like Don Pedro de Granada, Miguel and I are descendants of Muslims. After the war in the Alpujarra, where I worked as a translator first for the Marquis of Mondéjar and then for Prince John of Austria, I was asked by King Philip to look after the Arabic books and manuscripts in El Escorial monastery. He wanted me to translate them, to catalogue them . . . Another task the King set me was to search for and acquire new books in Arabic. I found some in the Córdoba region: a couple of copies of the Koran the royal library was not interested in, and some copies of prophecies and lunar calendars.'

The translator fell silent. No longer struggling to free his arm, Hernando had a moment to think. What did these two renegades want from him? They had collaborated with the Christians! Their forebears were the ones who surrendered Granada to the Catholic monarchs, and they had no problem admitting that they themselves had been on the side of the Christians in the Alpujarra war. They were nobles, scholars, physicians or poets who wanted to convert others, just like Don Pedro de Granada. Castillo even worked for the Inquisition! What if this invitation had simply been to unmask him?

'In the end I did not buy them.' This sudden affirmation by the translator put Hernando on his guard. 'They were written on coarse modern paper and interspersed with *aljamiado*, as if—'

'Why are you telling me all this?' Hernando interrupted him. 'What is it you are telling my guest?'

Hernando turned round and found himself face to face with Don Pedro de Granada.

'We were telling him about the work Alonso does in the royal library,' explained Luna, 'and we said we knew Don Julián, the librarian at Córdoba cathedral.'

'He was a good man,' the nobleman said. 'A person dedicated to the defence of religion . . .'

The lord of Campotéjar left his final words floating in mid-air. Hernando could feel the attention of all three men on him. What could he have meant? Concealed beneath his priest's habit, Don Julián was a Muslim.

'Yes,' he lied. 'Don Julián was a good Christian.'

Don Pedro, Luna and Castillo exchanged glances. The nobleman nodded to Castillo, as if giving him permission. Checking to see that no one could overhear, the translator went on: 'Don Julián told me it was you who made copies of the Koran,' he announced solemnly, 'so that they could be distributed around Córdoba . . .'

'I didn't—' Hernando began.

'He also told me', Castillo said, increasing the pressure on Hernando's arm as he spoke, 'that you were fully trusted by the council of elders along with Karim, Jalil and . . . what was his name? Yes: Hamid, the holy man from Juviles.'

Surrounded by the three men, Hernando had no idea what to say or where to turn.

'Hamid was a descendant of the Nasrid dynasty,' Don Pedro said. 'We were distantly related. His family chose another destiny: they followed Boabdil into exile in the Alpujarra, but chose not to follow the "Little King" when he fled to Barbary.'

Hernando tugged and finally freed his arm from Castillo. 'Gentlemen,' he began, making as though to leave the group, 'I don't understand what it is you want from me, but—'

'Listen,' Castillo interrupted him, at the same time stepping aside as though to indicate that Hernando was free to leave the group if he so wished, 'do you really believe that Don Julián would have betrayed you and told us everything we have just said to you if we were nothing more than a group of mere renegades as you think?'

Hernando paused. Don Julián? A thousand memories flashed through his mind. He would never have done that! He would have preferred to die under torture first, as Karim had done. Not even the Inquisition had been able to get the name they wanted out of him: his own name, Hernando Ruiz of Juviles! True Muslims did not denounce one of their own.

'Think about it,' he heard Luna say.

'I know a lot about you,' Castillo insisted. 'Don Julián held you in high esteem, and had great respect for you.'

Why had the librarian found it necessary to tell them anything? Hernando wondered. If he had, that could only mean these three men were fighting for the same cause as him. But was he himself still fighting for anything? Even his mother had repudiated him.

'I have nothing to do with any of that now,' he said weakly. 'Our community in Córdoba turned its back on me when they found out that I helped Christians during the war.'

'We have all played that game,' Don Pedro de Granada said. 'Myself first and foremost. Look,' he went on, pointing to a large chest behind Miguel de Luna, who stepped aside so that Hernando could see it more clearly. 'Can you see the coat of arms? That is of the House of the Granada Venegas: we bore it when we fought with the Christian monarchs against our people. But can you see its motto?'

'*Lagaleblila*,' Hernando read out loud. 'What does that mean . . . ?'

He himself answered, as he deciphered the meaning: *wa la galib ilallah.* 'There is no victor but God!' The motto of the Nasrid dynasty that was repeated throughout the Alhambra to the honour and glory of the one God: Allah.

'We are not interested in what old people in the Morisco communities think we should do,' Castillo said. 'They are all in favour of either armed insurrection or conversion to the true faith. All of them are expecting the Turks, Berbers or the French to come to their aid. But we don't think that is the answer. Nobody will come to our aid, and if they did – if anyone finally decided to do so – the Christians would annihilate us: we Moriscos would be the first to fall. And in the meantime, peaceful coexistence between the two communities grows more impossible by the day. The Moriscos in Valencia and Aragón are rebellious, and those from Granada are no more than a people without a homeland! Six months ago four thousand five hundred Moriscos who had gone back secretly to their previous homes were expelled from Granada a second time. There are many voices now clamouring for all the Moriscos to be expelled from Spain, or for far more cruel, bloodthirsty measures to be adopted against them. If things go on like this—'

'Then what?' Hernando cut in. 'I know we don't stand much chance in any armed conflict against the Spaniards and that it would be a miracle if anyone came to our aid. But that means all that is left is to be converted as the Christians require of us.'

'No!' Castillo protested vigorously. 'There is another possibility.'

'We have to go back to Córdoba!'

Don Sancho burst into the study where Hernando was trying for the umpteenth time to explain what had happened in Juviles during the uprising. A few days earlier he had read over what he had written so far, then torn everything up. He raised his eyes from a sheet of paper that had remained blank since he had sat down at the desk more than an hour earlier, and saw the hidalgo striding towards him, grim-faced.

'Why? What's wrong?' he asked.

'What's wrong?' shouted Don Sancho. 'You tell me! All the servants in the house are talking about you. You have sullied the honour of a judge in the royal chancery of Granada! If Don Ponce were to find out . . . How dared you do something like that? The gossip could spread through the whole city. I don't want to even think about it! A judge!' Don Sancho scratched the sparse grey hairs on his head. 'We have to leave! To get back to Córdoba at once!'

'What are the servants saying?' Hernando asked casually, desperately trying to gain time.

'You ought to know better than anyone: Isabel!'

'Sit down, Don Sancho,' Hernando said, but the hidalgo waved his hand dismissively, and continued pacing up and down in front of the desk. 'I can see you're angry, but I've no idea why. Isabel and I have done nothing wrong. I have not sullied anyone's honour.'

Don Sancho stopped pacing, rested his fists on the desk and studied Hernando as a teacher would his pupil. Then he looked over the Morisco's shoulder at the garden behind him. Isabel was not there.

'That's not what she says,' he lied.

Hernando turned pale. 'You've . . . you've spoken to Isabel?'

'Yes. A moment ago.'

'And what did she tell you?' Hernando's voice contradicted the self-assurance he was trying to project.

'Everything,' Don Sancho almost shouted. Taking a deep breath, he forced himself to speak more quietly. 'Her face told me everything. Her sense of shame is confession enough. She almost fainted!'

'And how do you expect a pious Christian woman to react if you accuse her of adultery?' Hernando tried to defend himself.

Don Sancho pounded the desk with his fist. 'Don't try to be clever. I know what went on. One of the Christian maids tried to convince a Morisco slave to show her the pleasure that you apparently give her mistress. She wants to be taken "like the Moors do", as she put it.'

Hernando could not hide a tiny smirk of self-satisfaction. It had taken him days and repeated furtive meetings with Isabel to persuade her to give herself to his caresses.

'Satyr!' the hidalgo shouted at him when he saw the Morisco was pleased with what he had heard. 'You have not only taken advantage of the innocence of a young girl who most probably fell into your arms out of a sense of gratitude, but you have perverted her in an obscene, shameless way, violating all the precepts of the Holy Mother Church.'

'Don Sancho!' Hernando objected, trying to calm him.

'Don't you realize?' the hidalgo silenced him again, this time speaking slowly and deliberately. 'The judge will kill you. With his own bare hands.'

Hernando stroked his chin. Behind his back the rays of the sun filtered down into the courtyard.

'What are you thinking?' insisted Don Sancho.

That this was not the moment to stop, Hernando would have liked to tell him. That he was succeeding in making Isabel's eyes look dreamy, and for her to sigh more and more deeply as he caressed her and bit her playfully: sure signs that she now actively wanted to make love. That at each new meeting Isabel left routine ever further behind, rising above guilt, prejudice and Christian teachings. That she was almost ready to experience an ecstasy she had never even imagined. And that, thanks to the pleasure her body showed, he himself would perhaps reach the heavens as he once had with Fátima. Hernando could sense his member stirring in his breeches. In his mind's eye he saw Isabel naked, desirable and voluptuous, straining at the touch of his fingertips and tongue, avid to discover the world.

'I don't think I can leave for Córdoba now,' he told the hidalgo. 'The bishop is expecting my report and, as you know, your friends in the Casa de los Tiros want to see me again.'

'What you should know', Don Sancho roared, 'is that according to law, once Don Ponce has ended your life, he is obliged to kill her as well.'

'Possibly he will not kill either of us.'

'I'll write to my cousin telling him what is going on,' the hidalgo threatened him.

'You will be very careful not to call a lady's honour into question.'

'Is she really worth so much you would risk your life for her?' Don Sancho retorted, striding out of the room before Hernando had time to reply.

What is my life worth? Hernando asked himself after the hidalgo had left, slamming the door. He owned nothing more than a good horse, which he could not ride anywhere because he had nowhere to go and nobody waiting for him: not even his own mother! The duke would not allow him to work, but was sending him out to help the same King who had humiliated his people and expelled them from Granada. He had agreed to work for the bishop's men. 'Keep on drawing up the list of martyrs,' Castillo had advised him in one of their talks. 'We have to be more Christian than the Christians,' he had stressed. The same thing that Abbas had once said! What was the life worth of someone who was always pretending to be something he was not? What was his goal? To allow his life to flow along comfortably thanks to the duke's generosity, as his fawning relations did?

After they had got to know him better, Don Pedro de Granada, Castillo and Luna had revealed their plan to Hernando: to convince the Christians of the good qualities of the Muslims living in Spain, so that they would change their opinion of them. Luna was writing a book entitled *The True History of King Rodrigo*. This was based on the events described in an imaginary Arab manuscript found in El Escorial library, and was intended to show that the conquest of Spain by Muslims from Barbary had been to liberate the Christians suffering under the tyranny of their Goth kings. After the conquest, as he pointed out, there had been eight centuries of peace when the two religions had coexisted side by side.

'Why can't we achieve the same now?' Luna had asked himself rhetorically.

'We have to combat the image the Christians have of the Moriscos,' said Don Pedro. 'Their writers and priests are creating the fiction that we Moriscos are extremely fertile because our women marry as girls and have lots of children. But that's not true! They have the same number as Christians. They also say our women are promiscuous and adulterous. And as for us men, they say since we do not have to do military service or go into the Church, the new Christian population is increasing out of all proportion, and is amassing gold, silver and all kinds of possessions, and so ruining the kingdom. But that's false! They say we are perverted, and murderers. That in secret we profane the name of God. It's all lies! But when it's repeated over and over, when it's shouted out in sermons or published in books, they start to believe it. So we have to use the same weapons to convince them the opposite is true.'

'Listen,' added Castillo. 'If a Berber crosses the strait to come and live in Spain and convert to Christianity, he is received with open arms. No one is suspicious of these new converts, although they may have little real intention of embracing the Catholic faith. But Moriscos who have been living for almost a century as baptized Christians are not accorded the same privileges. We have to change these deep-rooted ideas. To do that we need educated people like you who know how to read and write and who can fight alongside us.'

This had been the story of Hernando's life ever since he was a boy in Juviles, when he had been chosen to guard their goods and look after their livestock in order to avoid paying taxes. And it had been the same in Córdoba. Where had all that got him? To try to win the Christians round seemed as crazy to him as trying to defeat them in a new uprising.

He dropped the quill he still had in his hand on to the blank sheet of paper.

'Yes, Don Sancho,' he murmured towards the closed door of the room, 'it is probably worth risking an absurd life even if it is only for a single moment of pleasure with a woman like her.'

But, he thought, he would have to be careful from now on.

That night after dinner Don Ponce de Hervás withdrew to his study to work. Shortly afterwards, a servant hoping to earn a few coins for supplying his lord with such important information knocked hesitantly at the door. The judge listened to the man's stammered account just as impassively as he listened to the litigants in the chancery.

'Are you sure of what you are telling me?' he demanded when the servant had finished.

'No, your excellency. I only know it is what is being said in the kitchens, the vegetable garden, the servants' bedrooms and your stables, but I cannot vouch for the truth of it. I thought, though, that you would wish to know.'

Don Ponce sent him on his way with his reward and instructions to keep him informed. When the servant had left, he screwed the piece of paper on which he had been writing up into a ball. His fists clenched, he trembled with rage in the very same chair where a few hours earlier Hernando had decided to risk his life for the sake of the hope of ecstasy with Isabel. And yet, although he was accustomed to taking decisions, this time he choked back his anger and stifled his first impulse to get up, give his wife a thrashing, and then kill the Morisco.

The silence of the night enveloped house and garden. Don Ponce still sat there, punishing himself with visions of Isabel in the arms of the Morisco. 'They try to give each other pleasure,' the servant had told him, 'they ... they don't fornicate,' he had managed to stammer, bowing in front of the judge, the knuckles of his hands white as he clenched them. The whore! Don Ponce breathed into the night. Just like a common prostitute in the bawdy house! He knew what the servant had been referring to: the forbidden pleasure he himself sought in the brothel. For hours Don Ponce imagined Isabel as the blonde girl he enjoyed in a bed there: obscene, painted and perfumed, revealing her body to the Morisco dog while she kissed and caressed him. In the brothel he had chosen a girl because she looked like Isabel, and now the Morisco was savouring the pleasures he himself had never known with his wife. The thought of killing them filled his mind.

However, in the early hours, as the night breeze wafted in from the garden, refreshing his sweat-slicked body, Don Ponce decided not to do anything as drastic as killing the two of them. If he slew Isabel, he would lose the substantial dowry provided by the Los Vélez; even more importantly, he would lose his influence in the circles around the King and in the various royal councils, which were vital to his interests. Fighting for their honour was something that only the very rich, the very poor or stupid people could contemplate, and he was none of those. He therefore decided that to accuse someone who was protected by the marquises was both a risky as well as a dishonourable move. At the same time, however, there was no way he could allow adultery in his house . . . that cursed Morisco son of a whore! He had treated him like a gentleman, had organized a celebration in his honour . . . and yet he could not even take his legitimate revenge on him without causing ribald gossip. The Morisco was a hero! The saviour of the Christians! The Duke of Monterreal's protégé . . .

Don Ponce found it impossible to sleep the whole night, but by dawn the next day, his mind was made up: Isabel was not to leave her apartments; he told the household she was suffering from a fever. She remained in her room until later that morning, when in response to an urgent call, his cousin Doña Ángela, a dry, grim-faced widow, arrived. As soon as she entered the house she took charge of the watch over Isabel.

After a short conversation with her cousin, Doña Ángela set to work immediately. Isabel's young chambermaid disappeared that same day. Someone said she was later seen in the dungeons of the chancery, accused of theft. That afternoon Doña Ángela had the other maid, the one who'd sought sexual pleasure with the Morisco slave, flogged, using the excuse that she had shown her disrespect. She also ordered that another servant should lose part of his salary for not working to her satisfaction.

Within a single day, therefore, the judge and his cousin had sent all the servants a clear message. There was very little they could do about it: according to the law, unless they were expressly dismissed, they faced a penalty of twenty days in jail and banishment for a year if any of them left Don Ponce without permission to serve in any other household in the city of Granada or its surroundings. If anyone did leave without his agreement, they would either be obliged to emigrate or to find work as a day labourer, and there was no denying that in the judge's house they never went hungry.

It was not only the servants who were given a swift demonstration of the cousin's harsh character: neither Don Sancho nor Hernando escaped her attentions. Doña Ángela made sure that all her decisions were made in the open, so that the Morisco immediately saw what was going on. Late in the afternoon, just before sunset, she told Isabel to leave her room. Dressed in black, the two women strolled round the gardens of the property, in full view of everyone but in particular Hernando, who was thus given to understand he would never again be able to approach his lover in private.

It was not only Hernando who saw that Isabel was now being kept under close watch by Doña Ángela. Don Sancho saw it too, and realized that the judge had uncovered the affair. When he twice met Don Ponce during the day, the judge cut him dead; Don Sancho immediately went to have it out with Hernando.

'We will leave tomorrow morning, without fail,' he ordered him. Hernando didn't reply. 'Don't you understand?' Don Sancho shouted at him. 'What are you thinking of? If you have any respect – or whatever it is you feel for that woman – you have to get away from her. You'll never see her on your own again! The judge must have found out, and is taking steps to prevent it.' The hidalgo let a few seconds go by. 'As your own life seems to matter so little to you, at least consider that if you continue to behave in this way, you will be ruining hers.'

Hernando was surprised to find himself agreeing with his companion. How briefly his determination had lasted! But it was true; the hidalgo was right. How could he get near to Isabel? When he saw her dressed in black and walking, head bowed, through the gardens alongside the haughty, defiant figure of Doña Ángela, he realized it would be impossible. Besides, if the rumours had reached the judge, it would be madness!

'All right,' he agreed. 'We'll leave first thing tomorrow.'

That night Hernando began to pack up his things for the journey. Among his clothes, he found the rich garments the judge had provided him with for the celebration in his honour. The night he had worn them, Isabel . . . He tried to convince himself it had all been a foolish adventure. As Don Sancho said, what right did he have to ruin the life of an honest woman? He might well feel that she desired him with increasing intensity, but perhaps it was true that he had taken advantage of someone who was merely grateful to him. He looked round him: was he forgetting anything? What about those clothes? He took them and threw them as far away as he could, in a corner of the room. It was not true that he had taken advantage of Isabel's innocence, as Don Sancho had accused him. She was the one who had pressed against him during the fireworks display, and she had stretched out her hand to him. What did it all matter now anyway? He was on his way back to Córdoba.

Hernando collapsed into a chair adorned with decorated, beaten silver. He stared out at the Alhambra and the play of light from the braziers and the moon on its red stones. It was past midnight. The house and gardens were silent: so it seemed was the whole of Granada! A wandering breeze cooled the room and helped make up for the day's stifling heat.

Hernando relaxed, closed his eyes, and took a deep breath. 'This will be the first time we have the moon with us.'

The words woke him with a start. Dressed only in her night-shift, Isabel was standing on the balcony. She looked beautiful and sensual, with the Alhambra outlined behind her.

'What are you doing here?' asked Hernando, rising from his chair. 'What about your husband?'

'I could hear him snoring from my bedroom. And Doña Ángela retired hours ago.'

As she told him this, out on the balcony, Isabel let her shift slip down from her shoulders, until she stood naked before him. She stared straight at him, a proud look in her eyes, inviting him to enjoy her.

Hernando was amazed: it seemed as though even the moonlight was caressing her marvellous body.

'Isabel . . .' whispered Hernando, unable to take his eyes off her breasts, her hips, her thighs . . .

'Ponce tells me you are leaving tomorrow,' she said. 'All we have left is tonight.'

Hernando went towards her and with outstretched hands pulled her into the room. He picked up her night-shift and closed the doors out on to the balcony. He turned back to her and was about to say something, but she laid a finger on his lips as if to tell him not to. Then she gave him a gentle kiss. He reached out to caress her, but Isabel caught hold of his hands and kept them away from her body.

'Let me do it,' she begged him.

She started to unbutton his shirt. They only had that night and she wanted to take charge! She was anxious to explore the pleasure Hernando had so often promised her. He was surprised at the sure way her hands caressed his shoulders as she slipped off his shirt. She kissed his chest and dropped her hands to his breeches. After hesitating a moment, she knelt in front of him.

Hernando sighed.

Isabel explored Hernando's body, kissing and licking him,

and then they went over to the bed. For a long while, the light from a single lantern cast the silhouettes of the sweating, shining bodies of a man and a woman who were whispering to each other as they kissed, caressed and gently bit one another to their hearts' content. Finally it was Isabel who encouraged him to come inside her, as if at last she was ready, as if she now understood the meaning of all that Hernando had been telling her. They fused into one single body. Isabel's quiet moaning became louder and louder until Hernando had to stifle it with a prolonged kiss, still thrusting inside her until he sensed, rising from deep inside her, a guttural cry that Isabel would never have imagined she was capable of, a cry that mingled with his own moment of ecstasy. For many minutes afterwards they lay quietly, sated, still joined as one.

'I'm leaving tomorrow,' Hernando finally said.

'I know,' was her only reply.

There was silence again between the two of them, until Isabel almost imperceptibly shook her head and rolled away from him.

'Isabel . . .'

'Don't say anything,' she told him. 'I have to return to my own life. You have appeared in it twice, and twice you have saved me.' Sitting up in bed, she stroked Hernando's cheek with the back of her hand. 'I have to go back.'

'But—'

She again raised one of her fingers to his lips, urging him to be quiet. 'God be with you,' she whispered, fighting back her tears.

Unable to watch her leave, Hernando lay on his back and stared up at the ceiling. Eventually, when he could hear the night-time sounds of the city once more, he got up and went out on to the balcony. He lost himself again in contemplation of the Alhambra. Why had he not insisted? Why did he not run to her and promise her eternal happiness? Despite Don Sancho's warnings, he had risked his life for her. Was the mere fact of enjoying such sensual pleasure with her enough? Was what he felt for her love? he wondered, confused and miserable. After a while, the wonderful red fortress on the far side of the Darro seemed to offer him the answer: he remembered how in his youth in the gardens of the Generalife he had dreamt of dancing with Fátima. Fátima! No! What he felt for Isabel was not love. Thoughts of his wife's big black almond-shaped eyes brought back memories of the nights of love they had shared. Where was that sense of completeness, of absolute joy, of the thousands of silent promises with which those nights always ended?

Hernando used what little time there was left before dawn to finalize his preparations for departure. Then he went down to the stables, catching the stable lad by surprise before he had even had the chance to muck out the horses' stalls.

'Get Volador ready for me,' he ordered the boy. 'Then prepare Don Sancho's mount and the mules. We are leaving.'

Next he headed for the kitchen, where the staff were still half asleep and having their breakfast. He took a piece of stale bread and bit into it.

'Tell Don Sancho we are going back to Córdoba,' he said to one of the servants. 'Be ready by the time I return. I have to go to the cathedral.'

He rode from the Albaicín down to the cathedral. Granada was waking up, and people were beginning to leave their houses. Hernando rode on without looking to right or left. When he reached the cathedral he could not find the chapter clerk, only a priest who assisted him and who did not seem at all pleased to see the Morisco. If he was going back to Córdoba he would need a safe conduct allowing him to travel through the different regions, similar to the one he had been given by the Bishop of Córdoba to move freely around that city.

'Kindly tell the clerk I have to return to Córdoba,' he said to the priest after they had exchanged cold greetings that Hernando would have preferred to avoid altogether. 'Tell him I find it hard to work here in Granada as it is a place so involved in the events I have to relate. I will personally bring him my report and anything else that might be of interest to the dean or archbishop. Tell him also that being a Morisco I will need a safe conduct from the bishop's office, or whoever else grants such things, authorizing me to travel freely throughout the region. He should send it to me in Córdoba, to the Duke of Monterreal's palace.'

'But an authorization—' the priest started to object.

'Yes, that's what I said. Without one there will be no reports. Do you understand? I'm not asking you to pay me for my work.'

'But—'

'Haven't I been clear enough?'

Hernando had only one more piece of business to attend to. The streets of Granada were already full of people, and the silk market by the cathedral was teeming with those who had come to buy or sell silk or other fabrics. Hernando thought Don Pedro de Granada must surely be awake by now.

The noble received him on his own in the dining room as he made short work of a capon. 'What brings you here at such an early hour? Sit down and join me,' he said, waving towards all the other delicacies spread on the table.

'Thank you, Pedro, I'm not hungry.' Hernando sat down next to the nobleman anyway. 'I'm leaving for Córdoba, but before I do I needed to talk to you.' Hernando gestured towards the two servants who were waiting on them. Don Pedro told them to leave.

'What is it then?'

'I need you to do me a favour. I've had a falling out with the judge.'

Don Pedro stopped eating and nodded as if this was no great surprise. 'Like all legal men, he's a twisted sort.'

'So much so that I'm afraid he will want revenge on me.'

'Was it such a serious matter?'

Hernando nodded.

'He's a bad enemy to have,' said Don Pedro.

'I'd like you to find out what he does or says regarding me, and to keep me informed. He could try to influence the cathedral chapter against me. I thought you should know.'

The lord of Campotéjar leant his elbows on the table and cupped his chin in his hands. 'I will be on the alert for any news. Don't worry,' he promised. 'Am I allowed to know what the problem was?'

'It's not hard to imagine, when one has to live so close to such a beauty as the judge's wife.'

Don Pedro's fist pounded the table so hard the sound echoed all round the hall and knocked over a couple of glasses. Smiting the table a second time, the noble guffawed. The servants came rushing back in, but Don Pedro dismissed them again, still laughing.

'That woman was as impregnable as the Alhambra! So many men have tried and failed to conquer her. I myself—'

'Please be discreet,' Hernando said, trying to calm his companion down. He was wondering whether he had done the right thing in telling him of his conquest.

'Of course. So someone has finally put the judge in his place,' said Don Pedro, chortling again. 'And hitting him where it hurts the most. Did you know that a large part of his fortune comes from the way the legal clerks robbed the Moriscos by digging out ancient documents and demanding legal titles to lands that had been theirs for centuries? In those days, his father worked in the chancery, and like many others took advantage of the situation. He already has the money, now he wants power through the Los Vélez family. He won't want any scandal of this sort.'

'I'm not putting you in a difficult position, am I?'

Don Pedro stopped laughing. 'We all have difficulties, don't we?'

'Yes,' Hernando agreed.

'You'll be in touch with us?'

'Don't doubt it.'

50

What more relics do you want than the ones in those hills? Pick up
a handful of earth, squeeze it, and the blood of martyrs will pour
out.

Letter from Pope Pius IV to the Archbishop of Granada, Pedro
Guerrero, who was asking him for relics for the city

I F HERNANDO had been hoping that on his return from
Granada the Morisco community in Córdoba would have
relented a little in its attitude towards him, he soon discovered
this was not the case. Thanks to the letter the judge had given
Don Alonso, news of his role in the study of the Christian
martyrs of the Alpujarra had travelled ahead of him. The archbishop's request was commented on in the duke's court, and it
was not long before Abbas came to hear of it through the
palace's Morisco slaves.

A few days after his return to the city, at Hernando's insistence his mother agreed to talk to him. She looked old and
stooped.

'You are the man,' she explained in a dull voice when
Hernando arrived at the silk-weaver's. 'The law demands I obey
you, whatever my wishes.'

They were standing out in the street a short distance from
where Aisha worked.

'Mother,' Hernando almost begged her, 'it's not your
obedience I wish for.'

'You were the one who arranged for them to increase my daily wage, weren't you? The master did not want to give me any explanation,' said Aisha, motioning towards the workshop door. Hernando turned and saw the weaver, who waved from a distance and stayed in the doorway watching them, as if waiting to talk to Hernando.

'Why can't we return to our—?'

'I've heard that now you're working for the Archbishop of Granada,' Aisha interrupted him. 'Is that true?' Hernando hesitated. How had they learnt that so quickly? 'They say that you are devoting your efforts to betraying your brothers in the Alpujarra—'

'No!' he protested, his face flushed.

'Are you working for the papists or not?'

'Yes, but it's not what it seems.' Hernando fell silent. Don Pedro and the translators had demanded he keep their project a complete secret, and he had sworn by Allah to do so. 'Trust me, Mother,' he pleaded.

'How can you expect me to do that? Nobody trusts you any more!' With this they both fell silent. Hernando felt the urge to embrace her, and stretched out his hand towards Aisha, but she moved away from him. 'Is there anything more you want from me, my son?'

Why not tell her everything?

'Never tell a woman!' Don Pedro had almost shouted when he raised the possibility of confiding in his mother. 'They talk. All they do is gossip shamelessly. Even your mother.' After that he had obliged Hernando to swear to it.

'Peace be with you, Mother,' he said, withdrawing his hand.

With a lump in his throat, he watched her walk off slowly down the street. He coughed, and headed towards the master weaver, who was still waiting for him. After the customary greetings, the weaver demanded he fulfil his promise: the duke's household should buy goods from him.

'I promised I would make sure the duke showed an interest in your wares,' Hernando told him. 'If he buys or not is not for me to say.'

'If they come here, they will buy,' said the weaver, pointing into his workshop.

Hernando glanced inside: it looked like a well-run establishment. As was stipulated, light came flooding in through open windows that were not covered in any way so that potential buyers could clearly see the weaver's wares. The velvet, silks and damasks were displayed without any tricks to deceive the public.

'I'm sure of that,' said Hernando. 'I thank you for what you have done for my mother. As soon as I see the duke—'

'Your lord could take months to return to Córdoba,' the weaver protested,

'He is not my lord.'

'Tell the duchess then.' Hernando's obvious reluctance caused the weaver to frown. 'We made an agreement. I've kept my part of it. Now it's your turn,' he demanded.

'I'll keep mine,' said Hernando.

Of course he would. That was what he told himself as soon as he had turned his back on the master weaver. His mother would never accept money from him, but he could not allow her to live in poverty while he was given such a generous allowance. She was all he had left, even if she rejected him. Some day he would be able to tell her the truth, he told himself to try to raise his spirits as he walked by the stone benches lined up along the blind wall of the San Pablo convent. A group of young boys were staring open-mouthed at the corpse of a young woman found out in the fields by the Brothers of Mercy. Hernando was reminded of the time when he used to come here day after day expecting to see the body of Fátima or one of his children on public display.

Fátima had come back into his thoughts and dreams with renewed intensity. A few days earlier as he rode out on to the fertile plains outside Granada, he had turned his horse round to stare at the city of the Nasrid dynasty. That was where Isabel lived. Yet the capricious clouds forming in the skies above the mountaintops, whose changing shapes the old men had once used to make prophecies, now showed him the face of Fátima.

Someone, probably Don Sancho, had made a noise at his back, as though to remind him that they should continue on their way. The hidalgo was cold and distant towards him now. Hernando did not turn round, but remained absorbed in the cloud that seemed to be smiling at him.

'You carry on. I'll catch you up.'

It had been three years since Ubaid had murdered Fátima and the children, thought Hernando. He had just met another woman with whom he had tried to reach the heaven he could now see stretching above the cloud, but it was with Fátima that he had been there. It was as if Isabel, in that Granada he could almost reach out and touch, had set him free and opened the doors to feelings he had kept hidden within him all that time. Three years. Hernando did not weep as he had done on hearing the news of his wife's death. Neither tears nor pain distorted his memory of her laughter, Inés's sweet words, or Francisco's revealing blue eyes. He stared up at the cloud, and went on gazing at it until the shape gradually merged with another one. Then he patted the horse's neck and made it turn round again. Don Sancho and the servants were some way ahead. Hernando thought about spurring Volador on to catch up with them, but then changed his mind and followed them at a walk.

The Duke of Monterreal's valet was called José Caro. He was almost forty years old, ten years older than Hernando. Caro was a serious, haughty man who was extremely scrupulous in his dealings with others, as befitted someone who had started out as a page boy to Don Alfonso's father at a very early age. The valet, who in the household hierarchy was second only to the chaplain and the personal secretary, was the man responsible for the duke's wardrobe and other personal effects, as well as everything to do with the decoration and maintenance of the palace. It was José Caro whom Hernando had to convince to go and see the master weaver's silks, but in all the time that he had been living in the palace he had hardly exchanged a dozen words with him.

Hernando saw him one afternoon in one of the halls, impeccably dressed in his livery as he supervised the work of a carpenter repairing the hinges on a sideboard. Next to him a young maid was sweeping up the wood shavings even before they touched the floor.

Hernando paused in the doorway. 'I need you to go to the master weaver Juan Marco's workshop to buy . . .' he rehearsed. 'I need you to?' 'I would like you to . . . I beg you to . . .' 'Why?' Caro was bound to ask. How would he answer a question like that? 'Because I'm the duke's friend,' he could answer, 'I once saved his life.' He imagined having to repeat that argument to the duchess, and immediately rejected it. Don Sancho had taught him many things, but he had definitely never shown him how to behave towards the servants with the authority the others seemed to show so naturally. He also considered going directly to the hidalgo, but the old man had refused to speak to him since their dispute over Isabel.

All of a sudden Hernando felt himself being watched. The valet was staring straight at him. How long had he been standing there in the doorway?

'Good afternoon, José,' he said, twisting his lips in what he hoped looked like a smile.

The maid stopped sweeping and also gazed at him in surprise. The valet merely nodded briefly in his direction and turned back to oversee the carpenter's work.

Seeing the young servant look at him in that way confused Hernando, and made him decide not to go ahead. He realized he had not established any personal relationship with the household servants in the three years he had been there. He turned round and dawdled in the palace courtyards until he saw the maid emerge.

'Come here,' he said. As she approached, Hernando felt in his purse. 'Take this,' he said, handing her two silver coins. The girl took them with some suspicion. 'I want you to keep an eye on the valet and tell me if he leaves the palace at night. Do you understand?'

'Yes, Don Hernando.'

'Does he go out at night?'

'Only if his excellency is not in the palace.'

'Good. You'll get another coin when you report to me. I'll be in the library after supper.'

The maid nodded as if she already knew this.

Hernando went out riding every day. He tried to rise as early as possible, partly to avoid the hidalgos, who got up in mid-morning, but especially so as not to run into Doña Lucía. He had reached the conclusion that Don Sancho must have told her about his love affair with Isabel, because her disdain for him had turned into undisguised animosity. On the few occasions when they met in the palace, Doña Lucía turned her head away, and at mealtimes she made sure Hernando was seated at the far end of the table, almost out of reach of the food. The hidalgos smiled when they saw Hernando trying to get at least some scraps.

Given this state of affairs, Hernando made sure he had a good breakfast, then left Córdoba to enjoy the morning in the pastures. He often spent hours in with the bulls, walking his horse at a distance and neither challenging nor making them run. He was haunted by the memory of Azirat throwing himself on to the bull's horns, and could not bring himself to watch the nobles fighting them in the city. Sometimes he would meet the riders from the royal stables and watch nostalgically as they broke in that year's colts. In the evening, he would shut himself up in the library after the meal. He had plenty to do. First there was the transcription of the gospel of Barnabas, which he had fetched from Arbasia's house. He would probably have to share his discovery at some point and did not want to have to hand over the original. He read the chapters in Arabic, but it was only when he was transcribing them that he understood the concepts' true meaning. In the Annunciation story, the angel Gabriel did not say to Mary that she would give birth to a divine being, but to someone who would show the way. The way where? he wondered, pausing in his task. Show whom the way? The true Prophet, he said, answering his own question. As in the Muslim world, neither Jesus nor his mother could drink wine or eat unclean meat, and the angels did not tell the shepherds that it was the Saviour who had been born, but simply another prophet. Unlike the later evangelists, Barnabas affirmed that Jesus Christ, whom he had known personally, never called himself God or the son of God, nor even the Messiah. He only considered himself as someone sent by God to herald the arrival of the true Prophet: Muhammad.

In addition Hernando was still writing his report on what had happened at Juviles for the Archbishop of Granada. He was reminded of his promise when the special safe conduct in his name arrived. Whatever Abbas, his followers, or even his mother thought, he had no intention of betraying his people. He wrote that it had been El Zaguer, a Morisco, who had prevented the murder of all the Christians in the village. Besides, he added, if there had been a massacre in Juviles, it was the murder of a thousand women and children by Christian soldiers. He relived the agony of his desperate search for his mother, and the accidental rescue of Fátima and her little Humam in the midst of the explosions and clouds of smoke from the harquebuses in the dark village square.

He also fulfilled his promise to gather information from the vast network of Morisco muleteers for the book on Don Rodrigo, the King of the Goths, that Luna was writing. Hernando's contribution consisted in providing facts about the peaceful coexistence of Christians and Muslims in the Córdoba of the caliphates. The aim was to show that during the period when Muslims ruled the city, the Christians (then known as Mozarabs) were not only allowed to live in their realms but more importantly still were permitted a certain freedom of worship. Hernando was able to confirm that the

Mozarabs had kept their churches and other places of worship, their ecclesiastical organization and even their own justice system. To the contrary, how many mosques were still standing in the lands of the 'Prudent King'? The Mozarabs were not forced to convert, as the Moriscos were.

He supplied information about the churches dedicated to Saint Acisclus and Saint Zoilus, Saint Faustus, Saint Cyprian, Saint Ginés and Saint Eulalia, all of which had remained standing within the city of Córdoba during the years of Muslim rule. He did however remain silent about the subjugated state of the Mozarabs (Hernando told himself that at least they were allowed to keep their own beliefs) during the terrible period when the vizier Almanzor was in power.

Whenever he grew tired of all this work, he refreshed himself by practising the art of calligraphy. The treatise he had found in the casket together with the gospel was nothing less than a copy of the famous work *A Typology for Scribes*, written by Ibn Muqla himself, the greatest of all the officials serving the caliphs of Baghdad. As he wrote, Hernando tried to make each stroke perfect, and found himself stimulated spiritually in a way that was close to prayer.

'You have offended God with your images of the holy word,' he accused himself one evening in the silence of the library, only too aware of how imperfect his writing was and the lack of magic in the characters he penned in the copies he made of the Koran. He did not so much draw as scribble them.

He needed a supply of reeds to make his quills, and to learn how to cut their ends sharply and slanted to the right, as Ibn Muqla recommended: Christian quills were not good enough to serve God. Hernando thought it would not be difficult to find the necessary implements.

Yet he also needed to keep his increasingly prolific work hidden, which meant he paid regular visits to the minaret tower. He did so under cover of darkness, for fear of being seen, and aware that the slightest slip could have disastrous consequences. He also took the hand of Fátima out of its hiding place in the tapestry and concealed it again in the hidden chamber in the tower wall. He made sure he burnt all his calligraphy exercises so that there would be no trace of them. The only thing he left out was his report for the Granada council, which was soon read, as the chaplain began to share his solitary breakfasts and to take an interest in Hernando's opinion, which seemed to him so out of tune with the cause of the martyrs of the Alpujarra.

'How can you possibly compare an unfortunate misunderstanding which resulted in the deaths of a few Morisco women in the square at Juviles with the premeditated, vile murder of Christians?' the priest asked him quite openly one morning.

'I see you are spying on my work,' said Hernando, still eating. He did not even bother to turn towards the chaplain.

'Working for God means having to do many strange things. The Marquis of Mondéjar has already meted out punishment for those deaths,' the priest insisted. 'Justice was done.'

'El Zaguer went further than the marquis,' Hernando argued. 'He stopped the killing, and prevented the deaths of many Christians in Juviles.'

'But they happened all the same,' the priest declared.

'Are you trying to compare the two?' Hernando asked boldly.

'You are not the one to do so.'

'Nor are you,' Hernando retorted. 'The archbishop must be the one to do that.'

One night as he was finishing work on the report the young maidservant poked her head round the door.

'His excellency's valet has just left the palace,' she announced.

Hernando gathered up his papers. He stood up from the desk, searched for the coin he had promised her, and handed it over.

'Take these papers to my bedroom,' he said, handing her the report. 'And thank you,' he added when she took them from him. She smiled shyly back at him. Hernando noticed she had a pretty face. 'Do you have any idea what he usually does, where he goes?' he asked.

'It's said he likes to play cards.'

'Thanks again.'

He hurried out. When he reached the courtyard next to the duchess's favourite room, he heard one of the hidalgos reading out loud to the others. Hernando crossed the yard quickly and without being seen, thanks to the shadows from the gallery on the far side of the building. He went out into a cool autumn night, suddenly feeling the lack of a cape. It was more than ten years since he had set foot in any gambling den, and he did not want to lose sight of the valet in the dark streets of the city. Would the places still exist where he had acted as a tout enticing innocent gamblers inside to be fleeced? The valet would have to be heading for either the Corredera or the Potro district, and to do that he would have to cross the old Arab wall separating the medina from the eastern part of the city. The only two places he could do that were through the El Salvador or the Corbache gates. Hernando chose the first. He was lucky, and soon saw the valet's silhouette as he was accosted by the destitute vagrants who slept beneath the royal arch. By the light of candles permanently lit in honour of a statue of Christ Crowned with Thorns kept behind a grille underneath the arch, he caught sight of José Caro waylaid by a group blocking his path and asking for alms. Hernando felt for a penny, and as soon as the valet managed to struggle free of the beggars and continue on his way towards the El Salvador gate, he strode towards the royal arch.

He found himself surrounded as the valet had been. Hernando showed them the penny, then tossed it over his shoulder. Four of the men ran to fight for it, and it was easy for him to break free of the other two who were begging for another coin.

José Caro was aiming for the Potro district. Where else could he be going? thought Hernando with a smile, following him at a distance, listening for his footsteps in the darkness and catching occasional glimpses of him when he passed by a lit roadside altar. But he almost lost him when they came out into Plaza del Potro, with all the hustle and bustle of people in it. How long had it been since he spent a night in the Potro? He searched for the valet in the crowd. He took a step to follow him, but was immediately intercepted by a youngster.

'Is your excellency looking for a gaming house where you can win good money? I can show you the best—'

Hernando smiled. 'Do you see that man?' he interrupted the lad and pointed towards the valet, who had just turned a corner into Calle Badanas. The boy nodded. 'If you tell me where he goes, I'll give you money.'

'How much?'

'He'll get away from you,' Hernando warned.

As the lad ran off, Hernando allowed himself to be carried away by his memories: the bawdy house and Hamid; Juan the mule-driver; Fátima broken and defeated, spitting out the broth Aisha was trying to force her to drink; he himself, running after clients for the gaming houses . . .

'He's gone into Pablo Coca's den.' The boy's words brought Hernando back to reality. 'But I can take you to a better place: they cheat on people there.'

'Are there any where they don't?' Hernando asked ironically. He did not know the one the lad had mentioned: it hadn't existed when he frequented the area.

'Of course! I can take you—'

'Don't bother. We'll go to the one Coca runs.'

'We'll go?' asked the lad, confused.

'In a few moments. You show me where it is. Then I'll pay you.'

They waited long enough for it to appear to be a chance meeting, then the boy showed Hernando a dark, narrow entrance. Hernando showed the doorkeepers a couple of gold sovereigns and then slipped inside the gambling den. It was a sizeable room concealed at the back of a workshop making carding brushes. About fifty people, including card sharps, swindlers, curious onlookers and other people playing cards or dice, were scuttling between several gaming tables. If it were not for the noise outside in Plaza del Potro, the racket from inside the gambling den would have been enough to keep the city governor awake.

Hernando surveyed the room until he caught sight of the valet sitting at a table. He already had a couple of cheats standing behind him. Was he an experienced gambler, or an ingenuous beginner they would allow to win a few times so that they could fleece him when he had more funds? A girl offered Hernando a glass of wine, and he took it. The house paid: it was in their interest that someone coming in with gold sovereigns should drink and stay to play. He went from table to table to see what each one was offering: dice, card games like Thirty, the First Lady of Germany, or Mix and Match. He came to José Caro's table and watched from the far side. He looked to see what the game was: Twenty-one. Hernando soon realized José Caro was nothing more than a novice. A cheat was standing behind him, wearing a doublet and a broad belt decorated with shiny metal ornaments. The card sharp on the other side of the board, who was the bank for the game, kept glancing at the reflecting mirrors on his accomplice's doublet and belt to see what cards José Caro had. Hernando shook his head slightly: everyone else playing at the table seemed to be in on the swindle, and they would all get their share for helping the cheat fleece the customer. The chamberlain revealed his hand: an ace and a court card. Twenty-one! He won a sizeable amount. So they wanted him to trust them.

'You're very hard to find.' Hernando turned to face the man talking to him, and frowned as he tried to place him. 'When you disappeared I thought something must have happened to you, but obviously not. You come back dressed like a noble, and with gold coins in your pocket. '

'Palomero!'

Several of the gamblers, including the valet, looked up to see who this newcomer was who was speaking to the place's owner like that. Pablo Coca signalled to Hernando not to call him that.

'I'm the owner here,' he whispered. 'I have to consider my reputation.'

'Pablo Coca,' Hernando murmured to himself. He had never known the name of the youngster who had been able to hood-wink the most suspicious customer. The players returned to their cards. Intrigued to see the Morisco there, the valet kept glancing at him out of the corner of his eye. 'You have a fine place here,' said Hernando, adding: 'It must cost you a small fortune in bribes to the magistrates and officials.'

'The same as always.' Pablo laughed. 'Come on, leave that vinegar and I'll pour us some decent wine.'

Hernando accompanied him to a corner away from the tables. Here, behind a rough table, a man protected by two guards with weapons tucked in their belts was counting money and doing the accounts. Pablo served two glasses of wine and they made a toast.

'What brings you here?' asked Pablo after they had clinked glasses.

'I need a favour from that man playing Twenty-one over there,' Hernando told him frankly.

'The duke's valet?' Pablo cut in. 'He's one of the most gullible players who comes here. If you don't talk to him soon, they'll take all he has and he won't be in any mood to hear about favours.'

Hernando looked over at the gaming table. The valet was putting down a bet against the bank. Another man was arguing about the game, and began a fight with a third player. Two men immediately came up to the table, separated them, and told them to calm down. Hernando could not bear to think of how far away he was from Muslim law: drinking in a gaming house . . . Why was it so hard to remain faithful to his religious beliefs?

'If you want to catch him in a good mood, let him lose a little more. They've seen you with me. When you sit down, the dealers will change, and you'll be able to do as you please. Do you know any tricks? Is that how you've been making a living? In Seville?'

'No. All I know is what a good friend once taught me,' said

Hernando, winking at Pablo. 'Things can't have changed that much since then, can they? And beyond that . . . let's see what luck brings.'

'You're being naive,' Pablo warned him.

They carried on talking for a good while, and Hernando told him about his life. Then they went over to the card table, where the valet had lost almost all his money. Pablo gestured to the player seated to the right of the valet, and he stood up to give his seat to the Morisco. José Caro made as if to stand up as well, but Hernando put a hand on his forearm to keep him seated.

'From now on you will only have luck to contend with,' he whispered in his ear.

Some of the other players stood up, but were immediately replaced by new ones.

'What do you mean?' said the valet as the players changed. 'I've been keeping my eyes open for any cheating.'

'I didn't mean to offend you. What I'm trying to say is that this is not like playing with the duchess for a ducat a time. For a start, never sit in front of a man with mirrors on his coat.' Hernando lifted his chin towards the man with the decorated doublet, who was receiving his share from the winner a few feet away from the table. Other gamblers who had seen what was going on and said nothing were waiting for their rewards.

The valet made to slam his fist on the table, but Hernando stopped him.

'You won't get any comeback now. That game has finished.'

'What do you want? Why are you helping me?'

'Because I want you to show an interest in the fabrics that the master weaver Juan Marco produces. Do you know his workshop?' The valet nodded, and was about to say something, but Hernando beat him to it: 'You don't have to buy. All I want is for you to go there.'

The board was now full, with nine players. One of them picked up the cards and was about to deal, but Hernando stopped him.

'A new pack of cards,' he demanded.

Pablo already had one to hand. Hernando took the old one, which the player had thrown on to the table in disgust. He handed it to the valet.

'Keep it. Later on, I'll show you a couple of things.'

The change of cards led the man who wanted to deal and another card sharp to get up and leave. With Pablo Coca looking on, they began to play Twenty-one. Each player was dealt two cards, with one for the bank. The player who got closest to the number twenty-one (with the ace counting as one or eleven, the court cards ten, and the others their face value) won against the bank if he came closer to a total of twenty-one, or if the bank went beyond it. Luck changed, and the valet managed to recoup his losses. He even offered to buy a drink for Hernando, who was neither winning nor losing.

There came a moment when Hernando was hesitating about how much to wager. He'd had a run of uninspiring hands and was getting bored, and he fingered his stake money. He looked over at the dealer. Pablo was standing behind him, erect and serious-looking, keeping a close eye on the game. Then the lobe of his right ear moved almost imperceptibly. Hernando tried not to show his surprise, and placed a large wager. He won. He smiled, remembering what his friend had once told him: they had it in their blood!

'I see you finally learnt from the Marshal,' Hernando said to him at the end of the game, when he and the valet were saying farewell to Pablo Coca. The Morisco had won a large sum; his companion had managed to recoup some of his previous losses.

'What's that about a marshal?' José Caro wanted to know.

The two old friends exchanged glances, but neither of them said a word. Hernando smiled as he recalled the young Palomero's grimaces as he tried to move his right earlobe. He shook hands with him, and the valet did the same.

'This money wasn't honestly won,' Hernando said to Pablo, feeling the weight of his purse.

'Don't torment yourself. Don't imagine it was a fair game.

They all tried some trick or other. The thing is, you're as gullible as your friend. You didn't even notice. Times change, and the tricks get more and more sophisticated.'

'I can't right now' – Hernando looked towards the valet, who was already several yards away – 'but some other day I'll pay you your share.'

'I hope so. That's the rule in gaming, as you know. Come back whenever you like. The Marshal and his accomplice died a long time ago, and took the secret with them to their tomb. So now only you and I know about how I move my ear. I've never wanted to tell anyone about it or even to use the trick; I would never have been able to buy a gaming house. Nobody will spot us. It cost me heaven and earth to learn the trick.' He sighed, pointing to the valet, who had stopped and was waiting for Hernando.

Hernando said goodbye again, and caught up with José Caro. The two of them walked back to the palace together.

'Will you go and see the weaver?' he asked as they were crossing Plaza del Potro, which was just as lively as he remembered it.

'The moment you show me how that pack of cards was rigged.'

51

THAT YEAR Queen Elizabeth of England 'permitted' the execution of Mary Queen of Scots, the Catholic Stuart monarch. Indignant, and seeking to defend the true faith, Philip II decided finally to put into practice his idea of equipping a great armada under the command of Álvaro de Bazán, the Marquis of Santa Cruz, to conquer England and punish the Protestant heretics. Despite the surprise attack that the intrepid pirate Sir Francis Drake made on the fleet in the bay of Cádiz, when he sank or burnt almost thirty-six Spanish ships, and then continued to harass the boats taking supplies out to the Spanish vessels, Philip II pressed on with his plan.

The Great and Most Fortunate Fleet, which by God's will, according to the Spanish ambassador to Paris, Philip II was to launch against the English, also stirred the religious fervour of the Spanish nobles and ordinary people. They were always keen to defeat their ancestral enemies the English in the name of God, especially as they had also become allies of the Lutherans in the Low Countries in their wars against the Spanish throne. Don Alfonso de Córdoba and his eldest son, who by now was in his twentieth year, made preparations to embark together with the Marquis of Santa Cruz on this new crusade.

However, at the same time as the country was preparing for

war against England, there was more bad news for the Moriscos. Ever since the meeting held in Portugal six years earlier, when Philip II had considered the possibility of putting them all on ships and then scuttling them on the high seas, several reports had been drawn up recommending the Moriscos be detained and sent to the galleys. And then in this year of preparation for war one of the most influential voices in the kingdom of Valencia, that of the Bishop of Segorbe, Don Martín de Salvatierra, made another proposal. With the support of several others of the same opinion, he sent a report to the Council of State proposing what to him seemed to be the only solution: the castration of all male Moriscos, be they adults or children.

Hernando shuddered and felt a tightening in his testicles as he read the letter sent him by Alonso del Castillo from El Escorial, informing him of what Bishop Salvatierra had suggested.

'The cowardly dogs!' he muttered to himself in the silence and solitude of the duke's library.

Would the Christians really be capable of such an act of barbarity? 'Yes. Why not?' was the answer Castillo gave in his letter to that same question. Only fifteen years earlier Philip II himself, forever fomenting trouble and supporting the Catholic cause in France, had reacted enthusiastically to the news of the Saint Bartholomew's Day Massacre, when French Catholics had massacred more than thirty thousand Huguenots. If King Philip could publicly express his joy and satisfaction that in a quarrel between Christians thousands of people had been killed (they might not have been Catholics, but they were still Christians), what mercy could mere Moriscos expect from him? Hadn't the Spanish King considered drowning them all out at sea? Would the Catholic monarch so much as lift a finger if the Christians rose up and, following the new report's advice, started to castrate all male Moriscos?

Hernando read the letter over again before crushing it in his hand. Then he destroyed it, as he did with all his communications from the translator. Castrate them! What kind of madness was that? How could a bishop, a leading figure in a religion that prided itself on showing mercy and piety, advise such a barbaric course of action? All at once the work he was doing for Luna and Castillo seemed to him pointless: events were moving far too fast for them, and by the time that Luna had completed his panegyric about the Muslim conquerors, obtained the necessary licence to publish it, and finally managed to bring it to the attention of the Christians, the Moriscos would have been wiped out, one way or another. What if Abbas and the other Moriscos who favoured an armed revolt were right after all?

Hernando got up from behind his desk and paced up and down the library. He was confused, and wrung his hands muttering oaths as he walked. He would have liked to discuss this latest news with the painter Arbasia, but he had left Córdoba a few months earlier to go and paint in the Del Viso palace, commissioned by Don Álvaro de Bazán, the Marquis of Santa Cruz. He had left behind a magnificent painting for the sacrarium chapel in the cathedral, in which Hernando was still intrigued by the enigmatic figure next to Jesus Christ at the Last Supper.

'Fight for your cause,' he recalled the master encouraging him from the mule he was leaving on, led by a muleteer.

How could he fight against the proposal that they should be castrated?

'Hypocritical dogs!' he shouted in the silence of the library.

A hypocrite! That was how Arbasia had described King Philip II during one of their meetings. 'Your pious king is nothing more than a hypocrite,' he had told him quite openly.

'Only a very few people know that your King Philip owns a series of erotic paintings he personally commissioned from the great master Titian. I saw one of them in Venice. In it a naked Venus is clinging lasciviously to Adonis. Titian painted several more for the Christian monarch, all of them with nude goddesses in different poses. "So that they are more pleasant to look at," the master wrote to your King. A Christian woman would never fling herself on her husband in the way Titian's

Venus does.' For a brief instant, Hernando's mind flew back to memories of Isabel. 'What are you thinking?' the painter asked, seeing his attention wander.

'About Christian women,' Hernando said by way of an excuse. 'In their situation . . .'

'You Muslims do not value your women greatly either. They are your prisoners, unable to do anything on their own account. Isn't that what your Prophet said?'

Hernando nodded. 'Yes,' he agreed after a few moments' thought. 'Both religions have dismissed them. They are alike in that. So much so that we even agree about the Virgin Mary: Christians and Muslims believe in her in a similar way. But it is as if the fact that they agree about a woman, even if she is the mother of God, is somehow unimportant . . .'

Remembering the conversation he had had with Arbasia, Hernando paused in his agitated walk around the library. The Virgin Mary! She truly was a link between the two religions. Why try so hard to show the benevolence of the Arab conquerors of Spain towards the Christians, as Luna would have it, when there already was an undeniable relationship that both communities recognized? What better argument could there be? Even the gospel of Barnabas agreed with the distorted version put forward by the popes, which the Christians defended as the truth! Why not use the figure of the only person they all seemed to agree about as the starting point on the path towards a unity that would allow the two religions to coexist? The whole of Spain was experiencing an almost fanatical period of devotion to Mary; there were constant demands that Rome declare the virgin birth a dogma of faith. Not even God, the god who was God for both religions, the God of Abraham, could produce such unanimity: the Christians had clouded that issue with their doctrine of the Holy Trinity.

For several days afterwards, Hernando found he could not concentrate on his work. He had already sent his report on the killings at Juviles, and to his surprise – because he thought that when they read it the council would not ask him to do anything more – they now wanted information about what had happened at Cuxurio, where Ubaid had torn out little Gonzalico's heart. How could he possibly excuse such butchery? No Morisco leader had halted the massacre there. Leaving aside his transcription of the gospel of Barnabas and what he was writing for Luna, Hernando concentrated on his calligraphy. He had found some excellent reeds to fashion quills out of, with their point slanting slightly to the right as Ibn Muqla recommended, and yet he was still not sure of exactly where he should cut the reed to achieve this. In the mornings, while Volador was grazing in the pastures, he would lean against a tree and start to cut the ends off reeds he tried out later on in the library.

However, his exercises in calligraphy were not enough to calm his anxiety. He was not in a proper state of mind to find God through drawing characters. The day after he thought he had found the solution, thanks to Maryam, Hernando began to have fresh doubts. How could he do it? Was he right? How could he present this to the Christians so that it would have sufficient impact? How could he embark on such a project all on his own?

His daily life was very different. Since the evening when he had visited Pablo Coca's gaming house to talk to the valet, Hernando had been to gamble on several other occasions. The valet had kept his promise and visited the weaver when Hernando showed him the tricks the card sharps used with the pack of cards: making tiny black marks on them, using cards that were almost invisibly different in size from the rest of the pack and so on. Sometimes Hernando took him along, at others he went on his own. He knew he was breaking the commandment that prohibited gambling, but what was one more among the many he was forced to break in this foreign land?

One night he was trying to adjust the proportions of his letters to match an *alif* he had already drawn. He drew a circle round this first letter of the Arabic alphabet, using the height of the *alif* for the diameter, and then tried to fit all the following letters into the same dimensions. He had hardly been at the exercise half an hour when he realized that, however hard he tried, he could not make the letter *ba*, which was horizontal and curved, fit into this circumference or occupy the space it was meant to fill horizontally next to the *alif*.

Hernando tore up the sheets of paper, stood up and decided to go and gamble at Pablo Coca's gaming house, despite the fact that he knew he would lose. He had lost on the two previous nights, but according to his friend he'd have to do so once again.

'You can't always win,' Pablo had warned him. 'Although nobody might spot our trick, they are bound to think something odd is going on if you always win, and they would soon associate you with me. However much I go from one table to another, they know I am your friend. Let the money go where it will.'

From that moment on, Pablo always told him the days when he would win, and the winnings always far outweighed the losses he had accumulated. Hernando enjoyed gambling, whatever the result. However much he learnt, he still played like a complete novice, betting indiscriminately until the instant he saw his friend's ear moving. Also, whenever he left the gambling house he headed for the brothel, where he enjoyed the favours of a young redhead with an exuberant body and lusty appetite. That night, before leaving the palace, he enquired after the valet, because he liked having him for company when it was his turn to lose; at least it meant he had someone to talk to. The duke was still away, planning the invasion of England at the Madrid court, so José Caro was happy to accompany him.

'You don't seem in very good spirits,' the valet commented after they had walked a good way in silence.

'I'm sorry,' said Hernando.

Their footsteps resonated through the deserted alleyways of the Santo Domingo neighbourhood. They were striding along;

the valet allowed the sheath of his dagger to clink against his belt, to warn anyone who might be lurking in the dark corners that they would have to face two strong, armed men. Hernando had a small knife hidden in his tunic, as Moriscos were forbidden to carry weapons.

It was true he was not in good spirits. The idea that he could use the figure of the Virgin Mary to bring the two communities closer was still going through his mind, but he had no idea what to do with it, or whom he could talk to about it. One of the multitude of altars that lit up Córdoba at night-time came into view at the end of the street they were walking along. Whereas during the day all the statues, niches and religious paintings attracted the prayers and pleas of devoted Christians, at night they became beacons that seemed to indicate the way through the surrounding darkness. This one was an altar on the front of a house, lit by candles and with flowers and ex-votos on the ground beneath it. Hernando came to a halt in front of the painting: Our Lady of Mount Carmel.

'Our blessed Virgin,' murmured José Caro.

'Untouched by sin,' whispered Hernando, unconsciously repeating the words of the Prophet contained in his teachings.

'That is so,' the valet replied, crossing himself. 'Pure and spotless, conceived without sin.'

They continued on their way, with Hernando still bound up in his thoughts. Could his Christian companion even imagine that his affirmation about the Immaculate Conception came from the Sunna, the collection of the Prophet's sayings? What would he think if it were explained to him that the elevation to dogma that the Spanish Christians were fighting for so keenly was already contained in the Koran? What would the valet think if he were told it was the Prophet who maintained that the Virgin was never touched by sin? What would he make of the esteem in which the Prophet held Maryam? 'You will be mistress of the women in paradise . . .' Muhammad told his daughter Fátima when he saw the hour of his death was drawing near '. . . after Maryam.'

Hernando quickened his pace. That was the path they had to take to bring together the religions and win the respect Don Pedro and his friends wanted to see accorded to the Moriscos! He had to do it!

Still obsessed with his idea, Hernando learnt that in that same year of 1587 another conspiracy by Moriscos in Seville, Córdoba and Écija had been uncovered. The Moriscos had plotted to take advantage of the lack of defences to overrun Seville during Saint Peter's Night. The leaders were summarily executed; Abbas was not one of them, but various members of the Córdoba community were. Arms! They would never achieve anything through the use of arms apart from enraging the Christians and their King even further, thought Hernando. They wanted to castrate them! Did the Morisco community and the elders leading it not realize that?

He had finally worked out a plan. The Christians of Granada were searching for martyrs and relics – they needed them to make their city a cradle of Christianity comparable to the great centres of pilgrimage in the rest of Spain: Toledo, Santiago de Compostela, Seville – so why not provide them with what they wanted? That was what he wrote in a long letter to Castillo:

We believe in the same God, the God of Abraham. To us, their Jesus Christ is the Messiah, the word of God and the spirit of God: the Koran affirms this often. Isa is the Sent One! as Muhammad, peace be upon him, said. But do the Christians know that? They take us for dogs, or ignorant mules. None of them has ever bothered to find out what our true beliefs are, while polemicists on both sides in their writings and debates concentrate on all that separates us rather than on anything that might unite us. We all know that three hundred years after his death, Jesus's divine nature was distorted by the popes. He, Isa, never called himself God or the Son of God. All he did was defend the existence of one single God, just as we do. If Jesus's divine nature was falsified by the popes, the same cannot be said of his mother. Perhaps her condition as a woman relegated her to a secondary role, so that they were not concerned about her; even today, despite popular fervour, they refuse to make the Immaculate Conception a dogma of faith. So it is in Mary that our two religions still coincide, and perhaps through her we can bring our two communities closer together. The arguments about the Virgin are concerned with her genealogy, not the esteem in which she is held. If the Christians and their priests who now see us as heretic dogs came to understand that we too venerate the mother of God, then perhaps they would reconsider their views. Devotion to Mary is second nature among the ordinary people; they cannot possibly hate those who share the same feelings as them! Could this be the basis of the understanding for which we are so desperately searching?

Hernando then went on to tell Castillo about his discovery of the gospel of Barnabas, as if it had just taken place:

Doubtless a document such as this gospel would immediately be dismissed as apocryphal, heretical, and contrary to the beliefs of the Holy Mother Church if it were released without a prior strategy. We should start by convincing the Christians what our beliefs are and how we are forced to live; if we prepare them for the gospel's existence, we could one day reveal it so that it can at least sow doubt in their minds and lead them to treat us more benevolently and mercifully.

The royal translator soon replied. One morning a muleteer sent especially from El Escorial met Hernando on the outskirts of Córdoba and handed him a letter. He galloped out to the pastures, looked for a spot where he could hide, dismounted, and then eagerly began to read Castillo's reply.

In the name of Allah, the most gracious, the most merciful, He who indicates the right path. In order to stand against the Christians, many of our brothers have forgotten the things you point out in your letter. But you are right: with God's help, this could be a good way for the two communities to be brought together, and for peace to reign between us. I anxiously await the possibility of reading the gospel you speak of. In the sixth century *Decretum Gelasianum* on 'approved and non-approved books' the Church has already made mention of a gospel by Saint Barnabas, which it describes as apocryphal. I also agree with you that to reveal its existence without preparation would get us nowhere. Granada is the place to do this. Start there. Supply them with evidence of the Christian tradition they so desperately long for, and at the same time provide clues of what one day might lead them to the Truth. The Virgin, of course, but do not forget Saint Caecilius. He was the first Bishop of Granada, who was supposedly martyred during the rule of the Roman Emperor Nero. Saint Caecilius and his brother Saint Ctesiphon were Arabs. Make sure therefore that you employ our divine tongue, so that the Christians discover their past through our universal language, but do so ambiguously, in such a way that what you write will give rise to different interpretations. Remember that in those ancient times there were no vowels or diacritic signs in Arabic writing. When you are ready, send me word. Peace be with you, and may God be your guide.

Hernando tore up the letter and climbed back on to Volador. A storm was brewing. Could he do all that? He had been deceiving people all his life. In his youth, he had taken money so that he could exchange Fátima for a mule. Now he was making more money by betting when he saw Pablo waggling his earlobe ... but to deceive an entire realm, to deceive the Catholic Church! A cool rain started to fall. Hernando continued at a walk, imagining that he was involved in a huge game all by himself. A game that required all his intelligence: this was not a game of cards with simple tricks. Chess! It was like a great game of chess: he was on one side of the board; on the other was the whole of Christianity.

That night he excused himself from the evening meal. He

needed to be alone. The garden by the mosque was the same as ever: hundreds of penitential garments, with the names of those punished written on them, still hung from the walls of the cloister. Some of the thieves seeking sanctuary there were wandering about, oblivious to the rain, while others sought shelter. Hernando briefly wondered what had become of his erstwhile companions. There were also dozens of young and old priests among a gaggle of believers; many of them were running inside to avoid the persistent downpour. Hernando went into the cathedral and paused for a moment outside the grille to the San Bernabé chapel. He bent over, as if he had dropped something: the keys to the chapel were still hidden where he had left them, tied to the bottom of the grille. 'Saint Barnabas!' murmured Hernando. His gospel! What other sign did he require? He picked up the keys, wondering whether or not they had changed the lock. He would not know until he tried, and for that he would have to wait for the doorkeepers to shut the cathedral. As he walked towards the sacrarium, he looked closely at the lock. Was it the same? All he could do was wait. He did so in rapt contemplation of Arbasia's paintings in the new chapel, especially the figure alongside Jesus Christ in the Last Supper. Why? he asked himself for the umpteenth time.

The keys did open the grille to the San Bernabé chapel. Hernando slipped inside and opened the cupboard. He climbed inside as best he could, and piled the paraphernalia for celebrating mass at his feet. Then he crouched inside, and waited once more.

In the early hours, with the cathedral empty and the guards gathered in the distant Punto chapel, the storm broke over Córdoba. The flashes of lightning repeatedly lit the figure of a man prostrate in front of the mihrab of the most marvellous mosque in the world. A man whose mind was fixed on a plan that might, just might, bring about the reconciliation of the two religions.

52

H ERNANDO FOUND lodging in the Casa de los Tiros, at the invitation of Don Pedro de Granada. He had left Córdoba with the excuse that he was visiting the cathedral chapter with information about the Alpujarra martyrs and so, armed with his safe conduct, he set out along the tragic route that had seen so many deaths during the exodus of the Moriscos. As he was forced to travel alone, he considered changing his route to avoid painful memories, but the detours made his journey twice as long. The month of March was bringing life back to the fields, and when he visited little Humam's grave, which was for him where all his own family were buried, the fresh scents of a spring night accompanied his prayers.

Already informed that he was coming, Luna and Castillo had travelled from El Escorial to see him.

When they had locked themselves in the Golden Stable, Hernando showed them a tar-covered lead casket. Opening it, he solemnly took out a piece of cloth, a small tablet with the image of the Virgin on it, a bone and a parchment. He placed them all on a low inlaid table.

The four men stood in silence for a few moments, staring down at the objects on the table.

'I found an old parchment in the minaret of the duke's

palace,' Hernando started to explain. 'It must date from the time of the caliphs, when al-Mansur was terrorizing the peninsula,' he went on, smiling at Luna. 'I only had to cut the outside part to find a clean fragment.'

Saying this, he unfolded the parchment. He took hold of the top corners and held it up to his companions. 'It's like a big chess board,' he said.

In the centre of the parchment were two rectangles, one on top of the other. The top one, which had 48 columns and 29 rows, contained an Arabic letter in each square. The lower rectangle, which had 15 columns and 10 rows, and where each individual square was much larger, contained an Arabic word in each one. Luna and Castillo leant towards the parchment to study it as closely as possible and noted that none of the letters or words (written in red or brown ink) contained any vowels or diacritic signs.

' "Prophecy of the apostle John",' Castillo read out from an introduction written in Arabic in the margin above the rectangles, ' "on the destruction and judgement of the peoples of the earth and the punishments that will follow, as revealed in his worthy gospel deciphered from the Greek by the scholar and holy servant of the faith Dionysius the Aeropagite."' The translator leant back. 'Excellent! What do the other inscriptions say?' he added, pointing to further lines of writing at the foot and sides of the parchment.

'By combining letters and words, it can be deduced that it is a prophecy translated by Saint Caecilius from the Greek after it was given to him by Dionysius, the Archbishop of Athens. In it are foretold the arrival of Islam, the Lutheran schism and the evils the Christian Church will suffer, dividing into a multitude of sects. It says a king will come from the East to dominate the world. He will impose a single religion, and will punish all those who have wallowed in vice.'

'Bravo!' Pedro de Granada applauded him.

'Whose is the signature at the bottom of the parchment?' asked Luna.

'Saint Caecilius, Bishop of Granada.'

'And the other things?' Castillo enquired, pointing to the objects laid out on the table.

'According to the parchment, this is the Virgin's veil,' said Hernando, pointing at the triangular piece of cloth. 'She used it to dry Jesus Christ's tears in his Passion. The tablet shows the Virgin, and this is one of Saint Stephen's bones.'

'What a shame!' Don Pedro said. 'The Christians will not be getting the relics of Saint Caecilius they so desire.'

'Saint Caecilius could hardly be writing this and bring his own bone along at the same time,' Hernando said with a smile.

'It's a simple-looking veil,' Castillo said, feeling the cloth. Hernando nodded. 'Might I ask how you did all this?'

'I borrowed the tablet from an ex-voto beneath an altar to the Virgin in Córdoba. Out in the fields I wrapped it in a cloth and put it in a hole with manure to make it seem ancient.'

'A good idea,' Luna admitted.

'I know a little about the effects of manure on things,' Hernando explained. 'As for the bone and the piece of cloth, I paid some poor wretches in the Potro district to dig up bodies from the common graves in the Campo de la Merced, until I found the cloth and a clean bone—'

'Could they recognize you again?' Castillo cut in.

'No. It was at night, and I was hooded the whole time. They thought I wanted it for some witchcraft. No one can link it with our plan. I left loaded down with bones!'

'What now?' Don Pedro asked.

'Now,' Castillo answered, 'we have to find a way to get our first message to the Christians. As I understand it, this is no more than the first move in a much more ambitious plan, isn't it?' Hernando nodded at the translator. 'Let's see how the Church reacts when it finds its venerated bishop and patron of Granada expressing himself in Arabic . . .'

'And to the prophecy,' added Hernando.

'They will interpret the prophecy as they see fit. Have no doubt about that.'

'You told me to make the message ambiguous,' Hernando complained.

'Yes, that's essential. The important thing is to sow doubt. Some will interpret it to suit the Church, but there will be others who do not see it in the same way. They will start to argue. We are good at that in this country of ours. If someone says something, the other will say the opposite, just for the sake of it. Doubtless Miguel and I will be called upon to translate the document; we can adapt it as we see fit. If we did it scrupulously and sent a message that was openly in favour of Islam, it would immediately be denounced as heresy, and there would be no room to argue; a lot of people know Arabic. That message, the one contained in the gospel you have discovered – by the way, did you bring it? I would very much like to read it.'

'No, I'm sorry,' Hernando apologized. 'I still haven't finished transcribing it, and I don't want to risk the original.'

'You're right. Well, as I was saying, that message, the Truth, must arrive at a moment when we have succeeded in spreading as many doubts as possible. We need to prepare carefully for its appearance. The problem now is what to do with all this.' Castillo pointed to the objects on the table. 'How can we conceal them for the Christians to find?'

'They are knocking down the old tower, the Turpian tower,' Don Pedro informed them.

'That would be ideal for our purposes,' Luna agreed. 'The old minaret of the main mosque.'

'When?' asked Castillo.

'Tomorrow is the feast of the Archangel Gabriel,' smiled Hernando.

The four men looked at each other. Gabriel was Jibril, the Muslims' most important angel, the one who took it upon himself to show the revealed word to the Prophet.

'God is with us, there's no doubt about that,' Don Pedro said happily.

Castillo looked for something to write with, asked permission from Hernando, who waved him on, and then added a few phrases in Latin and Castilian to the parchment, among which was the order to hide it high up in the Turpian tower.

The others looked on in silence.

'More uncertainties for the Christians,' Castillo said as he finished, blowing on the ink to dry it. 'Tomorrow night we can visit the tower.'

As with the Turpian tower, the main body of the bell tower of San José church in the Albaicín had once been the minaret of the Almorabitin, the oldest mosque in Granada. Here, though, it was the mosque that had been destroyed, while its minaret survived. The day dawned with a promise of sunshine and heat. Hernando was up early, and went for a walk around the environs of the church. The previous night, before going to bed, he had taken Don Pedro to one side and asked him about Don Ponce de Hervás: he wanted to know if his love affair with Isabel had had any repercussions.

'None at all,' replied the nobleman. 'As I told you, the magistrate does not want any scandal. You can be reassured on that score.'

Hernando stopped to admire the uneven stones and patterned brickwork of the minaret. He was particularly struck by an obviously Muslim horseshoe arch in one wall. Trying to imagine days gone by when the Muslims were called to prayer from this minaret, he almost failed to recognize two women who were leaving the church with the congregation at the end of mass. But Isabel's shining blond hair could not be hidden, even by the delicate lace of the black mantilla covering her head and face. Hernando shuddered as he watched her pass by, proud, erect, inaccessible. Sour-faced, Doña Ángela kept a vigilant eye on her. Neither of them noticed him as they walked on, staring straight ahead of them. Hernando hid in the low doorway of one of the nearby Morisco houses, and saw them head back towards the villa. The previous evening, the sight of the Alhambra lit up had reawakened his passion. He kept Isabel in sight as they moved through the passers-by. What could he do? Doña Ángela would not allow him to talk to Isabel, and when they arrived home there was no way he could even get close to her. He met four youngsters playing in the street. Taking a real out of his purse, he showed it to them; they immediately crowded round him.

'Do you see those two women?' Hernando asked, trying to make sure none of the passers-by heard him. 'I want you to run after them and to bump into the smaller one. Then keep her busy for as long as you can. But don't even touch the other one, understood?'

The four of them eagerly agreed. The eldest grabbed the coin, and they ran off without even discussing what they were going to do. Hernando hastened after them, dodging other men and women. He was worried he might have gone too far: the judge's cousin was an elderly woman . . .

A cry of shock echoed round the narrow street as Doña Ángela was bowled over and fell full length to the ground. Hernando shook his head. There was no changing his mind now! The street urchins didn't have to try to distract Doña Ángela's attention: a crowd of passers-by rushed to gather round the two women while the youngsters escaped to a chorus of curses and threats. Hernando went up to the group. Two people were helping Doña Ángela back to her feet; others were looking on, and a couple of men were still shaking their fists at the boys in the distance. Isabel was leaning over her companion. While Doña Ángela was being helped up, Isabel seemed to realize she was being watched. She straightened up and peered round until she saw Hernando standing opposite her between a man and a woman who had stopped to see what was going on.

They stared intently at one another. Isabel glowed in the sunlight. Hernando did not know whether to smile, blow her a kiss, rush round the group of bystanders to catch her arm and drag her away, or simply shout how much he wanted her. In the end, he did nothing. Nor did she. They simply devoured each other with their eyes until Doña Ángela was able to stand without any help. Hernando was distracted by the sight of a woman trying to brush the sand from Doña Ángela's dress, although the chaperone pushed her off as if she were in a hurry to get away. When he looked back again at Isabel, he saw there were tears in her eyes; her chin and lower lip were trembling. Hernando made a move towards her, as though to push his way through the crowd, but Isabel's lips tightened, and she shook her head slightly in a way that froze him solid. Then, together with the woman who had tried to clean Doña Ángela's dress, the two of them continued on their way: the cousin limping and complaining, Isabel trying to hold back more tears.

Hernando pushed his way through the people who were already dispersing and followed them, until Isabel turned her head and saw him.

'You go on, cousin,' she said, indicating to the other woman she should help Doña Ángela back to their house. 'I think that in all the commotion I lost a pin from my mantilla. I'll catch up with you.'

Watching her draw near, Hernando tried to spot the slightest sign of joy in Isabel's face, but when she was by his side he could see only the tears in her eyes.

'What are you doing here, Hernando?' she whispered.

'I wanted to see you. To talk to you, to feel—'

'That's impossible,' she said, choking with emotion. 'Please don't come back into my life. It's been so hard for me to forget you . . . No, don't say anything, for God's sake!' she cried when Hernando leant over to whisper something in her ear. 'Don't make me suffer again. Leave me, I beg you.'

Isabel did not give him the opportunity to respond. She turned her back on him and hurried off to catch up with Doña Ángela.

Isabel's refusal stayed with Hernando throughout the rest of the day. As night was falling, together with Don Pedro, Castillo and Luna, he walked round past the silk market to the Jelices gate, from where he could see the building work being done on the cathedral. The silk-weaving quarter was behind them: almost two hundred shops crammed into its narrow streets. At night it was almost deserted. The ten entrance gates were closed, and a bailiff guarded the businesses and the customs house where the traders paid duty on their goods.

Beyond the Jelices gate stood the Turpian tower. This had once been the minaret of the great mosque in Granada, and whilst the mosque had been turned into a place of Christian worship, its square tower, a little over thirteen spans in height, had become the cathedral bell tower. However, in January of that year a majestic new tower on three levels had been built to house the bells, so that the Turpian tower, now redundant, remained simply as an impediment to the works in the midst of the bishop's cathedral seat.

From the gateway where the four men stood they could see the whole area, dimly lit by the torches of the watchmen guarding the building works and those of the colleges opposite, on the far side of a square. On the left were the Colegio Real and the Santa Catalina college; on the right, set back from the square, was the cathedral. Only the central dome and the ambulatory had been completed, as well as the new belfry. This gave on to the square, leaving a large empty space between it and the other new buildings. A few yards away, at the opposite extreme to the new bell tower, stood the old mosque and its minaret.

The Turpian tower was being carefully taken down, stone by stone, so that the materials could be reused and to make sure the new cathedral roof was not damaged in any way. The four men surveyed the tower, listening hard for the conversation and laughter from the guards, who were out of sight in the main part of the cathedral.

'They mustn't see us,' whispered Castillo. 'Nobody should be able to link our presence here with the discovery of the casket.'

'There are too many guards,' Don Pedro said, discouragement in his voice. 'They're bound to see us.'

Silence reigned once more, broken only by the cries of the guards inside the cathedral. With the tar-covered casket well hidden under his cloak, Hernando breathed in the smell of silk that permeated the whole of the network of narrow streets of the silk-weaving district. It brought back to him a similar smell he had so often met back in the Alpujarra, when the cocoons were being boiled and the precious product was being spun. *It's been so hard for me to forget you,* Isabel had told him. He imagined her in Don Ponce's arms once more . . .

'Hernando!' Castillo whispered urgently in his ear. 'What shall we do?'

Yes, what shall we do? Hernando asked himself. What he most wanted to do at that moment was to run off, climb the wall into the judge's house, slip back into Isabel's bedroom and . . .

The translator shook him.

'What shall we do?' he repeated, more loudly this time. Hernando returned his attention to the square in front of them.

'There are too many guards,' Castillo warned him.

A nobleman and two scholars! What clever ruses could he expect from them?

'Yes,' he admitted, 'there seem to be quite a few of them. But they won't be guarding the Turpian tower. They're not interested in it. They'll be concentrating on the cathedral; that's why they're there.' He thought it over for a few moments. 'You three go round the cathedral, and on the far side, beyond Calle de la Cárcel, make sure your faces are covered and start a quarrel. As soon as I hear your voices, I'll go across and get into the tower.'

The three others could not hide their sense of relief at Hernando's suggestion. They hurried off towards Plaza de Bibarrambla until they reached Calle de la Cárcel, beyond the cathedral. As soon as they had left him, Hernando's thoughts again turned to Isabel. Did her refusal mean he would never be able to talk to her again? Did he really *want* to see her again? Or were his feelings merely a mirage created by the enchanting glow from the Alhambra? He closed his eyes and gave a deep sigh.

Shouting in the distance brought him back to reality. 'Santiago!' he heard someone call. He did not think twice. A couple of bounds took him to the mosque wall. He pressed his back against it so that he could glide along in its shadow. There was no entrance to the tower from the square; it must be inside the mosque itself. He crept out from behind the Turpian tower and found himself in the open ground where the cathedral transept and nave were being built. There were several bonfires near the building works, and he could see that the guards were all looking in the direction of Calle de la Cárcel, where the sounds of men's raised voices and the clash of swords could be heard. Hernando went round the tower and at its base discovered the entrance. He edged sideways up a narrow staircase barely more than a couple of handspans in width, and then suddenly found himself out again in the cool night air. Don Pedro and his companions were still carrying on with their fight, but up there he could no longer hear them: he could see the Alhambra and the whole of Granada! How often the faithful must have been called to prayer from this very spot! 'Allah is great!' he exclaimed, clasping the casket. By the light of the moon he searched for a stone that had already been loosened prior to being dismantled. When he found one, he pulled it apart, scraped away the lime sealing the blocks together, and pushed the tarred casket into the gap. Then he pushed the stone back into place. He climbed back down the staircase and retraced his steps to the silk exchange. From there he headed to Bibarrambla and Calle de la Cárcel to put an end to the staged quarrel.

53

Early in May 1588, only a few days before the Spanish armada was to set sail from Lisbon to conquer England, Philip II wrote to the Archbishop of Granada thanking him for the gift of half of the veil of the Virgin Mary that he had sent to El Escorial, and in the name of his subjects expressed his satisfaction at the discovery of such precious relics. As soon as the workmen dismantling the Turpian tower had found the casket Hernando had hidden there, and inside it discovered the parchment signed by Saint Caecilius, the Virgin's veil and the relic of Saint Stephen, Granada exploded with Christian fervour. This was the first, longed-for news of Saint Caecilius. With it came proof that before the arrival of the Muslims, Granada had been as Christian as any other capital city in the Spanish kingdom. This caused an outburst of passion and mysticism in the ordinary people that the Church was careful not to restrain in any way. From that moment on, countless people said they had witnessed miracles, mysterious lights, apparitions and all kinds of extraordinary phenomena. Granada cathedral had its relics, and the faith of its inhabitants could be based on something more than words!

Aisha was taken aback when one of the only two Morisco beggars in the city closed his filthy, trembling hand with surprising speed just as she was about to drop a penny into it. They were in Calle de la Feria, near the Corbache gate. She was left holding the coin as the beggar spat at her feet and turned away from her. At once, several Christian beggars pressed round her to claim the money. Aisha hesitated. The law of the Prophet said that one should give alms, but not to Christians. But she was so perturbed when she saw the man who had refused her charity return to begging a little further down the street that she let the penny fall into one of the hands insistently clasping hers.

Not even beggars respected her! She dragged herself towards Juan Marco's weaving workshop. 'The Nazarene woman', some of them even called her, after the news spread through Córdoba that Hernando was betraying his brothers and collaborating with the Church in the investigation into the crimes committed in the Alpujarra. In recent years, the economic situation of the deported Moriscos had improved considerably. The fact that they worked hard, compared to the lazy Christians, had brought them prosperity, so that many of those who at first had been obliged to sell their labour for wretched day wages now had businesses of their own. Most of them supplemented their incomes by cultivating small plots on the outskirts of the city down by the river Guadalquivir. So successful were they that the guilds in Córdoba, as in many other Spanish cities, implored the authorities to stop new Christians opening shops or having a trade, and ensure that they only did paid work for others. Their requests fell on deaf ears, because the city councils were pleased with the competition the Moriscos brought to the economy. All this meant that the relations between the two communities were more strained than ever.

Aisha was by now almost forty-seven years old. She felt old and alone: especially alone. The only son she had left was an enemy to their faith, a traitor to his brothers. What could have become of her other children? she wondered, as she entered the door of the master weaver's light and airy workshop. Shamir. Fátima and the children. What was Fátima's life like with Brahim? At night, as she lay still and anguished on her straw mattress, Aisha tried to drive away the images that kept appearing of Fátima being violated by Brahim; of her own son and her grandson Francisco being whipped on one of the ships, forced to become galley slaves. Yet the tragic images kept coming back again and again, assaulting her senses as she tried to sleep. Musa and Aquil! It was common knowledge that all those children who had been handed over to the Christians after the uprising had been forcibly converted or sold as slaves. Were her children still alive? Aisha raised her forearm to her face and staunched the tears that had begun to flow. More tears! How could her weary eyes still weep so much?

She earned a good wage, yes, but everyone seemed to know this was thanks to Hernando, and ever since she had heard the people she shared her house with calling her 'Nazarene' in whispers, this extra money was of no use to her. None of them spoke to her. First some of her food started to disappear. She said nothing. Then, in the place where she kept her supplies, she found dry chunks of millet bread. Still she said nothing, and continued to buy things the others ate. One day she found her room taken over by a family with three children. Again, she said not a word and went on paying as if she were living in it on her own. What if they threw her out? Where would she go? Who would take her in? She might have money, but she was nothing more than the Nazarene woman; at least there she had a roof over her head. Another day when she returned from work she found all her belongings piled in the front doorway. From then on, she slept out there.

In the back room of the weaver's workshop, where the taffeta was woven on four looms, Aisha made for her post opposite a series of baskets where the dyed strands of silk were piled. They were divided into colours: blues, greens and many other shades, including gold, the famous Spanish red, and the valuable crimsons, made from cochineal that came from tiny insects that lived on the holm oaks. She had to sort out the threads and then prepare the warp of the loom by gathering all the ones of the same length and winding them round the iron spindle used for the weaving. She picked up a stool and carried it across the room, raising her hand to her lower back to ease the pain. She sat down in front of a basket. Why had all-powerful God abandoned her? she complained to herself as she started to work on another skein of coloured silk.

On the far side of the strait separating Spain from Barbary, in a rich palace in the Tetuan medina, Fátima was dictating a letter to a Jewish trader. She promised him a large sum of money to write it in Arabic, deliver it to Córdoba with someone he trusted, and then bring back the reply.

'Beloved husband,' she began, her nervousness evident from her voice, 'peace and the blessings of the Magnanimous, He who judges with truth, be upon you . . .'

Fátima paused. What could she say to someone she had not seen for seven years? How could she find the words? She had it all prepared, she had thought it over as she remembered the past with joy and tears, but when the moment of truth came she could not find the words.

The patient old Jew raised his eyes from the sheet of paper and stared at her: she was beautiful, proud-looking and self-possessed, but there was something hard and cold about her, a severity that now seemed to be giving way to doubt. He watched her pace up and down the room, go out through the arches leading to the courtyard and then almost immediately come back in; raise her ring-laden hands to her lips, then cross them under her breasts or wave one in the air as if this would help her find the fluency she seemed to have lost.

'My lady,' said the trader turned secretary, 'may I help you? What is it you want to say to your beloved?'

Fátima fixed her shining cold eyes on the Jew. What she wanted to say would never fit into a letter, she wanted to tell him. She wanted to tell him something as simple as the fact that Brahim had died and she wished above all that Hernando would come to be with her in Tetuan. That nothing now stood in the way of their happiness, and that she was waiting for him. But what if he had married again? What if he had already found happiness? It had been seven years . . .

Seven years of complete submission! Fátima came to a halt in front of the old Jew, who went on observing her, quill poised.

'It was a shout,' she whispered. The old man made as if to dip his quill into the ink, but Fátima stopped him. 'No, don't write it down. It was a shout that woke me up and brought me back to life.'

The old man put the quill down on the desk and settled back in his chair, encouraging Fátima to go on with her story. He knew about Brahim's murder; all Tetuan knew he had been killed.

'Filthy dog!' Fátima continued. 'That was what I heard Shamir shouting at Nasi. It was then I realized that the boy of fifteen had become a man, toughened by his life at sea, the attacks on Christian ships and raids on the coast of Andalusia. It happened right here in this courtyard,' she added, pointing to the marvellous fountain surrounded by a circular mosaic of brightly coloured tiny stones forming a geometric pattern, which shot a jet of water from ground level. 'I watched how Nasi, ten years older than him and a feared, cruel corsair, dropped his hand to the hilt of his scimitar when he heard this insult. I trembled, and shrank into myself as I had done ever since I first set foot in this wretched city. My little Abdul, his blue eyes opened wide, was standing next to Shamir. When Nasi unsheathed his scimitar and brandished his weapon in their faces, I thought I was going to faint.' Fátima fell silent as she relived those moments; the Jewish trader did not dare move. All of a sudden she stared intently at him: 'Do you know something, Ephraim? God is great. Shamir and Abdul took a few steps back, but not to escape, as I was willing them. No, they too drew their swords, both at the same time, and stood there side by side, their feet firmly planted on the ground, as if they were a single person. They did not show the slightest sign of fear. Shamir ordered Abdul to step aside, to leave him on his own. My little one obeyed, but moved to protect his back as if it were something he had done thousands of times. "Dog!" Shamir insulted Nasi a second time, thrusting his scimitar at him. "Flea-bitten swine!"

'Blind with rage, Nasi launched himself at the lad, but Shamir, agile as a cat, avoided his lunge, struck Nasi's scimitar and parried the blow. I remember ... I remember that the sound of the clash of steel made the pillars round the yard shake. The noise was like a signal to my little Abdul. He wheeled round from behind Shamir and also slashed at Nasi's scimitar. The corsair could do nothing to stop it, only watch as his weapon flew out of his hand. In the blink of an eye my two boys were back in position, weapons at the ready, a smile on their faces. Yes, they were smiling! As if they had the world at their feet. "If you don't want to die like the pig you are, pick up your sword and try to fight like a true believer," Shamir told Nasi.'

Fátima fell silent. She gazed out at the courtyard, reliving the fight.

'My lady ... carry on,' the Jew begged her when the silence became prolonged.

Fátima smiled nostalgically. 'The commotion woke my husband,' she resumed. 'He came waddling out into the court-yard to stop the fight and chastise Shamir and Abdul. "What makes you think you can attack my lieutenant in my own house?" he shouted at them. "Scum!" he muttered, spitting at their feet.

'But by then I had caught a glimpse of the universe opening before my son and Shamir, the world they had smiled at so proudly and confidently like the grown-up men they now were ... Day by day, encouraged by the virility of my children, I gradually recovered my self-esteem. One night soon afterwards, while the four of them were eating, sitting on cushions around a low table without any weapons, I burst into the dining room. The first thing I did was dismiss the servants and slaves. I can still see Brahim's look of surprise. Little could he guess what was coming. "There's something urgent I need to discuss with you," I said brazenly. With that I pulled out two daggers I had hidden under my clothes. I threw one to Shamir, and seized the other. Nasi leapt to his feet, but Brahim was unable to react. Before his lieutenant could reach me, I plunged the knife into Brahim's chest.' Fátima broke off and stared defiantly at the old Jewish man. Her voice was cold, expressionless. 'Shamir did not immediately realize what was going on, but when he did, he seized Nasi and threatened him with the dagger; Abdul also threw himself on the corsair.'

Fátima fell silent again for a few moments. When she spoke once more, her voice was barely a whisper. The old man watched her, intrigued: what other secrets were hidden behind those beautiful black eyes?

'My husband did not die from that first wound. I am only a weak, inexperienced woman. But it caused him so much pain he was unable to defend himself. I stabbed him in the mouth so that he could not cry out, then hacked at his stump until I almost reached his elbow. He took a long while to bleed to death. A very long while . . . He was pleading with me. I remembered the life of suffering he had given me as I saw his life drain away. I did not look away until he breathed his last. He died like a stuck pig.'

'Mother! What have you done?' shouted Abdul.

The boy was staring wide-eyed at Brahim, who was lying sprawled on the cushions with his left hand pressed against the wound in his chest; the blood was gushing out all over him.

Fátima said nothing, and gestured for them to be quiet as Brahim slowly bled to death on the rich silk rugs covering the floor of the room.

'Shamir,' she said firmly when her despised husband had finally expired, 'from now on you are the head of the family. Everything is yours.'

Shamir, who was still standing behind Nasi with his dagger pressed to his throat, was unable to take his eyes off his father. Abdul held his breath, his gaze darting between Brahim and Shamir.

'He was not a good man,' Fátima insisted, faced with Shamir's silence. 'He ruined your mother's life, and mine. Both of yours too . . .'

The lad reacted when he heard Aisha named. 'What shall we do now?' he asked, increasing the pressure from his knife on Nasi's throat, as if he wanted him to share the same fate as Brahim.

'You two,' she said, addressing Shamir and Abdul, 'take Brahim's treasure and go and hide in the port. Have all your men and ships ready to depart. Wait there for my instructions. You,' she added, going up to the corsair, 'are to go straight to the house of the governor Muhammad al-Naqsis. You are to inform him that Shamir, the son of Brahim of Juviles, who is now the head of the family, swears his loyalty to him and places all his ships and men at his disposal.'

'What if I refuse?' Nasi retorted.

'Kill him!' said Fátima, turning her back on him.

The sound of the dagger slitting the throat of Brahim's second-in-command took her by surprise. She had expected to hear the corsair pleading for his life, but Shamir did not give him the chance. Fátima turned back to see Nasi slumping to the floor, his throat cut.

'He was not a good man,' Shamir said simply.

'All right,' Fátima agreed. 'This does not change anything. Do as I told you.'

At first light, Shamir and Abdul set off for the port with all Brahim's gold, jewels and documents. Fátima had told two slaves to prepare the corpses and to clean the dining room. That same night she had visited the wing of the palace where Brahim's second wife lived her lonely existence. She told her that Brahim had died without giving her any more details, but emphasized that it was Shamir who was the new head of the family. The other woman looked at the floor and said nothing. She knew that her fate now depended on the generosity of the young man who loved Fátima like a mother.

The next morning, Fátima dressed and headed for the house of Muhammad al-Naqsis. Earlier in the sixteenth century, Tetuan had been part of the kingdom of Fez, which was subsequently taken over by Morocco; after a period of independence, it was conquered a second time. Power at the centre was weak, however, and insistent rumours had reached Brahim's palace to the effect that the al-Naqsis family wanted to declare their independence. Brahim himself had talked about the possibility, angry that his commercial rivals might take control of the city. Even though she was a woman, the governor agreed to see Fátima. The al-Naqsis family were at loggerheads with Brahim over the division of the spoils of piracy, and so a visit by his adversary's wife aroused Muhammad's curiosity.

'What about Brahim?' Muhammad al-Naqsis asked when Fátima swore loyalty to him in the name of Shamir.

'He's dead.'

The governor looked Fátima up and down, unable to conceal his admiration. Before him stood the most beautiful, and now the richest, woman in all Tetuan.

'And his second-in-command?' he asked, pretending to have accepted her terse response.

'He also has passed away,' Fátima replied. Her voice was firm, although as befitted a submissive Muslim woman she did not raise her eyes from the floor.

Passed away? thought the governor. Is that all? What did you have to do with those two deaths, I wonder?

He looked at Fátima with increased respect. She spoke again, briefly and to the point. It took him only a few seconds to decide not to ask her any more questions, and to accept the aid that this generous widow seemed willing to offer him so that he could win independence.

The next day Fátima, accompanied by women hired to mourn dressed in coarse garments, their faces daubed with soot, listened as verses and songs were recited in honour of the dead. After each verse, the mourners cried out, beat their breasts, scratched their cheeks until the blood ran and tore out their hair. These funeral rites were repeated for seven days.

The old Jewish man looked up. His eyes met Fátima's. They both knew that the confession she had just made would never be repeated anywhere else. He had long since learnt to see, listen and keep quiet. His own people had not only survived but grown rich, thanks to the virtue of discretion.

'My lady . . .' he murmured, pointing to the still-blank sheet of paper.

Fátima sighed. Yes, the moment had come. In a strong, clear voice, she started to dictate: 'Beloved husband, peace and the blessings of the Magnanimous, He who judges with truth, be upon you . . .'

54

He blew with His winds, and they were scattered.

Medal inscription ordered by Queen Elizabeth of England

After spending two months in the port of La Coruña, and despite several attempts at peace negotiations and various meetings where the advice was not to go ahead with the enterprise, the great armada finally set off for the conquest of England. It was commanded by the Duke of Medina Sidonia, who had taken over from the Marquis of Santa Cruz after his sudden demise.

Don Alfonso de Córdoba and his eldest son, together with twenty servants including José Caro, as well as dozens of trunks containing their belongings, clothing, books and two complete dinner services, embarked on one of the leading ships.

The news of the fleet that began to reach Spain soon afterwards was not what had been expected after the blessing from God with which they had undertaken the war against England. The aim had been to join up with the Duke of Parma's regiments in Dunkirk, embark them on the ships, and then to invade England. However, after the fleet had dropped anchor in Calais, only twenty-five leagues from where the Duke of Parma's troops were stationed, the Spaniards found that the Dutch had blockaded the bay at Dunkirk. This meant that the Duke of Parma had no way to skirt round the Dutch blockade and join the fleet. The English admiral Lord Howard took full advantage of the opportunity offered by having the enemy fleet confined in a small space at Calais, and attacked it with fire ships.

On the night of 7 August, the Spaniards saw eight burning supply ships bearing downwind on them from the English side. Two of the dreaded 'hellburners' were diverted by means of long poles from small boats, but the other six drifted into the Spanish fleet, bursting into flames, their guns firing at random as they exploded. The Spanish captains were forced to cut their anchor cables and scatter, thus breaking the crescent formation the fleet had adopted from the start. Seeing that the enemy's usual tight formation was now in tatters, the English attacked and a bloody battle ensued. The Spaniards found themselves pushed by the wind towards the north of the English Channel. However hard the Duke of Medina Sidonia tried to get back to the coast of Flanders, the atmospheric conditions made this impossible. The English stood off without attacking, simply making sure that their enemy did not return.

Some days later, the Spanish admiral ordered that all the animals the fleet was transporting be thrown overboard. The fleet's supplies of water and food were soon spoilt because of the poor quality of the barrels in which they were kept (they had been made from cheap staves and hoops after Drake had burnt the more solid ones at Cádiz the year before), and many of the ships were by now in poor condition, with their crews dying of typhus or scurvy. Nevertheless, the Duke of Medina Sidonia decided to continue north around Scotland and the unknown coasts of the west of Ireland in order to return to Spain.

On 21 September the Duke of Medina Sidonia's flagship, bound together by three huge cables to prevent it coming apart (as though it were some macabre gift), and with the admiral himself dying on a litter, arrived back in Santander with another eight galleons. Only thirty-five of the original 130 that had made up the great armada succeeded in reaching different ports of Spain once more. Some had been sunk during the

Channel battle; many more were lost on the Irish coasts, where storms had battered the dilapidated ships, wrecking them on the shores of the west of the island. Still others met an unknown fate. Some days after the admiral's arrival, a letter was dispatched to Córdoba: the ship Don Alfonso and his son were sailing on had not returned.

When she received the news, Doña Lucía gave instructions for everyone in the duke's palace – hidalgos, servants, slaves, and Hernando as well – to attend the three daily masses that the priest of the palace chapel organized. During the rest of the day the silence was interrupted only by the murmuring of rosaries being said at all hours by the hidalgos and the duchess, gathered in the gloom of one of the main rooms. They all had to adhere to a strict fast; reading, dancing and music were forbidden; and none of them dared leave the palace except to go to church or to attend the constant rogations and processions that had been organized all over Spain following the disaster and the lack of information about so many ships and their crews.

'*Maria, Mater Gratiae, Mater Misericordiae . . .*'

Kneeling behind the duchess, the entire household recited the rosary over and over again. Hernando repeated the interminable prayers mechanically, but all around him he could hear the voices of the proud, haughty courtiers praying with real devotion. He could see from their faces how concerned, even anxious, they were: their future depended on Don Alfonso's life and generosity, and if he were dead . . .

'Don't worry, cousin,' Don Sancho said one day over their midday meal: the table had an austere look to it, with black bread and fish, and none of the wines or delicacies usually served in the palace, 'if your husband and his first-born were taken prisoner on the Irish coast, their captors will respect them. They represent a large ransom. No one will harm them. Trust in God. They will be well looked after until the ransom is paid; that is the law of honour, the law of war.'

The glimmer of hope that had shone in the duchess's eyes when the old hidalgo said this turned to tears as the news from

Ireland began to reach Spain. Sir William Fitzwilliam, at that time commander of the English forces in Ireland, had only 750 men to protect the island from the native inhabitants, who were still fighting for their freedom. As a consequence he could not contemplate having to deal with such a high number of enemy soldiers. His orders were categorical: any Spaniard found on Irish territory, be they noble, soldier, servant or galley slave, was to be arrested and immediately executed.

Philip II's informers and those soldiers who, with the help of Irish lords, managed to escape through Scotland were told endless stories of ghastly massacres of Spaniards. Without compassion or chivalry, the English killed even those who surrendered.

Hernando's concern for the fate of a man who had treated him as a friend turned into worry about his own future. His relations with the duchess had worsened still further when she had found out about his love affair with Isabel. As was the case with Don Sancho, Doña Lucía refused to speak to him: she never even looked in his direction; and the entire palace treated him as if he were nothing more than a hindrance left by someone whose fate they knew nothing of. Perhaps in other circumstances he would not have been so concerned, since he hated the hypocrisy such an idle kind of existence implied. But the duke's favour, and access to his library with dozens of books in it, as well as the possibility of devoting himself completely to the Morisco community's cause following the spectacular success of the discovery of the parchment in the Turpian tower, were things that Hernando would not and could not renounce, however awkward his continued presence in the duke's palace was proving to be. The cathedral chapter had commissioned Luna and Castillo to translate the parchment. He had finally worked out how to cut the end of the reeds he used for writing into a slight rightward curve, and, as if his hand were guided by God, he could now inscribe the most beautiful Arabic letters he had ever imagined on to the sheets of paper.

*　*　*

In September of that year, while the whole of Spain, including the King, was weeping over the defeat of the great armada, a young Jew from Tetuan carrying fake papers declaring him to be an oil merchant from Málaga arrived in Córdoba as part of a caravan he had joined in Seville.

The young man passed the customs house at the Calahorra tower. As he was crossing the Roman bridge with a string of mules beside him, he stared up at the vast building works going on almost opposite, beyond the bridge and the entrance gate to the city. He remembered what his father had told him before he left Tetuan: 'On the far side of the bridge you will find the great mosque on which the Christians are building their cathedral.' His father was in turn repeating the instructions he had received from Fátima. He spoke to his son in Spanish, to remind him of the language they used only for doing business with the Christians who came to Barbary. Now he had reached his goal!

Ephraim's son (and namesake) came to a halt in front of the monumental structure rising above the mosque's low roof. Rows of majestic flying buttresses stood waiting for the completion of the dome that would be the cathedral's crowning glory.

'By the cathedral front, on the far side of the river, where the bell tower stands,' his father had continued, 'you'll come across a street that leads up to Calle de los Deanes, which in turn takes you to Calle de los Barberos, and then, higher up, becomes Calle Almanzor . . .' The old Jewish man's voice trembled.

'What's the matter, Father?' Ephraim asked with concern. He reached out to rest his hand on his father's arm.

'The district you are to aim for', the old man went on, after clearing his throat, 'is what used to be Córdoba's Jewry, from which the Christians expelled us less than a century ago.' His voice quavered again. Fátima had explained to him about the house with a courtyard where the family lived. He listened patiently to her. How often had he heard the description of those same streets from his grandfather's lips! 'That's where your roots are, my son. Breathe the air in deeply, and bring me back some of it!'

The woman who received him in the house knew nothing about Hernando Ruiz, a new Christian from Juviles to whom Ephraim was supposed to give the letter he had carefully concealed under his clothing. In fact, she threw him out when the Jewish boy insisted that a Morisco family had lived there in the past.

'No heretic has ever set foot in this house!' she shouted at him, slamming shut the door in the entranceway.

'If by any chance you don't find him there,' his father had told him, 'you should make for the royal stables. According to my lady, they are bound to have news of him there.' Ephraim asked where the stables were, went back through the city and past the fortress where the Holy Inquisition had its head-quarters, and finally reached them.

'I've no idea whom you're talking about,' he was told by a lad he bumped into as soon as he entered the yard. 'But if he's a new Christian, ask in the smith's forge. Jerónimo is bound to know of him; he's worked here for years.'

Ephraim went on, through the horses' stalls and the central ring, where several riders were training colts. The Jewish lad stopped for a few moments. How different these horses were from the small Arab steeds of his country! The lad called out to him from the entrance to the yard, telling him to carry on to the forge. Why would this Jerónimo know about a new Christian? he wondered as he made for the building. He found his answer in the blacksmith's dark complexion and Arab features. The man greeted him with a smile, which vanished as soon as he learnt of the reason for his visit.

'What do you want from Hernando?' he growled.

Ephraim hesitated: why such suspicion? The smith straightened up, surrounded by anvils, the roaring forge, his tools and bars of iron. He looked massive, and was breathing heavily through his bulbous nose.

'Do you know him?' the young man asked firmly.

This time it was the blacksmith who hesitated.

'Yes,' he admitted finally.

'Do you know how I could find him?'

Jerónimo took a step towards him. 'Why?'

'That's my business. All I'm asking you is if you know where I can find this Hernando. If you do, and want to tell me, that's fine; if not, I don't mean to trouble you, and I'll ask elsewhere.'

'I know nothing about him.'

'Thank you,' Ephraim said by way of goodbye, convinced that the Arab was not telling the truth. Why would that be?

The blacksmith had no wish to tell him anything about Hernando, but then again, perhaps it would be useful to discover what the visitor was doing in Córdoba.

'I do know where you can find his mother though,' he admitted.

Ephraim halted. 'The lady demands that the letter be handed over to him personally, or to his mother. Her name is Aisha. You are not to give it to anyone else,' his father had warned him.

What was happening with that family? Ephraim wondered when he reached the door of Aisha's house in a narrow alleyway in the Santiago district, at the opposite end of the city. It was obvious from his eyes that Jerónimo had lied to him, and when he asked some women working with pots and flowers in the courtyard of the building about Aisha, they looked at him with contempt. Ephraim was a strong young man, perhaps not as strong as the blacksmith, but more so than the Morisco who answered the women's calls. And he was tired. He had walked for days from Seville, where he had arrived in a Portuguese boat that had sailed from Ceuta, and he had spent all day going from place to place looking for Hernando Ruiz or his mother, running the risk that any argument might lead to his arrest and reveal either that he was a Jew or that his papers were false.

'Why are you looking for Aisha?' the Morisco asked him disdainfully.

That was enough! Ephraim cast aside all caution, scowled and swung his hand to the dagger hilt at his belt. The Morisco's eyes could not help but follow the movement of the young Jew's hand.

'That's none of your business,' Ephraim said. 'Does she live here?' The Morisco hesitated. 'Does she live here or not?' Ephraim shouted, making as if to draw his dagger.

She did. She slept right there, behind where Ephraim was standing, in the entrance gateway. He turned and saw the crumpled blanket the Morisco pointed to with a tilt of his chin. However, at that time of day she was still at the weaver's workshop.

Ephraim waited out in the narrow alleyway leading to the house. A short time later, something told him that the stooped woman coming slowly towards him, staring at the ground and with her clothes hanging loosely from her shoulders, must be the person he was looking for.

'Aisha?' he asked as she walked past him. She nodded, showing her sad, sunken eyes in lined, discoloured sockets. 'Peace be with you,' Ephraim greeted her. She seemed surprised at his courteous tone. To the young Jew she seemed like a hurt, defenceless animal. What was going on? 'My name is Ephraim, and I've come from Tetuan . . .' he whispered in her ear.

Aisha reacted with unexpected energy. 'Be quiet!' she warned, gesturing towards the interior of the house beyond the entrance. Ephraim turned and saw several faces peering out at them.

Without another word, Aisha set off towards the river. Ephraim followed her, trying to walk as slowly as she did.

'I've come—' he repeated when they were some distance from the house, but Aisha again gestured for him to be quiet.

They went through the Martos gate down to the banks of the Guadalquivir, by the mill that belonged to the Order of Calatrava. When they had reached the riverbank, Aisha turned to him.

'Have you brought news of Fátima?' she asked in a faint voice.

'Yes. I have—'

'What do you know of my son Shamir?' she interrupted him, forcing him to come to a halt.

Ephraim thought he could detect a glimmer of life in her dead-looking eyes. 'He is well.' Before he had left, his father had explained the situation. 'But I know little more about him,' he added. 'I've brought you a letter from Fátima. It's for your son Hernando, but it's also addressed to you.' He searched in his clothes for it.

'I don't know how to read,' said Aisha.

Ephraim stood holding out the letter. 'Give it to your son so that he can read it for you,' he said, moving towards her for her to take it.

Aisha gave a sad smile. How could she possibly tell her son she had lied to him and that Fátima, Francisco and Inés were still alive? 'You read it.'

Ephraim hesitated. 'To Hernando or his mother,' his father had told him. In the background he heard the incessant noises of the millstones crushing the grain as the waters of the Guadalquivir flowed by.

'All right,' he agreed, and tore open the seal. ' "Beloved husband," ' he started to read, ' "peace and the blessings of the Magnanimous, He who judges with truth, be upon you . . ." '

The sun was beginning to set, picking out their silhouettes on the riverbank. Concentrating on reading the letter, Ephraim did not notice Aisha's smile of satisfaction when he told of the moment when Brahim died, bleeding like a stuck pig. He had to clear his throat several times as he read the details of the murder written in his father's familiar hand.

The letter addressed to Hernando went on:

Your son is well. He has turned into an intelligent young man and has become hardened through piracy against the Christians. How is your mother? I trust that the strength and courage she showed when looking after me have helped her overcome all the trials God has put us through. Tell her that

Shamir is also a grown man, who in addition is very rich now after his accursed father's death. Both of them, brave and free, plough the seas in the name of the one true God, our strength and hope, the one who brings life and death, fighting and causing harm to the Christians who have brought so much evil upon us. Inés is growing in good health. Beloved husband, I do not know what your mother told you about the kidnap of your son, Inés and me, your slave, but I have come to think she told you we were all dead. Otherwise I am convinced you would have come to find us. The boys never realized this, and for many years were expecting you to come. I wondered whether I should tell them, but decided that the possibility, the hope, would help them on what seemed to be a cruel and difficult path. Now it is too late to tell them. You yourself will have to do so. They will forgive you, I am sure; as I am also certain that you forgive your mother. I was the one who asked her to do this, to prevent you from following us to this den of corsairs where Brahim was waiting with a whole army to kill you.

At this point, Ephraim had to pause in his account because Aisha was sobbing so much. He avoided looking at her, taken aback by the grief she made no effort to hide.

'Go on,' Aisha urged him in a trembling voice, and the Jew read:

Hernando, we have many nights to catch up on. Tetuan is our paradise. We can live here with no problems and in the true faith, without having to hide ourselves from anything or anyone. And yet I do not know whether you have married again. I would not reproach you for it, as it is understandable. If that is the case, come here with your new wife and children, if you have any. Like the good Muslim woman I am sure she is, she will understand and accept the situation. Bring Aisha as well: Shamir needs her. We all need both of you! May God guide the bearer of this letter, find you in good health, and bring you back to my arms and those of your children.

Aisha stood without speaking for a long while, staring at the already darkening waters of the Guadalquivir.

'That's all,' said Ephraim eventually.

'Does she expect a reply?' Aisha said, turning to confront him.

'Yes,' Ephraim said uncertainly, surprised at her forcefulness. 'So I've been told.'

'I don't know how to write either.'

'Your son . . .'

'My son doesn't write in Arabic any more!' Aisha retorted, her voice sharp with rancour. 'Remember well what I am going to tell you, and make sure Fátima hears it: the man she once loved no longer exists. Hernando has abandoned the true faith and betrayed his people; no one in our community either talks to him or respects him. His Nazarene blood has won out. In the Alpujarra he helped the Christians and in secret even saved some of their wretched lives. He is now living in the palace of a Córdoba nobleman, one of those who killed so many of our people. Hernando has become just like them, living a life of ease. Instead of making copies of the Koran or prophecies, he works for the Bishop of Granada praising the Christian martyrs of the Alpujarra, those who stole from us, spat at us . . . abused us.'

With this, Aisha fell silent again. Ephraim saw her tremble, and watched as tears fought to flow from furious, sad eyes.

'Hernando is no longer my son. He is not worthy of you or of my grandchildren,' she murmured. 'I, Aisha, tell you this, the woman who conceived him after being cruelly abused, who carried him in her womb, and who gave birth to him in pain . . . all the pain in the world. Fátima, my beloved Fátima, may peace be with you and yours.' Aisha grabbed the letter from Ephraim's hands and tore it into pieces. She went to the river's edge and dropped the pieces into the water. 'Did you understand all that?' she asked, her back towards him.

'Yes.' It cost him a great effort just to get out this single word.

He swallowed what little saliva was still in his throat. 'And you, what will you do? The letter said—'

'I no longer have the strength. God cannot ask me to set off on a long journey like that. Go back to your country and give my message to Fátima. May God be with you.'

Then, without so much as turning to look at him, Aisha walked away slowly along the very same path she and Hernando had taken one day, alongside the river that had swallowed up Hamid.

A few days before the feast of Saint Luke on 18 October, the Córdoba authorities put up posters all over the city announcing the great rogation for the return of the armada ships that had still not arrived. More than seventy still had not reappeared! At the same time, criers from the city council read out proclamations in the busiest spots calling on all inhabitants to join in the procession, everyone, having confessed and been to communion, to carry their cross, flail or candle. The procession was to start from the doors of the cathedral an hour after noon, so that the Christians of Córdoba spent the morning confessing and taking communion as though it was Easter Thursday.

In the Duke of Monterreal's palace, Doña Lucía, her daughters and her son were all ready, dressed in the strictest black and each of them carrying a big candle. The hidalgos and Hernando, also dressed in black, supplied themselves with torches to carry in the procession and began to gather in Doña Lucía's room to wait for the tolling of all the city's bells. The bishop had ordered that even those in the convents and hermitages around the city should join in. A haggard-looking Doña Lucía was sitting with her children murmuring prayers as she clicked her rosary beads. The others were in a state of tense expectation. Then Don Esteban made his appearance. He was barefoot, stripped to the waist, and wearing only a pair of breeches. Carrying a big wooden cross over his good shoulder, he went up to the duchess and greeted her with a slight bow of the head. The old invalid sergeant still had a strong body, criss-crossed by many scars. Some were no more than big or small lines in his skin; others, like the one that began at his left shoulder, were deep furrows. Doña Lucía returned the sergeant's greetings, her thin lips tightening into a line and her eyes suddenly moist. At that moment one of the hidalgos slipped out of the room to find another cross he could carry in the procession. The others exchanged glances and one by one followed the first man's footsteps.

'If you commend yourself to God, you can save Don Alfonso's life a second time.' These were the first words Don Sancho had addressed to Hernando in many days. 'Or is it all the same to you if he dies?'

Did Hernando want the duke to die? No. He recalled the days they had spent in Barrax's tent, and their escape. The duke was a Christian, but he was his friend; perhaps the only one he could count on in all Córdoba. Besides, was it not he, Hernando, who defended the existence of a single God, the God of Abraham? He followed the hidalgo, determined to do penance for Don Alfonso. What did anything matter now? His brothers in faith were convinced of his betrayal. Nothing he did could make the contempt they felt towards him any worse.

'How will we find a wooden cross now?' he heard one of the hidalgos complain. 'We don't have time to . . .'

'Swords, iron bars or planks of wood will do if we tie them to our backs and keep our arms outstretched to make a cross,' the man beside him said.

'Or a penance,' another hidalgo said. 'A whip or a hairshirt.'

There was no lack of swords in the duke's palace, but Hernando remembered the large old wooden cross hanging in a corner of the stables. The stable lad had explained that the duke had decided to replace the magnificent bronze Christ that hung in the palace chapel for one made from mahogany brought from the island of Cuba. The old cross, stripped of its figure, had ended up in the stables.

It was a sunny, cold day. To the sound of all the bells in the city and the surrounding villages, the huge rogation procession left Córdoba cathedral by the Santa Catalina gate. It proceeded down towards the river, then crossed under the bridge between the bishopric and the cathedral until it reached the bishop's palace, where the bishop blessed it from his balcony. The procession was headed by the city governor and the cathedral master, followed by the councillors and the city magistrates with their banners. Behind them, in the midst of the members of the cathedral chapter, priests and sacristans, the figure of the Christ from the Punto chapel was carried on a bier. The friars from the many convents in the city carried floats with images of their churches, some of them under canopies. Then came more than two thousand people carrying candles or lit torches, with Doña Lucía and her children in the lead, consoled by the nobles who had taken up their places alongside the family.

In the rear of the procession were almost a thousand penitents. Carrying his cross, Hernando studied them while he waited to join in. Like him, most of them were barefoot and naked to the waist. Many were carrying crosses. Others had their arms outstretched, with swords or iron bars strapped on their backs. Still more penitents had spiked belts round their legs or waists, or had covered themselves in brambles or nettles, while a few had ropes round their necks with which their companions pulled them along. All of them murmured prayers as they walked, but the noise left Hernando feeling completely empty. What would the Moriscos think if they saw him? Perhaps they would not recognize him among all these people, and anyway, he told himself again, what did it matter now?

The inhabitants of the city fell to their knees as the procession went by, following a route through the streets that took it past all the churches and convents. Whenever it reached a church of any size, the procession entered, to be greeted by singing from the choir. The line of people was so long that the start of the procession was several hours ahead of the penitents. In smaller churches, the religious community came outside with their images and sang misereres from the doorways; the nuns in closed orders looked on from inside their sanctuaries.

They had walked a long way in the procession, which according to the proclamation should continue until nightfall, when Hernando began to feel that the weight of the cross was becoming unbearable. Why had he not simply tied on a sword like the hidalgos? What on earth was he doing there anyway, getting his feet torn to shreds, stepping in pools of mud and blood, praying and chanting misereres? In front of him the old infantry sergeant, who was carrying the cross with his only good arm, suddenly became stuck when the end of his cross fell into a pothole. Don Esteban pulled as hard as he could, but could not get it out of the hole. The penitents flowed past him, but those also carrying crosses found their path blocked and had to come to a halt. A young bystander jumped out of the crowd and lifted the end of the cross. The sergeant turned towards him and thanked him with a smile. The procession continued on its way, with both men hauling the cross. He would need help too, thought Hernando as they set off again, struggling to drag the heavy wooden beam. And there was still the whole afternoon to get through!

'Hail, Mary, full of grace, Our Lord is with thee . . .' Hernando added his voice to that of hundreds of others.

Hail Marys, Lord's Prayers, creeds, Hail Holy Queens . . . the noise was incessant. What was he doing there? Sung misereres. Thousands of candles and torches. Incense. Blessings. Saints and holy images everywhere. Men and women kneeling as he went by, some of them crying out and calling on God with their arms stretched to the skies in mystical ecstasy. The bloody backs of flagellants all round him. Hernando felt utterly out of place . . . he was a Muslim!

The pious Christians of Córdoba had been called to the procession by proclamations and street criers, but the same was not true of the Morisco community. Prior to Saint Luke's Day, parish priests, sacristans, magistrates and bailiffs consulted the census lists of new Christians and went from house to house demanding they take part. As if it were a Sunday, on the day itself they stationed themselves from first thing in the morning in the church doorways, censuses in hand, to make sure that none of the Moriscos was absent. None of them was to stay at home; they all had to witness the procession and to pray for the return of those ships of the great armada that had not yet reappeared. The whole of Spain was praying as one for their return!

'What are you waiting for, old woman?' said the Morisco baker, shaking Aisha roughly in the doorway.

Several men who had already left the house had also urged her to get up and go to confess and take communion. She ignored them. What did she care about the Christian King's dreadful ships? The baker was the last to emerge: he was not going to permit the woman to stay where she was.

'It's a procession of Nazarenes,' he shouted at her when she wrapped the blanket more closely round her. 'People like you and your son! The authorities are making sure we all go to the procession. Do you want to bring misfortune on this house and all of us in it? Get up!'

Two other Moriscos who also lived in the house but were now some way down the street came walking back towards them.

'What's wrong?' asked one of them.

'She won't get up.'

'If she doesn't go to confession, the bailiffs will come and check and will become suspicious about the house. They'll be on our backs the whole time.'

'That's what I told her,' said the baker.

'Listen, Nazarene,' the third man said, kneeling down beside Aisha, 'either you come of your own accord, or we'll drag you.'

So Aisha was taken to Santiago church by two young Moriscos who pulled her along roughly. When he saw her, the sacristan backed away from Aisha nervously, but crossed her name off his list.

'She's ill,' the young Moriscos said by way of an excuse.

What they could not do was to force her to confess. Nor did they dare take her up to the altar to eat the 'cake', but there was such a crush inside the church, and so many people standing in line for the confessional, that nobody noticed. The bailiffs simply noted that she had been to church. From there, under the watchful eye of a guard, the Moriscos of the Santiago parish were told to go to Calle del Sol, between their church and the nearby Santa Cruz convent, to wait for the procession to pass by. Aisha was dragged along with the rest, oblivious to everything going on around her. They all had to wait in the street for several hours, from the ringing of the bells to the moment when the procession passed through the Santiago neighbourhood by the city's eastern wall on its way back to the cathedral.

Aisha did not speak to anyone. She had not done so for days, even in the weaver's workshop, where she sat staring ahead of her without uttering a word even when Juan Marco took her to task for lining up her threads wrongly. As she worked, her mind was constantly on Fátima and Shamir. Fátima had done it! She had suffered years of humiliation, but she had kept quiet and endured it. Her willpower and single-mindedness had enabled her to take a revenge Aisha herself would never even have imagined possible. A paradise! she remembered it said in the letter. Fátima was living in a paradise. As for her, what had she done with her life? She was old, sick and all alone. She looked at her neighbours crowded around, as if they were trying to hide her. They were eating. They ate millet bread, cakes, almond sweetmeats and fritters they had bought. Not one of them offered her any, although she would not have been able to eat it if they had. Many of her teeth were missing, and her hair was falling out in clumps. She had to crumble the stale bread they gave her every night into crumbs so that she could eat it. What terrible sin could she have committed for God to treat her this way? Hernando was betraying his Muslim brothers, and Shamir was living far away, in Barbary. Her other children had been murdered or sold as slaves. Why, God? Why did He not take her once and for all? She wanted to die! She called out for death every night when she had to stretch out on the cold, hard ground in the doorway, but it never came. God could not decide whether or not to free her from her wretchedness.

Her legs were aching as the statue of Christ passed by her. The Moriscos all knelt on the ground. Somebody pulled at her skirt for her to do the same, but she refused and stood there silently, not praying, a shrunken old woman among the kneeling men. It took a long time for the penitents to appear. They had been round the entire city, and many of them were collapsing under the weight of their crosses, so that onlookers had to help them. Hernando was still carrying his, but the sergeant, who was alongside him, had abandoned his cross when they got past La Corredera and was simply walking in the group of penitents. His eyes were downcast, and he felt defeated now that the burden had been taken up by two young men. The bodies of the penitents with flails were by now covered in blood. The fervent Christians watching the procession were deeply moved by these shows of passion, adding their shouts and howls to those of the marchers. The nuns from the Santa Cruz convent began to intone the miserere, raising their voices so that they could be heard over the hubbub, encouraging the thousand penitents not to give up.

'*Miserere mei, Deus, secundum magnam misericordiam tuam,*' the mournful chant filled Calle del Sol.

Aisha was looking on dully as these unfortunates went by, when suddenly in among them, dragging an enormous cross and with his back bleeding from where the wood had rubbed his shoulder raw, his face contorted and purple, she saw her son. He was struggling along with the others; the sight of him reminded her of the hundreds of Christs in the churches and wayside shrines of the city.

'No!' she shouted. Her fingers clenched. When the baker turned to look at her, he saw the soft blue veins in her throat were tense and bulging beneath her chin. Her eyes glittered with hatred. 'No!' she shouted again. Another Morisco turned towards her. A third man tried to silence her, but this only caught the attention of one of the guards. Evading the man's grasp, thanks to strength born of anger, Aisha cried out: 'Allah is great, my son!' The guard began to make his way towards her.

'*Et secundum multitudinem miserationum tuarum, dele iniquitatem meam*,' the nuns of Santa Cruz lamented.

The Moriscos in the crowd shrank away from Aisha.

'Listen to me, Hernando! Fátima is alive! Your children as well! Come back to your people! There is no god but God, and Muhammad is the mess—'

She was unable to finish her profession of faith. The guard threw himself on her and silenced her with a slap that knocked out two more of her teeth.

Hernando, his mind a blank, delirious from pain, was muttering to himself the sorrowful chants he had been hearing all day: '*Amplius lava me ab iniquitate mea*.' His whole attention was concentrated on pulling his heavy cross. He did not notice the disturbance among the crowd of Moriscos. He did not even turn his face to see the commotion around the figure of his mother.

55

At THE END of October that year, King Philip addressed himself to all the bishops in Spain thanking them for their rogations, but calling on them to be suspended. He considered it impossible that two and a half months after the armada had entered the waters of the Atlantic, any other ship would now return. A few days later the King himself wrote a deeply felt personal letter to the wife of his cousin the Duke of Monterreal, grandee of Spain, to inform her of the death of Don Alfonso de Córdoba and his eldest son at the hands of the English on the Irish coast, where they had been shipwrecked.

Two sailors who had escaped the killings, thanks to help from Irish rebels, and who succeeded in fleeing first to Scotland and then to Flanders, had confirmed the deaths of the duke and his son beyond all shadow of doubt. According to them, a brigade of the English army had arrested the duke and his men as they were wandering through the Irish countryside after swimming ashore. With no regard whatsoever for Don Alfonso's rank – he had tried to argue that he was a nobleman – the English soldiers forced all the Spaniards to strip naked and then hanged them on the top of a hill like common criminals.

Hernando was not present on the morning when the palace secretary Don Silvestre read out the letter to all the hidalgos, after having first done so to Doña Lucía. For two days, Hernando had been going to the Christian monarchs' fortress, pleading to be received by the clerk, the notary or the inquisitor himself. He wanted to hear at first hand about his mother's detention, something he had learnt of when Juan Marco, the master weaver, sent him a message returning the money he received each month, telling him his mother had not been to work. It was the apprentice who brought him the money – little more than a boy – who spat the news at him scornfully.

'Your mother invoked the god of the heretics when the penitents in the procession passed by her.' The coins slipped from Hernando's fingers and fell to the floor with a strange tinkle. He felt his legs give way beneath him. She must have seen him in the procession! It must have been that!

'She has committed sacrilege!' the lad cried when the noise of the coins died away.

One of the servants agreed with him. 'She deserves the maximum penalty the Holy Office can impose: to be burnt at the stake is hardly punishment enough for someone who's blasphemed against a sacred procession.'

The only concession Hernando won from the Inquisition was to be allowed to pay for Aisha's food, although he had no idea that she had decided not to eat, and was rejecting the tiny, disgusting rations the jailers threw into her cell.

Don Esteban was the first to fall to his knees when the secretary ended his reading of the King's letter. Don Sancho crossed himself time and again, whilst other hidalgos imitated the infantry sergeant. The murmur of prayers, many and different, filled the room, until the chaplain's voice rose above them:

'How could Christ answer our prayers if at the same time as we were begging for him to intercede, the mother of the person on whom Don Alfonso had bestowed his favour and friendship was calling on the false god of the Muslim sect?'

Doña Lucía, who until then had been slumped in a chair, raised her head. Her chin was trembling.

'What use is a rogation when a sacrilege has been committed?'

The duchess turned her tear-filled eyes on the hidalgo who had just spoken. As she nodded in agreement, another of them took up the attack on Hernando.

'Mother and son plotted this together! I saw the Morisco give a signal.'

At this a storm of complaints was unleashed by the hidalgos, all denouncing Hernando:

'Blasphemy!'

'God was offended!'

'That's why He refused us His grace!'

Doña Lucía's eyes closed tightly. She was not going to allow the son of a woman who had committed such a sacrilege to go on living in her palace, enjoying the favour of someone who could no longer offer it him!

That same night when Hernando, unaware of the news of Don Alfonso's death, returned defeated yet again from the Inquisition after waiting in vain all day for someone to receive him, the secretary intercepted him in the palace doorway.

'Tomorrow morning you are to leave this house,' Don Silvestre told him. 'Those are the duchess's orders. You are not worthy to live under this roof. His excellency the Duke of Monterreal and his son died defending the Catholic cause.'

In his mind, Hernando heard once more the clang of the chains on his ankles as Don Alfonso brought his Toledo steel down on them while the two of them crouched beside a stream in the Alpujarra. Hernando rolled his eyes. With his death the duke had again set him free from a servitude he himself had been unable to put an end to.

'Please convey my condolences to the duchess,' he said.

'I don't think that would be appropriate,' the secretary said acidly.

'You are wrong there,' Hernando retorted. 'They could be the only sincere ones she receives in this house.'

'What are you implying?'

Hernando waved his arm in the air. 'What can I take with me?' he asked.

'Your clothes. The duchess does not want to see them. The horse—'

'The horse and its tackle are mine. I don't need to ask anyone's permission to take them with me,' Hernando said firmly. 'As for my writings . . .'

'What writings?' the secretary asked suspiciously.

Hernando gave a weary sigh. Were they going to humiliate him to the end? 'You know very well,' he said. 'The reports I am drawing up for the Archbishop of Granada.'

'Very well. They are yours.'

Hernando felt Don Alfonso's death keenly. He realized he had been counting on his return. He was genuinely fond of the duke, who had done so much for him, and could have wished for his help in interceding on his mother's behalf with the Inquisition. He had mentioned the duke's name a hundred times in order to see someone, but the Holy Office did not seem to set any store by the mention of Spanish nobles or grandees. No one, whatever their social rank, was greater than the Inquisition, or could put pressure on its members.

He hastened to the minaret tower where he kept hidden the gospel of Barnabas and his other secrets. Silvestre might well search him when he left the palace, so he decided to take only a few things with him. He took out the hand of Fátima and held it in his palm for a few moments, trying to remember how it used to shine just above his wife's breasts, and how it swayed with them. The jewel had lost its glow with Fátima's death, he thought, just like his life. He made a rapid decision about his books and writings: all he would take with him was the gospel of Barnabas; he would destroy everything else, including the transcription of the gospel he had made. Ibn Muqla's treatise on calligraphy would meet the same fate. He could not run the risk of it being found on him, and besides, he knew it by heart. The images of the letters and the drawings of their dimensions leapt into his mind as soon as he brought his quill to paper.

When he had done all this, he went back to his rooms. He opened the chest to take out the purse where he kept his savings, but could not find it. He searched among his scarce belongings. Someone had stolen it. 'Christian dogs!' he muttered. They had been quick to start their pillaging, just as they had done in the Alpujarra. All he had left was what little money he had on him.

Cursing himself for not having kept his savings in a safe place, he prepared a bundle of his clothes and hid the parchments of the gospel among his writings on the martyrs. No one would notice them. He dropped the tarnished hand of Fátima on top of his clothing: he planned to hide it on his body when he left. Finally, he washed before praying. When he had finished his prayers, he stood in the centre of his bedroom: what was he going to do now?

'I need money.'

Pablo Coca did not flinch at Hernando's words. The gambling house was empty; a Guinean slave was cleaning and tidying up after last night's play. 'We all need money, my friend,' he answered. 'What has happened?'

Hernando recalled the boy practising so hard to move his earlobe as the Marshal did, and decided to trust him and explain his situation. He also decided not to tell him how he had managed to get through the search Silvestre had submitted him to.

'What are they?' the secretary had asked, pointing to the papers Hernando was showing openly in his right hand. Silvestre had just been rummaging among his clothes as though he were a petty thief, in full view of the servants coming and going in the stable courtyard.

'My report for the Granada cathedral chapter.'

The secretary motioned for him to give him the papers. Hernando lifted them up, but did not hand them over.

'They are confidential, Silvestre,' he said, nevertheless allowing him to read the first page, which dealt with the killings in Cuxurio. 'I'm telling you they are confidential to the Church in Granada,' he insisted, challenging him to look further. 'If the archbishop found out . . .'

'All right!' the secretary conceded.

'And now, are you going to strip me naked?' Hernando scoffed, thinking of the hand of Fátima he had concealed in his breeches. 'Would you like to?' he challenged him again, holding out his arms. Silvestre blushed. 'Don't worry, I came poor to this palace and I'll leave as poor as I arrived.' Hernando smiled cynically at the secretary: was he the thief? ' "A miserable Morisco," as you all call me.'

The stable lad refused to saddle up Volador, putting into his refusal all the rancour accumulated over years of having to serve a Morisco. Hernando did it himself, although he soon had to unbridle the horse again at the Potro inn, where he found lodging. He chose it out of the many inns in and around the square because the innkeeper did not know him. Volador, bearing the royal brand and twice the size of any of the mules and donkeys resting in the inn-yard, as well as the distinguished-looking clothes he was wearing, quickly secured him the best room: a bedroom all to himself. A bed, two chairs and a table were the only furniture. Hernando paid in advance as if he were a rich man, despite the fact that when he took the money from his purse he realized all he had left were a few reales. The first thing he did was to get out some clean sheets of paper that he had brought from the palace and write a letter to Don Pedro de Granada Venegas, explaining what had happened to him and his mother, and begging for his help. There was little he could do for them and the Morisco cause, he argued, if he were forced to live in penury. In the same Potro inn he found a muleteer setting out for Granada that same day, and so his purse became completely empty.

'I gave most of the money I had to the Inquisition jailer to feed and look after my mother,' he explained to Pablo Coca. 'The rest . . .'

'You could make some tonight,' his friend tried to encourage him. Hernando waved his hand dismissively. 'It will help you get by,' Pablo insisted. 'At least you'll be able to pay at the inn.'

'Palomero,' Hernando replied, using his youthful nickname, 'I need much more money than that, don't you see? I have to buy off a lot of people in the Christian monarchs' fortress.'

'Money will get you nowhere with the Inquisition. When there was that witchcraft case with the two Camacha women, they arrested Don Alonso de Aguilar, of the House of Priego. An Aguilar! Bribes had no effect until the matter was finally resolved and he was released. They have even moved against archbishops.'

'But my mother is only an old Morisco woman of no importance, Pablo.'

Coca thought it over for a few moments, rubbing a finger round the top of his glass. They were sitting with a jug of wine the Guinean slave had served them.

'I am often asked to organize important gaming sessions,' he said doubtfully, as if unsure whether this would be of any real help. Hernando put down the glass he had been raising to his lips and leant towards him across the table. 'I don't like doing it. I agree sometimes, but . . . these are games for nobles, lawyers, bailiffs, sheriffs, proud, arrogant young men who are the sons of great families – even priests! The games are all cut and thrust, with huge sums wagered; they are very different from the slow bloodletting of nights in my gaming house. The gamblers are about as knowledgeable as the poor fools who come to my place, but they are quick to draw their swords if they are challenged on any of the tricks or sleight of hand they try to perform. It's as though the honour they make so much of is enough to excuse a marked pack of cards.'

'But why do they use you?'

'They always bring in a professional like me, for two reasons. First because they don't want to lower themselves by going to a gaming house; more importantly because, as you know, all gambling, apart from wagers to try to get food or of less than two reales, is forbidden. Until a few years ago, anyone who lost money in a clandestine game had a week to claim back any money lost. That's no longer the case: if you lose money, that's that, but if anyone denounces one of these illegal sessions, everyone goes to jail, and those who won money have to pay a fine equivalent to their winnings, plus a similar amount which is divided between the King, the judge and the person making the accusation. That's where we professionals come in: everyone who takes part in or knows about one of these illegal games is well aware that if they talk about it, their life is not worth a penny. Any of us in Córdoba, Seville, Toledo or anywhere else that person might escape to would carry out the punishment, even if we were not involved. That is our law, and we have the means to enforce it. A gambler always goes back to the tables some day or other . . .'

'Even so,' Hernando reflected, after thinking about Pablo's words for a few moments, 'wouldn't you like to fleece them?'

Coca smiled. 'Of course. But if we're found out, my business is at stake. We professionals also run a further risk: even if no one denounces the illegal game, any angry bailiff who has lost at one could make my life impossible; a resentful councillor could ruin me. If you're convicted of running a gaming house you face two years' banishment, and if you're caught with dice, you have all your possessions confiscated, receive a hundred lashes and five years in the galleys. And I do have dice at my place: they bring in good money . . .'

'There's no need for them to know you and I are in it together. I win, you lose, and afterwards we share it out. You took far too much trouble to learn the Marshal's trick to waste it on a few sad wretches. Remember the hopes we had back in those days.'

'Sometimes blood is spilt,' Pablo said reluctantly.

'Let's get their money!' insisted Hernando.

'Are you hoping to live off gambling then?' asked Coca. 'They're bound to link us at some point. You can't always be winning at games I organize.'

'I've no intention of turning into a card sharp. As soon as I

can get my mother out of this mess, I'll leave the city. We'll go
... to Granada, probably.'

Coca took a long swig of wine. 'I'll think about it,' he said.

That first night Pablo Coca did his trick several times, and
Hernando won enough to feel more comfortable. He returned
to the inn, and before going up to his room went to the stables
to see how Volador was. The horse was dozing between two small
mules at a shared manger. Several muleteers and guests who
could not pay for a room were also sleeping there. Volador
sensed his master's presence and snorted. Hernando went over
to pat him.

'What are you doing there, little man?' he exclaimed when he
saw a boy curled up on the straw between the horse's front legs.

The boy, who could not have been more than twelve years
old, opened a pair of huge brown eyes, but did not move. 'I'm
looking after your horse, sir,' he said, in a calm voice that belied
his years.

'He could tread on you while you're asleep,' said Hernando,
holding out his hand to help him up.

The lad made no attempt to take it. 'He won't do that, your
honour. Volador – I heard you call him that when you arrived
– is a good beast, and we're already friends. He won't step on
me. I'll take care of him for you.'

As if he had understood what the boy was saying, the horse
lowered his head until he was nuzzling the lad's tousled, filthy
hair. This tender scene was in sharp contrast to the shouts,
threats, dirty tricks, bets and greed of the gaming house that
Hernando felt were still stuck to his clothes. He hesitated.

'Come on, get out from under there. He could hurt you,'
he said finally. 'Horses sleep too, and without wishing to he
might . . .'

All at once he fell silent. The boy gave a sad smile, then he
clutched on to one of Volador's front legs in order to haul himself up. His own legs were shapeless stumps: they had been
broken in a ghastly way. Hernando bent down to help him.

'Goodness! What happened to you?'

The boy managed to stay upright by clinging on to Hernando's shoulders. 'What I find most difficult is staying on my feet,' he said with a smile that revealed a few sparse broken teeth. 'If you pass me those crutches, I could . . .'

'What happened to your legs?' Hernando asked with dismay.

'My father sold them to the devil,' the boy replied in all seriousness.

Their faces were inches away from each other.

'What do you mean?' Hernando whispered.

'My brother had his arms and hands smashed. With me it was my legs. My elder brother José told me that shortly after I was born I cried a lot when my father broke my bones with an iron bar. After that, they all wondered if I was going to survive. All of us are crippled in some way. I remember my parents blinded my little sister with a hot wire in her eyes only two months after she was born. She cried and cried as well,' the boy added sadly. 'You see, more people give alms if there's a crippled child with you.' Hernando could feel his hair standing on end. 'The problem is that the King prohibits beggars asking for money if they've got children aged over five with them. The bailiffs and parish priests can take away their permits to beg if they are found with any children older than that. I was allowed to carry on a while longer because I'm so tiny, but when I was seven they abandoned me. So you can see, your honour: my legs for seven years of alms.'

Hernando could not think what to say. His throat seized up. He knew that some parents abused their children cruelly in order to stir people's compassion enough to give them a wretched coin or two, but he had never seen the reality of this treatment so close to. *So you can see, your honour: my legs for seven years of alms.* The boy's words were so heart-rending . . . he had a sudden urge to hold him in his arms. How long had it been since he embraced a child? He cleared his throat.

'Are you sure Volador will not step on you?' he asked eventually.

The boy's broken teeth reappeared with his smile. 'I'm certain. Ask him.'

Hernando patted Volador's neck and helped the boy lie down again between his front legs.

'What's your name?' he asked as the lad curled up into a ball and closed his eyes for sleep.

'Miguel.'

'Look after him well, Miguel.'

That night Hernando did not sleep. After writing to Don Pedro in Granada he had only one clean sheet of paper left, one quill and a small pot of ink. He sat at the rough, dilapidated table, blew the dust off it, and by the light of a flickering candle started to write, with all his nerves stretched to the limit. His mother, Miguel, the gambling, that dark and dismal room, the noises from the other guests disturbing the calm of the night . . . the quill slid across the sheet of paper, tracing the most beautiful Arabic characters he had ever written. Without thinking about it, as if it were God guiding his hand, he wrote out in full the profession of faith that had led to his mother being locked in the Inquisition's dungeons: 'There is no god but God, and Muhammad is the messenger of God.' Then he prepared to continue with the prayer in the way the Moriscos did. He dipped the quill in the ink, the image of Hamid suddenly springing into his mind. He had made him recite it in the church at Juviles to show he was not Christian. What if he had died at that moment? 'Know,' Hernando added, reciting the Morisco profession of faith: 'Know that all people must understand there is only one God . . .' He would have been spared such a hard life, thought Hernando, dipping the quill into the ink once more.

The next morning Volador was not in the stables; nor was Miguel. Hernando shouted for the innkeeper.

'They went out,' the man told him. 'The boy told me you had given him permission to do so. One of the muleteers sleeping in the stable confirmed you asked him to look after the horse.'

Hernando ran in a rage to Plaza del Potro. Had the boy fooled him? What if Volador had been stolen? He came to a halt as he entered the square: Miguel was standing there, one arm on a crutch, his legs bent under him, watching the horse drink from the fountain basin. Volador's coat shone in the still-gloomy morning: he had obviously brushed him.

'He was thirsty,' the boy explained when he saw Hernando standing beside him.

The horse turned his head to one side and dribbled some of the water it had been drinking on to Miguel. The boy nudged his head back with the top of one of the crutches. Hernando looked on: they seemed to understand one another. Miguel guessed what he was thinking.

'Animals want to be with me as much as people want to avoid me,' he said.

Hernando sighed. 'I have things to do,' he said, handing him a two-real coin, which the boy took with eyes as big as saucers. 'Look after him.'

Hernando headed off towards Calle del Potro, then walked down it towards the fortress where his mother was being held. As he entered the street, he turned to look back, and saw the boy on his crutches playing next to the fountain, flicking water at Volador. Both of them seemed completely absorbed in their game. Hernando set off again when he saw Miguel decide to return to the stables. He did not hold the halter, but simply draped its rope over his shoulder. Although the horse was free, it followed him meekly like a dog. Hernando shook his head. Volador was a pure Spanish thoroughbred, lively and highly strung. Normally he would have been spooked by someone hopping along in front of him, but apparently not by Miguel, who was using his crutches to keep his feet off the ground, as if he might damage his wizened, deformed legs even more if they touched it.

Hernando reached the Christian monarchs' fortress, still impressed by the way Miguel hopped along and Volador meekly followed him. He was even more surprised when, on reaching the dungeons, the jailer (who until then had refused to let him see his mother) accepted the gold coin that Hernando had half-heartedly pulled out of his purse. He had won it the previous night in a game of Twenty-one, when his ace and king had provoked a thousand curses from the other players betting against him.

In this dazed state he followed the jailer into a big courtyard with a fountain surrounded by orange and other trees. The yard would have been beautiful had it not been for the moans and groans from the cells overlooking it. Hernando listened carefully: could some of them be coming from his mother? The jailer showed him to a cell in the far corner of the patio, and Hernando went in through a solid wooden door set in thick walls. No, there was no sound at all from this squalid, miserable place.

'Mother!'

Hernando knelt beside a motionless bundle on the dirt floor. His hands shook as he searched for Aisha's face in the folds of the rough tunic. He had difficulty recognizing her as the person who had given birth to him. The skin hung from her shrunken neck and cheeks. Her eyes were sunken and discoloured, her lips dry and cracked. Her hair was filthy and matted.

'What have you done to her?' he growled at the jailer. The man made no reply, but stood lurking in the broad doorway. 'She's only an old woman . . .' At this, the jailer shifted from one foot to another and scowled at Hernando. 'Mother,' the Morisco repeated, taking Aisha's head in his hands and bringing it up to his lips to kiss her. She did not respond. Her eyes were glazed over. For a moment, Hernando thought she might be dead. He shook her gently and she stirred.

'She's crazy,' said the jailer. 'She refuses to eat and hardly even drinks. She doesn't say anything, even to complain. She's like this all day long.'

'What did you do to her?' Hernando asked again, his voice faltering. He was scraping obstinately at a small patch of dirt on his mother's forehead as he spoke.

'We've done nothing to her.' Hernando turned to look at the man. 'It's true,' the jailer insisted, spreading his palms. 'The Inquisition judged that the bailiff's evidence was sufficient to condemn her. I've told you she won't speak, so they decided there was no point torturing her. She would have died.' Hernando turned back to see if his mother reacted in any way to this. She did not. 'No one would be surprised if she died . . . this very night . . .'

Hernando, cradling his mother in his arms with his back to the jailer, said nothing. What was the man suggesting?

'She could die,' said the jailer from the doorway. 'The doctor has already warned the tribunal of that. Nobody would think twice about it. Nobody would come to check. I would be the one to announce it, and to bury the body . . .'

So that was it! That was why he had allowed him to visit.

'How much?' he asked.

'Fifty ducats.'

Fifty! Hernando had been about to offer five, but bit his tongue. Was he going to bargain for his mother's life?

'I don't have them,' he said.

'In that case . . .' The jailer turned to go.

'But I do have a horse,' Hernando said in a low voice, staring into Aisha's lifeless eyes.

'I didn't hear you. What did you say?'

'That I have a good horse,' said Hernando, trying his best to speak louder. 'With the brand of the royal stables. He's worth far more than fifty ducats.'

The deal was for that same night. Hernando would exchange Volador for Aisha. What did he care about money? It was simply an animal against . . . against perhaps no more than the chance to bury his mother, for her to die in his arms. Perhaps God would permit her to open her eyes at that moment, and he should be there. He had to be at her side! Aisha could not die without him having the chance of being reconciled with her.

* * *

Miguel was back sitting on the ground by Volador, watching the horse eat some grass he had put in the manger.

'I'm sorry,' Hernando said, kneeling down and ruffling his hair. 'I'm selling the horse tonight.' Why was he apologizing? he wondered. Miguel was only a little waif who—

'No,' the boy replied, interrupting his thoughts but not turning towards him.

'What do you mean, no?' Hernando did not know whether to be amused or angry.

Now Miguel did look up at him, as Hernando straightened and stood next to the horse. 'Your honour, I've been with dogs, cats, cage-birds and once even a monkey. I always know when they are going to come back . . . and I always sense when it will be the last time I see them. Volador will come back to me,' he said solemnly, 'I know it.'

Hernando looked down at the boy's crushed legs stretched out on the straw. 'I won't argue about it. You may be right. But I'm afraid, if that is the case, it won't be with me.'

When the bells rang for compline, Hernando led Volador from the stables and headed up Calle del Potro to the mosque. They had agreed to meet in Plaza del Campo Real, next to the fortress. Hernando could not bear to ride the horse, but led it on a halter, without looking back. Miguel followed them as best he could. When Hernando reached the square, he aimed for one of the corners where, as almost everywhere else, there were big piles of rubbish. It was in the middle of this mess that the exchange was to take place. Miguel came to a halt a few yards away from the spot where Hernando was peering into the darkness, trying to make out the jailer carrying his mother. He attached no importance to the boy's strange way of standing, his legs oddly braced against the ground, leaning on one crutch and holding the other in his right hand above his head. Volador was nervous: he snorted, shifted, and even threatened to rear.

'Whoa, calm there,' said Hernando, 'calm down, pretty one.'

As he patted the horse's neck, Hernando thought Volador

must have realized he was going to be parted from him. Just at that moment an enormous rat squeaked and ran out between Hernando and Volador's legs. It was immediately followed by another, then another. Hernando leapt to one side. Volador bucked, pulled free and galloped off in terror. Balancing as best he could, Miguel tried to hit the rats with one of his crutches.

Volador's frightened neighing roused the attention of all the other horses in the royal stables next to the fortress. They soon added their snorts and neighs to the uproar. The gatekeeper and two stable lads came out to the street that gave on to Plaza del Campo Real and were astonished to see a magnificent dappled horse charging along, trailing its halter rope.

'A horse has got out!' one of the lads shouted.

The gatekeeper was about to tell him he was sure none of the horses had escaped from the stables, but he fell silent when by the light of one of the torches on the walls of the Inquisition headquarters he clearly saw the royal brand on the flank of the fleeing steed.

'Run after him!' he shouted.

Hernando was also chasing after Volador. How was he going to set his mother free with all this tumult going on? The jailer would never appear. Miguel had moved away from the rats and was standing still, admiring the strength and beauty of the galloping horse, yet again cursing his useless legs. 'He'll be back,' he whispered after Hernando. More people came pouring out of the royal stables, and from the fortress as well, through the gate where during the day a cloth market was held. Hernando stopped running when he saw that half a dozen men had succeeded in cornering Volador against one of the fortress walls.

Blowing hard, the horse allowed one of them to seize the halter.

'He's mine!' Hernando shouted, joining the group and cursing the rats as he did so. Why had he not thought of that when the jailer suggested the meeting place?

The staff from the royal stables soon verified that the horse was not one of their colts.

'You ought to be more careful,' one of them reproached him, 'he could hurt himself in the dark.'

Hernando did not bother to answer, but took the halter from him. What did those wretches know?

'Aren't you the one who comes to visit the madwoman every day?' one of the Inquisition guards asked.

Hernando frowned, but said nothing. How often had he asked this same man for permission to see his mother, only to be refused disdainfully, because instead of doing his job he was far more interested in what was being sold in the square?

'It's about time you came to collect her,' another of the guards said. 'If you wait another couple of days, she'll be dead.'

The halter rope slipped from Hernando's hand, but before it could touch the ground, it was intercepted by a rough wooden crutch. Hernando turned towards Miguel, who smiled his broken-toothed smile as he grasped the rope in his hand. Had the guard said it was high time he came to collect his mother? What did he mean by that?

'What . . . ?' he stammered. 'What about her punishment? And the auto-da-fé?'

'The Inquisition held a special tribunal a few days ago in the courtroom. They sentenced your mother to the wearing of a penitential cloak and to going to mass daily for a year, although given her state of health, I don't think she'll complete her sentence. And no one really wants a crazy woman like her to set foot on holy ground,' said one of the men. 'That's why they held the hearing. The Inquisition doctor told them your mother would not survive until the next general auto-da-fé, but they wanted to try her before she died. She's mad! Come and take her with you!'

'Yes, hand her over to me,' Hernando managed to stammer out, realizing as he did so that the jailer had tried to trick him.

Shortly afterwards, Hernando was walking back towards the Potro inn with his mother in his arms.

'There's no need for you to take her to church!' one of the guards shouted after him.

'My God, she's lighter than a feather!' Hernando cried out to the starry sky as he passed by the wall enclosing the mihrab of his mosque.

Miguel followed them, Volador's halter rope draped over his shoulder. The horse walked along placidly, as though anxious not to get ahead of him.

56

THE FUNERALS of the Duke of Monterreal and his eldest son were as sad as they were solemn, because of the impossibility of giving them a proper Christian burial. In the cathedral, the bishop invoked the name of the sheriff of Clare, Boetius Clancy (the man responsible for their deaths), and called on God never to let him out of purgatory. From that day on, he declared angrily, every seven years the same call would be made, in order to remind the Lord that the vile murderer should never escape punishment.

Another person unable to escape their own purgatory was Aisha. Hernando had still not heard from Don Pedro de Granada Venegas, and did not dare undertake such a long journey in winter when she was so ill. Everyone thought she was bound to die. He gave some money to the wife and daughter of the innkeeper so that they would wash her and change her clothes.

'She is nothing but skin and bone,' the innkeeper's wife commented when she came out of the room. 'You can almost see through her. She won't last long.'

At night Hernando played cards, winning sometimes and losing at others, as Coca had insisted. He spent his days trying to get Aisha to react, but she still lay motionless with her eyes rolled up, refusing to take any nourishment. Nor did she speak, and the only sound was of her wheezing breath. Hernando made her as comfortable as possible in the bed, and tried time and again to at least wet her lips with a little chicken broth so that something would find its way down her throat. He told her in a whisper all that he was doing for the Morisco community; how he had hidden the Turpian tower parchment. *It was written in Arabic, Mother – and the Christians are already venerating the Virgin's veil and Saint Stephen's bone!* Why had he not told her this before? Why did he not break his oath? Would God have punished him for saving his own mother's life? But he could never have imagined . . . He was to blame! He was the one who had abandoned her so that he could live the easy life of a parasite in the palace of a Christian duke.

As the days went by and Aisha showed no sign of reacting, it was Hernando who grew thinner and weaker, shedding tears and cursing himself.

'Let me try, your honour,' Miguel suggested one morning when he found Hernando at the foot of the stairs up to his mother's room, bowl of broth in his hand, uncertain whether to go up.

The boy clambered up the stairs hanging on to the railing and carrying his crutches in the other hand. Hernando carried up the broth.

'Put it there by the bed,' said Miguel.

Hernando obeyed, and withdrew to the doorway. Sitting down beside Aisha, Miguel brought the broth to her lips. He began talking to her in the same way as he did to Volador or to the cage-birds he said he had once lived with, as though she were a defenceless animal. Hernando stood for a long while in the doorway, watching this young boy with the crushed legs who knew when animals would leave or stay, and his mother lying supine beside him. He listened as Miguel told her stories, accompanying them with laughs and gestures. Where did a poor crippled boy whom life had denied everything get such optimism? What was he telling her now? An elephant! Miguel was hunting an elephant . . . in a boat on the Guadalquivir! He saw him imitating the animal's trunk by bending his arm in front of his mouth and folding back his hand, then twirling it before Aisha's expressionless eyes. Where could the boy have heard about an elephant? Hernando sighed painfully and left the room with the sound of Miguel's laughter ringing in his ears. The elephant had sunk when it reached the Albolafia mill! For the first time in many days, he saddled Volador and headed out to the pastures, where he launched into a breakneck gallop.

'You are to pay immediately against this letter, at six per thousand, to Hernando Ruiz, new Christian from Juviles, currently residing in Córdoba, the sum of one hundred ducats, at a rate of three hundred and seventy-five maravedís to the ducat . . .' Hernando studied the bill of exchange he had been handed by a muleteer in the Potro inn in the name of Don Pedro de Granada Venegas. A hundred ducats was a considerable amount. 'You cannot fail us now,' the nobleman wrote with the letter. The Turpian tower parchment had been an excellent first step. Luna and Castillo were translating the chequerboard of letters for the good of the cause, but the main objective had to be to reveal the gospel of Barnabas and to try to bring the two religions closer together, thanks to the figure of the Virgin Mary. This was all the more urgent, Don Pedro maintained, because petition after petition against the Moriscos was being sent to the King, each more drastic than the last. From Seville, Alonso Gutiérrez was proposing they be put in special neighbourhoods containing no more than two hundred families. They would be governed by a Christian official, who would control everything, including their marriages, and would be branded on the face in order to be recognizable everywhere. They would also be required to pay onerous taxes to the Crown. In addition to this, the letter continued:

a cruel, intransigent Dominican friar by the name of Bleda goes much further still. He maintains, using the doctrines of the Fathers of the Church to support him, that it would be morally acceptable for the King to dispose of the lives of all the Moriscos as he sees fit, for example to kill them or sell them as slaves to other countries; he therefore suggests they be used as galley slaves. In this way, the friar says, they could take the place of all those priests who are forced to row in them because their superiors punish their failings by sending them to galleys with the sole aim of not having to pay the costs of keeping them in prison. The Church, which considers itself the seat of mercy, is thus proposing to kill or enslave thousands of human beings. We have to get to work. All these proposals come to the attention of the Morisco communities, and only serve to inflame their anger: the more petitions that are sent to the King, the more uprisings are planned. Then when these are uncovered, the Christians have further reasons to seek a bloodthirsty resolution of the problem. Moreover, the defeat of the great armada also has to be taken into account. England has emerged greatly strengthened, and its support for the armies fighting in Flanders is bound to increase; in France, the Christian league promoted and financed by the Spanish King is in serious difficulties following the disaster to the fleet. As the Spaniards lose power in Europe, they will consider that the Moriscos might ally themselves with one or other of these countries, and adopt counter-measures. Circumstances are against us. Keep me informed of your situation and count on me; we need you.

Hernando burnt Don Pedro's letter and left the inn. He asked a guard where he could find Don Antonio Morales's bank – this was where Don Pedro's banker in Granada had addressed his bill of exchange – and set off towards it with this document and his own safe conduct. Morales's establishment was near the silk and corn exchanges, and Hernando, elegantly dressed, was received by the banker himself. He charged him the commission stipulated in the letter, opened a deposit of ninety ducats in Hernando's name, and gave him the rest in gold crowns, sovereigns and other smaller coins.

Hernando returned to the inn and paid the innkeeper generously, hoping that would silence his suspicions of him as a Morisco and card sharp. Matters had become even more complicated now that his mother, who had been sentenced to do penance by the Inquisition, was also staying there.

'I don't know if you have a permit to live in this neighbourhood,' the innkeeper had said a few days earlier. 'You have to understand my position. If the bailiff came . . . new Christians need permission from the parish priest to change their domicile.'

Hernando shut him up by showing him the safe conduct from the Archbishop of Granada. 'If I can move freely throughout the kingdoms of Spain, surely I can do so in a single city?' he argued.

'But the woman . . .' the innkeeper protested.

'The woman is with me. She's my mother,' Hernando answered him sharply, but gave him a few more coins to keep him quiet.

Hernando was aware that his present situation could not last for ever. Don Pedro had sent him money, but he had also asked him to continue to work on their plan, and he could not do that at the inn. He was sleeping on the floor, as he had given up his bed to Aisha, who remained in the same state as when she had left the Inquisition dungeons. Miguel was looking after her daily with great care and affection. He talked to her, told her stories, stroked her, and laughed – he laughed the whole time, except when he called the innkeeper's wife and daughter to help him wash her and change her position so that she did not get sores.

'Have you managed to get her to eat something?' Hernando asked him one day.

'She doesn't need it,' the lad replied. 'For now I'm still giving her chicken broth. That's nourishment enough for someone in her condition. She will eat when she wants to.'

Hernando was not so sure; he cupped his chin in his hand. He did not dare ask if the boy thought this little animal was going to leave them or stay, but he did realize that Miguel, standing there on his crutches in front of him, was well aware of what he was thinking.

Miguel smiled, but said nothing.

Hernando also knew he could not leave Córdoba with his mother in the state she was in. In the meantime, he could rent a house and look for work. With horses. He was a good rider. Possibly a noble would take him on as a horse-trainer or a groom, or even as a stable lad. Why not? If that did not work out, he also knew how to read and do accounts; somebody might be interested in that. And at night he could devote himself to working on the gospel, which he still kept hidden among his papers. At least in the inn, unlike in the duke's palace, nobody had shown the slightest interest in them: no one there could read.

Turning all this over in his mind, he made his way to Coca's gaming house. The Guinean slave let him in. Perhaps Coca would know of a house he could rent . . .

'Bless my soul!' his friend greeted him. He was busy counting the winnings from the previous night. 'I was just going to look for you.'

Hernando went up to the table where he was sitting.

'Do you know of any house to rent that is not too expensive?' he asked him straight out as he walked towards him. Coca raised his eyebrows. 'Why were you going to look for me anyway?'

'Wait.' Coca finished calculating the winnings, then told the Guinean slave to leave. When they were on their own, he gazed at Hernando, a serious expression on his face. 'There's an important game on tonight,' he told him.

Hernando hesitated.

'Aren't you interested?' Coca said in surprise.

'Yes . . . I think so. I . . .' He wondered whether to tell him about the hundred ducats he had received from Don Pedro. He had been the one who had insisted Pablo organize a game of this sort, but now . . . the hundred ducats gave him a security he had not felt then. The money guaranteed he could look after his mother, and rent a house . . . how could he possibly gamble the ducats his protector had sent him so that he could advance the Morisco cause? 'I've got a hundred ducats,' he finally confessed. 'An acquaintance of mine has lent them to me . . .'

'I'm not interested in your ducats,' Coca surprised him by saying.

'But . . .'

'I know you. In my line of business I've learnt how to distinguish between people. I can smell it, I know how they will react. When you first came to me, you said you had no money. If you have some now, and have to risk losing it, you won't do it. You're not a born gambler.' Coca bent down and picked up something at his feet: two bags full of coins. He dropped them on to the table. 'This can be our stake,' he said. 'Honestly, in normal circumstances I would never play with you as my accomplice, but you're the only person who knows my secret, and the only one who will ever know it. You're the only person I can use it with, and one of the few people – perhaps the only one again – to whom I feel any debt of gratitude. And tonight I want to win. A lot of money. The more the better. This has to be our night.'

'But this money of yours,' exclaimed Hernando, 'there's a fortune here.'

'Yes, there is. Forget what you have been wagering here at night. This is another world. If you count your money carefully they will find you out – and me with you. These are gold sovereigns: that is what they wager on each hand. You have to convince yourself that a gold sovereign is just the same as a silver penny. Can you do that?'

This time Hernando did not hesitate. 'Yes.'

'It's dangerous. I want you to understand that from the start. No one is to know we are friends.'

The game was to take place in the house of a rich cloth merchant who was as arrogant and snobbish as he was reckless when it came to placing bets.

After nightfall, Hernando nervously walked the short distance between the Potro inn and Calle de la Feria where the merchant lived. He was clutching the bag of money and trying to remember the instructions Pablo Coca had given him. They had to sit opposite each other so that Hernando could get a clear view of his friend's earlobe. He was to bet heavily even if Coca made no signal; it would be suspicious if he only bet a large amount when he won.

'Try to not speak more to me than to the others,' Coca also told him. 'But look straight at me as you do the other players, as if you are trying to judge from my face what kind of a hand I have. Remember, I won't be playing for myself, but for you. If we're lucky and they use our cards, I'll know what they are; if not, I'll only be able to help you with my hand. Play boldly, but don't imagine they're stupid; they know what they're doing and try to cheat as much as anyone else in ordinary gaming houses. Above all, remember one thing: these people's sense of honour leads them quickly to lay hands on their swords, and since these are illegal games, there is a pact of silence if someone wounds or kills anyone else.'

A servant led Hernando into a big, well-lit room that was luxuriously appointed with tapestries, embossed leather decorations and shiny wooden furniture. The Morisco's attention was caught by a large oil painting of a religious scene. Eight people were already there, standing in pairs and talking in low voices. Pablo was one of them.

'Gentlemen,' Coca called out to two pairs who were standing near the door where Hernando had just entered, 'allow me to present Hernando Ruiz.'

A tall, strong man whose rich attire marked him out even from all the other elegantly dressed men was the first to hold out his hand.

'Juan Serna,' Pablo introduced him, 'our host.'

'Have you brought money with you, Señor Ruiz?' the merchant asked slyly as they shook hands.

'Yes . . .' Hernando stammered, as several of the others guffawed at the comment.

'Hernando Ruiz?' queried an old man with sunken shoulders dressed entirely in black.

'Melchor Parra,' said Pablo, presenting him. 'Public notary . . .'

The old man signalled abruptly to Pablo Coca to be quiet. 'Hernando Ruiz,' he repeated, 'a new Christian from Juviles?'

Hernando avoided Pablo's gaze. How did this old man know he was a Morisco? Would they want to play with a new Christian?

'A new Christian?' he heard another of the players who had come up to him ask.

'Yes,' the Morisco replied. 'I am Hernando Ruiz, a new Christian from Juviles.'

Pablo tried to intervene, but the merchant stopped him.

'Do you have money?' he asked once more, as if the fact of him being Morisco was of little importance.

'By my life he does, Juan,' the old man suddenly announced as Hernando was going to show them his purse. 'He's a beneficiary of the late Duke of Monterreal, may God rest his soul. I myself opened and read his last will and testament a few days before the funeral. Don Alfonso de Córdoba made a provision outside his family. "To my friend Hernando Ruiz, a new Christian from Juviles, to whom I owe my life," it said. I remember it as if I were reading it now. Have you come to gamble away your inheritance?' he ended up asking sarcastically.

That night at the cloth merchant's house Hernando found it impossible to concentrate on his cards. An inheritance! What could that mean? The notary did not explain, and he had no time to take him aside to ask him, because now that he had arrived, Juan Serna decided the gambling should begin at once. Pablo Coca looked worried as he sat down. Hernando did not even try to sit opposite him, and in the end it was the gambler himself who had to change places so that they could see each other clearly. Yet as the hands followed each other, Coca began to relax: Hernando was playing almost absent-mindedly, betting heavily and losing quite a lot, but sweeping the table whenever he saw his companion wiggling his earlobe. The session went on all night without anyone suspecting they were in league. Hernando cleaned the others out. Serna, who like the notary had lost almost five hundred ducats, which he paid in gold to Hernando, demanded with no more than a veneer of civility that they have a rematch. The rest, including Pablo, had to pay him smaller but still considerable sums. One conceited young man, the scion of a noble house who during play had insulted Hernando (who had not reacted, still lost as he was in speculation as to what he might have inherited), had to swallow his pride and put his sword on the table, its hilt inlaid with gold and precious stones, as well as his ring, embossed with his family coat of arms.

'Sign a paper saying they are mine by right,' Hernando demanded when he saw the affronted young man getting up to leave swiftly.

The old notary also had to sign a document, although in his case it was to confirm that he owed Hernando money, since he did not have enough in his purse and had been allowed to play on trust. His hand shook as he signed the paper. He complained the whole time about the small fortune he had lost at the table, and pleaded for time to settle his debt. Hernando hesitated. He knew that promissory notes for gambling debts were not legal, and that no judge would demand they be met. However, Pablo signalled almost invisibly for him to accept: the notary would pay.

They left the house on Calle de la Feria. The sun was shining and the people of Córdoba were already going about their business. Escorted at a discreet distance by two armed guards Pablo had stationed outside the door, since he knew there would be substantial winnings that night, Hernando followed the old notary. He caught up with him in Plaza del Salvador.

'You did not have a lucky night, Don Melchor,' he said, falling into step alongside the old man, who was still clearly upset. 'You mentioned a legacy in my favour.'

'You will have to come to an arrangement about that with the duchess and the trustees appointed by Don Alfonso, may he rest in peace,' the notary snapped coldly.

Hernando grasped him by the forearm, forcing him to come to a halt. He pulled the old man round to face him.

Two women passing by at that moment glanced at them in surprise, then continued on their way, whispering to each other. Pablo Coca's two men came up.

'Listen, Don Melchor, I have an idea. You settle things for me with the duke's family. And do it quickly, do you hear me? Because otherwise I won't give you the grace period you asked for. If you do as I ask, I'll return your promissory note . . . for nothing.'

57

But the author of this tale, who has searched with great curiosity into the deeds that Don Quixote performed in his third adventure, has been unable to find any mention of them, at least in authentic writings. Only legend has reported, in the annals of La Mancha, that Don Quixote, the third time he left his house, went to Zaragoza, where he took part in the famous jousting tourneys held in that city, and things happened to him worthy of his courage and understanding. Nor could he discover anything relating to his end or destiny, apart from having the good fortune to find an old physician who had in his possession a leaden chest that according to him had been uncovered in the foundations of an ancient hermitage that was being demolished and rebuilt. In this chest were found parchments written in Gothic characters but in Castilian verses, which told of his feats, and told of the beauty of Dulcinea del Toboso, the figure of Rocinante, the faithful Sancho Panza, as well as the burial of Don Quixote himself, with different epitaphs regarding his life and customs.

Miguel de Cervantes in the words of Cide Hamete Benengeli,
Morisco. *Don Quixote Part One*, Chapter LII

A house with a courtyard in the Santa María neighbourhood, near the cathedral in Calle Espaldas de Santa Clara, as well as several plots of land near Palma del Rio belonging to an abandoned farmhouse, which brought in an annual rent of almost four hundred ducats, plus three pairs of hens, five hundred pomegranates, as many walnuts and three bushels of olives brought to him each week by his tenants, plums and winter or summer vegetables too. This was the legacy, along with sums of money to pay the dowry of deserving but poor young women, or for the redemption of captive Christians, that Don Alfonso de Córdoba willed in favour of the person who had saved his life in the Alpujarra. Melchor Parra and the trustees of the duke's will handed over the legacy without complaint, apart from the envy and insults that the notary, with a touch of sarcasm, assured him he had heard from the string of courtiers who had not received a penny – that was, all of them.

'It seems that none of them likes you very much,' said Parra, unable to disguise his satisfaction as the Morisco signed all the property deeds.

Hernando did not respond. He finished signing and straightened up in front of the notary. He searched for the promissory note in his clothing and handed it over to him, with the trustees as witness.

'The feeling is mutual, Don Melchor.'

After settling up with Pablo, who had his heart set on the young noble's sword and ring, and arranging to repay Don Pedro de Granada Venegas's hundred ducats, Hernando still had a considerable sum of money left to keep him going until he could start to enjoy his new house and his rents.

Life for him had taken yet another unexpected twist.

'It's rented out, your honour,' Miguel complained as the two of them stood outside the property in Calle Espaldas de Santa Clara. Hernando had told him to get everything ready to transfer Volador and his mother to the new house. 'You'll have to wait until the contract ends.'

'No,' Hernando declared. 'Do you like it?' Miguel whistled between his broken teeth to show what he felt about the magnificent building. 'Good, so here is what we are going to do.

I'll go back to the inn, and you stay here and ask for the mistress of the house. The mistress, Miguel: have you got that?'

'They won't allow me to. They'll think I've come begging.'

'Try. Tell them you're the new owner's servant.' When he heard this, Miguel almost lost his balance on the crutches. 'Yes, that's right. I don't think either my mother or my horse could find a better servant than you. Try – I'm sure you'll succeed.'

'And if I do?'

'Tell the lady of the house that from now on she will have to pay the rent to her new landlord: the Morisco Hernando Ruiz, from Juviles. Make sure she understands I'm a Morisco, one of those who took part in the Alpujarra uprising, and that I was expelled from Granada. And that in spite of all this, I am the new owner. Repeat it several times if necessary.'

The tenants, a wealthy family of silk merchants, took less than a week to return the house to Hernando, once they had confirmed with the duchess's secretary that he was indeed the new owner. What self-respecting old Christian could allow himself to have a Morisco as landlord?

The sunny courtyard, with the scent of flowers and the constant sound of water from the fountain, seemed to breathe new life into Aisha. A few days after they had moved in, as Miguel was looking after her, telling her stories out loud while he picked flowers to put in her lap, Hernando saw his mother move her hand slightly.

The memory of what Fátima had said the day he found his children taking classes in the courtyard of their first home came rushing back to his mind: *Hamid has said that water is the source of life.* The source of life! Could it be that his mother might recover?

With this fresh hope he walked over to the odd couple. Miguel was almost shouting out the story of an enchanted house.

'The walls rustled like reeds in the wind . . .' the lad was saying when his master came up to them.

Hernando smiled and looked down at his mother, slumped in a chair by the fountain.

'She's going to leave us,' he heard Miguel say to him.

Hernando spun round to face him. 'What? But she looks better!'

'She's going, your honour. I know it.'

They looked at each other. Miguel held his gaze, and then narrowed his eyes to confirm his premonition. Shaking his head slightly as if to share Hernando's pain, he went on with his story.

'The wall of the room where the girl was sleeping vanished as if by magic, Señora María. Can you imagine that? An enormous hole . . .'

Not paying any attention to the story, Hernando knelt in front of his mother and stroked her knee. Was Miguel really able to foresee death? Aisha seemed to react to her son's touch, and moved her hand again.

'Mother,' Hernando whispered.

Miguel came closer.

'Leave us, I beg you,' Hernando said.

Miguel withdrew to the stables, and Hernando took his mother's bony hand in his.

'Can you hear me, Mother? Are you able to understand what I'm saying?' he sobbed as he squeezed her frail fingers. 'I'm so sorry. It's my fault. If I had only told you . . . if I had done that, none of this would have happened. I have never stopped fighting for our cause.'

He told her all he had done, and explained the work Don Pedro had asked him to do: everything they were hoping to achieve!

When he finished, Aisha made no movement. Hernando hid his face in her lap and gave in to his tears.

Four days went by until Miguel's prediction came true. Four long days during which, alone with his mother, Hernando recounted the details of his life time and again, while she gradually slipped away, until one morning she peacefully breathed her last.

Hernando did not want to pay for any burial or funeral ceremony. Miguel grimaced when he heard his master telling this to the Santa María priest. He had deliberately only informed him when Aisha was already dead to come and give extreme unction and remove her from the list of Moriscos in the parish.

'Even though she was my mother, she was possessed by the devil, Father,' Hernando tried to excuse himself, giving him a few coins to perform ceremonies that were not going to take place. 'That was what the Inquisition ruled.'

'I know,' said the priest.

'I can't explain,' he told Miguel later, who was still shocked at what he had heard.

'Did you say she was possessed by the devil?' the lad protested, losing his balance on his crutches. 'Even if she said nothing, your mother suffered more than I did when my family used me to beg with! She deserved a burial—'

'I know what my mother deserves, Miguel,' Hernando cut him short.

He would not have achieved his aim if he had paid for Aisha to be buried in the parish cemetery, rather than in the common graves in the Campo de la Merced, where nobody looked after the bodies. Who cared about corpses whose relatives had not been able to give them a decent Christian burial?

'Go home,' he ordered Miguel after they had seen the grave-diggers throw his mother's body into the grave without the slightest respect.

'What are you going to do, your honour?'

'Go home, I say.'

Hernando went to the royal stables in search of Abbas. He was allowed in, and presented himself in the forge. He found the blacksmith had aged since the last time they had spoken, when the Morisco community refused to accept his charity. The smith also saw how grief had left its mark on Hernando's face.

'I doubt if anyone will be willing to help you,' Abbas said curtly when Hernando explained the reason for his visit.

'They will do if you tell them to. I'll pay well.'

'Money! That's all you're interested in.' Abbas stared at him scornfully.

'You're wrong, but I don't want to argue with you. You know that my mother was a good Muslim. Do it for her. If you won't do it, I'll have to look for a couple of drunken Christians in Plaza del Potro, and then we run the risk of people getting to know how we bury our dead and of the Inquisition investigating. You know the priests would be capable of digging up the whole burial ground.'

That night two strong young men and an old woman went with him. They would not accept any money, but refused to talk to him. They left the city for the Campo de la Merced through a derelict gate in the old walls. By moonlight in the deserted cemetery the two young Moriscos dug up Aisha's body on Hernando's instructions. They handed the corpse over to the old woman and began to dig a long, narrow hole in virgin ground to the depth of a man's waist.

The old woman had come prepared. She stripped the body and washed it. Then she rubbed it with soaked vine leaves. 'Lord! Forgive her and have mercy on her,' she recited over and over again.

'Amen,' Hernando responded. He was standing with his back to her, his eyes veiled with tears as he gazed at a darkened Córdoba. The law forbade anyone not washing the corpse from looking at it, and Hernando would never even have considered infringing the rule.

'Lord God, forgive me!' the old woman said when she accidentally touched the body after purifying it. 'Did you bring the cloths?' she asked Hernando.

Without turning to face her, Hernando passed the woman several white linen cloths to wrap Aisha's tiny body in. The two young men, who had finished digging the hole, came to take the body and bury it, but Hernando stopped them.

'What about the prayer for the dead?' he asked them.

'What prayer?' he heard one of them ask.

They were probably twenty years old, thought Hernando. They had been born in Córdoba. All of these young people shunned study, knowledge of the revealed book or prayers. Instead they professed a blind hatred for all Christians, hoping in this way to appease their souls. They probably only knew the profession of faith, he lamented.

'Put the body by the grave and leave if you wish.'

Then in the moonlight he raised his arms and began the lengthy prayer for the dead: 'God is great. Praise be to God, the giver of life and death. Praise be to God, who resurrects the dead. He only is great, He only is sublime, He has the power . . .'

The two young men and the old woman stood behind him while he recited the prayer.

'Is this the man they call the Nazarene?' one of the young men whispered to the other.

Hernando finished the prayer. They placed Aisha on her side in the grave, facing the kiblah. Before covering her body with stones, on to which they would shovel earth in order for the burial not to be visible, Hernando slipped the letter of the dead inside the linen shroud. He had written it that afternoon with perfect lettering in saffron ink, in close communion with Allah.

'What are you doing?'

'Ask your holy scholar,' Hernando said gruffly. 'You can go now. Thanks.'

The young men and the old woman left with grunted farewells. Hernando was on his own at the graveside. His mother's life had been one of great hardship. Memories of her came to his mind, but unlike previous occasions when they had flashed by chaotically, now they appeared slowly and clearly. He stood by the grave for a long time, tears alternating with nostalgic smiles. She was at peace now, he consoled himself before heading back to the city.

When he had climbed through the opening in the wall, he heard a muffled but familiar sound behind his back. He stopped in the middle of a narrow alleyway.

'Don't hide,' he said into the night. 'Come out here with me, Miguel.'

The lad did not obey.

'I heard you,' insisted Hernando. 'Come on.'

'My lord.' Hernando tried to identify where the voice was coming from. It sounded sad. 'When you took me on as a servant, you said you needed me to look after your mother and your horse. Now María Ruiz has died, and . . . I can't even reach up to put a bridle on Volador.'

Hernando felt a shudder go through his whole body. 'Do you think I would turn you out of my house just because my mother has died?'

A few moments went by until the clicking sound of crutches filled the silence that had followed his question. Miguel appeared out of the darkness. 'No, your honour,' he said. 'I don't think you would do that.'

'My horse appreciates you, I know that, I can see it. As for my mother . . .' Hernando's voice failed him.

'You loved her very much, didn't you?'

'Yes.' Hernando sighed. 'But she didn't . . .'

'She died comforted,' said Miguel. 'She died in peace. You can be assured that she heard your words.'

Hernando tried to make out the features of the young lad in the gloom. What was he saying?

'What do you mean by that?' he asked.

'That she understood your explanations and knew you had not betrayed your people.' Miguel spoke with his head bowed, not raising his eyes from the ground.

'What do you know about that?'

'You must forgive me.' He raised his sincere eyes to Hernando's face. 'I am nothing more than a beggar, a vagrant. Life for people like me depends on what we hear in the streets, round a corner . . .'

Hernando shook his head.

'But I am loyal,' Miguel hastened to add. 'I would never denounce you. I swear I wouldn't, even if they broke my arms.'

Hernando said nothing for a few moments. How could the lad be sure his mother had died comforted?

'I have wished for death many times,' said Miguel, as if reading his thoughts. 'I've been at death's door many times when I've been ill on the streets, all alone, scorned by people who stepped aside so as not to go near me. I have been in the same state as her, and in that limbo I have known dozens of souls like Señora María's, all of them on the threshold of death. Some are fortunate and are allowed in; others are rejected and have to carry on suffering. I know it. I could hear them. I can assure you I know what she felt.'

Hernando still said nothing. Something about the lad made him trust him, believe in his words. Or was it simply his own wish that his mother had died in peace? He sighed and put his arm round the boy's shoulders.

'Let's go home, Miguel.'

'I confirmed it, my lady.' Back in Tetuan, the young Ephraim raised his voice when faced with the constant cries of disbelief from Fátima as he gave her Aisha's message. His father, who had gone with him to Brahim's palace, put his hand on his son's forearm to calm him down. 'I confirmed it,' Ephraim said again, less agitatedly this time, while Fátima continued to pace up and down the luxurious room giving on to the palace courtyard. 'When I had finished talking to Aisha, the blacksmith from the royal stables came looking for me—'

'Abbas?' Fátima blurted out.

'A man called Jerónimo. He was the one who told me where the woman lived. He must have followed me and waited for me to finish with her before he intercepted me and assailed me with questions—'

'Did you tell him anything about me?' asked Fátima, interrupting him once more.

'No, my lady. I told him what my father and I had agreed to say if things did not turn out well: that I was looking for Hernando because I had an excellent thoroughbred Arab horse I was given as payment for a shipment of oil, which I wanted him to train for me.'

'Well?'

'He didn't believe me. He insisted on wanting to know about the letter he had seen Aisha tear to pieces and throw into the Guadalquivir, but I refused to say anything about it. I swear it.'

'What did Abbas say?' asked Fátima, coming to a halt nervously in front of the young Jew. She had just listened to him tell her about the state in which he had found Aisha: he had spoken of her obvious broken health, how old and ill she looked. Perhaps . . . perhaps she had gone mad? Fátima thought. But Abbas would not lie! He was Hernando's friend. They had worked side by side, putting their lives at risk for the community. Not Abbas. He could not lie.

Ephraim hesitated. 'My lady, that Jerónimo, or Abbas as you call him, confirmed everything the mother had said to me. That night, he invited me to stay in the house of someone called Cosme, a friend of his held in great respect by the Morisco community in Córdoba. Both of them confirmed in greater detail what Aisha had said. Soon after they believed you were dead – because they think you are dead, my lady, both you and your children . . .' Fátima acknowledged this with a sigh. 'Well, less than a year after that, your husband went to live in the palace of the Duke of Monterreal. They oozed hatred for the Nazarene, my lady.' His father stirred uneasily when Ephraim talked of Hernando in this way, but it seemed only to make Fátima more resolute: her expression hardened and she clenched her fists even tighter. 'The entire Morisco community hates him for what he has done and how he has betrayed them. I could see that from several of Cosme's neighbours. I'm sorry,' the young man concluded after a few moments' silence.

During Ephraim's lengthy journey from Tetuan to Córdoba and back, Fátima had considered a thousand possibilities: that

Hernando had rebuilt his life and would refuse to leave the caliphs' capital – she could have accepted that! She even came to think he might have died: she had heard of the terrible outbreak of plague that had hit Córdoba six years earlier. He might also not have wanted to give up the position as horse-trainer in the royal stables that he enjoyed so much, or could simply have decided that the Morisco community needed him there, in Christian lands, to copy the revealed book, the calendars or the prophecies . . . She would have understood that as well! But she would never have imagined that Hernando could betray his brothers and his beliefs. Hadn't she given up her own freedom to allow the money to be used to redeem a Morisco slave?

'And you say . . . ?' Fátima hesitated. Those were the days when they were living together, the years of the uprising in the Alpujarra in which they had both suffered a thousand misfortunes for their God, when Ubaid and Brahim had abused and humiliated them. How could he have kept his actions secret? Hernando had told her about how he had escaped from Barrax's tent with that Christian nobleman, but how had he kept the whole truth hidden from her after all the sacrifices she had made to secure marriage to him? She had lost her little Humam in that holy war! 'You say he saved the lives of several Christians in the Alpujarra?'

'Yes, my lady. It is known for certain that he saved the life of the noble who took him into his palace, and that of the wife of a judge in the chancery of Granada, but people talk of many others as well.'

Fátima exploded. The shouts and insults that poured from her mouth resounded round the room. She strode angrily out into the courtyard, raised her arms to the skies and howled with rage and grief. The old Jewish man gestured to his son, and they both slipped out of the palace.

A few days later, Fátima called in Shamir and her son Abdul and told them all she had heard about Hernando.

'The dog!' was all Abdul growled when she had finished.

She watched as they left the room, serious and determined.

The trappings on the scabbards of their scimitars clinked as they left. They were corsairs, thought Fátima, they were used to living with cruelty.

From that day on, Fátima devoted herself to administering with an iron hand all the profits and wealth the family possessed, while the two young men roamed in their pirate ships. Nothing distracted her from her work, although alone at night she still remembered Ibn Hamid with a mixture of anger and sorrow. Thanks to her offer of a splendid dowry, she married Maryam to a young man from the al-Naqsis family, who by now were lords of Tetuan. She also looked for appropriate brides for Abdul and Shamir. The alliance she had entered into with the al-Naqsis family after Brahim's death was very profitable, and the fact that she was a woman did not stop her occupying a prominent place in the business world of the corsair city. She was not the first woman to play such a role in the history of Tetuan. After being conquered by the Muslims, its first governor had been a one-eyed woman who was still remembered with great respect. Like her, Fátima was feared and revered. Like her, Fátima was alone.

PART FOUR

IN THE NAME OF OUR LORD

And I say to you that the Arabs are one of the most excellent of peoples, and their tongue one of the most excellent tongues. God has chosen them to convey his law in recent times . . . as I was told by Jesus, who has renounced the children of Israel, who were unfaithful . . . they will never wear the crown. But the Arabs and their tongue will return to God and his law, to his glorious gospel and his Church in the time to come.

The Lead Books of the Sacromonte: *The Book of the History of the Truth of the Gospel* (ed. by M. J. Hagerty)

58

THE DAY had dawned cold and overcast. Hernando, who by now was forty-one years old, seemed to have awoken in as grey a mood as the sky seen from his courtyard. Miguel could not help but be worried about his master and friend. He could see he was nervous, out of sorts, a prey to anxiety, which was unusual in someone who for the past seven years, from the time he came back from riding to the early hours, was in the habit of retiring quietly to a room on the second floor that had become his library. The books, papers and parchments in there were more numerous than the leaves that fell from the trees in winter.

It was the climax of seven years' work that was causing the anxiety that Miguel had noticed in Hernando. Seven years' study. Seven years dedicated to imagining and then putting into practice a scheme that he hoped would bring the two great religions closer, and would completely alter the perception the Christians had of those who had been lords of the Spanish kingdoms for eight centuries, but now found themselves reviled. Hernando had even taught himself Latin in order to be able to read certain texts. His one aim was to reconcile the two religions. He no longer indulged in gaming, and only occasionally allowed himself to visit concubines.

'The seven apostolic brethren!' Hernando had exclaimed in the courtyard one day, startling Miguel as he was preparing the beds for flowers that would bloom the next spring. 'If I use that legend as a reference point, all the other pieces will fall into place, including the story of Saint Caecilius that Alonso del Castillo told me.'

Miguel, who had heard of Hernando's plans when he had revealed them to his dying mother, was both indifferent and sceptical about his master's intentions.

'Do you really expect me to trust in any God?' he remarked bitterly when they discussed the matter one day. 'What kind of God can He be, whether He is yours or theirs, if He allows people to smash children's legs to earn a few more coins?'

In spite of this attitude, it was to Miguel that Hernando turned when he wanted to voice his doubts or the progress he thought he was making. He had to talk to someone, and Luna, Castillo and Don Pedro were many leagues away.

'So who are these apostolic brethren?' asked Miguel impatiently, but willing at least to try to please his friend.

'According to the legend in some writings,' Hernando explained, 'they are the seven apostles sent by Saint Peter and Saint Paul to bring Christianity to ancient Hispania: Torquatus, Ctesiphon, Indaletius, Secundus, Euphrasius, Caecilius and Hesychius. The remains of four of them have been found and are venerated in many places, but do you know something . . . ?' Hernando left the question floating in mid-air.

Leaning on one of his crutches as he pulled off a dry twig with his other hand, Miguel glanced at his master. When he saw how brightly his eyes were shining, he no longer felt annoyed, and revealed his broken teeth in a smile. 'No, what should I know? Tell me . . .'

'That of the three apostolic brethren who have yet to be found, one of them is Saint Caecilius, who was said to have been the first Bishop of Granada. All I have to do is use the legend and make sure that Saint Caecilius's remains are discovered in Granada. It would even tie in with the parchment in the Turpian tower! It could—'

'But, my lord,' Miguel objected, letting go of the twig and grasping both of his crutches, 'don't the bishops maintain that the person who brought Christianity to Spain was Saint James? Even I know that, but you haven't named him as one of the seven.'

'That's true,' Hernando admitted. 'I know what I'll do. I'll unite the two legends!' Saying this, he immediately ran upstairs, as though he were about to do so there and then.

Miguel saw him trip over a step and stumble to recover. 'I'll unite the two legends,' he said mockingly as he bent over a bed of what would be beautiful roses. 'I'll unite the two religions,' he added, as he had often heard Hernando say, busying himself pruning some dead shoots. 'There's only one thing that really needs uniting,' he said, raising his voice almost to a shout in the empty garden, 'and that's the smashed bones in my legs!'

That freezing January morning, as he heard Hernando scolding María, the Morisco woman who did their housework, Miguel remembered his words of frustration. As he looked down at the flower bed where the previous year the roses had grown and filled the courtyard with their sweet perfume, he could not help feeling for an instant that nature was mocking him. Why was everything but his legs reborn so beautifully each year? He had never resented his handicap so much in all his life as in the previous month, when he realized that their neighbour Rafaela was casting her innocent eyes at his crippled legs and hurriedly looking away. She was not the slightest bit curious, and yet could not avoid glancing at them from time to time, although she always quickly stammered some excuse and looked him in the face instead.

Although he had seen her coming and going many times from the house next door, he had not really noticed her until a few weeks earlier. It had been one night, when he had gone to the stables to check that the new colt that Toribio had brought from the stud farm was settling down properly. Five years earlier, realizing that Volador was growing old, Hernando had decided to set up the farm at Palma del Río with the intention of mating him with some of the rejected mares he had bought at the royal stables. He had also taken on another horseman: Toribio, who since then had been put in charge of training the new colts, something he did with limited success. When Toribio considered they were properly trained, he sent them on to the stables in Córdoba.

That evening Miguel went to look at a colt called Estudiante, which, like César, the other colt they kept in the stables at the house, was a son of Volador and a chestnut mare. Hernando was worried about the colts, which meant that Miguel often went down to see they were all right, at any time of the day or night. The fact was that neither of them was happy in their stalls. They were both difficult and mistrustful, and when they were ridden it soon became obvious they had been trained using violence rather than skill. Hernando had been forced to admit to Miguel that Toribio lacked sensitivity. One positive result, however, was that the Morisco came down more often to the stables to try to correct these faults, and was soon spending every morning riding. From then on, Miguel could see that his master had recovered his appetite, and that the fresh air of the meadows where he rode had got rid of the ashen look on his face that came from spending so many hours shut up in his library.

It was when Miguel went down to see that Estudiante was settled next to César that he first met Rafaela. He had just wheeled round on his crutches to return to his bedroom when he heard the muffled sound of sobbing. Could his master be crying? He listened more closely, and looked up in the direction of the library where Hernando was still at work. The light from the lanterns spilled out on to the gallery above the courtyard: there seemed to be nothing wrong there. He realized the sobs were coming from the opposite direction, from where the stables adjoined the next house's yard. That was where the magistrate Don Martín Ulloa lived. Miguel was about to dismiss the sounds as unimportant, and to continue on his way, but the muted distress reminded him of the way his brothers and sister had tried desperately to contain their tears at night, for fear of receiving another beating. He went over to the adjoining wall. Someone was crying their heart out. He could hear quite clearly now how the person was imploring the heavens for help, just as his brothers and sister used to do . . . and so had he.

'What's wrong?' He sensed it must be a girl on the other side of the wall. Yes, no doubt about it. Those were the sighs and tears of a young girl.

There was no answer. Miguel could hear someone trying to choke back their sobs and stifle their moans, which only set off uncontrollable hiccoughs.

'Don't cry, my child,' Miguel insisted, but in vain.

Miguel gazed up at the starry night sky above Córdoba. How old could his blind sister be now? The last time he had seen her she must have been five or six: old enough to realize her life was different from that of the other children playing happily in the streets. Miguel whispered the same words as he had used to her, years earlier, in the darkness of the dank, foul-smelling room they all shared with their parents:

'Don't cry, my child. Do you know, there was once a little blind girl . . .' Leaning against the wall, he sadly remembered, word for word, the first story he had made up for his little sister. '. . . who stretched her arms up in the air and jumped up to touch the marvellous starry sky that everyone said was above their heads, but which she could not see . . .'

For several nights, they communicated in this way through the wall. Miguel told stories that brought smiles to her face, even though he could not see them; the girl was happy to be lulled by his voice into forgetting her misfortunes for a brief while.

'You are the . . .' she whispered one night.

'Yes, the cripple,' Miguel sighed sadly.

A few days later, they finally met. Miguel asked her to come and see the colts he had told her so many stories about. Rafaela sneaked out of an old gate that was hardly used any more, but which gave on to the exit to Hernando's stables. Setting his mouth in a firm line, Miguel waited for her on his crutches. Even though she only had to travel a few steps, she came to the stables wrapped in a black cloak. Miguel had never seen her close to before: she must be about sixteen or seventeen years old. She had long chestnut-coloured hair that curled over her shoulders, a gentle smile and a snub nose above her thin lips. That night she finally told him face to face why she was so sad. Her father, the magistrate Martín Ulloa, did not have enough money to offer his two daughters a dowry while at the same time paying for his two sons' extravagant ways.

'They think they're noblemen,' Rafaela said bitterly, 'when really they are nothing more than the sons of a needle-maker whose father weaselled his way into the law through trickery. My father, my brothers, even my mother, behave as though they were all blue-blooded.'

Don Martín had therefore decided that Rafaela, his eldest daughter, who did not seem to him beautiful enough to attract a suitable husband, should go into a nunnery. If she did, he could bestow the entire dowry on his younger daughter, who was more attractive and by common consent more flirtatious. But he did not have enough money to offer the religious orders he was trying to persuade to take his daughter, so Rafaela could see she would end up in a convent as a maid for the more well-to-do nuns. This was the only solution for a pious, unmarried young Christian woman who had no money.

'I heard my father and brothers discussing it. My mother was there too, but she didn't say a word in protest at the way they were trying to get rid of me. If only one of them saved some of the huge amounts they spend. They treat me as if I had the plague!'

Night after night from then on, Miguel was amazed at how the bad-tempered colts allowed Rafaela to stroke and whisper in their ears. One evening, with the girl sitting on the straw opposite him, for the first time in his life he found words failed him. All he wanted was to get closer to her and embrace her, but he did not have the courage: how could he with those crushed legs of his? After she had gone, he spent the rest of the night thinking about it: what could he do for that poor girl? She deserved a far better future.

59

The angels said, 'O Mary! Indeed God has chosen you, and purified you, and has chosen you above all other women of all nations.'

Koran 3, 42

ONE MORNING in that January of 1595, Hernando prepared to saddle up Estudiante. 'I'm going to Granada,' he told Miguel.

'Wouldn't it be wiser for you to ride César?' the other man replied. 'He's more—'

'No, Estudiante is a fine horse, and the journey will do him good. I'll have time to teach and train him – which will give me something to do along the way.'

'How long will you be gone?'

Hernando was holding the bridle, and was just about to insert the bit. He smiled at Miguel: 'Aren't you the one who is supposed to know when animals and people will reappear?' he said, as he always did whenever he was leaving on a journey.

Miguel had known he would say this. 'You know very well that is no use with you, my lord. There are things that have to be done, decisions to be made, rent to be collected from our tenants, and so I need—'

'And you need to meet your night-time friend,' Hernando said, taking him by surprise.

Miguel flushed. He mumbled an excuse, but Hernando would not listen. 'I've nothing against it, but beware of her father. If he finds out, he's capable of stringing you up from a tree, and I'd like to find you here safe and sound when I return.'

'She's a very unhappy young girl, my lord.'

Hernando had finished inserting the bit, and Estudiante was champing vigorously on it. 'That Toribio will never understand how to use sticks with honey,' Hernando complained when he saw the colt's attitude. 'Why is your friend so unhappy?' he asked off-handedly.

When there was no reply, he paused, lifting the saddle in his arms. He sensed that Miguel wanted to tell him something; in fact, he had been wanting to for several days now, but he had always had other things on his mind. Seeing Miguel's sad face, he sighed and went over to him.

'I can see you are worried,' he said, looking him in the eye. 'I cannot stop now, but I promise that as soon as I'm back we'll talk about it.'

The youngster nodded silently. 'Have you finished what you were writing, my lord?'

'Yes, I've finished. Now,' he said, pausing for a few moments, 'it is for God to get to work.'

But Hernando did not head for Granada as he had said. Instead of crossing the Roman bridge out of Córdoba, he left by the Colodro gate and took the route towards Albacete and the Mediterranean coast. He intended to ride as far as Almansa, and there turn north for Jarafuel. From the outset, Estudiante was difficult and skittish. While they were going through the busier areas outside the city, Hernando gave him his head and allowed him to lean on the bit. Further on, when they had gone past the crossroads with the Camino de Las Ventas leading to Toledo, he spurred his mount on until the horse was going at a full gallop, controlled only by his rider's strength. Two leagues were enough. Despite the winter chill, Estudiante was in a lather by the time they crossed the Alcolea bridge, and was panting through his nostrils, but he was responding to the spurs. From then on they went at a walk: there were still almost sixty leagues to Almansa, and the journey was long and arduous, as Hernando had discovered a few months earlier when he had gone to Granada to discuss the question of the martyrs. The new archbishop, Don Pedro de Castro, asked him for reports just as his deceased predecessor had done.

It had been Castillo who had advised him to visit Jarafuel. Together with Teresa and Cofrentes, this village was on the western edge of the kingdom of Valencia, situated to the north of Almansa in a fertile valley with a river that flowed into the river Júcar. On the far side was the Muela de Cortes mountain. Most importantly, however, these villages had a predominantly Morisco population.

'I don't have any ancient parchments,' Hernando had complained during his last visit to Granada. He was meeting Don Pedro, Miguel de Luna and Alonso del Castillo in the Golden Stable, with green and gold reflections glinting in the roof vaults. 'At the moment I am writing everything on normal paper, but—'

'We shouldn't use parchments,' Luna argued. He had just published the first part of his work *The True History of King Rodrigo*, which had stirred up a fierce debate amongst intellectuals throughout Spain. Unfortunately for the author, the strongest opposition to his positive view of the Arabs came from someone who was himself a Morisco, the Jesuit Ignacio de las Casas. 'Some authorities have claimed the parchment from the Turpian tower is a fake, because they say it's not old enough—'

'It was certainly old,' Hernando cut in with a smile, 'it dated from the time of al-Mansur at least.'

'Yes, but that's not old enough,' Castillo declared. 'We need to employ something that is not paper or parchment: gold, silver, copper . . .'

'Lead,' Don Pedro asserted. 'It's easy to get hold of. It's used a lot by goldsmiths.'

'The ancient Greeks wrote on lead sheets,' said Luna. 'It's an excellent choice. No one will be able to tell whether it is old or not, especially if we put it through a manure bath, as our friend did with the Turpian tower document.'

Hernando smiled along with the others.

'In Jarafuel in the kingdom of Valencia,' said Castillo, 'I know a goldsmith who secretly creates Morisco jewellery despite the prohibition. I also know the village holy man. They are both completely trustworthy. Binilit the goldsmith makes hands of Fátima and patens with moons and Arabic inscriptions for baptizing the newly born. He also makes bangles, bracelets and necklaces on which he engraves verses from the Koran and magnificent Morisco patterns just like the ones our womenfolk used to wear before the Christian conquest. I'm sure he'll be able to copy what you've written on to lead plates.'

'Some of the work is in Latin,' Hernando explained, 'but for the ones written in Arabic I've used odd, pointed letters in a style of calligraphy I myself invented. I've based it on the images of the points of the Seal of Solomon, the symbol of unity. I wanted to avoid any style invented after the birth of the prophet Isa.'

Don Pedro nodded contentedly; Luna rewarded the idea with polite applause.

'I can assure you that Binilit the goldsmith is sufficiently skilled to inscribe any kind of writing we may give him on the lead.'

Hernando had been able to appreciate Binilit's skill on his previous visit to Jarafuel. He looked for the holy man Munir – someone who was surprisingly young for the responsibilities he carried on his shoulders. The two of them made their way to the goldsmith's tiny workshop. When they arrived, Binilit was working on a hand of Fátima he had been asked to make for a wedding. He placed a strip of silver in a hollow mould, then placed another strip of lead on top of it and began to hammer delicately until he could pull the moulded jewellery out cleanly. Then he began tracing geometrical designs on it. As he was working, the holy man explained what they wanted from him.

'It's something on which the whole future of our people in these lands depends,' Munir concluded.

Binilit nodded, and for the first time raised his eyes from the jewellery he was creating.

Hernando had been watching him work, fascinated. He congratulated him on his efforts. Binilit encouraged him to pick it up, and Hernando was immediately reminded of the hand of Fátima he kept so carefully hidden in his library. He weighed this one; it seemed slightly lighter than the one he had. He stroked the unfinished patterns. Who was the girl who would wear it in secret? What adventures would befall it? His memories of all he had lived through with Fátima and their own piece of jewellery brought a nostalgic smile to his face.

'Do you like it?' asked Binilit, bringing him back to reality.

'It's marvellous.'

The two men stood contemplating it for a few moments.

'Let me see what you have written,' the goldsmith said.

Hernando put the hand of Fátima down and handed him the sheets of paper. The goldsmith examined them. At first he seemed unconvinced, but when he saw the Seal of Solomon on several of them, the pointed Arabic letters, and began to decipher some of the phrases at random, his eyes narrowed. He began to concentrate on them as if he considered them a real challenge.

'There are twenty-two pieces of writing,' Hernando explained. 'As you can see, some of them are only one page, but others are longer.'

The goldsmith examined the sheets of paper several times. He spread them out on his small work bench, mentally calculating how much writing they contained, imagining what they would look like inscribed on lead plates. All at once his attention was drawn to several sheets with unreadable letters that were not written either in Latin or in the curious Arabic script Hernando had devised.

'What's this?' he wanted to know.

'I call it the Mute Book. It has no meaning. As you can see, the letters are completely indecipherable. I had a really hard time trying to invent all those meaningless characters. In another of the books,' Hernando said, rummaging among the papers, 'this one here – the *History of the Truth of the Gospel* – it is said that the meaning of the Mute Book will be revealed at a later date. The two complement each other,' he explained. He hesitated, wondering whether to tell them that the meaning of the book was none other than the gospel of Barnabas, but decided not to. 'The revelation will only come once the Christians are prepared to receive the true message, the one that has not been distorted by their Church, the one that shows there is only one true God.'

Binilit murmured his approval. Hernando thought through the guiding principle of his efforts: the writings were an ingenious puzzle constructed around a central figure, that of the Virgin Mary. Together they pointed to an apparently irreconcilable conclusion: the Mute Book, the gospel of the Virgin, written in an incomprehensible language that would defeat any scholars who tried to interpret it. Yet, as Hernando had just explained to Binilit, another of the plaques would announce the appearance of a text that would resolve the mystery. That text would be the gospel of Barnabas, which he himself kept closely guarded. Once the lead plates were accepted, together with the enigmatic Mute Book, the gospel of Barnabas and its acceptance of Islam would shine out as the only, unquestionable truth.

'All right,' the goldsmith agreed, rousing Hernando from his thoughts. 'I will get word to you when I've completed them.'

Hernando searched in his bag for money to pay him, but Binilit stopped him.

'I only charge enough for my jewellery to help me live a sober, frugal life; I'm an old man now. All I want is for we Muslims to be able to wear the ornaments our ancestors wore. So you can pay me when the Christians accept the revealed word.'

* * *

In his second journey to Jarafuel, it took Hernando four days to reach the village. He joined the caravans of traders and muleteers he met each night at the wayside inns. Travelling such roads he risked unfortunate encounters with bands of outlaws, but he also met a wide variety of other people: endless numbers of friars and priests going from monastery to monastery; puppeteers travelling to villages with their shows; foreigners and gypsies, rogues and countless beggars thrown out of the cities asking for alms from travellers and pilgrims.

Hernando spent the third night in the village of Almansa. It was here that he had to leave the busy Roman road and head inland for five leagues along smaller tracks, and so he wanted to travel by day.

When he set out the next morning, it was Estudiante himself who became suspicious and warned him of danger. He was riding at a walk along a solitary path through a fertile valley surrounded by mountains. The castle of Ayora stood high on a crag a league away. All he could hear were his own horse's hooves, when suddenly Estudiante pricked up his ears and stopped dead. Hernando looked all around him, but could not see anything moving. Estudiante, however, had stiffened and laid back his ears, which were twitching nervously. Hernando had decided to trust to the animal's instinct, and was about to spur him on, when of its own accord the horse leapt forward and began to gallop. Hernando flattened himself on its neck. A few paces further on, several armed men suddenly appeared from both sides of the path. Hernando did not even have time to see their faces properly: one of them stood menacingly in the middle of the path, brandishing an ancient sword. Hernando cried out and spurred Estudiante on. The man hesitated, and then decided to jump out of the way of the horse's mad career. Even so, seeing the rusty blade flashing in the air, Hernando pulled the horse to one side and aimed straight at the man to prevent him slashing at his back. Estudiante responded in an agile fashion, almost as if he were dancing round a bull's horns in the ring, and the outlaw was sent flying. Estudiante began to gallop off again, and Hernando flattened himself on his back, just in time to avoid two harquebus balls that whizzed through the air close by him.

'Volador would be proud of you,' he said, patting the horse's neck as they drew close to Ayora castle.

He continued on his way to Jarafuel, which he reached without further incident. He found the young holy man, and the two of them headed once more to Binilit's workshop. They left Estudiante tethered in the small garden behind Munir's house.

'Did you come alone?' Munir asked him as they walked towards the workshop.

'Yes. And I had a lucky escape near Ayora—'

'That wasn't why I was asking you,' the holy man interrupted him, 'although I will find someone to accompany you on the way back at least as far as Almansa, or go with you myself. No, I was asking because I don't know how you on your own are going to be able to carry everything that Binilit has prepared for you. He has done a magnificent job.'

Hernando had not considered that it was one thing to transport papers, but something entirely different to have to carry lead plates. In Córdoba he had simply slung a couple of saddlebags over Estudiante's back. When he reached Binilit's workshop, he could not help whistling in surprise at the sight of all the work the goldsmith had done: there must be between a hundred and two hundred lead plates – perhaps more! They were plaques of about half a hand span in width, where Binilit had inscribed all Hernando's texts. They were piled up high in one corner of the workshop. It would be impossible for him to carry all that weight in his saddlebags!

He picked up the topmost plaque from one of the piles. Hernando had called it *The Book of the Foundations of the Church*. He weighed it in his hand, and then examined the goldsmith's work. It was wonderful: Binilit had carefully transcribed all the pointed letters on to the small plate of metal.

'Mary did not commit original sin,' said the holy man.

Hernando turned towards him. 'I've spent many days here,' explained Munir, 'reading . . . or rather, trying to interpret what you have written. You've left out all the punctuation and the vowels.'

'That's because they were not used in those days.' The holy man made as if to say something, but Hernando went on speaking. Binilit was listening attentively. 'Besides, our message ought not to be direct; it should be ambiguous. If it were not, the Christians would reject the books straight away.'

'But the references to Mary are clear,' said Munir.

'That's because there is no problem with those. The Christians will accept the Virgin's intervention without questioning it,' Hernando asserted. 'The figure of Mary is probably the only link between the two religions that has not been tarnished. In addition, in Spain there is great pressure for the Church to make it dogma once and for all that Mary conceived without sin. My texts support this view, so they will accept them. As you will have noticed, Mary is the central point of all the books. She is the one in possession of the divine message, which she conveys to Saint James and the other apostles following the death of Isa. She tells James to take Christianity to Spain, and she is the one who gives him a new gospel, the Mute Book. Although this cannot be deciphered now, its meaning will be revealed on the day that the Christians realize the popes have distorted God's message. All this will come about thanks to an Arab king.'

'What do we gain if the Christians cannot understand the message?' the goldsmith asked. 'They could interpret it as they see fit.'

'And they will do so. Have no doubts about that,' said Hernando.

Binilit spread his hands towards the piles of plaques, as if he felt cheated after all the work he had done.

'That is what we want, Binilit,' Hernando said, trying to re-assure him. 'If the Christians interpret the books to their advantage, they will have to admit that both Saint Caecilius, the patron saint of Granada, and his brother Saint Ctesiphon were Arabs. They both came with Saint James to convert Spain. Granada's patron saint, an Arab! However hard they try, they cannot accept some parts of the books as true and ignore others that might cause problems. They will also have to admit, as the Virgin Mary herself says, that Arabic is the most sublime of all languages. If they want to use the books to their advantage, they will have to accept these ideas and many more that appear there. It's a good way to bring our two peoples together; perhaps we could even get them to lift the prohibition on us speaking our own language. Besides, if Saint Caecilius was an Arab, what justification is there for all this hatred towards our people?' Munir nodded thoughtfully. 'Many authorities will have to reconsider their teachings and opinions. We Muslims and Christians believe in the same God! That is something most ordinary people do not understand, and their priests hide the truth from them, constantly attacking the Prophet. But in any case, Binilit, all this is simply one more step following the Turpian tower parchment; it's not the end. Once the true meaning of the Mute Book is revealed – the gospel whose meaning has not been distorted by the popes – all the ambiguous aspects contained in many of the texts of these books, such as for example the series of professions of the Muslim faith and the true identity of Isa, will have to be interpreted in accordance with our beliefs.'

'But how can the contents of an illegible book be revealed?' the jeweller asked.

'The book cannot be read,' Hernando explained. 'It's sufficient for it to be acknowledged as the gospel the Virgin wrote. If the Christians recognize these lead books, they will also have to recognize the appearance of the Arab king that is foretold in them, the one who will make known the true gospel, the one that no pope or evangelist has been able to falsify. And no one will be able to claim that this gospel contradicts whatever is in the Mute Book. In this way, we come full circle: the Mute Book, or the Virgin's gospel, which will always have been a mystery, will be ratified by the gospel coming from Arab lands. No one will be able to challenge this new book without calling all the others into question – and they will already have been accepted.

'No one will be able to challenge the gospel of Barnabas,' Hernando added to himself.

Hernando spent the night at Munir's house, where for the first time in many years he could pray alongside a Muslim holy man. The two men then became involved in an intimate and profound discussion that lasted until the early hours of the morning. Muslim beliefs survived almost intact in these distant regions of the kingdom of Valencia. The Christian lords were concerned only with the money the Moriscos brought in, and so were indulgent towards their way of life. Nor were there any priests capable of converting them.

The next morning, Munir himself and two young Moriscos accompanied Hernando to the outskirts of Almansa, which they reached as night was falling. Hernando entered the town to find an inn and companions for the journey on to Granada. Despite the cold winter night, the Moriscos chose to sleep out in the open, because they did not have permits to leave Jarafuel.

'May the one who indicates the right way accompany you and show it to you,' the holy man said in farewell.

It took Hernando four days to reach Granada. He was accompanied by traders, friars and soldiers, who were headed either for Murcia or the city of the Alhambra. In his saddlebags Hernando was carrying twenty or more of the lead plaques that he had chosen among the many Binilit had made. He had chosen two of the books: *The Foundations of the Church* and *The Essence of the Gospel,* as well as more plaques that spoke of the martyrdom of several of Saint James's disciples, among them Saint Caecilius. In them Hernando had included a reference to the discovery in the Turpian tower, hoping in this way to lend the parchment the credibility that some scholars still refused to give it.

Before leaving Jarafuel he promised the goldsmith that either he or his friends in Granada would make sure they took all the remaining plaques. Throughout the four days of his ride, he boasted to all and sundry of the work he was doing for the Archbishop of Granada, showing the signed permit that allowed him freedom of movement, and telling everyone that he was carrying documents referring to what he called the atrocious crimes committed in the Alpujarra in his saddlebags. In this way he hoped to keep the lead plaques safe: who would search in the bags if they contained documents about the Alpujarra martyrs?

To make doubly sure, he never let the saddlebags out of his sight, and even used them as a pillow when he went to sleep in the inns along the route.

He wasted a whole day in Huéscar, which he reached on a Saturday evening. On Sunday morning he attended high mass and had to wait around for the rest of the morning so that the priest could sign the document saying he had fulfilled his religious obligations, which he would need to present to the Santa María parish on his return to Córdoba. While he was waiting inside the church, three barefoot Franciscan friars sought out his company after hearing from the priest that like them he was headed for Granada.

'As you will no doubt understand,' he said, when he explained that his trip was related to the martyrs of the Alpujarra and the friars asked to see the documents he had collected, 'they are confidential. Until the archbishop has given his blessing, no one is to read them.'

So Hernando completed the final part of his journey accompanied by the three Franciscans. Despite the intense cold, all they wore was the coarse brown woollen habit that was the colour of earth and a symbol of humility. On the way they showed him the special dispensation they had received from the provincial of their order that allowed them to wear special open sandals instead of going barefoot. In the two days he spent in their company, Hernando was amazed at the austerity and extreme poverty these 'barefoot' friars demonstrated, although they asked for alms from anyone they met. He admired the frugality of their meals and their stoic attitude towards life, which even meant they slept directly on the ground.

Hernando bade farewell to the Franciscans once they had reached the outskirts of Granada and gone through the Guadix gate above the Albaicín. From there he rode down Carrera del Darro, the road that ran alongside the river towards the Plaza Nueva and the Casa de los Tiros. On the hillside to his right he could see the houses and gardens of the Albaicín, shrouded in mist on this winter's day. What could have become of Isabel? He had not seen her for seven years. On the rare occasions he had travelled to Granada during that time to see Don Pedro, Miguel de Luna or Alonso del Castillo, or to hand over a report about the Alpujarra martyrs, he had not wanted to insist, but had respected the tearful refusal she had given him when she had said goodbye the last time they had met, on the steps of the church.

He spurred Estudiante on so that he would go faster. Seven years! Yes, he enjoyed the redhead in the bawdy house, and several other women too, and yet he had never managed to forget the last night he had spent with Isabel when the two of them had seemed to touch the heavens. He thought he could see the terrace of her garden up on the hillside above the river Darro. Staring up at it, he suddenly felt his whole body go weak. He leant back and rested his hands on Estudiante's withers. The horse took advantage of him relaxing his grip to nibble at the grass growing at the roadside. Hernando had worked hard on behalf of his God, but what had he got out of it? Only memories . . . of Isabel, and how beautiful and sensuous she was; of his loved ones who had died: his mother, Hamid . . . Fátima and the children. His life had been focused on a dream: to reconcile two religions that were opposed to each other, and to demonstrate the supremacy of the Prophet. What for? Who for? Who would thank him for his efforts? The community that rejected him? The next step after the Turpian tower had been taken: what now? What if he did not succeed? Fátima! Her black almond eyes came alive in his memory; her smile; her determined nature; the golden necklace between her breasts, and the nights of love he had lived with her. Hernando felt a tear running down his cheek and did nothing to stop it as his thoughts flew back to Francisco and Inés playing in the courtyard of their house in Córdoba, studying with Hamid, learning, laughing, or gazing at him in silence, attentive and happy.

He had to say it out loud. He had to hear himself admitting the truth.

'Alone. I'm alone,' he murmured, his voice choking with emotion. He took hold of the reins once more, obliging Estudiante to stop eating the grass and start on his way again.

While he was absent, Miguel continued to meet Rafaela every night. Now, though, the stories he told her were no longer about fantastic beings, but always had the same protagonist: Hernando, his lord and master. Rafaela listened to him entranced: Hernando had been a hero; he had saved countless young girls during the war; he had fought and survived many dangers. She was almost reduced to tears when she heard about the death of his wife and children at the hands of cruel bandits. Miguel's smile was tinged with sadness when he saw how without her realizing it she was slowly coming under the spell of the hero of his tales.

60

HERNANDO HAD decided not to stay in Granada any longer than necessary after handing over the lead plaques. Following seven years of work, at the very moment when he entrusted them to Don Pedro, Luna and Castillo, who were waiting for him in the Casa de los Tiros, he was suddenly assailed by doubts as to the effectiveness of what he had done.

The three men took the plaques solemnly and passed them from hand to hand, studying the inscriptions closely. Hernando left them to it, and walked away until he was by one of the windows in the Golden Stable. He became absorbed in contemplation of the Franciscan monastery that stood opposite. Is it all a fantasy? he asked himself. The entire country was full of legends, myths and fables. Not only had he read and studied them, but had himself copied hundreds of Morisco prophecies. Yet they only influenced the credulous minds of ignorant people, both Christian and Muslim, who liked to believe in all kinds of magic and witchcraft.

Only a few days earlier in Jarafuel, with the Muela de Cortes mountain in view on the far side of the valley, Munir had told him a prophecy Hernando had not heard before, even though it was widely believed by the local Moriscos. The prophecy said that they would one day be rescued by the Moorish knight al-Fatimi, who had been hiding in the mountain since the days of James I the Conqueror, three hundred years before.

'What no one here can agree on', the young holy man

complained, 'is whether the Moorish knight is green, or if it is his horse. Some even say that both horse and rider are green.'

A three-hundred-year-old green knight who would come riding to their rescue . . . How naive!

Hernando turned back to look at his companions in the Golden Stable, who were still examining the lead plaques. He shook his head and looked out of the window once more. This was something very different. The lead books were not simple prophecies. They were intended to change the entire religious world by undermining the foundations of the Christian Church. Bishops, priests and friars, as well as intellectuals, doctors of the Church and other learned men, would scrutinize them. News of them would be bound to reach Rome! This was something he had not even contemplated while he was at work. He had allowed his imagination to soar, thinking he could unite traditions, stories and legends around the figure of the Virgin, weaving in the lives of saints and apostles, exploiting the ambiguities inherent in both religions, making deliberate mistakes here and there. Who was he to change the course of history? Had he received inspiration from God? Him? An apprentice muleteer from a poor village in the Alpujarra? How pretentious! How arrogant of him! He thought of all that he had written on these plaques, and it seemed to him crass, vulgar, oversimplified, too ambiguous . . .

'Magnificent!'

Startled, Hernando turned back to face the others.

Don Pedro, Luna and Castillo were smiling. 'Magnificent!' Alonso del Castillo repeated. The other two men joined in the congratulations. Why could he not share in their enthusiasm? He told them they should go and fetch the remaining lead books that were still in Binilit's workshop. He also told them that the plaques would need to be accompanied by bones and ashes that he had not been able to bring from Córdoba. He begged them to hand over to the cathedral council on his behalf the documents on the Alpujarra martyrs that he had collected. When Castillo again asked him for his transcription of the gospel of Barnabas he had to tell him he did not have one. He had destroyed it when he was thrown out of the duke's palace, and had not bothered to make another one because it had not seemed that important. Studying and writing the texts for the lead plaques had taken up all his time.

'We have to send the gospel to the Sublime Porte. Why don't we use the original? The Sultan is the obvious person to make it known,' Don Pedro argued, as if this were an urgent matter.

Luna calmed him down: 'It will be years before that is necessary. For now, we must simply make sure it is kept in a safe place. And you, Hernando, now you have finished your magnificent work with the lead plates, you could devote your time to copying the gospel again so that we can all study it. I have a burning desire to read it.'

'I don't think it is a good idea to send it to the Sultan at the moment,' Hernando agreed. 'We should do it only when we hear that he is willing to back our plan. Up to now, the Turks have not exactly distinguished themselves in their support for our people.'

Then, as the other three were busy speculating about the best moment to reveal the existence of the lead plaques to the Christians, Hernando announced that he was returning to Córdoba.

'You've been distracted all day,' Castillo said. 'You don't seem to share our enthusiasm. All this', the translator added, sweeping his hand towards the lead plates on a table, 'is the fruit of your labours, Hernando, work that has taken you many years. An exceptional effort. What's wrong?'

Hernando made no reply. He hesitated. Stroking his chin with his hand, he looked his companions up and down. 'I can't help having doubts. I need . . . I don't know. I don't know what I need. But perhaps it would be best if I don't interfere in the work you have to do now . . .'

'Our work?' Don Pedro protested. 'But you're the one who—'

Hernando lowered his hand to calm the nobleman. 'It's true.

Of course I'm not going back on everything I've done, but I have the feeling that I would not be of much use to you at this stage—'

'Empty,' Miguel de Luna suddenly said. Hernando fixed his blue eyes on him. 'You must feel completely empty. You've worked so hard it's only natural that's how you feel. Have a rest. It will do you good. We'll see to everything.'

'My mother went to her grave because of this plan of ours,' Hernando said, taking them by surprise. The three men saw his features grow taut and that he was struggling not to cry in their presence. Don Pedro looked down at the floor; the other two exchanged glances. 'She could not bear to think her son had gone over to the Christians, and I had sworn not to reveal anything about our idea.'

Taking a deep breath, he finished in a quavering voice: 'For now, my friends, that is all I have achieved with these lead plaques.'

Hernando clicked his tongue to speed Estudiante up on the way back to Córdoba. He had left Granada at dawn, without seeking any company for the long journey. As he rode through the plains beyond the city, he stood up in the stirrups and looked back towards the snowy peaks of the Sierra Nevada he was leaving behind. Juviles: that was where he had lived his childhood, with his mother . . . and Hamid. He almost had to duck as a flock of starlings flew close by his head. He watched them soar into the sky, as though they wanted to reach the mountaintops, but then suddenly they all wheeled and swooped down on the cultivated fields. He sat back in the saddle and let the reins drop on Estudiante's back. He rubbed his hands vigorously, cupped them and blew his warm breath into them. Houses and farms were dotted about the fertile plains, with here and there people working out in the fields. In the distance, he could see some of them straightening up to get a look at him as he rode by. Hernando peered at the horizon and sighed at the thought of the long, lonely journey ahead of him. The steady clip-clop of Estudiante's hooves on the earth hardened by the cold seemed to be his only companion.

As soon as he saw him, Miguel could tell how sad and distressed his master felt. He had been anxiously awaiting his return so that he could talk to him about Rafaela, as they had agreed before his departure, but when he saw the state he was in, he could not bring himself to broach the subject. Instead, for the next few days he tried to awaken his interest in all that had happened during his absence in the house, on his lands and at the stud. He had argued with Toribio over the violent way he was treating one of the colts, he explained angrily to Hernando on one occasion.

'He was punishing it for no reason!' he shouted. 'Jabbing it with spurs when the poor horse had no idea what he wanted from it.'

Not even news of this argument seemed to interest Hernando, who remained immersed in melancholic nostalgia despite his horse riding and several night-time visits to the bawdy house.

'Do you know the story of the cat that wanted to ride on a horse?' Miguel asked him another time, hopping up to him on his crutches in the gallery beside the courtyard. Hernando came to a halt, and the sound of the crutches also ceased abruptly. 'It was a grey cat—'

'Yes, I know the story,' Hernando said, interrupting him. 'I heard you tell it to my mother at the Potro inn. It's about a noble knight who's turned into a cat by some wicked witches and who can only reverse the spell if he succeeds in mounting and controlling a warhorse. But I don't remember the ending.'

'If you already know that one, perhaps I should tell you about the knight who lived shut up in a tower, always alone . . .' Miguel deliberately let the words float in the air.

Hernando puffed his cheeks out. A few seconds elapsed. 'I don't think I would like that story, Miguel.'

'Perhaps not, but you should listen to it. The knight—'

Hernando motioned to him to be quiet. 'What are you trying to tell me, Miguel?' he asked, looking grim.

'That it's not good for you to be on your own!' Miguel replied, raising his voice. 'You've finished the work you set yourself: what are you planning to do now? Spend the whole day in that library of yours, surrounded by papers? Wouldn't you like to marry again? To have children?'

Hernando did not reply. Waving his arm in an irritated fashion, Miguel turned his back on him and hobbled off.

And Hernando did seek refuge again in his library. In the privacy of the room he contemplated the thirty or so books he had accumulated during his seven years' work on the lead plaques, all neatly arranged on shelves. He tried to read one or another of them again, but soon gave up. He also tried calligraphy once more, but could not get the quill to trace any letters properly. It was as though he had lost the spiritual link that ought to bind him to God as he set out to write the characters praising Him. Hernando tenderly picked up the last quill he had prepared. He saw it was properly cut, with a curving nib . . . and, all at once, it came to him: his link with God. He thumped his fist on the desk. That was it!

The very next morning, after performing the prescribed ablutions, he set off for the mosque. Had he been neglecting his God? he wondered during the short walk to the Perdón gate. He had spent seven years writing about the Virgin, Saint James the Apostle and countless other saints and martyrs of Spain. He had meant well, but could all that effort have undermined his own beliefs, or the purity of his convictions? He felt the need to stand in front of the mihrab, however badly the Christians had desecrated it, and to pray there, even if he had to stand upright and do it silently. If the *taqiya* permitted them to conceal their faith without it being seen as a sin or a renunciation of their beliefs, why should he not also pray secretly in the mosque? There, behind the sarcophagus to Don Alonso Fernández de Montemayor, a past governor of the frontier provinces, was to be found one of the most splendid places of worship ever created by the followers of the Prophet. He entered through the Perdón gate and crossed the cathedral garden. The walls of the cloisters were still hung with hundreds of the penitential garments that those punished by the Inquisition had been forced to wear, with their names and sins written on them. The cloisters also offered shelter to many people who were trying to escape the biting cold of that leaden morning. The sight of the forest of marvellous arches of the original mosque calmed Hernando somewhat, and his step lightened as he walked through the cathedral. Priests and worshippers moved about the interior, while masses and holy offices were being celebrated in some of the side chapels. Work on the transept and the choir had been suspended for a number of years, awaiting the completion of the dome and the vaults around it. The Christians were miserly towards their God, thought Hernando as he wandered through the unfinished sections: bishops and kings lived opulently, but preferred to waste their money on luxuries rather than spend it on their places of worship.

'O ye who believe!' he thought he could read, when he reached the mihrab, the phrase just visible through the plaster moulding the Christians had added in order to hide the revealed word. These words were the start of the Kufic inscriptions from the fifth sura of the Koran engraved on the cornice leading to the holy of holies. He went on silently reciting: 'When ye rise up to prayer . . .'

As Hernando prayed, it came to him, as though God had rewarded his act of devotion. The truth, the word that had been revealed and was chiselled into hard, beautiful marble, had been concealed beneath a vulgar layer of plaster that would crumble at the slightest of blows. Was that not the same situation he was fighting against with his lead books? The unique truth, the supremacy of Islam, was concealed by the false words and trickery of popes and priests, a fiction that would collapse with the revelation of the Mute Book, just as the weak coating of plaster hiding the revealed word could do in the mihrab of the Córdoba mosque. Then he raised his eyes to the double arches built on top of single ones and ending in slender marble columns: the power of God descending with all its weight on the faithful, unlike the Christians, who sought firm foundations for their beliefs. The weight of divine will on simple believers like him. He filled his lungs with this incredible certainty, stifling the shouts of joy with which he would have liked to continue praying to the one God, forcing his lips closed so that not so much as a murmur could be heard.

That very same day, on the hill of Valparaíso in Granada, two of the many treasure hunters who roamed the area in search of the valuable possessions the Moriscos had left behind in their hasty flight from the mountains found in one of the caves of an abandoned mine directly above the Albaicín a strange and useless lead plate with inscriptions on it in an almost indecipherable Latin.

Finding no use for their discovery, the treasure hunters soon handed the plate over to the Church. Eventually it came to the attention of a Jesuit priest who, after translating the inscription, concluded it was indeed a valuable treasure. It was a funeral inscription declaring that this was the burial site of the ashes of Saint Mesiton the martyr, who had been put to death during the reign of Emperor Nero. Mesiton's remains had never been found. The archbishop of Granada, Don Pedro de Castro, immediately ordered that all the ashes found in the cave be gathered, and that the entire mine workings were to be excavated and cleaned in order to facilitate further explorations. In March of that same year, another plaque was found, this time referring to the burial of Saint Hesychius, together with more ashes and some charred human bones. Before the month was out, *The Book of the Foundations of the Church* and shortly afterwards *The Book of the Essence of God* were also discovered. On 30 April, in the midst of the religious fervour of Holy Week when the people of Granada experienced the passion of Christ in their own lives, a young girl by the name of Isabel found the plaque confirming the martyrdom of Saint Caecilius, the patron saint of Granada and the first bishop of Roman Illiberis. Alongside the plaque appeared the ardently desired and sought-after relics of the saint.

The whole of Granada exploded in an outburst of religious joy.

Following his visit to the mosque, Hernando seemed to Miguel like a changed man. He was smiling again, and his blue eyes sparkled as they had done in the past. Miguel was desperate to talk to him: Rafaela's situation had become impossible. Her father, the magistrate Don Martín, was on the verge of coming to an agreement with one of the many convents in the city. One evening after supper, Miguel struggled upstairs to the first-floor library. He found his friend and master absorbed in his calligraphy.

'My lord, there's something I've been wanting to talk to you about for a long while.' He remained on the threshold out of respect for this space that he considered almost holy. He waited for Hernando to raise his eyes from his writing.

'Well? Is something wrong?'

Miguel cleared his throat and came limping into the room. 'Do you remember the girl I told you about before you left for Granada?'

Hernando gave a sigh. He had completely forgotten the promise he had made. He had no idea what Miguel might want of him, or why the girl was so important to him. He could tell, however, from his friend's worried face, so different from his normal happy expression, that it must be something serious.

'Come in and sit down,' he said, smiling. 'I can sense this is going to be a long story . . . So tell me, what is the problem with this young girl?' he added, watching Miguel fight with his crutches so he could sit on a chair.

'Her name is Rafaela,' Miguel began, 'and she is in despair. Her father the magistrate wants to shut her away in a convent.'

Hernando spread his hands. 'Many Christian girls end up wearing the habit quite happily.'

'But she has no desire to do so,' Miguel retorted, laying his two crutches down beside the chair. 'The magistrate does not want to give the convent any money, which means all she can look forward to is being a maidservant to the other nuns.'

Hernando had no idea what to say; he studied his friend's face. 'What do you want me to do? I don't think I have any—'

'Marry her!' Miguel cried, not daring to look his master in the face.

'What?' Hernando's expression was one of utter incredulity. He did not know whether to laugh or be furious. When he saw from Miguel's face that he was struggling to hold back tears, he decided neither was appropriate.

'It's a good way out!' the cripple argued, encouraged by his master's silence. 'You are alone, she has to get married if she doesn't want to be shut away in a convent . . . it would be perfect!'

Hernando listened to him in utter astonishment. Could he be serious? He realized he was. 'Miguel,' he said slowly, 'you, more than anyone, know this is not an easy matter for me.'

The young man held his gaze defiantly.

'Miguel,' Hernando said again, trying to find an adequate response. 'Even supposing that I were willing to marry this young girl – whom I do not even know – do you really think that an arrogant city magistrate would agree to it? Do you think he would allow his daughter to marry a Morisco?' Miguel started to reply, as if he had the answers, but Hernando cut him short. 'Wait,' he said.

He had suddenly realized what was really going on. He had been so caught up in his own thoughts of late that he had not noticed the transformation in his friend.

'I think there's another problem which is even harder to solve,' he said, his blue eyes fixed on the person who was possibly his only friend. He paused, then went on: 'You . . . you are in love with that girl, aren't you?'

Miguel stared down at the floor for a few seconds, but then raised his eyes and looked Hernando directly in the face. 'I don't know,' he said with determination. 'I don't know what it means to love someone. Rafaela . . . Rafaela likes my stories! She calms down when she strokes the horses and whispers to them. As soon as she comes into the stables she stops crying and forgets her worries. She is a sweet, innocent creature.' Miguel's head dropped again. He shook it, and then cupped his chin in his hand. Seeing his friend's dismay, Hernando did not have the heart to protest. 'She's . . . very delicate. She's beautiful. She's—'

'You do love her,' Hernando asserted. He cleared his throat several times before he went on. 'How could we all live together in this house? How could I marry a woman I know you are in love with? We'd see each other every day, be around each other. What would you think or imagine at night?'

'You don't understand.' Miguel was still staring at the floor, and talked in a whisper. 'I don't think anything. I don't imagine. I don't have desires. I can't love a woman as a husband. They have never had any respect for me. I'm nothing but the dregs. My life is worth nothing.' Hernando tried to protest, but this time it was Miguel who stopped him. 'The most I have ever hoped for is to have a bone or a hunk of stale bread to put in my mouth. So what does it matter if I love her or not? What does it matter if I desire her? Throughout my life all my hopes have been crushed, like my legs are. But now I have a new hope. And it's the first time in my wretched life that I believe, with your help, that I can see it achieved. Do you realize what that means? In the nineteen years I think I have been on this earth, I have never – never! – had the chance to see one of my desires fulfilled. Yes, you took me in and gave me work. But I'm talking about my dearest wishes. Something that is all mine! All I really wish for is to help that girl.'

'Does she love you?'

Miguel looked up and grimaced. 'Love a cripple? A servant? It's you she loves.'

'What?' Startled, Hernando rose from his seat.

'I've told her so much about you that, yes, I think she does love you; at the very least, she has a great admiration for you. You were the knight in all my stories, the rescuer of young maids, the tamer of wild beasts, the snake charmer—'

'Have you gone mad?' Hernando's eyes seemed about to start out of his head.

'Yes, my lord,' said Miguel, his face flushed. 'It's a madness I've been living with for some time now.'

That same evening, Miguel climbed up to the library again. Hernando was busy making another copy of the gospel of Barnabas, as his friends in Granada had requested. If they were so insistent that he sent them the original he kept hidden in his library, he would need to make another transcription. He had managed to convince them that the time was not ripe for him to send it to them, but he might not be so lucky on another occasion. Hernando could not help but have his doubts about the Sultan. Would the Great Turk be able to help the Moriscos? This time all he would have to do was make known the gospel that the Mute Book announced. He would not be expected to launch his armada against the King of Spain's realm, but simply to be the king of kings the Virgin Mary spoke of and reveal the lies of the popes through the ages.

'Hernando,' Miguel said from the doorway, 'I'd like you to come and meet Rafaela.'

'Miguel . . .' the Morisco began to complain.

'Please, come with me.' His voice sounded so imploring that Hernando could not refuse. Besides, deep down he was also rather curious.

Rafaela was waiting next to Estudiante. She had one hand entwined in his long, thick mane, while with the other she stroked his muzzle. The stables were only dimly lit by the light of a single lantern hanging well away from the straw. Hernando could see the girl had her head timidly sunk on her chest.

Miguel stayed back, as if to give the two of them room. Hernando hesitated. Why was he nervous? What had Miguel told her, apart from making him the hero of all his stories? He went up to Rafaela, who was still staring down at the straw. She was wearing a petticoat tucked up at her waist, which revealed underneath an old skirt that reached down to her shoes. Her upper body was covered by an open bodice with sleeves on top of a blouse. All her clothes were a dull brown colour, and hung from her body as if they could find nothing solid to give them shape. What had Miguel promised her? Perhaps . . . Could he have gone so far as to tell her Hernando would marry her before he had even mentioned it to him?

All of a sudden he wished he had never come down to the stables. He turned on his heel to leave, but found himself confronting Miguel, standing firmly on his crutches in the doorway.

'Please, I beg you,' said Miguel.

Hernando relented, and turned back to Rafaela. He found her staring at him with bright brown eyes that even in the semi-darkness spoke eloquently of her distress.

'I . . .' he began, trying to excuse his attempt to leave.

'I thank you for what you are willing to do to help me,' Rafaela interrupted him.

Hernando jumped. He was startled by the gentleness of the girl's voice: but what was it she had said? Miguel! He had told her . . . He was about to turn accusingly towards him when Rafaela went on:

'I know I am not much to look at; my parents and brothers tell me so the whole time, but I am healthy.' She smiled as she said this, revealing perfectly straight white teeth. 'I have never been ill, and in our family we are very fertile,' she went on. Hernando could hardly believe his ears. The sincerity and vulnerability in her voice took him aback. 'I am a good, pious Christian and I promise you I will be the best wife you could find in all Córdoba. I will repay you a hundred times for the fact that my father cannot offer you any dowry,' she finished.

The Morisco did not know what to say. He waved his hand and fidgeted uneasily. Yet . . . the girl's innocence aroused his tenderness. Her sad brown eyes radiated such desolation that even Estudiante, standing strangely peacefully beside her, seemed aware of it. The only discordant note came from Miguel's wheezing breath behind him.

'I'm a new Christian,' was the first thing he could think of to say.

'I know you have a pure and kind heart,' she said. 'Miguel told me so.'

'Your father will not allow—' stammered Hernando.

'Miguel thinks he has a solution.'

This time Hernando did wheel round to look at the cripple. He was smiling! His jagged teeth, so different from Rafaela's, were exposed. Hernando looked at both of them in turn. They seemed to be drilling him with their eyes. What solution could Miguel have in mind?

'It's not against the law, is it?' he asked.

'No.'

'Nor against the Church?'

'No.'

How could Don Martín Ulloa possibly allow his daughter to marry a Morisco who was the son of someone condemned by the Inquisition? It was completely inconceivable. He did not even have to apologize to Rafaela, because her father would be the one to prohibit the marriage. That meant he could listen to whatever it was that Miguel was planning without there being any possibility of him being the one who dashed their hopes.

'I'm tired,' he said. 'Let's talk about it tomorrow, Miguel. Good night, Rafaela.'

'Wait, please,' Miguel implored him as he brushed past him.

'What do you want now, Miguel?' he asked in a weary voice.

'You have to come and see for yourself. I'll only keep you from your rest a few moments longer.' Hernando sighed again, but Miguel's insistence made him give way once more. He nodded. 'Follow me,' said the cripple, 'we have to go up to the first floor.'

Saying this, he turned on his crutches and made to leave the stables.

'What about Rafaela?' protested Hernando. 'She is an unmarried young woman. She cannot come to my house.' Miguel paid no attention, as if he took it for granted she would wait for them where she was. 'Go back home,' Hernando urged her.

'She can't do that now,' he heard Miguel say as he hopped towards the door. 'It's too dangerous.'

'What do you mean?'

'She can wait for us here, with the horses.' His words floated into the air as he rushed out across the courtyard.

Hernando turned back towards Rafaela, who smiled at him. He set off after Miguel. Why could she not go home? What danger was she in? Miguel was already climbing the stairs, clinging on to the handrail. Hernando caught up with him near the top.

'What's this about, Miguel?'

'Quiet,' his friend warned him. 'They mustn't hear us. You'll soon see.'

They walked along the upper gallery to the corner where Hernando's house gave on to the alleyway at the stable exit. Miguel hobbled along, trying not to make any noise. When they reached the corner, both of them flattened themselves against the wall and peered down.

'I think they'll be here soon,' Miguel whispered as they stood shoulder to shoulder against the wall. 'This is when they usually come.' Hernando could not bring himself to ask what this was all about. 'Congratulations,' Miguel also whispered. 'You are taking the best woman in all Córdoba. And more than Córdoba – in all Spain!'

Hernando shook his head. 'Miguel—'

'There they are!' the young man cut in. 'Now be really quiet.'

Hernando leant forward and in the darkness saw two figures halt outside the gate that Rafaela always escaped through. Now he understood why she had to stay in the stables. After a few moments, a man carrying a lantern opened the gate from the magistrate's side. The light shone on the faces of two women as they went up to Don Martín Ulloa, whom Hernando immediately recognized. The women handed something over to him, then they vanished back up the alley. Don Martín closed the gate, and the glow from his lantern gradually died away.

Hernando spread his hands in bewilderment. 'Well? Is that what it was so important for me to see?'

'Two weeks ago,' Miguel began to explain as soon as he judged that the magistrate must be back inside his house, 'while you were away in Granada, Rafaela and I almost bumped into those two women and her father one night. Every night since then I have had to check they have left before Rafaela can get back home.'

'But what does it mean, Miguel?' Hernando stepped away from the wall and confronted his friend.

'Those women are beggars, like many others who turn up at the house. I recognized one of them once; Angustias, they call her. I went out into the streets and mixed with . . . with my people. I wasn't given a single penny, not even a fake one.' He smiled in the darkness. 'I must have lost my touch.'

'Oh, get on with it,' Hernando protested, 'it's late.'

'All right. So I asked a few questions here and there. Those two you saw tonight are called María and Lorenza. Lorenza was the shorter one . . .'

'Miguel!'

'They hire children to beg for them,' Miguel exclaimed.

'From the magistrate?' Hernando asked after a shocked pause.

'Yes. It's a good deal. The magistrate is a member of the guild that looks after foundlings. He's the one who decides which family they should go to. The orphans are handed over to women of Córdoba who are paid a few ducats a year to wet-nurse them if they are still suckling, or to bring them up if they are a little older. Those women in turn hire them out to the women you saw so that they can go begging in the streets with them. A lot of them die . . .' Miguel's voice failed him.

'What does the magistrate have to do with all this?'

'Everything,' said the young man, encouraged by Hernando's interest. 'The statutes of the guild stipulate that an inspector should periodically check that the foundlings are living with the family who are being paid for their services; and if they are alive and well. Don Martín and that visitor are in league with each other. The magistrate chooses the women, and the inspector turns a blind eye. Every week the beggar women come to pay Don Martín his share; they do the same with the inspector. Rafaela has told me her father needs lots of money to pay for all his luxuries and to appear to be as rich as the other councillors. I could tell you the names of the last dozen children handed over in this way, the names of those they were given to, and the names of the beggar women who drag them around the streets with them.'

Hernando's eyes narrowed. 'Did you say a lot of them die?' he asked, shaking his head sorrowfully.

'It's nothing more than a business deal, my lord. I know how it works. Some children are good at making people weep and stirring their compassion; others aren't. These last don't survive. It's no good using plump, well-fed children to beg for money either; that's one of the basic rules of the trade. They are all kept starving. And, of course, many of them die of hunger, or from the slightest of fevers, gnawed at by rats, and of course none of this figures in the guild's registers.'

Hernando raised his eyes to the dark, heavy sky. 'And you want me to blackmail Don Martín with this so that he allows me to marry Rafaela?' he asked finally.

'That's right.'

61

D ON MARTÍN ULLOA, needle-maker and magistrate of Córdoba (the post inherited from his father), refused to receive him. A fat old Morisco slave, pretentiously decked out in a uniform that had seen better days, gave him the message: the first time disdainfully, the second peremptorily, the third time angrily.

'Tell your master', Hernando retorted after this last refusal, raising his voice because he was well aware somebody was listening behind the door, 'that it was Angustias and other friends and companions of hers who sent me. Did you hear that? Angustias!' he repeated loudly and clearly. 'Tell him also that I shall be expecting him at my house on a business matter of interest to him. I will not give him another opportunity before I pay a call on the governor or the bishop. In case he is not aware of it, I live in the house next door,' he added ironically.

Later that day, alone in his library, Hernando could not stop pondering on the whole affair. Did he want to marry Rafaela?

'You're on your own! You need a woman beside you to look after you. Someone who loves you and can give you the warmth of a family,' Miguel had shouted at him the morning after they had met Rafaela in the stables, when Hernando had told him he was sorry but that he had to find some other solution because he was not willing to marry the girl. What they had to do, he said, was to expose the question of the foundlings to the judicial authorities.

'Don't you see what's happening?' Miguel had protested. 'For years, you've been shut up with your books and writings. What about children? Wouldn't you like to have children to pass your properties on to? Would you like to have a new family? How old are you? Forty? Forty-one? You're growing old. Do you want to spend your old age alone?'

'I have you.'

'No.' There was an embarrassed silence between the two men. 'I have thought about it a lot. If you don't marry Rafaela, if you don't rescue her from the convent, I'll go back to begging myself.'

'It's not fair for you to threaten me like that,' said Hernando, frowning.

'Yes, it is,' Miguel insisted, his mouth tightening in a line as he shook his head, aware of how serious the matter was. 'I told you that my one aim was to set that girl free. God knows that if it were possible, if there were the slightest chance of it, I would not bring you into this. I can respect the fact that you do not want to marry. But I couldn't go on living here if you refused me the help I'm asking you for.'

'But you're asking me to get married!'

'So? Those people you call your brothers in faith want nothing to do with you. Are you going to go out and look for another Christian woman to marry? What is so bad about marrying Rafaela? You will have a good woman to serve you, look after you, and give you children. You're rich. You have a house, rents from your tenant farmers, lands and horses. Why not get married?'

'I'm a Muslim, Miguel!'

'So what? Córdoba is full of marriages between Morisco men and Christian women. Bring up your children in the two religions you claim you want to unite. What else has all your work been for? For those who reject and insult you? What do you want now? What future do you have? Marry Rafaela and be happy.'

Be happy. Those two words had pursued him all the next day before he decided to present himself at the magistrate's door. Had he ever sought happiness? Fátima and the children had once given it him. How long ago that was! It was fourteen years since they had all been killed. And since then? He was all alone. Suddenly he recalled how desolate he had felt during his last trip to Granada, when Estudiante had been nibbling at the grass by the river Darro and he had looked up at Isabel's garden. Miguel was right. Who had all his work and efforts been for? *Be happy!* Why not? Rafaela had seemed like a good woman. Miguel adored her. And what if Miguel left him? If his only friend were to leave as well . . .

What did he stand to lose if he married? He imagined the house full of children scampering about, their chatter and laughter providing a joyful backdrop to his work in the library. He saw himself leaning over the gallery handrail watching them play in the courtyard, just as he had once done with Francisco and Inés. Fourteen years! He was surprised to find he did not feel guilty about considering the possibility: Rafaela was so different from Fátima . . . Nobody was saying it had anything to do with love; very few marriages were for love anyway. There was no passion in it either; simply the chance to escape the melancholy solitude he had to admit he often felt engulfed by. Thinking of the possibility of having more children suddenly brought him a sense of peace.

'What are you after, you filthy Moor?'

Don Martín Ulloa did not wait until the next day. He came to see Hernando that same evening. Hernando received him in the gallery in the courtyard. The magistrate refused his offer of a seat, and spat out his question leaning menacingly over him. Hernando caught sight of the sword he had at his belt. Behind the stable door, Miguel was listening in.

'Do sit down,' Hernando offered again.

'In a Moor's seat? I do not sit down with Moors.'

'In that case, step away from this Moor whom you find so

offensive.' The magistrate stepped back a couple of paces. Hernando remained seated. 'I would like the hand of your daughter Rafaela in marriage.'

Don Martín was a corpulent man, getting on in years but still with a haughty demeanour. The white of the little hair still on his head and of his thick beard suddenly contrasted even more vividly with the scarlet flush that spread over his face. He launched an incomprehensible insult, guffawed twice, and then returned to further insults.

Alarmed, Miguel stuck his head round the stable door.

'My daughter's hand! How dare you even mention her name? Your dirty lips stain her honour—'

'It is your honour that would be destroyed for ever', Hernando butted in threateningly, 'if the city council heard of your dealings with the foundlings. Yours, that of your wife, and that of your children. Your grandchildren too . . .' Don Martín reached for his sword. 'Do you take me for a fool, magistrate? On this very spot, those Moors you detest so much created a splendid culture, and that was no coincidence.' Hernando spoke calmly, despite the half-drawn sword. 'At this very moment there is a sealed document in the hands of a public notary,' he continued, lying, 'which contains all the details of your dealings with the foundlings. It includes the names of the children and all those involved. If anything happens to me, that document will immediately be passed to the judicial authorities.' Hernando saw the other man hesitate, although part of the sword blade was still glinting outside the scabbard. 'If you kill me, your future is not worth a thing. Do you remember a little girl by the name of Elvira?' he went on, to show how accurate and serious his information was. The magistrate shook his head briefly. 'You gave her as a newborn baby to a wet-nurse called Juana Chueca. You remember her, don't you? Then Elvira was passed on to go begging on the streets with Angustias. She died about six months ago – but none of this is to be found in the registers of your guild.'

'That's a problem the inspector must face,' Don Martín argued.

'Do you think the inspector would be willing to take all the blame? Or that the nurses and beggar women will say nothing about your participation, or about the money they take to your house at night?' He could see doubt begin to cloud the magistrate's face. 'You have a daughter whom you intend to get rid of by sending her to a convent, without any dowry. Is it worth risking your and your family's honour for her sake?'

'How do you know my daughter?' the magistrate asked suspiciously. 'When have you seen her?'

'I don't know her, but I have heard her story. We are neighbours, Don Martín. Think of the offer I am making: my silence in exchange for that daughter of yours who is such a burden to you . . . and your word of honour that you will cease in your trafficking of those children. I swear I will keep a close eye on that! I may be a new Christian, but I have close links with the archbishop in Granada. Look at this.' Don Martín sheathed his sword, and Hernando handed him the commendation the archbishop had signed for him. The magistrate, however, could not read, and so handed it back once he had seen the cathedral council's seal. 'You need not feel ashamed in front of your peers. You know I was under the protection of the Duke of Monterreal—'

'And that you were thrown out of his palace,' Don Martín muttered disdainfully.

'The duke would never have done that,' Hernando replied. 'He owed his life to me. Think it over, Don Martín, but I expect your answer by tomorrow night at the latest. If I do not hear from you . . .'

'Are you threatening me?' Don Martín took another step back. Real concern had crept into his eyes.

'Have you only just realized that? I've been doing so ever since you arrived,' said Hernando with a sarcastic smile.

'What if my daughter doesn't agree?' the magistrate muttered between clenched teeth.

'For your sake and that of your children, make sure that she does.'

With these words, Hernando put an end to their conversation. He accompanied the magistrate back to the entrance, making sure he did not turn his back on him. Don Martín seemed lost in thought, and when he stumbled in the doorway, Hernando was convinced he had won. He walked back into the courtyard and found Miguel standing outside the stable door. Tears were streaming down his cheeks, but as he had both hands on his crutches, he could not wipe them away or stop them falling. Hernando realized with a shock that this was the first time he had ever seen him cry.

The wedding took place at the end of April in that same year. Through Miguel, Hernando learnt that Rafaela had played a very clever trick on her father. She had refused to accept his suggestion that she be married to a Morisco. 'I'd rather go into a convent!' she had shouted at him. Fearful of compromising his honour and his social position because of the foundlings, Don Martín was even more incensed by his daughter's refusal, and so shrieked at her until he got his way.

The marriage took place without any celebration, without the bride's insulted brothers and sisters, and also without any dowry. After the ceremony was over and they were walking back from the church, Hernando began to realize what a huge step he had taken. Rafaela went into what was to be her new home with bowed head, scarcely daring to say a word. They both fell into a tense silence. Hernando studied her; the poor girl was trembling. What was he going to do with this frightened little thing, who was almost twenty-five years younger than him? He was surprised to find that he felt nervous too. How long was it since he had been with a woman other than the ones in the bawdy house? He sighed, and accompanied her to a bedroom alongside his own. Blushing, Rafaela went in, murmuring something so softly he did not understand what she had said. He looked down at his wife's hands: she had been rubbing them so hard the skin was raw and torn.

Hernando sought refuge in his library.

The day after the wedding, Miguel came to talk to him. Red-faced, he stammered as he announced his intention of leaving the Córdoba house and going to stay at the stud farm. His excuse was that he wanted to keep an eye on Toribio and the twenty pregnant mares they had, as well as the newly born foals. Both of them knew the real reason for his decision, though: he was getting out of the way, and leaving Hernando and Rafaela room to get to know each other. His master had kept his promise and married her, and now Miguel did not want his presence in the house to put any kind of obstacle between the new couple.

There was no getting him to change his mind, and so Hernando and his wife saw him off. When the two of them went back inside the house, Hernando suddenly felt himself strangely alone. He ate with Rafaela in a silence interrupted only by the occasional polite phrase, and then retired to the library. From there he could hear Rafaela cleaning the rooms and working around the house. He sometimes even thought he heard her humming a tune, which she herself then interrupted as if she did not want to make any noise.

The weeks went by. Hernando grew accustomed to having Rafaela around, while she felt increasingly comfortable in her new home. She went with María to the market, cooked for him, and did not seem at all bothered by the time he spent shut up in his library; she did not even ask what he did there. Summer had brought a bloom to her pallid cheeks, and her timid, quickly stifled murmurs had given way to songs that could be heard all over the house.

'Why does this horse have a different bit from the one you use with the other colt?' Hernando was surprised to hear her ask in the stables one morning as he was setting out for his daily ride.

Rafaela had never before appeared in the stables when he was preparing to go out. Now she pointed towards the tackle hanging on the wall. Although Hernando usually said very little to her, on this occasion, almost without realizing it and without pausing as he got his mount ready, he found himself giving his wife a lesson.

'It all depends on what kind of mouth they have,' he told her. 'Some of them are black, others white, and still others pink. The best are the ones with black mouths – that's the most natural, as with this one.' Hernando tightened the girths. 'With them you only need to use an ordinary, soft bit that's not too wide . . .' He came to a halt for a moment behind Rafaela, but went on speaking: 'The others need bits that are much thicker and longer . . .' He turned towards his wife. 'And the curb needs to be thicker and rounder too,' he concluded, now looking her full in the face.

Rafaela gave him one of her sweetest smiles.

'Why are you interested in all this anyway?' he asked.

They stood facing each other for a few moments. In the end, it was Hernando who took a step towards her. He grasped her by the shoulders and kissed her gently on the lips. He felt her whole body quiver.

That evening, Hernando watched her while they ate. She was in a lively mood and told him a funny story about something she had seen on the way to market. When she opened her thin lips in a smile, her white teeth appeared; her voice was soft and innocent. For the first time, Hernando found himself laughing with her.

After their meal, they both went out into the courtyard. The night sky was filled with stars, and the roses gave off a sweet perfume. They stared up at the bright moonlit night. She asked him in a whisper: 'Don't you want to have children with me?'

Taken aback, Hernando looked her up and down. 'Is that what you want?' he asked.

Rafaela's courage seemed to have deserted her with her first question.

'Yes,' she murmured, her eyes on the ground.

They climbed silently up to his bedroom. Her immense

shyness seemed contagious, and Hernando approached her gently, anxious not to harm her. He forgot the kind of pleasure he had enjoyed with Fátima and Isabel and made love in the way that Christians did. Rafaela lay on the bed, her body covered in her long tunic so that she would not be committing a sin.

A year and a half later, their union was blessed with the first of their children: a boy, whom they called Juan.

62

IN THE YEAR 1600, Don Pedro de Granada Venegas summoned Hernando to his city. The moment to send the gospel of Barnabas to the Great Turk was fast approaching. The lead plaques containing what Hernando had written, which Don Pedro, Luna and Castillo had been concealing in the caves of Monte Valparaíso for the Christians to find, had achieved their first objective.

That year Archbishop Don Pedro de Castro, ignoring the voices denouncing the discoveries as fakes and calls from Rome to be cautious over them, declared that the bones and ashes found with the plaques on what was now popularly known as the Sacromonte were authentic relics. At last Granada had the relics of its patron saint, Saint Caecilius, as well as of other martyrs who had accompanied Saint James the Apostle. At last Granada could throw off the stigma of being the city of the Moors, and become the equal of all the other important sites of Christianity in Spain! Granada was just as Christian (and perhaps even more) as Santiago, Toledo, Tarragona or Seville. Many saintly men had suffered martyrdom on its sacred mountain.

Although Archbishop de Castro had the authority and legitimacy to declare the relics authentic, he was not in a position to do the same with the lead plaques, or to affirm the truth of what was written on the tablets and medallions. Only Rome could decide such matters, and so the Vatican had asked they be sent there. The Granada prelate had refused to do so, with the excuse that first the arduous task of translating them had to be completed, by the very same Luna and Castillo.

This was the situation Hernando found in Granada. The relics had been declared authentic, while the lead plaques that said the relics were those of this or that saint were still being studied. But these formal questions of authority did not seem to affect the fervent Christians of Granada or the new King Philip III, who had come to the throne two years earlier after his father's slow, painful death. King Philip III was delighted with this reborn Granada.

Hernando went to visit the Sacromonte in the company of Don Pedro de Granada; both Castillo and Luna excused themselves. Followed by two servants, the men took the road along the river Darro, turned at the Guadix gate and climbed up towards the sanctuary along a path that led from a gap in the old walls surrounding the Albaicín. Hernando did not know this way up. He had not been to Granada for three years, since the moment when he had taken his eagerly awaited transcription of the gospel of Barnabas for Luna and Castillo to study in detail. The discovery of the lead plates had also meant that the cathedral council was no longer so interested in the Alpujarra martyrs, and had therefore not asked him to draw up reports on the matter.

Since the appearance of the first plaque there had been a constant stream of miracles and visions. A great number of people in Granada, including one entire convent of nuns, testified to the archbishop that they had seen strange lights in the sky over the sacred hill, and even witnessed ethereal processions lit by holy fires making their way to the caves. 'Can you imagine it? An entire convent of nuns!' When he saw Hernando shaking his head, Don Pedro went on: 'You don't believe me? Listen: a young crippled girl prayed inside the caves and came out cured. The daughter of a chancery official who had been laid up in bed for four years was carried on a litter to the caves, and returned walking by herself. Dozens of people have testified as much in the inquiry verifying the authenticity of the relics. Even the Bishop of the Yucatán came from the Indies to pray to the martyrs to cure his *herpes militaris*! He said mass, then he mixed earth from the caves with holy water, spread it on his herpes, and was cured on the spot! A bishop! He testified to this miracle as well. And there are many more cures and miracles that the ordinary people say they have witnessed on the Sacromonte.'

'Don Pedro—' Hernando began sarcastically.

'Just look . . .' the nobleman interrupted him. By now they were drawing near to the part of the hill where the caves stood. Hernando followed his gesture as he waved at the scene confronting them. 'This is the result of your work.'

A forest of more than a thousand crosses rose all round the entrance to the mine where the caves were to be found. This was where the crowds of pilgrims gathered in front of tiny shrines or the huts where the priests lived. The two men reined in their horses; Hernando's high-spirited mount tossed its head impatiently. The Morisco's eyes roamed over the hill, coming to a halt at the sight of all the crosses with the pilgrims kneeling beneath them. Although some were simple wooden constructions, others were made from carved stone and rose high in the sky from solid pedestals. 'The result of my work,' Hernando whispered to himself. When he had come to Granada to hand over the first plaques, he had doubted whether he would succeed, but the credulity of the Christians was far greater than any errors he might have made.

'It's astonishing,' he said admiringly, twisting his head upwards to try to see the top of a lofty cross standing right next to him.

'Most of the churches in the city have put up crosses,' Don Pedro explained, following the direction of Hernando's gaze. 'So have all the convents, the city and parish councils, the guilds and religious brotherhoods – the candle-makers, blacksmiths, weavers, carpenters. The chancery and the legal clerks have theirs too. Everyone. They come up here in procession with their crosses, escorted by guards of honour to the sound of fifes and drums, chanting the Te Deum. And there are constant pilgrimages.'

Hernando shook his head. 'I can't believe it.'

'Yet I know Castillo is having real problems translating the plaques.'

Hernando was confused: what possible problems could the translator have?

'The archbishop personally supervises his work,' Don Pedro explained. 'Whenever there's an ambiguity which seems to favour the Muslim doctrine, he changes it to something he prefers. That man is determined to make Granada a holier city than Rome. But in the end, on the day the Great Turk reveals the gospel to the world, the truth will come out and all these people' – he gestured in front of him – 'will be forced to recognize the error of their ways.'

The Sultan? Hernando asked himself doubtfully. 'I don't think we should send the gospel to the Great Turk,' he objected. Don Pedro looked at him in surprise. 'No, I really don't think so,' he insisted. 'The Turks have done nothing for us—'

'The gospel isn't just about us,' said Don Pedro. 'It involves the entire Muslim community.'

Hernando went on speaking, as if he had not heard what the nobleman had said: 'For years now, the Turks have failed to equip any fleet to attack the Christians in the Mediterranean. They are only concerned with their problems to the East. There is even talk that things are so quiet that the new King of Spain might be able to attack Algiers, and that preparations for the expedition are already under way.'

'But you were the one who suggested we send the gospel to the Turk!'

'Yes,' admitted Hernando. 'But now I think we need to be more cautious. Didn't you just tell me that the lead plaques haven't been translated yet?' Don Pedro nodded. 'In the references to the Mute Book it simply said that the revelation would come from an Arab king. At first I did think that could be the Great Turk, but he is increasingly distant from us. And there are other Arab kings who are just as important as the Ottoman Sultan, if not more so: in Persia Abbas I is on the throne; in India there is Akbar, known as the Great One. There are Jesuits at work in those lands, and I have heard that, despite being a convinced Muslim, Akbar is tolerant of the other religions practised there. Perhaps he is better suited to making the doctrine of the gospel of Barnabas known to the world.'

Don Pedro weighed up what he had heard. 'We could wait until the translation of the plaques is finished,' he admitted. 'Once that is done we can decide whom to send the gospel to.'

Hernando was about to agree when one of the servants told his lord that they could advance into the caves. The crowd drew back to let the lord of Campotéjar and chief magistrate of the Generalife through. A priest led them through the intricate tunnels, lighting the way with a taper along long, dark, low passageways that came out in the different caves. They pretended to pray with great religious fervour at the altars that had been erected where the remains of the martyrs had been found, now contained in stone urns. The priest was a young man endowed with a heightened sense of mysticism. As they walked, he explained to the respected nobleman's companion what was written on the plaques. Don Pedro watched out of the corner of his eye to see how Hernando was reacting: he should know what was written there – he had created them!

'The books and treatises that were found are far more complex than the plaques that spoke of the martyrdom of the saints, which are still being translated,' the young priest said almost apologetically as they reached a small, round cave. 'By the way,' he said, as another man got to his feet after praying at the altar, 'let me present you to someone from Córdoba, who, like you, is paying us a visit. The physician Don Martín Fernández de Molina.'

'Hernando Ruiz,' said the Morisco, taking the hand the doctor was holding out to him.

After respectfully greeting the nobleman, Don Martín joined

their party and accompanied them on their visit to the caves and on the way back to Granada. Hernando rode quietly in front of the other two, absorbed in his own thoughts. He was dumbfounded by all that had arisen out of seven years' hard work aimed at getting the Christians to change their view of the Morisco community. Would they achieve their goal? For the time being, it was the Christians who seemed to have taken over . . .

As they were riding along Carrera del Darro, Hernando looked up at Isabel's garden. Don Pedro had avoided mentioning her. What could have happened to her? Hernando was surprised only to have confused memories about their time together. Silently wishing her luck, he continued on his way, as she had once told him to do. It was only when he saw Don Martín jump to the ground at the Casa de los Tiros that he understood he had missed the conversation between the doctor and Don Pedro.

'He is going to eat with us,' the nobleman explained, as the grooms took care of the horses. 'He is very interested in meeting Miguel de Luna and Alonso del Castillo. I told him that as well as being translators they are medical doctors. Don Martín says there is an outbreak of the plague in Granada.'

While they were eating, Don Martín revealed that he had been sent on a mission by the Córdoba city council to investigate reports of the plague having struck Granada. All the big Spanish cities refused to admit officially there was a problem until their streets were piled with bodies. To declare there was an outbreak meant that the city was immediately isolated and all trade with it was halted. That was why as soon as there was any suspicion of the plague striking, other city councils sent a doctor they could trust to see for themselves if there was any truth to the rumours.

'The president of the chancery has authorized me to investigate,' Don Martín explained over their meal. 'He assures me it is nothing serious, and that the population is healthy.'

Both Luna and Castillo expressed their surprise.

'The Granada council is organizing fiestas and dances to entertain the people,' said Castillo, 'but they have been taking precautions against the plague for some time now.'

'I know, but they are palliative rather than preventive measures,' insisted Doctor Martín Fernández. 'I've seen the covered chairs they are taking the plague victims out of the city on, and squads of soldiers patrolling the neighbourhoods. I've visited the hospital where the sick are kept, and the doctors working there talk of nothing but the plague.'

'It won't be long before they're obliged to recognize officially there is an epidemic,' agreed Miguel de Luna.

Hernando could scarcely believe his ears. 'Wouldn't it be better to take action at once?' he asked. 'What do they gain by denying reality? It's the people who will suffer, and the plague makes no distinction between lords and vassals. What do you mean by "palliative measures"? Is there any way to avoid the disease?'

'I call them palliative', explained the physician, 'because they are only taken with those who already have the plague. Traditionally it has always been believed the disease is spread through the air, although theories that it can also be spread by clothing and personal contact are gaining ground. The most important thing is to purify the air by burning aromatic herbs in all corners of the city, but the streets should be kept clean too, and people should be encouraged to stay at home rather than organizing dances and bringing crowds together. And if a case is confirmed, the house should be boarded up and all those showing symptoms should be kept apart from everyone else, including their families. Unless measures like these are taken, the contagion will spread until there is a real epidemic.'

'But—' Hernando started to protest.

'And most important of all,' Don Martín interrupted him, as Luna and Castillo nodded their agreement, knowing what he was about to say, 'the city must be sealed off so that the epidemic does not spread any further.'

* * *

The epidemic in Granada was confirmed shortly afterwards. The plague reached Córdoba the next year, in the spring of 1601. Despite the conclusive evidence that Doctor Martín Fernández presented about the negligent attitude of the authorities in Granada, the council in the city of the caliphs behaved in exactly the same manner. At the same time as auctions and the sale of second-hand clothes were suspended, and the beds of the victims taken outside the walls and burnt, the eight city doctors signed a declaration declaring Córdoba to be free of the plague or any other serious contagious disease.

Hernando had two wonderful young children: Juan, aged four, and Rosa, who was two. He adored them, and they had gradually transformed his life. 'Be happy,' he told himself each night as he watched them sleeping. The mere idea of losing his family again terrified him, so on his return from Granada he laid in sufficient provisions so that they could survive shut up in their house for however many months were necessary. As soon as he heard that the plague had struck in nearby Écija, he sent for Miguel, who was living at the stud farm with the horses. At first he said he had too much work to do and refused to come to the city, but when Hernando went out to talk to him he had to yield, and in spite of his protests he too was brought back to the house.

'There's so much to do here,' the cripple insisted, pointing to the mares and colts.

Hernando shook his head. Miguel had done a good job: Volador had died several years ago, but the young man had used his habitual astuteness to find other excellent stallions to improve the breed. By royal decree, horse breeding was controlled by the bailiffs of the area where the stud farms were located. No horses from Andalusia could be taken north of the river Tagus for sale in Castile, and the mares were to be covered by properly registered stallions. Miguel had succeeded in making sure that the animals born in Hernando's stables were highly prized.

Hernando realized what his friend was afraid of, and was less open in his affection towards Rafaela during the time he was living with them. Over the past few years, the two spouses had led a quiet, peaceful existence, getting to know each other little by little. Hernando had found her to be a gentle, discreet companion; Rafaela considered him a caring, considerate man who never put pressure on her. He was much better educated than her father and brothers and sisters. The birth of their two children had made her completely happy. Rafaela, who had filled out after having babies, turned out to be exactly what Miguel had predicted: a good wife and an excellent mother.

They all spent several months shut up in their house in Córdoba, where a fire of aromatic herbs was kept permanently lit in the courtyard. They went out only to attend mass on Sundays. It was then that Hernando, cursing under his breath the fact that the Church insisted on bringing people together for mass or on rogation days, could see to his horror the effects the plague was having on the city: all the shops were shut, and there was no commercial activity of any kind; bonfires of herbs were being burnt beneath the street corner shrines and outside churches and convents; houses were marked and boarded up; entire streets where the most cases had occurred were sealed off; whole families were expelled from the city while a sick relative was carted off to the San Lázaro hospital and all their clothes burnt; previously decent women whose sense of honour forbade them to beg in the streets publicly offered their bodies in order to make some money to feed husbands and children.

'It's absurd!' Hernando whispered to Miguel one Sunday when they came across one of these women. 'They can become prostitutes, but not beggars. How can their menfolk accept the money?'

'It's a question of honour,' replied Miguel. 'In times like these the religious brotherhoods that help the "proud poor" no longer function.'

'In the true religion,' said Hernando, lowering his voice still further, 'there's nothing wrong with receiving alms. The

Muslim community believes in solidarity. Say your prayers and give alms, the Koran tells us.'

It was not only the Church that defied the plague by calling together its congregations. Oblivious to all advice, at the height of the epidemic the city council itself organized bull runs in the Plaza de la Corredera in order to raise the people's spirits. Neither Hernando nor Miguel was able to see how two sons of Volador that they had raised and then sold danced away from the bulls' horns, defiant and agile, to the applause of a public which, even if they managed to forget their sorrows for a few moments, seemed unable to understand that by crowding together so close to each other they would only make them worse.

During these months of seclusion, Hernando devoted himself to his two children. He avoided even looking at Rafaela, who for her part behaved prudently and with great modesty. In the long, tedious evenings, it was Miguel who entertained them with his stories, making little Juan smile at his antics.

'Why don't you teach me about accounts?' Miguel asked Hernando, who practically lived shut up in his library.

The years Hernando had spent writing the lead plaques had awakened in him an insatiable desire for learning. He tried to satisfy this urge by reading about all kinds of topics, but always with one aim in mind: to find something that could help bring about the peaceful coexistence of the two cultures in Spain. His friends in Granada were happy to provide him with as many books as they could find that might interest him. He understood the reason for Miguel's request, and with all the addition, subtraction and sums they did together, Miguel also became almost a recluse in the library. In this way they overcame the inconvenience of being immured in the house, while outside the epidemic decimated the population of Córdoba.

The magistrate Don Martín Ulloa was one of the victims. In each parish the magistrates were obliged to check the houses to see if there were any plague victims inside, and if there were, to send them to the San Lázaro hospital and drive their families out of the city. Don Martín came many times to Hernando and Rafaela's house, demanding that the doctor who came with him carried out unnecessary tests that were far more stringent than those he performed on the other parishioners. He was no longer afraid of the Morisco; the affair of the foundlings had happened so long ago that nobody was concerned about it any more. Don Martín did not bother to hide his desire to find symptoms of the disease even in his own daughter.

So Hernando was surprised one morning when he found not the magistrate at the door but his wife Doña Catalina and Rafaela's younger sister.

'Let us in!' Doña Catalina demanded.

Hernando looked her up and down. She was trembling and wringing her hands, her face contorted with anxiety.

'No. I am obliged to let your husband in, but not you.'

'I order you to!'

'I will tell your daughter,' Hernando said, backing away. He realized that only something very serious could have led a woman like her to humiliate herself by coming to knock on his door.

Hernando and Miguel could hear the conversation between Rafaela and her mother from inside the doorway.

'They'll throw us out of Córdoba,' sobbed Doña Catalina, after quickly telling her daughter that her father had caught the lethal disease. 'What are we to do? Where will we go? The plague is devastating the countryside. Please let us take refuge in your house. We will shut ours up so that no one will know. As is his right, your elder brother Gil will become the new magistrate. He will keep our stay here a secret.'

Hernando and Miguel raised their eyes from the ground and gazed at each other in astonishment when they heard the tone of Rafaela's reply.

'You have not been to see us in all this time. You have not even bothered to come and meet your grandchildren, Mother.' The older woman did not reply. Rafaela continued, in a clear, firm voice: 'Now you want to come and live with us. I wonder why you don't want to go to Gil's house. I'm sure you'd feel much more at home there.'

'By all the saints!' Doña Catalina insisted, her words sharp and angry. 'Why are you reproaching me now? I'm begging you. I'm your mother! Have pity on me.'

'Or perhaps you have already asked him?' Rafaela went on, ignoring her mother's pleas. Doña Catalina again said nothing. 'That's it, isn't it, Mother? I should have known you would only come here if you had no other choice. So, my brother is afraid of being infected, is he?'

Doña Catalina stammered an answer.

Rafaela's voice rang out again: 'Do you really think I would put my family in danger?'

'Your family?' her mother snorted indignantly. 'A Moor—'

For perhaps the first time in her life, Rafaela raised her voice to her mother. 'Get out of this house!'

Hernando breathed a sigh of satisfaction. Miguel allowed himself a smile. They watched as Rafaela passed in front of them, walking along silently, head erect. She crossed the courtyard, with her mother's pleas and sobs still resounding in the street.

The Morisco and his family survived the plague. Together with many other Córdoban families, Doña Catalina returned to the city as soon as it was declared free of the epidemic and its thirteen gates were opened once more. She was half starved and still full of anger at Hernando and Rafaela.

As the crowds of people began to re-enter the city and return to their houses, Miguel hastened to return to their stud. He said a quick, halting goodbye to his master and his wife.

More than six thousand people had perished in the epidemic.

63

TOGA WAS A small village north of Segorbe, set deep in a valley on the far side of the Espadán mountain range. Hernando headed there, via Jarafuel, on a magnificent four-year-old chestnut, which was so high-spirited that it trotted more than it walked and had to be constantly reined in. It always held its broad, proud Spanish head high, snorted even at butterflies, and shifted nervously whenever any insects flew by, its ears erect and alert at all times.

Nine years after his last visit to Jarafuel, Hernando found that the Muslim scholar Munir had aged prematurely. Life was very hard in the mountains of Valencia, especially for someone who was trying to keep alive beliefs that were increasingly persecuted. The two men embraced and then openly studied each other. Munir's wife served them a frugal meal, which they ate sitting on unadorned mats. They immediately began to discuss the meeting to be held in Toga, a small, hidden village still several days' ride away, where, as in much of the region, the Muslim population were in the majority. The meeting concerned the most serious attempt at revolt to have been planned since the uprising in the Alpujarra, a revolt that was said to have the backing of King Henry IV of France as well as that of the now deceased Queen Elizabeth of England.

The rebellion had been brewing for three years now, and Don Pedro de Granada Venegas, Castillo and Luna had asked Hernando to accompany Munir to this meeting, which was meant to finalize all the preparations. The three of them thought that the lead plaques were on the point of bearing fruit; the authentication process must finish soon, and they did not want a fresh uprising to reduce all their efforts to naught.

The Jarafuel holy man listened closely to Hernando's arguments.

'That may be true,' he said, 'but it's nigh on ten years since the lead plates first appeared, and you have to admit that so far you have achieved nothing. Without Rome's blessing, they are worthless. That is the reality. On the other hand, the situation of our brothers in faith has grown considerably worse in these kingdoms. The Dominican Friar Bleda is continuing to insist on our annihilation by whatever means possible. He is so extreme that the Inquisitor General himself has forbidden him to speak about us, but he keeps travelling to Rome, where he has the ear of the Pope. Even more worrying is the way that the Archbishop of Valencia, Juan de Ribera, has changed his opinion.'

Munir paused; his lined face was etched with worry.

'Until recently,' he went on, 'Ribera was a fervent supporter of the idea of converting our people, to the extent that he paid the wages of the parish priests assigned to carry out this task from his personal fortune. That was in our favour: the priests who come here are nothing more than a band of ill-educated thieves who are not concerned about us in the least. All they ask is that we go and eat their "cakes" in church every Sunday. The only church in the entire valley of Cofrentes is the one here in Jarafuel, and even that is the former mosque! But after years of trying to convert us without success, and after spending a huge amount of money, Ribera has changed his mind. He has sent a report to the King arguing that all the Moriscos should be enslaved, sent to the galleys or forced to work in the mines in the Indies. He claims that God would favour a decision of this sort, which means that the King's conscience should be clear. Those were his exact words.'

Hernando shook his head in disbelief. Munir nodded gravely.

'I'm not worried about the friar, because there are many like him. But Ribera does frighten me. Not only is he the Archbishop of Valencia, he is also the Patriarch of Antioch and, most important of all, the captain-general of the kingdom of Valencia. He wields great influence in the circles of the King and the Duke of Lerma.'

The scholar fell silent again, this time for a long while, as if he needed to think carefully before going on.

'Hernando, you know I supported your plan with the lead plates, but I also understand our people. They are afraid the day will soon come when the King and his council decide to adopt some of the drastic measures that are being talked about now. If that happens, we only have one choice: war.'

'Ever since the revolt in the Alpujarra I've heard of many attempted uprisings. Some made no sense, and they all failed.' Hernando was not willing to give up so easily. 'More war? More deaths? Haven't we had enough already? Why should it be any different this time?'

'It is completely different,' the scholar replied firmly. 'We have promised . . .' Seeing Hernando raise his eyebrows, Munir repeated: 'Yes, I include myself with them. I support the revolt. It's a holy war,' he said solemnly. 'We have promised that if the French invade this kingdom, we will help them with an army of eighty thousand Muslims and will hand over three cities to them, including Valencia.'

'Do . . . do the French believe you?'

'They will. They are to be given a hundred and twenty thousand ducats as guarantee.'

'A hundred and twenty thousand ducats!' Hernando exclaimed.

'That's right.'

'But that's a fortune! How ...? Who has managed to raise such an amount?' Hernando recalled the serious difficulties the Morisco community had faced in trying to pay the special taxes the Christian kings imposed on them – the same kings who now wanted to exterminate them. After the defeat of the Great Armada, they had been forced to pay – 'gladly', as the documents put it – two hundred thousand ducats to the royal coffers. They were ordered to pay a similar sum when the English sacked Cádiz, and were constantly required to make special extra contributions. How could they find such an enormous amount now?

'They are the ones paying,' laughed the scholar, imagining how bewildered his companion must be.

'Who do you mean by "they"?' asked Hernando.

'The Christians. King Philip himself.' Hernando gestured impatiently for him to explain. 'Despite all the riches pouring in from the Indies, and all the property taxes it imposes, the royal treasury is empty. Philip II suspended payments several times, and his son Philip III will soon have to do the same.'

'What has that got to do with it? If the King has no money, how is he going to pay you a hundred and twenty thousand ducats? Even if he ... It's ridiculous!'

'Be patient,' the scholar begged him. 'Because of his financial situation, King Philip II debased our coinage.' Hernando nodded. Like everyone else in Spain, he had been affected by the change. 'Where once the coins had four or six parts of silver in them, now they are minted with only one.'

'Yes, and people complained because they were obliged to exchange coins with a high proportion of silver in them for others that had much less. So for every coin they lost three or more parts of silver.'

'That's right. Thanks to this ruse, the royal treasury recovered all the old coins and made huge profits. But the officials had not thought of the effect this would have on people's confidence in our currency, especially in the smaller, most common coins. Then, two years ago, King Philip III decreed that the metal for coins should not have any silver in it at all, but be made entirely of copper. Since there was no precious metal in these new coins, they did not even bear the mark of the assayer of the mint where they were struck. And our community has had more than enough practice at making coins!' Munir smiled. 'Binilit is dead now, but in his workshop, the apprentice who used to make Morisco jewellery now spends all his day minting fake coins. Many others are doing the same. Nowadays the coins do not even have to be made of copper. Lead ones are accepted, and so are even the heads of nails that have been stamped with something vaguely resembling a castle and a lion on each side. For every forty fake coins, the Christians are paying us up to ten silver reales! It's been calculated that there are hundreds of thousands of ducats in fake coins in circulation throughout the kingdom of Valencia.'

'Why don't the Christians fake the coins themselves?' Hernando asked, although he already suspected what the answer was.

'Because they're afraid of the penalties against counterfeiters, and because they don't have our secret workshops,' said Munir, with a smile. 'But mostly out of laziness: it demands hard work, and you know not even the poorest Christian craftsmen are fond of that.'

'But why do people, and traders in particular, accept coins they know to be fake?' Hernando asked. He remembered how careful Rafaela always was that the coins she used were authentic, although it was true that in Córdoba it was not as common to find counterfeits as it seemed to be in Valencia.

'Because they couldn't care less,' the scholar explained. 'It's what I told you before. Ever since Philip II stole the three parts of silver from them, they have no faith in the currency. With all the fakes it's as though they are doing the same as the King, and getting their own back. So the fakes are accepted. It's a new system of exchange. The only problem is that prices are rising, but even that doesn't affect us as badly as it does the Christians. We don't buy as much as them, because we have fewer needs.'

'So that is how you raised the hundred and twenty thousand ducats?' Hernando was still amazed this had been possible.

'Most of it,' said the scholar, beaming. 'The rest came from Barbary, from our brothers who have settled there but share our hopes of recovering the lands that belong to us.'

By now they had finished the meal Munir's wife had prepared. Rising to his feet, the holy man invited Hernando to go out into the small garden at the back of the house. The moon and a cloudless starry sky above the Muela de Cortes mountain offered them magnificent views.

'But tell me about you,' said Munir, as he guided Hernando out into the garden. 'Now you know what my intentions are: to fight and win . . . or to die for our God. I know that is not your way of doing things.' The scholar leant on the railing at the far end of the garden, high above the town of Jarafuel, with the valley spread out beneath them and the dark mass of Muela de Cortes on the horizon. 'But what has become of you since we last met?' he asked as Hernando came and stood beside him.

The Morisco looked up at the sky, feeling the chill winter air on his face. Then he began to tell Munir of all that had happened to him since his return to Córdoba after taking the first lead plates to Granada.

'You married a Christian woman?' Munir interjected when he heard about Rafaela. There was no note of reproach in his question.

The two men stood staring out in front of them. Two figures silhouetted in the night, high above the valley, all alone.

'I'm happy, Munir. I have a family again, with two beautiful children,' Hernando replied. 'All my needs are more than satisfied. I ride horses, and train colts. They're highly prized in the market,' he said proudly. 'I dedicate the rest of the day to calligraphy or to studying my books. I think that the serenity I have acquired through this new family permits me to unite with God the moment I dip my quill in ink and guide it over the paper. The letters flow from within me with a perfection I have only rarely achieved before. I am writing what I hope will be a fine copy of the Koran. The Arabic characters look harmonious, and I enjoy colouring in the diacritical marks. I also pray in the mosque, in front of the caliphs' mihrab. Do you know something? When I stand there and whisper my prayers, I feel something akin to what I feel now, staring at the spectacle the night is offering us: just like all these stars, I see the gleam of the gold and marble that went into the construction of that sacred place. And yes, I did marry a Christian woman. My wife ... Rafaela is sweet, good and modest. And a wonderful mother.'

Hernando gazed once more up into the starry sky. The figure of Rafaela appeared in his mind's eye. The skinny, fearful young girl had blossomed into a mature woman. Following the birth of her children, her breasts were fuller, her hips broader. Munir refrained from interrupting his companion's thoughts; he guessed they must be focused on the wife who seemed to have won his heart.

'Besides, there are the children,' said Hernando with a smile. 'They are my life, Munir. I spent fifteen years without hearing the laughter of a child. Without feeling the touch of a tiny hand seeking protection in mine, without seeing in their innocent, truthful eyes all they do not know how or dare to say. Their faces alone are the most beautiful poetry there is.

'We suffered a lot when our third child died before it had even begun to walk. I had already lost two, but this was the first child whose life I saw slipping away through my fingers without being able to do anything about it. I felt a huge void: why was God taking this innocent being? Why was He punishing me so harshly yet again? As I said, this was not the first child I had had taken from me, but Rafaela . . . it almost destroyed her. I had to be strong for her, Munir. Even though part of me also died with the little boy, I had to keep going to help her get over it. Since then, Rafaela has not become pregnant again, but now Allah has blessed us: we are expecting another child!'

Hernando gazed up into the night sky once more. Rafaela and he had watched their son die, each silently praying to their own God. They were at their third child's side until he breathed his last. They cried over him together. They buried him together according to the Christian rites, overwhelmed with despair. They returned to their home together, leaning on each other. When they were finally alone, Rafaela broke down in tears. It had been a long time before he had seen her smile again, or heard her singing around the house. But little by little the other two children and Hernando's support had brought joy back to her face. It pained Hernando to remember those sad months, and yet at the same time he felt proud: they had both survived the misfortune, and their marriage, which had started out on weak foundations, was now much more solid. There were only two things that had not changed since those cold, distant beginnings: Rafaela continued to respect the library, where she knew he wrote in Arabic, and Hernando, although they had decided to sleep together, also respected his wife's beliefs and did not try to persuade her that she was not sinning when they had sexual relations. He was surprised to discover a new kind of pleasure: one that derived from the love she offered him every night. It was a silent, calm love far removed from passion and the pleasures of the flesh, as though both of them knew that nothing and no one could spoil the beauty of their union.

'But tell me, do you educate your children in the true faith? Does your wife know about your beliefs?' Munir wanted to know.

'Yes, she knows,' said Hernando. 'It's a long story. Miguel, the crippled groom who plotted to bring us together, told her about them. She . . . she does not say much, but when we look at each other we can read one another's thoughts. When I pray in front of the mihrab she stands next to me as if she is fully aware of what I am doing. She knows I am praying to the one God. As for the children, the eldest is only seven. Neither of them is old enough to know how to pretend, and it would be dangerous if they gave the game away in public. A tutor comes to the house to give them lessons. For now I am happy just to tell them the stories and legends of our people.'

'Will Rafaela agree to their instruction when the time comes?' the holy man probed.

Hernando sighed. 'I think . . . I am sure we've reached a tacit agreement. She says her prayers with them; I tell them stories about the Prophet. I would like to . . .' Hernando paused. He did not know whether the Muslim scholar would understand his dream: to be able to bring up the children in both cultures, respecting and tolerating each of them. He decided not to go on: 'I'm sure she will.'

'She's a good woman then.'

They went on talking for a long while in the starlight, taking advantage of the brief pauses in their conversation to drink in the splendid night air surrounding them.

Three days before Christmas 1604, sixty-eight representatives from the Morisco communities of the kingdoms of Valencia and Aragón met as planned in a clearing in the middle of a wood above the river Mijares, close to the small, isolated village of Toga. They were joined by ten or more Berbers and a French nobleman by the name of Panissault, sent by the Duke de la Force, one of Henry IV of France's marshals. Night was falling by the time Hernando and Munir, who was representing the Moriscos of the valley of Cofrentes, were allowed through by the guards and arrived at the meeting place. In order not to raise suspicion, Hernando left his horse in Jarafuel and rode a mule, as did Munir. It took them seven days to reach the spot, days spent deep in conversations that served to strengthen their friendship.

The clearing was dimly lit by several bonfires. The nervousness of the men gathered there was almost palpable. Yet there was also a sense of determination in the air: as soon as he greeted some of the other Morisco leaders, Hernando could tell they were all set on going ahead with the rebellion.

What would become of all his efforts with the lead plates? he wondered when he heard the Moriscos' rousing calls for a fight to the death. As Munir had explained to him along the way, they were no longer counting on the Turks. The most they were hoping for was some help from the Berbers on the far side of the strait.

The lead plates would prove their worth! Hernando told himself. The time would soon arrive to send the copy of the gospel of Barnabas to the Arab king who would make it known to the world. That was what Don Pedro, Luna and Castillo had promised – but these people were not willing to wait any longer. Hernando sat on the ground next to Munir, among the Morisco delegates. Standing opposite them were the French noble Panissault, disguised as a merchant, and Miguel Alamín, the Morisco who had been negotiating for two years with the French. Which was the better path for them to choose? Was Hernando right, or were they? He was still mulling this over when Alamín presented the Frenchman to the group. In agreement with Hernando were a nobleman from Granada who had close links with the Christians, two physicians who translated from the Arabic and himself, a simple Morisco from Córdoba. On the other side were the representatives from the majority of the regions of the kingdoms of Valencia and Aragón. They were all in favour of war. War! Hernando recalled his childhood and the uprising in the Alpujarra; the help from across the strait that had never come, and then the humiliating and painful defeat. What would Hamid say about this new call to violence? And Fátima? What would her view have been? With the shouts of the Morisco leaders ringing in his ears, Hernando could not help but feel dejected. All that effort, all that sacrifice, simply to have another war! He could understand why the others defended the need to take up arms. But something told him that, yet again, it would not be the solution. Perhaps I'm too old, thought Hernando. Perhaps the peaceful life I'm leading now has weakened my resolve . . . And yet deep inside him, something told him that violence would lead nowhere.

'The Inquisition is bleeding us dry!' he heard one Morisco leader shout behind him.

It was true. During the ride to Toga, Munir had explained what was happening. Hernando had not seen it in Córdoba, but in these lands where the Moriscos were a majority, the number of sins committed in theory by these new Christians were so many and various that the Inquisition fined them in advance, so that each community was forced to pay them a large sum every year.

'The Christian lords as well!' another man cried.

'They want to kill us all!'

'To castrate us!'

'To enslave us!'

The shouts of protest and defiance multiplied all around him with increasing fervour.

Hernando stared down at the ground. Wasn't all this true? Surely they were right? The Moriscos were unable to live, and the future . . . what future could their children look forward to? Yet faced with this threat he, Hernando Ruiz from Juviles, shut himself up in his library and led an affluent, easy life . . . and naively sought to undermine the foundations of the Christian religion by finding an answer in books!

He shuddered when he heard the details of the agreement reached after lengthy discussions: on the night of the Thursday before Easter 1605, the Moriscos would rise up in Valencia and burn the churches to attract the attention of the Christians. Coinciding with this, Henry IV would send a fleet to the port of El Grao. In the rest of the region, the Morisco chiefs would lead their people in an armed uprising. But what if the King of France failed to keep his promise, as those in the Albaicín had failed to do when the revolt broke out in the Alpujarra? If that happened, the Moriscos would find themselves alone again to face the Christians' wrath at their profanation of the churches.

Just like all those years before. The Moriscos were putting their future in the hands of a Christian king. He might be an enemy of Spain, but he was still a Christian! How many of those who were so keen to fight now had lived through the war in the Alpujarra? Hernando wanted to say something, but the clamour was deafening. Even Munir was on his feet, his arm raised high, shouting excitedly in favour of a holy war.

'*Allahu Akbar!*'

After this the Moriscos proceeded to appoint a new king: Luis Asquer, from the village of Alaquás, was the man chosen. The new monarch was robed in a scarlet cape. He buckled on a sword and took the oath according to Morisco customs. Everyone acclaimed him and crowded round him. Hernando stood up and walked away from them. So the decision had been taken: war was inevitable. Either they would be victorious, or they would be wiped out! He moved further away from the acclamations and noise, remembering how often he had heard similar shouts in the Alpujarra. He himself—

All at once Hernando felt a sharp blow to the back of his neck. He felt as though his head was about to explode. He began to topple. As he did so, he dimly sensed that several men had seized him by the arms and were dragging him away from the clearing and the bonfires. He was pulled into the trees and then dropped to the ground. Although his head was ringing and he could hardly see, he thought he could make out three ... four men standing round him. They did not harm him any further, but began talking in Arabic. Hernando tried to get to his feet, but was too dizzy. He could not hear what they were saying above the applause and ovations for the new king.

'What ... what do you want?' he managed to stammer out in Arabic. 'Who are—?'

One of them threw the freezing contents of a waterskin over his face. The cold water revived him. He tried again to get to his feet, but this time a boot on his chest pinned him to the ground. He could make out the silhouettes of the four men against the background of flames from the fires, but their faces were still in shadow.

'What do you want with me?' he asked, more coherently.

'To kill a renegade dog and traitor,' one of the men said.

The threat echoed through the night. Hernando could feel the edge of a scimitar blade at his throat. He tried to think quickly. Why did they want to kill him? Did one of them know him from Córdoba? He had not recognized anyone from the city in the meeting, but ... The tip of the scimitar pressed against his Adam's apple.

'I'm neither a renegade nor a traitor,' he said loudly. 'Anyone who told you I was that—'

'The person who told us knows you well.'

The scimitar was jabbing into his skin, making it hard for him to speak.

'Ask Munir!' he stuttered. 'The holy man from Jarafuel! He will tell you . . .'

'If we found him and told him all we know about you, I'm sure he himself would kill you, and that's something we must do. Vengeance . . .'

'Vengeance?' gasped Hernando. 'What harm have I done you for you to seek vengeance from me? If it's true I am a renegade and a traitor, let our King judge me.'

One of the men squatted beside him. Hernando could see his face only a few inches from his own, and feel his hot breath. His words dripped hatred.

'Ibn Hamid,' he whispered. Hernando shivered when he heard the name. Were they from the Alpujarra, then? What did it mean? 'That was how you liked to be called, wasn't it?' the voice whispered.

'Yes, that's my name,' he said.

'The name of a traitor to his people!'

'I have never betrayed them. Who are you to voice such lies?'

The man signalled to one of his companions. He ran into the clearing and came back with a lighted torch.

'Take a good look at me, Ibn Hamid. I want you to know

who is going to put an end to your life. Look at me . . . Father.'

The other man lowered the torch. The darkness receded, and Hernando could make out a pair of huge, enraged blue eyes staring at him. His features, his face . . .

'My God,' he murmured with bewilderment. 'It can't be true!' His head began to spin again. At the mere sight of that face, thousands of memories flooded through his mind, one on top of the other. It had been more than twenty years . . . 'Francisco?' he mumbled.

'I've been called Abdul for many years now,' his son replied harshly. 'Shamir is here too – do you remember him?'

Shamir! Hernando tried to pick him out among the other three men, but none of them emerged from the shadows. He was totally confused: so Francisco was alive . . . and Shamir too. Had they escaped from Ubaid? But his mother . . . Aisha had assured him they were dead, that she had seen with her own eyes how the muleteer had killed them in the mountains.

'I was told you were dead!' Hernando cried. 'I looked . . . I looked for you for weeks. I roamed the mountains to try to find your bodies. And those of Inés . . . and Fátima.'

'Coward!' Shamir insulted him.

'My mother waited . . . we all waited years for you to come and help us,' Abdul went on. 'You dog! You didn't lift a finger for your wife, your daughter, for your half-brother. Nor for me!'

Hernando felt as though he could not breathe. What had his son just said? That his mother had waited . . . His mother! Fátima!

'Is Fátima alive?' he asked faintly.

'Yes, *Father*,' hissed Abdul. 'She is alive . . . with no thanks to you. We have all survived. We had to endure Brahim's hate, and to feel it in our own flesh. Our mother most of all! And meanwhile, you forgot your family and betrayed your people. I can assure you that Brahim has already paid with his life, the dog. Now you must pay too!'

Brahim! Hernando closed his eyes, allowing the truth of what he had heard to seep into his mind. So Brahim had fulfilled his threat: he had come back for Fátima and taken his revenge on his stepson by stealing his children, his wife, everyone he loved . . . How had he not suspected as much? He had come for them and taken them away . . . but if that was the case, what about Fátima's white shawl? He had seen it wrapped round the neck of Ubaid's dead body! How was that possible? Ubaid and Brahim together? A thought flashed through his mind. His mother must have known all this! Aisha had told him Ubaid killed them all. Aisha had sworn time and again that she had seen Fátima and the children die . . . Aisha must have deceived him. Why? The idea that his mother had lied to him was appalling, unbearable. In spite of the scimitar at his throat, Francisco, and the man thrusting the torch into his face, Hernando curled up on the ground. He could feel his heart throbbing in his chest as if it were about to explode. God! Fátima was alive! He wanted to cry, but the tears refused to come. He began to shudder uncontrollably, curling up even tighter on the earth, as if he were trying to shake himself to pieces. A whole lifetime believing his family had been murdered by Ubaid!

'Fátima!' he almost shouted.

'You are going to die,' Shamir declared.

'In death, hope is everlasting,' Hernando replied instinctively.

Abdul took a dagger from his waist. Back in the clearing, the Moriscos were watching the crowning of their King in respectful silence. 'I swear to die for the one true God,' Hernando heard in the distance as the man with the torch seized him by the hair to expose his throat. The dagger blade glinted in the darkness.

Fátima! The memory of her flashed into Hernando's mind.

'Who are you to decide to kill me?' he protested. 'I will not die before I've had the chance to speak to your mother! I won't let you kill me before I've begged her forgiveness! I thought you were all dead. Only God knows how much I've suffered from losing you. Fátima must be the one who decides whether to forgive or punish me, not you. If I must die, let her be the one to say so.'

In a fit of sudden rage, he pushed his son away. Caught unawares, Abdul fell to the ground on his backside. Hernando tried to get up, but Shamir's scimitar pressed against his chest. Hernando grasped the weapon, the blade cutting into his palm.

'Are you afraid I'll escape?' he spat. 'That I'll try to fight you?' He spread his arms to show he had no weapon. 'I want to be handed over to Fátima. She has to be the one who sinks the knife into me, if she truly believes I was capable of abandoning her, or all of you, had I known you were still alive.'

For the first time, Hernando could make out his half-brother's features, and could see his likeness to Brahim. Shamir looked enquiringly at Abdul. After a few moments' hesitation, Abdul nodded: it was right that Fátima should have her revenge, in person, as she had done with Brahim.

At that very moment in the clearing the coronation came to an end, and all the Moriscos burst into cheers and applause.

Most of the delegates and leaders took advantage of what remained of the darkness to begin the journey back to their villages. The Frenchman Panissault left with the promise that the 120,000 ducats would be handed over to him in the city of Pau, in French Béarn, where the Duke de la Force was governor. At first, with all the commotion of people saying farewell and leaving, Munir had not even noticed that Hernando was no longer with him. Gradually, however, he began to worry about him. He looked all round the clearing, but saw no sign of him. He went back to where they had left the mules: they were both tied up as before.

Where could Hernando be? He would not have left without saying goodbye to him, or taking the mule: his horse was in Jarafuel. Munir asked several Moriscos, but none of them could help. One of the Berbers collaborating in the planned revolt rushed by him, weighed down and in a hurry. What would a Berber know . . . ?

'Hey there,' Munir called to him nonetheless. 'Do you know Hernando Ruiz, from Córdoba? Have you seen him?'

When he heard the name of the person the holy man was looking for, the man, who at first had seemed to pause when Munir tried to attract his attention, stammered an excuse and continued on his way.

Why had he reacted like that? Munir wondered as he watched him head into the wood. After taking a few steps, the Berber turned to look back at him. When he saw Munir was still staring after him, he speeded up. Munir did not think twice about it, but headed after him. What was the Berber trying to hide? What was happening to Hernando?

He did not have time to ask himself any more questions. As soon as he entered the wood, several men leapt on him and held him prisoner; someone else threatened him with a dagger.

'If you call out, you're a dead man,' Abdul warned him. 'What do you want?'

'I'm looking for Hernando Ruiz,' said Munir, trying to stay calm.

'We don't know anyone called Hernando Ruiz...' Abdul began.

'Well then, who is that you're trying to hide over there?'

Even in the darkness of the wood, he could see Hernando's boots sticking out between the legs of a group of four Berbers who were trying to keep him out of sight. They were all wearing soft slippers best suited to life on a ship. Abdul turned to where Munir was pointing.

'Him?' said Abdul, when he saw it was impossible to deny there was someone else there besides the Berbers. 'He's a renegade, a traitor to our faith.'

Munir could not help laughing. 'A renegade? You don't know what you're saying.' Abdul frowned, a shadow of doubt appearing in his intense blue eyes. 'There are few people alive in Spain who have done more for our faith than him.'

Abdul wavered. Shamir left the group hiding Hernando and came over to them.

'Who are you to make such a claim?' he asked when he reached them.

For the first time, the holy man caught a glimpse of Hernando. His friend looked defeated; his head was down and his expression vacant. He did not show the slightest interest in the conversation going on only a short distance from him.

'My name is Munir,' he said. What had happened to Hernando? 'I'm the holy man of Jarafuel and the valley of Cofrentes.'

'We know this man collaborates with the Christians and has betrayed the Moriscos. He deserves to die.'

Hernando still did not react.

'What would you know?' Munir objected. 'Where do you come from – Algiers, Tetuan?'

'We are from Tetuan,' replied Abdul, grudging respect for the holy man in his voice. 'The others—'

Munir took advantage of this hesitation to free himself from the Berbers holding him. He interrupted Abdul: 'You live on the far side of the strait, where you can practise the true faith freely.' He closed his eyes and slowly shook his head. 'I myself go to mass every Sunday. I confess my Christian sins in order to keep the permit that allows me to move around. I often find myself obliged to eat pork and drink wine. Do you think I'm a renegade too? All the Moriscos you've met tonight have to obey the orders of the Christian Church! How would we survive otherwise and keep our faith? Hernando has worked for the one true God as much, if not more, than any of us. Believe me, you do not know this man.'

'We know him very well. He's my father,' said Abdul.

'And my half-brother,' Shamir added.

Munir tried to convince the two young Berbers of the secret efforts Hernando made on behalf of the Morisco community. He told them about all that Hernando had written, the years of labour, the lead plates and the Turpian tower, the Sacromonte and Don Pedro de Granada Venegas. He mentioned Alonso del

Castillo and Miguel de Luna, the gospel of Barnabas and what they were trying to achieve. He explained that Hernando thought they had all been killed by Ubaid.

'His mother knew nothing about the work he was doing,' he told Abdul when he spoke of how Aisha had replied to the letter Fátima had sent to Córdoba with Ephraim. 'Hernando had to keep it a secret, even from his mother. To her, like everyone else, her son was a renegade, a Christian. Hernando thought you were dead. Believe me! He never knew about that letter.'

He also told them that, despite being married to a Christian woman, he must be the only Morisco who still prayed in the mosque at Córdoba.

'He says he swore to your mother he would always pray in front of the mihrab,' he added, speaking directly to Abdul. He was worried that his mention of Hernando's Christian wife might only increase the corsairs' desire for vengeance.

He fell silent, and for a few moments the sounds of those saying goodbye and preparing for departure could clearly be heard from the clearing. Munir could see Abdul and Shamir looking towards Hernando. Had he managed to convince them?

'He helped Christians in the Alpujarra war,' Abdul suddenly growled. His expression was harsh; his blue eyes icy.

'He was only trying to escape slavery, and used a Christian to do so—' the holy man tried to excuse his friend.

'After that, he collaborated with the Christians in Granada,' Abdul interrupted him. 'He denounced the Moriscos who had rebelled.'

'What about the other Christians whose lives he saved?' Shamir put in. Munir flinched: he did not know about any other Christians. The corsair noted his reaction, and saw an opportunity to free himself from the sense of respect he felt for such a renowned holy man. 'Yes, he saved many more of them. Didn't you know that? Didn't he tell you? He's nothing more than a coward. Coward!' he shouted in Hernando's direction.

'Traitor!' Abdul added.

'If he thought it was Ubaid who had killed us, why didn't he pursue him to hell and back?' Shamir went on, gesticulating in front of the learned man. 'What did he do to gain revenge for what he thought was the death of his family? I'll tell you what he did: he sought refuge in the luxurious palace of a Christian duke.'

'If he had insisted, if he had sought vengeance as every self-respecting Muslim ought to,' Abdul shouted, 'perhaps he would have discovered it was not Ubaid but Brahim who was the cause of all his misfortunes.'

A few paces away, Hernando felt these words as blows. He did not even have the strength to defend himself. To say out loud that he had seen Ubaid's body, that the desire for revenge had left him when he saw him dead. That he had scoured the mountains looking for the bodies of his family so that he could give them a proper burial . . . What was the point of that now? As his mind whirled with all the accusations his child and half-brother made, he could think of only one thing. Why? Why had Aisha lied to him? Why had she let him suffer when she knew the truth? He remembered her tears, her face contorted with grief as she said she had seen how Ubaid had butchered them all. Why, Mother?

His son's words interrupted his thoughts.

'And besides, he is married to a Christian! I want nothing to do with you, you dog!' Abdul went on, spitting at his father's feet.

Unconsciously, Munir followed the gob of spittle. He looked at Hernando, who had not even stirred at his son's insult. Even in the darkness, his body looked broken, crushed by guilt, overwhelmed by everything that was going on around him.

'But the lead plates—' insisted the holy man, filled with pity for his friend.

'The lead plates – what are they worth?' Shamir butted in. 'What have they achieved? Have any of our people benefited from them?' Munir did not want to concede this, and tightened his mouth in a firm line. 'Those tricks are only useful to the rich, those nobles who betrayed us and now want to save their own skins. Not a single one of our brothers, the poor, those who continue to believe in the one God, those who hide to pray in their houses or out in the fields, will gain anything from them! He has to die.'

'Yes,' Abdul agreed, 'he must die.'

The death sentence echoed through the woods, above the fading sounds from the clearing. Munir shivered as he saw how cruel the two corsairs could be. He knew they were accustomed to playing with people's lives as though they were mere animals.

'That's enough!' he shouted, in a last, desperate attempt to save his friend's life. 'This man came to Toga as my responsibility, under my protection.'

'He will die!' Abdul exclaimed.

'Can't you see he is dead already?' replied Munir, pointing sadly towards him.

'There are thousands of Christians like him piled in the dungeons of Tetuan. Save your pity. We're taking him with us. Let's go,' Shamir ordered the Berbers.

Munir drew strength from his despair. He took a deep breath before he spoke again. When he did so, his voice was firm and resolute, with no trace of the fear he felt inside.

'I forbid you to do so!'

He stood unflinching in front of the corsairs. Abdul's hand went to his scimitar, as if he had been insulted, and had never been given such an order in his life. Munir continued, trying to make sure his voice did not tremble.

'I am Munir. I am the holy man of Jarafuel and all the valley of Cofrentes. Thousands of Muslims accept my decisions. According to our traditions, my authority is the second highest in the principles our world is governed by, and in matters of law I am to be obeyed. This man is to stay here.'

'And what if we don't obey?' asked Shamir.

'Unless you kill me too, you will never embark on your vessels. I can guarantee that.'

All the corsairs and Berbers stood staring at the holy man.

Only Hernando still sat on the ground, head in his hands, lost in thought.

'Brahim paid for his crimes,' Shamir said. 'This treacherous dog is not going to escape punishment.'

'You have to respect the authority of those more learned than you,' Munir insisted.

One of the Berbers lowered his head when he heard this, and at that moment Hernando seemed to wake up. What had Shamir said?

Abdul realized two things: his men would respect the laws, and he could not bring himself to kill a holy man either. His blue eyes met those of Hernando, who was gazing at him enquiringly. Brahim was dead . . . The corsair stepped towards his father.

'Yes,' he spat. 'My mother killed him. She has more courage in one of her hands than you have in your whole being. Coward!'

At that moment one of the Berbers guarding Hernando shook him roughly, while another hit him in the kidneys with the butt of his harquebus. Hernando fell to the ground again and they began to kick him. He did nothing to defend himself.

'Enough, for God's sake!' Munir implored.

'By that same God your holy man is invoking, by Allah,' growled Abdul as he gestured to the men to stop beating Hernando, 'I swear I will kill you if you ever cross my path again. Never forget that oath, you dog!'

Brahim! Fátima could see him in the shouts and threats that Shamir made. But he was much more powerful than that simple muleteer from the Alpujarra, much more cunning. Fátima shuddered when she recognized the same voice, the same gestures, the same angry face in his son.

As soon as they returned from Toga, Abdul and Shamir went to the palace to see her. Both looked grim and serious, but refused to tell her what had gone so badly. Fátima knew why they had travelled to Toga: she herself had helped raise a large sum of money from the Berbers for the new uprising. She listened to their news with interest, but there was something in her son's expression that disturbed her.

'Abdul,' she said at last, laying her hand on her son's muscular arm. 'What's the matter?'

He shook his head and muttered something incomprehensible.

'You can't fool me. I'm your mother, and I know you too well.'

Abdul and Shamir caught each other's eye. Fátima waited expectantly.

'We've seen the Nazarene,' Shamir confessed finally. 'That treacherous dog was in Toga.'

Fátima's jaw dropped. For an instant she could not breathe. 'Ibn Hamid?' As she said his name, she could feel her heart shrink, and lifted a bejewelled hand to her breast.

'Don't call him that!' Abdul protested. 'He doesn't deserve it. He's a Christian and a traitor! He dragged himself away like the cur he is.'

She looked up in consternation. 'What . . . what have you done to him?' She tried to stand up from the divan, but did not have the strength.

'We should have killed him!' Shamir cried. 'And I swear we will do so if our paths ever cross again!'

'No!' Fátima's voice was a hoarse cry of fear. 'I forbid it!'

Abdul stared at his mother in surprise. Shamir took a step towards her.

'Wait. What was he doing in Toga? Tell me everything,' Fátima demanded.

They did so. They spoke with hatred of the Nazarene, told her in detail what had happened in Toga, including the holy man's pleas that had saved the traitor's life. While she listened closely to every word they said, Fátima was busy thinking. Ibn Hamid was in Toga with those who were planning the revolt. He had dedicated years of his life to producing those texts. That meant he had not renounced his faith. As the two men spoke, her eyes came alive. If only it were true! If it were true that Ibn

Hamid was still a believer! Then Shamir's final, stinging words hit her like a slap to the face.

'And you should know he has remarried ... a Christian woman. So you are free, Fátima. You can marry again too. You are still beautiful.'

'Who do you think you are to tell me what I can or cannot do? I will never marry again!' she flung at him.

It was when Shamir realized what emotions lay behind this vehement denial that Brahim's demons resurfaced in him. He faced her threateningly.

'You will never see him again, Fátima. If I ever hear there is any kind of communication between the two of you, I will kill him, do you hear me? I'll tear his heart out with my own bare hands.'

He went on raging in this way for several minutes. She was only a woman! A woman who ought to obey. The palace, the slaves, the furniture, the food, even the air she breathed: all of them belonged to him, Shamir. How could they allow her to be in contact with that cowardly dog who had not defended them in their childhood? If they did so they would forfeit the loyalty of their men and the entire community. They were all aware of the oath he had sworn in Toga about Hernando: the Berbers had told anyone who cared to listen. What authority would they have to impart justice to their men if they agreed to the slightest link with the Nazarene? What power would they have to ask their men to risk their lives in dangerous raids when behind their backs, in Shamir's palace, a mere woman could disobey them? They would keep their promise if they ever saw him again. They would kill him like a dog.

Fátima stood up to Shamir proudly, just as she had done on the night when she told Brahim he would never possess her again. She did so without turning to Abdul for help. She did not so much as look at him, anxious not to put her son in a dangerous position, to pit him against his companion, with whom, when all was said and done, he was the owner of everything.

'Remember what I said: don't do anything stupid,' growled Shamir before he turned on his heel and left the room.

After he had gone, Fátima tried to find a hint of understanding and support in her son's face, but his eyes were cold, and his weather-beaten features were as harsh as those of the other corsair. She watched as he strode out of the room equally determinedly. Only when she was alone did she allow the tears to well up in her eyes.

64

Many Moriscos have been imprisoned in Valencia because of
certain letters sent by the King of England. These letters were
found amongst the papers of the former queen, whom the
Moriscos had written to, asking for her to look favourably on a
revolt by them and saying they would give the order for her to lay
waste to the said city if she sent a fleet from England. Many of
these Moriscos have been tortured to find out what happened in
this affair, and some will be punished in order to set an example
to the rest.

Luis Cabrera de Córdoba, *Relation of Events Occurring in the
Spanish Court*

FOLLOWING THE death of Queen Elizabeth, Spain and
England had signed a peace treaty at the end of August
1604. Amongst other undertakings, the Spanish King promised
to relinquish his efforts to help put a Catholic king on the
English throne. Perhaps for this reason, a few months later, as a
token of gratitude after the signing of the treaty, James I sent
Philip III a series of documents found in his predecessor's
archives. They revealed the Spanish Moriscos' proposal to enlist
the help of the English and French in a rebellion against their
Catholic monarch in order to reconquer the kingdoms of Spain
for Islam.

The viceroy of Valencia and the Inquisition set to work as
soon as the Council of State made the plot known. Hundreds of

Moriscos were arrested and tortured until they confessed to the plan. Many of them were executed in the manner customary in Valencia. The prisoner was asked whether he wanted to die in the Christian or Muslim faith. If his answer was the former, he was hanged in the market place. If he insisted on remaining true to his faith, he was taken outside the walls of the city to the Rambla, and in accordance with the divine punishment laid down in Deuteronomy for idolaters, he was stoned and his body burnt.

Apart from a few exceptions, the Moriscos chose the quicker death. They chose to die as Christians, but at the moment the rope was pulled tight around their neck, they cried out their allegiance to Allah. This trick became so well known that the townspeople went to executions armed with stones to throw at the hanged man just as he was calling on the Prophet. Afterwards, the Morisco families would collect up the stones and keep them as a memento of the death of their loved ones.

Three months after his return to Córdoba, Hernando learnt that the attempted revolt in Toga had been suppressed. Throughout those three months, the only thing to relieve his permanent feeling of despair was the letter he had managed to write to Fátima.

He and Munir had made the journey back from Toga in silence. Hernando's mule plodded along behind Munir's, as if it were being pulled along to Jarafuel. His mother had deceived him. Fátima was alive, and had killed Brahim. His son had sworn to kill him if their paths ever crossed again. To kill him! His own son! Wouldn't he have done so in Toga if he had been able to? Hernando recalled Francisco's innocent, expressive eyes in the courtyard of their house in Córdoba. And what could have become of little Inés? Hernando's head was still spinning from all the revelations of the past few hours. Images and questions crowded into his mind. Every short step his mount took seemed to bring a fresh stab of pain.

Fátima! His wife's features appeared and disappeared in his memory as if mocking his suffering. What could she have thought of him? Had she been expecting him to come and find her? How long – how many years – had she thought he would come to her aid? His stomach clenched as he imagined her in Brahim's power, waiting for him to come. His Fátima! He had betrayed her.

Why did you do it, Mother? He raised his eyes to the heavens a thousand times. *Why did you hide the truth from me?*

The journey to Toga had taken them seven days, but on the way back they covered the same distance in four. Munir, who stubbornly refused to say a word, only stopped when strictly necessary, and they travelled at night by the light of the moon. Hernando did nothing more than obey his travelling companion's instructions: let's have a rest here; let's eat something; let's water the mules; tonight we'll halt close to this village . . . Why had Munir saved his life?

In Jarafuel, the holy man made him wait outside his house without asking him in. After a while, he reappeared, leading Hernando's horse.

Hernando tried to explain: 'Apart from the duke, I only saved a young girl's life. The rest are rumours—'

'I'm not interested,' Munir cut in sharply.

Hernando scanned his face: Munir was staring at him harshly, and yet after a few moments Hernando thought he could detect a glint of compassion in his eyes.

'I have saved your life, Hernando, but it is God who will judge you.'

During the rest of his journey back to Córdoba Hernando avoided any contact with the friars, pedlars, minstrels or travellers who were usually to be met on the main roads. He kept himself to himself, wrapped up in his own thoughts. Guilt weighed on him like a tombstone, and there were moments when he thought he could bear it no longer. As he drew nearer to the city, his troubles gave way to an even greater concern: he had no wish to arrive. What was he going to tell Rafaela? That his marriage to her was a fraud? That his first wife was still alive?

He delayed his arrival for as long as possible. He was afraid of confronting Rafaela, who was pregnant again. He was equally afraid of having to face up to himself if he were obliged to confess the truth. When he finally crossed the threshold into his home, he could not bring himself to look at her.

He saw out of the corner of his eye how Rafaela's welcoming smile vanished as she ran towards him. When she saw the cuts and bruises the Berbers had given him she came to a sudden halt.

'What happened to you?' she said, reaching out to touch his injured face. 'Who . . . ?'

'It's nothing,' he replied, instinctively brushing her hand away. 'I fell off my horse.'

'But are you all right?'

Hernando turned his back on her, leaving her speechless. He went to the stables to unbridle his horse, and then walked across the courtyard to the gallery stairs.

'I'll eat my meals in the library,' he told her coldly as he passed by.

He slept there too.

So the days went by. Hernando put aside the Koran he was working on and forced himself to write a letter to Fátima. It took him a long time to finish it; it was hard for him to express all he felt on paper. Whenever he tried to concentrate on the words, he was overwhelmed by feelings of guilt and pain. He rejected and tore up many sheets. In the end he wrote to her about Rafaela, his two children and the third about to be born. 'I didn't know! I didn't know you were still alive!' he scratched with trembling hand. When he had finally written it, he decided to turn to Munir to get the letter to Fátima. Despite the scholar's cold dismissal of him, Munir was a holy man and would help. Besides, the Moriscos bound for Barbary all left from Valencia. He needed his help! He wrote a second letter to Munir begging him to do so.

One day when he heard Miguel was in Córdoba he called

him to the house. He wanted the cripple to find him a trustworthy Morisco mule-driver: he himself was still regarded as an outcast by the community in Córdoba, and had lost all contact with the network of thousands of muleteers who travelled the length and breadth of the country. Miguel, though, was a regular client of the muleteers, from whom he bought and sold all he needed for the horses.

'I need to get a letter to Jarafuel,' he said abruptly to the cripple. He was seated at his desk; Miguel stood in front of him, trying to imagine what had made him speak in that way. He had spoken earlier to Rafaela, and she had told him how worried she was about her husband. 'What are you waiting for?' snapped Hernando.

'I know a story about a messenger who brought bad news,' Miguel replied. 'Would you like to hear it?'

'I'm not in the mood for stories, Miguel.'

When Miguel left, the sound of his crutches bumping along the gallery echoed in Hernando's ears. Now what? He took out the beautiful Koran he was working on; he had not the slightest desire to continue with it. Even so, he murmured some of the suras he had already copied.

'Whatever he was doing, it looks as though he's finished.'

Miguel had gone to Rafaela after leaving the library with his master's instructions to find a muleteer who would take his letter to Jarafuel.

Rafaela looked at him inquisitively, her eyes red with tears.

'Go and see him,' Miguel insisted. 'Fight for him, and for yourself.'

During all the days Hernando had shut himself in the library, Rafaela had not been able to see him once. She had thought she could do so when she took him his food, but he told her to leave it outside the door. Hernando had also asked for a pitcher of clean water for his prayers, which he also left outside the door once he was finished with it. Rafaela found herself constantly listening for the sound of the library door opening so that she could go and change the water. Five times a day.

What had happened to her husband? Rafaela asked herself yet again as she struggled up the stairs to the gallery. Her latest pregnancy was proving more difficult than the others. She hesitated outside the library. Through the open door she could hear the murmur of suras. What if Hernando became angry? She halted and was about to retrace her steps, but the days the two of them had shared before Hernando had left for Toga – the tenderness, laughter, joy and happiness, the love they had declared to each other – made her go in.

Hernando was sitting at his desk. He was following the letters of the Koran while he murmured his prayers, oblivious to everything else. Rafaela came to a halt again: she did not want to destroy what seemed like a magical moment. When Hernando finally became aware of her presence, he saw her still standing on the threshold, her eyes brimming with tears, both hands resting beneath her prominent belly.

'I don't think I've done anything to deserve this treatment. I need to know what's happening with you . . .' Rafaela managed to stammer before her voice failed her completely.

Hernando nodded, somewhat coldly, his eyes still fixed on the desk. 'More than twenty years ago . . .' he began. But what was the point of telling her? He had never said anything about Fátima or his children to her; she had learnt what she knew from Miguel. 'You're right,' he conceded. 'You don't deserve this. I'm sorry. They're things from the past.'

But the simple fact of apologizing seemed to liberate Hernando. The letter to Fátima was already in Miguel's hands: who could predict what results it might bring or what Fátima might reply, if indeed she did so? Rafaela wiped the tears from her eyes with one hand, the other still clutching her stomach.

All at once, Hernando realized something: yes, he had failed Fátima, and he would never be free from his sense of guilt about that . . . but he was not going to make the same mistake twice with the person he loved. Without a word, he stood up, came round the desk and enveloped his wife in a tender embrace.

Despite his best efforts to hide his concerns from Rafaela, Hernando could not stop thinking about the revelations his son had made. Rafaela, however, made no further mention of his behaviour, as though the days he had been shut up in the library had never happened. Hernando looked for consolation in his children and in the baby yet to be born. One day he even went to the La Merced cemetery and walked through it until he came to his mother's grave. He spoke silently to Aisha.

Why did you do it, Mother?

He tried to find the answer within himself. His mind raced through a thousand possibilities until one thought overtook them all, insistently, that did not really have anything to do with Aisha's actions. *They are alive.* Fátima was alive. So were Francisco and Shamir; Inés had probably survived as well. Would he have preferred them all to have died just to alleviate his sorrow? He felt ashamed of himself. Until that moment he had been thinking only of himself, of his guilt, of the cowardice that Francisco had repeatedly accused him of. But the important thing was that they were alive, even if they were distant from him. The idea gave him some respite, but he still needed to know that Fátima forgave him. He anxiously awaited news from Munir, but his expectations turned to bitter disappointment when the holy man returned his letter to Fátima. He had refused to send it on to Tetuan.

Fátima could not help but notice: after Shamir and her son's visit, three giant Nubian slaves, carrying swords, became part of the household at the palace.

'It's for your safety, my lady,' one of the servants told her. 'These are troubled times, and your son thought it was a good idea.'

For her safety? Whenever she went out into Tetuan, two of the Nubians followed a couple of paces behind her. Fátima put her suspicions to the test. One morning, accompanied by two slaves whom she gave bundles to carry, she strode towards the Bab Mqabar gate in the city's northern wall.

Before she could pass through it, the two Nubians stopped her.

'You cannot leave the city,' one of them said.

'I only wish to go to the cemetery,' Fátima said.

'It's not safe, my lady.'

On another day she left her bedroom at first light. She had not got halfway down the corridor before the immense figure of one of the Nubians loomed out of the semi-darkness.

'Is there something you want?'

'Water.'

'Don't worry, I'll see that some is brought to you. Get some rest.'

So she was a prisoner in her own house! She had not intended to run away, yet she had no idea what to do or think. All she did know was that after years of believing that Hernando had betrayed her, the mere possibility that this had not been the case had stirred up emotions she had pushed to the furthest corners of her mind. Following Brahim's death, she had devoted herself to running her businesses and saving money with the same cool determination with which Abdul and Shamir attacked Christian ships or the coasts of Spain. She had even forgotten she was a woman. But now something had been reawakened inside her. At night, as she gazed towards the horizon where she thought the mountains of Granada must be, she felt almost imperceptible stirrings that reminded her she had once been capable of loving with her whole being.

One afternoon Ephraim came to discuss some business matters with the great lady of Tetuan. After the death of his father, the Jew had become her closest associate in the family business.

'I need to ask a favour of you, Ephraim,' she said as he tried to talk numbers and commodities with her.

'You should know that your son has been to see me,' the astute Jew whispered in response.

Fátima fixed her beautiful black eyes on him.

'But it is you I am loyal to, my lady,' Ephraim added, after a few moments' silence.

65

In death, hope is everlasting.

The Book of Morisco Ballads, 'The Ballads of Aben Humeya'

JUAN AND ROSA had a tutor who came every day to give them lessons. As Rafaela was seeing him out one day, she saw a stranger approaching the house. Although Hernando appeared to have recovered his usual calm, Rafaela, who was nearing the end of her pregnancy, was still shaken by any unexpected event. The man, who looked to be aged around forty and was wearing Spanish-style clothes soiled from a long journey, asked if this was the house of Hernando Ruiz. Rafaela nodded, and sent Juan to give his father the message. Hernando did not take long to come to the front door.

'Peace be with you,' he greeted the man, thinking he must be one of his tenant farmers or someone interested in buying a horse. 'What is it you want?'

Ephraim hesitated before speaking. Fortunately this time it had been easy to find Hernando.

'Peace,' the Jew replied, staring straight at Hernando.

'What is it?' the latter repeated.

'Can we talk somewhere in private?'

At that moment Hernando realized that this man was more than a horse dealer. Although his accent sounded rather strange, something about him inspired confidence.

'Come with me.'

They left the doorway and crossed the courtyard.

'I don't want to be disturbed,' Hernando told Rafaela.

They went up to the library, where Hernando could not help but notice the Jew gaze admiringly at the books that were his most precious treasure.

'I congratulate you,' Ephraim said, referring to the books. He sat down at the desk. Hernando accepted the compliment, and for a while both men were silent.

'Your wife Fátima sent me,' said the Jew at last.

A tremendous shudder ran the length of Hernando's body. He found himself unable to say a word, and the other man realized it.

'Fátima needs to know what has become of you,' Ephraim continued. 'Many rumours reach Tetuan, but she refuses to believe them unless she hears it from you. First of all, though, I should tell you that about fifteen years ago I came to look for you here in Córdoba, also sent by my lady—'

'How is she?' Hernando interrupted him.

They talked the whole day. Hernando told Ephraim all that had happened to him, openly and without omitting the slightest detail. He even told him about his love for Isabel. This was the first time he had opened his heart to anyone with such sincerity. He justified the fact that he was living like a Christian, although he did admit that on occasion, because of the circumstances, he had made the mistake of taking this too far. Why for example had he walked in procession carrying a cross?

'If I had not shown off like that, my mother would not have died,' he said, his voice choking with emotion.

After that he told the Jew all about the lead plates.

'Shamir said that the poor would never benefit from them,' he admitted. 'He was probably right.'

'Perhaps one day the gospel you mention will see the light of day,' said Ephraim.

'Perhaps.' Hernando sighed sadly. 'But I don't know what our situation will be by the time that happens. We Moriscos seem to be cursed: the Christians want us all dead, and none of the Muslim rulers has ever done anything to help us. We're constantly scanning the horizon in the hope of glimpsing an armada from Turkey or Algiers that never comes.'

Ephraim was tempted to argue. Cursed? His own people really were that, in Spain and all the other European kingdoms. The Jews did not even have the consolation of scanning the horizon: there was nobody who could come to their aid. In the end, though, he said nothing. That was not why he was here. Fátima had given him strict instructions: he was to watch and judge Hernando's words and demeanour. Based on this, he himself had to decide whether to give him her message or to leave without mentioning it. 'I put all my trust in you,' Fátima had told him before he left. The Jew had seen enough by now to make up his mind.

'In death, hope is everlasting,' he said.

Ephraim could feel the Morisco's blue eyes staring straight at him, just as his son Abdul had done some time ago when he went to warn the Jew he was on no account to help Fátima in anything related to the 'miserable traitor'. They had the same eyes, but what a different message they conveyed! The corsair's eyes flashed with hatred and rancour; Hernando's showed only an infinite sadness.

How often had Fátima put her trust in death in order to find hope? Hernando thought when he heard that phrase once more. Why was she doing so again?

'Your wife is a prisoner in her own house,' said Ephraim, as though he had guessed what was going through the other man's mind. 'There are Nubian slaves guarding her day and night.'

'Because of me?' Hernando asked faintly.

'Yes. If you go anywhere near Fátima, they will kill you, and she—'

'Francisco would kill her as well?'

'Abdul? I don't think he has it in him . . . but I'm not sure,' the Jew corrected himself, remembering the threats the corsair had made. 'But we mustn't forget Shamir. The truth is, I don't know what he might do. In any case, she would be the one to suffer, that's for sure.'

Ephraim talked to him about Fátima. Hernando finally learnt why his mother had behaved as she did: it was Fátima herself who had asked her to do so. They both wanted to protect him from certain death. He learnt about how Brahim had been murdered, and of the journey Ephraim had made many years before, of Fátima's letter that Ephraim had read to Aisha when he had been unable to find Hernando, Aisha's harsh words and the insults he had received from Abbas and the other Moriscos. As he lauded Fátima and praised her beauty, courage and determination, his gaze wavered; Hernando saw in his face feelings that went beyond admiration and felt a sudden pang of jealousy towards this man who lived so close to her. Ephraim also told him about Abdul and Shamir; Inés, now called Maryam, was well: she had married and had several children. He praised his mistress's skill in business affairs, and insisted on how admired and desired she was in Tetuan. As he held forth, Hernando let his mind wander through his memories, nodding and smiling at the other man's descriptions.

'My lady trusts you will keep the oath you once made to her: to bring the Christians to her feet, to the feet of the one God. She wants you to go on working for the cause of your faith in Spain, in the same way you did when you were married,' he concluded. 'Her happiness depends on it. It is only through this communion of ideas that she will find peace; that is all she wishes and hopes for. She says that God will unite you again . . . after death.'

'And until then?' Hernando muttered under his breath.

Ephraim shook his head. 'She will never put your life at risk.' Hernando made as if to reply, but the Jew cut him short with a gesture. 'You mustn't put hers under threat either.'

Both men fell silent.

'I wrote her a letter,' Hernando eventually said, 'and tried without success to get it to her.'

'I'm sorry,' said Ephraim, 'I cannot take it now, and she can't be in possession of it either. I made the excuse that my journey was for business purposes. If your son or Shamir or the Nubian guards were to discover a letter on any of us . . .'

'But I have to explain to her!' Hernando butted in, almost pleading. 'There's so much I have to say to her!'

'And you can: through me. You know Fátima.' The Jew shook his head. 'Of course you know her – far better than I. She was worried about you, but now I'll be able to give her the happiness I know she craves most of all: don't you think she'll make me repeat every last word that you say to me?' Hernando could not avoid smiling at the thought of Fátima's impetuous character. Ephraim saw his reaction. 'She'll make me do it a thousand times!'

'And you must do it, and more than a thousand times if need be. Tell her . . . tell her also that I still love her, that I have never stopped doing so. But life . . . Fate was cruel to us both. I've spent half my days crying over her death. Ask her for forgiveness for me.'

'Why do I need to do that?'

'I have married again . . . and have other children.'

The Jew nodded. 'She knows already, and understands. Life has not been easy for either of you. Remember: in death, hope is everlasting. That was the first thing she asked me to tell you.'

That night, before he left to return to Tetuan, Ephraim was received as an honoured guest in Hernando's house. Warned by his host that Rafaela was not at any moment to suspect the real reason for his being there, Ephraim was extremely discreet and perfectly behaved. Behind his courteous appearance, however, he was interested in finding out as much as possible about Hernando's Christian wife to tell Fátima. What is the woman he has married like? Does he love her? she had wanted to know.

That night, caught up in his memories of Fátima, Hernando was very cold and distant towards Rafaela.

A few days later, with Hernando busy copying the Koran and praying in the mosque, hoping that this would provide the communion at a distance that Fátima was asking him for, Rafaela gave birth to her third child. Lázaro, as the boy was baptized in the presence of Christian godparents (whom Hernando did not even know; they were chosen by the parish priest), broke with the family tradition and was born with huge, clear blue eyes. The newborn bore the stigma with which a Christian priest had poisoned an innocent Morisco girl! Hernando could not stop this thought leaping into his mind as soon as he saw his new son. It had to be a sign from God.

'He is to be called Muqla, in honour of the renowned calligrapher,' he announced to Rafaela and Miguel on the day of the baptism, using warm water to wipe away the oils poured over the baby in church. 'That will be his name in this house.'

Lowering her gaze, Rafaela agreed with an almost inaudible murmur.

'Won't that be dangerous?' said Miguel, alarmed.

'The only dangerous thing is to live with your back turned to God.'

From that day on, Hernando decided it was time to tell his children something other than Muslim legends. He dismissed the tutor and took personal charge of educating Juan and Rosa, whom he renamed Amin and Laila. He began to teach them the Koran, the Sunna, Arabic poetry and language, the history of their people and mathematics. Little Muqla lay in his cot beside them, and was lulled to sleep listening to the suras whispered by his father. At eight, Amin already had some knowledge of these things, but the girl, who was only six, suffered.

'Don't you think you should wait until Rosa is a little older, to give her time?' Rafaela tried to tell him.

'Her name is Laila,' Hernando corrected her. 'In these lands, Rafaela, women are called on to teach and spread the true faith. She has to learn. They both have to know many things. When will they do that if not now? They are of an age to learn our laws. I think . . . I think I've made too many mistakes in the past.'

This answer did not satisfy Rafaela. 'It's not that simple,' she said. 'You're endangering our family. If anyone were to hear about this . . . I can't even bear to think about it.'

Hernando said nothing for a few moments, staring at his wife's face.

'You knew, didn't you?' he said eventually. 'Miguel told you before we were married. He told you I professed the true faith.' Rafaela nodded. 'So when you married me, you accepted that our children would be brought up in the two cultures, the two religions. I'm not asking you to share my faith, but my children—'

'They're my children too,' she retorted.

Yet she did not insist, or interfere in their education. At night, however, she prayed to the Christian God on their behalf as she had always done, and Hernando said nothing. Every day, when he had finished teaching the children, he would wash and purify himself, then go to the mosque to pray facing the mihrab. Sometimes he stood quietly in front of the spot where the holy marks should be carved into the marble; at others, if he thought his presence there might arouse suspicion, he hid some distance away. 'Here I am, Fátima,' he would whisper to himself, 'I'll be with you whatever happens.'

The mosque was a reminder to him that anything could happen. By now the Christians had taken it over completely. The chancel, the transept and the choir had recently been completed, and the dome rose high above the buttresses to show the whole world the magnificence of this longed-for church. Even the former kitchen garden where criminals had sought asylum had been renewed. The penitential costumes of those condemned by the Inquisition still hung from the walls of the surrounding gallery, adding a macabre note, but the space had now become a proper garden, with paved paths and fountains among orange trees: for this reason, it was now known as the Patio de los Naranjos.

Clergy, nobles and poor alike were proud of their new cathedral. Every expression of astonishment or pride that Hernando heard from one of the Christian faithful about this masterpiece of architecture only served to irritate him more. This heretical building, which had profaned the greatest Muslim temple in the West, was a symbol of what was happening throughout Spain: the Christians were trampling on his people, and Hernando had to fight back, even at the risk of his own and his children's lives.

Occasionally he would stand at the doors to the tabernacle of the cathedral and contemplate the Last Supper by Arbasia. He remembered all the days he had spent there with Don Julián when it was the library, fooling the priests while he worked for his brothers in faith. What could have become of the Italian painter? He looked at the figure beside Jesus, the one he thought must be a woman. He, too, had chosen a woman, the Virgin Mary, and put her at the centre of the story of the lead plates in the Sacromonte. A story that seemed to have failed to reach its desired conclusion, if what he had heard from Granada was true.

Whenever he was not praying or teaching his children, Hernando loved to ride. Miguel did an excellent job, and the colts born at their stud were increasingly sought after by the wealthy and nobles throughout Andalusia. They even sold some to courtiers in Madrid. Every so often, Miguel would send a pair of trained young horses to Córdoba. He chose the best, the ones he considered would benefit most from the lessons his master could give them. Hernando rode them out in the countryside for hours, putting them through their paces. He also taught Amin to ride, on the back of his horse Estudiante, who by now was old and docile and seemed to understand he was not to make any sudden movements with the boy astride him. And Hernando ran the bulls in the pastures once more, enthusiastically watched and cheered on by Amin; his sad experience with Azirat was a thing of the past. When he judged the colts had been properly trained, he gave them back to Miguel for him to sell. Hernando looked on with pride as some of them later faced the bulls in the La Corredera bullring when there was a feast day. The horses' fortunes depended on the skill of the Córdoban nobles riding them, but they never failed to show their nobility and good temperament.

At night Hernando shut himself in the library to experience again the union with God born of his skill in calligraphy, tracing suras of the Koran in magnificent coloured characters. Then he would make further copies in simpler lettering, interspersing the lines with his translation into *aljamiado*, just as he had done alongside Don Julián in the cathedral library. He gave the completed books to Munir for free. Despite his cold farewell in Jarafuel and his refusal to send Fátima the letter, Munir was prepared to accept them on behalf of the community, as Miguel told his master through the muleteer who took the holy man the first copies. Hernando was fighting back! Yes, he was still in the struggle, Hernando whispered to Fátima a few hundred leagues away. He was at peace with God, himself and with all those around him. In his mind's eye he saw her as beautiful and as proud as ever, fanning his religious ardour, urging him to keep going.

66

A letter could be sent to the viceroy of Catalonia saying that with regard to the Moriscos crossing into France, they are to make themselves known, and if there are any rich and distinguished persons among them, they are to be detained and kept securely in order to determine their intentions, while the ordinary people are to be left alone and allowed to pass, because the fewer who remain the better.

Decree of the Council of State, 24 June 1608

BY THIS TIME, Miguel was more than thirty years old, although his lined features and crippled legs made him appear much older. He had no teeth, and his legs seemed to have refused to continue growing the way the rest of his body had. The bones in his legs that had been crushed at birth had developed from the point where they had been broken, but had no muscles to help them move. This meant that as time went by he looked increasingly like a grotesque puppet. Yet he continued to tell stories and tales, making the children laugh and delighting Rafaela in the few moments of rest she allowed herself. It was as though God, whichever one He might be, had exchanged Miguel's ability to walk or run for an endless supply of imagination and fantasy.

It was Miguel who, because he was always in the know about well-to-do families – those who could afford to buy the magnificent horses they bred at their farm – commented to

Hernando that many rich Moriscos were leaving for France. He said it in a way that suggested Hernando was one of them and should think about doing the same.

In January of 1608 the Council of State, headed by the Duke of Lerma, had unanimously agreed to suggest to the King that he expel all the new Christians from Spain. The news spread quickly, and the wealthy Moriscos began to sell their properties before the drastic measure could come into force. Since they were forbidden to cross to Barbary, they all cast their eyes towards the neighbouring realm to the north. France was Christian, so they were allowed to cross the frontier.

When Miguel told him all this, Hernando looked at him and then shook his head.

'My place is here, Miguel,' he answered, and thought he heard a sigh of relief from his companion. 'This is not the first time we've heard talk of expulsion. Let's wait and see if the order is carried out. At least they are not proposing to castrate us, or slit our throats, turn us into slaves or throw us into the sea. If they expelled us, the nobles would lose a lot of money. Who would work their lands? The Christians don't know how to, and would not stoop to it.'

Yet during that year King Philip failed to act on the proposal his Council had recommended. Apart from the patriarch Ribera and a few other extremists, who continued to call for the killing or enslavement of the Moriscos, most of the clergy rent their garments at the thought of thousands of Christian souls reaching Moorish countries where they would renounce the true faith. There was no denying that their attempts to convert the Moriscos had failed time and again. And yet – as the Knight Commander of León pointed out – priests and saints were being sent all the way to China to take the word of Christ to those mysterious peoples. Given that was the case, why were they prepared to give up trying to convert the non-believers in their own realms?

If it was forbidden to flee to Muslim countries, it was also against the law to take gold or silver out of Spain, even to another Christian country, so the Council ordered that all rich Moriscos should be detained at the border. The flow of wealthy people to France dried up. The Morisco communities throughout Spain were wary now, and on their guard: the poor, who were in the majority, remained chained to the land; those with more resources began to look for ways round the royal decree, should it be proclaimed.

Hernando, like his brothers in faith, was worried. After the birth of Muqla, Rafaela had had another fine son, Musa, and then a girl, Salma (whose Christian names were Luis and Ana). Neither of them had blue eyes. Hernando now had a large family and the fact that the rich Moriscos who knew all the inner workings at court were fleeing Spain made him realize there were grounds for concern. As a result, he decided to go to Granada to find out what was happening with the lead plates.

He got out the carefully hidden safe conduct the Archbishop of Granada had given him. No one was concerned about the martyrs of the Alpujarra any more: enough saints and martyrs of antiquity, disciples of Saint James, had been discovered in the Sacromonte for them not to worry about a few peasants tortured by the Moriscos only some forty years earlier. Yet no bailiff or other official of the Holy Brotherhood would dare question the document Hernando showed them firmly whenever anyone asked him what he was doing. Concealed with the safe conduct was the completed copy of the Koran, the copy of the gospel of Barnabas from the time of the great Almanzor, and the hand of Fátima. As Hernando did each time he opened the hiding place, he picked up the jewel and kissed it, thinking of Fátima. The gold had lost its lustre.

It was not good news in Granada. Just as the Christians had taken over the mosque in Córdoba, so in Granada they had made the Sacromonte their own. As usual, Hernando met with Don Pedro, Miguel de Luna and Alonso del Castillo in the Golden Stable of the Casa de los Tiros.

'There is no point in trying to get the gospel of Barnabas to the Sultan,' Don Pedro argued. 'We need the Church to recognize the books' authority, especially the lead plate that refers to the Mute Book, the one that announces that some day a great king will appear with another text, this one decipherable, which will outline the Virgin Mary's revelation as described in the book that cannot be read.'

'But the relics . . .' Hernando cut in.

'That's a battle we have won,' said Alonso del Castillo, who looked much older now. 'The relics have been approved as authentic and are venerated as such. Archbishop de Castro has decided to build a large collegiate church on the Sacromonte. He has appointed Ambrosio de Vico to be in charge.'

A collegiate church! Hernando sighed. 'That cannot be right. The doctrine in those books is Muslim!' his voice rang out. 'How can the Christians build a church on the spot where lead plates have been found that praise the one God?'

'The archbishop isn't allowing anyone to see the plates.' This time it was Luna who spoke. 'Despite knowing no Arabic, he is personally supervising their translation. If there's something he doesn't agree with, he changes it, and ignores the translator. I've experienced it myself. Both the Holy See and the King are demanding he send them the books, but he refuses. He is keeping them under his control as though they belonged to him.'

'In that case', Hernando observed, 'the truth will never be known.'

Defeat filled his voice. The golden reflections from the paintings on the ceiling danced in the silence that fell between the four men.

'We'll not be able to do it,' he insisted dejectedly. 'We'll be expelled or killed before we can.'

None of the others responded. Hernando could see the three of them were ill at ease: they shifted in their seats and avoided his gaze. Then he realized: yes, they had failed, but they were not risking expulsion. One was a nobleman; the other two worked for the King.

He was alone in his fight.

'We can see to it that you and your family are saved from expulsion or whatever other measures are taken against our people, if in fact they are implemented one day,' Don Pedro said to Hernando, who, seeing no point in continuing the conversation, had made to get up from his chair and leave the Golden Stable.

He looked closely at the nobleman, grasping the arms of his chair to rise to his feet. 'What about our brothers in faith?' he asked, unable to stop a note of resentment entering his voice. 'And the poor?' he added, remembering Shamir's prediction.

'We've done all we could,' Miguel de Luna replied calmly. 'Or don't you agree? We've all risked our lives, you more than anyone.'

Hernando fell back into his seat. It was true. He had risked his life in their undertaking.

'For the moment,' the translator went on, 'God has not rewarded us with success. He in His infinite wisdom will know why. Perhaps one day . . .'

'If the expulsions or any other drastic measures occur,' said Don Pedro, 'we must continue to live in Spain. Our seed must always be here, in these lands of ours. A seed always ready to grow, multiply and recover al-Andalus for Islam.'

For a few moments, Hernando sat trying to take in all he had heard. His life of sacrifice and suffering passed through his mind. Had it been worth all the misfortunes? He was fifty-four years old. He felt old, immensely old. And yet, his children . . .

'How would you save me from being expelled?' he asked faintly.

'By petitioning for you to become a nobleman,' Don Pedro replied.

Hernando could not avoid a cynical laugh.

'Me, a nobleman? A Morisco from Juviles? The son of a woman condemned by the Inquisition?'

'We have many friends, Hernando,' the nobleman insisted. 'Nowadays everything can be bought, including a title of nobility. The records of entire villages are forged. You have an excellent position with the Church in Granada. You have collaborated with them. You saved Christians during the Alpujarra uprising! All that is well known to everyone.'

'Besides, aren't you a priest's son?' Castillo added, knowing this was a delicate topic. 'Titles are granted through the male line, not the female.'

Hernando snorted and shook his head. That was all he needed: for that dog of a priest who had raped his mother to be his and his family's salvation now!

'Many bloodlines have been washed clean,' Luna said, trying to convince him. 'Everyone knows that the grandfather of Teresa de Jesús, the founder of the barefoot Carmelites, was Jewish. And now they want to make her a saint! There are hundreds if not thousands like her. All kinds of Christians are seeking to become nobles so that they are exempt from paying taxes, and now many Moriscos are doing the same to avoid being expelled. While their cases are being studied, nothing will happen to them – and the process could take years.'

'What if they are refused in the end?' Hernando asked.

'By then times will have changed,' replied Castillo.

'Trust us,' Don Pedro insisted. 'We'll see to everything.'

Before leaving Granada, Hernando hired a lawyer to present his case to the Royal Chancery.

These plans were overtaken by events. Desperate at the rumours of expulsion, the Moriscos called on the King of Morocco to come to their aid. A group of fifty of them travelled to Barbary to persuade him to invade Spain with the help of the Dutch, who had already agreed to supply enough ships to form a bridge across the strait. The proposal was similar to all those they had made in the past: all Muley Zaidan had to do was to take a coastal city with a port, bring in twenty thousand soldiers, and they would guarantee that another two hundred thousand men would rise up to take over kingdoms that were already weak.

Although he was a bitter enemy of Spain, the Moroccan King

laughed at the Morisco proposal, and sent the ambassadors packing. The person who did not laugh was Philip III. He was sick and tired of conspiracies and increasingly concerned that one or other of them might actually come to fruition, and his territories be invaded by a foreign power supported by the Moriscos. In April 1609 the King sent the Council a request in which he called on its members to take definitive measures against the Morisco community, 'without shrinking from slitting their throats, if necessary'.

Five months later a decree was issued in the kingdom of Valencia for the expulsion of all the Moriscos. The intransigent views of the patriarch Ribera and other Christian extremists had won the day. The only possible opposition, from nobles afraid their lands would suffer because they would lose cheap, skilled labour, was silenced with the promise that they would be given titles to all the lands and properties the Moriscos were forced to abandon. The only goods the Moriscos were allowed to take from Spain were whatever they could carry to the designated embarkation ports, which they had to reach within three days. Everything else was to be left for the benefit of their Christian lords, under penalty of death for anyone who destroyed or concealed any possessions.

Fifty royal galleys with four thousand soldiers on board, the Castilian cavalry, the Valencian militia and the Atlantic fleet were given the responsibility of supervising and carrying out the expulsion of the Moriscos from Valencia.

Even though it had been expected, the royal decree nonetheless dealt a severe blow to Hernando and all the Moriscos in the different kingdoms of Spain. Valencia was only the first: the others would soon follow. Every new Christian was to be expelled, and their possessions requisitioned either to the benefit of the Christian nobility, as in Valencia, or the Spanish Crown.

Hernando had not yet fully taken in the significance of the decree when he spied two soldiers on guard outside his house.

The first time he noticed them, he didn't think it was important. Just a coincidence, he thought. But when he saw they were posted there day after day he realized they must be watching his movements.

'It's by order of the magistrate Don Gil Ulloa,' one of the soldiers answered mockingly when Hernando finally asked what they were doing there.

'Gil Ulloa!' he muttered, turning his back on the sneering soldiers. Rafaela's brother, who had inherited the post of magistrate from his father. A bad man to have as an enemy.

In Córdoba, the Christians celebrated when they heard of the royal decree. To avoid any disturbances the city council threatened to punish anyone who mistreated the new Christians with a hundred lashes and four years in the galleys. At the same time, it threatened the Moriscos of the city with two hundred lashes and six years in the galleys if more than three of them met at any one time.

However, the decision that most affected Hernando's interests was one passed immediately afterwards: the prohibition on Moriscos selling their homes or lands.

'I can't sell the horses either,' Miguel told him one day. 'I had a couple of sales agreed, but the buyers have backed out.'

'They're waiting for us to have to sell them at any price.'

Miguel nodded silently. 'Our tenant farmers are refusing to pay their rents,' he finally admitted.

Miguel knew these payments were essential to the family. It was he who, the year before, had convinced Hernando to make improvements to the farm buildings. They needed new stables, a new ring for the horses and a hayloft: the old ones were falling down. Hernando took his advice, and also invested a large part of his savings in livestock. What Miguel did not know was that Hernando had spent the rest of his money on his petition for ennoblement. He had to pay his lawyer, the lawyer in Granada, and for all the documents required to present his case to the Royal Chancery.

'They will pay them,' he reassured Miguel. 'I'm not going to be deported. I've started a petition to be made a nobleman,' he explained when he saw the look of surprise on Miguel's face. 'Tell the tenants that. If they don't pay they will lose their lands. Tell that to anyone who wants to buy my horses too.'

He had spoken firmly, but all of a sudden he looked and sounded exhausted. 'I need money, Miguel,' he murmured.

News of what had happened to the Moriscos of Valencia began to reach Córdoba. The city had become one huge market place where speculators from all the Spanish realms flocked to buy the Moriscos' possessions for next to nothing. The hatred between the two communities, previously latent or held in check by Christian lords defending the people who worked for them, now exploded into the open. The King's threats to punish anyone attacking or robbing the Moriscos proved useless: it was not long before the roads to the ports they had to embark from were littered with dead bodies. Long columns of men and women, children and old people – some of them sick, all of them weighed down with bundles of goods like a vast group of defeated pedlars – set off for exile. The Christians made them pay to sit in the shade of trees or to drink water from rivers that for centuries had belonged to them. Many of them were starving, and some even sold their children to buy food that would keep the rest of their family going. More than a hundred thousand Moriscos from Valencia began to congregate, closely guarded, in the ports of El Grao, Dénia, Vinaroz and Moncófar.

Startled, Hernando lifted his head. Something serious must have happened for Rafaela to disturb him in the library without even knocking. She only rarely visited his sanctuary, where he was busy making another copy of the Koran, but whenever she did it was to discuss an important matter. She came in and stood at the far side of the desk. Hernando stared at her in the lamplight. She must be a little over thirty, and the frightened little girl he had first met in the stables had grown into a mature woman. Even so, to judge by her face, she was as terrified now as she had been then.

'Do you know about the decree expelling the Moriscos from Valencia?' she asked.

Hernando could feel her eyes fixed on him. He hesitated before replying. 'Yes . . . well,' he stammered, 'I only know what everyone does: that they have been expelled from the kingdom.'

'Don't you know the details of the decree?' she insisted.

'You mean about the money?'

Rafaela waved her hand impatiently. 'No.'

'So what do you mean, Rafaela?' It was unlike her to be so nervous.

'I was told in the market that the King has imposed specific conditions on couples made up of new and old Christians.'

Hernando leant forward in his chair. He knew nothing about this. 'Go on,' he signalled to her.

'Morisco women who are married to old Christians are permitted to remain in Spain, and so are their children. Morisco men married to old Christians have to leave Spain . . . and take with them all their children aged over six. Those younger than that are to stay here with their mothers.' As she said these last two sentences, Rafaela's voice began to quaver.

Hernando put his elbows on the desk, clasped his hands together, and dropped his forehead on to them. This meant that if the royal decree were applied in his case, Amin and Laila would be expelled with him. Muqla and the two younger children would stay in Spain with Rafaela, and live . . . on what? His lands and house would be seized, and his possessions . . .

'That will not happen to our family,' he swore. Tears were streaming down his wife's cheeks. She did nothing to stop the flow. She was trembling all over, her eyes fixed on him. Hernando could feel his stomach churn. 'Don't worry,' he added gently, getting up from his chair. 'You know I've begun a petition to be made a noble. I've received the first documents from Granada. I have important friends there who are close to the King. They'll plead on my behalf. We won't be expelled.' He went over to her and pulled her into his arms.

'Today . . .' Rafaela sobbed, 'this morning I met my brother Gil round the corner from our house.' Hernando frowned. 'He mocked me. He laughed – so cruelly. I could hear it echoing behind me as I tried to get away from him as fast as I could.'

'Why was he laughing?'

'"A noble?" he shouted at me. When I turned back towards him, he spat on the ground.' Rafaela burst into tears once more. Hernando urged her to go on. '"That heretic husband of yours will never become a noble!" he told me.'

So they knew, thought Hernando. It was to be expected. Miguel would have told his tenants and the nobles who were thinking of buying horses from him, and the news must have travelled from mouth to mouth.

'Rafaela, even if I am not granted my petition, the mere fact of starting the process means they cannot expel me for years. Afterwards . . . afterwards, we'll see. Things change.'

Nothing he said could stop her weeping. She raised her hands to her face as her sobs broke the silence of the night. Hernando, who had turned away from her anguish, came up behind her and started to gently stroke her hair, trying to project a calm he was far from feeling.

'It's all right,' he whispered in her ear. 'Nothing will happen to us. We'll all stay together.'

'Miguel has had a feeling about this,' she began, still weeping.

'Miguel's presentiments do not always come true. Everything will be all right. Stay firm. Nothing will happen . . .' he murmured. 'Calm down. The children shouldn't see you like this.'

Rafaela nodded. She took a deep breath, but clung to him. She was so afraid that only contact with Hernando could reassure her.

When she finally dried her eyes and left the library, Hernando was overwhelmed by a strong feeling of tenderness. He had learnt to live with two women, Fátima and Rafaela. He was with the former when he prayed, or in the mosque, when he was copying the holy texts, or when he heard Muqla whisper words in Arabic, his huge blue eyes fixed on him, hoping to win his approval. He was with Rafaela during his daily life, when he needed warmth and affection. She looked after him lovingly, and he returned her regard. Fátima had become no more than a kind of beacon he followed in the moments when he communed with God and his religion.

The expulsion of the Valencian Moriscos went ahead, though not without difficulty. To carry more than a hundred thousand people meant that the ships had to come and go from Spain's east coast to Barbary time and again. Despite only having been given three days to leave, the whole process of expelling the Moriscos took several months to complete. This delay meant that, thanks to the crews of the ships making the journeys and the malicious cruelty of Christians who liked to repeat the stories, reports of how the new arrivals in Africa were treated soon began to reach the ears of the Moriscos still left in Spain. The most fortunate among them, the ones who disembarked in Algiers, were immediately transferred to the mosques. Once there, the men were made to line up; their penises were examined and they were circumcised on the spot, one after another. After that, they became part of the lowest caste of this pirate port ruled by the janissaries, and were sent to work the land in subhuman conditions.

Those less fortunate fell into the hands of the nomad tribes or Berbers, who lost no time in attacking, robbing and killing people they saw as nothing more than Christians: men and women who had been baptized and had renounced the Prophet. The rumour spread that almost three-quarters of the Moriscos from Valencia had been murdered by the Arabs. Even in the cities of Tetuan and Ceuta, where many Moriscos from al-Andalus lived, the new arrivals were tortured and executed. Declaring their allegiance to their faith, entire communities crowded round the walls of the Spanish prisons in the African enclaves, demanding protection. Hundreds of terrified, disillusioned Moriscos found their way back to Spain, where they handed themselves over as slaves to the first man they met, because slaves were exempt from deportation.

It was also said that entire shiploads of Moriscos were stripped of their possessions and thrown overboard.

News of the killings and other misfortunes spread like wildfire among the Valencian Moriscos still waiting to be expelled. Two communities rose up in revolt. Munir led the men of the valley of Cofrentes, who, under a new king called Turigi, took to the mountains and made a stand on the heights of Muela de Cortes. Several thousand other men and women in the Vall de Laguar did the same, under the command of King Melleni. But al-Fatimi on his green horse did not come to their aid, and the battle-hardened soldiers of the Spanish King's army had no problem dealing with the uprisings. Thousands were executed; thousands more ended up as slaves.

Before the end of the year the decree ordering the expulsion of the Moriscos from the two Castiles and Extremadura was issued. The people of Andalusia knew it was their turn next.

One cold, uncomfortable morning in January of the following year, Hernando was in his library correcting the letters Amin had written on the blank tar-covered tablet he used as his notebook. He had tried giving his son a quill, but the boy just smudged the paper with ink, so he preferred him to write on the tablet, which he could wipe clean and then get him to write characters over and over again. Amin had managed to write a graceful, correctly proportioned *alif*. Hernando picked up the tablet and congratulated his son, ruffling his hair. Muqla came over and looked jealously at his elder brother.

'If you carry on like this, you'll soon be able to use the quill, and choose the point that most suits your hand.'

His son looked up at him with eyes full of hope, but just as he was about to say something they heard a loud pounding at the street door. The sound echoed across the courtyard and up into the library. Hernando froze on the spot.

'Open up in the name of the council of Córdoba!' they heard from out in the street.

Gesturing hastily to his son to hide everything on the desk, Hernando went out to the gallery, leading Muqla by the hand. Before he left the library he made sure Amin had tidied the desk and put a book of psalms on it: they had rehearsed this move many times.

'Open up!' they heard, the blows raining on the door again.

Hernando gripped the gallery railing and looked down into the courtyard. Rafaela was standing in the middle. She gazed up at him, terrified, asking him what to do.

'Answer it,' he said, and then ran down the stairs.

He caught up with his wife as she was undoing the bolt on the inside of the door. Out in the street, a bailiff and several soldiers stood behind a richly dressed man of about thirty. Behind them bobbed the head of a smiling Gil Ulloa, and beyond him stood a small crowd of curious onlookers. Hernando pushed in front of Rafaela, who was staring at her brother. He himself was trying to recognize the nobleman: his features . . .

'Open in the name of the Córdoba council and the councillor Don Carlos de Córdoba, Duke of Monterreal,' the bailiff shouted once more, despite the fact that Hernando was already out in the street.

Don Alfonso's son! He had his father's features, mixed with those of his mother, Doña Lucía. The duchess! The mere thought of her and the hatred she had shown towards him was enough to make Hernando's legs go weak under him. He knew then that nothing good could come of this visit.

'Are you Hernando Ruiz, a new Christian from Juviles?' asked Don Carlos with the haughty, authoritarian voice nobles always used to speak to someone of lower rank.

'Yes, I am he.' Hernando smiled wanly. 'As your excellency well knows.'

'By order of the Royal Chancery of Granada I am delivering their decision regarding the petition for a title of nobility that you so presumptuously embarked upon.' A clerk stepped forward and handed him a scroll. 'Can you read?' asked the duke.

The document seemed to scorch Hernando's hand. Why had the duke taken the trouble to come to his house to hand it to him personally, when he could have simply called him to the council chamber? When he saw more and more people crowding round to see what was going on, he understood: the duke wanted this to be a public act. Out of the corner of his eye, Hernando could see Rafaela swaying: he had promised her the process would last for years!

'If you cannot read,' Don Carlos insisted, 'the clerk will proceed to read the resolution in public.'

'I read Christian books to your excellency's father,' Hernando lied, speaking out loud for all to hear, 'as he lay dying in a corsair chief's tent, before I risked my life to set him free.'

A murmur ran through the ranks of the onlookers, but Don Carlos's expression did not change. 'Keep your insolence for when you are in the lands of the Moors,' was his only reply.

Hernando managed to catch Rafaela just as she fainted. The bundle of papers crumpled in his hand as she fell into his arms.

'Thus resolves Don Ponce de Hervás, chief magistrate of the Royal Chancery of Granada, and head of the College of Arms.'

Hernando settled Rafaela into a chair on the gallery, splashed water on her face and gave her some to drink. He could not wait for her to recover completely, though, because he wanted to read the document properly. Don Ponce! Isabel's husband! The magistrate had thrown out his petition *ad limine*, without even bothering to consider it.

'A new Christian, as he himself has publicly declared on many occasions to the archbishopric of this city of Granada. His obstinate defence of the killings in Juviles of those pious Christians who became the martyrs of the Alpujarra amply demonstrates his adherence to the sect of Muhammad.'

Hernando remembered the first document he had sent to the archbishop in Granada, in which he had indeed tried to justify the murders committed by the outlaws and Moriscos in the Alpujarra. Why were all his enemies seemingly conspiring to persecute him now? Don Ponce, Gil Ulloa and the Duke of Monterreal's heir, brought up by a woman who hated him. Who else was left?

'The outline of events and circumstances by which the petitioner attempts to support his claim before this tribunal is nothing more than a gross and clumsy distortion of reality, and as such does not merit the slightest attention.'

Hernando recalled the promises made by Don Pedro, Luna and Castillo. They had assured him everything could be faked. What use had that been to him? Don Ponce de Hervás had taken his revenge! He crushed the document in his fist.

'That cuckold whoreson!' he cried, and then fell back in his chair, defeated. All of a sudden he seemed weighed down by the years. Next to him, Rafaela stretched out her arm and rested her hand on his thigh. Her touch made him feel even worse. He looked down at his wife's long, slender fingers, the skin roughened by years of housework. He turned to look her in the face. She was still pale. He felt paralysed, as though he could not move. Rafaela knelt at his feet and laid her head in his lap. They stayed like that for some time: silent, their eyes closed, as if reluctant to open them to a reality over which they had no control.

The threat of expulsion cast its shadow over their home. From that day on, Hernando paid closer attention to Rafaela's movements around the house, her conversations with the children. He could hear her crying when she was alone. One night, when he took her in his arms, she pushed him away.

'Leave me, I beg you,' she said as he started to caress her.

'Now more than ever, we need to be united, Rafaela.'

'No, for the love of God!' she sobbed.

'But—'

'What if I become pregnant? Have you thought of that? What would we do with another child?' she murmured bitterly. 'Only to see you expelled in a few months' time, and having to leave me here pregnant?'

Soon after this Hernando, ashen-faced and prematurely aged, decided to make one last effort: he would go to Granada, talk to Don Pedro and the others – to the archbishop himself if necessary.

The next morning he told Miguel of his decision. As soon as he had learnt of the failure of his master's petition, the groom had moved into their house in Córdoba, but Hernando had not heard him telling any of his stories, even to the children. The little ones could sense that something awful was about to happen, and went around sadly and silently. That morning, Miguel opened the doors for him to ride out on one of the colts, a fast, strong young animal. Hernando was ready to gallop all the way to Granada and ruin the horse's health if necessary. As it was, he got no further than the street outside his house.

'Where do you think you're going?' one of Gil's soldiers said, stepping in front of him.

'To Granada,' Hernando replied, reining in his horse. 'To see the archbishop.'

'On whose authority?'

Hernando handed him the safe conduct. The soldier glanced at it dismissively. 'You don't even know how to read!' Hernando felt like shouting at him. Instead he tried to explain: 'It's a permit signed by the archbishop of—'

'It's not valid,' the soldier cut in, tearing it up in front of him.

'What are you doing?' It was his last hope! Hernando could feel his blood boil. 'You dog!'

Hernando instinctively spurred the horse at the man, and then leapt off to pick up the pieces of the document. Before he had even touched the ground, the other soldier was threatening him with his sword.

'Just try it!' the soldier challenged him.

Hernando wavered. The first soldier had recovered from the horse's charge and was standing alongside him, also with a drawn sword. The colt was tugging at its reins. Hernando realized there was nothing to be done.

'I only . . . I only wanted to pick up the pieces . . .'

'I've already told you; it's no use to you. You are not to leave Córdoba.' He trampled on the archbishop's safe conduct.

'Go back inside,' the other soldier ordered him, waving his sword in the direction of the house.

Hernando walked slowly back, leading the horse. Miguel was waiting for him by the still-open doors. He had seen the whole thing.

Hernando tried to send a letter to Granada but could not find a way to do so. All the muleteers from Valencia had been expelled; so too had the ones from Castile, La Mancha and Extremadura. The mule-drivers in the other kingdoms were forbidden to make any journeys.

'They stop and search me whenever I leave the house,' a sorrowful Miguel confessed. 'And Rafaela is followed all the time. It's impossible . . .'

'Why don't they get in touch with me?' Hernando complained out loud. There was a note of desperation in his voice. 'They must know my petition was rejected.'

'No one can come anywhere near the house without passing through the cordon of the magistrate's men,' Miguel explained, trying to calm him. 'They might have tried and been turned back.'

Hernando knew that neither Don Pedro nor any of the translators would dare come to Córdoba in person. He was aware that the year before a book had been published, entitled *The Antiquity and Excellences of Granada*. In it the lineage of the Granada Venegas family was outlined, claiming that its members could trace their Christian roots back to the time of the Goths. And they were one of the most important families in the Muslim nobility! How ironic! The book, which had escaped the royal censorship, maintained that following the capture of Granada by the Catholic monarchs, Don Pedro's ancestor Cidiyaya had seen a vision of Jesus Christ in the form of a miraculous cross in mid-air. The vision had called upon him to embrace the religion of his Goth forefathers. The Granada Venegas family renounced the Nasrid *wa la galib ilallah* ('There is no victor but God'), which until then had been their motto, and instead substituted the extremely Christian '*Servire Deo regnare est*'. Who was going to call into question the purity of the blood of a family that, like Saint Paul, had been singled out by a divine hand?

'They have already ensured their salvation,' Hernando muttered. 'Why should they be worried about a simple Morisco like me?'

Hernando and his family had run out of money. Their larder was bare: the tenant farmers did not bring any provisions, and Rafaela was finding it difficult to buy food. Nobody would offer her credit, neither the Christians nor the Moriscos. And yet these daily hardships and the fact that her children were going hungry seemed to have given her the strength her husband increasingly lacked.

'Sell the horses. At any price!' Hernando ordered Miguel one day, after hearing Muqla complain in tears that he was hungry.

'I've already tried,' the groom replied to his surprise. 'No one will buy them. A dealer whose word I trust has told me I wouldn't even be able to sell them for a handful of coppers. The Duke of Monterreal has forbidden it. Nobody wants to get into difficulties with a councillor and a Spanish grandee.'

Hernando shook his head dejectedly. 'Perhaps they'll recover their value once all this is over,' he said to console himself. 'Then Rafaela will be able to sell them at a fair price.'

'I doubt it,' said the other man. Hernando spread his palms in a gesture of helplessness. What further misfortunes could befall them?

Miguel went on: 'My lord, we have not been able to pay for the straw or the barley, the blacksmith or the saddler for some time now. And we can't pay the wages of the day labourers and the grooms. The day you're no longer here – if not before – all our debtors will come running, and a woman alone . . . well, you can imagine what will happen.'

Hernando did not reply. What could he do? How were they going to survive?

Miguel looked away. How did his master think he was keeping the farms and the horses going if not by getting into debt? It was Hernando himself who had ordered him to transfer the horses in the stables out to the stud, because they could not feed them any more.

They tried to sell the furniture and Hernando's books for whatever they could get in a Córdoba that had become one vast market place. Thousands of Morisco families were trying to auction off their possessions in the streets, surrounded by old Christians who amused themselves by underbidding each other. They laughed at men and women who had to contain their anger while they waited to see if any Christian would buy a piece of furniture they had bought with so much effort and hope a few years earlier, or beds where they had slept and dreamt of a better life. The Morisco artisans and merchants, cobblers and food-sellers begged their Christian competitors to buy their tools and machinery. Not a single Christian even turned up to look at the books and furniture Hernando brought out of his house, which Rafaela and the children kept a close eye on so that at least they would not be stolen.

One night in despair Hernando went to try to find Pablo Coca. He was hoping he might at least win something at gambling, but his old friend was dead. As a last resort, even though he did not have a permit, Miguel went on to the streets to beg. The soldiers on guard outside the house laughed and joked when they saw him return each evening hopping along on his crutches with a few rotten vegetables stuffed into the satchel on his back. For his part, Hernando tried every day to gain an audience with the bishop, the dean, or any of the prebends who were part of the Córdoba cathedral council. The bishop could save him if he endorsed the fact that he was a Christian: after all, he had done a lot of work for them, hadn't he?

He stood waiting for days in the courtyard at the entrance to the great building, together with many other Moriscos who had gathered for the same reason.

Day after day the cathedral attendants snapped at them: 'You won't get anyone to see you.'

Hernando knew this was true, that none of the priests who passed by would pay the Moriscos the slightest attention. Some looked straight through them; others scurried across the courtyard to avoid them. But what else could he do apart from wait for a show of the mercy that the Christians were so proud of? He could not think of any other solution. There was none! Rumours about the date for the expulsion grew more fervent day by day, and unless he received the backing of the Church, Hernando was condemned to leave Spain with Amin and Laila.

What would happen to the rest of his family? That was the question he asked himself every night as he returned crestfallen to his house, piling up in the doorway the same pieces of furniture and the same books he had taken out that morning with Rafaela's help.

His children waited for him as if by his mere presence he could resolve all the problems they had faced during the long, tedious day of trying in vain to sell their belongings. Hernando forced himself to smile and allow them to rush into his arms. He longed to break down in tears, but forced himself instead to utter words of encouragement and affection, and to listen closely to the urgent, innocent tales they gabbled to him. The older ones must know what was going on, he thought to himself amid all the disruption; they could not escape the tension and fraught atmosphere that filled the entire city, and yet they probably had little idea of the consequences of the expulsion decree for a family such as theirs. They all waited anxiously for whatever scraps Miguel had managed to beg for supper; then when the children were asleep and Miguel had discreetly left them to themselves, Hernando and Rafaela talked over the situation. Neither of them dared say what they really thought.

'I'll see someone tomorrow,' Hernando assured her.

'Of course you will,' Rafaela replied, feeling for his hand.

The next day dawned, and they once more dragged furniture and books out into the street. Clustered round their mother, the children watched the two men set off: Miguel to beg, Hernando heading for the bishop's palace.

'By the nails of the Holy Cross, help me!'

Hernando sprang forward from the crowd of Moriscos and knelt on the ground as the cathedral dean went by. The prebend stopped and looked down at him. He could tell by Hernando's clothes who he was; his problems with the city council were well known.

'You are the one who sought to excuse the deaths of our martyrs in the Alpujarra, aren't you? You're the son of a heretic!' the dean said dismissively.

Hernando crawled on his knees with arms outstretched to try to get closer to the church official. The man drew back in horror. The cathedral attendants came running over.

'I . . .' is all Hernando managed to say before they grabbed him under the arms and pushed him back into the crowd.

'Why don't you ask your false prophet for help?' he heard the dean shout behind him. 'Why don't you all try that? Heretics!'

67

ON SUNDAY 17 January 1610, the feast day of Saint Anthony, the decree expelling the Moriscos of Murcia, Granada, Jaén, Andalusia and the town of Hornachos was published and proclaimed. The King forbade the new Christians to take any money, gold or silver, jewels or bills of exchange out of the country, apart from what was needed for their journey to the port of Seville (for the Moriscos of Córdoba) and the cost of their sea transport, which they themselves had to pay. The wealthier deportees were supposed to help those without means. After selling what they could of their possessions and tools of their trades for next to nothing, the Moriscos rushed to buy any lightweight goods they could find – cloths, silks, or spices – at inflated prices.

Hernando and his family were in their kitchen. Rafaela was trying to scrape the mould off some bits of unleavened bread, while he tried to find a way to tell his sons and daughters what would happen to them now that the expulsion was imminent.

'Children . . .'

His voice failed him. He looked at each of them in turn: Amin, Laila, Muqla, Musa and Salma. He tried again to speak, but the tension of the past few months proved too much for him. He buried his face in his hands and burst into tears. For a few moments none of the others moved: the children stared terrified at their weeping father. Laila and little Salma began to cry as well. Miguel struggled to his feet and made as though to take the two youngest out of the room.

'No,' Rafaela stopped him. She looked exhausted, but her voice was calm. 'Sit down, all of you. You need to know', she went on once Miguel had collapsed into his chair again, 'that in a little while your father, Amin and Laila will be leaving Córdoba. The rest of you will be staying here, with me.'

Rafaela reached deep inside herself to be able to raise a smile. Unable to understand what was going on, Salma smiled as well.

'When will they be back?' asked little Musa.

Hernando finally looked up and caught Rafaela's eye.

'It's going to be a very long journey,' she told her son. 'They're travelling to somewhere far, far away . . .'

'Mother?' The voice of their eldest son broke the silence that had followed her words. Amin had listened closely to the proclamation and understood what it meant. He knew they were being expelled from Spain, and that this was not a journey they could come back from. 'If the case should arise', the crier had proclaimed, 'that for whatever reason they do not carry out this order and are found in my realms and dominions beyond said date, they will face the pain of death and confiscation of all their possessions. They will be so punished for this simple fact without any possibility of trial, sentence, or declaration.' They would be killed if they came back! He had understood perfectly: any Christian had the right to kill them if they returned, without the need for any trial or even any explanation. 'Why can't you come with us: you, Uncle Miguel and the little ones?'

'That's right! We'll all go!' Musa agreed.

Rafaela sighed, touched by her little boy's innocence. How could she explain it to them? She looked to her husband for help, but he was still sitting in silence, staring into space, almost as though he was not there.

'Because that is what God has decided,' she told Amin.

'No! It was the King!' Laila contradicted her.

'No!' They all turned to stare at Hernando. 'It was God, as your mother says.'

Rafaela thanked him with a smile.

'Children,' Hernando went on, recovering his composure, 'God has decided we must go our separate ways. You little ones are to stay here in Córdoba with your mother and Uncle Miguel. The older ones will come with me to Barbary. Let us all pray,' he said, staring at Rafaela. 'Let us pray to the God of Abraham, the God who unites us, that one day in His kindness and mercy He allows us all to be together again. And pray to the Virgin Mary; always commend yourselves to her in your prayers.'

As he finished speaking he felt Muqla's blue eyes on him. The boy was only five, but seemed to understand.

As dusk fell that afternoon he sat with Rafaela by the fountain in the centre of their courtyard. When the stars came out, he called the two eldest children over to explain further about the separation.

'The Christians will not allow your mother, who is an old Christian, or your brother and sister who are younger than six, to go with us to Barbary. They think any children aged more than six cannot be saved for Christianity and must therefore be expelled with their parents. That is why we are being split up.'

'Let's all run away together!' Amin insisted with tears in his eyes. 'Come with us, Mother,' he begged her.

'Your mother's brother, the magistrate, will never allow it,' said Hernando. 'Oh, my son, there are things you cannot understand.'

Amin said no more. Trying to hold back his tears because he was the eldest, he nevertheless went over to his mother so that she could comfort him. Laila had sat at her feet. Hernando looked at the three of them: Rafaela took her boy's hand and stroked her daughter's hair. It was a moment to treasure. How many similar ones had he missed over the years by being shut in his library studying, writing, fighting for the peaceful co-existence of the two warring religions? All at once he recalled the lullabies his mother sang on the rare occasions when she could openly show him her love. He started to sing the first notes. Surprised, Amin and Laila looked up at him; Rafaela tried to stop her lips quivering. Hernando smiled at his children and went on singing the lullabies, as the water splashed softly from the fountain.

Later, after they had got the children to bed, they sat there quietly, trying to hear each other's breathing.

'I'll make sure you get enough money,' Hernando promised after a lengthy silence. Rafaela was about to say something, but he cut her short with a gesture. 'Our lands and this house will become the property of the King: you heard what the crier said. The horses will be seized to pay our debts. That's all we have, and you will be here with three children to feed.' The fact of saying it like that, out loud, made it more real, more tangible and more terrible.

Rafaela sighed. She could not allow Hernando to lose heart now. 'I'll manage,' she whispered, snuggling close to him. 'How can you send me money? It will be difficult enough for you as it is trying to get by with our two eldest. What do you intend to do? Train horses? At your age?'

'You mean you think I couldn't do it?' Hernando had stiffened, but tried to say the words lightly; Rafaela responded with a strained smile. 'No. I don't think I'll work with horses. Those small Arab ponies: they might be fine for the desert, but they're nothing like our Spanish thoroughbreds. I know classical Arabic and how to write it, Rafaela. I think I can do it very well, especially if our children's lives are at stake . . . and yours. God will guide my pen, I'm sure of it. Muslims hold scribes in high esteem.'

Rafaela was at the end of her tether. She had spent the whole day putting a brave face on things for the children's sake. Now in the darkness of the night she gave vent to her anguish. 'But they kill everyone who reaches Barbary! And anyone they don't murder, they force to work in the fields! How do you imagine—?'

Hernando again motioned for her to be quiet. 'That is in the cities controlled by the corsairs, or on the Barbary coast. But I know the Moriscos who reach Morocco are well treated. It is a backward kingdom, and the King has understood that the knowledge the people from al-Andalus bring can be of help to him. I'll find work at the court, and perhaps one day you . . .'

Rafaela stirred restlessly. He knew what she was thinking: they had only rarely spoken of their beliefs, their different religions. The thought of having to live in a Muslim country terrified her.

'Don't go on,' Rafaela interrupted him. 'I've never interfered with your beliefs, Hernando, even when you taught them to our children. Don't ask me to renounce mine. You already know that when you are no longer here, your children will be brought up in the Christian faith.'

'All I ask of you', Hernando said, 'is that when Muqla comes of age, you give him the copy of the Koran I've made. I'll hide it in a safe place until that day.'

'By then, he'll be a Christian, Hernando,' his wife murmured.

'He'll still be Muqla, the boy with blue eyes. He'll know what to do. Promise me.'

Rafaela didn't answer.

'Promise me,' Hernando insisted.

She sealed her promise with a kiss.

From the moment that the two of them accepted there was nothing to be done about the situation, the days went by in a strange sense of harmony. As always, Hernando went on visiting the mosque to pray in secret. Something had changed, though. He no longer tried to achieve communion with Fátima: now, his prayers called on God to come to the aid of Rafaela and the children who had to stay in Córdoba. He had thought of going to Tetuan with Amin and Laila, finding Fátima and asking her for help. He was even about to send a message to Ephraim, but something the Jew had said stopped him: they will kill you. What if they killed his children too?

Tetuan had not received the Moriscos kindly: Shamir and Francisco would doubtless be on their guard against this massive influx. Hernando's stomach churned at the mere thought of his two little ones being cut to pieces by corsairs.

He walked round the mosque. He decided that he should hide his priceless Koran among the magic forest of columns where the echo of true believers would always be heard. One day he was sure little Muqla would find it. But where could he conceal the holy book?

'Have you gone mad?' Miguel exclaimed when he heard his plan.

'It's not madness,' Hernando replied, with such determination that the cripple had no doubts he was being entirely serious. 'It will be the best story you've ever told. I need you . . . and Amin.'

'You want to get the boy mixed up in this?'

'It's his duty.'

'You do realize that if we are found out, the Inquisition will burn us alive?' said Miguel.

Hernando nodded.

That same morning, the three of them headed for the mosque. Hernando was carrying a strong iron bar and a mallet, hidden in his clothes. Amin was clutching the unbound leaves of the Koran to his chest under his tunic. Miguel hopped along beside them on his crutches. Father and son stood reverentially outside the chapel dedicated to Saint Peter, which had replaced the mihrab, pretending to pray. Miguel was some way behind them, doing the same between the Royal Chapel and the one dedicated to Villaviciosa. Time went by, and Hernando could feel the hand holding his tools becoming covered in sweat. He stared straight ahead of him towards the chapel where he had so often prayed to his own God. Most of the front was blocked by a rough masonry wall built in the interstices of the mosque's columns. At one end of this wall, exactly opposite the mihrab, the chapel was enclosed behind two grilles that reached the capitals. Behind the wall and the grille lay the sarcophagus of Don Alfonso Fernández de Montemayor, a former governor of the frontier provinces. It was a big, simple sepulchre of white marble, with no carving or decoration apart from a raised band across the top. Half the sarcophagus was visible beyond the grille; the other half was hidden from view behind the wall. Hernando turned to Amin several times, but the boy did not look at all nervous. He stood quietly beside him, straight, solemn-looking and proud as he muttered the Lord's Prayer and Hail Marys. Was this really madness? thought Hernando. There were so many people . . .

He did not have long to ask himself this, because as usual the attendant of San Pedro's chapel came up to unlock the grille and prepare for mass. Hernando hesitated. When he looked round he saw Miguel smiling at him, encouraging him to take the plunge. Amin nudged him with his shoulder to indicate that the priest had opened the grille. Hernando nodded to Miguel.

'God!' came the cry, resonating throughout the mosque. People began to turn round and saw a cripple dancing excitedly on his crutches. 'He was here! I saw him!'

Some of the worshippers crowded round Miguel. He went on shouting that he had seen a vision. Hernando glanced first at him, and then at the chapel grille. Alarmed, the priest had emerged and stood by the iron rails.

'His merciful face appeared over a white dove!' Miguel was shouting.

Hernando could not stop himself smiling. As ever, he was amazed at people's credulity. In front of him, an old woman fell to her knees and crossed herself.

'Yes! I see him! I can see him too!'

Several others joined in, drowning out Miguel's voice. Many dropped to their knees and pointed to the dome above the high altar, in the opposite direction to the chapel, where Miguel was still proclaiming that he had seen a white dove. The priest ran towards them, joining a group of other clergy, their surplices fluttering as they ran.

'Now,' Hernando whispered to his son.

It took only a few strides for them to get inside the chapel. Hernando went to the head of the sarcophagus, which was hidden from view. As he thought he had noticed the day before, the sarcophagus was not sealed, but when he pulled out the iron bar and wedged it under the lid, it seemed impossible to lift. Wrapping the end of the bar in his tunic to muffle the sound, he hit it with the mallet. Flakes of marble came off the lid, but eventually he succeeded in pushing the bar far enough inside to make a lever. It was too heavy: he would never do it. He could hear the din outside the chapel, and realized just how old he was: fifty-six years old. He was an old man, and yet he thought he could lift the enormous, weighty lid on a marble sarcophagus. Amin was waiting patiently by his side, the sheaves of paper in his hand. Hernando was convinced he would never do it.

'Allah is great!' he muttered.

He pushed down as hard as he could, but the lid would not budge. Amin watched his father struggle. 'Allah is great,' he also whispered. He threw himself on the lever alongside his father.

'You who give strength,' Hernando prayed, 'O Strong and Constant One, help us now!'

The lid was raised a finger's breadth.

'Push the sheets of paper in!' he urged his son through gritted teeth, his face purple from the effort.

Still pressing down on the lever, Amin started to push small bundles of paper through the gap; there was no way he could get the entire book in at once.

'Keep going!' Hernando encouraged him. 'Quickly!'

There were still a few pages left. The only noise behind them was now coming from Miguel, who was ranting on as loudly as he could.

'Father!' Hernando suddenly heard from close to the chapel grille.

Hernando almost let go of the bar. Amin stopped pushing pages inside. It was Rafaela's voice!

'Father!' they heard again at the entrance to the chapel.

Rafaela fell to her knees in front of the priest as he made his way back to the chapel. She gripped the hem of his cassock firmly to hold him up. 'Save my husband and children from deportation!' she begged. Hernando motioned for Amin to hurry. There were only a few pages left. The boy's hands were trembling so much he could not get the last sheets into the gap. 'They are good Christians!' Rafaela pleaded.

'What are you talking about, woman?'

The priest tried to push past her, but Rafaela flung herself at his feet and kissed them.

'In God's name!' she sobbed. 'Save them!'

Rafaela tried to prevent the priest moving, until eventually he tugged himself free of her and slipped inside the chapel. She ran after him, closing her eyes as soon as she was beyond the grille.

'What are you doing here?'

Rafaela could feel her stomach clench as she opened her eyes again: she was greeted with the sight of Hernando and Amin kneeling by the altar, praying to the painting hanging over it at the head of the sarcophagus. Hernando was trying to stuff his tools back under his clothing, while with the other hand he swept the chips of marble that had fallen to the floor back under the sarcophagus. Amin saw what he was doing and imitated him.

'What does this mean?' the priest insisted.

'They are good Christians,' Rafaela repeated behind him.

Hernando rose to his feet. 'Father,' he began, pushing the last bit of marble away with his foot. 'We were praying for God to intercede on our behalf. We do not deserve to be expelled. We, that is, my children and I—'

'That's not my problem,' the priest answered drily, casting a rapid eye over the altar to make sure nothing had been stolen. 'Now get out of here,' he snapped when he was satisfied nothing was missing.

The three of them walked out. When they had gone a few paces, Hernando realized he was trembling. He closed his eyes tight, took a deep breath, and tried to regain control of himself. When he opened his eyes again, he saw his wife staring at him.

'Thank you,' he whispered. 'How did you know what I was going to do?'

'Miguel thought his help might not be enough, so he asked me to come as well.'

Inside the San Pedro chapel, the priest trod on some of the marble dust on the floor. He muttered a curse about filthy Moriscos. Outside, surrounded by an ever-increasing crowd of the faithful, some on their knees, others praying and ceaselessly crossing themselves, Miguel was continuing with his endless story, jerking his head towards where he had seen the tremendous flaming sword Christ was wielding to celebrate the expulsion of heretics from Christian lands. As soon as he saw Hernando, Rafaela and Amin, he fell to the floor as though he had fainted. Curled up in a ball on the ground, he went on with his pantomime, convulsing violently all the while.

They crossed the mosque towards the Patio de los Naranjos. The Christians might expel them from Spain and the lands where they had lived for more than eight centuries, but in front of the mihrab of the Córdoba mosque, the Word revealed in honour of the one God was still at work.

As soon as they had emerged through the Perdón gate, Rafaela came to a halt, as if she wanted to say something.

'You know where it is hidden,' her husband forestalled her.

'But how is Muqla going to recover it?'

'God will find a way,' he said, taking her by the arm and leading her affectionately back to their home. 'Now the Word is where it should remain until our son takes over my work.'

In mid-afternoon, Miguel reappeared. 'When I came round in the sacristy,' he explained, winking broadly at them, 'I told them I couldn't remember a thing.'

'And?' asked Hernando.

'And they went crazy. They repeated everything I told them back to me. Those priests have so little imagination! Even though they had heard my story, they could not get it straight.

They said I had seen a golden sword! I almost corrected them and told them it was a flaming sword, but that would have given me away. Gold is all they can think of! But they did give me some good wine to revive me and to see if I remembered anything.'

'Thank you, Miguel.' Hernando was going to tell him that the next time he should not say anything to Rafaela, but then he checked himself. What next time? he said to himself sadly. 'Thank you,' he repeated.

As if God wanted to reward them for what they had done, one night Miguel appeared with half a goat, fresh vegetables, oil, and small quantities of spices, herbs, salt, pepper and some white bread.

'What ... Where did you get all this?' Hernando asked, rummaging in the satchel Miguel carried on his back.

Rafaela and the children also crowded round.

'It looks as if fickle fortune has smiled on us for once,' said Miguel.

The deportees needed a means of transport for the goods they were allowed to take with them, as well as for their wives, children and old people on what was going to be a long journey. Few of the almost four thousand muleteers who used to roam the trails of Spain remained; most had already been expelled, and those still in the country were hiding in their houses waiting to leave, and had sold the mules and donkeys they could not take with them.

'People are offering a fortune for just one mule,' Miguel explained, his eyes fixed on Rafaela and the children as they ran to the kitchen with the food.

While he was begging, Miguel had seen several men jostling each other to hire a simple mule for the journey. And they had sixteen good horses! They were big, strong animals, capable of carrying a lot more weight than a donkey or mule.

'They've never been beasts of burden,' Hernando said doubtfully.

'They could be, though, by God they could!'

'They'll buck and kick,' objected Hernando.

'I won't feed them. I'll keep them on water for a few days, and then if they buck . . .'

'I'm not sure.' Hernando had a picture of his magnificent steeds laden down with goods and with two or three people on their backs, struggling in the midst of a flood of people that would be much bigger than the one that had set out from Granada at the end of the war in the Alpujarra. 'I'm not sure,' he repeated.

'Well, I am,' said Miguel. 'I've already done the deals. Some people are willing to pay up to sixty reales per day, there and back. We'll make many ducats out of this.'

Still not convinced, Hernando stared at the other man.

'I've already settled the debts we had with our suppliers and hired people to help on the journey. When the horses arrive back from Seville, there'll be no debts to pay off, so Rafaela will be able to sell them – if the duke allows her to. She'll also have money while all this is going on, and you'll have enough for the journey and for what you're permitted to take out of Spain.'

Hernando thought it over, yielded to his friend's arguments, and finally slapped him on the back. 'I've been thanking you a lot recently,' he said.

'Do you remember when you found me at the feet of Volador in the Potro tavern?' Hernando nodded. 'Ever since that day, you have nothing to thank me for . . . Still, I like to hear you say it!' he added, smiling at the emotion his lord and friend was showing.

68

LESS THAN a month after the expulsion of the Moriscos of al-Andalus had been proclaimed, the ones living in Córdoba were forced to leave the city. The interval was so brief there had been little chance of any appeal to the King to modify the ruling. Worse still, the city council agreed not to approach His Majesty with any demand for clemency towards the new Christians: the order was to be carried out to the letter.

The strength of character Rafaela had shown throughout the wait disappeared the day before the one the authorities had chosen for the expulsion. She broke down in despair. She no longer masked her grief from the children, and they soon were weeping alongside her. Contrary to what he had said a few days before, Hernando now told the youngest a lie: they would soon be back, he assured them; they were only going on a short journey. Almost at once he had to turn away so that they would not see him crying as hard as their mother. He encouraged them to play games, or told them stories they had first heard from Miguel. He gave little Muqla the small waxed tablet to write on. Now five, the boy drew a delicate *alif* with his stick, copying the way he had seen his brother do it. Why are you doing this, O God? Hernando asked himself before he rubbed the letter out.

After he had prepared a bundle with the few belongings they were permitted to take with them, the last thing Hernando did was to reach inside the hiding place behind the false partition and take out the hand of Fátima and the copy of the gospel of

Barnabas he had found in the old minaret in the duke's palace. He stuffed the gospel into the bag (he planned to hide it under the saddle blanket of one of their mounts, as they used to do with the paper they received from Xátiva), and was about to do the same with the hand of Fátima when he raised it to his lips and kissed it. Although he had done the same many times before, this time he pressed his lips to it as if he never wanted to let go.

That night, when the two of them were in bed together and Rafaela's tears had dried up, they let the hours go by in silence, as though trying to absorb all the memories of that moment: scents; the night-time creaking of the wooden floors of their house; the water splashing in the fountain down below in the courtyard; an occasional cry from the streets that disturbed the city quiet; the regular breathing of their children they thought they could still hear in the distance.

Rafaela pressed herself against her husband. She refused to think that this would be the last night they would share this bed, that from now on she would have to sleep alone. She spoke almost without thinking: 'Take me,' she said.

'But . . .' Hernando protested, ruffling her hair.

'One last time,' she whispered.

Hernando turned to face her. She had sat up in the bed, and to his surprise, began to take off her nightshift, showing him her full breasts. Then she lay down again, all shyness gone.

'I'm here for you. No man will ever see me the way you see me now.'

Hernando kissed her on the lips, at first gently, and then was carried away with a passion he had not felt for many months. Rafaela drew him to her, as if she wanted to keep him there for ever.

After they had made love, they remained entwined until dawn. Neither of them could sleep.

The sound of shouting in the street and banging on their front door made the whole family fall silent. They had just finished breakfast and were all gathered in the kitchen. Piled in the corner were the bundles of those who had to leave. Hernando had chosen to take very little for such a long journey, Rafaela thought to herself when she surveyed the small trunk and the cloth bundles. She was determined not to burst into tears again. Before she could turn her attention back to the family, Amin and Laila had thrown themselves on her, clinging to her waist as if they would not allow anyone to part them.

Choking with emotion, words and tears came tumbling out. Then they heard fresh banging at the door.

'Open in the name of the King!'

Little Muqla was the only one who seemed unaffected: his blue eyes stared at his father's face while the two smallest children also burst into tears. Rafaela succumbed once more, and wept as well, clutching her children to her.

'We have to go,' said Hernando after clearing his throat and lowering his gaze to avoid Muqla's insistent stare. Nobody paid him any attention. 'Come on,' he insisted, trying to pull the two eldest from their mother's side.

He only succeeded when Rafaela pushed them away. Hernando lifted the trunk and one of the bundles on to his back; Amin and Laila took the others. The narrow passageway outside the house offered a desolate spectacle: the Córdoban militias had spread out through each of the parishes according to the instructions of the church officials, and were going from house to house rounding up all the named Moriscos. Outside the house, behind Gil Ulloa and his soldiers, stood a long line of deportees weighed down by all they were carrying. They crowded round, waiting for Hernando and his children to join the column before it set off for the next dwelling.

'Hernando Ruiz, a new Christian from Juviles, and his children Juan and Rosa, who are older than six.'

These words were spoken by a clerk who accompanied Gil and his soldiers with the parish census in his hands. The Santa María priest stood beside him.

Hernando acknowledged the call, checking that his children were not trying to rush back into their mother's arms. Rafaela was standing in the doorway, but Amin and Laila could not take their eyes off the column of Moriscos being deported. They stood silently in a submissive, humiliated line behind the soldiers.

'Go and join the others!' Gil ordered them.

Hernando turned back towards Rafaela. After their last night together they had nothing more to say. He embraced the three little ones who were staying with her. My children! he thought as he kissed them over and over with aching heart.

'Get moving!' insisted the official.

His eyes red with tears, Hernando clenched his teeth: there were no words with which he could say goodbye to his family. He was about to obey the order when Rafaela leapt on him, flung her arms round his neck and kissed him on the mouth. The chest and bundle he was carrying fell to the ground. Her kiss was so passionate it infuriated her brother Gil. The soldiers looked on, some of them shook their heads, feeling sorry for their captain: to see his sister, a true Christian, kissing a Moor that avidly. And in public too!

Gil Ulloa went up to the couple and tried in vain to push them apart. Several of the soldiers rushed to help him and started to rain blows on Hernando. He tried to turn to face them, but the blows only fell more heavily still. Rafaela collapsed wailing to the floor. Amin went to his father's aid and kicked one of the soldiers.

Overpowered and bleeding from the nose, Hernando was pushed in front of Gil Ulloa for him to strike the final blow. Amin also had a bloody lip.

'Moorish dog!' Gil growled, punching him as hard as he could in the face.

Rafaela was back on her feet by now. She rushed to defend her husband, but Gil pushed her away.

'Requisition that house in the King's name!' he ordered the scribe.

Still dazed, Hernando attempted to protest, but the soldiers struck him again, then dragged him away to join the group of Moriscos who had witnessed the scene. Amin and Laila were forced to follow him. Gil gave the order to move off, and the deportees started on their way again. Hernando and his children picked up their things as the Moriscos, escorted by the squad of soldiers, passed in front of them.

'My God! No!' shrieked Rafaela as her husband walked away. 'I love you, Hernando!'

In the midst of the other Muslim faithful, Hernando tried to reply, but the crush of people bore him away before he could say a thing. It was impossible for him even to turn round. Father and children were swept away by the crowd.

By the end of the morning, some ten thousand Córdoban Moriscos had been rounded up on the outskirts of the city in the Campo de la Verdad on the far side of the Roman bridge. The local militias kept a close watch on them. Miguel was there too, his mule and horses weighed down with the Moriscos' possessions. He wanted to oversee the arrangements he had made for the horses: he would be coming back from Seville with the animals and the money.

'Why not?' Fátima allowed herself to ask the question out loud in mid-air. She was alone in the hall. 'Why not?' she mused again, a delicious shiver running down her spine. Ephraim had left the palace some time earlier after giving her the latest news from Córdoba. When the first Moriscos from Valencia started to arrive in Barbary, she had urged him to find out what would happen to Ibn Hamid, and the Jew moved quickly to enquire among commercial networks that cared nothing for religion.

He had returned with the news she had been anxious to hear: that the Moriscos of Córdoba were also to be expelled, and Hernando would soon be deported from the port of Seville. There was nothing Hernando could do to prevent it. Ephraim had learnt that Hernando Ruiz had made many enemies among the most prominent people in Córdoba and in Granada, where his petition to become a noble had failed. His Christian wife was to stay in Spain with the children under six.

It was when the Jew left the room that the idea occurred to Fátima. She looked round the ample hall. The inlaid furniture, the cushions and pillows, the columns, marble floor and carpets spread over it, the lamps . . . it all appeared to her in a new light, and reinforced her determination. For some time now, she had been drowning in all this wealth: Abdul and Shamir had been captured by a Spanish fleet, which had set a trap for them as they tried to board a merchant ship that had been deliberately put there as bait. How could they have fallen for such a trick? Perhaps they had become overconfident? The sailors from a pinnace that had managed to escape brought confused and contradictory versions of what had happened. Some said the two men were dead, others that they had been captured; one even claimed he had seen them dive into the sea. Then yet another person claimed they had been sent to the galleys, but no one could prove this with any certainty. Fátima shed tears over her sons' fate, although she had to admit that their relationship had suffered after what had happened in Toga between the corsairs and Ibn Hamid.

Shamir's widow and children had lost no time in laying claim to the substantial inheritance he had left behind. The judges showed no hesitation in backing up their claims.

Fátima's links with Shamir's family were very distant. She was nothing more than the wife of their Christian half-brother. Shamir's parents-in-law soon gave her notice to quit the palace. What would she do after that? Live on the charity of Abdul's wife or that of one of her daughters?

There was another possibility. She had talked it over with Ephraim, who had first suggested it when he saw the predicament she was in. Without his help, Shamir's family would never know the extent of the investments he had made in the corsair's name throughout the Mediterranean. Fátima could use the money for her own purposes. The Jew himself had no wish to lose the control and the profits from all those businesses, of which he was sure that Shamir's relatives would want to deprive him. So Fátima could still be rich, although not in Tetuan, where nobody would believe her story of how she had come by such wealth.

Fátima walked round the room, lightly stroking the pieces of furniture with her fingertips. Without Abdul and Shamir she was alone, but at last she was completely free. There was nothing to keep her in Tetuan. Why not leave there for ever? Ibn Hamid was going to be expelled from Spain, and his insipid Christian wife would have to stay behind. Who but God Himself could have sent her such a clear signal?

She went out into the courtyard and stood staring at the water in the fountain. She would soon be seeing it for the last time. Constantinople! That was where she would live! For once, she allowed herself to think of Ibn Hamid, something she had tried to avoid for many years now. He must be fifty-six years old by now, a year older than she was. What could he look like? How would the years have treated him? All at once her doubts vanished. Yes! She had to see him! Destiny, which had so cruelly separated them, was now offering her another chance. And that was something which Fátima, a woman who had suffered and killed, loved and hated, had no intention of letting pass her by.

'Call Ephraim!' she shouted to her slaves, her mind made up.

The Jew had told her the Moriscos would be deported from Seville. She had to get there before they were unloaded somewhere where they might fall into the hands of the Berbers. She had heard how the deportees from Valencia had been massacred. Those who managed to reach the port of Tetuan were not well received either: many people saw them as Christians who had been obliged to come to Barbary, and killed them. She had to reach Seville before he was put on board a ship! She needed a vessel that could then take them on to Constantinople. She needed papers to be able to search for him in the Spanish city. First though she had to settle her affairs. She would have to win over many people. Ephraim would look after everything. He always did. He always got what he wanted ... however much gold it cost.

'Where is Ephraim?' she howled.

Rafaela and the younger children were allowed to stay in the house until the magistrate Gil Ulloa returned from Seville and decided what to do with them. Throughout the following day, Rafaela watched as a clerk and a bailiff made a detailed list of all the objects and possessions left in their home.

'The edict . . .' Rafaela stammered when she saw the clerk rummaging in the chest where she kept her clothes. 'The edict states that only the property is to be handed over to the King. All the other things are mine.'

'The edict', the other man replied harshly, while the bailiff raised a white embroidered petticoat to the light with a lascivious gesture, 'gave the Moriscos the opportunity to take their belongings with them. Your husband did not do so, and therefore—'

'But those are my clothes!' Fátima protested.

'As I understand it, you came to your marriage without a dowry. Isn't that so?' the clerk asked, without turning towards Rafaela as he noted the petticoat on his list. The bailiff threw it on to the bed and bent to pick up the next item. 'You have no possessions,' he added. 'The city council or a magistrate will have to decide whom all this belongs to.'

'They are mine,' Rafaela insisted, but her voice was faint. She felt exhausted, overwhelmed by all that had happened.

At that moment the bailiff held aloft a delicate bodice, spreading his arms out wide in Rafaela's direction as though he were trying it on her breasts for size from the far side of the room.

Rafaela rushed out. The bailiff's cackle pursued her down the stairs and into the courtyard where her children were gathered.

'How could Our Lord allow these things to happen?' Rafaela asked herself time and again that night as she lay in bed staring up at the ceiling, her three children curled up on top of her. None of them had wanted to sleep in their own beds, and she had let them into hers. The hours went by as she stroked their backs and heads, twisting their hair around her fingers. That afternoon she had heard from a soldier who came to talk to the bailiff that the column of deportees had set off for Seville, hastened on their way by the jeers and insults of the people of Córdoba. She imagined Hernando, Amin and Laila among them, weighed down by their bundles. Perhaps the children could get a ride on a mule with Miguel; she knew that all the horses had been taken by other Moriscos. Her children! Her husband! What would become of them? On her lips she could still feel the passion of the last kiss she had given Hernando. Oblivious to her brother, the soldiers, and the dozens of Moriscos looking on, Rafaela had quivered like a young girl, her whole body trembling with despairing love until her brother had tugged her away. Where was the pity she had so often heard in the mouths of priests and pious Christians? Where was the forgiveness and compassion they preached all the time?

Little Salma, who was lying across her legs, stirred in her sleep and almost fell on to the floor. Struggling to an upright position, Rafaela lifted her up to her stomach and settled her between her two brothers.

What did the future hold for the poor little thing? The convent, which she herself had managed to avoid? A servant for some well-to-do family? A bawdy house? What about Muqla and Musa? She recalled the lewd look on the bailiff's face as he handled her clothes: that was the treatment she could look forward to. She was nothing more than the abandoned wife of a Morisco, and her children were the sons and daughters of a heretic. The whole of Córdoba was aware of it!

And yet in spite of everything she, Rafaela Ulloa, had decided to remain in these Christian lands, jealous of her faith and her beliefs. Now after less than a day her world was tumbling down around her. Where was the rest of her family? Her horses would be taken from her just as they planned to do with her clothes and furniture. How would they live then? She could not expect any help from her brothers and sisters: she had besmirched the family's honour. Would any Christian come to her aid?

She sobbed and held her children even more tightly. Muqla opened his blue eyes, and even though he was still half asleep, gazed up at her tenderly.

'Go back to sleep, my little one,' she whispered, relaxing the pressure and gently rocking him in her arms.

Gradually his breathing became steady once more. As she so often did, Rafaela sought consolation in prayer, but the prayers would not come. Pray to the Virgin, she had been told. Hernando believed in Mary. She had heard him talking to the children about the Virgin, explaining that Mary was the one thing that unified two religions at war with each other. Respect for her immaculate conception had survived the centuries undiminished among both Christians and Muslims.

'Mary,' Rafaela murmured in the night. 'God save and protect you . . .'

It was while she was whispering the prayer that her heart showed her the way: it was a decision as sudden as it was decisive. For the first time in days her lips widened in a smile and her eyes gave way to sleep.

Dawn the next day found Rafaela, with Salma in her arms and Musa and Muqla trotting beside her, walking across the Roman bridge with all those who went out each day to work in the fields. All she was taking with her was a basket with food and the money Miguel had given her, which she had managed to hide from the greedy clerk.

'Where are we going, Mother?' Muqla asked after they had been walking a good while.

'To find your father,' she replied, staring straight in front of her at the long road stretching ahead of them.

Mary would unite her family again, just as Hernando always said she did for the two religions, Rafaela decided.

The Arenal in Seville was a large stretch of land between the river Guadalquivir and the magnificent walls surrounding the city. At one end it stretched as far as the Gold tower on the riverbank. This was where all the work was done to maintain the city's important river port, the point of departure and arrival for the fleets to the Indies, the ships that brought all the riches the conquistadores had plundered back to the kingdom of Castile. Caulkers, carpenters, stevedores, boatmen, soldiers . . . normally, hundreds of men worked in the port or repaired and fitted out ships. But in February 1610, the Arenal was heavily guarded by soldiers stationed at each end and at the gates leading into the city, and had been turned into a prison for thousands of Morisco families waiting with all their possessions to be deported to Barbary. Some of them were rich, because no exceptions had been made either in Córdoba or in Seville when the royal edict had been executed. In their luxurious attire, these families did all they could to keep as far away as possible from the thousands of poor Moriscos. Hundreds of children aged under six had been left behind, in the hands of a Church obsessed with the idea of achieving something they had not succeeded in doing with their parents: converting them to Christianity. Bailiffs and soldiers prowled among the dejected crowds of people, searching for any hidden gold or coins the deportees might be carrying. They searched men, women, children, old people and the sick, rummaging among their clothes and possessions. They even unpicked the ropes the Moriscos were carrying to make sure there were no necklaces or jewels hidden among the strands.

Galleys, caravels, carracks and myriad other smaller vessels lay at anchor on the river, ready to take on board the close to twenty thousand Moriscos who had to leave Seville. Some of the ships were from the royal fleet, but most had been specially commissioned for this one-way trip. Unlike the Moriscos from Valencia, the ones from al-Andalus had to pay for their own deportation, and the ship owners smelt an opportunity in this gruesome affair: they charged more than double the normal rates.

On board one of these ships – a Catalan caravel with a square mainsail – which was anchored at some distance from the shore, Fátima stood by the gunwale and observed the crowds on the Arenal. How was she to find Hernando among so many people? She had heard that the deportees from Córdoba had arrived and were mixed in with those from Seville. The previous night she herself had seen the endless column snaking round the city walls down to the Arenal. Since first light, barges had begun to transport people, goods and possessions from the shore to the boats on the river. Fátima surveyed the grief-stricken faces of the Moriscos they were carrying: some of them seemed to be still wet with tears. Mothers whose children had been stolen from them; men forced to abandon dreams and years of effort to sustain homes and families; sick old men who had to be helped into the barges and then again into the larger ships. Others, though, appeared happy, as if they saw this as a liberation. Fátima did not recognize her husband among these first passengers, but she knew it was too soon for anyone from Córdoba to be boarding. During the voyage to Seville she had allowed her imagination to run riot. She saw Ibn Hamid rushing into her arms, swearing he had never forgotten her, declaring his eternal love. Then she checked herself: nigh on thirty years had gone by. She was no longer young, even though she knew she was still beautiful. Had she not earned the right to be happy? Fátima was lulled by a vision that filled her with hope: she and Ibn Hamid, together in Constantinople until the end of their days. Was that madness? Perhaps, but never had madness seemed to her so alluring. Now that she had reached her destination, she felt increasingly anxious. She had to find Hernando among this throng of desperate men and women who had lost everything and were facing an uncertain future.

'Tell the pilot to prepare a skiff for me to go ashore in,' Fátima ordered one of the three Nubian slaves Ephraim had bought for her. Her previous slaves, brought in by Shamir to protect her, had performed their task well; there was no reason that these new ones under her direct command should not do the same. 'Go on!' she shouted at one of them who was staring doubtfully at her. 'You can accompany me. No,' she changed her mind, thinking of the commotion that the three giant Negroes would cause. 'Tell the pilot to find four armed seamen to come with me.'

She had to get off the ship. She would only find Hernando if she could look directly among the crowds on the Arenal. She had the necessary papers and authorizations. As ever, Ephraim had done all she had asked, she reflected with a smile. The lady from Tetuan figured as the owner of the caravel, with permission to take her human cargo to Barbary. Nobody would cause her any trouble on the Arenal, she thought, but just in case – she felt for the purse full of gold coins she had hidden under her dress – she had enough money to bribe all the Christian soldiers patrolling the shore.

She slipped agilely into the skiff, and was soon seated on one of its benches, together with a servant woman and four Catalan seamen whom the pilot had placed at her disposal.

Once on shore, the seamen cleared a way for her, and Fátima began to go round the Arenal, fixing her big black eyes on anyone who stared at her with curiosity. What would her husband look like now?

Exhausted, defeated, Rafaela collapsed on to a tree stump by the side of the road to Seville. She set Salma and Musa down, but they kept on crying even though they had travelled the last part of the way in their mother's arms. Only five-year-old Muqla had withstood the ordeal in silence, as if he really understood the importance of their journey. But Rafaela could not go on. They had been walking for several days, trying to catch up with the deportees from Córdoba, who were only half a day ahead of them, and yet they were still behind them. Half a day! The two little ones could not go even half a league further. The slow progress exasperated Rafaela, although she sensed that the exiles were probably travelling equally slowly. She had thrown away the basket of food when she picked the two children up. With one on each arm she had tried to make more rapid progress, but now she too felt she could not go on. Her legs and arms were aching. Her feet were cut, and the muscles on her back seemed to be on the point of exploding. And still the little ones were wailing!

Time passed, with the empty fields silent all round her, and the children sobbing by her side. Rafaela stared at the horizon, imagining where Seville must be.

'Come on, Mother. Get up.' It was Muqla insisting, just as she buried her face in her hands. She shook her head. It was impossible!

'Get to your feet,' the boy repeated, tugging at her arm.

Rafaela tried to stand up, but her legs gave way as soon as she put any weight on them. She had to sit down once more.

'We'll just rest for a while,' she said, trying to reassure him. 'Then we'll set off again.'

She looked closely at him. His blue eyes shone brightly, but the rest of him – his clothes and his worn-out shoes looked as wretched as those worn by any of the street urchins begging in the streets of Córdoba. But those eyes of his . . . could it be that Hernando was right to put so much faith in this young boy?

'We've already rested a lot,' Muqla complained.

'I know.' Rafaela opened her arms wide for her son to seek shelter there. 'I know, my love,' she whispered in his ear when he came to her.

The rest did not help her recover. The winter cold seeped into her body, and instead of relaxing, her muscles contracted in painful spasms until they had completely seized up. The two little ones were playing happily in the grass of a nearby field. Muqla was keeping an eye on them, although he was also watching his mother, ready to renew their march as soon as he saw her get up from the tree stump.

They would never do it, sighed Rafaela. Tears were the only thing that came easily to her stiff body. They slid freely down her cheeks. Hernando and the older children would board a ship headed for Barbary. She would lose them for ever.

Her anguish made her forget her physical pain. Her body was racked with sobs. What would become of them? She was starting to feel faint when all of a sudden she heard a clamour in the distance. Muqla appeared as if from nowhere by her side, staring back along the path.

'They'll help us, Mother,' he encouraged her, feeling for her hand.

A long column of people and horses appeared in the distance. These were the Moriscos expelled from Castro del Río, Cañete and many other villages. They were also headed for Seville. Rafaela dried her tears, fought the pain in her body, and stood up. She hid with her children a few paces back from the path, and when the column passed in front of them and she could check there were no soldiers guarding them, she picked up the little ones and slipped in among the others. A few Moriscos looked enquiringly at them, but did not regard them as important: they were all headed for exile, so what did it matter if a few more joined them? She did not think twice about it, but took money from her purse and gave a generous amount to a muleteer to allow Salma and Musa to perch on top of the huge bundles on one of the mules. They might reach Seville in time! The mere thought gave her the strength to put one foot in front of the other. Muqla walked alongside her, hand in hand, a smile on his face.

Fátima had to endure the stench of thousands of people forced together in the worst conditions imaginable. But the shouting, the smoke from fires and cooking, the way she was jostled despite being protected by the seamen, having to slide around in mud, fight her way past some groups lamenting their lot and others consoling themselves with wild dancing and singing, and wander aimlessly up and down, often finding herself going round in circles, eventually convinced her this was not the way to find Hernando. She had been shut away within the golden walls of her luxurious palace for too long, and now found that she was perspiring freely. She tried to control her nerves: the last thing she wanted was to appear filthy and unkempt before Ibn Hamid after all these years.

She asked some soldiers if they knew Hernando. They

stared at her as if she were mad, and then burst out laughing.

'They don't have names. All these dogs are the same!' one of them spat.

She found a stone bench to sit on close by the city wall.

'You,' she said, pointing to three of the Catalan seamen, 'go and look for a man called Hernando Ruiz from Juviles, a village in the Alpujarra. He's come with the people from Córdoba. He's fifty-six, and has blue eyes.' Wonderful blue eyes, she thought to herself. 'He has a boy and a girl with him. I'll wait here. I'll pay you handsomely if you find him – all of you,' she added, to satisfy the one who was staying to guard her.

The men split up and hurried off in different directions.

While in the port of Seville these Catalan seamen were mingling with the Moriscos, searching everywhere and shouting if anyone had seen Hernando, shaking those they thought were not paying them attention, Rafaela was trying to contain her impatience and match the slow pace of the column of deportees. Hope had eased her pain, but she seemed to be the only one in a hurry. The others dragged their feet in silence, heads sunk on their shoulders. 'Take heart!' she would have liked to shout at them. 'Run!' As if he could read her thoughts, little Muqla, still clutching her hand, raised his face to her. Rafaela squeezed his hand, using the other to stroke the other two, who were dozing up on the mule's load.

'The man you are looking for is over there, my lady,' said one of the seamen, pointing towards the Gold tower. 'He's with some horses.'

Fátima got up from the bench where she had been sitting. 'Are you sure?'

'Yes. I talked with him. He told me he is Hernando Ruiz, from Juviles.'

Fátima felt a shudder run down her body. 'Did you tell him . . .?' Her voice quavered. 'Did you tell him someone was looking for him?'

The seaman hesitated. Someone from Córdoba had pointed out a man who was standing with a group of horses, his back to them. The seaman had simply seized the man by the shoulder and turned him round. He had asked his name, and when he had replied, set off as quickly as he could to claim his reward. 'No,' he admitted.

'Take me to him,' Fátima ordered.

The seaman pointed him out: he was the man who was facing away from them and talking to a cripple on crutches. People carrying bundles on their backs constantly blocked her view. When she reached near the spot where he stood, Fátima trembled and came to a halt. Incapable of going a step further, she waited for him to turn round. The seaman halted by her side: what was the matter with her now? He gestured once more at the Morisco. Miguel, who was facing them, recognized the man who had spoken to Hernando a few moments earlier. He nodded to his companion, and said: 'I think someone is looking for you.'

Hernando turned round. He did so slowly, as though already expecting something out of the ordinary. He saw the seaman a few paces away from him. Next to him stood a woman. He could not see her face because at that moment someone crossed in front of them. Then he saw a pair of black eyes staring straight at him. He could not breathe . . . Fátima! Their eyes met, and locked. Hernando felt an uncontrollable rush of emotions paralysing his senses. He could not move. Fátima!

When the walls of Seville came into sight, it was Muqla who had to tug on his mother's hand to stop her speeding up still more. The Moriscos were going even more slowly! She heard sighs all around her. A woman's terrible wailing rose above the sound of animals' hooves and thousands of shuffling feet. An old man walking close beside them shook his head and clicked his tongue just once, as if incapable of expressing any more pain than with this one feeble complaint.

'Walk!' one of the soldiers shouted.

'Keep going!' cried another one.

'Get a move on, you dumb beasts!' a third soldier taunted them.

Rafaela glanced down at her son as the other soldiers laughed at the joke. Stay with the rest of them, the boy seemed to be saying silently to her. Don't stand out in any way now. We'll get there! He smiled reassuringly, and then immediately wiped all trace of emotion from his face. But Rafaela did not want to give in to the despair that seemed to have overtaken the Moriscos. She let go of Muqla's hand and gently shook Musa.

'Come on, little one, wake up!' she said, before realizing that the mule-driver was staring at her in surprise.

She hesitated, but then shook Salma as well. 'We've arrived,' she whispered in her ear, trying to hide her anxiety from the muleteer.

The little girl muttered a few words and opened her eyes, but then closed them again, overwhelmed by tiredness. Rafaela lifted her down, and held her tight in her arms.

'Your father is waiting for us!' she whispered once more, this time concealing her lips in the girl's tousled hair.

It was Fátima who broke the spell. She shut her eyes and pressed her lips together. At last! she seemed to be saying to Hernando. She walked slowly towards him, her black eyes filled with tears.

Hernando could only stare at her. Thirty years had not diminished her beauty. A jumble of memories fought their way to the surface of his mind. As she reached his side, he began to tremble like a child. 'Fátima!' he whispered.

She stared at him for a moment, her eyes running tenderly over his features. His face was very different from the one she remembered. The years had left their mark, but the blue of his eyes was the same as when she had fallen in love with him in the Alpujarra.

She did not dare touch him. She had to clasp her hands to stop herself throwing her arms round his neck and smothering him in kisses. Without meaning to, a passer-by bumped into her. Hernando caught hold of her to prevent her falling. She felt his hand on her skin and shuddered.

'It's been such a long time,' he murmured at last. He still had hold of her hand, the same one that had stroked him on so many nights.

Fátima sighed and the two of them came together in a tight embrace. For a few seconds, in the midst of all the noise and confusion, they stood immobile, listening to each other's breathing, caught up in a thousand and one memories. He drank in the perfume of her hair, clutching her to him as hard as he could, as if he never wanted to let her go again.

'I've dreamt so often—' he started to say into her ear, but Fátima would not let him go on. Pulling her head back, she kissed him on the mouth: an ardent, sad kiss, which he encouraged by slipping his hands round the back of her neck.

Emerging at that moment from among the horses, Miguel and the children looked on in utter amazement.

The column of deportees from Castro del Río skirted the city walls and made their way past the company of guards stationed at the points of access to the Arenal. They started to mingle with the other Moriscos, while Rafaela halted to get her bearings. She knew what to look for. It must be easy to spot sixteen horses even in this crowd: that was where Hernando and the children would be.

'Keep your eye on your brother and sister and stay close to me. Don't get lost,' she warned Muqla, setting off towards a cart drawn up nearby.

As soon as she reached it, she climbed up on to the driver's platform without so much as a by-your-leave.

'Hey,' shouted a man, trying to stop her. Rafaela had already foreseen that, and slipped determinedly past him. 'What are you doing?' the driver insisted, pulling at her skirt.

A few seconds were all she needed. Resisting his tugs, she stood on tiptoe on the seat, staring all round the Arenal. Sixteen horses. It can't be that difficult, she told herself. The man made to climb up as well, but Muqla reacted and flung himself round his legs. As the driver tried to kick himself free of the little urchin's grip, a crowd of curious onlookers gathered round them. Sixteen horses! Rafaela kept repeating to herself, only half listening to the man shouting and the efforts her son was making to hold him back.

'There they are!' she cried out in surprise.

The horses stood out clearly at the foot of a magnificent tower that rose from the shore at the opposite end of the Arenal.

She jumped down from the cart like a young girl. She did not even feel the pain in her feet when she hit the ground.

'Thank you, kind sir,' she said to the cart-driver. 'Let the gentleman go, Muqla.' The boy relaxed his grip, and scampered off to avoid another kick. 'Come on, children!'

Forcing a path through the onlookers, she made her way proudly towards the tower. She smiled as she crossed the Arenal, pushing people aside when she had to.

'We've done it, children!' she repeated.

She was carrying the two smaller ones in her arms again, while Muqla struggled to keep up beside them.

'I don't want to be parted from you ever again,' Fátima had exclaimed as they separated after their prolonged kiss.

They were still standing close to one another, searching each other's faces and trying to smooth away the lines age had brought to them. For a few moments they were once again the young muleteer from the Alpujarra and the girl who had waited for him. The time that had gone by since then seemed to evaporate. The two of them were there, together again; the past was lost in the emotion of their reunion.

'Come with me to Constantinople,' said Fátima. 'You and your children. We will lack for nothing. I have money, Ibn Hamid, a lot of money. There is nothing and no one to stop me. Neither of us will face any dangers. We'll be able to start all over again.'

As Hernando heard this, a shadow of doubt flitted across his face.

'We'll have money sent to the rest of your family,' Fátima said hurriedly. 'Ephraim will take care of it. They won't want for anything either, I swear.' Fátima gave him no time to think, but went on talking hastily, passionately. Amin and Laila stared at each other open-mouthed, unconsciously creeping closer to Miguel as they listened to this strange woman who had kissed their father. 'I have a ship. I have all the permits necessary to transport our brothers in faith to Barbary. Then we two can continue on to the East. We'll soon be installed in a huge house – no! A palace! We deserve it! We'll have all we want. And we'll be happy the way we used to be, as if all these years had not happened, discovering each other again every day . . .'

Hernando was caught up in an endless whirl of sensation and emotion. Fátima! The memories swept back into his mind in a tumultuous flood. The distant communion he had felt for Fátima in recent years, like a faint beacon lighting his way, had suddenly become a tangible, marvellous reality. It was . . . it was as though his body and spirit had both suddenly reawakened to life, allowing feelings he had deliberately suppressed to come to the surface. How much they had loved each other over all those years! Fátima was there, in front of him, pouring out her hopes in an impassioned, endless stream. How could he ever have thought that all their love had vanished into thin air?

'No one will ever keep us apart again, ever!' she said again. Hernando turned to glance at his children.

What about them? And Rafaela? And the little ones left behind in Córdoba? An almost imperceptible shock of dismay ruined the magic of the moment. Was he going to betray them? Amin and Laila were still staring at him, silently posing a thousand questions and as many reproaches. Hernando felt their condemnation like sharp needles in his flesh. Who is this woman who is kissing you and whom you embraced with such passion? That was the accusation his daughter seemed to be flinging in his face. What life is it that you want to resume far from my mother? Amin demanded to know. Miguel . . . Miguel was staring at the ground, his legs more crumpled than ever. It was as if his whole life, all the efforts he had made and all he had been forced to renounce, was concentrated in that patch of mud beneath his crutches.

Fátima had fallen silent. The hubbub and laments of the thousands of Moriscos in the Arenal could be heard once more. The real world was back. The Christians had expelled them from Córdoba. Exile awaited him, and an uncertain future for him and his children. Perhaps it was God who had placed Fátima in his path at this very moment! Only He could have brought his first wife here.

He was about to say something to her when Laila's voice caught him by surprise.

'Mother!' she suddenly shouted, then set off at a run.

'Lai—' Hernando began. Mother? Had she said 'Mother'? He saw Amin running off to catch her.

Words failed him. He stood rooted to the spot. Only a few paces away from them, Rafaela was hugging Amin and Laila, showering their faces and heads with kisses. Next to her stood the three youngest, staring expectantly at him without a word.

Rafaela freed herself gently from the children and came up to her husband. She smiled at him, her lips stretched in a triumphant gesture. I did it! Here you are! they seemed to be saying. Hernando could not react. His wife was nonplussed, and felt her clothing, in case it was her appearance that had shocked him in this way. She knew she looked ragged and filthy. Feeling ashamed, she tried to smooth down her skirt.

'Is this your Christian wife?'

To Hernando, Fátima's words sounded more like a reproach or a lament than a question. He nodded without turning round.

It was only then that Rafaela became aware of the presence of a beautiful, richly dressed woman beside her husband. She came closer to him, her eyes on the stranger.

'Who is this woman?' she demanded.

'Have you never told her about me, Hamid ibn Hamid?' Fátima asked him, although she could not take her eyes off the dirty, dishevelled figure coming towards them.

Hernando was about to answer, but Rafaela forestalled him, with the same determination she had shown when she turned her mother out of their house in Córdoba when the plague had struck.

'I am his wife. What right do you have to question us?'

'The right which comes from being his first and only wife,' Fátima responded, pointing her chin at Hernando.

Rafaela's confusion was evident from her face. Hernando's first wife had died, hadn't she? She remembered Miguel's sad story about it. With her eyes tight shut, she shook her head as if to drive away what she had heard.

'What are you saying?' she gasped. 'Hernando, tell me it isn't true.'

'Yes, tell her, Hamid,' Fátima said defiantly.

'When I married you, I thought she was dead,' was all Hernando managed to utter.

Rafaela shook her head violently. 'When you married me!' she cried. 'And since then? Did you learn she was still alive? Holy Mother of God!'

She had abandoned everything for Hernando. She had walked leagues to find him. She was in rags, filthy, and her shoes were torn to pieces. Her feet were still bleeding! Where had this woman come from? What did she want from Hernando? What was she doing here among these thousands of defeated Moriscos, abandoned to their wretched fate? She could feel her strength ebbing away. The sense of determination that had driven her on was lost amidst the tears and laments of the others.

'I have walked and walked,' she sobbed, as if giving up entirely. 'The children would not stop crying! Only Muqla was strong. I was afraid we would not get here in time . . . and all for what?' At this, she half raised one of her arms in the air. As if this were a signal, Laila ran over to comfort her. 'We've lost everything: house, furniture, all my clothes . . .'

Hernando went up to her, his hands spread out in the hope that they would speak for him. His face, however, betrayed his confusion. 'Rafaela, I—' he began.

'I could arrange it so that she came too,' Fátima interrupted him in a loud voice. What was the Christian woman doing there? She herself was not going to renounce her dreams, even if that meant . . . She would find a way.

Hernando turned back to Fátima. Rafaela could see him hesitating. Why was that? What was the woman talking about? Go where? Why with her?

'What is this madness?' she asked.

'That, if you so wish,' Fátima calmly replied, 'you and your children could come with us to Constantinople.'

'Hernando,' Rafaela said coldly to her husband. 'I've given my life to you. I am . . . I am willing to renounce the teachings of my Church and to share a belief in Mary and in your destiny with you, but never – do you hear me? Never – will I share you with another woman.' As she finished speaking, she pointed towards Fátima.

'What choice do you have, Christian?' Fátima replied. 'Do you think they'll allow you to sail to Barbary with him? They will not. And they will take your children from you! Both of you know that. I've seen it while I was waiting here: they tear them mercilessly from their mothers' arms . . .' Fátima left her words floating in the air. Her eyes narrowed when she saw how Rafaela's expression changed at the thought of losing her little ones. She could understand what she was going through. She could feel her pain when she thought of her own son, killed by these same Christians, and yet remembering this only made her angry once more. This was a Christian; she did not deserve her compassion. 'I've seen it!' she insisted. 'When they discover she has no papers proving she is a Morisco they will arrest her, accuse her of apostasy, and take the children from her.'

Rafaela raised her hands to her face.

'There are hundreds of soldiers on guard here,' Fátima went on.

Rafaela burst into sobs. The world was collapsing around her. Her exhaustion, the intense emotion, the shock . . . everything fused into one. She felt her legs give way. She could hardly breathe. All she could hear were this strange woman's words, which were getting fainter and fainter, more and more distant . . .

'There's no escape for you. You'll never get out of the Arenal. I'm the only one who can help you . . .'

Rafaela stifled a moan, and fainted.

The children ran to her, but Hernando pushed them away and knelt by her side. 'Rafaela!' he cried, patting her cheeks. 'Rafaela!' He looked desperately around him. For a fleeting second his eyes met Fátima's. That was enough for her to understand, even before he did, that she had lost him.

'Don't abandon me,' Rafaela begged Hernando, still feeling dazed. 'Don't leave us.'

Miguel, the children and Fátima looked on at the couple from a few paces away. Hernando had carried his wife to the riverbank. Her face was still pale, her voice weak and tremulous. She could not bring herself to look at him.

Hernando still had the smell of Fátima on his skin. Only a few minutes earlier he had given himself to her, desired her: for a few short moments he had even dreamt of being happy as she had suggested. But now . . . He looked down at Rafaela: tears ran down her cheeks, mingling with the dust of the roads that caked her face. He saw her chin tremble as she tried to control her sobs, doing her utmost to show him she was a tough, resolute woman. Hernando grimaced. He knew she was not that: she was the girl he had saved from the convent, the one whose sweet nature had won his heart little by little. She was his wife.

'I'll never leave you,' he heard himself say. He took her hands gently, and kissed her. Then he put his arms round her.

'What are we going to do?' he heard her ask.

'Don't worry about that,' he muttered, trying to sound convincing.

They were soon surrounded by all their children.

'First there's something I must do,' Hernando said.

Miguel moved away when he saw Hernando coming towards him and Fátima.

'I came to find you, Hamid ibn Hamid,' she said solemnly as he reached her. 'I thought that God—'

'God will decide.'

'You are right. God has decided this,' she added, gesturing towards the multitude crammed into the Arenal.

'My place is with Rafaela and my children,' said Hernando. The firmness of his voice brooked no argument.

Fátima shuddered. Her face had become a beautiful, hard mask. She made to walk away, but before she had even taken a step, she turned and looked back at him: 'I know you still love me.'

Having said that, Fátima turned on her heel and began to walk off.

'Wait a moment,' Hernando begged her. He ran over to the horses and came straight back, carrying a package. When he was near her again, he searched inside it. 'This is yours,' he said, handing her the old gold necklace. Fátima's hand shook as she took it. 'And this . . .' Hernando gave her the copy in Arabic of the gospel of Barnabas from the time of Almanzor. 'These are very precious writings. They're very old, and belong to our people. I was meant to see that the Sultan received them.' Fátima refused to take the sheets of paper. 'I know you feel cheated,' Hernando admitted. 'As you said, it will be difficult to escape from here, but I'll try, and if I succeed, I will go on fighting in Spain for our one God as well as for peace between our peoples. I hope you understand: I can put my life at risk, as well as that of my wife and children, I can even renounce you . . . but I can't put our people's heritage at risk. I cannot keep this, Fátima. The Christians must not get hold of it. You keep it, in honour of our fight to preserve our Muslim laws. Do with it whatever you see fit. Take it for Allah and the Prophet's sake. Take it for all our brothers.'

Fátima stretched out a hand towards the bundle.

'Remember, I loved you,' Hernando went on, 'and I will go on doing so until my . . .' He cleared his throat, and was silent for a few moments. 'In death, hope is everlasting,' he whispered finally.

Before he could get the words out, Fátima had turned on her heel.

It was only after he saw Fátima disappear into the crowd that Hernando realized how true her words had been. As he looked round the Arenal, his stomach clenched. Thousands of Moriscos were trapped on the muddy expanse. Soldiers and clerks were shouting orders all the time; some people were being rowed out to board ships; merchants and pedlars were trying to get the last pennies out of all these destitute men and women; priests were there making sure no one escaped with young children . . .

'What shall we do, Hernando?' asked Rafaela. She sounded relieved to see the other woman walking off. They were together again, one family. The children pressed round them eagerly.

'I have no idea.' Hernando could not take his eyes off Rafaela and the children. He had been on the verge of losing them. 'Even supposing we found some way to get you on board ship as a Morisco, they would never let us take the little ones. They would steal them from us. We have to escape from this nightmare, and there is no time to lose.'

The evening sun was glinting off the tiles of the Gold tower as Hernando surveyed the city walls. Rafaela and Miguel did the same. Directly behind them there was no way out: the wall and the fortress blocked their exit. A little further on stood the Jerez gate, but that was guarded by a company of soldiers. So were the Arenal and Triana gates. Only the river Guadalquivir offered an escape. Rafaela and Miguel saw Hernando shake his head. It was impossible! The officials and priests were keeping such a close watch on the riverbank that they had no chance of reaching a boat. The only way out was by the same way they had got into the Arenal, at the far end, where there were no walls, although this access was heavily guarded too. How could they manage it?

'Wait for me here,' Hernando ordered them.

He strode across the Arenal. The entrance was guarded by a company of soldiers, who were sheltering in some temporary shacks put up to supervise the arrival of the columns of Moriscos. Hernando could see, however, that the soldiers were passing the time talking or playing cards. No more Moriscos were arriving, and none of the people on the shore would dare try to break out. The Christians in the Arenal left by one of the city gates, not this distant gap in the walls. And yet . . . they had to get out!

Night was drawing in by the time Hernando returned to the foot of the Gold tower. It was the hour for prayer. He looked up at the sky, calling on God for help. Then he told Rafaela and Miguel, as well as Amin and Laila, to gather round. It was risky, very risky.

'Where are the men who accompanied you with the horses?' he asked Miguel.

'In the city. There's one left on guard.'

'Tell him to go with his colleagues. Tell him . . . tell him I'd like to spend my last night with my horses. On my own. Will he believe that?'

'He won't care much about the reason. He'll be happy to go and have a good time. I've paid them. They have money to burn, and the city is very lively.'

They waited where they were for Miguel to reappear. 'Done,' said the cripple.

'Good. As a Christian, you can walk out of here . . .' Miguel started to object, but Hernando cut him short. 'Do as I say, Miguel. We will only have one chance. Get off the Arenal by any of the gates, cross the city, and leave it on the far side. Wait for us outside the walls.'

'What about Rafaela?' said the cripple, pointing to her. 'She's Christian as well. She could leave with me.'

'With the children?' Hernando objected. 'She would not get past the guards. They'd think she was trying to smuggle them out, and we'd lose them. What excuse could a Christian woman have for being in the Arenal with her small children? They would be sure to arrest her.'

'But . . .'

'Do as I say, Miguel.'

Hernando embraced his friend, and then helped him up on to the mule. This might be the last time he saw him.

'Peace, Miguel,' Hernando said as the cripple set off. Miguel muttered a farewell. 'Don't cry, Rafaela,' Hernando added, turning back towards her and seeing she had tears in her eyes. 'We'll manage it . . . with God's aid we will. Children, there's a lot to do and little time to do it,' he warned Amin and Laila.

He went over to the horses, which were resting after their exhausting journey. Miguel had told them he had given them less feed to weaken them so that they would carry their loads of goods, women and old men more placidly. Most of them had cuts and sores from all they had carried. Hernando gathered their halters and ropes.

'Tie them all together at their heads, as close together as you can,' he explained to his children, handing them the halters but keeping back some long lengths of rope. 'No,' he corrected himself, realizing how hard it would be to control sixteen horses roped together, 'tie . . . ten horses at most. Rafaela, I want you to take the three little ones and head for the far end of the shore. You'll take longer than us. When you get there, stay as close to the guards as possible, but make sure they don't see you or suspect what you're doing. I'm going to launch the horses at them.' Rafaela looked startled. 'It's all I can think of, my love. When you see me doing that, cross the lines of soldiers as quickly as you can, and then hide in the bushes by the riverside. But don't stay still: get as far away as possible. Carry on along the bank until you leave the city behind and meet up with Miguel.'

'What about you three?' she asked in astonishment.

'We'll get through. Trust me,' Hernando said, though the tremor in his voice belied his confidence. Giving her a tender kiss, he urged her to set off across the Arenal. Rafaela hesitated.

'We'll do it. All of us,' Hernando insisted. 'Trust in God. Go on. Hurry up.'

It was little Muqla who pulled on his mother's hand to make sure she got started towards the far end of the Arenal. For a few moments, Hernando stood and watched as part of his family disappeared into the crowd. Then he turned resolutely to help his other children.

'Did you hear what I said to your mother?' he asked the two eldest. They nodded. 'All right then. One of you is to stand on either side of the horses. I'll steer them. It will be hard to push our way through all these people, but we have to do it somehow. Fortunately most of the soldiers are off having a good time in the city, so they're not patrolling. We shouldn't be stopped.' He spoke forcefully as he tied the horses together, so that the children would not have time to think about what they were going to do. 'Keep them moving from behind and the sides,' he ordered Amin and Laila. 'Hurry them along, and don't worry what anyone says. We have to get across this sand, whatever it takes. Do you understand?' The two children nodded once more. 'When we are close to the way out, keep behind them, then run past the soldiers as I told your mother to. All right?'

He did not wait for their answer. The ten horses were already tied together. Hernando took the two long ropes and tied them to the front legs of the two that would take the lead. Finally, he grasped the halter of one that he wanted to keep apart from the others.

'All right?' he repeated. Amin and Laila nodded again. Hernando smiled to encourage them. 'Your mother is waiting for us! We can't leave her on her own! Let's go!' he said, without pausing for breath. Amin was only thirteen; his sister two years younger. Would they be able to do it?

He pulled at the three leading horses. Roped together, the seven others spread out in a line.

'Go on! Get on with you, my beauties!'

At first it was hard to make them move: they were not used to being tied together in this way. The ones at the back kicked, reared and bit each other, refusing to budge. And he himself? he wondered. Would he be able to do it at his age? He kicked a horse as hard as he could in the belly.

'Get a move on!'

'Go on!' he heard someone shout behind him.

Through the milling animals he saw that Amin had picked up a piece of rope and was using it to hit the hindquarters of the rear horses. Almost immediately he heard Laila's voice as well, hesitant at first, but soon as strong as her brother's.

They would do it! Hernando smiled, his children's shouts ringing in his ears.

Once all the horses had begun to move, they were like an unstoppable army. Hernando was afraid he would not be able to control them, but his children ran here and there behind and alongside them, urging them on and keeping them in line.

'Be careful! Stay well away!' he warned them constantly.

The children were shouting as well. The Moriscos they knocked out of the way complained and insulted them. Ignoring them, the horses trampled on possessions, and clattered over tents. When they leapt over a small bonfire, Hernando realized just how blindly the animals were plunging on. They would never have done anything like that in normal circumstances.

'Careful!'

He had to pull fiercely on the lead horses to give an old woman the chance to escape without being trampled, but several Moriscos were sent flying through the air by the horses on the flanks.

Even though the Arenal stretched a long way, they crossed it in no time. Hernando saw the guard post, with the soldiers trying to work out what all the fuss was about.

'Now, children! Off you go, as fast as you can!'

He no longer had any need to urge the horses on. As soon as

they saw open ground between the last Moriscos and the guards, they broke into a furious gallop. Hernando ran a couple of paces alongside the steed he had kept free from the others. He grasped it by the mane to mount it. It was hard going: his muscles creaked from the effort. He failed in his first attempt, getting his leg stuck halfway up the animal's rump, but he rebounded from the ground, pulled hard, and this time succeeded in swinging his leg over. Now that Amin and Laila were no longer driving the other horses on, they fanned out. Horrified, the soldiers watched as eleven crazy, unbridled horses came hurtling towards them.

'*Allahu Akbar!*'

No sooner had he called on his God than Hernando pulled on the two ropes he had tied to the front legs of the other two lead horses. They both stumbled, crashed to the ground, then turned a cartwheel in the sand. In the torchlight Hernando caught a glimpse of the soldiers' terrified faces as the horses collided with each other and fell on top of them and their shacks. He himself, on his free horse, was able to gallop out of the Arenal, leaving the guard post in ruins.

He jumped off the horse as quickly as he had mounted, and ran to the riverside bushes. The night was filled with the neighing of horses and the soldiers' anguished cries.

'Rafaela? Amin?'

It was a few endless moments before he heard a reply.

'Over here.'

Even in the pitch dark he recognized his eldest's voice.

'And your mother?'

'Here,' Rafaela answered from a little further on.

When he heard her voice, Hernando's heart leapt. They had done it!

69

THEY ESCAPED to Granada, knowing full well that if they were stopped they faced death or slavery. The captains of the Córdoban militias must have known it was he who had escaped: Hernando was the owner of the horses and his name and his children's would be on the list of deportees embarking on the ships. He decided to head for the Alpujarra. There were many abandoned villages up in the mountains. Miguel had no problem getting out of the Arenal on his mule. He met up with the others beyond the city walls. His only regret was leaving behind those sixteen magnificent horses. But what did that matter?

After a long journey from Seville to the Alpujarra, avoiding roads, hiding from people, stealing whatever food they could from the winter fields or lurking outside villages while Miguel tried to beg some alms, they found refuge in Viñas, near Juviles. Viñas had been deserted ever since its inhabitants had been expelled following the earlier revolt.

It was still bitterly cold and the peaks of the Sierra Nevada were covered in snow. Hernando surveyed them, then looked back at his children. This was where he had spent his childhood. He forbade them to light fires except at night. They took over a tumbledown house that Rafaela and the children tried hard to clean, without much success. Hernando and Miguel watched them: they looked like beggars.

The two men left the house, and found themselves in a

narrow lane flanked by ruined dwellings. When Rafaela saw them leave, she told the children to carry on, and followed them.

What now? her enquiring gaze seemed to say as she caught up with them. Are we going to live in hiding here for the rest of our lives?

'I have another favour to ask of you, Miguel,' Hernando said hastily, not turning towards the cripple but meeting his wife's gaze and stretching out a hand towards her.

'What is it you need?'

Hernando went as close as he dared to Granada with Miguel, then returned to the Alpujarra with the mule: a beggar should not possess such an animal. Miguel managed to get through the Rastro gate after the guards yielded to his incessant stream of incomprehensible talk. From there he headed straight for the Casa de los Tiros.

During the days Miguel was absent, Hernando entertained his children and tried to teach them to catch little birds. He found a piece of dried-out rope, unpicked the strands, and with his children watching him closely, made several traps they hung in tree branches. They did not catch any birds, but the children had a good time. They also had enough to eat. Hernando knew this region well, and apart from meat, he was able to find all they needed to keep them going. After a week in Viñas, when not another soul had appeared, he told Rafaela he was going away for a few days with Amin and Muqla.

'Where are you going?'

'I have to show them something.' A worried shadow flitted across his wife's face. 'Don't worry,' he reassured her. 'Keep your eyes open, and if you see anything strange, go and hide with the children in the caves close to where we tried to catch birds. Laila knows where they are.'

Just as Hernando remembered it, the castle of Lanjarón stood proudly on top of its hill. They waited at the bottom for night to fall before they began the climb. Hernando had timed their journey to coincide with the full moon, which shone like a huge disc in a cloudless, starry sky. With his children scampering behind him, he headed for the fortress's southern tower.

'There is no god but God, and Muhammad is the messenger of God,' he whispered into the night.

With that he knelt down and started to dig. He soon came upon Muhammad's sword. He lifted it carefully out of the ground and showed it to his two boys, reverentially undoing the cloths he had used to wrap it in.

'This', he told them, 'is one of the swords that belonged to the Prophet.'

How he wished that the gold scabbard and the metal strips would shine in the moonlight just as they had done all those years ago when he had first set eyes on the sword in Hamid's humble shack. Instead, he saw a similar gleam in his children's eyes. He drew the scimitar. As it emerged, the blade made a grating sound, and Hernando was startled to see that the edge of the rusty blade still bore traces of dried blood: it must have come from Barrax the corsair leader's neck! For a few moments he was lost in memories and, despite himself, Fátima's black eyes appeared to him yet again, like stars in the night sky.

A few timid coughs brought him back to reality. He glanced at Amin, then found himself staring at Muqla: even by moonlight he could see how his eyes shone.

'For years,' he said vehemently, 'Muslims cherished this sword. At first, when we ruled these lands, it was exhibited proudly and wielded with great courage. Then, when our people were subjugated, it was hidden to await a new victory that must come one day. You can be sure of that. Today we are more defeated than ever; our brothers have been driven out of Spain. If my plans succeed, we will have to go on behaving like Christians, even more convincingly because there will be few Muslims left. We will have to talk like them, eat like them, and pray like them. But don't despair, children. I will probably not live to see it, and perhaps you won't either, but one day a true believer will appear, take this sword, and . . .' He hesitated for a moment, recalling the words Hamid had spoken all those years ago. What was he going to say? That the sword would be raised to wreak revenge for injustice? In spite of the anger he felt, he did not want his children to grow up with an image of hatred in their minds. '. . . and will brandish it in the light as a symbol that our people have regained their freedom.

'Always remember where that freedom will come from and, if it does not happen in your lifetimes, transmit the message to your children so that they can do the same. Never give up in the fight for the one God! Swear it by Allah!'

'I swear,' said Amin, looking solemn.

'I swear,' Muqla copied him.

As the three of them headed back to Viñas, Hernando reflected on what he had just made his sons swear. He had worked all his life for the Christians to accept the Moriscos, to allow them to talk in Arabic, and yet now he had stirred his boys up against them – to what end? He felt confused. Alongside the images of thousands of defeated Moriscos herded together on the sands of the Arenal at Seville, he remembered the day when Hamid had presented him with the sword. Back then it had been a fight for survival, and they were ready to die to preserve their laws and customs. How different this humiliating expulsion from Spain was! They and a few more Moriscos hidden in the countryside and the cities were probably the only ones left. What had happened to the mutual understanding he had fought so hard for? He put his arms on his boys' shoulders and drew them closer in the night. They would keep the flame of hope alive for their ill-used people. It might be only a feeble glow, but didn't huge fires start from the tiniest spark?

It was almost three weeks before they saw Miguel again in the Alpujarra. When he reappeared he was riding a new mule, and did not come alone. Accompanying him was Don Pedro de Granada Venegas, who rode on his own, without any servants.

The nobleman said they could take shelter in lands he was lord of in Campotéjar, on the borders of the provinces of Granada and Jaén, but they must pretend they were Christians who had come there from the city of Granada. Don Pedro had seen to it that they had fake documents stating they were inhabitants of the city, and old Christians. Hernando's new name was Santiago Pastor; Rafaela was Consolación Almenar. No one would be surprised at their move. The expulsion of the Moriscos had left the fields empty, with no one to work them. This was especially true in the kingdom of Valencia, but it also affected many other regions, including the lands where the Granada Venegas family were lords. Don Pedro also gave them two letters: one was addressed to the steward who looked after his estates. The other was a letter of introduction to the parish priest at Campotéjar. In it he praised the religious spirit of a family who he said were his devoted servants, and whom he guaranteed as people fearful of God. Miguel had papers showing that he was a close relative. Don Pedro assured them that if they made no mistakes, nobody would bother them.

'What has become of the lead plaques?' Hernando asked him in private before the nobleman mounted his horse once more and headed back to the city.

'The archbishop is still keeping hold of the books and personally supervising their translation. He will not tolerate the slightest reference to any Muslim teachings. A collegiate church is being built on the Sacromonte, as well as a school for religious and legal studies. We have failed.'

'Perhaps one day . . .' Hernando said, a note of hope in his voice.

Don Pedro looked him up and down and shook his head. 'Even if we were successful, even if the Sultan or any other Arab ruler made the gospel of Barnabas public, there are no Muslims in Spain any more. It would be of no use.'

Hernando wanted to argue, but thought better of it. Didn't Don Pedro see how important it was that the truth saw the light of day, whatever had become of the Moriscos in Spain? The converted nobles had managed to escape being expelled. Don Pedro had discovered his Christian roots thanks to an apparition of Jesus Christ, which had been told of in a book in a way that had only increased his standing. He might be offering them help, but did he still believe in the one true God?

'I wish you long lives,' the nobleman added as he lifted a foot into the stirrup. 'If you have any problems, make sure I hear about it.'

With that, he galloped off.

Epilogue

Many of them remain, especially where there are communities and they are protected . . .

Letter from Count Salazar to the Duke of Lerma, September 1612

Campotéjar, 1612

A LMOST TWO years had gone by since that conversation and, as predicted, Hernando and his family had encountered no problems in installing themselves in an out-of-the-way farmhouse in the lands of the Granada Venegas family. Because they had once been in his employ, they were still protected by Don Pedro. Their way of life had changed. Hernando no longer had any books to take refuge in, nor any paper or ink to write with. Nor did he have any horses. The scarce funds the family possessed could not be wasted on such things; even if he had had the money, Hernando could not have spent any time on calligraphy – they were in such close contact with the other families living in this backwater that their neighbours would soon have realized what was going on and become suspicious. The house doors were always open, and the low murmur of the women endlessly reciting rosaries became a characteristic of the hamlet. Sometimes, however, when they were alone in the fields, Hernando would almost unconsciously trace Arabic letters in the earth, which Rafaela and his children quickly rubbed out with their feet. It was only the seven-year-old Muqla (who increasingly had to become used to being called Lázaro) who fixed his blue eyes on the written shapes, as though trying to memorize them. He was the only one of his children to whom Hernando continued to teach the Muslim doctrine, remembering the copy of the Koran he had hidden in the mihrab of the Córdoba mosque, which he hoped to recover some day.

Apart from this exception with Muqla, Hernando avoided talking about religion. He did not give any classes to the other children for fear they might be found out. There was a great deal of unrest in the region, and there were constant denunciations of Moriscos who had managed to avoid being expelled. Any Morisco arrested was destined for death, slavery, the galleys, or work in the mines at Almadén. Hernando could not put his children's lives at risk! But Muqla was different. He had exactly the same colour eyes as him: the legacy of the Christian priest who had violated his mother, and the symbol of the injustice that had led the people of the Alpujarra to rise up in revolt.

Hernando puffed out his cheeks, rested the long pole on the ground, and paused in his work. He was about to put a hand to his aching back when he saw Rafaela looking his way and desisted.

'Have a rest,' his wife told him for the umpteenth time, although she herself was still bent over picking olives from the ground and dropping them into a big basket.

Hernando clenched his teeth and shook his head, but he did give himself a few moments to survey his children. Amin (who in the village was known as Juan) was jumping from branch to branch of the olive tree. Just as he himself had done with an old tree that survived the frosts on the terraces up above Juviles, his son scampered up the gnarled branches to reach the olives that the pole could not dislodge. The other four were helping their mother pick up the ripe windfalls and the ones Hernando had knocked to the ground. His eldest son was fifteen, and could wield the pole with great skill, but if Amin was the one who banged the trees to dislodge the late olives, what was left for him to do? There was no way he could climb trees at close to sixty.

He lifted the pole again to strike the branches of the tree. Rafaela saw him and shook her head.

'Stubborn mule!' she shouted.

Hernando smiled to himself as he hit the branch. She was right, but they had to pick the olives. Like many other families in the region, they were faced with dozens of trees in lines that seemed to stretch for ever. The sooner they got the olives to the oil-mill, the better quality oil they would produce, and the more they would earn for their work.

At dusk they returned home exhausted. They lived in a tiny, tumbledown two-storey house, which together with five other equally ramshackle dwellings made up the farming hamlet some distance from the village of Campotéjar.

This was where they had been for the past two years. They worked in the fields for wretched daily wages that were scarcely enough for them to feed their five children. Like all those who worked the land, they often went hungry, but at least they were together, and took strength from that.

On Sundays and days of obligation they attended mass in Campotéjar, where they gave the appearance of being more religious than anyone. Since 1610, Archbishop de Castro, a passionate defender of the lead plates, had left Granada and installed himself in Seville. From there, thanks to his immense private fortune, he continued his labour of translating the plaques and lead plates and with the construction of the collegiate church above the caves. At the same time, he became the chief proponent of conceptionism, making the purity of the Virgin Mary the banner of his archbishopric. The doctrine of the Immaculate Conception spread throughout Spain, reaching even the smallest, most remote parishes such as Campotéjar.

Hernando and Rafaela listened to the fervent homilies about Mary, that same Maryam the Prophet had decreed to be the most important woman in heaven, in whom the Koran and the Sunna saw identical virtues to the ones now being praised in Christian churches. From the perspective of their own faiths, Hernando and Rafaela were united through her figure: he with respect, she with devotion.

Often on those occasions they sought out each other's eyes from their separate places inside the church. When their gazes met, they spoke volumes. The Virgin Mary was the vital link between their two beliefs, exactly as suggested by the lead plates, although nothing had come of Hernando's efforts on that score. As Rafaela commented when they were alone at night, how, if not thanks to her intercession, had a Morisco and a Christian woman managed to escape Seville? How, if not thanks to the intercession of Mary, had God permitted such a happy marriage between a follower of the Prophet and a devout Christian?

On those holy days, whenever Hernando saw a horse of any description, Rafaela trembled to see how his eyes narrowed nostalgically. She could not help wondering whether she had done the right thing in deciding to flee with him, if she had not condemned him to a sterile, monotonous life. Far from his books and his projects, he must be bored, if not miserable.

And yet without fail on those days of obligation, her husband showed her she had not made a mistake. He played with little Musa and Salma, tenderly hugging and kissing them. When they were out in the fields where no one could see them he also tried to teach them numbers and arithmetic, and whatever else he could think of that did not need paper or writing tablets. The little ones soon grew tired of lessons that could not possibly be of any use to them, and instead demanded he sit with them to listen to the stories Miguel told. Then at night when they were back in their home, the two adults talked about their children, the future of Amin and Laila, who had almost reached adulthood, as well as about the work in the fields, life in general, and a thousand other things. Afterwards they would retire to the small bedroom they shared and make tender love.

They rose at dawn one working day to continue with the arduous labour of the olive harvest. Hernando had to shake the children, who were curled up asleep on a straw mattress, to wake them. After a frugal breakfast, they set off for the fields through the morning mist, before the sun had time to burn it off. As they set to work, none of them spoke. Rafaela was worried: against her wishes, her body was telling her she had become pregnant again. How could she bring another child into this world of poverty and suffering?

At mid-morning they paused for something to eat. While they were doing so, they caught sight of Román, a lame old man who always stayed behind in the hamlet, walking slowly towards them with the aid of a rough stick. They saw him in the distance pointing towards them to direct two men on horseback.

'Don Pedro,' Miguel said in surprise when he saw the strangers.

'Who's that with him?' Rafaela asked, concern etched on her face.

'Don't worry, Don Pedro would never do anything to harm us,' her husband reassured her, although his voice was not completely steady.

The two men cantered over to them.

Hernando stood up and stepped a few paces in front of his family to receive them, just in case. His fears were calmed when he saw the smile on the nobleman's lips, and so he motioned for Rafaela to come and join him.

'Good day to you,' Don Pedro greeted them, jumping from his horse.

'Peace,' replied Hernando, casting a glance at the other rider. He was of average height and richly dressed, but not in the Spanish style. His beard was neatly trimmed, and he had a penetrating gaze. 'Have you come to see what's going on in your lands?' said Hernando, holding his hand out to Don Pedro de Granada.

'No,' the nobleman replied, taking Hernando's hand and gripping it tight. His smile broadened still further. Rafaela clung to her husband while Miguel tried to keep the children away from them. 'I've brought good news.'

With that, Don Pedro searched in his garments and pulled out a document. He passed it to Hernando.

'Aren't you going to open it?' he queried when he saw his friend standing with the letter unopened in his hand.

Hernando looked down at the document. It was sealed. When he looked more closely at the seal, he saw it was the royal coat of arms. He hesitated, and began to tremble. What could it be about?

'Open it!' Rafaela urged him.

Miguel could not resist seeing what was going on, and struggled laboriously over to them, his crutches sinking in the soft earth. The children ran alongside him.

'Open it, Father!' Turning towards his eldest son, Hernando nodded and broke the seal.

He began to read the document out loud: '"Don Felipe, by the grace of God King of Castile, León, Aragón, the two Sicilies, Jerusalem, Portugal, Navarre, Toledo, Valencia, Galicia and Majorca . . ."' Without realizing it, his voice fell to a murmur as he read out the long list of Philip III's titles: '"Archduke of Austria . . . Duke of Burgundy . . ."' until eventually he was reading it under his breath.

No one dared interrupt him. Her hands clasped tightly together, Rafaela tried to guess at the contents by the almost imperceptible movements of her husband's lips.

'The King . . .' Hernando began, his voice thick with emotion. 'The King personally exempts us from the expulsion decree, that is, Hernando Ruiz from Juviles and his children. He acknowledges that we are old Christians, and therefore restores to us all those properties seized on his behalf.'

Rafaela could not contain a sob that was a mixture of

laughter and tears. 'What about Gil and the duke?' she managed to stammer.

Hernando began to read again, in a loud, firm voice: '"We so decree in the name of our sovereign lord to all the nobles, prelates, lawyers, barons, knights, judges and sheriffs of the cities, towns and other places in our realm, together with His Majesty's bailiffs, governors, all other ministers, citizens and residents of his kingdoms."'

He showed Rafaela the letter: she burst into tears. Hernando opened his arms wide and she flung herself into them.

'Your new son will be born in Córdoba,' Rafaela whispered tearfully in his ear.

'How has this come about?' Hernando asked.

Don Pedro gestured him to one side. As they walked in the olive grove, he presented his companion: André de Ronsard, an ambassador at the French embassy at the court of Spain. 'The honourable lord has another letter for you.'

The three men came to a halt in the shade of a gnarled old olive tree. Feeling inside his cloak, the Frenchman handed him a second document. 'It's from Ahmed I, the Sultan of Constantinople,' he announced. Hernando looked enquiringly at him, and the Frenchman explained, 'As you must know, following the expulsion of your people from Spain, many Muslims escaped to France. Unfortunately, our population often robbed, mistreated, or even killed these exiles. These out-rages came to the ears of Sultan Ahmed, who immediately dispatched a special ambassador to the French court to inter-cede with the French monarch on behalf of the deportees. Agí Ibrahim, for that is the ambassador's name, succeeded in this effort, but while he was in our country he also received another request, which he transmitted to the French embassy at the Spanish court. That was to win a pardon for you and your family . . . whatever the cost. And I can assure you, it cost a great deal.' Hernando waited for a further explanation. 'That's all I know,' Ronsard said by way of excuse, 'I was merely informed that when we achieved this we were to seek out Don Pedro de Granada Venegas; and that he would probably know your whereabouts because of the lead plates. I was simply told I should accompany him to give you the Sultan's letter.'

Hernando opened it. The neat, brightly coloured Arabic characters were stylishly written by an expert hand. He shuddered, and then started to read the letter silently. As she had planned, Fátima had travelled to Constantinople, where she had handed the gospel to the Sultan in person. Ahmed I thanked him for his defence of Islam and for having sent the gospel of Barnabas to him. Above all, though, he was grateful for the way he had kept the spirit of Islam alive in the Córdoba mosque by praying before the mihrab. Who in all the Muslim world had not heard of him?

The Sultan, as the letter went on to explain, was building the world's largest mosque in honour of Allah and his Prophet in the city of Constantinople. It was to include six tall minarets and a vast dome, and was to be covered in a mosaic made up of thousands of blue and green stones. Even so, the Sultan recognized that however beautiful the new mosque might be, it would never reach the heights of the symbol of the victory over the Christian realms of the West.

The Sultan continued:

It is my wish and that of all Muslims that you continue to praise and glorify the 'peerless Creator' within the walls of what once was the greatest mosque in the West; that, even if it is in whispers, the prayers to the one God continue to be heard from your mouth, and when you are no longer there, from the mouths of your children and your children's children. That your prayers mingle with the echoes of the murmurs of the thousand upon thousands of our brothers who have prayed on that spot, so that on the day that God so decrees, through you and your family the past will join the present which, with the help of the All-powerful, must surely arrive.

The doctors of religion consider it vital to find the original of the gospel that the copyist claims to have hidden back in the time of al-Mansur. God willing, we will do so. We would give anything to have it in our hands, because the Christians will never give credence to a mere copy.

Your wife greets you, wishes you happiness, and encourages you to continue with the fight you began together. We will take care of her until death unites you once more.

Fátima! She had forgiven him!

The sound of his children's laughter brought him back to reality. He looked across at them: they were running and playing among the olive trees. Miguel was encouraging them, while his wife watched with a smile on her face. Yes, his family was his greatest achievement ... Hernando sighed. Why had it not been possible for the two peoples to live together in peace? It was then that he noticed Muqla, who was standing apart from the others. He was quiet, and looked serious as he regarded his father. They were all his children, but Muqla was the one who had inherited the spirit forged out of eight centuries of Muslim history in these lands. He would be the one who carried on his work.

At that moment, Rafaela saw how close father and son were and, as if realizing what was going through her husband's mind, went up behind Muqla and rested her hands on his shoulders. The boy leant back against her and entwined his fingers in hers.

Hernando gazed tenderly at his family, then raised his eyes above the tops of the olive trees. The sun was high in the sky. In the clear blue heavens, for a brief moment he saw clouds forming a huge hand of Fátima that seemed to be protecting each and every one of them.

Author's Note

The history of the Morisco community in Spain, from the conquest of Granada by the Catholic monarchs to their final expulsion, is one of the many episodes of xenophobia in our history. Other examples include Almanzor's attacks on Jews and Christians and the infamous expulsion of the Jews by the Catholic monarchs. The conditions for the surrender of Granada established very generous terms for the Muslims. They were allowed to keep their language, religion, customs, properties and authorities; eight years later, however, Cardinal Cisneros imposed the forced conversion of the Moriscos, as well as the elimination of their culture, the establishment of new, onerous taxes, and the curtailment of their administrative autonomy. The so-called 'new Christians' became increasingly exploited and reviled, while their previous rights were severely restricted.

The Morisco revolt in the rugged, beautiful region of the Alpujarra was a direct consequence of that people's constantly deteriorating situation. We know about it thanks to two detailed accounts by the chroniclers Luis de Mármol Carvajal (*Historia del rebelión y castigo de los Moriscos del reino de Granada*) and Diego Hurtado de Mendoza (*Guerra de Granada hecha por el Rey de España Don Felipe II contra los Moriscos de aquel reino, sus rebeldes: historia escrito en cuatro libros*). This was a war that both sides pursued with the utmost cruelty, although the atrocities committed by the Moriscos are better known, owing to the incomplete nature of the Christian accounts. In spite of this, one of the few voices raised to explain, though not to justify, these excesses was that of the Spanish ambassador in Paris, who, in the letter quoted on page 18, related how an entire village was complaining that its women were raped by the priest, and that their children were born with the stigma of his blue eyes – as is the case of the protagonist of this novel. However, the Christian side also committed atrocities. Massacres (the worst example of which took place in the village of Galera), the forced enslavement of the defeated Moriscos and extensive pillaging were common. For this reason we should give credence to events such as the deaths of more than a thousand women and children in the square at Juviles, and the sale of a similar number of both groups at public auction in Granada, as related in these chronicles.

This butchery was carried out by soldiers and commanders who were not part of the regular forces, and whose sole aim seems to have been personal enrichment. The chronicles constantly give prominence to the efforts to win spoils and share them out, to ambition being the only strategy, and to desertion by men satisfied with the booty they had accumulated.

Together with this, I have also tried in my novel to present an image of the conflicts and conditions within the rebel camp until the Moriscos, abandoned to their fate by Algiers and the Turks (as they had been before and would be again), were defeated by the professional Spanish soldiers. The taking of hashish to instil courage, the use of aconite as a poison on arrow tips, the arrogant attitude of the squad of janissaries sent from Algiers, the corsairs and the inclination some of them had for young boys: all this appears in the books of the chroniclers of the time. Also, in the work *Mahoma* by Juan Vernet, it is noted that according to Arab legend, several of the Prophet's swords reached al-Andalus, as I describe in my novel.

The Alpujarra uprising ended with the deportation of the

Moriscos of Granada to other kingdoms in Spain. In the case of those taken to Córdoba, like the protagonists of the novel, their exodus led to the death along the way of a seventh of those expelled, as seen from the study *Los Moriscos en tierra de Córdoba* by Juan Aranda Doncel.

The defeat, the dispersal of the Moriscos, the discriminatory laws (which also had the result of rendering useless any attempts at assimilation) did not resolve the problem. There are many reports and opinions from the time which not only made this clear, but proposed terrifying 'final solutions'. As a consequence, there were also many plots, all of which failed. Among the most serious was the one at Toga, which is recounted in the novel and which was thwarted as a result of the documents the King of England sent to the Spanish monarch following Elizabeth I's death and the Anglo-Spanish treaty. In his book *The Moriscos of Spain: Their Conversion and Expulsion*, the historian Henry Charles Lea states that the 120,000 ducats the Morisco community promised to pay on that occasion to secure the support of the French King for the insurrection were in fact handed over in Pau; while Domínguez Ortiz and Bernard Vincent, in their *Historia de los Moriscos; vida y tragedia de una minoría*, maintain that this never in fact happened. However, the payment, or the offer to make it, does seem to be true. For plot purposes, I have decided the payment was made, and have fictitiously put this down to the profits made from counterfeiting money – a real economic scourge which occurred above all in the kingdom of Valencia, where in 1613 the municipal treasury was bankrupted, leading to the withdrawal of hundreds of thousands of fake ducat coins. The Moriscos were directly accused of this counterfeiting. Several Berbers were present at Toga, but the aid was not meant to come from Algiers or the Sublime Porte, but from Christians.

The sufferings that the children went through – and here I am referring to the Morisco children, innocent victims of their people's tragedy – merit an in-depth study. There is a wealth of references for this: first and foremost, there is proof of the slavery into which children under eleven were forced during the Alpujarra uprising, despite the royal edicts. From our viewpoint, it is also hard to consider all those over eleven as being adult. In second place, once the war had finished, there was the handover of the children of deported Moriscos to Christian families; there are documents that confirm legal processes in favour of these children who were trying to recover their freedom once they reached the age of majority. Third, there was a fresh enslavement of children after the rebellions in the Valencian mountains (Vall de Laguar and Muela de Cortes). Finally, there exists documentation on those children aged under six who were kept in Spain when the definitive expulsion of the Moriscos took place. There are accounts that some families managed to send these children to France (the prohibition was on sending them to Barbary) and that others succeeded in getting round the royal decree by setting sail for Christian countries and then changing course at sea for the African coast. In the novel, several hundred of these children are said to have been detained in Seville. In Valencia, almost a thousand of them were handed over to the Church, and the viceroy's wife used her servants to abduct an unknown number of them and looked after them to prevent them falling into the hands of Satan, as would have happened if they had gone to 'Moorish lands'.

Following their expulsion, the Moriscos from the village of Hornachos, an enclosed, warlike community, settled in and later took control of the corsair port of Salé, next to Rabat. In 1631 they negotiated with the King of Spain to hand over the town to him on several conditions, including that of the return of the children of whom they had been robbed. From kingdom to kingdom, village to village, there are many examples of communities where the youngest children were taken from the Moriscos.

* * *

As far as the exact number of Moriscos expelled from Spain is concerned, the figures quoted vary so widely it would be really unhelpful to name those authors who suggest one or other figure. Perhaps, following Domínguez and Vincent, the closest we can come is their total of approximately three hundred thousand. Moreover, most of the authors who have studied the Moriscos (Janer, Lea, Domínguez and Vincent, Caro Baroja . . .) speak of the killings that took place when those deported reached Barbary. Some of them affirm that almost a third of the Moriscos expelled from Valencia were killed on arrival. In this they are following Philip III's chronicler, Luis Cabrera de Córdoba, in his *Relaciones de las cosas sucedidas en la corte de España desde 1599 hasta 1614*: 'and they [the Moriscos] are so horrified at the mistreatment and harm that the people of Valencia have received in Barbary, since a third of those who left have died, that very few of them wish to go there.' King Philip, however, celebrated the operation and gave a gift of a hundred thousand ducats in Morisco possessions to the Duke of Lerma on the occasion of the royal adviser's wedding to the Countess of Valencia.

After the first expulsion, a series of edicts was issued that insisted on the deportation of any Moriscos who might have remained in Spain or returned there, permitting and even rewarding the murder or enslavement of anyone found. It should also be recognized that the expulsion edicts varied according to each kingdom, although basically these different orders varied only slightly. In the novel, I have used the first of these that was passed, in the kingdom of Valencia.

Among the exceptions, the city of Córdoba is particularly interesting. On 29 January 1610 the city council petitioned the King for permission to allow two old, childless harness-makers to stay in the city 'for the general good and for the sake of the riders'. I have no evidence to suggest that apart from these two old Moriscos, who were to carry on looking after the horses, there were any other exceptions; nor do I know what His Majesty's reply was to the request.

* * *

In 1682, following the death of Archbishop Don Pedro de Castro, Pope Innocent XI took possession of the Lead Books of Sacromonte and the parchment from the Turpian tower, and declared them to be forgeries. Yet the Vatican said nothing about the relics, which had been certified as genuine by the Church in Granada in 1600, and which have continued to be venerated to this day. It is a situation similar to the one experienced by the protagonist of this novel: the documents – even if they were made of lead – affirming that this bone or those remains were of a specific martyr were rejected as forgeries by the Vatican; but the relics themselves, whose credibility was based precisely on those documents (how otherwise could ashes found in an abandoned mine on a hill be attributed to Saint Caecilius or Saint Ctesiphon?), were still considered authentic by the Church in Granada.

Today, most researchers agree that the Lead Books and the Turpian tower parchment were forged by Spanish Moriscos in a desperate attempt at syncretism between the two religions. In this way they hoped to find common bonds that could bring a real change in the view that the Christians held of Muslims, without renouncing their dogmas of faith.

There is also almost complete unanimity that these inventions were the work of the physicians and official Arabic translators Alonso del Castillo and Miguel de Luna, who wrote a *Verdadera historia del rey Rodrigo* in which they offered a sympathetic view of the Arab invasion of the Iberian peninsula and of the peaceful coexistence of Christians and Muslims. Hernando Ruiz's participation in these events is fictional, but that is not the case with Don Pedro de Granada Venegas (mentioned in several of the studies), who eventually changed his family motto, originally the triumphant 'Lagaleblila' or *wa la galib ilallah* of the Nasrid rulers, to the Christian '*Servire Deo regnare est*'. In 1608, shortly before the expulsion, the book *Antigüedad y excelencias de Granada* was published. Written by the academic Pedraza, it glorified the conversion of Cidiyaya, a

Muslim prince who was one of Don Pedro's forebears, as a result of the miraculous apparition of a cross in mid-air in front of him. Many Muslim noble families, in ways similar to the Venegas, succeeded in becoming integrated into Christian society.

The link between the Lead Books of Sacromonte and the gospel of Barnabas, originally upheld by Luis F. Bernabé Pons in *Los mecanismos de una resistencia: los Libros Plúmbeos del Sacromonte y el Evangelio de Bernabé* and *El Evangelio de san Bernabé: un evangelio islámico español,* is based on the discovery in 1976 of a thirteenth-century partial transcription of the supposed original, written in Spanish, to which there are several historical references, especially from Tunis. It is now in the University of Sydney. This modern theory could however call into question the purely syncretic aim that the Lead Books are said to represent. It seems logical to suppose that the authors of the Mute Book of the Virgin – whose contents, according to the prologue and another of the books (which is legible), were to be made known by an Arab king – foresaw the appearance of another text, although there is no proof this ever came to light. Whether or not this new text was the gospel of Barnabas (which bears many similarities to the Lead Books), it remains no more than a hypothesis. What is not hypothesis, but the exclusive fruit of the author's imagination, is the link between the gospel and that fictitious copy saved from the burning of the magnificent library of the caliphs of Córdoba ordered by Almanzor, an event which unfortunately was only too real, like so many other barbaric bonfires, painful to recall, in the history of humanity when knowledge becomes the object of the anger of fanatics.

Moreover, it is also true that studies were made about the Christian martyrs in the Alpujarra, although these were carried out much later than described in the novel. The first recorded attempt, according to information collected by Archbishop Pedro de Castro, dates from the year 1600. In the annals of Ugíjar (1668), where most of the killings of Christians that occurred in the Alpujarra are recorded, a boy by the name of Gonzalico is mentioned. He described his sacrifice for God as 'beautiful' before he was martyred. Tearing the heart out through the victim's back as described in the novel is repeatedly cited by Mármol in his chronicles as a sign of the Moriscos' cruelty towards their Christian victims.

Córdoba is a marvellous city, as a consequence of which it is the largest urban area in Europe to be declared a World Heritage site by UNESCO. In some parts it is still possible for the imagination to take flight and conjure up the splendid epoch of the Muslim caliphate. One of these places, of course, is the mosque/cathedral. We do not know for certain if the Emperor Charles V actually said the words attributed to him when he saw the works he himself had authorized in the interior: 'I did not know what this was, otherwise I would not have allowed you to touch what was here before; because you are doing something that could have been done anywhere, and have undone something that was unique in the world.' The truth is that the cathedral, as it was conceived in various stages and squeezed as it is into the forest of columns of the mosque, is a work of art. It is undeniable that the light of the Muslim place of worship was obscured, its pure lines were broken and its spirit tamed, and yet despite all this a goodly portion of the caliphate construction still exists. Why was it not demolished, as was the case with many other mosques, in order to build a completely new Christian cathedral in its place? Perhaps, leaving aside any possible interests the councillors and the nobility may have had, it is worth recalling the death sentence that the city council pronounced against anyone who dared work on the new cathedral.

Around one of the courtyards of the Christian monarchs' fortress the ruins and marks on the ground from the former cells of the Inquisition can still be seen. Next to it is another building that can transport the visitor back to those days: the royal stables, where Philip II dreamt up and carried out the creation of a new breed of court horses, a breed which even today ennobles and defines the Spanish horse.

The hand of Fátima (*al-hamsa*) is an amulet in the shape of a five-fingered hand. According to some theories, these represent the five pillars of faith: the profession of faith (*shahada*); the five daily prayers (*salat*); the giving of alms (*zakat*); fasting (*sawm*); and the pilgrimage to Mecca at least once in a lifetime (*haj*). However, the same amulet also appears in the Jewish tradition. This is neither the place nor the moment to enter into a discussion of its real origins, still less the efficacy of amulets in general. Books on the period insist time and again, however, that not only the Moriscos but society as a whole in that period believed in all kinds of witchcraft and spells. Even by 1526, the Council of the Chapel Royal in Granada made reference to 'hands of Fátima', forbidding silversmiths to make them and Moriscos to wear them; similar precepts were adopted at the synod of Guadix in 1554. There are many examples of the hand of Fátima in Muslim architecture, but perhaps the most representative within the scope of this book is the hand with the five outstretched fingers carved in the keystone of the first arch in the Puerta de la Justicia (Justice gate) which forms the entrance to the Alhambra of Granada, built in 1348. Therefore the very first symbol that any visitor to that marvellous monument sees is none other than a hand of Fátima.

I could not end this note without offering my thanks to all those who, in one way or another, have helped and advised me in the writing of this novel. A special thanks goes to my editor, Ana Liarás, whose personal commitment, advice and hard work have been invaluable, as have those of all the staff of Random House Mondadori. And my gratitude goes, of course, to my first reader: my wife, a tireless companion, and to my four children, who took it upon themselves to remind me forcibly that there are many important things beyond work. It is to them that I dedicate this book, in homage to all those children who suffered and unfortunately continue to suffer the consequences of the problems of our world: problems we seem incapable of resolving.

Barcelona, December 2008

Cathedral Of The Sea

Ildefonso Falcones

A spell-binding drama of love, war, greed and revenge
in medieval Barcelona . . .

A YOUNG SERF IN fourteenth century Spain, Arnau is on the run
from his feudal lord. Through famine, plague and thwarted love he
struggles to earn his freedom in the shadow of the mighty Cathedral
of the Sea: a magnificent church being built by the humblest citizens
of the city.

Arnau's fortunes begin to turn when King Pedro makes him a baron
in reward for his courage in battle. But his new-found wealth
excites the jealousy of his friends, who begin to plot against him, with
devastating consequences.

A page-turning historical epic, the tale of Arnau's journey from slave
to nobleman is the story of a struggle between good and evil that will
turn Church against State, and brother against brother . .

'Falcones' intricately plotted noveL.binds you into its thrall. A bold
work of imagination, which pays homage to lives gone by as well as
to the great church itself'
DAILY EXPRESS

'An exciting, very readable adventure novel, enriched by realistic
descriptions of medieval life, work, finance and politics'
INDEPENDENT

9780552773973

The Poet's Wife

Judith Allnatt

IT IS 1841.

Patty is married to John Clare:
Peasant poet, genius and madman.

Travelling home one day, Patty finds her husband sitting, footsore, at the side of the road, having absconded from a lunatic asylum over eighty miles away. She is devastated to discover that he has not returned home to find her, but to search for his childhood sweetheart, Mary Joyce, to whom he believes he is married.

Patty still loves John deeply, but he seems lost to her. Plagued by jealousy, she seeks strength in memories: their whirlwind courtship, the poems John wrote for her, their shared affinity for the land. But as John descends further into delusion, hope seems to be fading. Will she ever be able to conquer her own anger and hurt, and reconcile with this man she now barely knows?

'A fascinating, compelling novel about the wife of John Clare, and the bewildering effects of her husband's madness'
CLARE MORRALL

'A subtle and sympathetic portrayal of losing a loved one to mental illness ... at once homely and poetic'
TIMES LITERARY SUPPLEMENT

'This novel will have you reaching for the nearest copy of John Clare's powerful poems'
DAILY MAIL

'Affecting and beautifully written'
THE TIMES

9780552774437

The Book Thief

Markus Zusak

HERE IS A SMALL FACT
YOU ARE GOING TO DIE

1939. NAZI GERMANY. The country is holding its breath. Death has never been busier.

Liesel, a nine-year-old girl, is living with a foster family on Himmel Street. Her parents have been taken away to a concentration camp. Liesel steals books. This is her story and the story of the inhabitants of her street when the bombs begin to fall.

SOME IMPORTANT INFORMATION
THIS NOVEL IS NARRATED BY DEATH

It's a small story, about:
a girl
an accordionist
some fanatical Germans
a Jewish fist fighter
and quite a lot of thievery.

ANOTHER THING YOU SHOULD KNOW
DEATH WILL VISIT THE BOOK THIEF THREE TIMES

9780552773898

Q & A: Slumdog Millionaire

Vikas Swarup

'This brilliant story, as colossal, vibrant and chaotic as
India itself . . . is not to be missed'
OBSERVER

A young tiffinboy from Mumbai, Ram Mohammad Thomas, has just
got twelve questions correct on a TV quiz-show to win a cool one
billion rupees. He is brutally slung in a prison cell on suspicion of
cheating. Because how can a kid from the slums know who
Shakespeare was, unless he has been pulling a fast one?

In the order of the questions on the show, Ram tells us which
jaw-dropping event in his street-kid's life taught him the answer.
From orphanages to brothels, gangsters to beggar-masters, and into
the homes of Bollywood's rich and famous, *Slumdog Millionaire* is
brimming with the chaotic comedy, heart-stopping tragedy, and
tear-inducing joyfulness of modern India.

'A rollicking read as well as being a polished, varnished, finished
work of impressive craftsmanship'
HINDUSTAN TIMES

'*Q & A* is a poignant, funny, rich, beautifully written novel with an
utterly original and brilliant structure at its heart'
MEG ROSOFF, author of HOW I LIVE NOW

'Swarup is an accomplished storyteller'
DAILY MAIL

'An inspired idea . . . a broad and sympathetic humanity
underpins this book'
SUNDAY TELEGRAPH

NOW A MAJOR MOTION PICTURE,
filmed as *SLUMDOG MILLIONAIRE*

9780552775359